A SECRET REFUGE

THREE NOVELS IN ONE

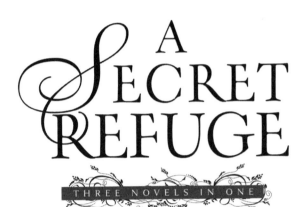

A SECRET REFUGE

THREE NOVELS IN ONE

LAURAINE SNELLING

DAUGHTER of TWIN OAKS

SISTERS of the CONFEDERACY

THE LONG WAY HOME

BETHANYHOUSEPUBLISHERS

Minneapolis, Minnesota

A Secret Refuge
Copyright © 2000, 2001
Lauraine Snelling

Previously published in three separate volumes:
   Daughter of Twin Oaks © 2000
   Sisters of the Confederacy © 2000
   The Long Way Home © 2001

Cover design by John Hamilton Design

Published by Bethany House Publishers
11400 Hampshire Avenue South
Bloomington, Minnesota 55438

Bethany House Publishers is a division of
Baker Publishing Group, Grand Rapids, Michigan.

Printed in the United States of America

ISBN 978-07642-0651-1

Library of Congress Cataloging-in-Publication Data

Snelling, Lauraine.
   A secret refuge : three novels in one / Lauraine Snelling.
      p.   cm.
      ISBN 978-0-7642-0651-1 (hardcover ; alk. paper)   1. Kentucky—History—Civil War, 1861–1865—Fiction. 2. Women horse owners—Kentucky—Fiction. 3 Sisters—Fiction. 4. Overland journeys to the Pacific—Fiction. I. Snelling, Lauraine. Daughter of Twin Oaks. II. Snelling, Lauraine. Sisters of the Confederacy. III. Snelling, Lauraine. Long way home. IV. Title.

   PS3569.N39S43   2008
   813'.54—dc22

                                                                        2008028773

LAURAINE SNELLING is the award-winning author of over sixty books, fiction and nonfiction, for adults and young adults. Her books have sold over two million copies. Besides writing both books and articles, she teaches at writers' conferences across the country. She and her husband, Wayne, have two grown sons, a basset named Chewy, and a cockatiel watch bird named Bidley. They make their home in California.

Books by

Lauraine Snelling

DAUGHTER
of TWIN OAKS

DEDICATION

To the Brown Family and
all the others at Family Circle.
Y'all made our visit the highlight of the trip,
and your help on things southern will carry on.
Thank you for the hugs and joy-filled love.
Donny, Jenny, Sarah, Jonathan, Rebekah, and Suzanne,
you make our lives richer, and we thank you for that.

Acknowledgments

My thanks goes to the Historical Societies of Wyoming, Kansas, Missouri, and Kentucky. People there know how to research and taught me much. So many compilations of diaries, letters, and other books helped me research both the era and the area. My special thanks to Tom at Joseph Beth bookstore in Lexington and to Bryan S. Bush, who wrote *The Civil War Battles of the Western Front* and let me run my plot line by him at the Old Bardstown Civil War Museum and Village, where he is assistant curator. The folks at Fort Laramie, Fort Kearney on the Platte River, the Oregon Trail Museum in Independence, and the Wilson Creek Battlefield in Missouri all provided more blocks to add to my building novel.

I am blessed to have some of the best editors and readers who keep my time lines clear and my facts straight. Sharon Asmus and Helen Motter are two of God's gifts to my writing, along with all the others at Bethany House who work so hard to publish these books.

Husband Wayne says he never knew he wanted to know so much about the Civil War, but with each book I've written, he has contributed more and more in the research and development of the stories. Thank God for someone who remembers where places are on the map and where he read whatever it is I need at the moment and loves to travel the backroads to find all the sites mentioned in our research.

Thanks to all my readers who let me know how much they enjoy my books. Without readers I couldn't do what I love—write stories. I'd hate to have to go flip hamburgers at McDonald's. What a mighty God we serve.

Hugs and blessings,
Lauraine

Prologue

Midway, Kentucky
Spring 1860

"Jesselynn, what you doin' wit dem britches on?"

Jesselynn Highwood scrunched her eyes closed as if by not seeing Lucinda's scowl, Lucinda couldn't see her.

"You heard me, chile." Lucinda moved silently in spite of her bulk, a habit acquired during years of slave training. "What yo' mama gonna say?"

"What Mama doesn't know won't hurt her." Jesselynn spun away from the restraining hand on her arm. "You don't have to tell her every little thing, you know." *And besides, I'm not a "chile" any longer.* Sometimes Jesselynn thought she should have accepted one of those suitors who'd come callin' on her daddy, just to get out from under both Mama's and Lucinda's thumbs. Jesselynn squared her shoulders. "If you must know, I'm goin' down to the stables to ride Ahab for his morning works."

"Young ladies don' ride stallions, young ladies don' wear britches, and . . ." Lucinda drew herself up to her full imposing height by sucking in a lungful of air. "Young ladies don' disobey dey mama." She let a silence lengthen for effect. " 'Sides, what happen to that lazy pup Abe? Dem horses him responsibility for running 'round de track."

"His arm still isn't strong enough from when he broke it. You know that."

Lucinda's harrumph said she might know it but in no way agreed.

Jesselynn continued, ignoring her mammy's mutterings and knowing she could be accused of impudence. Lucinda could be as stubborn as one of those old field mules at times.

"Zachary's at school, Adam is too heavy, and we all know I can get more out of those horses than anyone else." Jesselynn sneaked a peek from under the tan porkpie hat she wore pulled down over her brow. Lucinda hadn't budged. The frown on her shiny black brow looked deep enough to plant tobacco in.

"Dey's other boys down in de quarters a'wantin' to ride. Now you just get yo'self back up dem stairs and change yo' clothes before yo' mama come down dem stairs. State she in, you want her to feel worse?" She pointed back up the carved walnut staircase with one hand and reached to turn Jesselynn by the shoulder with the other. Miriam Highwood, coming close to term, spent much of her days lying down either in bed or on the lounge in the parlor. Feeling so ill with this baby forced her to depend more on others, her eldest daughter especially.

Jesselynn glared at the old woman with all her sixteen years of practice but turned and made her way to the first landing, her back straight. She refused to allow herself to stomp on each tread as she wanted to. She had outgrown that at least. *You should have known better than to come down the front stairs,* she scolded herself. Out the window by way of the live oak tree would have been better. Joseph needed her down at the stables. She'd have to talk to her father about this again. He had said she could ride. But she had to be honest. He hadn't said she could ride Ahab—in britches.

Even he had bowed to her mother's edict that Jesselynn was no longer a child, that she was close to marrying age, and it was long past time for her to learn to act like a lady.

"Piffle." Jesselynn knew that if she didn't get down to the barns quickly, the entire day's routine would be in an uproar. What was all the ballyhoo about women wearing pants after all? It certainly made more sense than those bulky skirts and hoops and petticoats—and confining corsets. After all, she had nothing that needed squeezing in or pushing up. Because she was tall and wore britches and a hat that hid her sun-kissed hair, she'd been taken for a boy more than once. She peeked down over the banister. Lucinda hadn't moved from her guard at the newel-post, and the glare she sent upward made Jesselynn continue on to her room. She plopped down on the edge of the bed. Outside she could hear the robin's morning song, echoed by the cardinal's. Everyone, or rather, everything was outside but her.

She crossed to the window and pushed aside the lacy curtains. No one was in sight. Lucinda had stayed at her post, or at least was still in the house. Jesselynn pushed the window higher and bent to crawl out, reaching with one leg for the thick branch she'd used as an escape hatch for years. She found her footing from long practice, hand over hand guided herself down the tree, and dropped from the last branch to the thick lawn.

Young ladies shouldn't have to go out their windows and down the tree, either. She threw the thought over her shoulder as she trotted down the dirt road to the stables. *One of these days I'll have a plantation of my own to manage, and then we'll see who rides what.* After all, that's what all well-bred southern gentlewomen did, marry and manage their husband's house as well as a good part of the plantation. She knew there had been two young men asking her father's permission to court her. But when her father asked her about them, she'd shrugged and shaken her head. They were just boys, after all. He hadn't insisted.

"Piffle. I'd rather ride than be married any day." Ignoring the thrust of guilt that reminded her she should be at her mother's side for the day's instructions, she trotted past the slave quarters, a row of small houses with gardens in back. She knew her father provided better houses for the slaves than most of the plantation owners. And while some of the younger slaves had been in the classroom with her, she wasn't supposed to know that he taught all his people to read, write, and do sums too. It was against the law for slaves to read, but Major Joshua Highwood was a farseeing, godly man who believed the law was wrong and he had to follow his own conscience. Jesselynn argued that slavery was also wrong, but so far he hadn't written the manumission papers for his slaves.

She missed him when he was gone, as he had been the last week, off to Frankfort, trying to keep the South out of war. Or at least Kentucky. Both of her brothers, Adam, the elder at twenty-two, and Zachary, at nineteen, were all-fired sure the South would win the war in a week—three at the most.

She'd heard so many rantings of the wonders of southern chivalry, she was sick of it. Why should the women just smile and say how wonderful the men were? How glorious to go off and fight—for what, she wasn't sure after eavesdropping on their near-to-fisticuffs discussions. She had a feeling many of the hotheaded young men weren't too sure either. The glory of fighting was all they could talk about, how they would run right over the enemy. Maybe they didn't think about getting shot, injured, or killed. Men's wounds wouldn't be much different than a deer's, for pity's sake. She'd cried buckets the first time she saw a deer that had been shot. The bullet hole that tore open its heart still showed up sometimes in her dreams.

It was all a conundrum to her. She smiled to herself—that was her newest word. She liked to be able to use a new word three times in the next day. Then she would remember it forever—or so the boys' tutor had said. After Adam and Zachary went off to school, he'd stayed on to teach the three younger girls, another of her father's wars against the mores of the day.

"Hello, handsome," she greeted the fiery red, or blood bay, stallion, Ahab, who bobbed his head and nickered as soon as he saw and heard her.

"How you this mornin', Missy Jess?" The soft voice of Joseph, their head groom, floated out from the stall where he was giving the stallion one last brushing. "This ol' son surely be ready to run."

"Good. I am too." Jesselynn inhaled the fragrance of clean horse, which was better in her mind than any perfume, even those made in Paris. She rubbed the stallion's ears and smoothed his black forelock. "You been behavin'? You know I got in a mighty lot of trouble this mornin' to come ride you, so don't you go givin' me any sass, that clear?" The Thoroughbred nodded as if he understood every word.

Joseph gave her a leg up. "If'n I din' know better, I'd think you was a boy, up der like dat." Joseph shook his head. "What this world a'comin' to?" He led the prancing stallion out to the half-mile track, all bounded with white board fences and dug every week to keep the sand loose so as not to injure the legs of the Thoroughbreds that trained on it. Twin Oaks Farm had turned out some of the top winners at Keeneland Track in Lexington, and buyers came from all around the South when the Twin Oaks' yearlings went on sale every November.

Jesselynn let the old man ramble. He'd been the one to pick her up after she fell off her first pony. Her brothers had been laughing too hard to help. She lifted her face to the sun, barely peeking over the horizon, too new to burn off the morning coolness. Why would anyone want to waste this perfect part of the day in bed? Of course that was why she was able to sneak out the way she did. Her mother slept so poorly of late that she no longer rose at first light. Her two younger sisters liked to lie abed, then, though they were barely old enough to put their hair up, play at dressing up and weddings before joining Jesselynn in the schoolroom. When Jesselynn had called their preferences "rot" and a few other choice phrases, Miriam Highwood had admonished her eldest daughter to never again use those words—a southern gentlewoman did not even *think* them.

Life was a conundrum, it certainly was. After trotting once around the track to warm the stallion up, Jesselynn leaned forward and stroked her mount's neck. "Okay, old son, let's see what you can do. You need to be really tough for the running of the Futura next month." She leaned over his withers and loosened the reins. Ahab leaped forward, gaining speed with every stride. Fence posts blurred and other horses being worked by young slaves in training flashed past. She pulled him up when she saw the entrance to the track flash past the second time.

Her eyes watered and her heart sang. Bit by bit she eased him back down to a hand gallop and then to an even canter. She'd pulled him down to a trot before they stopped in front of Joseph, who waited with stopwatch in hand.

The five-year-old stallion tossed his head, speckling her chest and face with globs of foam. Jesselynn wiped her eyes and brushed the bits of white away. "He did real fine, didn't he?"

"Yessum, dat he did. I surely do wish you could ride him at de track. We'd have us a winner fo' sho'." He checked the stopwatch again and chuckled. His grin flashed white in the sun against his dark face.

"Maybe that can be arranged." Jesselynn leaped to the ground and started walking the horse out.

"Now, don' you be gettin' any ideas, chile."

"Oh, I wouldn't do that." The words may have been correct, but the expression in her green eyes told the old man she was cooking up a scheme. Everyone knew what good schemes she brewed.

Hounds baying made her look toward the long oak-lined drive. "Father's home. Come on, horse, let's get you washed down and . . ."

Joseph took the reins. "You go on up dere. We takes care of Ahab here." The groom nodded toward the house.

Jesselynn shot him a smile of gratitude. He never broke her father's rule that when you rode the horse, you made sure he was cared for, no matter if you were half starving or bleeding. But today was different. Something was in the air—they all sensed it.

She found her father slumped in a rocking chair on the shaded front portico. He'd leaned his head against one of the white pillars and closed his eyes. The lines of fatigue etching his face made him look much older than his forty-five years. He looked as though he'd been days and nights without sleep. Love for him welled up in her heart, so painful it brought tears to the back of her throat. The thought of a world without her father was beyond comprehension.

She sank down on her knees beside his chair and laid a gentle hand on his arm. "Father, what is it?"

He covered her hand with his own. "War, my dear. There will be war, and there's nothing more I, or anyone else, can do to prevent it."

Chapter One

"You have . . . to get our . . . horses out of Kentucky. You're . . . the only one left who can." Major Joshua Highwood, brought home by his slave Benjamin after they'd been wounded in the battle at Kingston, lay in his own bed, being eaten alive by gangrene. He raised himself up on one elbow. The struggle to get closer to his daughter's face brought sweat to his brow and an even greater weakness to his voice. "Jesselynn, I told you to take them away two years ago, and you didn't do it." He sank back on his pillows and closed his eyes, every breath a struggle. The stench of putrid flesh permeated the room. "I know . . . far too much to ask . . . of a young . . . woman."

Jesselynn felt as if she'd been stabbed through the heart with one of her father's swords. "I know, but Adam and Zachary said . . . and you were already off fighting . . . and Mama so—oh, Father, forgive me." At this point she wasn't sure which Father she needed forgiveness from most, heavenly or earthly.

"I know child. I do. T-too much . . ."

She leaned closer to hear him.

"Your mother, right there at the foot of the bed. And a man in white standing right behind her." He rose up, a smile breaking over his entire face. "I'm coming, my dear. Only a moment." He lay back and turned his head to look directly into Jesselynn's tear-filled eyes. "Promise me."

"Yes, I will, I will. Oh, Father, don't leave me." But it was too late. She could tell he'd already left her. All that remained was his broken body and the smile he wore to greet the woman he'd loved since childhood.

Jesselynn laid her head on the sheet and let the tears she'd been holding back for two long years pour forth. She cried for the father just gone to meet his God and his dear wife. If Jesselynn hadn't believed in a life after death, she surely did now. She cried for her brother Adam, who was killed in action, and for Zachary, if alive. Only God knew where he was. She cried for the man who'd captured her heart and then been ordered out before they could marry, he, too, a casualty of the tragedy they called war. But mostly she cried for her mother, who'd died not long after the birth of baby Thaddeus. No longer could she hold the grief at bay.

"God, it is too much. I cannot bear this, I cannot." Heavy, pushing her down like a huge man with strong arms, the weight of her grief seemed to crush her beyond repair.

With her tears finally spent, she pushed herself to her feet, staggering about with a weakness beyond belief. She'd have to tell the others. She paused. The keening from the slave quarters had already begun, so the word, in a way known only to the black slaves, would pass from one plantation to another. One by one the house slaves tiptoed in to say good-bye to their master. Tears flowed freely, and Lucinda left the room with her apron over her head, sobs shaking her rounded shoulders.

Jesselynn thought about going to wake her little brother, Thaddeus, the son born not long before Major Highwood left to prepare for war. Poor child might only remember meeting his father when the man was too ill to do more than pat the boy's cheek. She chose to let him sleep. Tomorrow would be soon enough to tell him that they now had neither mother nor father. While he was too young to understand, he must be told. She sank down in the leather armchair in her father's study. Here was where she'd been conducting what little business the plantation had done since the war started. She'd shipped tobacco last fall, but this year, thanks to the drought, the crop looked meager. Picking and drying should start soon. That first November they'd had their annual yearling sale too, netting a goodly sum that carried them through. There would be none this fall. Both armies in the war were conscripting all the horses they could find.

"Take the horses and leave," her father had said. *How can I? What about Thaddeus? Go to Uncle Hiram's? I don't know the way.* Thoughts raced through her mind like the foals romping in the springtime. Surely her father didn't really expect this of her. He'd been ill, that's all. It had been the ravings of a dying man.

But she had promised.

She and the remaining slaves had been hiding what horses they had left in case a patrol came by and demanded all the horseflesh available. So many men and fine animals used for cannon fodder. Even Adam, on his first and only leave, couldn't get over the mindless brutality of war. She'd never forget the look in his eyes that said he'd faced the devil himself, with his fellowmen caught in the crossfire. He had never come home again. Was buried in some unmarked grave, she supposed. All she knew for certain was that he'd been identified as killed in action. She sometimes wondered if his slave, Sammy, had died too or had run off to fight for the North. Knowing the name of a battle site wasn't important to her either. They were all casualties—sons and fathers, brothers, cousins, and friends.

If she left, what would happen to Twin Oaks? Who would care for the slaves remaining? Who would oversee the harvest, the spring planting? Maybe she could come back in time for that. Surely the war would be over by next spring. Surely.

"Can I get you anythin' else, Missy?" Lucinda, with her dignity pulled around her like the shawl she wore in the winter, stopped just inside the doorway.

Jesselynn shook her head. Since her mother died, Lucinda had appointed Jesselynn head of the household and deferred to her accordingly. Sometimes Jesselynn wished for a scolding like former days. More often she wished for her mother's lap, a place of refuge where she could pour out her hopes and fears and be comforted by that loving hand on her head. But no more. And now Father was gone too. "You go on to bed. Tomorrow will be a busy day with neighbors coming to call. I'll send one of the stable hands 'round with a note, not that there are many left to come calling. I'm sure Reverend Benson will conduct the funeral on Friday. He was surprised Father lived this long."

"You not gonna wait for de young missies?"

Again Jesselynn shook her head. "They're safer where they are. Carrie Mae will have her wedding at Aunt Sylvania's, and Louisa is more help there in the hospital than she ever could be here." Jesselynn propped her head on her hand and rested her elbow on the rolled arm of the chair where her father had so often done the same. If she thought about it, she could still smell his cigar smoke. But it was a dream. He hadn't sat here smoking for over two years. Ever since he left before the war began. A fire that had been smoldering in her breast unbeknownst to her flickered, and a thin flame reached for air. The war—always the war. How could a loving God countenance something so destructive?

"Have some lemonade, Missy. Might be you feel better wit a cool drink." Lucinda crossed her arms across her bosom.

Jesselynn gave in. No matter how hard she tried to make life easier for this woman, she failed every time. If Lucinda believed lemonade would be a help, it would be. And she'd better get used to it. "Thank you, and then you go on to bed."

The harrumph that floated back to her told her exactly what the woman thought of going to bed before her mistress.

What would she do about Lucinda and the other house slaves? Could they stay here, or would some lowlife steal them and sell them down the road?

Jesselynn rose. The decisions to be made were too momentous to undertake sitting down. Crickets sang outside the window when she stopped to peer into the darkness. "God, what am I to do?" She waited, but no answer seemed to be forthcoming. Who could she ask for advice? Her mother would say to ask the

Lord. She just had. Her mother would say to wait for an answer. She hadn't—unless you called five minutes waiting. Perhaps He'd give her an answer in a dream overnight. Her father always said, "The Lord guides His children in mysterious ways, but He guides them." Tears choked her throat. She'd never hear either of their beloved voices again.

She thanked Lucinda for the lemonade and, after blowing out the lamp, carried her glass up the stairs, sipping as she went. Lucinda was right. A cool drink did help, even when watered by a renewed burst of tears. They were never coming back. None of them.

———

She came down in the morning to find her father lying in state in the parlor, resplendent in his best uniform, which had been cleaned and patched so the bullet holes no longer showed. Lucinda and her helpers had created a long table by covering sawhorses with boards and draping them in black. Her father appeared to be sleeping peacefully, a pleasant dream giving him a slight smile. She remembered the glory of his face just before he died. Had the man in white been his Savior?

She crossed the hall to the study and sat down at the desk, then began writing: a note for one of the slaves to carry around announcing the death, letters to the dear sisters so far away, and a note to Reverend Benson reiterating her request for a simple burial service to be performed the next afternoon.

A longer letter went to her father's brother, Hiram Highwood, who owned a large horse farm in southern Missouri. Had her father ever written his brother, as he said he would, and asked permission for them to take the horses there? They had never received an answer if he had.

The more she thought about it, the more certain she felt that she should keep her promise to her father. Surely no soldiers that far away would care about the few remaining horses of Twin Oaks. Missouri seemed at the western edge of the world, even though she'd read about California and Oregon. Gratitude welled up in her heart for a place of refuge. Missouri it would be. Far out in the country, away from all the scouting patrols of either blue or gray. Safe until the end of the war. She called Meshach to harness a wagon and take the letters to Midway to mail and pick up supplies at the general store.

The singing and wailing from the slave quarters continued all through the day as local friends and dignitaries came to pay their respects. Lucinda and her helpers kept the dining room table covered with food, much of which Jesselynn was surprised to discover they still had in the larder. Lucinda had been known to work miracles, and this seemed to be another one. When Jesselynn tried to catch the black woman's eye, Lucinda looked the other way. Some things Jesselynn had learned to leave well enough alone, and the kitchen was one, even if she was the mistress now.

Jesselynn joined a group of men to thank them for coming, and listened to their talk of the war.

"I knew Kentucky shoulda seceded, along with the other states. But at least we are in Confederate hands, where we belong," one man was saying.

"Those bumbling idiots in Frankfort—they don't have no idea what we all want," another added.

"You mark my words, there'll be fighting even in Lexington if we don't watch out. You want soldiers battling right here on our lands?"

One of the men turned to her. "I'm sorry, Miss Jesselynn, this isn't polite conversation for womenfolk to hear. So sorry about Joshua. We lost a fine man."

"Thank you." She nodded, glancing around at the men gathered. "Thank you for coming." She stepped back. "Now, if you'll excuse me, I . . ." She had to leave before she told them what she *really* thought about the war.

"If Governor Hughes would . . ."

"Get that nigger lover out of the White House . . ."

Their discussion followed her across the room to a gathering of women.

"Jesselynn darlin', how are you holdin' up?" A slender woman, her hair now silvered and wearing black mourning for her own son, put her arm around Jesselynn's waist.

Jesselynn swallowed and forced a smile to lips that would rather quiver. "I'm fine." She could feel tears threaten to erupt. *Fine? What do you mean fine?* If she didn't get out of here she would make a spectacle of herself. "Excuse me, please, I think . . . I . . ." She nodded around the circle and fled.

She kept the sobs at bay by walking to the rose garden, all the time ordering herself to behave, to be brave and act as her mother would have wanted. She blew her nose, returned to the house, and picked up a tray of small cakes before returning to the front portico. Offering food kept others from getting too close.

Through sheer will, Jesselynn kept a smile on her face, feeling like a ghost in the black dress of mourning. Thaddeus clung to her, refusing her suggestion that he go out and play with the neighbor children who came calling with their parents. Finally she had Ophelia, the boy's nursemaid, come and carry him off for a nap. He was far too young to understand what was going on anyway.

"Thank you for coming. No, I haven't heard from Zachary. Yes, it was a miracle Father was able to come home to die." Her answers became rote, leaving her mind free to run through her plans. Thank heaven her mother had instilled in her gracious manners and a backbone of iron, both required of a woman of her station.

By the time the last carriage and wagon rolled down the oak-lined drive and the last horse and rider trotted after, she felt like lying down on the floor and wailing, just as she could hear Thaddeus doing. Ophelia carried him down the stairs, his tear-streaked face flushed and sweaty.

"I can't make 'im stop cryin'. He won't shush fo' nothin'." The slender woman with skin the color of strong tea patted his back, but the child pushed away from her, his attention focused on Jesselynn.

"Come here, baby." Jesselynn stepped forward and took him in her arms. Like a fledgling coming home to roost, Thaddeus buried his face in the softness of her neck. She propped him on her hip and patted his back with her other hand. "There now, you mustn't treat Ophelia so. You hurt her feelings." A sniff greeted her teasing voice. "Come, let's have a smile." She kissed his cheek and blew back a lock of soft golden hair. Would John's and her child have looked like this—a cherub right off a Raphael painting? Jesselynn closed off the thought. John Follett was dead, like so many others. She thought of the discussions she'd overheard that afternoon between several of the young women. She agreed with them. There wouldn't be many men of marrying age left in the South when this war was over.

Besides not being the world's greatest beauty, she had an annoying habit of speaking her mind, something no southern gentleman tolerated well. She knew what she looked like. Skin that freckled when out in the sun, where she'd spent much of her time planting, hoeing, and, lately, harvesting the garden. Sometimes she helped in the fields when necessary. While John had said her hair was the color of honey fresh from a beehive and her slightly tilted eyes when laughing sparkled like dewdrops on spring green blades of grass, she had a hard time believing that now. The mirror told her that her hair looked more like straw and her eyes more gray than green of late. There hadn't been much to laugh about for the last two years. Too, she'd been graced with a figure that lacked the prerequisites of womanhood. Instead of blossoming, it remained stick straight and nearly flat to boot. Her mother always said it was her chin that would get her in trouble—square and determined. She'd learned to not lead with it, thanks to her brothers. Boxing lessons had not been for the girls, but Jesselynn had watched and let her brothers practice enough on her that she learned the basics. Learning to shoot a rifle had come about the same way, but much to her brothers' delight and consternation, she could outshoot both of them. Bagging a squirrel leaping from limb to limb brought her high accolades.

She buried her face in the little boy's tummy and made splattery noises to hear him laugh. If only she could switch from tears to tickles as fast as he.

"You charm him like nobody else." Ophelia now wore the relieved smile of someone who'd turned her charge over with gratitude. "He don't know him daddy gone."

"He didn't know his daddy at all, more's the pity." Jesselynn tickled Thaddy's tummy when he raised his shirt. And again. One thing with this one, once you started something, he kept it going long past anyone else's desire. Jesselynn enjoyed the game as much as he. How could she take a child this young with her to Missouri?

It wasn't as if they were going to load up the carriage and travel in comfort as they used to. Would Ophelia go along? She'd been trading flirty glances with Meshach, formerly second to Joseph down at the stables. Jesselynn had appointed him overseer of the fields and the hands who worked them. Though Meshach could manage the plantation while she was gone, he would have to go along with her to Missouri. There was no one else she trusted to keep them safe. And Ophelia would go anywhere if she thought it would give her time with Meshach.

Jesselynn gave the boy in her arms an extra squeeze and handed him back to his nursemaid. A headache had started at the base of her skull and was working its way around to the front. "Too much thinkin'," Lucinda would say, but as far as Jesselynn could tell, thinking never hurt anyone. In fact, her father had spoken highly of it, for both men and women, including his wife, daughters, sons, and slaves. Why did every thought weave its way back to her father? And every time, tears followed the same thread.

She sniffed and dug for a handkerchief in the pocket of her black silk mourning dress. After blowing her nose, she forced a smile onto lips that would rather tremble and took in a deep breath. "Well now, Ophelia, let's light the candles in the parlor, and after supper we can all gather there and I'll read from the 'Good Book,' as Father called it. We will rejoice that he has gone home to be with his Lord and my mother. At least, we will try to rejoice." She led the way into the kitchen, where one of Lucinda's grandchildren was snapping beans.

"Henry, go on down to the quarters and tell everyone we will have a hymn-sing tonight after supper."

"An' don' you dawdle." Lucinda's admonition made him pick up his feet even faster. "Supper be ready soon, and, Missy, you needs to rest up a spell. Ophelia come git you when we's ready."

Jesselynn nodded. Did she look as bad as she felt? She mounted the stairs to her room and collapsed on the rose-sprigged counterpane. White lace suspended by the four posters of the bed created a roof above her head. She'd tied the mosquito netting back this morning as she had every morning for years. All her life she'd gone to sleep in this room except for the times she'd been visiting a friend or relative. She'd never been farther than Lexington, twenty miles away, and that only for the races at Keeneland. Would life ever be the same again? She rolled her aching head from side to side. Stupid question. Of course, it never would. While today was bad, tomorrow would be even worse.

———

"Dust to dust, ashes to ashes . . ." Reverend Benson poured a handful of rich Kentucky soil in the shape of a cross on the pine box. "In the name of the Father, Son, and Holy Spirit, amen." He signaled the mourners, and together they turned and filed out of the iron-fenced family plot. A live oak, centuries old by the size of it, shaded the final resting place of Joshua Highwood, his wife Miriam, and the two children who died before the age of five. Two field workers remained and began shoveling the dirt back in on top of the box.

Jesselynn heard the thuds echo on the wooden cover. She would return in the evening with a spray of roses from the garden and dust grass seed on the mound so it wouldn't be so harsh. The graveyard had become a place for rest and contemplation for many of the family members. Squirrels raced through the overhanging branches of the oak, pelting the ground with shells, while birds sang their courtship arias. A camellia bloomed in the spring, dropping pale pink petals over the graves. Through the benevolence of Mother Nature, helped along by the women of the Highwood family, the burying plot had become a place of peace in spite of the sadness.

Jesselynn looked back again. This too she would be leaving, her parents, grandparents, and great-grandparents, along with various uncles and aunts and more cousins than she cared to count. Her family history. *Please, God, don't let anyone ransack this sacred place as they have others.* She breathed the prayer and clutched her Bible in trembling fingers. God promised to watch out for orphans, and now that's what they were.

Coming out of her reverie, Jesselynn recalled her manners and stopped the preacher before he could climb into his buggy. "Won't you stay for a cool drink and some of Lucinda's lemon cookies, Reverend Benson?"

"Why, thank you, Miss Jesselynn, I most certainly would." The white-haired cleric placed his Bible and prayer book on the seat of the buggy and turned to follow his hostess to the portico, where she gestured him to one of the rocking chairs. He settled himself with a sigh and pulled the clerical band away from his perspiring neck. "Thank the good Lord for shade, breeze, and a tall glass of lemonade of Lucinda's secret recipe. I've sat here many a time and enjoyed all three." He looked across the braided rug to the young woman in the opposite chair. "Your father sat in that chair, telling me of his dreams for his family and for Kentucky. What a loss for all of us." He shook his head. "Such a waste."

His gentle voice made Jesselynn fight the tears again. She had made it to this point of the day without a tear shower, but if he kept on like this, another wasn't far away.

"What do you plan to do now?"

His question caught her up short. She couldn't tell him they still had horses on the plantation, for someone might ask him, and he'd be obliged to tell them. She was sure he didn't lie well, as neither did she. But she had to start practicing sometime, and now was as good a time as any.

"I-I'm not sure." That part was certainly the truth. "I might go visit my aunt in Memphis." Jesselynn cleared her throat. "She's been ailin'."

"Is that where Carrie Mae and Louisa are staying?"

"Ah, no. They're with Aunt Sylvania in Richmond." Truth again. Maybe that was the trick, mix truth and stories, so one couldn't tell where one began or left off.

"You are fortunate to have family to turn to. I know these years have been terribly hard for you."

"But no more than for all the others around here. The war is draining everyone, and as my father so frequently said, 'It will get nothing but worse.' If only heads like his had prevailed instead of those foolish hotheads who thought we would win the war in a matter of weeks." Pictures floated through her mind of her brothers cheering the news of Fort Sumter being fired on, thinking war was glory and honor instead of death and destruction. While some of their friends and relatives were Union sympathizers, like her father, most of the young men she knew talked secession. She brought her attention back to the man beside her.

"Yes, even if God is on our side, war is—"

Jesselynn tossed her manners over the white-painted railing, interrupting with a decidedly unladylike snort. "You don't really believe that drivel, do you?"

"What is that, my dear?"

"That God is on our side? This is war, Reverend Benson. God is on neither side. He is stepping back to let us destroy each other, and when we're finished, He will need another flood to wash the blood away—the blood that brothers fighting brothers shed." She clenched her fingers over the curved arms of the rocker. "This is no holy war, Reverend." She turned at Lucinda's throat clearing.

Looking at her old mammy's face, she knew she'd overstepped the bounds of propriety.

"Excuse me." Jesselynn pulled a handkerchief from her sleeve and rose to her feet. "Please make yourself comfortable, and I'll be back in a few minutes. Ah . . . pardon me. I-I'm not myself." She took three steps before Reverend Benson made it to his feet.

"I'm sure if you feel that way, there is no more use for me here." He clapped his hat on his head and thundered down the three steps. "Good thing your mother and father weren't here to listen to such sacrilege. All our brave boys fightin' for our very existence." He glared at her one more time. "I do pray you will come to your senses, Miss Jesselynn."

Whatever had gotten into her? Ignoring the sense that she should make things right, she entered the study and closed the door, willing herself to calm down. She could feel her heart racing, pumping blood to her face so that hours spent in the sun couldn't have made it hotter. She took several deep breaths, bracing her hands on the flat surface of her father's desk. Well, so much for propriety. She'd practiced lying, gone on a political tirade, and deeply offended her pastor, all in a few short minutes.

She was glad he left. The thought of facing him again made her cheeks burn hotter. What would her mother say to this?

"Missy Jesselynn!"

She raised her head. The call came again. She could tell by the panic in the tone that the child calling her needed her now. She spun around and hurried to the back steps.

"Missy Jess, Yankees comin' up the drive. Dey's gonna murder us all." The child's eyes rolled white in his round black face.

"Nonsense. You run to the stables and make sure the horses are hidden. Go now!"

The little boy took off as if the Union soldiers rode right on his heels.

Jesselynn took a deep breath to compose herself and walked back to the front portico. Sure enough, a group of horsemen were riding up the drive. Even if she hadn't been warned, from this distance she could see they wore uniforms of blue.

Chapter Two

"Lucinda, go make more lemonade."

"Yessum."

Jesselynn looked around to find Meshach striding through the door as Lucinda hurried back to the kitchen. She knew the smile she gave her black field overseer went no further than barely turned-up lips, but she knew too that he understood. Or else he wouldn't be backing her up like this.

She whispered without moving her lips, "The horses?"

"Safe."

Her heart settled back to only double time. The Union soldiers trotted up the circular drive and stopped their horses ten feet from the portico steps. *At least this man has the manners to not ride all over the lawn.* The last officer to come calling hadn't been so courteous.

"Evening, ma'am." The officer in charge tipped his hat. "I'm Captain James Dorsey of the United States Army, and there have been rumors that you might have more horses to sell to the Union army." He patted the shoulder of the sorrel Thoroughbred under him. "I appreciate Roanoke here. He comes from Twin Oaks, I believe."

Jesselynn cocked an eyebrow. "Sell, sir? I don't recall evah receivin' the money promised when *that* group was taken." She deliberately deepened her accent, speaking more slowly, giving herself more time to think.

The man had the grace to look uncomfortable. "I'm sorry to hear that. I know a requisition was turned in."

"Seems, then, there was a break somewhere in the line between requisition and payment. I could surely use the money that officer promised." She nodded to the black bands circling the white pillars. "As you can see, we are in mournin' over the death of my father, so if there is nothin' else?"

"I'm sorry to hear that."

He repeats himself. He must be uncomfortable. My mother would offer them lemonade and cookies. But then my mother is dancing on the clouds of heaven with my father, and I'm the one left here.

"Would you and your men care for some lemonade?" she said and heard Meshach suck in a breath behind her. "I trust y'all would find these chairs more comfortable than your saddles." She indicated the rocking chairs and padded lounges grouped so invitingly off to either side of the front door.

The captain tipped his hat again. "That we would, and we appreciate your hospitality." He nodded to the officer mounted to his left.

"Dismount!" The crisp command cut through the settling dusk. Doves cooing in the magnolia trees by the house set up a startled cry, and a flurry of wing flapping spoke of their agitation.

At the rattle of sabers and jingling harness, a black-and-tan hound came growling around the corner of the pillared white house with teeth bared, the hackles raised on the back of his neck.

Jesselynn felt like doing the same but kept her best company smile in place. She could barely hear the ratcheting song of the cicadas above the beating of her heart.

Meshach crossed the porch in silent strides and, murmuring to the dog, took him back behind the house. Within seconds the man was back, always standing to the rear of Jesselynn but an imposing presence nonetheless.

Jesselynn knew he would do everything in his power to protect her should there be any aggression on the part of the Union soldiers. All five of them, spurs and sabers clanking, strode up the two wide steps and took a seat.

Her face a mask of resentment, Lucinda passed around a tray of glasses, already sweating from the September heat. Ophelia followed her with a plate of cookies left over from the funeral.

Neither of the women responded to the polite thank-yous from the blue-coated men.

"I appreciate your hospitality, ma'am, but I have to ask again. Do you have any horses remaining here at Twin Oaks?"

Such audacity when this is Confederate country. She glanced toward the horses being held by one of her own slaves. "Those were the last, other than a team of mules we use in the fields and to pull our wagon. Would you take everything that helps to keep us alive?"

"No, ma'am, I don't want to do that, but I'm sure you wouldn't mind if I send a couple of my men to search the stables and barns?"

Jesselynn smiled sweetly. "Why no, sir, we wouldn't mind that one little bit. But this time, please leave the hens alone. Took them three weeks to start layin' again after your last visit."

A snort from one of the men made her smile more widely. "Other than that, we have nothin' left to hide."

"You understand, this is not my . . ." The captain stopped and nodded to three enlisted men. "And don't disturb anyone or anything not connected to the horses."

A considerate Yankee. Now, if that isn't an oxymoron. In spite of all that had gone on, Jesselynn still enjoyed using a new word when she could. Now was a good opportunity. As the three left the portico, she nodded for Lucinda to pass the tray again. "Please, help yourselves. Not many bl—" She cut off the term "bluebellies" and reframed her sentence. "I reckon not many of those from the North have an opportunity to taste Lucinda's secret recipe for lemonade."

The captain's eyes twinkled, but he answered gravely. "Then we are all the more grateful that you would share this with us." He lifted his glass.

Lucinda harrumphed behind Jesselynn's chair. Without looking, Jesselynn knew the expression on the woman's face was anything but pleasant. The thin cry of a restless child floated down from the open upstairs window.

"Excuse me, please. My little brother has had a terribly hard day, and I must go to him." Jesselynn stood as she spoke, causing the Union officers to rise also. Again she was surprised at their manners. The patrol who came before had shown none.

"Please, Miss Highwood, accept our condolences on the death of your father. And of course you must see to your brother."

Jesselynn almost choked on her smile. If it hadn't been for the war, her father would still be alive, along with her brothers. And this man had the gall to offer condolences? "Well, I reckon I must say thank you, sir. I'll return as soon as I can. Please, make yourselves comfortable." *Mama, if you only knew what your training is costing me.* With a glance at her two slaves that conveyed an order to not only remain where they were but to behave properly, she left the porch in a swirl of skirts. While she no longer wore hoops due to the war, she had donned extra petticoats that morning, so she was closer to fashionable dressing than at any time in the past year.

After all, an old maid like herself didn't need to dress in her finest, as if there were such gowns available any longer. She'd dyed two of her dresses black when her mother died and kept them for mourning. She had already put them to repeated use what with all the funerals in the vicinity.

"Thank you, Thaddy, for getting me away from them," she muttered as she swiftly climbed the curving walnut staircase to the second floor.

"Lynnie." His cry came more pitifully. He had yet to be able to say her full name.

She pushed the door to his room all the way open and crossed the woven reed rug to lift him from his net-draped crib. "Hush now, baby, I'm here."

He sniffled into her neck and stuck his thumb back in his mouth. "Eat supper?" He sniffed again.

She patted his back and swayed from side to side, calming him with the rocking motion. "Not yet, but soon." She stroked the soft golden hair from his sweaty forehead and kissed his flushed cheek. Crossing to the basin, she held him with one arm and poured tepid water into the bowl from the matching pitcher painted with pink roses. Then dipping a cloth and squeezing it dry, she wiped his face around the hand attached to the thumb in his mouth.

"Daddy home?"

"No, dear, Daddy's gone."

"To war?"

"No." Tears clutched her throat and watered her eyes. "Daddy's gone to heaven to be with Mama and Jesus." Sometimes she wished he didn't talk so well. Or that he was older and could understand. How do you explain death to a baby little more than two years old? Especially one who had now lost both his parents and never knew his mother at all. She set him down on the changing table and checked his diaper. "Good boy. You are still dry. How about tryin' the pot?"

Anything to keep from going back down to the portico.

"Good boy." She praised him when she heard the tinkle in the chamber pot and, after dressing him again, could think of no real reason to not join the officers down below. Other than that she didn't want to. She refused to think of them as guests. At least her mother had not had to deal with army officers on conscription forays. *But you would have known how to behave and would have charmed them so that they would have forgotten all about the horses. Oh, Lord, please help me. We can't lose the rest of the breeding stock or Twin Oaks stud will be no more.*

Sometimes she wondered if the Lord really cared about the carnage going on, let alone the horses. As her father had said in the beginning, this was a fight between brothers, not between warring nations. Sometimes she wished she'd been able to leave as her sisters had, to get away from making decisions here, to get away to safety. Which was the reason she had sent both Louisa and Carrie Mae to Richmond to be with their aunt Sylvania—to keep them safe from marauding soldiers.

She carried Thaddeus down the back stairs and left him playing on the kitchen floor with Lucinda's two grandchildren. She'd rather stay and play with them and the kittens than go back to being the hostess. She stepped through the front door as the three enlisted men returned from the stables.

"Nothing there, sir." One saluted as he spoke. "Except for the two mules like she said and a milk cow."

"Please don't take the cow. My little brother needs the milk." She tried to keep a note of panic from her voice.

"We aren't in the habit of leaving women and children destitute." The captain rose to his feet. He set his glass back on the tray Lucinda held and nodded his thanks. "Sergeant," he said, giving a silent order.

"Mount up!" The command cut through the air, all official once more.

Captain Dorsey set his blue felt hat back on his head and touched two fingers to the brim. "Ma'am, sorry to inconvenience you regarding the horses. But just in case you happen to find any running loose, we will be on the watch."

Was that a twinkle she caught in his eye or a trick of the light? Jesselynn didn't take time to ponder the thought. "I'm sure you will be, and if there were any horses running loose, why, Captain, what a surprise that would be to all of us." *As if we'd let our horses run loose!*

The men mounted, and the captain tipped his hat again. "Good evening, Miss Highwood, and I am indeed sorry about the death of your father. From everything I hear of him, he was a fine man."

Jesselynn swallowed hard. The tears she'd kept reined in all day now threatened to break loose. "Yes, sir, he was." She watched the straight-shouldered, blue-clad backs as they trotted their horses down the long drive. Speaking of fine men, she had a feeling she'd just met one. If only he'd worn gray instead of blue.

She shook her head and turned back to the house. As soon as they'd had supper, she needed to finish the letter to Uncle Hiram and begin the thank-you notes to those who'd left gifts today. How soon could she possibly leave? Who would she take? Who would stay? And who would protect those who remained behind?

She'd just sat down to the table when one of the young hands skidded through the door.

"Rider comin', Missy."

"Friend or . . ."

"Sojer, I thinks."

Jesselynn dropped her napkin on the table. "Blue or gray?"

"Too dark." But the boy shook his head. "Bad 'un, I specs."

"Benny, what do you mean?"

Quiet as a shadow, Meshach took his place behind her as soon as she stepped on the porch.

The horse's front feet nearly clattered on the first step as the rider yanked his mount to a stop.

"So, they didn't find 'em, did they?"

The sneering voice of their ex-overseer sent shivers chasing up her spine. "I was watchin'."

"Find what?" The thought of Second Lieutenant Cavendar Dunlivey of the Confederate army keeping a watch on Twin Oaks made her want to take out a gun herself.

Chapter Three

"My father told you never to set foot on this place again."

Dunlivey shook his head, his smile sinister in its beauty. "Yer *father* ain't here no more, Missy, and I come to get what is rightfully mine."

If only he was as handsome inside as out. The thought made her choke. All she could see now was evil. Jesselynn kept her hands away from protecting her middle with a burst of anger that she refused to let show. That was what he wanted, to see her cringe. She clamped her teeth together to keep the words she wanted to scream at him inside until she could speak civilly. Dunlivey had abused the slaves, stolen from her father, and then asked for her hand in marriage, claiming it was his right, since he had done so much to keep the plantation running. He knew every inch of the land.

She raised her chin, tightening her backbone at the same time. "If you don't leave now, you may never leave."

She heard a gasp from behind her while at the same time she felt Meshach move a step closer. She knew he carried the rifle at his side.

"Think yer better'n anyone else, that's what," Dunlivey said in a threatening voice. "But now I got you. Givin' succor to the enemy, you was." He narrowed his eyes and leaned slightly forward in the saddle. "I aim to get me those horses, Missy, and I aim to get you right along with them." His words hissed worse than a water moccasin. "Those slaves you try so hard to protect will work for me again, I promise you. Or they goes down the river. Bring in good money, they will."

"You want I should shoot him now?" The click of a hammer drawn back sounded loud as a rifle crack in the stillness. One of the other slaves whimpered.

"No, then we'd have to bury him, and I don't want to soil our hands handling varmints like him." She watched as the fury built within the man and exploded.

Yanking his horse back, he screamed at her, froth erupting in spittle that bathed his mount. "I'll get you, all a'you, if it's the last thing I do."

"I reckon it just may be that if you don't turn and head on back the way you came. Next time we catch you on Twin Oaks land, there won't be any talkin' first."

"Next time, Missy, I won't be alone. This time was a warnin' outa the goodness of my heart."

"I sincerely doubt your body contains such an organ." She beckoned Meshach, who raised the gun. "If you've forgotten, we're all trained to shoot." She nodded to her slave. "Make sure you hit him in the heart so we can keep the horse."

Dunlivey's glare was so filled with hate, she almost stepped back. She wanted to run and hide, but she kept her place.

He spun his horse, applied spurs, and tore down the curving drive. "The South needs those horses of yourn, so now you can be shot as traitors." His diatribe trailed behind him.

Jesselynn blinked at his final scream that seemed to echo through the trees. Traitors. Was that what they were, simply for trying to keep something that would ensure their livelihood when this terrible calamity was finally over? *Who'd believe it?*

"Dat man be the hate-fullest man I ever knowed," Lucinda said with a huff. "Never in my life be so glad to see someone daid."

"That's not the Christian way," Jesselynn said, turning with a gentle smile. "At least that's what Mother would have said."

"Yo' daddy shoulda shot him long time ago." Meshach shook his head. "Some men born mean and jus' get meaner. He one." With dusk faded to night, Meshach could disappear into the darkness as long as he didn't smile. "He might could have a accident 'tween here and town."

"No. There'll be no killin' around here. This war has done enough of that." Jesselynn turned and entered the house. "We have some figurin' to do. Dunlivey will *not* get our horses." *If only I had done what Daddy said back in the beginning, we'd have all the horses left, not just the few. Why, oh why, did I listen to those brothers of mine? "The war'll be over in three weeks. The South can't be beaten. God is on our side."* "Ha!"

But who am I to take the horses out of here? A woman traveling with five Thoroughbreds? Fine bet that I'd get anywhere. Entire plantations have been lost on bets less than that. Oh, God, what am I to do?

After putting Thaddy to bed, she returned to her father's study, positioning the lamp so she could work at his desk. Though she'd been managing the plantation since her mother died and the men were at war, deciding to leave it was the most difficult decision she'd ever had to make.

"Oh, Lord, who should stay? Who will keep them safe? Who should go with us? Should I take them all?" While waiting for answers, she penned another letter to her sisters, describing the funeral and ordering them to stay where they were. There was nothing they could do at Twin Oaks. She didn't tell them her fears for their home. Other great houses had been burned to the ground, and no one knew for sure who was responsible. The South said it was the northern soldiers who burned and looted and vice versa. She had a feeling the burnings were more the work of scum like Dunlivey. He wore the uniform of the South. Why hadn't he been ordered elsewhere like her father and brothers?

They could only hope Zachary was still alive, since there had been no word of his death. She shuddered at the thought of Zach being confined in a Yankee prison. The rumors they'd heard were near impossible to believe.

"Remember," she wrote, "our God is in His heavens and taking care of us here, no matter how terrible things are. All He asks is that we love and trust Him. I trust Him to care for you and for all of us here, and to bring us back together again soon." After signing the letter, she studied the words while the ink dried, wondering if she'd written the last more for herself than for them.

The lamp was flickering by the time she'd gotten through the thank-you letters from the funeral. As she stuffed the last one in the envelope, tears threatened to overflow her burning eyes.

"Daddy, why? What am I to do?"

Lucinda pushed open the door, shaking her head. "Missy, you git yourself on up to bed. De roosters be crowin' befo' you close yo' eyes." She laid a hand on her young mistress's shoulder. "Things always look better in de mornin'."

Jesselynn shook her head. "I don't see how. I really don't see how." Nevertheless, she blew out the kerosene lamp and followed Lucinda and her candle out the door and up the stairs, neither one of them needing the light, they'd trod these familiar halls and stairs so many times.

A breeze fluttered the white curtains at her window and the mosquito netting that had been let down to curtain her bed. Using the light from the moon, she undressed and slid between the sheets, grateful for the cooling breezes of approaching fall.

"Father, in your Word you promise to be a father to the fatherless and a husband to the widow. I need the guidance of a father and the wisdom to know what to do. You say you will both guard and guide. All of these people here depend on me—for everything. And I have nothing. I couldn't sell the planta-tion if I wanted to until we prove whether Zach is dead or alive. Besides there is no one to buy it anyway."

"Get the horses out." She could hear her father's voice as if he were in the room with her. And she had promised. Was a promise made on a deathbed really a vow? After all, she was just a girl. Well, eighteen and once betrothed might be considered basis for womanhood. Others her age were married and had children by now.

"Get the horses out." She flipped over on her other side. *"How* do I get the horses out?"

There was no answer but the breeze billowing the curtains and the call of the nighthawk foraging for insects.

———

"Britches, that's what I need!"

Dawn had barely stained the horizon lavender when she threw back the covers and brushed aside the netting. She dug in the back of the chifforobe and pulled out the trousers she used to wear when exercising the racehorses. Some more digging yielded the long-sleeved white shirt. But she knew she'd outgrown her boots. Donning the pants and shirt, she stood in front of her mirror. From her neck down, she'd pass as male. But her hair.

Scooping it up she pinned the rich mass on top of her head. A hat. Without making a sound, a skill she'd learned years earlier when exiting by the live oak, she strode down the hall to Zach's room. Surely between her two brothers' gear, there was a hat that would cover her hair. Or one of her father's would do.

She located the tan felt hat hanging in her father's closet. The odor of pipe smoke and shaving soap brought back every memory of her father. She crushed the hat to her breast and fought the tears that threatened to overwhelm her. Hadn't she already cried enough?

But no matter. The tears overflowed her lashes and rained down her cheeks, spotting the tan felt like raindrops. She buried her sobs in the bed pillows lest anyone hear and come seeking to help.

There *was* no one to help.

No one. The responsibility was all hers.

God, where are you? You were here when Mother died. Why have you deserted me now?

Birds broke the dawn hush with their morning gossip. A rooster crowed. Another answered. A horse whinnied.

Jesselynn leaped to her feet. Was it one of their horses, or was someone coming? She dashed to the window, but the long curved road remained empty.

She grabbed a handkerchief from her father's dresser drawer and wiped her eyes and nose. Ignoring the desire to let the tears flow unchecked, she sniffed and looked in the mirror. Repinning her hair, she set the hat in place, but every time she tried to pull it snug, a loop of hair drooped from the confining band.

"Fiddlesticks!" She whipped the hat off her head and jerked out the pins, letting the curls tumble down her back.

She stared in the mirror. Could she do it? While her sisters were truly lovely, she knew her hair was her best feature. Thick and glossy with curls that were the envy of both her sisters and her cousins. She glared at a chin that could only be called stubborn and eyes that still wore the red marks of her tears. At least she no longer had the milky skin so prized by ladies. Her face, neck, and arms had picked up a golden hue from working in the sun, even while wearing a hat. At least the freckles had run together to a tone of tan.

"It has to come off."

"Missy Jess, dat you in dere?"

Jesselynn rolled her eyes. Leave it to Lucinda. She glanced down at her shirt and britches. Might as well get the caterwauling over with. Touching her forehead in a one-finger salute, she strode to the door and jerked it open. "Get the scissors."

"What you aimin' to do?" Lucinda looked her up and down, shaking her head and moaning, "What yo' mama think?" over and over.

Jesselynn paused. What if someone came calling and she had no hair? She'd give the whole plan away and someone sure as shooting would notify the authorities. Cutting her hair would have to be one of the last things she did before leaving.

"I'll change right away. Just trying to make some plans," she said, pulling off the shirt and pants and tossing them on her bed. She knew better than to let Lucinda know ahead of time what would be happening. While the older woman would try to cover her feelings, her sniffs and sad eyes would announce clearly that something bad was about to happen. The speed with which news traveled from the big house to the slave quarters was nothing short of miraculous as far as Jesselynn was concerned. She donned her dress and let Lucinda button it up.

"Breakfast ready half hour," Lucinda said.

"Good, that'll give me time to check on things at the barn. Let Thaddy sleep as long as he can. Yesterday was mighty hard on him, and I don't want him sick again if we can help it."

"Yessum."

"And, Lucinda, I think it is time to bury the silver."

"I 'specs so." The tips of her knotted kerchief fluttered as she shook her head. "I been feared dis was comin'."

"Well, at least we had things nice for Daddy's funeral." Jesselynn swallowed her tears again. All she had to do was say his name or think it and her eyes burned clear back of her nose. She choked back a sigh too. Pretty soon she and Lucinda would be crying on each other's shoulders again if they kept this up.

"Dem Yankees take ever bit dey see."

"If what I've been hearing is true, it's not just the bluebellies that have been raiding the plantations. Thieves are thieves no matter what color the uniform. Dig the holes in the rose garden like we decided, and make them plenty deep enough so no saber can find them."

"Yessum. I takes care dat."

"Good. We'll eat as soon as I get back. Bake up those two hams hanging out in the coolhouse too, please."

"Dem's de last."

"I know." Jesselynn headed for the stairs, tying her straw hat under her chin as she went. "I'll be back as soon as possible." The sun had already burned the mists off the hollows when she reached the stable doors. Meshach had Ahab, their oldest stallion and son of the foundation of the Twin Oaks stud, crosstied in the hard-packed aisle so he could be cleaned of the mud from the hiding place.

"Leave him dirty. In fact, take him back and get him filthy, him and all the others. We need to disguise them somehow."

"We leavin' den?" He dropped the brushes in the bucket.

"Tonight."

"Ever'body?"

"Oh, how I wish we could stay." She unclenched her hands at her sides. "But we can't. We'll leave the house slaves and the field hands and just take the horses. I hope we will be able to come back in time for spring planting."

"Who take care dem?"

"I reckon they'll have to take care of themselves. You think Joseph can make sure the tobacco is picked and dried? I'll write and ask Embers to take care of selling it when he does his." Tod, the eldest Embers son, had come home minus a leg, but at least he came home. His father didn't.

"Dat work. I tell dem shifless niggers to get da work done or . . ."

"I wish I could leave you in charge here, but Benjamin and I can't protect the horses alone. Maybe, if things go well, we can leave them safe at Uncle Hiram's and come right back."

"Daniel good tracker. You take 'im?"

"If you think so. Lucinda will manage the house slaves and gettin' the rest of the garden put by."

"You takin' Marse Thaddy?"

"If only there were some way to send him back to Richmond to the girls." She shook her head and moved to stroke the stallion's neck. "He's so little to take along." But she knew in her heart she couldn't leave him behind. She'd never forgive herself if something happened to her baby brother. The thought of Thaddy made her think of her older brothers. Adam so young and already cannon fodder. The tears that hovered so near the surface threatened to overflow again.

"That means we take the wagon. Can you train one of the mares to harness so we can leave at least one mule here?"

"Today?" His eyebrows shot up.

"By dark."

"Lawsy, Miss Jesse, she might spook easy."

"We'll trade off as we go and get them all broke to harness. No one looks at a horse pullin' a wagon." She rubbed Ahab's ears and stroked down his cheek. "We'll get you through, old son, we will." She studied the bright white star between his dark eyes. "Better dye all their white markings and do everything you can to rough up their coats." For the first time in her life, she felt sad at the beauty and spirit of the Twin Oaks' Thoroughbreds.

Back at the house, she took the portico steps in one leap and entered the dining room just as Lucinda was setting the platter of ham and eggs in the center of the table. While Lucinda still hovered, the remainder of the household slaves took their places at the table. Jesselynn had decreed she didn't want to eat alone, and since Lucinda insisted on using the dining room, they all ate together. Meshach took his place just in time for the platter to reach him.

Jesselynn bowed her head and paused for the settling. "Heavenly Father, we thank thee for this food prepared by loving hands. Bless this day and keep us, thy children, safe from harm. Please, if Zachary is still alive, watch over him and bring him home again. In Jesus' name we pray. Amen."

She'd almost said her father's name too, as she had at all the meals in the two years he'd been gone. But now they knew where he was, in his heavenly home, along with his beloved wife and eldest son and all the other saints gone before.

Sometimes she envied them. Their troubles were over, while she had a feeling that hers were about to get worse.

An hour later, she had an inkling of how bad "worse" could get. After hours searching for the secret drawer her father told her about in one of his more lucid moments, she finally found it. When she discovered how to open it, the manumission papers she thought her father had signed were blank. He hadn't signed them as he said he had. Why? Was it all delirium? What could she do now?

Chapter Four

"Oh, Lord, what am I to do?"

As she was beginning to think was usual, no answer came forth.

Who can I ask for advice? She ran the list of neighbors through her mind, but none of them could know she still had horses. Besides, she'd already offended most of them with her forthright views on the war. *Why can't I keep my mouth closed like Mama would have?*

"So who can I get to look after things around here for me?" *God, if you'd bring Zachary back, at least part of my burden would be solved.* She felt the tears burning her eyes again. All she wanted to do right this moment was to lay her head on the desk and bawl.

The picture of Cavendar Dunlivey screamed its way into her mind, jerking her upright. His vow branded itself on her brain.

"You will not get the horses, nor me or my people." A shudder made her teeth rattle at the remembered evil in his eyes. Her stomach clenched, and she tightened her jaw.

"You be needin' somethin'?" Lucinda appeared in the doorway.

"Ah, no. Thank you." Jesselynn's heart hammering against her ribs like steel on an anvil, she forced a smile to lips too dry to stretch. *Lucinda. How can I leave Lucinda?*

But how could she take her and the other slaves who'd been part of her life since she was born? Her father had not traded in slaves. He'd inherited them from his father, and when children were born in the slave cabins, they became part of Twin Oaks. None had ever been sold, although several had been hired out to work for another planter. Tom the blacksmith was right now over at the Marshes' fixing machinery. Sarah, who had healing in her hands with herbs, often served as a midwife around the parish, and Aaron, whose woodworking skills rivaled those of fine furniture makers, had spent the last six months at a cabinet shop in Lexington.

As her father had, Jesselynn gave those who worked out a part of their wages. The remainder had helped keep Twin Oaks going.

Could she sign the papers, copy her father's signature?

She drew paper from the drawer and uncapped the ink bottle. Using one of his letters, she drew over the signature with a dry quill over and over to get the flow and feel of his hand. Then she tried it with ink. And tried again.

Bit by bit the signature drew closer to that of her father's. Sweat trickled down her spine, and once a drop from the tip of her nose blurred the last line.

"Fiddlesticks!" She felt like hurling pen and pot across the room. Getting up, she strode to the window and looked out across the tobacco fields, the large leaves rustling in a breeze. If only she could stay until the field was picked and hooked across the rods in the barn for drying.

A horse whinnied, then the sound was cut off, most likely by a hand clamped on the muzzle.

She spun back to the chair. She had to leave tonight. Before they were discovered.

Tying her hair back, she returned to the desk. She wrote on both fronts and backs of precious paper, on old envelopes, and on the empty pages at the back of the journal she kept for housekeeping expenses and for recording the amount of preserves made, meat smoked, and eggs laid.

Her hand cramped. Again she rose and went to stand at the window. The sun stood directly overhead.

Lucinda appeared in the doorway. "Dinner ready." She glanced at the mess of papers by the desk and back to Jesselynn.

Jesselynn closed the walnut doors to her father's study and followed Lucinda to the dining room, where everyone was already gathered. When she took her chair at the head of the table, they all sat and bowed their heads. No one laughed or whispered or shifted on a chair. The song of a mockingbird followed the cadence of her prayer. At the amen no one moved, they all sat staring at the plates before them.

"Is there somethin' here that I'm not aware of?" She looked up as Lucinda set the platter of corn bread in front of her, the old woman's eyes gazing straight forward. "Lucinda?"

"No, ma'am."

Jesselynn felt like looking around to see who else the solemn-faced woman could be speaking to. "Where's Thaddy, Ophelia?"

"I let 'im sleep." Ophelia looked as though someone had whipped her, her eyes staring out of her drawn face.

"All right." Jesselynn slapped her palms on the table. "What is goin' on here?"

Button, Lucinda's youngest grandson, jumped and started to wail. Ophelia shushed him, giving Jesselynn a look that screamed pure terror.

Jesselynn looked down the table to Meshach, who was studying his plate as if to memorize each green bean and corn kernel. Arms rigid, holding herself up as if all strength had drained from her legs, she turned slowly to look at Lucinda.

"What . . . is . . . it?" The pause between each word lasted seconds that crawled like hours hoeing tobacco.

"You goin' to leave us." Lucinda tied her apron in knots.

Jesselynn sank down in her chair, sure now that the escaped strength in her legs would never return. She should have known better than to think she could keep something like this a secret.

"I thought we would talk about this later today." The weakness traveled up her body, making her head float like a magnolia petal on the water. "I . . . I'm tryin' to do what is best for all of us. Go on, eat your dinner, and then we'll talk."

"You not goin' to sell us to dem slave traders." Lucinda's words snapped Jesselynn's head around.

"Lord above, whatever gave you that idea? Of course I'm not goin' to sell anyone. I'm tryin' to puzzle out how I can set y'all free."

"Don' wanna be free. Wanna be here, like always."

Jesselynn looked around the table to see all the heads bobbing. Lucinda indeed spoke for them all.

"I understand, I guess, so eat your food and then we'll talk." She knew she was probably the only woman in the parish, nay, in the entire state of Kentucky, who planned on discussing her plans with her slaves. She looked at the faces before her. Not too many others shared the dining table with black faces either. Such a thing hadn't happened while her mother and father were alive. White folks ate in the dining room, and the others in the kitchen or their cabins.

A collective sigh rose, and then bit by bit, normal mealtime chatter picked up, starting with Ophelia and passing around the table from one to the next.

Jesselynn forced the corn bread, sliced string beans, and fried ham past the lump in her throat. Even the redeye gravy over new potatoes had a hard time going down. How could she explain to them what she needed to do? Meshach knew. Thoughts beat in her head like a broody hen beating off anyone come to steal her eggs.

"You don't like de ham?" Lucinda paused in the gathering of plates.

"No, it's fine. I just . . ." Jesselynn handed her plate up.

As soon as the table was cleared, everyone looked at Jesselynn. The time had come. Lucinda sat down and took a little one on her lap.

The silence vibrated like a plucked guitar string.

Oh, Lord, help me. Please give me the words.

"Y'all heard Dunlivey yesterday." At their gasp she knew she'd started on the wrong tack. She took in a deep breath and began again. "When my father died, he made me promise I would take the horses out of Kentucky before the soldiers, either gray or blue, could conscript them, er, take them away. If we lose the horses, we will have nothing to start over with again after the war. Joseph and Meshach have been hiding them, as y'all know, but Dunlivey knows this place. If anyone can find them, he can."

A gasp leaped from mouth to mouth.

"So, I will do as my father said. I promised him, and a promise is a promise."

"Where you go?" Lucinda continued as speaker for all.

"I can't tell you that. Not because I don't trust you, but to help keep you safe. If you don't know where I've gone, then . . ."

"Den we can't tell no one."

"That too."

"One thing I can do to keep you all safe is give you your freedom papers. Then no one can sell or buy you." Chatter started, but she raised her hands for quiet. "You don't have to leave here. I will pay you wages for stayin'." Where she would get the money, she had no idea. Other than the tobacco crop. "Life will go on like always here. You all know what to do, many of you better than I do. Then when the war is over, we will raise horses and plant tobacco and soybeans and other crops, just like we always have."

She hoped they believed her words, because right now all she could think of was leaving. She, who had never been beyond Lexington, had to find their way to Uncle Hiram's in Missouri.

"Who goin' and who stayin'?" Lucinda rocked the child she held to her bosom.

"Good question. I'd take all of you if I could, but we have to travel fast and at night so we don't get stopped." Fear tasted like blood in her mouth.

"I wisht I shot Dunlivey right 'tween the eyes." Meshach muttered so quietly Jesselynn barely heard him, but the gasp from Lucinda confirmed her suspicions.

"There'd only be others." Jesselynn looked from face to face. Tear-streaked, shaking, eyes pleading, all of them were her people, her family. Leaving them defenseless—the thought made her eyes burn, and the tears running down Ophelia's cheeks called for her own tears.

She sucked another deep breath into lungs that refused to expand. The lump in her throat grew. "God will keep us all safe. The Bible, it—" She could go no further. "Excuse me." The chair rocked behind her as she left the table.

———

"De wagon loaded," Meshach said from the doorway to the study.

Jesselynn finished the final signature, each one appearing more like her father's as she wrote out the twenty manumission papers. Her hand cramped, and she was nearly out of ink.

"We'll leave an hour after full dark. No one should be on the roads then." She folded and slid the last sheet of paper in an envelope and wrote Meshach's name on the front. "Here."

He crossed the faded oriental rug and took it from her. "I don' need dis."

"You might."

"Joseph out here like you said."

"Good. Bring him in."

In a moment the two black men stood before her, one as tall and broad shouldered as the other was skinny and stooped. Both of them clutched their hats in their hands, wringing the life out of the brims.

"Joseph, keep this someplace safe." She handed him his envelope.

"Laws, Missy, I . . ."

"Now, Joseph, as a free man, you can leave Twin Oaks if you want, or you can take over Meshach's job as overseer and make sure the tobacco is harvested and dried." *Please, God, let him stay.*

"Where would I go? Dis my home."

Relief attacked the stiffening in her spine. A momentary slump, a swallow, and she smiled around her clenched teeth. "Thank you, Joseph. Between you and Lucinda, I know you can keep Twin Oaks together. With the garden and the hogs to butcher, you'll have enough to eat." *If you can keep it all out of the hands of either soldiers or scum.* "We will leave you guns and lead for hunting." *And to keep off the scavengers.*

"Supper ready." Ophelia, a white cloth tied around her head, spoke from the doorway.

Jesselynn scooped the remaining envelopes into a pile and straightened them. She'd give out the rest at the table and down in the cabins.

When she entered the dining room, her gaze automatically noticed the empty sideboard. No three-branched silver candlesticks, no shiny servers. Lucinda and her helpers had done as instructed. Her father's picture no longer hung on the wall, nor did her mother's. Samuel Morse had painted them both years before.

Supper passed in a flurry of tears, instructions, and questions, many of which had no answers. Thaddy sensed the tension and insisted on sitting on Jesselynn's lap, crying and shaking his head when Ophelia tried to take him.

"Ophelia, I want you to come with us to take care of our boy here."

She glanced down the table to where Meshach was eating as if nothing untoward were happening. "I goes."

Jesselynn followed Lucinda into the kitchen. "I have a mighty big favor to ask you."

Lucinda turned, arms crossed over her ample bosom.

"Lucinda." The words wouldn't come. Jesselynn fought the tears and tried again. "While I want you to come with me, there's no one else I can trust to stay here and take care of things. You are free now. . . ."

Lucinda's harrumph said more than a string of words. "Don't need be free. Twin Oaks my home."

"Mine too." *Oh, God, why do I have to leave?* "Please, Lucinda, will you take care of things here for me?" Jesselynn knew if she let the tears come, they'd both be crying. "Please." Her whisper barely squeaked around the lump in her throat.

Lucinda wiped the tears from her eyes. "I never see you again."

"No, we'll be back in time for spring planting."

Lucinda shook her head slowly from side to side as if a great weight lay atop her knotted turban.

God, I can't stand this. You know how often she has been right. She listens when you speak and hears what you say. Please, please say we will come back.

"I stay. And I pray for you ever day, and for us." She swept her arm to the side, including all those to be left behind.

"Thank you. I will write."

Lucinda nodded.

Jesselynn stood still a moment before heading for the door. She paused, looked back. "Winter will go fast and when spring comes, watch for us."

They began loading the wagon after dark.

"Food all in de wagon. I packed a carpetbag for de baby. Yo' dresses in de trunk." Lucinda wiped her eyes with the corner of her apron.

"Thank you." Jesselynn couldn't bear to tell her right now that there would be no need for dresses. "Just in case anyone is watching this place, we must go on like nothing is changed. Those of you who stay here, you have to do the same." Jesselynn looked at June, Lucinda's daughter, whose skin wasn't much darker than her own. While June was more rounded, they were about the same height.

If she could become a boy, surely June could become her.

"June, come with me."

"Yessum." Eyes rolling, the young woman rose from the table where she'd been plucking a chicken.

"Now, there's nothing to be afraid of," Jesselynn said as they mounted the stairs. "I have an idea that might make things look normal around here. After I'm gone, I mean."

"Don' want you to go." The whimper lashed at Jesselynn's shoulder blades.

"I know. I don't want to go either." She crossed her room to the chifforobe and pulled out the other of her mourning dresses. "Put this on."

"Can't do that." June took three steps back, folded hands clasped to her breast. The shaking of her head made her kerchief shudder.

Jesselynn breathed deep and sighed. "Yes, you can. You and I are about the same size, and if you wear my clothes and a straw hat like I always do, anyone watching this place will think I am here." *And not come hotfooting it after us. Anything to buy time.* Every time she thought of Dunlivey watching the big house, she wanted to hide under the bed.

"But you be gone. I can't be you."

"Please, June, for the sake of everyone at Twin Oaks, try the dress on." She held the dress out until June reached for it as if she were being told to put her hand into flames. Jesselynn dug in the chest of drawers for a camisole and petticoat and handed them to the shaking woman beside her.

"Come now, you and I used to play dress-up together, remember? You've worn my clothes before."

"I know, but dat was playtime. This for real thing."

"Just be glad I'm not making you wear that corset."

When June finally stood dressed in the black silk dress and a white apron, Jesselynn looked at her with eyes slitted. "You fill it out far better than I do." She motioned to her chest area. Taking the straw hat off its peg, she clamped it onto June's head. "Sure do wish now I'd worn a sunbonnet. That way no one could see your face at all." She stepped back and, hands on hips, nodded. "Go ahead, look in the mirror. What do you think?"

June fingered the material of the skirt. "I think I done gone to heaven, dis here stuff feels so fine." She smiled at the woman in the mirror. "Pretty dark for a nigger like me."

"Don't use that word, June. You are a beautiful free woman who is doing Twin Oaks a big favor."

Tears pooled in June's eyes and one slipped down her cheek. "Thank you, Miss Jesselynn, from de bottom of my heart." She smoothed the silk over her bosom and down to her waist. "I do my best till you gets home again."

Several hours later, Jesselynn was wishing Lucinda were half so cooperative. She breathed in wind for a sigh big enough to blow the woman down and let it out slowly. "Lucinda, no matter what we all think and want, I have to take the horses to Uncle Hiram's in Missouri like Daddy said. I promised. You know that." While Jesselynn thought this discussion had been taken care of in the kitchen, she was learning otherwise.

"Oh, lawsy, my baby get herself kilt fo' sure." Lucinda threw her apron over her head.

"Lucinda, please get the scissors."

One dark eye peeked over the white hem. "Why?"

"Just get them, please."

Jesselynn had tried on two pairs of her father's boots before Lucinda heaved her bulk back up the stairs. By stuffing the toes with cotton and wearing two pairs of socks, it looked like she had footwear more in keeping with her new life. Now for the hair. She pulled out the seat to her mother's dressing table and sat down.

Handing Lucinda the comb, Jesselynn sat with her eyes closed. "Cut it off short like a man's."

Lucinda took the scissors and comb, all the while muttering and shaking her head. She stepped back. "I can't do dis thing. Hair like dat, no way, Missy. Lucinda won' be party to such goin's on."

Jesselynn's eyes snapped open. She straightened her back and narrowed her eyes, sending sparks bouncing off the mirror and catching her mammy full force. "Will you help me or won't you? I have to save the horses, for without them we will have nothing after the war is over. You know what marauding soldiers would do to a young woman traveling with fine horses like ours."

"Laws, Missy, I can't cut yo' hair." Tears bubbled from her dark eyes and tracked down her cheeks.

Jesselynn spun on the bench seat and reached for the scissors. "I'll do it, then."

"Den yo' look like, like . . ." Lucinda shook her head. "I do it." Tears flowing, she cut the heavy tresses off at the neckline, then lifted it in sections with the comb and snipped some more.

Jesselynn gritted her teeth against the hurt as she watched her hair fall to the floor. John had loved her hair, said it reminded him of shimmering silk in the moonlight. All her life she'd had one vanity, and now it lay in pools around their feet. She closed her eyes, pretending it was her mother standing there as she'd done for so many years, combing her daughter's hair and telling stories of when she was a young girl.

Oh, Mother, if only you were here now to tell me what to do. I've needed you so these last years. Immediately she felt guilt jab her in the ribs. Poor little Thaddy had never known his mother. At least she'd had one for seventeen years.

Lucinda's repeated sniffing and harrumphs broke into her reverie. Jesselynn turned enough on the walnut bench that she couldn't see in the mirror.

"Hold still, lessen you want to look like a sheared sheep." Lucinda sniffed again. "Good thing yo' mama ain't here. Dis nigh to break her heart."

Better a broken heart than . . . But Jesselynn didn't want to think of the coming days either. How could she leave Twin Oaks, the only home she'd ever known, and head across country without her father or her brother or . . . ? She sucked in a deep breath and let it out as a heavy sigh.

Lucinda stepped back. "Dere."

Jesselynn looked up into her mammy's tear-filled eyes. "I'm sorry, Lucinda, dear, but I just can't see any other plan. Do I look like a boy?"

"Maybe if you use walnut dye on yo' face and hands and keep a hat on yo' head." She squinted her eyes. "Maybe dye yo' hair too."

"That's a good idea. Good thing I'm not as endowed as some of the others." She pulled her camisole tight across her chest. "I won't miss the corsets, that's for sure." She thought of the whalebone contraption hanging from a hook on her closet door. Up until yesterday for the funeral, she'd pretty much given up wearing one, as she'd had to do more of the outside work. Even though Joseph ran the stables and barns, someone as big as Meshach had needed to oversee the tobacco planting and hoeing, the haying, and the grain harvesting.

Could Joseph really take care of the tobacco picking? She'd planned to start that next week.

Could she trust the slaves left behind to keep things going? Perhaps one of the neighbors would check in once in a while.

Oh, God, this is too much. I can't leave Twin Oaks. And if I do, will there be anything left to come home to?

"Missy Jess, you all right?" Lucinda bent down to stare into her mistress's face.

Jesselynn nodded. "I will be. God will uphold and protect us." She wished she believed that as truly as her mother had. If God had been protecting them, why did her mother never recover from childbirth and her father and brother die in the war?

I will never leave you nor forsake you.

"Funny way you have of showing it."

"What dat you say?" Lucinda stopped on her way out the door.

"Nothing. Just muttering." Jesselynn got to her feet and ran her fingers through her hair. It barely covered the tops of her ears. She shook her head, and bits of hair flew free. But long tendrils did not slap her in the face, and her head felt strangely light. Maybe this wouldn't be so bad after all.

She returned to her own room and, after donning brown britches, a belt, and a white shirt, dug in the back of the closet for her porkpie hat, the one she'd worn when working the racing stock. It fit much better now that it didn't have all that hair to hold up. She eyed the two, broad-brimmed or porkpie. Of course she could take her father's straw hat . . . but she shook her head. Young boys didn't wear plantation owner hats.

She stared into the mirror. Did she look enough like a boy? She switched to the broader brimmed hat and pulled it lower onto her forehead. That was better. By lowering her chin, she could hide more of her face.

She'd have to deepen her voice too. When had her brothers' voices changed? Fifteen, sixteen? Earlier? With all that had happened in the last two years, somehow small facts like that had slipped away. She looked back in the mirror. How old did she look? She twisted her head from side to side. *After I dye my hair and skin, will that help?*

Whirling, she ran to the stairs, her boots clattering as she descended. "Lucinda?" She lowered her voice and tried again. "Lucinda!"

Lucinda came down the lower hall. "Comin'."

Jesselynn turned her body as if to study the empty space where her father's portrait had hung.

"Yessuh?" Lucinda stopped in the doorway.

"Is Miss Jesselynn to home?"

"Yessuh. Who I tells her is callin'?"

"Jonathan from Creekside."

"Wait here." Lucinda began to climb the stairs.

Jesselynn waited until Lucinda was halfway up the stairs before she looked up. "That's right kind of you, ma'am, but you won't find her up there."

Lucinda stopped with one foot on the upper riser. She looked down over the shiny walnut banister, rolled her eyes, and shook her head. "Well, I never . . ." Heaving a sigh, she came back down the stairs. "Such a trick to play on ol' Lucinda."

Jesselynn breathed a sigh of relief. If she could fool Lucinda, anyone else would be easy.

"Let's get the dye, all right?"

"Lawsy, what dis world comin' to?" Lucinda continued to shake her head as she made her way toward the back of the house. "I boiled up some walnut husks an' we see what happen." The sniff at the end made Jesselynn wonder if tears weren't clogging her mammy's throat as they were her own.

———

Jesselynn gathered the last of her things, her father's journal, and the precious ink bottle. When she walked by the mirror, she didn't even recognize herself. Were her hair not so straight and brown, she might have passed for one of the mulattos. She brushed walnut-colored hair back, but it fell forward onto her brow. Her hat would have to keep it back.

The grandfather clock in the hall struck eleven as they gathered for a final prayer. Sobs from some of the house slaves broke the silence as Jesselynn bowed her head. "Heavenly Father, we commit our lives into thy hands. Keep those of us on the road safe and those at home as well." She stopped and swallowed hard, trying to clear her throat and keep the tears at bay. She knew if she broke down, there would be such wailing that it would be heard clear to Lexington. "Please set your legions of angels in charge over us all. If it be thy will, bring Zachary safely home again." Oh, how she wanted to pray for God to take care of Cavendar Dunlivey in a permanent way. "Protect us from those who set to do us harm, we pray in thy holy name, amen."

"Missy Jesse?"

She whirled and, taking a step forward, glared up at Meshach. "You mean Marse Jesse!"

"Yessum—ah, suh." Meshach studied the wrinkled brim of his hat. The sound of a nighthawk called from the front portico. "Dat mean all is clear."

"All right." She turned to the others. "Now, you all know what you have to do. You will all refer to June as Miss Jesse, even when inside the house, in case Dunlivey makes it through those posted as guards. Everything will go on as usual here. If someone comes calling for me, say that I am indisposed or gone to town or something." She looked around the circle to make sure everyone nodded.

"All right, Ophelia, go get Thaddy. You and he will sleep in the back of the wagon."

"Yessum."

"What?" She spun on the slave as if to strike her.

"Yessuh." Ophelia ran up the stairs without looking back.

Dear God, if we manage this, it will be a miracle for sure.

Chapter Five

ON THE TRAIL
SEPTEMBER 18, 1862

Unlike Lot's wife, Jesselynn knew she didn't dare look back.

The squeak of the wagon wheels sounded like children screaming as they passed the two stone pillars and turned onto the road from the long drive of Twin Oaks. She didn't need to see the copper plaque posted on one to know what it said. TWIN OAKS. Established 1789 by Joshua A. Highwood. The two trees from which the plantation garnered its name stood sentinel at the junction as they had for longer than her family's memory. Story had it that her great-grandfather had picnicked under those trees the day his land grant was signed and delivered. His journal had described them as "two oaks, nearly perfect a match in size and shape, huge and majestic beyond description, offering shade for the weary, a home for birds and squirrels, and enough acorns to raise an entire herd of swine."

How his heart would break if he could see us now. Jesselynn wiped a tear from her eye with the back of her sleeve. *It's just too much—Father dying and now my having to leave. What will Zachary think when he returns? How can I do this? God, you are asking too much.*

She blew her nose and pressed the bridge between thumb and forefinger, anything to stop the tears. If her people—she refused to call them slaves any longer—if her people knew how she felt, they would not be able to go on.

Except perhaps Meshach. Since she'd given him his papers, he had become different. Always straight and broad shouldered, he no longer looked down at the ground when talking to anyone. He held his head high and looked a person in the eye. His speech too had changed some, but God help them if he called her "missy."

She flicked the reins for her team to pick up their feet. The mare on the right still hadn't quite gotten the idea of teamwork in wagon pulling, but at least she was willing. Ahab had not taken kindly to the harness, so Meshach was riding him. The mule didn't seem to care who pulled with him.

Why hadn't she thought to break them to harness earlier? She shook her head. Why so many things? Like her father had said, "If only you'd obeyed me two years ago . . ." The memory reopened the lacerations on her heart. Could one die of a broken heart?

"Riders up ahead," Daniel, who'd been riding point, whispered out of the darkness.

Jesselynn immediately pulled off the road under the bordering tree, the wagon wheels crushing brush as they hid. Thank God there was no stone wall or fencing here. She leaped from the wagon and ran to her horses' heads, clamping a hand over each muzzle so they wouldn't nicker.

Her heart made so much noise, she had a hard time listening for the riders. Grateful for the darkness, since the moon had yet to rise, she strained to hear, knowing Meshach and Daniel were near and doing the same thing. Benjamin would be ahead somewhere. Thank God she'd thought to give Thaddy a few drops of laudanum so he would sleep through anything. What if he cried out? Only soldiers or scum would likely be on the road at this hour. Once they were farther from home, they could disappear in among all the normal traffic. After all, what was one more wagon loaded with despair?

The clop of hooves, the jingle of spurs and bits, sounded like five or six horses. While one man said something, blood thundering in her ears kept her from picking out his words. The smell of tobacco smoke overlaid the fragrance of crushed leaves and bark. Her eyes ached and watered from trying to peer through the darkness. One of her horses stamped a foot.

Now she knew what a deer felt like when it suspected danger. Her mind wept *Oh, God, help us. Please help us!* over and over till she thought she would scream. They waited what seemed like half the night from the time they could hear even the faintest sound of the riders.

"Go now," Meshach said right next to her. She hadn't heard him moving at all. Her heart leaped back up in her throat, and she clamped a hand to her chest.

"Oh." Leaning her forehead against the warm neck of the mare, she waited for her heartbeat to settle back down and her knees to regain their strength before she climbed back up in the wagon. Right at the moment, she wasn't sure she could make it.

"Marse Jesse, you all right?"

"Yes, thank you." *At least I soon will be.* She patted the mare's neck and, in spite of nearly tripping over broken brush, got herself back up on the wagon seat.

"Oh, Mi-Marse Jesse, I skeered so bad I 'most wet my drawers." Ophelia's whisper made Jesselynn smile, then start to chuckle.

"Me too, Ophelia, me too."

A giggle from behind added to her chuckle, and by the time they had the wagon back up on the road and running straight again, all of them, except for the sleeping child, were choking, trying to keep from laughing so loud that any other stragglers out on the road might hear them.

Sheer relief, that's what it is. Jesselynn could no more cap the gurgling laughter than fly back home to Twin Oaks. Twin Oaks. She sobered as if she'd had a bucket of water doused on her head. Had that been Dunlivey returning to watch over the home place?

Watch! Ha! Spy! That's all he is. A spy, and one cruel beyond measure at that.

She flicked the reins, and the horses picked up a fast trot. They clattered over a stone bridge, echoes bouncing from the low stone walls. Before long they turned west onto the Lexington/Frankfort Pike and picked up the pace, needing to be off the pike before sunrise and miles from Twin Oaks.

Her eyes burned as if she'd been standing in the smoke from a fire, and her rump ached from the hard boards by the time Meshach cantered back to them just as the birds made their first twitterings. The sun had yet to reach the horizon, but already she could see the features of the landscape. The trees grew taller as they drew closer to the Kentucky River, and the gently rolling hills sported pastureland with plots of trees. Stone fences, their flat capstones set on a slant, looked like gray medieval fortresses in miniature. Mist hugged the hollows. Horses whinnied. Roosters heralded the rising sun.

"Dorsey up ahead. We takes a road off to de left," Meshach said.

She nodded and rubbed her eyes with the tips of chilled fingers. Tomorrow night someone else could drive the wagon and she would ride. She heard rustlings in the wagon bed behind her.

Ophelia yawned and climbed over the supplies until she sat beside Jesselynn. "We stoppin' soon?"

"Soon." They both kept their voices low so as not to wake Thaddy.

Jesselynn turned on the road Meshach had indicated and saw Daniel waving at her a hundred or more yards ahead. In spite of the weariness that dragged her down, she wished they could keep on going. Farther out, maybe they could travel some during the day, when they and their horses wouldn't be so easily recognized.

Although looking at the team in front of her, she doubted anyone would believe the mare pulling with the mule was the dam of four Keeneland Derby winners. Two of her progeny were at stud already. And paid for handsomely in spite of the war. They were probably dead on the battlefield by now if the armies had had their choice. Unless others had already done what her father had told her to do two years ago.

"Dey's water here and even pasture fo' de horses."

Daniel rode beside her, showing the way after they left the narrowing dirt road.

"Meshach say we be safe here."

"Good."

Mockingbirds trilled their morning arias when she stepped down from the wagon with a groan. Squirrels chattered from the oak trees, informing them and the world of the invasion.

Jesselynn stretched, kneading her lower back with her fists and leaning from side to side. There was indeed water. A creek burbled over moss-covered rocks and around knobby roots. Out in the open, where the sun was already stretching golden fingers across the grass, the blades sparkled green, like a welcome mat sprinkled with diamonds.

Ahab snorted at their arrival and dropped his head to graze again, his front legs hobbled so he couldn't run or even walk fast.

Meshach came out of the trees with an armload of dried branches and dumped them by a fire pit that showed others had used this glen for respite. " 'Phelia, you get dem fryin' pans and such out of de wagon. Since you slept all night, you get de breakfast."

"Do we dare start a fire?" Jesselynn listened for any nearby farm sounds. Only the creek's gurgling and the birdsong broke the early morning silence.

"I think yes. We off de main road a mile or so, and de next farm way down over dere." He pointed to the west. "Can't see de clearin' from de road."

"How did you find this place?"

Meshach studied the dusty toe of his boot. "Don' ask. Just say I heard tell of it."

"Oh." Was this one of those places where runaway slaves could stop in safety? And had her people ever thought of running off? What did they talk about down in the quarters when the marse wasn't around?

"Lynnie?" Thaddy's voice came thinly from the wagon bed. "Lynnie?"

Jesselynn trotted to the wagon and lifted her little brother out of his nest. "Shush. You musn't talk loud." She kissed his cheek, pink from sleep, and settled him on her hip. "Come, let's go."

She sent an inquiring look Meshach's way, and he nodded.

"Just stay close."

When trees and low bushes screened them from camp, she pushed down his diapers and let him pee in the creek, much to his delight. Then while he threw twigs and pebbles in the clear water, she relieved herself, thinking immediately of the niceties of home. She would have had a pitcher of warm water to wash with, one of the household slaves would have emptied the slop jar, and breakfast would have been ready when she descended the stairs. But that was home, and this was now.

Dipping her handkerchief in the water, she used it to wash Thaddy's hands and face.

"Cold." He pulled away, scrunching up his face. "No more."

"Be a big boy, Thaddy."

"Go home now?"

I wish we could. Instead she knelt down in front of him and, laying her hands along his cheeks, looked deep in his eyes. "Listen to me, Thaddy, and listen good. Call me Jesse from now on, you hear me?"

"Lynnie."

"Not anymore, little brother." She shook her head. "Not anymore, and don't you forget it. Now, what is my name?" She dropped her hands to his shoulders and shook him gently.

His lower lip came out, and his eyes narrowed. At that moment he looked so much like his older brother Zachary that she blinked.

"No. Jes-sie-lynn," he said slowly.

Jesselynn sighed and rocked back on her heels. Right enough, she'd approached him the wrong way. One thing this child didn't lack was southern backbone. He'd go along nice as you please until . . . She'd just come up against that until.

How much do you tell a two-and-a-half-year-old child?

Seeking to corral her thoughts, Jesselynn picked up a stick with a caterpillar attached. She handed it to Thaddeus, sure that it would distract him for a moment while she thought what to do.

He held on to the stick and giggled as the fuzzy caterpillar humped his back feet up to his front.

"Thaddy, how would you like to play a game with me?"

He studied the now extended caterpillar.

Jesselynn sighed and got to her feet. Dipping her handkerchief again, she washed her own face and hands, ran damp fingers through her shorn hair, and set her hat back in place. They were ready for the day, and all she could think of was a hot meal and a soft bed, or any bed for that matter.

She took her little brother's hand. "Bet you don't know what my new name is."

"Jesselynn Marie Highwood." He glanced from the stick up to her, then grinned. "Jesse. Me new name?"

She let out a sigh of relief. *Not a bad idea.* How could this child be so smart? "Sure, what would you like?"

"Meshach."

"Ah, that's a good name, but it already belongs to Meshach over there. Think of another." They wound through the trees as they talked, Thaddeus all the time careful to keep his caterpillar on the stick.

"Joshwa." He stopped walking and looked up at her. "My daddy gone to heaven name, huh?"

Her eyes flooded. Pain gripped her heart. She sank to her knees and pulled Thaddeus into her arms, hugging him close so he couldn't see her tears. "That's a fine name. One I'm proud to call you by." She sniffed and relinquished him when he squirmed.

"Oh, my catepiwar." He looked around on the leaf-strewn ground. "Find him."

Jesselynn rocked back on her heels just in time to see that the caterpillar had been smashed by her knee. She fluffed some leaves over it and, rising, pulled him to his feet. "We'll look for another one later. See, Ophelia has breakfast about ready."

"Want my catepiwar." The lower lip jutted out and his face screwed up in what Jesselynn knew could give rise to a wail fit to raise the soundest sleeper.

"You eat, I'll look. Come, Joshua, tell everyone your new name."

His face cleared, and he ran to stand by his hero, tugging on the man's pants. "Meshach. Meshach."

"What you wants, little marse?" Meshach picked Thaddy up so they were eye to eye.

"Me new name. Like Jessel—Jesse." He glanced over his shoulder to see her approval. When she nodded, he smiled and turned back to his holder. He thumped his chest. "Me Joshwa."

Meshach nodded slowly. "Yessuh, that a fine name. We all call you Joshua, little marse. How dat?"

"Good." Thaddy pushed back. "Eat now."

Jesselynn took the plate Ophelia brought her and sat down on the wagon tongue. "Thank you." Looking around at the sun-dappled ground, the hobbled horses grazing on the open glen, her people sitting cross-legged on the ground or on a hunk of wood and laughing softly while they ate—it all made her think more of a picnic than a flight for their lives. Or at least their horses' lives, she corrected her meandering thoughts. Her mind skittered away from thoughts of any of them really being in danger. Only the horses.

A crow flew overhead. His raucous announcement that there were strangers in his woods sent shivers up her back. What if they were indeed running for their lives?

She shook her head. *There you go, borrowing trouble,* she scolded herself and returned Ophelia's smile as she picked up Jesselynn's plate. One hint of superstition like that and they'd all be moaning and crying like death was at their very door.

She stared into the dregs of her cup. What she wouldn't give for a cup of real coffee. The ground chickory looked like coffee, but the semblance ended there. However, it was hot and not too bitter when laced with milk. If only they had brought the cow. Instead, she hoped to buy milk along the way. Surely there would be farmers with a gallon or so of milk to sell. The cow could never have kept the pace she hoped to set, not and produce milk too.

She emptied the sludge in the bottom of her cup out on the ground and got to her feet. One good thing, britches beat skirts any day for the walking and climbing around she needed to do to check their supplies.

"You take de bed under de wagon"—Meshach nodded to the pallet laid out—"and sleep now. We all take turns."

Jesselynn nodded. Somewhere along the line Meshach had assumed the leading role here, and if she weren't so tired, she'd talk to him about that. Right now, thoughts in any kind of order were beyond her.

———

She woke with the sun in the western sky and the sound of gunfire.

Chapter Six

❧

"Why'd you let me sleep so long?" She kept her voice to a hiss.

Meshach shook his head. "You needed sleep." He cocked his head, listening. "Dey goin' away." He nodded toward the east.

"You're sure?"

"Um. Been lis'nin'."

"Where's Benjamin?"

"Scoutin'."

Jesselynn glanced around the campsite. Ophelia and Thaddy were sound asleep on a pallet under a full-branched oak. Ahab raised his head, studied the sounds from the east, and dropped his muzzle to graze again.

"Ahab better'n a watchdog."

"Prettier too." The guns were indeed going the other way; even she could tell that by now.

"We cross the ferry at dusk tonight." She wasn't sure if it were a question or an order.

"Yes, Marse." A smile tugged at the edge of his full lips. "Benjamin say river low enough to swim horses. Only take wagon on de ferry."

"We could save money that way."

"And be safe."

Jesselynn knew it was her turn to smile — and nod. She reached back under the wagon to pull out her boots. Wide awake as she was, she might as well write in her journal. Someday someone might want to read what happened on their way west.

That afternoon when they pulled out, Jesselynn sat on the wagon seat beside Meshach, and Ophelia rocked a sleeping Thaddeus in her arms. As they drew nearer to Clifton, where the ferry crossed the Kentucky River, she pulled a sheet over his face and kept on rocking.

Jesselynn swallowed to keep the fear from knotting her tongue and strangling her throat. Would someone be watching for them? They waited while the ferry, nothing more than a flat raft, was pulled from one side of the river to the other by a hawser attached to a single tree and pulled by a mule. When they unloaded, the mule on the east side of the river took over, and the ferry returned.

A woman approached the wagon. "That'll be fifty cents."

Jesselynn dug the coins out of her pocket and handed them over. *Maybe we should have swum the whole rig at that price.*

"Thankee."

Meshach nodded. "Welcome." He slapped the reins, and the team walked up the ramp placidly as if they did so every day.

Jesselynn let out a sigh and felt her shoulders slump. So far so good. As the ferry glided to the other side and bumped against the bank, the man on that side shoved the planks in place and off they walked.

Meshach nodded again and touched the brim of his hat as they drove up the bank and onto the westering road. A mile or so later, Benjamin and Daniel rode up on wet horses, leading the other two.

"We did it." Jesselynn slapped her knees and let out a decidedly unladylike whoop. "Okay, Ahab, my turn to ride." She leaped from the wagon and beat Benjamin to the saddle, slinging it and the pad over the stallion's back with smooth motions. Once bridled, she mounted and grinned at her people. "Now, let's get outa here."

After looking toward Jesselynn for permission, Ophelia settled Thaddeus on the pallet and climbed up on the wagon seat, her smile pure pleasure at being able to sit closer to the man with the reins. With Meshach driving the wagon, Jesselynn nudged Ahab forward, and the trip took on an entirely new meaning for her. All the years she'd halfheartedly obeyed the strictures of young woman-hood, she could now hear Lucinda as if she rode right behind her. *"Young ladies don' wear britches. Young ladies don' ride stallions."* And, oh, if she could only hear her mother speaking again, telling her to speak softly, to walk not run, to work before taking pleasure.

But she couldn't, so she paid attention to what she was doing. The horse she rode wanted to run. That's what Ahab had been bred for, and he fought the bit and the strength of her hands. If only she dared let him run for a while, just to top him off, but she knew better. Nothing in the world would attract more attention than the two of them racing down the road.

She brought him to a standstill and patted his sweat-dotted neck. "All right, old son, you can do this the hard way or the easy way, but I'll warn you right now, it's going to be my way." The stallion snorted as the other members of the party pulled on ahead. He twitched his tail and shifted from foot to foot.

Jesselynn tightened the reins and kept up a murmur that would soothe any fractious critter, two-legged or four. Ahab sighed and, flat-footed now, shook his head, his burr-filled mane slapping from side to side. She ached to clean him up, but the rougher he looked the better. Gone was the sparkling white blaze down his face and the rear off-white sock. His coat, dyed with walnut husks like her hair, looked rough and patchy, no longer that striking blood bay of days before. Even the river bath hadn't removed the dye, another worry off her mind.

Joseph and Meshach had done a good job on all the horses. By tomorrow perhaps Ahab would tolerate the harness. Meshach had worked him under it in the afternoon.

She let him trot until they caught up and no longer had to fight her horse and the fear that rose at every sound. Horses whinnied when they passed a farm, and dogs barked, but no one ordered them to stop. She rode alongside the wagon, glancing over to check on Thaddeus—or Joshua, as he now insisted on being called. How their father would have loved to hear "Joshwa," as the boy said it.

They'd ridden for several hours when she heard a horse galloping their way. Benjamin pulled to a stop in front of them. "Sojers ahead."

With woods on both sides of them, they hurried along the road, searching for a place to get the wagon through the trees. Jesselynn rode ahead, her heart pounding louder than the sound of her horse's hooves. Since it wasn't full dark yet, they needed to hide quickly. Her heart hammered until she saw a lighter place between trees. She beckoned to Meshach on the wagon.

"They're just up ahead. Hurry."

They'd barely cleared the opening when she heard the horses coming toward them. All of them had dismounted to cover their horses' muzzles.

God, please make them blind. Surely our tracks lead in here. She could feel Ahab come to attention as he shifted his front feet. She kept one hand firmly over his nose and the other clamped to the reins under his chin.

Horses and riders passed, then wagons.

Mosquitoes buzzed and drank their fill, for she had no hands to slap them. Sweat trickled down her back, her legs, her forehead. The wet beads burned her eyes, eyes that already ached from staring through the darkness, wishing for a night so black they couldn't be seen.

Was it the entire Confederate army passing by?

Where were Daniel and Benjamin?

She needed a drink. To cough. Her throat tightened. She swallowed. She tried clearing it softly with gentle pressure. She clamped two fingers over her nose to keep from sneezing. Ahab shifted.

The canteen on her saddle might as well have been in Lexington.

Now that it was truly dark, she wished she could see.

An owl hooted off in the woods. A mockingbird sang his night song. No matter how hard she strained, she could no longer hear the jingle of harness nor the clump of hooves.

She sagged against Ahab's shoulder and finally coughed. Her shoulders ached, her fingers too. The bones in her legs felt about as stout as newly washed chitlins.

When she swallowed, the fear tasted metallic, as if she'd chewed a patch of skin off the inside of her cheek and it bled.

"You all right?" Meshach spoke right by her shoulder.

She jumped as if he'd leaped from behind a wall and shrieked "boo" as her brothers used to do to tease her. Clapping a hand to her racing heart, she swallowed again. "I-I'm fine. How are the others?"

"Thaddy sleepin'. 'Phelia done good wid 'im."

"Good." Jesselynn fumbled for her canteen. She felt like pouring it over her head but instead took only a few swallows. "Hold Ahab and I'll be right back."

"Don' go far."

"No, I won't."

Back in the saddle they waited what seemed like hours for Benjamin to signal the all clear so they could drive back up on the road. How many miles had they sacrificed? It felt like half the night. They picked up a fast trot and kept the pace until the team was blowing and even Ahab had worked up a sweat. In spite of the jolting, Thaddeus slept curled next to Ophelia on the pallet of quilts in the back of the wagon.

First light lent its silvery sheen to the woods and farms as they trotted along the road, now searching for a place to spend the day.

"How far to Bardstown?" Jesselynn pulled back to ride by the wagon.

"Don' know fo' sure." Meshach studied the area around them. "Maybe git dere tomorrow night. I think we bypassed Lawrenceburg."

"We've got to lay up soon." A dog barked off to the left. Farmers would be heading for milking and fieldwork at any time. If they came upon a racing farm, the horses would be out on the track for morning works.

Jesselynn shook her head at the thought. No, they wouldn't. Most all the horses had already been conscripted, and while she was sure other farms were hiding what horses they could, no one would dare use the tracks.

The dog continued to bark, setting the next farm's watchdogs to doing the same. They had to find a place to camp.

From the looks of things when they topped a long grade, their wood cover had about been overrun with farming. Tall barns with slatted sides that could be raised to let the airflow dry the tobacco outnumbered the horse barns crowned with cupolas.

Did they dare ask for refuge in a barn?

Jesselynn shook her head again. That would be a last resort.

The rising sun gilded the treetops, setting fire to those that had begun to don fall dress.

"De sojers get us?" Ophelia raised her head, fear widening her eyes.

"No, you and Thaddy just go right on back to sleep." Meshach smiled over his shoulder, his voice reassuring.

Jesselynn wished she could believe him. Her eyes burned and her head felt as if it might fall right off her neck. While she loved to ride, and britches made riding astride possible, riding for pleasure and riding all night to escape were two mighty different things. Her rear hurt, her shoulders ached, and even Ahab was drooping. She had to nudge him sometimes to keep up an even trot.

She felt jiggled to pieces.

The sun broke from the horizon and bounded into the sky.

God, hide us. You say you are our refuge. Help us find a place to hide.

Panic tasted as bad as fear. Ahab's ears pricked forward. A lone rider was coming toward them at a good clip.

"Benjamin come."

Jesselynn knew Meshach must be right, but it was several seconds before she was sure herself.

Benjamin waved, beckoning them to speed up, then turned back the way he'd come. They picked up their speed, but breaking into a canter would attract more attention. Jesselynn rode back to the wagon.

"Here, you take Ahab and the filly with you and get out of sight. A young man with a wagon and one slave won't attract as much attention."

"No, Marse, I not do dat."

"Yes, you will." She swung to the ground just in front of the team, causing them all to stop, harnesses jingling in protest. She handed the reins up to Meshach and mounted the wagon wheel. "Now hurry."

Meshach hesitated one more heart-stopping second, his dark eyes snapping fire and his jaw carved in rock.

Jesselynn held her breath, at the same time reaching for the team reins. "You know I'm right." She kept her voice low, trying to guard against Ophelia starting to whimper and wake Thaddeus.

When the big black took the stallion's reins and jumped to the ground, all the air left her lungs and she sank onto the wagon seat. Within seconds he had untied the filly, mounted Ahab, and galloped after Benjamin.

She could feel his anger carried back to her on the wind. But his years of slave training had held. Marse was always right. She clucked the team into a trot and followed the two she could barely see ahead. A man on a horse cantered past them, calling a greeting as he pulled even. When he went on without saying any more than that, Jesselynn felt she could breathe again. Had her voice sounded low enough for a young man? Slurring her words helped somewhat, adopting the softer sounds of the slaves instead of her own more perfect speech. Her father had insisted those in the big house speak properly, in spite of their Kentucky drawl.

About a mile farther, Benjamin sat his horse by the side of the road, and as soon as Jesselynn answered his wave, he trotted off down a side road. Since a loaded wagon was coming toward them, she kept her chin low as she gently pulled the team down to an easier turning pace. The man driving the wagon looked familiar, but she refused to look over her shoulder. She was sure the man was the overseer of the Tarlander Plantation to the east of Twin Oaks, but evidencing any interest could catch the other's attention.

Thank God Ahab and Meshach were out of sight. He'd worked for Tarlander more than once and would surely have been recognized.

"Was that who I think it was?" she asked Benjamin when he waited for her at a bridge crossing a wide creek.

"Yessuh." Benjamin shook his head. "Dat close." He turned his horse. "Not far now."

They gathered in a small clearing bordering the creek, where Daniel awaited them. He was already gathering sticks for a fire.

Jesselynn reached behind her to help a groggy Thaddeus climb up on the seat. "You been a mighty good boy. I'm right proud of you."

"Hungry?" He reached up and wrapped his arms around her neck. Burrowing into her chest like a little gopher, he repeated with more insistence. "Hungry. Want milk."

Jesselynn sighed. Where would they get milk? Other fresh food too, for that matter. Her eyes felt as if they'd been rolling in the Sahara Desert, and her rear felt permanently glued to the hard seat.

"I git some." Benjamin remounted his horse.

"You'd best take the mule, then," Jesselynn said.

"Oh." He dismounted with a nod. " 'Phelia, you got a jug?"

Meshach unhitched the team and removed the harness from both horse and mule, then slipped a bridle with short reins on the mule. "You hurry."

After handing Benjamin a couple of their precious store of coins, Jesselynn climbed over the wagon wheel and, when her feet felt solid ground, leaned against the wheel until her knees no longer felt like buckling. She propped her head on hands crossed on the iron wheel rim, thinking only of her bed back at Twin Oaks. The mosquito net draped just so, clean sheets cool to the skin, a mattress that molded to one's body and let sleep come like a welcome visitor.

Not like a sledgehammer against rocks.

At this point, however, the sledgehammer and rock base would be appreciated. But they had to eat first and take care of the animals. Good thing Ophelia could sleep during the night, so she could be awake with Thaddeus, who was at the moment running from tree to tree, peeking out and giggling as he dodged Ophelia's reaching hands.

Jesselynn wasn't sure who was having more fun, the boy or the woman just grown beyond girlhood. She watched, wishing she had the stamina to join in. Every bone and muscle creaked and groaned when she left the wagon-wheel prop. Meshach already had the horses all hobbled, and Daniel was starting a fire to cook breakfast.

She should be helping. She should be telling them what to do. After all, that's what the mistress of the plantation did—set the tasks for the day and then make sure everyone was working. Somehow there seemed to be a shift in positions here, and at the moment she didn't much care.

She dragged her protesting body over to the creek and lay down flat on her belly to get her face close enough to the water to wash it without too much effort. Skirts would have prohibited such an action with the ease she accomplished it. Britches were definitely more accommodating. The cool water on her face made her dunk again. She clutched her hat in one hand and swished her face back and forth in the water, scrubbing with the other hand. Her hair dripped water in her face, and it ran down her neck into her shirt when she twisted to a sitting position. Now for her feet.

Thaddeus ran up as she finished untying her bootlaces. "Me too."

Jesselynn grunted as she jerked her boots off and wriggled her toes.

Thaddy recognized a lap when he saw it and climbed in. Reaching up, he patted Jesselynn's cheek with one chubby hand, at the same time inching down her legs toward the goal.

"Wait a minute, wiggle worm." She reached for the buttons on his shoes. "You can't go in the water with your shoes on."

He giggled again, the merry sound flirting with the birdsong from the trees above.

"All right." She set him on his feet and gave his bottom a pat. "Now hang on to my hand and . . ."

Thaddeus already had his toes in the meandering water, giggling even louder. He leaned forward to catch a floating leaf.

Jesselynn snagged the back of his britches just in time. "I said wait." She set him on his feet, ankle-deep in the water. He squished his toes in the smooth gravel and leaned forward again. This time she held him steady with a firm grasp of his suspenders so he could splash water, and wade, and not tumble in.

"Coffee."

She turned at the call and loosened her grip just enough for him to sit splat in the shallow water. "Thaddy!"

"Me Joshwa." He held up his hand and let the water trickle down his arm, making him giggle again.

"Come, let's go eat."

"No." He slapped his palms on the water surface and chortled at the spray.

Jesselynn groaned. She could tell by the look on his face that he wasn't ready to be taken out of the creek. And when Thaddeus wasn't ready to be moved, his roar would be heard clear to the Mississippi.

"Ophelia has bread and jam for you."

"No."

"Butter and sugar on bread?"

"No." He slapped the water surface again.

How did he get so spoiled? But she knew. No one wanted to say no to a motherless, and now a fatherless, little boy or make him unhappy. There was too much sorrow in his life already. But she didn't dare leave him for one minute either. While the creek was shallow on the edges, the center clipped along at a good pace, and she hadn't really checked to see how deep it was. But babies drowned in buckets, and though Thaddeus surely didn't consider himself a baby, if he fell flat out, the current might keep him from getting to his feet again.

She waded out and, rolling up her pant legs, stood in water to her knees. Her mother might just as well have been watching from behind the trees, her voice came so clear. "*Jesselynn Highwood, young ladies do not show off their ankles like that, nor their knees. For shame.*" For a minute, Jesselynn wished for both her mother and Lucinda. She snatched her thoughts back from memories of home as if being stung by bees. "Only look forward, girl. Only forward."

"Huh? You talkin' to me?" Ophelia stood on the creek bank.

"Ah, no. To myself." Jesselynn took in a deep breath and let it all out. Now that she thought of it again, her aches hadn't really gone away. "Come on, Thaddeus, we are going for breakfast now."

He looked up at her, eyes squinting to judge if her face matched her tone. When he saw it did, he raised his hand and stood when she took it. "Up."

She swung him to her hip. "You're all wet."

He patted her cheek. "Water good."

She turned at the sound of a horse cantering toward them. If it wasn't Benjamin, they could be in a heap of trouble.

Chapter Seven

RICHMOND, VIRGINIA

"Wounded comin' off the train."

Louisa Highwood settled the patient down against the meager pillow. She'd been holding him up so he could take a drink of water. "I'll be back soon as I can," she told him.

"Thankee, Missy." His mountain dialect no longer felt strange upon her ears. These days she was grateful when the men that entered her wards could talk. Leastways that usually meant they weren't slipping through death's door.

"I will be back." The gratitude blazing from his eyes caused her to lay a hand on his shoulder. "Soon as possible."

He nodded, and his eyes drifted closed.

While Louisa had volunteered at the hospital to read to the wounded and perhaps write letters home for those who couldn't, in reality, she'd become more of a nurse's helper in the month she'd been there. The soldiers called her an angel of mercy. God knew this place needed huge doses of mercy.

At first the older nurses had tried to protect her from the ghastly sight of male bodies ripped by shrapnel and blown apart by bullets. The stench alone was enough to make a stalwart man blanch. They kept her from the operating room, but life on the wards was one horror story after another.

Keeping a smile in place took a chunk of her will. Sometimes she bathed wounds with her tears when there was no medicine available. The Yankees blew up enough railroad track to keep supplies low. A sailing ship had run the blockade to bring in much-needed supplies until the Confederates regained ground and rebuilt the tracks.

She spent much of her time washing faces ravaged by pain and bringing cooling cups of water. Walking swiftly down the center aisle, she promised to be right back to all who called to her. An empty bed made her shut her eyes and swallow. John, the man who'd occupied that bed yesterday had not gone home, at least not to his earthly home. The letter he'd shown her from his wife told about a son born after he went to war.

Like Thaddeus at home. Twin Oaks, where what to wear that day had been the morning's main decision, where her older sister Jesselynn tried to get Louisa and Carrie Mae to help her on the plantation after Mother died, and Daddy and her brothers had ridden off to war. Maybe if she'd been more helpful, Jesselynn wouldn't have banished her to Richmond.

"Hurry, Miz Highwood, we needs you." The call came from one of the helpers outside. It was their job to bring the stretchers in, if they could find a place, that is. In the meantime, heat and flies and untreated wounds added to the death toll.

Louisa wiped her hands on an apron already stiff with blood and other unmentionables and wished she had time to stop for a drink herself. Pushing hair the color of honey-laced molasses back in a loosening chignon, she paused only a moment at the top of the steps. Real air. At least compared to that inside. Using the back of her hand, she dried the sweat—she no longer referred to the rivulets as perspiration—from her broad forehead clear down to her slightly pointed chin. She'd been told her eyes were her best feature, amber with flecks of gold, but right now all she could think was that they ached and she had no use for long lashes. She never batted them at anyone anyway. More than once she'd been told with her slight figure that she wasn't strong enough to help lift heavy men, but she knew there was strength in leanness, and she used it well.

"Over here." Jacob, taller and stronger than most of the free black men who'd been hired to assist, reminded her of Meshach back home. He moved from stretcher to stretcher, cloaked in a gentle spirit and a heart that ached like hers at the carnage.

While the doctors tried to keep her out of the maelstrom of incoming wounded, Jacob recognized those who needed her hand to give them strength. Joining the ebony-skinned man, she looked down at the stretcher and the man whose field bandages were now soaked and crusty with blood. Either the doctors or the bullet had taken one leg off below the knee and bound both the stump and the man's head, leaving only part of his jaw visible. His right arm was taped to his body to protect better than a sling.

She knelt in the dust and laid her hand on the man's heart and felt the strong beat. "Let's move him into John's bed. That's the only one left on our ward."

Jacob nodded and beckoned another assistant to help him.

While there, Louisa checked the man behind her but knew before she even touched him that he was beyond help. Death had won again. She moved down the row, her low murmur as soothing as her touch.

"Am I in heaven?" A soldier squinted against the sun's glare. " 'Cause if there's angels around, can't be hell." He coughed, and pink drool leaked from the side of his mouth.

Oh, God, why do you let this continue? Louisa had long ago given up the dream of an easy victory for the South. There was no glory in war. Her brothers had lied to her and to themselves. She beckoned to another freeman and pointed at the dead man. "Take him over there, and bring this man to my ward. I'll find a place."

They did as she said while she turned to the muttering man on the next pallet.

"What are you doin' out here?" The man, outlined by the blazing sun, stopped behind her.

Why, I'm pourin' afternoon tea. What all did you think? She bit back the retort and rose to her feet. She still had to tilt her head to see his face, shielding her eyes with her hand. Between his size and the fiery aura surrounding him, he might have been God himself.

"This is surely no place for a woman of your tender years. Get on home now."

He had to be new. Most of the other doctors were so grateful for help that they ignored her obvious age. Or lack thereof.

"I'm sorry you feel that way, sir, but my—the men need water, and usually I'm reading to them or writing for them. Surely that is within the bounds of Christian charity. Christ himself said—"

"I know what Christ said, miss, but He wasn't in the midst of a military hospital."

"No, sir. His battle was much bigger." She kept her voice gentle, hoping she sounded more like her mother than the harridan she'd been accused of one day. She backed away, knowing that if he sent her home, there would be nothing she could do about it—today. And she wanted to get inside to help with the man Jacob carried in first. There was something about that man.

"Doctor, over here." The call caught his attention, and Louisa hurried for the ward.

"He just wants to protect you," one of the older women said in passing. "You mustn't take it to heart. If I didn't need you so bad, I would never let you help here like you do. It isn't seemly, I know, but these are terrible times, and 'seemly' seems not so important any longer."

"Thank you." Louisa heard one of her patients calling. "I must go."

Between her and Jacob, they had the two new men cleaned up and resting on fresh sheets before the doctor arrived on the ward. Louisa held the enameled pan to catch the discarded bandages, which would be taken out to the washroom and boiled clean, then rerolled and used again. The man in the bed groaned but never regained awareness.

"Just do what you can. The longer he stays unconscious, the better off he'll be. Then the pain won't kill him at least."

"What about his head?"

"Not as bad as it looks. Head wounds always bleed profusely. He won't be so handsome as before, but the bullet didn't puncture the skull. Not sure if we can save the eye or not. Hardheaded man, he." Captain Tate, one of the few doctors who thanked Louisa instead of trying to chase her away, finished tying off the bandages around the head of the wounded man and got to his feet, his knees creaking with the effort. He looked down at his patient. "He's one of the lucky ones. No more war for him. If you can keep him alive, he'll go home."

He took the basin from Louisa and handed it to Jacob. "See that this makes it back to the caldrons, boy." He checked the arm stub of the man in the next bed and then looked up to his standing helper. "Lead on, dear Miz Highwood. I heard you have another new recruit."

"Down here."

When the doctor left the ward, Louisa took her water pail out to the pump in back of the hospital and nodded to the helper who leaned on the pump handle and began the requisite number of pumps to bring the cool water up from the well.

At least the hospital had a well, and a clean one at that.

"Thank you." She picked up her bucket and stopped, staring up at the tall windows on the second-floor wing, her ward. Seen from the outside, the brick walls and white-painted window trim gave no hint of the suffering inside. But when one opened the door, a miasma of moaning, despair, and the stench of putrefying flesh smothered the air, making it not only imprudent but impossible to draw in a deep breath. The September heat lay like a featherbed over the building, trapping the heat in the bricks. Even the leaves of the elm trees hung limp, too tired to rustle.

She'd become adept at shallow breathing.

The cries for help, for God, for home, were a different matter.

At least she could bring water.

"Miz Highwood, ain't it time for you to git on home?" One of the men who could now sit up nodded toward the dusking window. "Not good for you to be out after dark. Ain't safe."

"Thank you, I'm about to go. Aunt Sylvania always sends one of her servants to fetch me." Her aunt had given up trying to keep Louisa from the hospital, and now that Carrie Mae's wedding was drawing nearer, she had other things on her mind besides a niece who might have coined the word "stubborn."

Louisa set her pail down on the bench designated for it and glanced around the room. So much more to do and never enough help. If only she could get Carrie Mae down here, but the day she did come at Louisa's importuning, she'd fainted dead away at the sight of the men on stretchers waiting to be seen by the doctor.

"You comin' back?" one of the other men whispered as she walked the middle aisle, stopping to adjust a sheet, a pillow, touch a shoulder.

"First thing in the mornin'." She stopped at the man lying in John's bed. She couldn't think of it any other way until they at least knew this man's name. But he never stirred when she touched his hand. If only they could keep him alive long enough to find out who he was.

She studied the line of his jaw. What did he look like under those bandages? Would he recognize himself in the mirror when he awoke? What was there about him that seemed familiar?

"You got the purtiest hair, ma'am." A soldier who looked too young to shave tried to raise his head but winced and let it fall back. "Please don't think I'm bein' forward."

"I won't if you promise to rest and get well."

He shook his head with the barest motion. "Them nightmares. They make sleepin' purt near impossible, but I'll try." Eyes, circled and crisscrossed with red and sunken back in his skull, pleaded for her touch.

She took his hand and patted it. "I'll bring my Bible with me again tomor-row and read you some."

"Thankee, Miz Highwood. You git on home now."

Louisa stopped at the doorway and looked back. How many of them would still be there when she returned in the morning?

Chapter Eight

ॐ

"Town up ahead, mile or so." Meshach trotted Sunshine, the mare, alongside the wagon.

"Can we go out around it?" Jesselynn straightened her shoulders. She'd been nearly asleep.

"Night dark like this make no nevermind."

Driving through a town, no matter how small, brought out the knots in her stomach. "How far ahead is Benjamin?"

" 'Bout half mile. He waitin' on us."

There'd have to be a direct confrontation on a moonless night like the one they were driving through for anyone to even get a glimpse of them. They didn't know anyone this far from home, so how would anyone know them? Besides, they'd only be sounds, dark as it was.

"What do you think?"

"Go on through. Save time. I tie up to de wagon and drive. Dat way someone see us, dey not 'spect some nigger stealin' de hosses and wagon."

Jesselynn thought of her team. Even Ahab looked more like a workhorse now. He was tired enough to plod along, head down, the arch gone from his neck and the lift from his tail. The horses had begun to take on the nondescript look needed to keep them safe in the daylight, let alone the night.

What to do?

A dog barked off to their right. Another answered, but there was no excited yip of a dog coming to see who they were. They were just doing their job, announcing someone going by.

"All right." She tightened the reins with a soft "whoa," and the wagon squeaked to a halt. They needed to get some grease for the wagon wheels. So many things she should have thought to bring. So many she hadn't been aware they'd need.

Meshach stripped the saddle from the mare and tied her to the tailgate along with the filly.

"We's a'right?" Ophelia's sleepy voice came from the pallet where she and Thaddeus slept each night.

"Sho' 'nuff, sugar, you g'wan back to sleep."

If only I could crawl back there and sleep too. Jesselynn felt like rubbing her rear. Riding horse or hard bench, either way her rump hurt by the end of the night. Never had she thought that walking would feel good. Or that running would feel better. But not with someone chasing them.

She scooted over and Meshach clucked the team into motion again. "Where's the rifle?"

"Right behind us."

Jesselynn reached back and grabbed the stock, then settled the gun at their feet. Better safe than sorry, as her mother had always said. But then Miriam Highwood hadn't been fleeing across the state of Kentucky either, not that she wouldn't have if it were necessary. But no way could she picture her mother donning britches. She would have worn an old dress and shawl, but no britches.

Once she'd opened the gate in her mind, thoughts of home scrambled through like runaway sheep. How were Lucinda and Joseph doing with the plantation? Was the tobacco all cut and drying? With the drought, the leaves were small anyway and drying in the field. While the fugitives had only been on the road a few days, it felt like a month and another world.

The final question leaped into her head like the wolf that chased the sheep. *What about Dunlivey? Did he come back?*

She shivered at the thought. He could be trailing them already, and he wouldn't have to hide during the day. He could travel as long as he pleased.

But he's in the army. He can't just leave like that. This thought brought her a measure of comfort. So easy in the dark of night to dream up bogeymen, and Dunlivey surely was the king of those. An owl hooted right over their heads, leaving her heart pumping and her hands shaking. Maybe it was a good thing Meshach was driving. Ahab would feel her fear.

She could hear her brother Zachary's put-out voice. *"Quit acting like a girl, Jesse, or you can't come with us."*

Or her mother. *"Jesselynn, you must be a lady. You are too old for climbing trees any longer."*

Or Lucinda. *"You break yo' mama's heart, actin' like dat."*

This was a night for voices.

"All quiet up ahead." Benjamin trotted up to the wagon side, seeming to come out of nowhere.

"Good."

When they drew even with the outbuildings of the town, Meshach slowed the horses to a walk. While they could see the outlines of the buildings, not a candle lit a window nor a sound spoke louder than the clop of the horses' hooves and the squeak of the wheels. Maybe the town had been abandoned. Had there been fighting in the area?

Where in thunder were they?

She didn't realize she'd been holding her breath until she felt light-headed as they left the town behind without incident. Jesselynn sucked in a deep breath and let it out on a sigh.

She swatted at a mosquito, tired of the incessant whine about her head. The long sleeves of her shirt and long pant legs saved all but her neck and face. As dawn neared, a breeze picked up, and the mosquitoes left.

The sky lightened slowly like a shy bride hiding her blushes. Birds twittered and fluttered, trying out voices roughened by the night. A cardinal burst into song as the sun pinked the clouds. A rooster crowed, cows bellowed from the farm off to the side of the road, a horse whinnied, and Ahab pricked his ears.

The road started down a hill, and off in the distance they could see the steam rising from a river that glinted between the trees.

"Stopping somewhere along the river?" she asked.

"I s'pose. Benjamin find us a good spot." Meshach raised his head, sniffing the breeze. "Some'un cookin' bacon. My, that do smell good."

Jesselynn sniffed. "You're making that up."

"No, suh. Close yo' eyes and sniff again."

She did as he said, and a smile stretched her cheeks. "You're right. Bacon and eggs and biscuits. Lucinda's biscuits. Now wouldn't that be fine?"

"We might could buy bacon and eggs. Gots to get milk fo' Thaddy, but . . ." He shook his head. "No one makes biscuits like Lucinda." It was his turn to sigh. "I sho' do miss her good cookin'."

"When we get to camp, you want to find a farm and get us some supplies? Or I could do it."

"Benjamin will. Lucinda tan my black hide if she hear we let you go off by yo'self."

Jesselynn started to argue but chose to leave it alone. The farther they got from home, the less hold Lucinda would have. She nibbled on her bottom lip. You'd have thought Lucinda was mistress of the house instead of her.

Please, God, let us see Lucinda and Twin Oaks again. Guilt caught her by the throat and squeezed. How many days since she'd read her Bible, either to herself or to the others? How long since she'd thanked her heavenly Father for keeping them safe? Did it really make any difference?

After Benjamin signaled them to the stopping place, she dug a few more coins from her leather drawstring bag and handed them to him. Soon they would be down to gold pieces, and those she could never give to a slave. It would be far too noticeable.

"Get milk, bacon or ham if they have some, and eggs." She paused to think. "And ask if they have any vegetables they can spare from their garden."

"You wants grain for de horses?"

She shook her head. "They'll have to do on grass. I'm sure Uncle Hiram will have plenty of grain to fatten them for the winter. Take the mule."

"Yessuh." Benjamin grinned at her. "Not Ahab, huh?"

"You git." Meshach stripped the harness off Ahab and draped it over a wagon wheel. "And hurry. We's hungry."

"And tired of mush." Jesselynn scooped Thaddy up in her arms and gave him a whirl around hugs and kisses on both cheeks, making him giggle.

"More." He patted her cheeks with both hands. "More Jesselynn."

"More who?" She stopped whirling and adopted her sternest face. "What's my name?"

Thaddeus looked down, one finger on his lower lip. "Jesse."

"Good boy. Now say it again."

"Jesse." He pooched out his lower lip. "Jesse!" His finger now pointing to his own chest, "Me Joshwa."

"All right, Joshwa! Let's go wash in the river."

Cold water has a way of waking one more fully. By the time she'd removed her boots and stuck her feet in so she and Thaddy could wade, feeling was returning to her legs and posterior. She looked across the water to see two deer drinking in the shallows. But when Thaddy slapped a stick on the water, they vanished into the shadows before she could point them out to him.

Catching Thaddy by the hands, she swirled him around as she waded out to her hips and then dunked them both. He shrieked with laughter until she heard Meshach announce breakfast behind her.

"Good. Come on in. The water feels fine." Dripping, she turned, Thaddy in her arms.

Ophelia appeared from behind Meshach. "Missy Lynn." Her eyes and mouth showed her shock.

"Don' call her dat!" Meshach lashed out at her, his laughter turned fierce in an eye blink.

"I's sorry." Ophelia cringed like a puppy about to be whipped. She looked at Jesselynn. "I know, Jesse. I jes' fo'git."

"Then don't call me anything at all. If we make mistakes with just us, that is one thing, but little mistakes can lead to our being caught, and if we're caught, you might be raped or killed or sold. Keep that in mind."

"And think, 'Phelia. Think! You got a brain under dat kinky wool, so use it." Meshach frowned at Ophelia.

Jesselynn looked at Meshach, shock making her hands tingle. He sounded so like her father he could have been standing there. How many times had she heard Joshua Highwood say the same thing to one of the slaves? He expected them to think, fully believing that God gave those with dark skin every bit as much intelligence as those with light. Needless to say, other planters didn't agree with him and frequently told him so, so he'd no longer shared that information.

The fear of *uppity niggers* permeated the plantations like miasma hovering over a swamp. But even though it became illegal to teach slaves, Highwood had continued and, therefore, so had Jesselynn.

The song of a cardinal broke up the exchange, and Meshach shook his head once more in Ophelia's direction before returning to the fire, where Benjamin was dismounting with the supplies. The cardinal's song had become their signal so that no one ended up at the wrong end of the rifle.

Within minutes, Ophelia had the bacon frying, and the perfume of it brought the others back to the campfire. Jesselynn, with Thaddeus on one hip, grabbed a dead branch on the way and pulled it up to the fire. She swung her baby brother to the ground and began breaking sticks off for the fire, motioning him to do the same. Gone were the days when small children were carried everywhere on the hip of their slave and played with continually lest they cry and be unhappy. At least with those of Twin Oaks.

"My, that smells downright heavenly." Jesselynn sniffed again in appreciation. They had used up their bacon, along with the rabbits Benjamin and Meshach managed to snare. If only there had been more in the storehouse at home for them to bring along, but she couldn't see letting those left behind be without food either. So they had split the stores, knowing that the money would need to be stretched until it pleaded for mercy and then stretched some more.

They would be eating squirrel and rabbit at home too, unless someone got a deer. She jerked her thoughts back to the matters at hand just in time to scoop Thaddeus up and away from the fire.

"No! You don't touch the fire. You know better." At the sternness of her voice, he screwed his eyes shut and puckered his mouth to let out a wail. "No, stop that. You are not hurt." She gave him a bit of a shake to catch his attention.

"I take him." Meshach dumped some more wood down by the fire and reached for the child.

"No, he has to learn to mind." She grasped the chubby chin and looked right into Thaddy's blue eyes, so like his father's it made her heart hitch. "When I say no, I mean no, and you have to stop what you are doing right then. Without another move." He blinked and stuck a forefinger in his round mouth. "You hear me?" He nodded, never taking his eyes from hers.

"Me be good."

"I know you can be good." She hugged him and kissed his cheek, tasting the salt of a tear that trekked downward. "And you must be." *For all of our sakes.*

"Sit yourself an' eat." Ophelia handed her a plate with one hand and took Thaddeus with the other. "I feeds him."

Jesselynn knew that she should do that herself and let Ophelia eat too, but like a bolt from the sky, her knees nearly collapsed, setting her down with more of a thump than she'd reckoned. Her plate tipped alarmingly, but she righted it before her two fried eggs slipped over the edge.

"Bread! Fresh bread?"

"De lady, she gived me dat." Benjamin's smile near to cracked his face. He pointed to a sack behind the log. "Dey's carrots, an' beets, an' some beans, 'longside de milk an' such. She one nice lady. She say we by Morgantown on de Green River."

"I set snares. We have rabbit stew fo' supper." Meshach handed Thaddeus another piece of bread to dunk in his milk.

Thaddy smiled, a white trickle off the side of his lip. "Good." He waved the bread, brushing it against Ophelia's cheek so she ducked back. That made the little boy chuckle and wave his bread again.

A leaf floated down and hovered in the smoke before drifting off to the side. The sun slanted through the thinning branches of the oak tree to her back. Jesselynn inhaled the scents of autumn—leaves falling to decay and make rich leaf mold so that the land might sleep and sprout again, fried bacon, coffee, the shoreline of the sleepy river, oak branches fired to coals.

If she closed her eyes, she could pretend they were on a picnic and that later they would drive home and . . . if there was any home left.

Better to keep her eyes open. She drank the last of the coffee, tossing the dregs into the fire, then rising, she set her cup and plate in the wash pan steaming over the coals. Staggering to the wagon and taking the pallet out felt beyond her strength, but she did it anyway and collapsed without a blink. Some time later she felt someone pull her boots off and throw a mosquito net over her, so she mumbled a thank-you and sank back into the well of sleep.

Her favorite dream returned.

The shade of the oaks lining the long drive to Twin Oaks dappled their faces as she and John Follett strolled the length and back.

"I talked with your father." John took her hand and tucked it around his bent elbow so he could press her closer to his side.

"I know." Surely he could feel her heart thumping clear to her fingertips.

He stopped and, turning her to face him, took both of her hands. "I . . ." He cleared his throat and tried again.

She felt as if she were swimming in his eyes, stroking deeper to reach the fine soul she saw shining there. No suitor had ever made her feel like this.

"I love you, Jesselynn Highwood, and I want to marry you, the sooner the better." He didn't have to say before the war, but she knew what he meant. He squeezed her hands. "Tell me you feel the same."

"I do." Oh, how she longed to say those words in front of the minister.

He kissed her then, her first kiss, and the sweetness of it made her yearn for more. She nestled into his chest, both his arms around her. Such a safe place, like the nest she'd never known she searched for.

Turning her face up to his, she kissed him back, her parasol tipping over her shoulder and shielding them from any spying eyes. If Lucinda caught them . . .

"Jesselynn." The voice no longer matched that of the man in her dreams.

"Jesselynn!" The hand on her shoulder brought her back from her euphoric dream. She sat upright and banged her head on the wagon bed.

"What? What's wrong?"

"Bluebellies crossin' de river."

Chapter Nine

❧

ON THE BANKS OF THE GREEN RIVER
SEPTEMBER 24, 1862

"Hide the horses," Jesselynn ordered.

"Did dat." Ophelia sank back on her haunches, her eyes wide.

"Where's Thaddeus?" Jesselynn rubbed the spot on her head as she crawled out and sat to pull her boots back on.

"Sleepin'." Pointing to another pallet in the shade of a tree, Ophelia's hand shook.

"Good." Jesselynn dug under the mosquito net for her hat and clamped it back on her head, feeling as if she became a young man in that single motion.

No more Jesselynn, who'd enjoyed being kissed under the oak trees. She was Jesse, younger son of Joshua Highwood, on a mission.

She could hear laughter, horses splashing, men calling orders. How far from the ford had she set up camp? She glanced up to see the sun way past the high point. It was later in the afternoon now. Would they dare cross the ford at dusk with Yankees in the area?

Of course the soldiers could be miles up the road by then. Or they could camp just on this side of the river.

"Go on as if nothing is wrong," she whispered to Ophelia. "We have every right to be here, and as long as the horses are hidden . . ."

"But dey might cotch me." Ophelia looked like a rabbit who wanted nothing but to bolt back down its hole.

"Not with me here." She reached back in the wagon bed for the rifle they kept under the seat. A rifle and one pistol. Not much ammunition if they needed to frighten off a rover or two. Meshach wore the pistol tucked in his waistband.

She watched Roman, the mule, grazing in the sunlight, his long ears swiveling to keep track of the noises around him. When he raised his head, looking off to the north, she held her breath, only releasing it when the animal dropped back to cropping grass. A blue jay flew overhead, announcing its displeasure at the invasion of its territory.

The wait continued. Her mind raced through the things she should do if a blue-coated soldier rode into their camp. Shooting him would be stone-cold stupid, unless he tried to take a slave or a horse. Could she pull off her disguise as a young man? She'd already figured what to say about their traveling. Going to Uncle's for a visit, that's what. Was there a law against traveling?

She scrubbed her palms down the sides of her pants. Wet hands did not a sure shot make.

Silence felt like the kiss of heaven. She swallowed and patted Ophelia on the shoulder. "We'll be all right now." Birds twittered and flitted in the trees. A dog barked some distance away. All the normal sounds of woodland life carried on.

A bit later Benjamin and Meshach led the horses out of the woods and hobbled them again to graze. Roman nickered when his friends returned and fell to grazing again. Peace lay over the campsite.

Benjamin slipped out of the woods moments later. "Six, eight sojers on a patrol. Dey not lookin' for trouble."

"I surely do hope not." *But they always need horses.*

"Think I try fo' a mess a fish." Meshach slouched against the wagon wheel.

"Did you sleep?"

"Enough. Benjamin better sleep now. Daniel too."

Ophelia set about scrubbing vegetables for the rabbit stew, the savor of the cooking rabbit already tantalizing Jesselynn's taste buds. She dug in the sack for a carrot, since she had slept through dinner, and supper wouldn't be until near dark.

Carrot in hand, she took out her father's journals and flipped to the blank pages. After all the years he'd kept a journal, she had decided to follow suit when he went off to war, and she had kept them up until their flight. But now there would be no account of food put by or crops harvested unless Lucinda or Joseph thought to keep records at home. Hers was about their journey. She sharpened a quill and shook the ink bottle. Soon she'd need to make ink.

Jesselynn snugged her back against a tree trunk and, with journal on her knees, set to her task. After filling in the date, she swiftly described their travels through the nights, the patrols they'd avoided, the money they spent, and now the condition of the mares, who would soon need grain.

She watched them grazing so peacefully, then went back to her journal. If they had brought everything they might need, they would have had three wagons, not one. She fingered the Bible she kept in the leather satchel with the journals. Tonight she would read to them all before supper. She couldn't keep her eyes open long enough in the morning. How long would it take her to get used to staying awake all night and sleeping during the day? And feel rested?

She woke with a crick in her neck and the ink bottle unstoppered. The sun glowed red on the tree trunks as it sank toward the hilltop. Rubbing her neck, she stuck the cork back in the ink, mentally scolding herself for being so lax. She looked around the campsite and saw Thaddy playing in a pile of leaves, Meshach cleaning a harness, and Ophelia stirring the cooking pot.

Her stomach rumbled as the fragrance of the stew drifted past. Pushing herself to her feet took more energy than she thought possible, but once she had stretched and yawned, she could bend over to pick up her satchel and stow it back in the wagon. Scratching a mosquito bite on her neck, she wandered over to where Thaddy played with a carved wooden horse in the dirt and leaves.

Meshach had been busy.

"See horse?" He held his toy up for her admiration. "Good horse."

"That he is. You been eatin' dirt?"

He shook his head, but his mouth showed otherwise.

"Come on, let's go to the river and wash."

"Play in water?" He boosted himself to his feet, rear first, horse clutched in one fist. With the other he reached for her hand and together they strolled toward the water. The trip took longer than usual as Thaddeus admired three sticks and two patches of leaves, giggled in a flickering shadow, inspected a burl on an oak tree, insisted they walk around the *other* side of a tree, and found two rocks that went in his pocket.

Carrying him would have been ten times faster, but not as entertaining. Thanks to her sharp eyes, they watched ants carrying crumbs back to their soil home and a beetle digging for whatever beetles dig for.

When he sat in the water, she let him splash while she took off her boots. How wonderful a swim would feel. But if it washed the walnut dye out of her hair, she'd have to boil more husks to make new, and that took too long for this evening's entertainment.

Gold still streaked the river that looked more like a big creek with wide beaches and gilded the outlines of the trees on the far side. Fording this so they needn't go into town would be easy. The water didn't appear to be up to the horses' bellies even. They'd have to pitch or tar the wagon bed before they got to a river where they had to swim the horses. So many things to think of.

She rubbed her forehead. Most likely she'd slept a cramp into her neck, which caused the headache, not the thinking.

She studied the far shore. Upriver some cows stood drinking in the shallows, so obviously there was a farm there. Downriver all she could see were trees, some still green, others touched with fall paint. How far had the Union soldiers gone before camping? Or had they headed north to Louisville? If only she had any idea what was happening with the war.

"Jesse, look."

She glanced down to see Thaddy, water running down his arm, holding up something shiny. Bending over, she grasped his waving hand. A gold button, once closing an army uniform, lay in his palm.

Was it Union or Confederate? And how had it come to be here?

"My button." Thaddy grasped her rolled-up pant leg and pulled himself upright, reaching for the treasure.

"All right. But keep it out of your mouth, you hear?" He nodded and closed his fingers over the button.

"Mine."

"Put it in your pocket, then, so you don't lose it." She watched while he did so, then looked out again to the riverbanks.

A rifle shot popped in the distance and then another. Someone hunting or—

The barrage that followed answered her *or*. The shots came from the north-west and far enough away to keep her from running to hide, but if there were both gray and blue ahead of them, perhaps they'd best stay right where they were.

The volleys continued, a bugle blew, then silence fell. One more shot erupted, and that was it. She waited, but even as the sky shifted from fire to ember gray and the evening star peeked out, only the sound of birds gossiping off to sleep broke the stillness. A fish jumped and smacked the water on return.

"Come an' eat." Meshach spoke from off her right shoulder.

She hadn't heard him arrive. She looked down to find Thaddeus covered with mud from the hole he'd been digging in the bank.

"Oh, Thaddy." She shook her head, grabbed him up, and, holding his arms, soused him up and down in the water to wash the mud off. His giggle brought smiles to both her and Meshach. "Now we'll have to get you in dry clothes again."

———

"So, do we stay or go?" The question had been chewed on by each of them, with everyone but Jesselynn saying go. The thought of running into either patrol made the hair on the back of her neck stand at attention. They could lose everything.

"I take Roman and go scout." Benjamin leaned forward. "No one sees us."

"All right." She shook her head, wishing she felt braver. Here in this copse and small meadow with the river at their door, she felt safe for some inexplicable reason. The other side of the river spelled danger.

While they waited, she helped Meshach check on the horses, digging dirt and a rock or two out of their hooves and inspecting for any harness galls, all the while listening for Benjamin's signal. When it came, the sigh of relief originated in her toes and worked its way upward.

"No sign of sojers. Road clear." He swung off Roman and joined them in the firelight. "I followed a road some an' see signs a patrol go dat way." He pointed to the north. "But de road we take is clear."

"Good." She stood and dusted off the back of her pants. "Let's go, then."

Within minutes they had Ahab and one of the mares harnessed together, Jesse riding Domino, the younger stallion, and Meshach driving the wagon. As they headed out, she glanced back to the clearing, seeing the glint of the river through the tree trunks. Was it wrong to want to hang on to a moment of peace?

When they reached the ford, she waited on the bank for the wagon to go ahead. Glancing upriver, there appeared to be a log floating in the middle.

"Meshach, you see that log?" She raised her voice to be heard over the splashing horse hooves. Water was past their knees and heading for belly-deep. Would the wagon have to float?

"I sees it. Come on across." The horses were pulling the wagon into shallow water. Jesselynn nudged Domino into the river. He snorted and tossed his head but at the pressure of her legs continued forward, ears flicking to catch her encouraging words. He snorted again as they drew level with the log.

What she'd thought was a log. Where the face should have been, only a black hole gaped at the sky, and the gray-clad soldier floated on past. Jesselynn kicked her horse forward, her stomach fighting the urge to erupt.

Chapter Ten

RICHMOND, VIRGINIA

"But I have to go back to the hospital. The men need me."

"It's just not proper for a young girl like you to be working in that . . . that place, and you not even married. I don't see how the doctors ever let you in the door." Aunt Sylvania had said these words far too many times before for Louisa to pay a great deal of attention. Nor would she tell her aunt that the doctors and officers understood her to be a widow and several years older than her actual age. They knew her as Mrs. Zachary Highwood. Adopting the name of her missing brother had seemed like a good idea at the time.

And it still was. Getting a wedding ring hadn't been difficult, since she'd taken her mother's out of the strongbox at home. She kept it on a chain around her neck until after she left the house.

Louisa smiled gently at her aunt, whose chin had a tendency to quiver in righteous indignation. Out of the three girls of her family, only one did as any proper young lady would. Carrie Mae sought and found a fine young man to marry. No matter that he was missing part of an arm. His old family heritage more than made up for that, and being a successful lawyer had nothing to do with how many arms he had. In fact, his loss made him a more sympathetic character in the courtroom.

Louisa knew all this and understood Aunt Sylvania's concern, but . . . that was the word. But. What about the suffering right down the street? *What if Father were to come to my hospital and there was no one there to give him a drink, read to him, or write letters home if he couldn't use his hand? Or Zachary?* She already knew that Adam was beyond her care. She hoped he and their mother were enjoying each other's company and looking out for those left here on earth.

"Louisa, you are not listening to me." The spoon clattering onto the saucer let Louisa know that she had missed something important. When had she gotten so adept at appearing to be listening when her mind roamed off elsewhere?

"I'm sorry, Aunt. What was that you said?"

Sylvania sniffed, setting the ribbons on her morning cap to fluttering. She *tsked* with more force than necessary, another indication of her rising indignation.

Louisa laid her fork down on her plate and gave her aunt her full attention. Excuses would not help. Life here was so different than at Twin Oaks. Why, oh why, had Jesselynn sentenced her to so-called safety with Aunt Sylvania? Until she'd found a place at the hospital, the boredom of society in Richmond had more than once brought her to tears. As the capital of the Confederacy, Richmond held more balls and concerts and soirees than she ever planned to attend in a lifetime. Playing at dressing up and attracting beaus those years at home were vastly different than reality. Such a waste of time. She kept herself from shaking her head just in time.

"I . . ." Sylvania paused, beetling her brows at her niece. "I believe it is time for us to have a small soiree. I hear young James Scribner has returned from the war, and I believe you and he would . . ." She paused again and lifted one eyebrow.

Louisa forced a smile, making sure that both sides of her mouth lifted and, along with a nod, encouraged her aunt to continue. *Oh, Lord, no, please not another one. Now I have an idea what the slaves felt like on the auction block, but at least no one has checked my teeth.* "Are you sure you have time for that, what with gettin' ready for the weddin' and all?"

Long-suffering looked at home on Sylvania's time-spotted and wrinkled face. "I will manage. Your happiness is of utmost importance to me." Another sniff followed, and this time the bit of cambric touched the tip of her rabbity nose.

Louisa used every bit of training her mother had instilled in her. Her eyebrow stayed where it belonged. "Thank you, Aunt, I'm sure it is." Why can't

Carrie Mae get up early enough to distract her? Thoughts of what she would like to do to her sleeping sister took her mind off on another trail.

"More biscuit, Missy?" The soft voice at her shoulder made Louisa turn with a smile. Abby, her woolly hair covered with a white kerchief, held out a basket covered with a white napkin, the fragrance going before it.

"Thank you, I will. These are even better than Lucinda's at home, but I know you will never tell her I said that."

"No'm." The smile that caused dimples in her ebony cheeks made Abby chuckle too. "I knows Lucinda be one fine cook."

"Yes." Louisa took a golden brown biscuit and set it on her plate. *If only I could take some of those with me, they might tempt Sergeant Wilson's appetite.* But she knew if she asked, her aunt would launch again into her oft delivered speech on the unsuitability of her niece working at the hospital. Louisa had it memorized—*well* memorized.

"Message, madam." Reuben, who used to be the butler but now was more man of all trades, set a silver salver, worn bare in spots, on the table in front of his mistress.

"Oh, now what?" Sylvania set her coffee cup down only the least bit harder than necessary, showing that her displeasure had not totally abated.

Louisa used the distraction to lay her napkin on her plate and push back her chair. "Thank you, Abby, I must hurry." She spoke low enough that Aunt Sylvania wouldn't hear. She kept her pace sedate as "befitted a young woman of breeding"—her aunt's words—until she reached the hall, then flew up the stairs.

Coming out of her room, she nearly bumped into Carrie Mae, yawning and stretching as she crossed the hall.

"Goodness, need you be in such a rush?" Carrie Mae patted back another yawn with a delicate hand. Her hair, much the same rich color as Louisa's but curly instead of straight, looked charmingly tousled instead of sleep flattened. Sleepy eyed, she gazed at her sister. "I suppose you're all done with breakfast too and off to the hospital?"

"How did you ever guess?" Louisa patted her sister's cheek, feeling years older and wiser. "How was the cotillion last night?"

"Last night? I barely got to bed before the sun rose." Carrie Mae yawned again. "Excuse me, oh, did Aunt mention the soiree? It is about time we returned some of the invitations, you know."

Louisa shuddered. "If she drags out one more—"

"Now, sister dear, meeting the right people is important. You know that well as anyone. What would Daddy say?"

"Daddy would say what our Lord said—a cup of water for the thirsty, bandages for the wounded, and given as soon as possible." She smiled at her sister, who was already shaking her head.

"I have rolled enough bandages for the entire Army of the Potomac. You think I do nothing all day. Why"—she held out a needle-roughened finger— "see how often I've stuck myself, yet that uniform still looks like it belongs on a slave rather than a Confederate soldier."

"If you could sew as well as you play the piano, there would be more uniforms maybe, but think how many hearts are lifted by your music." Louisa leaned over and kissed her sister on the cheek. "How is Mr. Steadly?" Jefferson Steadly had asked Carrie Mae to be his wife after a minimal courtship, having declared himself so smitten by her he couldn't wait.

"Oh, Louisa, I only wish for you the happiness that I've found. I believe he loves me like Daddy loved Mama."

"Then that is our wish come true for you." Louisa squeezed her sister's hand. "I must hurry. I have much to do."

"Don't forget . . ."

The rest of the sentence was lost in the rustling of her skirts descending the stairs. Unbidden, a thought of the scarecrow on crutches, as the men called Lieutenant Lessling, passed through her mind. *Hmm, he'll hardly even talk to me. I wonder why.*

She picked up the basket that contained her Bible, a copy of Shakespeare's comedies, paper, quill and ink, and a packet of lemon drops for her men; then setting it on the entry table, she paused at the mirror to tie her bonnet. Once she had left the house without one, and the weeks of sniffing reminders weren't worth repeating the mistake.

"Here, Missy." Abby slipped a napkin-wrapped packet into the basket. "You must eat befo' you fades away."

Louisa raised an eyebrow in question.

"Not to worry. Dey's extra for de gentlemens." Abby ducked to hide a grin. "I fix a basket for dat Reuben to carry too." She stepped back a step. "But I not does it again 'less you promise me to eat yo'self."

Louisa fought the tears that burned at the back of her throat. "Thank you. I know our Father sees in secret."

"He better keeps the secret too." With that Abby headed to the back of the house, throwing a conspirator's smile over her shoulder as she pushed against the door leading to the outside kitchen.

"You ready, Missy?" Reuben held open the door, a much larger basket at his feet.

Knowing she had extra gifts to take lent speed to Louisa's slippers as they traversed the blocks to the two-story brick building that housed more suffering than the residents of the once fine but now aging houses in this part of the city cared to know.

Louisa couldn't understand how so many could go about their business as if the yard lined with wounded soldiers on pallets didn't exist. In fact, she had heard two matrons complaining one day that the screams heard from the hospital were just not to be tolerated.

It was all Louisa could do to keep from screaming at the two of them herself.

But in spite of those few, most women supported the war, rolling bandages, sewing uniforms, taking recuperating soldiers into their homes so they could be tended, knitting wool socks, and collecting what medicines and medicinal herbs they could for the soldiers' relief. Some contributed by earning money for supplies. The Ladies Aid at the church Louisa had chosen to attend did all of that and more.

Of course Aunt Sylvania had thrown a fit at that move too. The church Louisa chose was definitely not fashionable. How would she ever meet a young man of the proper quality there? What would her dear Joshua say if he saw his youngest daughter attending a Quaker meetinghouse, of all things?

As they neared the brick edifice, the low moans that sounded like a flowing river hummed louder than the cicadas thrumming in the elm trees.

The smell met her at the door like a heavy curtain.

"Where you wants dis?" Reuben nodded to his basket.

"Right here in this closet. That way I can parcel things out." She hung her bonnet on a hook and donned the white apron hanging beside it. At the same time, she scooped two bloodstained aprons out of another basket and, bundling them together, handed them to Reuben. Unbeknownst to Aunt Sylvania, Abby had been laundering the aprons since Louisa began her hospital service. Another secret she and the slaves kept between them. How would she ever be able to help with the soldiers if her aunt discovered their duplicity?

Reuben checked the water bucket and shuddered. "I gets fresh."

Louisa nodded and smiled her gratitude. As he left for the pump out back, she checked the contents of both baskets. Hard-boiled eggs, already peeled for ease of eating, a packet of salt, biscuits slathered with butter and honey, a loaf of bread all sliced and buttered, sliced cheese to add to the bread, cookies, and a jar of chicken soup. Surely something here would help Private Rumford take more than two bites at a meal. No matter how she encouraged him, she got the feeling that all he wanted to do was die, if not from his wounds, then of starvation.

Reuben returned and she reached for his bucket, but a shake of his silvering head made her smile again. Lately he'd taken to staying with her while she took dippers of fresh water around to the men.

"Thank you, but I don't want you gettin' on the wrong side of Aunt."

"Not you worry, Missy. Let's get goin' now."

They stepped into the ward, and silence fell like a featherbed floating into place. Greetings bounced around the room, one patient passing the news of her arrival on to the next who might not see or hear.

"Good mornin'." She began on the right side, taking turns each day so no one always received her assistance first. The man in the bed raised himself on one elbow.

"I was 'fraid you wasn't comin'." He scooted back to brace against the wall.

"Why? Am I late?" Her smile made the man in the next bed chuckle.

"I . . . I don't know. The nights are so long, seems like mornin' fergits to come." He drank his fill and lay back. "Thankee, ma'am. Just seein' you so purtylike makes the water taste pert near as good as the spring at home."

"Hey, don't spend all mornin' with that worthless mountain castoff." The laughter in the tone made others laugh, one to the point of coughing as if he might not stop.

"Now, y'all just wait your turn." She spoke to the room and held the dipper for the man in the next bed. "How are you this mornin'?"

"Toler'ble." He hawked to clear his throat and spat into a towel left by his head, a towel already spotted with red.

Louisa kept her smile intact and slipped him one of the slices of bread with cheese. "I'll be back with more water soon as I can." If only she could bring him something hot to drink, perhaps he could better fight the infection raging through his body. But he did look more alert today.

As she made her way around the room, smiles followed her like butterflies after blossoms. For those too sick to raise themselves up to drink, she put her arm behind them to give them support. Several men were unconscious, so other than laying a hand on their shoulders and breathing a prayer for healing, she passed them by. Later she would come by with a basin of warm water and wash hands and faces.

The man in bed seventeen was such. She studied the rise and fall of his chest. He was breathing well at least. "Has he been awake at all?" The man in the next bed shook his head.

"Nary a sound outa him. Not even a groan. Doc says it's the head wound."

"Is he in a coma, then?"

The nod made her wince. "Do you know anything about him?"

"No'm, not a thing." He eyed her basket. "I sure would appreciate some o' that cheese you brought t'other day."

"With bread, or would you rather have one of cook's biscuits?"

"Mighty hard decidin'." He closed his one eye, the other an empty socket with a scar that ran from his hairline to his chin. That early wound had healed, so he was sent back to the front. He wouldn't be returning to battle again, not missing a leg.

When she held out the bread and cheese, he took it, his hand shaking so the bread almost fell to the floor. With a quick hand for his advancing years, Reuben handed the bread back without looking the man in the face.

"Here you goes, suh."

When the soldier failed to say anything, Louisa frowned at him and smiled at Reuben. "Thank you. Some of us seem to have forgotten our manners."

A hoot from the men around him made the culprit flush and stop chewing long enough to mumble, "Sorry. Thank you, boy."

"His name is Reuben, and he is far too old and valuable to be a boy." The ice in her voice cooled the air around them by several degrees. She waited, one slipper tapping the floor, counting the seconds.

It took more time than she'd liked, making her wonder if her strictness with these wounded men made any difference in the way they thought.

"Ah, Frank, give in."

"Now, you dumb—" At the collective gasp, the remonstrator cut off the rest of his sentence, earning him a smile from their angel. While she was on the floor, they all knew she tolerated no swearing, crude language, or cruelty in general. Her method of punishment to those intrepid cursers changed many minds. She just ignored them, walking by as if they did not exist.

By the time she and Reuben had circled the room, one of the doctors arrived, along with an assistant who helped change the dressings. While they started at one end, she waved good-bye to her helper and started at the other end, this time with a basin of warm water, washcloth, soap, and a towel. Those who could wash their own hands and faces did. The others received her gentle touch with sighs of appreciation.

"I heard you know how to shave a feller," one of her men said, raising both his hands swathed in bandages.

"I do, but it will be some time before I can get back."

"No problem, Miz Highwood. I ain't goin' nowhere."

She smiled at his gentle joke. "Not today, but soon."

"Home? You think they might send me home?"

"That'd be my surmise, but the doctor there has the last say." No one without usable hands would be sent back to the fighting, that she knew for certain, and from the looks of him, this young man, a boy really, would be going home soon. They needed his bed for those much worse off than he. Her gaze wandered over to the man who had yet to regain consciousness. The doctor would be seeing him next.

What was there about him that drew her? She ignored the puzzlement and eased her way to stand by the foot of his bed.

"How are you today, Miz Highwood?" The physician stopped beside her, studying her face. "Child, how long since you've taken a day off?"

"Oh, last week, I think." She shot him a piercing look. "How about you?"

"Last week. Must have been last week." His smile and headshaking said he knew they were both lying. He patted her shoulder and turned to the patient, who showed no signs of impatience at the wait, unlike some of the others.

Louisa screwed up her courage. "Do you know anything about him?"

Dr. Fremont shook his head. "No, he had no identification and hasn't been able to answer questions. I was hoping he would be conscious by now, but then maybe this is better. At least he isn't feeling any pain, and with those wounds, the pain would be severe." He picked up the man's hand and checked the pulse. "His heart is strong. He's goin' to need that."

Louisa studied the man in the bed, what she could see of him. She promised herself to come back later because, conscious or not, warm water on his hands and face would feel good. And getting the blood washed off him would make her feel good. Knowing that the doctor would not tend his patient until she left the bedside, she returned to her errands of mercy, and the next time she looked up, the doctor and his assistant had left the ward.

With all of her men washed and some sleeping again, she searched out the razor she'd hidden away behind some boxes and filled her pan with hot water again. The razor needed stropping to get an edge back on it, but she hadn't found a suitable leather strap at Aunt Sylvania's. Short of asking Reuben to buy one for her, she'd made do up until now.

"I know this is dull, so if you'd rather wait . . ." She shrugged and raised her eyebrows as she spoke.

"Ah, she at least won't cut your throat and might get the worst off," the man in the next bed advised. "I could do it but . . ." He pointed to his bandaged eye.

"That's all right. I trusts her." The man lay back and raised his chin.

Louisa used the cloth to rub the soap so she could lather his face. The act brought back a vision of her father standing in front of a mirror in his bedroom, the brush in his hand full of lather, the razor glinting in the early morning sunlight. Her nose wrinkled at the memory. The soap had smelled nothing like this, and a rag didn't lather like the brush that fit in the mug designed just for that purpose.

Father, where are you? And where is Zachary? Is someone helping Zachary this morning?

She bent to her task, the rasp of the razor against the whiskers sounding loud, as if all the men were waiting with held-in breath to see if she would draw blood. With the razor she was using, it wasn't a case of *if,* but *when.*

By the time she'd finished, she had said "I'm sorry" so often that each new protestation brought chuckles that swelled to laughter from those around. If they only knew how good it made her feel to hear them laugh, even if it was at her expense.

She wiped off the remaining lather, shook her head at the leftover stubble, and stepped back.

"Looks to me like a rat been chewin' on 'im." One of the men who'd graduated to crutches offered his opinion from the foot of the bed.

"Thank you, Sergeant Arthur. Next time you can do the honors."

"Next time I'll make sure that razor got an edge on it. Give it here, and I'll take care of it."

"Now, why didn't you say that before?" Louisa picked up her pan of soapy water, draping the towel over her arm.

"You didn't ask."

She rolled her eyes and pushed on past him. "Tomorrow you're in charge of shavin'."

"Miz Highwood, you gonna read to us again?" The question came from another who could no longer see.

"Yes, that I am. Right now, as a matter of fact." She knew that if she didn't sit down fairly soon, she might just fall down.

By the time she headed for home in the evening dusk, her back ached, her feet felt like she'd walked miles, which she had, and the man in bed seventeen still hadn't awakened.

Chapter Eleven

❧

"Jesse, me go home."

Jesselynn picked up her little brother and hugged him close. "I know. I want to go home too."

Thaddeus patted her cheeks with both of his hands. "Then go." He turned to grin up at Meshach. "We goin' home." The smile lit up his face, and he laid his cheek against his sister's. "Go home now."

Jesselynn first tried to swallow the boulder blocking her throat, then at least swallow around it. *Home, where the hip bath can be filled with hot lavender-scented water, and I can soak for a week, then sleep in my own soft bed until I feel like waking up. Where Lucinda or one of the others will bring me coffee or tea in bed if I so desire, where the doves will coo in the tree outside my window and I can hear the horses whinny on their way to the track.*

She hid her smarting eyes in Thaddy's shoulder and rocked from one foot to the other, crooning under her breath. *Home . . . oh, Lord, I want to go home.* A shudder started in her heels and worked its way up until she clenched her teeth. All she had to do was tell Meshach to turn the horses around and head back to Twin Oaks. She clamped her teeth shut and her arms around Thaddeus. The words bubbled in her head and up her throat. *Home, let's go home.*

"Ow! Jesse, you hurtin' me." The boy leaned back and stared into his sister's eyes. He patted her cheek again. "You cryin'?"

She shook her head and, setting him down, rubbed the corner of her eye. "Just got a speck of dirt in my eye, that's all. You go on and help Ophelia find firewood so we can have breakfast."

"Home?"

"Someday." The look of such utter sadness that he sent her before he trudged off behind Ophelia made her swallow hard again. Like their father, Thaddeus could say more with one glance than most people could with their mouths in an hour.

Home, she thought as she settled down to sleep some time later. *Home . . . sometimes I wonder if I ever even lived there or if I made it all up.*

———

"Thaddeus. Thaddeus!"

The sound of Ophelia calling brought Jesselynn awake long before she was ready.

"Thaddeus!" Meshach had joined her.

Jesselynn rolled out of bed and slid into her boots in a motion getting smooth with practice. She grabbed her hat on the way out from under the wagon and jogged to the edge of the woods, listening for another shout.

If Thaddy is lost, I'll never forgive myself. What happened? "What happened?" Jesselynn grabbed a sobbing Ophelia by the arm as soon as she found her.

"I was . . . I was . . . oh, Marse Jesse, he be gone. Thaddy be gone. Dey snatch him away."

"Who? What?" Jesselynn gave the keening woman a shake. "Tell me, Ophelia! Tell me what happened." She could hear the others calling in the woods.

"How long ago?"

Ophelia shrugged. "I . . . he was right beside me, then gone. Lawsy, our boy be lost. Oh, Lawd, help us find 'im. Please, Lawd."

"Thaddeus Joshua Highwood, come out wherever you are." *He can't be lost. He must think we are playing a game.* But no matter how hard she listened, he didn't answer.

Meshach made his way through the woods and stopped beside her. "Dis brush be so thick, he could fall in a hole, be anywhere."

Jesselynn felt like someone had stabbed her in the heart. Not Thaddy, not her baby brother. For all she knew, her only brother. Why had she slept so long? Turning brimming eyes upward, she shook her head. "Not Thaddeus."

"We find 'im. He not get far."

"He got farther than we can see, didn't he? What was Ophelia doing? Taking care of Thaddy is the most important thing she does."

"She know dat."

"Could someone have snatched him?"

Meshach shook his head. "Can't see how. Who? Why? No one know we here."

Dunlivey. The name exploded in her head. *Dunlivey.* He would take Thaddy knowing that nothing could hurt her more. But if he'd been there, he'd have taken them all. No, that couldn't be it.

"We just got to find 'im."

Jesselynn swallowed hard and sucked in a deep breath. Fainting wouldn't help, that was for sure, but she felt so light-headed right now, she could float off into the woods. She leaned against a tree trunk. She could hear the others calling his name. They sounded so far away. Surely he couldn't get that far.

"Thaddeus, the game is over. Come out now!" Her voice didn't carry beyond her nose. She took another breath and tried again. *God, I'll do anything you ask. Just keep him safe. Bring him back. Please God, please let us find him.*

"Tha-dde-us!" Better. Taking more air in, she screamed his name.

Meshach walked not ten feet from her, alternating with her, calling the child's name.

"Shh." Jesselynn froze. Was her mind playing tricks on her?

"What?" Meshach leaped to her side.

"Shh. Listen." Benjamin called Thaddy's name some distance away. Jesselynn froze, wished she could stop her heart. It was making too much noise. She held her breath. Could that be him?

She looked at Meshach, who nodded back. He pointed off to their left.

Together they pushed through the brush, stopping every couple of feet to call and listen.

The child's crying sounded clearer.

"Thaddeus?"

"Jesse."

"Call again, baby."

"Jesse."

They changed their angle and pushed on. Meshach grabbed her arm before she slid down the embankment. At the bottom lay a badly injured horse with Thaddeus stroking his neck.

"Horse hurt bad."

"Yes, darlin', I can see that." She turned to Meshach. "You got your gun?"

He nodded. "Thank you, Lord, you takes care of our boy."

Together they made their way down the slope and, when the horse started to thrash, stopped. Jesselynn hunkered down and slipped into her gentle crooning.

"Thaddeus, baby, you come on away from there now. Come to me, baby."

"Make horse better?" Thaddeus stood. The horse tried to raise his head and knocked the boy over.

"Easy, Thaddy, come on now." But Thaddeus squatted back down by the horse's head and began stroking his nose again.

"Good horse. Be good, nice . . ."

If Jesselynn didn't know better, she'd have thought it was herself sitting by the downed animal, singing the song that quieted. The horse settled back, a rumble coming from his throat.

"He bad hurt on chest. Legs look all right. Maybe lost too much blood," Meshach observed.

Jesselynn had been cataloging the injuries while she motioned for Thaddeus to come to her. He shook his head.

"Help horse."

"Yes, Thaddeus, we will help the horse. You come away now."

"Comin'." He patted the horse's nose again and backed away. The horse lay still, but they could see how he watched the small child, as if trusting in his care.

When Thaddeus reached Jesselynn, he patted her cheek. "See horse. He bleedin'. You fix."

Jesselynn wasn't sure if she wanted to hug him or wallop him one first. "All we need is a wounded horse." She shook her head. If she could get Thaddy away, Meshach could put the animal out of its misery.

Slowly Meshach moved in on the animal, all the time singing the same song Jesselynn used so well. He extended a hand for the horse to smell, then sat down in front of it and rubbed up its white blaze. "You one fine-lookin' horse to be hurt so bad like dis. How we gonna get you outa here?"

Jesselynn groaned. With Thaddy in the circle of her arm, she watched Meshach calm the beast. The blue saddle blanket told them which army the horse belonged to. The carbine was still in the scabbard, the saddlebags tied on behind the army saddle. The rider must have been blown right off his horse.

"How long you think since he was hit?" It looked like the shell had taken half his chest off.

"Day or two. Got to clean dis up, stitch a bit, get 'im some warm water. Sure do wish we had some oats to mash."

"You want me to send Benjamin for some?" She said it with every ounce of sarcasm she possessed.

Meshach shook his head. "Cornmeal will work."

Jesselynn groaned.

"Meshach fix." Thaddy sighed. "Me hungry. Go find 'Phelia." He stood and started up the bank, but Jesselynn grabbed him before he got more than an arm's reach away.

"I'll go with you, young man. You stay with me, you hear?" She looked up to see Ophelia, Benjamin, and Daniel looking down at them, shaking their heads. Tears ran down Ophelia's face to stop at the smile that cut off their track.

Thaddeus broke away and scrambled up the grade. "Meshach fix horse. Hurt bad. Joshwa hungry."

Ophelia met him partway, snatched him up, and, clenching him to her bosom, scolded and cried over him all at the same time.

When Jesselynn broke clear of the trees, she expected to see dusk settling, but the sun hadn't moved that much at all. It just seemed like a lifetime they'd spent hunting for Thaddeus.

Ophelia had him seated on the wagon tailgate, threatening his life if he moved, when Jesselynn reached them.

"Jesse." He raised his arms to be picked up.

"You just sit there till I get done talkin' to you." She shook her finger in front of his nose. "Don't you ever, you hear me, ever go in the woods by yourself. You stay with me—"

"You was sleepin'."

"Or Ophelia or Meshach. You do not go off by yourself. Do you understand?" She clipped off each word, using the words to keep from smacking him on the behind—and hugging him to bits.

A finger went in his mouth. His head drooped. He nodded. "Yes." A sniff drew up his shoulders. "But—"

"No! No 'but.' I'll wallop your butt till you can't sit down."

"Thaddy sorry."

Jesselynn rolled her eyes heavenward. How come he already knew to say sorry? It had taken her forever to learn that. More than one lickin' as she recalled.

"Thirsty."

"Yeah, me too." She scooped him up in her arms and settled him on her hip. "Let's get a drink."

"Get horse a drink?"

"Benjamin is doing that." She hadn't heard a shot from that general area so she figured they were doctoring the horse. All she needed right now was one more mouth to feed. And one too sick to graze from the look of him. Surely they should just shoot him and get on their way.

Two days passed before Meshach deemed the horse they now called Chess because of his wounds ready for any kind of travel. "Will have to be slow and not go too far."

Jesselynn just shook her head and swung aboard Ahab. Chess and the filly were tied to the back of the wagon, the scabbard and saddle left where someone was sure to find them. The supplies in the saddlebags had added to their stores, and the gold piece tucked in a small pocket now resided in Jesselynn's pouch. All in all, they'd gotten good return on their time and caring.

"Keep Chess." Thaddy stroked the horse's nose from the wagon bed.

"No, Thaddy. We have enough horses."

"Chess my horse."

"Thaddeus Joshua Highwood, listen to me."

He looked up at her with a smile that came straight from the angels. What could she say?

"We'll talk about this later."

Benjamin kicked Domino into a canter in order to do his usual scouting to keep them out of the clutch of soldiers, didn't matter which color uniform. He waved once and disappeared around a bend in the road.

Jesselynn thought of the crude map the younger man had gotten in one of his scouting forays. According to the map, they were to head south for a time and then pick up a road heading west again. As the days passed, she wished at times they had followed the more heavily traveled road to Louisville, but they had decided against it. The possibility of boarding a keelboat to take them down the Ohio River and onto the Mississippi still carried far more appeal than the overland trek. But they'd have to pass the fort at Cairo, where General Grant was stationed with his army. "Army of the West," she'd heard it called.

Meshach clucked forward the team consisting of the two mares this time. Daniel rode the mule. Jesselynn glanced over her shoulder at the clearing they were leaving behind. Such a terribly close brush with tragedy. They would have to be more careful, that's all.

She pulled her coat more tightly around her. Clouds hung low and smelled like rain. Lightning splintered the sky off to the north. This promised to be a bad night if the clouds had anything to say about it.

It wasn't long after full dark that the clouds gave up and released their burden on the travelers below. Within minutes, Jesselynn's wool coat smelled wet and rain dripped from her hat brim down her neck. She turtled herself as much as possible, but the wind first nipped at her hat, then turned to tearing at it and shaking her furiously, like a dog shaking himself off. The frigid drops blew into her face, and when she tucked it into her coat, they ran down the back of her neck.

"Tain't fit fo' man nor beast," Meshach declared when Jesselynn trotted alongside the wagon. Already puddles disguised the road in a muddy stream when they climbed a rise and slid down the other slippery side. He set the brake some to keep the wagon from running over the horses and hushed Ophelia when she squealed at a slip.

They climbed another grade and were back on a westering ridge. At least she hoped it was westering. She couldn't even see Ahab's ears, let alone far enough ahead to get an idea where they were going.

The longer the rain persisted, the more she longed for home. So her father had made her promise. They gave it a good try. How would he know if they turned around, anyway? She shook her head, her hat flopping about her ears. Maybe this was God's punishment for leaving home. Surely they'd been on the road long enough for dawn to be coming soon.

Ahab snorted and, arching his neck, whinnied before she realized what he was doing. "No!" She tightened the reins in retaliation for being jerked from her somnolence. The horse sidestepped, his entire body at attention. Something was coming toward them.

She reined Ahab to the side of the road under the overhanging trees, praying that Meshach was doing the same. She could hear a harness jingling, and when that fell silent, a horse galloping toward them. She swung off her horse and clamped her hand over his nostrils. Others followed, barely heard above the rain on the leaves overhead and her heart thundering in her chest.

A shot and then another.

The lone rider raced by them, water splashing from the horse's hooves.

Was it Benjamin?

Her eyes hurt from straining to see what was happening.

Horse hooves fading, others charging on. Two riders splashed past, then two more. Another shot was fired, this time so close she saw the flash of the gun.

All the hoofbeats faded into the distance. The rain picked up again, as if the brief interlude had been to tantalize them. Who was the fugitive? Who was chasing him? Confederate, Union, or deserter? What lay ahead?

Her ears ached from listening, and her eyes burned in spite of the drenching. Ahab stamped a front hoof and pushed her in the back with his nose. She stumbled one foot forward, almost surprised that she'd been able to move. She felt rooted to the soil like the oak tree that kept only the worst of the downpour from her head.

"Jesse? Jesse?"

"Here." Clamping Ahab's reins tight in her fist, she followed the sound, discovering the wagon no more than twenty feet away. She stopped by the front wheels. "You think that was Benjamin?"

"Uh-huh. He run like de devil himself be after him. Patrol musta cotched him."

"Or tried to."

"Domino, he outrun army horses anytime. You watch, Benjamin be back soon," Meshach said.

"I hope so, but they were shooting at him."

"No matter, he too far 'head to get shot."

Jesselynn hoped he was as sure as he sounded. "So we wait?"

"We gets us off'n dis here road, dat's what. Daniel, you found any other trail or road?"

"I thinks so. Dey's a dark spot in de woods. You wants me to look it out?"

"An' be quick. Dem sojers might be comin' back."

Another wait set her skin to crawling under the soaked coat and dripping hat. At least Thaddy was dry in the wagon bed under the tarp. He and Ophelia were so quiet, either sleeping or too scared to make a sound. If only she could see. Another part of her mind reminded her, *If you could see, then they could see you.* Gratitude for the rain surged through heart and mind, the intensity of it turning the drops to steam. Or at least that's what it felt like.

She let Ahab listen for her. As long as he dropped his head and dozed beside her, she leaned against him, her eyes heavy but the frequent shudders from the cold keeping her awake. Besides, she had yet to perfect the art of sleeping standing up. When her horse raised his head, she clamped her hand over his nostrils to keep him from whinnying. As soon as he relaxed, she knew the arrival to be Daniel.

"Follow me." The rain nearly drowned his words.

Cold, wet, and tired didn't begin to describe the misery that made fitting her foot in the stirrup and pulling herself aboard her horse a near impossibility. When Ahab snorted and shifted away from her, she fought tears that would only add to the water funneling off her soggy hat and streaming down her face. Leaning against the saddle, she fought the despair that threatened to overwhelm her.

"Get on the horse! Now!" she commanded herself. "Ahab, stand still!" She punctuated her words with a slap on his shoulder. Instead of obeying, he nickered and took a couple steps forward. She knew he resented being left behind, and even though she couldn't hear the others, she knew he could. "Ahab, stand!" This time her voice snapped in the sodden air. Ahab stamped one front hoof but stood still until she swung into the saddle, it, too, soaking wet. The last remaining dry part of her shivered in the cold wet. Shrieking took more effort than she had available.

"You all right, Marse Jesse?" Meshach asked when she trotted even with the wagon. "We was 'bout to go back for you."

Marse Jesse indeed. Right now this *young man* couldn't wrestle a flea.

"You can git under de tarp wid 'Phelia and Thaddy."

"Thanks, but no thanks. Did Daniel say how far?"

"Over here!" The voice came from their left.

Never had night seemed so dark or rain so wet as they pulled the wagon under what smelled like an oak tree. The canopy cut off the worst of the torrent so they could hear each other talk without shouting.

"Sojers 'bout half mile ahead on de road. Farm mebbe down dis here one." Daniel sat his horse next to Jesse. "I think we be safe here."

Jesselynn could do no more than nod.

They waited out the night, huddling together under the tarp with the horses on long lines to graze on what they could find. The wind let up as the sky eased into gray. Torrents reduced to drizzle, tree trunks took on form, and one of the horses shook all over, his mane flapping like a soaked rag.

We'll never get a fire started, Jesselynn thought, trying to keep the shudders from making her teeth clack.

"We dare start a fire?" Meshach dug at a tooth with his tongue, studying the dripping landscape.

"Sojers close by," Daniel answered.

What about Benjamin? Did he get away? If I'm supposed to be the leader here, we are in worse trouble than ever before.

"Go on foot and see where de farm be." Meshach pointed back along the trail they had obviously come in on.

A bugle sounded some distance away but close enough to raise the hair on the back of her neck. Jesselynn heard Ophelia stirring behind her. At least someone had slept, and the longer Thaddy slept, the easier on all of them.

A hound bayed somewhere to the north of them. As the sky lightened, birds twittered in the branches overhead. Cold hard biscuit would be all they had if they couldn't get a fire going. A cup of hot coffee or even hot water sounded like ambrosia.

Daniel slipped back into camp like a shadow, appearing out of the trees without a sound. "Farm 'bout a quarter mile away. Dere's dogs 'round it. Saw a man go to the barn to milk."

Meshach returned from the trees carrying an armful of dry branches and pulled crackling leaves from his pocket. "Dey's under a rock." He took the tinderbox from under the tarp and set to making a fire. Within minutes the flames licking the branches brought a whole new feeling of cheer to the group.

Jesselynn felt hope climb over the despair that weighted her down.

"Is . . . is a fire safe?"

"Smoke won't go far in rain. I kin—" The sound of the bugle cut off his words as they all strained to hear anything else.

A horse whinnied. A cow bellowed. Drops smacked the sodden mat of leaves on the woods floor. Another horse whinnied, this time closer.

Jesselynn stopped moving as if someone had shouted an order to halt. The others did the same. She and Meshach reached for the rifles at the same time.

Ahab nickered. The mare did also. Benjamin rode into the clearing wearing a smile wide enough to crack his face.

"Mornin', Marse Jesse. Meshach, you kin put de guns down now."

"Benjamin, you're alive." Jesselynn dropped the rifle back down in the wagon bed and grabbed Domino's reins.

He slid off his horse and stood in front of her. "No dumb sojers gonna cotch me and Domino here. We outrun dem fo' sure."

"How'd you find us?" She wanted to check his arms and shoulders for the wounds she was sure he'd received with the shots fired.

"I puts bit o' cloth on a low branch to mark our turnin' places." Daniel slapped Benjamin on the back. "And he finds 'em."

A whimper from the sleeping pallets brought her attention back to the wagon. Ophelia was stirring a pot over the fire so Jesselynn pulled back the tarp, being careful to keep the puddling water from seeping into the bedding. "How's our boy this mornin'?"

"Hungry." He climbed up her side and nestled against her.

"Ophelia is makin' breakfast."

"Don't want mush."

"Too bad. This mornin' we're lucky to have anything hot." She glanced up at the skies that hung right about the treetops. While the gray was lighter, it was still gray and drizzling.

He clung to her more tightly, his voice turning to a wheedle. "Joshwa want bacon—and egg."

"Well, Joshwa better go on away and bring back Thaddeus, who is much more agreeable." She kissed his cheek and nuzzled his neck.

"You wet." He scrubbed his cheek dry.

"And cold. Get your clothes, and I'll help you get dressed."

"Me do it."

"Thaddy, please just do as I tell you." She took her hat off and slapped it against her thigh to get some water off it, then set it back on her head, pulling it low so the drip didn't go directly down the back of her neck. While he stood glaring at her, looking so much like a miniature version of her father that laughter warred with tears, she shifted things around until she found his clothes, dry but like everything else, carrying the feel of damp.

"Breakfast ready." Ophelia held out a bowl of steaming corn mush with a dollop of sorghum in the center.

Jesselynn pulled a wool sweater over Thaddy's curls and set him down to put on his shoes. He grabbed his stockings.

"Me do it!" The glare he gave her could have roasted a goose.

Since Jesselynn had been reared on stories of her own independence, she shook her head. *How did Mother put up with me?* "All right, Joshwa, you do one, and I'll do the other. Race you."

He took up the dare and tried cramming his toes into the stocking, which promptly slipped out of his hands and headed toward the wet ground. Jesselynn stopped rolling hers and snatched the sock before it hit the mud puddle. When she handed it back to him, Thaddy grinned up at her and handed the sock back.

"You do it." She nodded and within a minute had his socks on and was buttoning up his shoes. *Life sure would be easier if he had boots that just pulled on or laced without a button hook.*

Since puddles still dotted the ground, they ate leaning against the wagon gate and the wheels. Talk died while everyone made short work of the mush, dunking their biscuits in the coffee to soften them.

"Baby cryin'." Thaddeus cocked his head and looked off toward the west.

"There's no babies clear out here."

"Sho 'nuff is." Meshach stopped chewing to listen.

The cry came again, so sad it nearly tore her heart out. When the cry stopped, then picked up again, Jesselynn scraped the last bit from her bowl and set it down on the tailgate. "I'll go see."

"Not widout me." Meshach waved the others to stay where they were as he and Jesselynn headed into the woods. "Maybe dey's a cabin up ahead."

"Could be." A branch snapped underneath her feet. *Why was she making so much noise when Meshach seemed to move without touching the ground?*

They stopped to listen again, then angled some off to the right. The cry seemed weaker.

"Are we goin' the right direction?" she asked.

"Yessuh." He shot her a smile that in the dimness seemed even brighter than normal.

They stopped again, waiting, but no cry came.

A chill rippled up her back. Was this a trap to separate them all, make it easier for someone to steal the horses? She looked over her shoulder, but there were no sounds of attack from the direction of the wagons. Surely no one could sneak up on them so easily that Ophelia didn't even shriek.

She took in a breath and held it, listening so hard her ears buzzed.

A whimper. A hiccup. A cry.

Relief poured through her like a warm shower, soaking clear to her toes. There was indeed a baby. Now just to find it.

"Keep cryin', little one," she whispered as she and Meshach pushed aside branches and made their way toward the sound.

The ground dropped away at the lip of a hollow. Trees marched down the steep bank, a fallen granddaddy oak lying crosswise partway down. Mists feathered the trees and obscured the bottom, where she was sure a creek meandered downward between rocks and logs. How far to the water she had no idea. They ghosted from tree to tree, dancing with the fog that splattered when an errant breeze tickled the upper branches.

Once around the rotting log, she caught her breath.

Meshach shared her look of horror before stopping at the end of the log, just out of the child's sight.

Wearing a tattered shift and covered in mud, the child rooted at the breast of the woman lying dead in the lee of the log. From the looks of her, she'd died at least the day before. A newborn lay between her legs, also dead.

"Runaway slave." Meshach hunkered down where he was, shaking his head all the while.

"How do you know?" She kept her voice low also, not wanting to frighten the child.

"See de brand on her face."

Jesselynn recognized it now. Her father had forbidden such atrocities.

"Hey, baby, we come for you." Meshach's voice carried the same gentle cadence he used for the skittish horses.

The little one whipped around, screwed up his face, and, sitting in the muck, raised his arms to be picked up.

Jesselynn reached him first, crooning all the while, then picked him up and hugged him to her chest. "Ah, baby, how'd you make it through the night without wild animals gettin' you?" She rocked from side to side, watching as Meshach checked out the body of the woman and the dead infant. "We have to bury her," she said.

"I know." He held up a pitifully small sack. "She been on de road some time."

"And died in childbirth." Jesselynn looked around them. While in the sunlight this would be a lovely shaded glen, in the rain and fog, dismal was the only word she could think of. When she saw the scars of the whiplash on the woman's arms and chest, she hugged the baby tighter, making him wail instead of whimper.

"Think you can find de way back?" Meshach had placed the infant on its mother's chest. "Send Benjamin to help here."

She nodded. "We didn't come too far. I can call if I need."

"Or whistle like a robin?"

"Oh, I guess not." She picked up the tow sack and, with the child on her arm, made her way back around the ancient tree. "I'll have Benjamin bring the Bible."

"Yessuh, thanks."

As she climbed higher, she felt a rush of warmth down her side before she could hold the child away from her. "Well, thanks for that little gift. You could have warned me."

The boy whimpered and stuck his thumb and forefinger in his mouth, hiccuping at the same time.

"Wonder how long since you've been fed." She stopped at the top of the bank to catch her breath. He might be just beyond babyhood. She doubted he was even a year yet, but lugging him up the steep hill made him seem heavier with every step.

By this time too she was fairly certain he was running a fever. What might she be bringing into camp?

Chapter Twelve

THE MILITARY HOSPITAL
RICHMOND, VIRGINIA

"Do you think he is ever goin' to wake up?"

"I certainly hope so, Miz Highwood." The doctor shook his head. "But every day he remains comatose, the less chance . . ." His voice trailed off. "Maybe if you spent some time talking with him, reading to him, that might help."

"You think he can hear me?"

"I've heard tell of folks who woke up knowin' things they could only have heard while asleep. Makes me think ears are more important than we give them credit for. Let's see if Corporal Shaddock there might read to him. Missin' a leg won't hurt his tongue any."

If he can read. Louisa was careful not to voice the thought. Corporal Shaddock didn't need anything else to make him feel worse. Some men seemed to handle the loss of a limb better than others, but no one accepted living on one leg easily.

She studied the man wrapped in bandages and lying so still. Who was he? Why did he seem familiar? Was it because she had seen so many bandaged men by this time, or was it something else? Could he hear them and was just not able to respond?

But he wasn't paralyzed. The doctor had made sure of that. What was keeping him in some no-man's-land?

She thought back to her early morning time reading her Bible. This soldier had come into her mind even then, and so she had prayed for him as she did for so many others. That thought led to another, as so often happened. She'd prayed those at home too. What was going on at Twin Oaks, and why hadn't they heard from Jesselynn after the letter she wrote telling them that Father had died?

Sometimes the urge to go home was almost more than she could bear.

Instead of succumbing to the tears that threatened, she pasted a smile on her face and took the few paces to stand beside Corporal Shaddock's bed. "I know you are awake, so just open your eyes and take this little treat I have for you."

He blinked and cracked one eyelid. "Go 'way."

"Now, you know me better than that."

"Be nice to the lady, son, if ya know what's good for ya." Lieutenant Lessling leaned on his crutches, another victim of losing a leg but choosing to make the best of a bad situation. Said he had a plantation to run as soon as they released him from "this miserable example of a house of healin'." This he repeated more than once to whoever happened to be in the vicinity.

The general in charge hadn't thought too kindly of the rebuke.

Louisa had a hard time keeping a straight face when Lessling went on a diatribe. She'd heard much worse.

"So, Corporal Shaddock, shall I go on to someone else?" Her smile made him blink twice and flush once. He was young enough that he hadn't lost the ability to blush, and his fair skin shone like a rose in full bloom.

"No, ma'am." He winced as he rolled flat on his back and pushed himself up against the wall. He tried glaring at her, but the cutting glance from the man on crutches changed his glare to a grimace meant to be a smile—perhaps.

Louisa waited until he was about as comfortable as he would be, then handed him two molasses cookies in a napkin. "Wish I could offer you coffee too, but . . ." She shrugged. "You slept through breakfast."

"Warn't neither sleepin'." The act of growling made him cough and clench his treat tight enough to break the cookies into small pieces. He opened the napkin and gave her an apologetic look. "Sorry, missus."

"They'll taste just as good, but don't you go tellin' all the others what you have there. They might get jealous."

He ducked his chin, but she could see the beginnings of a true smile stretch his lips. She patted his shoulder before bending closer. "Now if you could do me a favor, perhaps?"

He nodded. "If'n I can."

"Would you mind talking with the man in that bed?"

"But he don't say nothin'."

"I know that, but Doc said this might help. I'd read to him if I had time." She touched the Bible she always kept in the pocket of her apron.

"I don't read so good, ma'am, but I could surely give it a try if you could see fit to loan me your Bible."

Rejoicing in the spate of words from a man who hadn't strung more than two together before, she handed him her Bible. "Why don't you start with the Gospel of John? It's always been my favorite."

With the crumb-sprinkled napkin spread on the bed beside him and the Bible propped on his chest, he fumbled through the pages until he found John and began to read. " 'In the beginning was the Word, and the Word was with God, and the Word was God. The same was in the beginning with God. All things were made by him; and without him was not any thing made that was made.' "

Thank you, Father. She sent her prayer winging heavenward as she went on to the next patient.

"Shore do be fine to hear them words." The boy on the bed looked too young to begin shaving, let alone nearly die in a hail of bullets. "My ma read to us ever night."

"Mine too, when my daddy wasn't there." Louisa handed him a lemon drop. "Thought this might help that frog in your throat." While she knew the frog would live there permanently due to his neck injury, sucking on the candy would be soothing.

"Thankee."

By the time she'd finished one side of the long room, the men on the other were getting restless. The heat and the flies ripened as the sun reached the midpoint, turning the second floor of the hospital into a miasma of sickness, smells, and sweat.

"You go on, take a minute under that shade tree out there." The lieutenant stopped beside her after his self-imposed traversing of the center aisle. While she'd tried to get him to take it easier, he insisted that walking not only made him stronger but also helped pass the time.

She'd noticed that much of his time was passed assisting those who were worse off than he. "Thank you. I think I will." She wiped her perspiring face with the underside of her stained apron. "I'll get a bucket of cold water at the same time."

"You let Jacob bring the water. Better him carrying those buckets up the stairs than you."

Louisa gave him an arched eyebrow look that clearly said, "Who made you my boss?"

"Sorry." A tiny smile quirked one corner of his well-defined lips. But he didn't back down, even leaning on crutches and looming over her. "That's what he was hired for. You want to take an old man's job away from him?"

Louisa sighed. "Now that you put it that way, of course not, but it doesn't look to me like he has extra time on his hands." She glanced over to where the corporal continued reading. Several other ambulatory patients had taken up the spare spaces on the beds. *Why didn't I think of that before?*

"You can't think of everything."

Her attention snapped back to the lieutenant. "How . . . ?"

"Your face is like an open picture book. One needn't even know words to read it." He cleared his throat. "I better get back to . . ." Without finishing his sentence, he turned and clump-thumped his way back down the aisle.

She watched him go. Thin—no, emaciated was a better word for his build, his shoulder bones sticking out of his thin cotton robe like angel wings. His wrists and fingers could do with a better flesh covering; the bones showed so clearly. And his face . . . She'd seen a human skeleton once, and it didn't look too different from the man swinging on his crutches. Yet his eyes hadn't lost their piercing blue nor his mind its sharpness. Both courtly manners and a keen intellect, quickened by a good education, were evidenced by every word he spoke. She'd be willing to bet he came into the world as officer material, and the war only honed it.

What would he do now?

None of your business, my girl. Now get on about your chores and quit lollygagging over something that has nothing to do with you. He's one of your patients, that's all. On her way out, she grabbed both buckets and headed on down the stairs.

A slight breeze made pumping the water a pleasure, and when the first gush hit the tin bucket, she wished she could stop and splash it on her face but kept pumping instead. Stopping would only prolong the effort. The clang and suck of the handle and pump sang a song peculiar to hand pumps, the gush turning to a gurgle as the bucket filled.

"You don't want to do dat, Missy." Old Jacob took the handle from her with a reproachful shake of his grizzled head.

Louisa glanced up to see the lieutenant looking down at her from the window. She put two fingers to her forehead in a saucy salute and stepped back as Jacob took the first bucket from under the spigot and set the other in place, all the time keeping the handle in motion. She dipped her handkerchief under the waterspout and used it to wet her face. If he weren't watching, she might have wiped her neck and down her bosom also. If only she dared defy Aunt Sylvania and go without her corset, the cool air could at least reach her skin.

She sneaked an upward peek, but no, he hadn't moved. *Drat and tarnation!* Taking the dipper that hung on a hook beside the pump, she filled it with water and drank, making sure that some of it dribbled down her front. The remainder she poured over her hands and wrists. She thought of plunging her hands in the bucket up to her elbows, but who'd want to drink water she'd had her hands in?

"I takes dese up now."

"Yes, thank you."

She watched him go, the weight of the full buckets rounding shoulders already curved from heavy toil. But as the lieutenant said, the man's job was important to him. She wondered whose slave he had been before and when he had been freed. Had Jesselynn freed all their slaves as she'd threatened to? Or had Father done it himself? Oh, the questions of home. When would a letter come through? Thaddeus would be so grown up by now that she would hardly recognize him, and he wouldn't even know who she was. They must be cutting the tobacco. Lucinda would have the kitchen in an uproar putting up pickles and jams and jellies.

Louisa leaned against the rough bark of the elm tree. *Home, Lord. Oh, please, I want to go home.*

"Miz Highwood, come quick." The lieutenant's voice propelled her into a decidedly unladylike run.

Chapter Thirteen

❧❧

"He one sick baby." Ophelia frowned in concern over the little tyke they had rescued.

Jesselynn nodded. Ophelia wasn't exaggerating this time. "We've got to get his fever down." The baby twitched in her arms. Thaddeus sat leaning against her, forefinger and thumb both in his mouth. He didn't look too good either at the moment.

It had taken them two days to get all dried out after the rainstorm, but the roads were still too muddy to make decent time, so they decided to stay where they were for another night. Right now she was wishing they didn't have the wagon — or the extra horse that needed to stop for rests. Riding, they could have been long gone and able to cover the country faster. But riding with Thaddeus would be miserable, near to impossible. Besides, they didn't have enough horses to pack all their supplies, meager though they were.

"See if you can get some more milk in him while Thaddy and I go search for some willow bark. A tea of that should help bring his fever down." *If only I'd brought more of Mother's simples.* But now was the time to be out harvesting things like ginseng, Solomon's seal, wood sorrel, and the like. If she didn't have to sleep during the day, she could be searching for them in the afternoon. How much easier it was at home where she knew where the best patches of everything grew.

Here it was hit or miss, although Meshach had brought in a fine mess of cress and dandelion to boil up for dinner. Stewed with the rabbit he'd snared and the wild onion, it tasted mighty fine. That was one good thing about Kentucky — one could live off the land if need be. While Benjamin and Daniel were catching some much needed sleep, Meshach seemed to need little rest. When she asked him about it, he shrugged her off.

"I gets enough, Marse Jesse. Not to worry."

But worry she did in spite of her good intentions. While she knew they were heading west, they'd had to detour so often she wasn't sure where they were or if they were traveling the best way. She rubbed her forehead, the ache behind her eyes getting worse instead of better. *What if that baby has something we can all catch? How do I care for all these people if I get sick? Or Meshach?*

The last time she remembered being sick she had the chicken pox, but Lucinda and her mother had cosseted her back to health in spite of the itchy bumps all over her body. While Louisa and Zachary had gotten off lightly, she and Carrie Mae had had bad cases. Her mother had always said it was amazing she didn't have more scars on her face.

Lucinda had warned her that if she scratched, her skin would all fall off and she'd be nothing but bones.

That picture kept her from digging at the sores.

But what did this baby have? Other than being out in the rain and wind by himself. No wonder he whimpered every time they put him down, poor thing. Too easily the picture of the dead mother came to her mind. She was trying to escape with her babes, and look what it got her. The scars covering her body said she'd gone under the lash more than once. It didn't take too strong an imagination to see the horrors she must have endured.

Jesselynn shuddered. While she'd heard many stories, she'd never seen one human beaten by another, other than the whipping Dunlivey had given one of the field hands. That had been Dunlivey's last act at Twin Oaks. Later on they'd learned that he'd beaten others, but by threatening them with worse, he'd never been caught at it.

What if he is searching for us now? The thought made shivers chase each other up and down her back. The sight of his snarling face made her stomach clench — and her headache worsen.

While she needed to be sleeping herself, she couldn't do that with the baby crying and coughing.

"Jesse, hold me." Thaddeus held up his arms. She wiped his runny nose with a square of cotton she used for a handkerchief and, picking him up, let him wrap his arms around her neck and his legs around her waist. He clung like a baby possum to its mother's back. She kissed his forehead and, sure enough, he felt warm too. Two sick children, muddy roads, and patrols going past not a quarter mile away. How were they to manage?

Now her headache felt like the drum of galloping horses' hooves on a wooden bridge. An entire platoon.

"He won't take no milk." Ophelia carried the baby on her hip, jiggling him gently but without much success. He cried anyway.

"Here, you take Thaddeus." Jesselynn tried to pull the limpet off her neck, but then he stopped whimpering and fell to out-and-out crying.

"Want you, not 'Phelia," he stammered between sobs.

"But the baby needs me." She tried prying again with no success.

"No-o-o-o." He scrubbed his runny nose against her neck.

"Hey, how 'bout we think of a name for the baby?"

"No. Don' like baby." He clung so tightly, he almost cut off her air.

"Thaddeus Joshua Highwood, you stop that this instant." She bounced him with a sharp jerk to get his attention.

"No!" He cried harder, stiffening his body and banging his head against her collarbone.

Wonderful. Now he was working his way up to a full-sized Highwood tantrum. She recognized it well, having thrown a few herself. One time Lucinda had dunked her in cold water. Trying to breathe around the shock made a screaming tantrum pretty near impossible, when she got her breath back, that was. She'd never thrown one again.

She hoped something like that wouldn't be necessary with Thaddeus.

But when he began shrieking and nearly threw himself out of her arms, she started looking for a bucket of water. When none was in sight, she thunked him down on the wagon bed. "Now you just stay there until you can behave. I will not hold a boy who kicks and hits me."

He rolled from side to side, arms thrashing.

Meshach came running from the woods. "What wrong?"

Jesselynn shook her head, disgust narrowing her eyes. "My little brother is throwing a tantrum, that's what. All because he is jealous of our new baby."

The poor baby was also screaming at this point, but stopping to cough brought his cries to a standstill. He coughed until he threw up what little milk Ophelia had gotten down him and then coughed some more. It sounded like he was coughing his lungs right out.

"You stay with him," she said to Meshach, pointing to Thaddy, then ran around the wagon to help Ophelia with the other one. She dunked a cloth in warm water and washed the baby's face and his nappy hair. His cries subsided, his eyes drifting closed and a hiccup jerking his entire body. While they had put one of Thaddy's shirts on him, she could still count every bone in his neck. His fingers looked more like claws than baby hands and his bowed legs didn't have the strength to hold him up yet.

Jesselynn thought back to the fat black babies tumbling around the little house where the babies stayed while their mothers worked in the fields. Twin Oaks had few women working alongside the men in the tobacco and hayfields, having them instead work the acre-sized garden and the orchards, and do the household tasks like spinning and weaving. Providing food and clothing for all the folks on the plantation took many hands and many hours. It seemed they never had enough of either.

She and Ophelia nursed the children through the afternoon and evening, but as the stars poked holes in the heavens, Meshach came to stand beside her. "We best be pullin' out."

"I know, but dare we travel with this one so sick?"

"Got to get away from sojers."

"I know." They'd heard another patrol just before dusk. "All right. You want to drive or ride?" Asking his preference was a real act of grace on her part. All she wanted to do was mount up on Ahab and ride free, gallop through the night far enough ahead so she couldn't hear children crying and coughing. If only she had some of Lucinda's elderberry wine or a hot toddy for the black baby. Her mother mixed honey, lemon, and whisky for sore throats and coughs. Surely there was something in the simples bag to help, but for the life of her, she couldn't remember. Why, oh, why hadn't she brought her mother's housekeeping journal along? It held all the recipes.

"I drive. 'Phelia can take care of both boys in de back of de wagon. They go to sleep and wake up better in de mornin'."

"What makes you think that?"

"I bin prayin' for dem."

Meshach's simple faith smacked her in the face. She had not thought to pray lately, other than a frantic "Oh, God" a few times. And how long since they'd read the Scriptures? She'd seen him reading in the early morning. Why hadn't she?

She squinted her eyes, staring at the fire until the flames seemed to fill her mind. *Because I'm no longer sure that God is listening.* She plundered her mind some more. Or cares.

"I'll saddle Ahab, then." Relief flooded her mind. She could get away. "And I hope your God is listenin'."

"He yo' God too, Marse Jesse, and He won't let you forget it."

"Yes, well . . ." She turned to Ophelia. "Let's fill that jug with hot water and wrap it in one of the quilts so you can use it as you need it." She tucked a quilt around Thaddeus, who had finally fallen asleep. When she felt his forehead, he didn't seem any cooler. *So much for God making them better. Maybe if I can find some willow bark by a stream that would help.*

Within minutes they were on the road, heading toward the evening star again. After the deluge the nights before, the air still smelled fresh and clean. A hint of woodsmoke, the tang of a long-departed skunk, ammonia of fresh horse droppings, the smells of forest and fall melded into a rich soup of aromas.

A rising half-moon cleared the treetops and sent their shadows leading them onward.

In spite of herself, Jesselynn dropped back to see how the babies were doing. Ophelia was rocking the black baby, and Thaddeus coughed in his sleep beside her.

"He burnin' up wid fever."

"Unwrap him from the quilt."

"Him get cold." But she did as Jesselynn ordered and loosened the covering. As the cool air touched his skin, the baby set up a howl.

"Here, hand him up here. Maybe the rocking of the horse will settle him down."

"With Ahab?" Meshach joined the conversation.

"Oh, you're right." Jesselynn felt like plugging her ears and riding hard—away. If she'd used her head earlier, they could have harnessed Ahab and she could have ridden the mare. "Up ahead, if he doesn't calm down, we'll switch the team around."

"Should do that anyways. De mud makes for heavy pullin'."

At least we're not hub-deep in it. That alone was something to be grateful for.

The moon floated high above them, silvering the trees and whitening the road. Jesselynn let herself slump in the saddle, riding far enough ahead so the fitful cries of their sick ones sounded more like bird twitterings.

"Halt! Who goes there!"

Her heart hit triple time before she could suck in a breath.

Chapter Fourteen

RICHMOND, VIRGINIA

"I'm comin'!" Louisa picked up her skirts and dashed back inside.

"No need to fret yourself." The old black man shook his grizzled head. "I gets de water."

"Sorry, no . . ." Louisa checked her rush up the stairs.

"You go on." He chuckled this time, still shaking his head. "Young ladies don' go runnin' like dat. Just not proper." But he made shooing motions with his hands, sending her on up the second set of stairs.

Louisa didn't need another invitation. She could hear laughter from her floor, laughter like she hadn't heard since she started volunteering over a month ago. Whatever could be so hilarious?

But when she burst through the arched doorway, silence fell with laughter choked off so quick it sent one patient into a fit of coughing. A snicker came from the region of the unknown soldier.

What in heaven's name is going on? She glanced over to the window where the lieutenant stood looking out as if he'd never ordered her to come back in with such urgency. Several others refused to look her in the eye, feigning sleep instead.

The low drone of Corporal Shaddock reading to the comatose man picked up again.

"All right, children, fess up. There's something going on here."

A snicker from the corner. She whirled to see who it was, but no one looked guilty even.

A moan came from a new man just returned from surgery. Lopping off limbs seemed the answer to most injuries, but a quick glance at two beds down on her right showed all four appendages in place.

"No more cookies until someone tells me what is goin' on."

Still no response other than a groan, this one forced enough to tell her it wasn't due to pain.

What could have happened? She hadn't been gone more than fifteen minutes, if that. Who could she intimidate the most?

Stopping at Corporal Shaddock's side, she cleared her throat. He stopped reading and sent a quick look her way, then glanced at the man whom she'd been calling the unknown soldier.

Shivers chased up and down her spine. The doc had changed the dressings, so one eye now showed. The dark brow above it arched in an oh-so-familiar way. The man was definitely conscious.

Her heart felt as though it had stopped. The whole world stopped only for an instant. She took four steps forward and sank to her knees, grasping the hand that lay on top of the sheet.

"Zachary?"

"None other." The hand squeezed hers back, weak but no weaker than the voice.

He's alive, my brother is alive. Oh, God, thank you, my brother is alive.

"At least what's left of me." The tinge of bitterness that underlay his words sounded so familiar that she laid her cheek on the back of his hand.

"But you're alive. That's all that matters. You're alive." *My brother who we feared was dead is alive.*

Hand clapping from those able and a cheer from others brought her back to the current place and time.

"How . . . how long have I been unconscious?"

"A week or so. You were muttering when they brought you in, but then we heard nothing more from you." She swiped away the tears that refused to stop. "We've been praying for you so long, never knowing if you were in prison, alive, or dead." She shuddered on the last words. *I can't tell him about Daddy yet. And Jesselynn. Or how they are at home.*

"Where . . . where am I?" He cleared his throat.

"Richmond. I'm visitin' Aunt Sylvania. Carrie Mae too."

"Why?"

"Jesselynn made us come here." She knew that wasn't altogether true. Carrie Mae had pleaded to go when the invitation arrived. And since Jesselynn wouldn't allow the younger sister to travel alone, they had both been sent off. Sometimes she still smarted under the injustice of it all. She thought a moment. "How did they all figure out—?" She stopped, not certain how much he knew.

"When I gave my name and rank, the lieutenant put two and two together."

"Really?" She kept herself from looking at the man still staring out the window.

"And figured out you are my wife. Mrs. Zachary Highwood, right?" At least he had the sense to whisper.

Chapter Fifteen

GORDONSVILLE, KENTUCKY
SEPTEMBER 30, 1862

Where was Benjamin, and why hadn't he warned them?

"Speak or I'll shoot!"

"Jus' some weary travelers, suh." She deepened her voice, masking the fear.

A man stepped out of the shadows, his uniform light in the moonlight, a rifle held across his chest.

She shot Meshach a look meant to keep him quiet and kept her hands in front of her. Not that she had anything to hide. The rifle lay safe behind the wagon seat. And of no use at all.

"Where y'all goin'?"

"Not far up yondah." She nodded toward the west, keeping her hat low over her face. The urge to tell him more caused her to bite her tongue. Benjamin had reminded them just before starting out tonight that the less said, the better.

"What are ya carrying?" The soldier stepped closer to the wagon, his rifle at the ready.

"Nothin' much." *What do I say?* "Jus' tryin' to gits home." She could tell by his accent he was southern, but a rifle pointed was still a rifle, no matter whose side held it.

"Where's home?" This time he looked at her directly.

She squared her shoulders and sucked in a deep breath trying to conceal the frenzy of her thoughts. Why hadn't she figured for this in advance? What town lay ahead? Where had they been?

The black baby let out a wail that made her spine tingle, it sounded so like a wounded animal.

The soldier stepped back.

An idea sizzled into her frozen mind. "Ah, you might not want to get too close, suh. That baby real sick. You might catch what he got."

"Sick?" The man stepped back again.

"Can you tell the smallpox?"

"S-smallpox?" He took three more steps back, moonlight glistening on the whites of his eyes.

"Well, we ain't sure what it is, but the baby be right sick. You know how to cure the pox, if that be it?"

"No. No, I don't." He waved his rifle. "You git on outa here now."

The baby wailed again.

"Right now, you hear me?"

"Yes, suh. Thankee, suh." Jesselynn put her heels to Ahab's ribs as Meshach clucked the team forward. They trotted down the road without looking back, even though for Jesse the temptation was nigh unbearable.

They caught up with Benjamin about a mile or so up the road when he whistled his presence.

"He din't stop me," the young man answered when questioned. "I din't know he was even dere."

"Most likely sleepin' at de post till we come by. Horses and wagon make more noise."

With the wagon moving again, the baby settled back down and fell asleep.

"How are they?" Jesselynn rode up next to Ophelia.

"Both sleepin'." She glanced over her shoulder to the two children in the wagon bed, then up at Jesselynn. "You really think him got de pox?" Her voice carried the same fear heard in the soldier's.

"No, not at all. I've never seen smallpox, but Mother told me what to watch for. You'd most likely be sick too if you spent the night in the rain like he did, naked, hungry. Poor baby."

Daniel rode up beside Jesselynn. "I 'bout wet my britches when dat sojer hollered."

Ophelia snickered. Meshach chuckled. And Jesselynn gave an undeniably feminine giggle before correcting herself with a deeper voice.

" 'Might be smallpox.' " Meshach imitated her comment, even to the hint of fear in her voice. Only the soldier didn't know that the fear had nothing to do with smallpox.

Their laughter rang through the night as they kept the horses at a trot to cover the ground they'd missed because of the sick boys.

But as they trotted on through the night, following the moon on its westward descent, thoughts continued to plague Jesselynn. What *was* wrong with the black baby? Had Thaddeus caught something from him so quickly, or was it the rain and traveling that gave him the grippe? By the time they could see individual trees instead of just a dark bank, she'd decided that she was going herself into the next town they came to. They needed supplies, and she needed information. Maybe there'd even be a newspaper to tell her what was going on with the war in general and Kentucky in particular.

As always, she would check the posted list of dead and missing. Never seeing the name of Zachary Highwood helped keep hope alive. Not much but enough.

When Benjamin whistled them off the road and into a clearing, she could finally give up the feeling that she needed to keep looking behind her in case the soldier changed his mind.

"All I seen is a couple of small farms," Benjamin said in answer to her question. "Man always up settin' out to milkin' him cows. You want I should go dere?"

Jesselynn nodded. That was another reason she needed to get to a town. They were about out of small coins. What farmer would be able to change a gold piece? And a young black man carrying a gold piece would be sure to create all kinds of suspicion.

While the others set up camp, Jesselynn took her little brother out behind the bushes and then down to the creek, still swollen from the rains, to wash. When she laid her cheek against his, no longer did the heat meet her. While his nose never ceased to run, and he coughed at times, she could tell he was on the mend.

"Stay here!" He pointed to the side of the creek when she tried to take him back to camp.

Yes, he was definitely feeling better.

"Aren't you hungry?"

"Want hot cakes and syrup."

She groaned inside. "Come, Thaddy. Jesse needs to eat and get some sleep." When his lower lip came out, she swung him up in her arms and tickled his ribs. With giggles floating behind them, they marched back to the fire.

"We need a name for that boy," she said after they'd finished eating and Ophelia went back to walking the baby. While he'd take milk from a spoon, drinking from a cup was not tolerable. And a sugar-tit took too long to make him content either. While she hated to give up one of the leather gloves, they might just have to do that. The leather would hold the milk and a hole in the end of a finger would make a nipple. If he would even suck on that.

"Call him ornery." Meshach dumped another armload of broken branches on the ground by the fire.

Ophelia sat on a log and commenced to spoon milk into the baby's mouth again. "Sho' wish him mama learned him better."

Jesselynn shuddered at the memory of the dead mother. All alone like that and having a baby. Often she'd assisted her mother in caring for a newborn baby and the proud mother down in the slave quarters. Birthing babies was a natural part of life, even to losing some, but to die alone like that, knowing there was nothing to be done for the older child must have terrified the woman.

She snagged Thaddeus, who was digging in the dirt at her feet, and gave him a loud kiss on the cheek.

He pushed back against her shoulder with both hands. "Down, Jesse. Me down."

She set him back on his feet, and he immediately plunked down to dig under the log again. When he had his mind on something, changing it was harder than stopping up a flooding creek.

———

The sun was well past the center point and the camp eerily quiet when Jesselynn woke again. *Where's everyone? Surely they didn't go off and leave me.* The nicker of a horse nearby made her shake her head at her crazy thoughts. She sat up and looked around, brushing away a persistent fly while straining to hear a voice, any voice, or rather any of the voices that belonged to her people. She scrubbed her face with her fingertips and brushed her hair back. Only two weeks on the road, and already it was falling in her eyes. No wonder men had to have their hair cut so often. Braiding it back would be a dead giveaway.

She smashed her hat onto her head, effectively solving the flopping hair problem, and stood, stretching out her body as she did so. She wasn't sure which was worse, riding all night, sitting on the wagon seat, or sleeping on the hard ground. Glancing around the camp, she saw Daniel sleeping soundly and left him to it.

Following the sound of another nicker, she found the horses hobbled in a small clearing, Ophelia lying asleep under a tree with the two boys curled against her like sleeping puppies, and Benjamin sleeping not far from her. As usual, Meshach was checking the horses' hooves. Still yawning, she wandered over to him and leaned against the mare's shoulder.

"Meshach, don't you ever sleep?"

"Sho'nuff. I slept myself plenty right after breakfast. Benjamin, he watch den." He picked up another of the filly's hooves and dug out the packed dirt and rocks. A rock caught between the frog and the inner part of the hoof could lame a horse faster than anything. "Ahab got him a loose shoe. I 'specs I better reset dem before we leave."

"You need the forge?"

"No, I just reset dem. Got plenty wear left."

They had the small hand-cranked forge with them that used to go to the track. While they had plenty of horseshoes, they didn't have much charcoal. One more thing that needed doing.

"What about the mule?"

"He fine."

"Did Benjamin find out if there was a town near here?"

" 'Bout five miles. Not much more den a store or two."

"No train station?"

"Didn't ask dat." He moved on to Domino, the younger stallion. "Stand still, you. I gots no time for you actin' up."

"How's Chess doin'?"

"Good. Him chest healin' good. I's thinkin' we might sell him soon as he's able."

Jesselynn nodded. "Good idea." She took hold of Domino's halter. "You just want extra attention, don't you?" She rubbed his ears and let him snuffle her neck. She inhaled the scent of horse. While her sister Carrie Mae might bewail the lack of Paris perfumes, she'd take honest horse aroma any day. That thought brought on another. How were her sisters managing with Aunt Sylvania? Jesselynn had visited Richmond and her aunt once and thought it enough to last for a lifetime—or two.

So then why did you send them back there? The voice in her ear sounded vaguely familiar, like a cross between her mother and Lucinda with a dash of Jesselynn thrown in for reality's sake.

Instead of arguing with herself, she went to saddle up the mule.

"I'll be back as soon as I can. Y'all go on and eat without me if I'm not here."

"You sho' might need one of us."

Jesselynn hesitated. It most likely would be a good idea to have one of them along, but the thought of being alone for a couple of hours was tempting beyond measure. Surely she'd be back before dark. And who would bother a rough-looking boy on an old mule?

Anyone needing a mule, that's who! The thought made her shake her head. "I'll take the pistol. It's not fair waking up one of the boys. And, besides, the horses need rest and time to graze too." She touched two fingers to the brim of her hat. "I'll be fine." She swung aboard the bareback mule and kicked him into a joint-cracking canter.

His trot was worse. By the time they rode the five miles to town, even her teeth hurt from the pounding.

"Grind you up for sausage," she muttered as she slung the reins over his long ears and tied them to the hitching post in front of the store. Several other places of business lined the street, empty but for a brown-and-white dog sniffing horse droppings. She walked around him, more to get her legs moving than to check out her mount, and took the four steps to the shed-roofed front porch in two. Two men, who looked older than the gnarly oak that shaded the west side of the building, nodded to her. *If they have three teeth between them, that would be sayin' some,* she thought.

"Hey, boy, you a stranger here?"

She kept herself from looking over her shoulder to see who the boy was they were talking to and nodded. "Yes, suh. Goin' west."

"Where ya from?"

She nodded over her shoulder. "Off thata way." She bobbed her head again. "Good day."

She knew she'd been rude, but the sun was racing for the horizon, and she had to get back so Meshach wouldn't worry. After telling the man behind the counter what she would need, she studied the jars of candy. Perhaps some horehound drops would help Thaddy's cough. Her grandmother used to keep a jarful for that very purpose. She added that to her list.

"They post a newspaper anywheres around here?"

The man nodded. "Only a day late too. Comes in on the train."

"Mind if I go read the casualty list while you get things together?"

"Not a'tall." But he paused, studying her through slightly squinted eyes.

"Don't worry, I kin pay." She pulled the gold piece from her pocket and held it up for him to see.

"Can't be too careful these days. Confederate dollars drop faster'n a pound of lead. Now is there anything else you might be needin'?"

"I'll be back." She strolled out the door like she had a month of Sundays to spend as she wished, greeted the two holding down the rockers and headed for the train station. Strains of "Dixieland" floated out the saloon door as she passed, and the smell of frying chicken from the hotel made her lick her lips and wish for some. The news had to be old already according to the folks around Gordonsville, since no one else was standing on the dock reading the paper. The name of the town could be found on either end of the station in fading white letters on an equally faded black sign.

She stuck her hands in her pockets and studied the paper tacked to the wall.

"General Buell Liberates Louisville" was one headline, but most of the page was taken up with Lincoln's proposed Emancipation Proclamation. She finally allowed herself to read the dead or missing-in-action lists, not breathing until she was positive Zachary Highwood was not listed. Thinking that the man had her order ready by now, she headed back for the general store.

A burst of laughter from the saloon struck her like a fist in the midsection.

Surely no one else on the entire earth laughed like that. Only Cavendar Dunlivey.

Horror tasted like blood on her tongue.

Chapter Sixteen

RICHMOND, VIRGINIA

"I can explain." She dropped her voice.

"I'm sure you can, but let me guess. You got bored at Aunt Sylvania's, and since you've always taken care of the wounded, be it bird, beast, or human, you decided to help out here at the military hospital. Only they would never let a young unmarried girl in the door to visit even, let alone care for the sick and dying, so you figured you needed a husband."

She nodded and looked at him from under her eyelashes. Was that a laugh she heard in his voice?

"But why me?"

"Because they say if you are going to tell a lie, keep as close to the truth as possible. So I just kept my name and added Mrs. Zachary in front of it." Her whisper was meant for his ears alone.

"So they call you Miz Highwood or Miss Louisa, which?"

"Don't you think you should take a nap or somethin'? You're lookin' mighty weary."

"It's wakin' up to find I have a wife that is wearyin'."

"You won't tell anyone, please?"

"Not unless that glowerin' lieutenant over there decides to beat me to death with his crutches."

"Zachary Highwood, why I never . . ." The heat rushed up her neck and over her face so fast it nigh to set her hair on fire.

"I know that, dear Louisa. Now why don't you get me a drink of that fresh water you went for, and I'll go back to sleep like a good boy—er, husband." He clenched her hand for a moment, then groaned. "Never try to yawn with a broken jaw. It hurts like . . ."

She could tell how bad by the way his hand shook. "I'll be right back."

But when she returned with the bucket and dipper, he was sound asleep.

After offering another drink to the men who were awake, Louisa returned to the closet where she kept her things and let the shock of Zachary being here roll over her. Her brother was alive. After the years of prayers and tears, here he was, in her hospital and on her ward, no less. The mercies of the almighty God were far beyond imaginable. If this didn't qualify as a miracle, what would?

Now, if only she could let Jesselynn know right today. Since the war began, letters took so long to get anywhere, and she hadn't heard from home in far too long. Up to this last month, her sister had been a faithful correspondent.

But she *could* tell Carrie Mae and Aunt Sylvania, and maybe when Zachary was well enough, they could all go home to Twin Oaks. Well, not Carrie Mae, since she would be living in Richmond with her newly wedded husband.

Her thought flickered to the walking rack of bones with the title of lieutenant. He might be handsome with some meat on his frame and a smile on that dour face. He stumped back and forth in front of the window like a sleek painter she'd seen caged once. All she'd thought of was opening the gate and letting the big tawny cat go free.

If only I could give the lieutenant back his leg and let him go free again.

That thought sent her scurrying back out with her copy of Shakespeare's *A Midsummer Night's Dream*. The tall stool was already set up for her, compliments of the lieutenant, she was sure. Since she'd started reading every afternoon, the men had taken to reminding her of it, just in case she forgot.

She glanced at her brother, who lay sleeping again as though he'd never been awake. *I could leave first to go home to tell the news.* The thought held certain possibilities. But when she looked up from finding her place, the eager looks on the faces of her wounded men drove the idea straight out of her mind.

She began with the words of Oberon:

> " 'I know a bank where the wild thyme blows,
>   Where oxslips and the nodding violet grows . . .' "

A cup of cool water appeared at her side when her voice began to creak. She glanced up to smile at the man who leaned on his crutches. "Thank you."

"You're welcome. At least I didn't spill it all."

The tone of his voice caught in her throat. Despair, disappointment, disillusionment, all words to describe the pain she could hear and see when he let her. Or accidentally when his blackness grew too dark to see or think or do anything but feel. She drank the water and handed the cup back to him, wishing she could do something other than read for him and the others caught in that same black hole.

"Go on, please, can you read longer?"

"Yes, of course." She smiled at the young private who shaved once a week whether he needed it or not. The smile on his face helped her forget that he'd lost one eye and most of the sight in the other.

Louisa continued her reading:

" 'Quite over-canopied with lush woodbine,
With sweet musk-roses, and with eglantine,
There sleeps Titania sometimes of the night . . .' "

When she closed the book, the private pleaded, "One chapter from the Good Book too, please?"

"Surely."

"Good, that comforts me more than about anything." The scars around his eyes puckered with his smile as he leaned his chin on his knees. He always sat on the floor a foot or so from her stool where she could lay her hand on his head when she moved on. One of the men had teased him about being more devoted than the spaniel he had at home until one of the other soldiers had warned him off. Neil had become a favorite around the ward because of his good spirits in spite of his wounds.

Corporal Shaddock handed over her Bible. "First chapter of John, please."

"But we read that yesterday."

"I know, but I'm tryin' to memorize it. My ma said if you memorize the Word and keep it in your heart, God will bring it to yer 'membrance when you need it. So if you read it, and I talk it with you, maybe it'll go faster."

Louisa glanced around the room and, at the shrugs of the others, began. " 'In the beginning was the Word, and the Word was with God, and the Word was God.' "

When she finished, the only sound to be heard was the mutterings of a man trapped in delirium. Ready to stand and go home for the evening, she smiled at each of the men looking her way.

Ask them if they'd mind if you prayed. She cocked her head as if that would help her hear better. *I can't do that, I . . .*

Ask them.

She bit her lip and closed her eyes for a brief moment.

"You all right, Miz Highwood?" Neil touched her hand gently.

"Yes, yes. I'm fine." She took in a breath, hoping it would stop the quivering going on in her chest. It didn't.

She cleared her throat. Then again. "Ah, would y'all mind if we said a prayer?" The words burst from her mouth like Thoroughbreds out of the starting gate.

A snort from a man several beds down caught her attention. "Prayin' don't do no good."

"Does so. I'm alive, aren't I? I prayed for someone to come for me, and they did, and I'm alive." Neil flung his hands wide, bumping her skirt-covered leg in the motion. " 'Scuse me, please." He looked up at her, his one eye pleading for her agreement.

"Of course." How easy it would be to wrap her arms around him and play at being the mother he missed so sorely. "Those of you who want to pray, join with me. The rest of you can put your pillows over your ears."

Several chuckles greeted her reply.

She bowed her head and closed her eyes. Some shufflings, throats being cleared, and then the room again grew silent. "God in heaven, Father of us all, we're all here through no fault of our own. These men fought for what they believed and now bear the scars. Jesus, thou bore our sins and wear our scars. Please, we beg of you, come into this room and lay thy healing hands on each man here. Give them strength to go on with their lives, to seek thy purpose. Father, help us all to know how wide and high and long and deep thy love is for us, for thy Word says we are precious in thy sight, our Rock and our Redeemer. In the name of Jesus, in whom we put our trust, we pray. Amen."

"That was plumb beautiful." Neil ducked his head to wipe a tear. "Thank you."

Other thank-yous came from around the ward as she took her books back to her closet. She glanced over to the window where the lieutenant kept his vigil. His jaw was clamped so tight the skin shone white over the bone.

"Time to go home, Missy." Reuben stood just inside the doorway.

"Yes, it is." *What can I do to help you?* she silently asked the lieutenant. She tried to smile at the face that had turned, but her lips wouldn't stop quivering. She waved instead, took up her basket with dirty aprons and empty napkins, and slipped out the door.

It took her better than a block to get the memory of his eyes out of her mind. Then remembering her joyful news, she burst out, "Reuben, I have wonderful news."

"What dat?"

"Zachary is alive, and he's in my ward."

"Don't make such jokes wit an old man, Missy. Tain't nice."

"I'm not joking. You know the man I told you about who lay unconscious for the whole week? Why, he woke up, and he's Zachary. My brother is alive!" She felt like whirling around in a circle and shouting for the entire town to hear.

"Praise de Lord for dat."

"Maybe as soon as he can get around good enough, we could go home."

"I wouldn't say dat to Missy Sylvania. She get right upset, she would."

"I know." Louisa took one skip and smiled at her companion. "And to think he's been there all week, and we didn't know." A couple steps later, she added, "But there was something about him. I came home thinking that two times at least. Something that seemed familiar, but all I could see was bandages."

"Miss Sylvania always like dat boy. She be right happy." He held open the door and motioned her through.

"Aunt Sylvania, Carrie Mae, where are you? I have wonderful news."

"She was here when I left." Reuben shook his head, confusion clouding his faded eyes. "Not tell dis ol' darkie she going somewhere."

Motioning Reuben to take her basket back to the kitchen, she climbed the stairs, one hand trailing on the carved walnut banister. *Where could Aunt Sylvania be? Ah, if only I could tell Jesselynn the wonderful news too.*

Chapter Seventeen

GORDONSVILLE, KENTUCKY

It can't be him. It can't be.

Jesselynn took the stairs to the store in a rush, checking herself before bursting through the door. *Don't call attention to yourself. Take it easy. Thank God those two old men are gone.* She pushed the door open to the sound of the bell tinkling above her and crossed the store to stand behind a woman wearing a dark shawl and chatting at the counter with the proprietor.

"Land sakes, you'd think they would know better, don't you think?"

"Yes, ma'am, I agree." He tied a string around her brown paper parcel. "Will there be anything else?"

Jesselynn almost grabbed the packet by the string and the woman by the arm and threw them out the door. What if indeed that man in the saloon was Dunlivey and he walked in here right this minute? What could she do?

She shifted from one foot to the other and cleared her throat.

The woman turned, gave her a dirty look, then shaking her head, picked up her package. "Thank you, Mister Charbonneau, and greet your dear wife for me. I do hope she is feelin' better soon."

Oh, please, just hurry and leave. Jesselynn could feel someone drilling holes in her back. Surely he was right behind her. But she knew no one had come in after her; the bell hung silent. But knowing and feeling had nothing to do with each other right now. Maybe she should have just left the order and headed out.

"I will do that. Thank you, and good day, Missus Levinger. I'll let you know when your order arrives."

Fine, good, now go.

The woman started to turn, checked herself, and leaned back across the counter. "You heard about . . ." Her voice dropped to a whisper that even Jesselynn couldn't hear, not that she wanted to. Sweat drizzled down her back.

The woman was shaking her head again. "Well, I better get on home and get some supper on the table."

Yes, your family is starving and your house is burning.

Missus Levinger gave her a baleful stare as if she'd been listening in on Jesselynn's thoughts, sniffed, and sailed out the doorway.

"Kin I help you? Oh yes, the young man with the order. I surely do hope there was no one on the casualty list that you knew." While he talked, he set her supplies on the counter and motioned to the white tow sack. "I saw that you rode in, so this will be easier for you to carry."

"Thank you." She kept from looking over her shoulder through sheer muscle-cramping determination. Digging her ten-dollar gold piece out of her pocket, she laid it on the counter.

"That'll be one dollar and seventeen cents, please." He took the coin and, turning to the cash register, pulled out Confederate dollars and change.

"Could I have that all in silver or gold, please?"

He looked at her over the tops of his glasses, raised an eyebrow, and went back for the change. "If you want a job, young man, you could come work for me anytime. You've got a head on those young shoulders of yours." He counted the change into her hand.

"Thank you kindly." Jesselynn shoved her money in her front pocket and took up the sack. Peeking inside, she glanced up at him again. "I didn't ask for any peppermint sticks."

"I know, but little ones like peppermint 'bout as good as horehound, and once they're feelin' better, this'll help."

"How'd . . . ?"

He tapped his head. "Just suspicioned. And your face says 'tis so. Call that my gift to you for bringin' me a gold piece."

"Thanks again." She took her sack, waved once on the way to the door, and stepped outside. This time she didn't dare just walk off. What if *he* was standing outside the saloon? But while the piano tune and laughter dressed in alcohol floated out the half door, all the men remained inside.

She didn't run the mule until she was far enough out of town to not be noticed. She didn't want to quit running him until they reached camp, but her father's training soaked through her fear-induced haze, and she tightened her reins enough to bring him to a walk. Once he caught his breath, they could trot again. Checking over her shoulder for about the fiftieth time still revealed only an empty road. Had it really been him? Was Cavendar Dunlivey following her, or did he happen to get stationed farther west? Could God be so cruel as to let that happen?

Ideas and fears tumbled around in her head just as her stomach was doing at the mule's gut-splitting gait. Surely she must have been hearing things. But no one else in the whole world could sound more like a braying jackass than Dunlivey, especially when he was drunk or whipping someone. That's why her father caught him. He could hear the man laughing and went to see what was so funny.

Strange how her mind could flip back to things like that in spite of the jolting trot. She kicked the mule into a canter, which wasn't a whole lot better. When she saw dark patches showing on his neck and shoulders, she pulled him down to a walk again. What could they do? No way on earth would she drive or ride through that town again. Benjamin would have to scout out a way around it, that's all.

When she rode into camp, she still felt like eyes were drilling her back. She flung herself off the mule's back and tossed the reins over his head.

"Where's Meshach?"

Ophelia turned from stirring a pot over the fire. "Gone to water de horses."

"Benjamin?"

"Wid him. Daniel fetchin' wood. Babies sleepin'." Her eyes grew rounder with each word.

Jesselynn plunked down the sack of supplies and swung back aboard the mule. "Thanks."

She trotted down the trail to the creek, ducking under the oak branches to keep from being slapped off.

"Hey, you back sooner den I guessed." Meshach's smile turned to a frown when she drew closer. "What wrong?"

"I think I heard Dunlivey laugh."

At the look of confusion he shot her, she continued. "I was walking from the store to the railroad station to check the casualty lists and had to go by the saloon. I heard men laughing, and one sounded just like Dunlivey. Who else in the entire world would laugh like that?"

"I don' know. He laugh mighty strange."

"I swear it was him." She slid off the mule and leaned against his shoulder. "We can't go through Gordonsville."

Meshach scratched his head. "Might be good idea to make certain." He studied Benjamin, who held the long lines so the horses could graze. "Send him in."

"They wouldn't let him in."

"He can look through de window, hang outside and see him come out."

"You think that's better than just heading out?"

Do I want to know or not? What difference does it make? She caught her breath in shock at the thought that whipped through her mind. *We could wait for him to come out and shoot him.*

"No, let's just get on the way again. Let Benjamin find us a way around town. There must be a back road somewhere." She led the mule down to the stream bank and let him have only a couple of swallows. "Sorry, boy, you'll get more later when you cool off."

Benjamin left shortly thereafter and returned later than she had hoped. All the while her mind played out scenes involving Dunlivey—his finding them, or getting killed in a skirmish, or baying on their trail like an old coonhound.

"Jesse?" Thaddy leaned against her knee when she sat by the fire.

"What?"

He climbed up in her lap with her belated help. Turning, he put his palms on either side of her face and looked deep into her eyes. "You mad?"

She shook her head.

" 'Phelia been cryin'."

"Oh."

He patted her cheeks. "Joshwa good boy."

"Umm." *Where was Benjamin? He should have been back by now.*

"Jesse!" He clapped his hands on her cheeks.

"Ouch!" She sat him on the ground with more than a gentle thump. "Thaddeus Joshua Highwood, you don't do things like that." Her cheeks smarted from the blows. "Whatever got into you?" Wagging her finger in front of his nose, she added, "Naughty boy."

"I not naughty." Hands on his hips, he met her glare with one of his own. "Me talkin' to you."

Jerked out of her stewing, Jesselynn swung between the desire to give him a swat on the rear or grab him and squeeze him tight. A little fighting rooster.

That's what he was. And it was her job to protect him better than she had before. She had almost lost him. She snagged one arm around him and snugged him up between her knees, the better to give him smacking kisses on both cheeks and a tickle on his belly.

"More," he insisted in between giggles.

Jesselynn did as he asked, trying to keep one ear clear for a returning horseman. *Oh, Lord, what if I sent him out to get caught? By Dunlivey?*

"We got to give dis baby a name." Ophelia stopped walking the sick child.

"I guess."

Thaddeus leaned back in Jesselynn's arms. "He Sammy."

"Sammy? How do you know?" Jesselynn stared at her baby brother.

Thaddeus shrugged. "Don't know."

"Why call him Sammy?"

"Dat's his name."

"He's too little to talk."

"He Sammy." This was said with the utmost assurance that he was correct and why on earth was his sister disputing his word?

You are so much like your father, I can't begin to believe it. "Sammy it is, then," Jesselynn agreed.

"Sammy is a fine name," said Meshach, flicking another curl of wood from his whittling into the fire.

All right, so you have a wait ahead. Get busy with your knitting. Wanting to argue with the voice in her head but knowing it was useless, she got to her feet and strolled over to the wagon. Digging down into a carpetbag of her own things, she retrieved her ball of yarn stuck on two knitting needles. When she got back to the fire, Ophelia sat on the log rocking Sammy, and Thaddy had climbed up in Meshach's lap.

"Tell me a story."

"Please." Jesselynn added without really thinking about it. No matter if they lived in the wilds of whatever, he needed to learn good manners. Every southern gentleman had good manners, and if he was to be the patriarch of Twin Oaks someday, he needed to know how to behave.

Zachary, where are you? You need to come teach your little brother how to be a man.

"All right," Meshach said to Thaddy, hugging him close. "Long time ago der lived a boy by name of David. David took care of his father's sheep way out in de fields. He kep' dem safe from de wolf—"

"What's a wolf?" Thaddeus asked the question around the thumb and fore-finger triangle that fit so perfectly in his mouth.

"Like a big ol' hound dog, only gray and lives wild in de woods."

"Like the woods here?"

"No, far away in Bible lands."

Jesselynn put down her knitting, the better to listen. Surely that was a horse she heard. Or was it more than one? She tried to block out Meshach's voice so she could hear better. One of the horses whinnied.

Another answered from not too far off.

Meshach stopped his storytelling. "Shush, listen," he whispered.

"Hey, is Benjamin."

Jesselynn let out a breath she had no idea she'd been holding. When she stood, she took a step forward to help settle her head, which felt as if it were floating off into the clouds. "What took you so long?"

Benjamin kicked his feet free of the stirrups and swung to the ground. "I found a way."

"Good."

"An' . . ."

Her breath caught in her throat. "And?"

"An' it be him. Cavendar Dunlivey be playin cards in de saloon."

Chapter Eighteen

RICHMOND, VIRGINIA

"Aunt Sylvania?" Louisa stuck her head into the sewing room. No one there, but she could tell they'd been busy sewing the wedding finery. Laces and ivory satin pieces draped the chair and hung over the three-paneled screen. A bodice fit perfectly on the dress form with a swath of lace pinned to one shoulder. Bits of thread and scraps of fabric littered the floor like the leaves that were falling from the trees in the yard.

She carefully shut the door and walked down the hall to her aunt's room. As usual the door was closed. She tapped once and waited. Nothing. Turning the handle gently in case her aunt was napping, she pushed the door open enough to peek in. The bed was made up with every pillow and bolster in place.

She pushed the door open a bit more and scanned the remainder of the room. Everything appeared neatly in place, including her aunt's wire-rimmed glasses sitting atop her Bible that lay in its usual place on the whatnot table beside the rocking chair.

She closed the door again and went into her own room to hang up her shawl and wash her hands. After tucking stray locks of hair back in the bun at the base of her head, she rubbed rose water and glycerin lotion into her hands and left the sanctuary of her room behind. How good it would feel to lie back on the chaise lounge and let the knots relax out of her lower back and shoulders. To pick up her book of poems by Henry Wadsworth Longfellow and dream of the love she knew God had waiting for her somewhere. While she refused to be paraded on the marriage block like Carrie Mae, she knew that someday her prince would come.

He didn't need any armor or a snowy white horse. Or a crown either. The thought of a tall, terribly thin man galloped through her mind and kept on going, crutches tied behind his saddle. That thought reminded her of her brother.

She *had* to share the good news.

"She out in de garden," Reuben said when he met her descending the stairs. "I was comin' fo' you."

"Thank you. Have Abby bring out some lemonade, would you, please?"

"Surely will do dat." He motioned her to go down the hallway first and followed close behind. "She lookin' a mite peaked. Dis cheer her."

But when Louisa opened the French doors and stepped out onto the slate patio, her aunt didn't look sad. She was sound asleep. *Something must be wrong, this is so unlike her.* She hesitated, taking her aunt's wrist and counting her pulse, something she'd learned from one of the assistants at the hospital. If Aunt Sylvania was coming down with something, perhaps she should just call the doctor, not that he had much time for house calls with all the wounded he tended at his house too. The military weren't the only ones wounded in this war.

Come to think of it, Aunt had been a bit pale lately. Was she moving more slowly too? Louisa tried to think back over the last weeks. When did she first notice a difference? Or maybe it was just the unseasonably warm weather.

So instead of saying anything, she sat down on the other chaise lounge, just as she'd wished to do upstairs, only now she could look over the garden. The roses still bloomed, scenting the air with a perfume all their own, from sweet to spicy and layers in between.

A fat bumblebee trundled from blossom to blossom, tasting the chrysanthemums and the fading petunias, then arising with pollen yellowing his legs. A pot of gardenias lent their heavy scent and glowed in the dimming light like pure beeswax candles. She stroked one of the blossoms, then leaned over to inhale their perfume. The creamy flowers against their dark glossy leaves always showed their best at this time of day.

When Abby brought out the tray, Louisa pointed to the table and touched her finger to her lips, glancing at the sleeping woman to signify silence.

Abby nodded, set the tray down with barely a tinkle of the filled glasses, and tiptoed back into the summer kitchen set off from the house. The peace of the garden seeped into Louisa's bones and calmed her as nothing else ever did. Doves cooing in the magnolia branches above the brick wall added one more layer to the contentment. No wonder God created a garden to wander in of an evening.

When she first came to Richmond, she had spent hours digging in the garden, transplanting daisies and irises, trimming the spent roses and tying up the honeysuckle that did all in its power to disguise the fence and overrun the plum tree. Taming the honeysuckle had helped keep the tears of homesickness at bay. Or else the salt of her tears had dampened its rampant growth. Either way, the garden had been her salvation until she answered the call to service at the hospital.

The irony of one of her aunt's friends helping her get on there had been lost on Aunt Sylvania. After hours of hand wringing, feigned sick headaches, and outright threats, she had finally given in. However, she had no idea what Louisa really did there, and the less said of it the better.

Studying the garden gave her mind a bit of an itch. If working in this one had helped *her* so much, what could it do for her broken soldier, Private Rumford? His body was gaining health by the day, but his mind—who knew where it wandered? There were gardens out behind the hospital in terrible disrepair. What if she took him and others like him out to restore the garden? Her gaze narrowed on the garden shed. There were enough tools in there to equip a platoon of garden lovers, and if they weren't that when they began, the garden itself would bring them to that feeling with time. And maybe, just maybe, would take them out of the shadowland that kept them prisoner.

She started to rise to check on the contents of the garden shed when her aunt harrumphed and sat up.

"Land sakes, child, what are you doing sneaking up on me like that? I just closed my eyes for a moment and—"

"Now, Aunt Sylvania, I just sat down here to enjoy the garden with you. And see, Abby brought us some lemonade." She got up and carried the tray over. "Here, have a sip while I tell you our most wonderful news." She carefully kept from looking at her aunt's face, so flushed now that perhaps she was running a fever. Instead, she set the tray down and took her own glass, holding it against her cheek as she sat back down. "My, doesn't that feel wonderfully cooling. Is it always this warm even when almost October?" She refrained from saying Kentucky would be cooler, because the last time she'd mentioned home, she'd received one of *those* looks.

"News? What news?" Sylvania took a sip of her lemonade and settled her glasses back on her nose, the better to stare over them at her niece.

"Well . . ." Louisa tipped her head to the side and shrugged just a bit, keeping the smile from bursting forth only with great effort. "Remember I mentioned the soldier who was so bandaged up we couldn't see what he looked like and had not regained consciousness since they brought him in?"

"Now, Louisa, you know that—"

Louisa did the unforgivable. She interrupted. "I know, Aunt, but listen. That man is Zachary. I knew there was something—"

"Our Zachary?" Some of the lemonade splashed out of the glass when Sylvania jerked upright so quickly. While dabbing at the front of her dress, she asked again, "Not *our* Zachary?" Her chin quivered on the name.

"Yes, Aunt. My brother Zachary is alive." She set her lemonade down on the slate at her feet and, rising, crossed to take her aunt's hands in her own and kneel in front of her. "Zachary is badly wounded, missing one leg below the knee, and I'm not sure what else, but he is alive."

"Hello, y'all. Sorry I'm late." Carrie Mae breezed through the French doors, stopping at the look on her aunt's face. "What's wrong? Aunt, are you all right? You're flushed as if you've been runnin' 'round the garden."

"You're just in time to hear the news." Louisa rose and turned to take her sister's hands. "Maybe you'd better sit down first."

"Stop teasing her." Aunt Sylvania harrumphed again but dabbed at her eye at the same time. "Our boy is here in the hospital, and he's comin' home soon."

"Zachary?" Carrie Mae took her sister's advice and sank down on the lounge. "You're not teasing?"

"No, he's the man who's been all bandaged and unconscious."

Carrie Mae shuddered when Louisa listed her brother's injuries. "But he's alive, oh, thank you, heavenly Father." She clasped her hands to her chest. "Ah, if only we could tell Jesselynn. I'll write to her tonight."

"I think we'd better bring Zachary home as soon as possible. We can take much better care of him here than they do in that pest hole." Sylvania clasped her hands in her lap and looked skyward. "Oh, thank the good Lord, at least one of the men in our family has made it through the war. I haven't heard from Hiram in months, and with Joshua still fighting, God only knows where." She took a bit of cambric from her pocket and dabbed her eyes, then straightened. "And why, Missy, did you not bring that news home to me as soon as you knew?"

Louisa sat back on her heels, shaking her head. *So much for that brief moment of shared joy.* She returned to her own lounge and sitting down, picked up her glass and took a long swallow. When she set it down, she met the hard line frequently seen on her aunt's face when directed at her.

While Carrie Mae could do nothing wrong, sometimes it seemed that Louisa could do nothing right.

Guilt sneaked up behind her and grabbed her around the throat. She should have come right home. She had thought of it at the time. But all the injured men needed her so much worse. Should she tell Carrie Mae about her concerns about Aunt Sylvania? What should she do?

Chapter Nineteen

GORDONSVILLE, KENTUCKY

Wish I had shot him when I had the chance, Jesselynn thought, but knew deep down she couldn't kill the man, no matter how evil he was.

"You want we go take care of him?" Meshach spoke softly enough that none of the others could hear.

The temptation to say yes was so strong she had to bite her lower lip to keep the words from rushing forth. "No, we will just get on around that town. Dunlivey has no idea we are here. He can't know that." She turned to Benjamin. "Were any other soldiers there with him?"

"Not dat I could see. Least no uniforms."

"Was he wearin' a Confederate uniform?"

"Had gray pants and s'penders. He din't have no jacket on."

Jesselynn thought back to the last meeting with Dunlivey at Twin Oaks. He'd worn an officer's jacket then, looking right resplendent. Was he still in the army, or had he deserted? She had a hard time believing that the Cavendar Dunlivey she knew would tolerate military discipline for long. But being in the army gave him permission to kill and maim, and that part he would love, along with taking advantage of the soldiers under him. The snake loved to hurt living things and especially people.

The thought that he'd been riding a Twin Oaks horse made her want to . . . to . . . she didn't dare contemplate the things that came to mind. She wondered what officer he had stolen the horse from. Why did God let scum like him live while fine men like her father and brothers died?

If anyone ever thought this life was fair, the war would surely prove them misguided.

Ahab nudged her shoulder.

"We best be goin' on, Marse Jesse." Meshach's soft voice brought her back from her wandering thoughts. She pried her clenched fingers loose from the reins and flexed them to get the blood flowing again.

"Yes, you're right. Let's move on." *And not stop until we're clear across the Mississippi.*

By the time they'd detoured around Gordonsville and picked up the road again some miles west, her ears and eyes ached from the strain of watching shadows and hearing night noises. When an owl hooted not far above her head, she jerked the reins so hard that Ahab reared. Calling herself all manner of uncomplimentary names, she stroked his shoulder and leaned forward to rub his ears. "Sorry, old son. That was uncalled for. I'm just lucky you're gentleman enough to not dump me on the ground."

When she finally got her middle settled back down, her thoughts kept returning to Twin Oaks. How had the tobacco harvest been? Had Joseph insisted on payment in gold as she'd instructed him? That would give those on the plantation something to live on in the months ahead and perhaps even send some money to her sisters. There would be enough to plant again in the spring, and when Zachary came home—she had to believe he was still alive—she could hand a thriving plantation over to him, in spite of the war.

If he comes home. That thought warred with the others.

She turned around, trotted back to the wagon, and rode alongside it for a while. At times Sammy still coughed until he threw up, making her wish she had bought some whisky in town. That and honey would surely help this poor baby. She heard Ophelia singing to the little one, a song that sang of glory in the by-and-by.

How can she really believe that glory by-and-by? With all the death and filth we've seen! Jesselynn scratched a mosquito bite on her neck. Sammy's crying brought back the horror of finding his dead mother. What terrible things had that woman endured to try to save her babies? And now Jesselynn had her people depending on her for their safety. She caught herself shaking her head. Riding in the dark, where even the scenery couldn't be a distraction, gave her too much time to think.

"Nudder river comin' up." Benjamin dropped back to ride beside her as dawn played hide-and-seek with the dark.

Jesselynn sighed and shook her head. "We just get dried out and there's another creek or river to cross. How big is this one?"

"Big."

"The Mississippi?" Hope leaped into her voice.

"Maybe."

But it wasn't. They crossed the Cumberland and then the Tennessee at Jenkins Ferry and kept on following the sun west.

————

A day later she rode the mule into a town crawling with blue uniforms. After tying her mount to a hitching post behind one of the stores, she strolled back and leaned against the wall of the local hotel.

Half the people in the streets wore blue uniforms. The other half swished their full skirts and simpered at the officers, twirling their parasols and giggling.

She ambled on down to where they had corrals for the army horses. A cloud of dust rose that made her sneeze as she climbed up on the corral posts to get a better look at the horses now cavorting around the corral, bucking and kicking, getting the kinks out. One trotted past that she was sure she recognized because of a twist of white hair on an otherwise deep red chest.

"Hey boy, get down from there." A heavy hand grabbed her shoulder, tore her off the rails, and thrust her down.

Her rear smacked the hard ground first with such a jolt her tongue got caught between her teeth. The metallic taste of blood filled her mouth and rage clouded her eyes. "Why you . . ." Just in time she caught herself from saying anything to draw unwanted attention. She stared at the shiny black boots planted beside her.

The hand reached down this time and, grabbing her shoulder, picked her up and slammed her against the corral bars. "Now you git yer carcass on outa here and don't be bothering our horses."

"Can't hurt lookin' at 'em." She remembered to lower her voice and spat a chunk of dirt at the ground. Good thing her brothers had taught her how to spit, another skill of hers that hadn't pleased her mother.

"Don't want no Johnny Reb hurtin' our horses."

"I ain't never hurt a horse, you—" At the memory of his giant hand on her shoulder, she thought better of calling him a bluebelly bushwhacker. He could pick her up and shake her like a dog with a rat. And he nearly had. Her head hurt from the slam against the corral bar, and her posterior still protested the abrupt contact with the ground.

He waved his hands as if shooing a fly. "Git on with ye now."

Jesselynn *got,* but her estimation of Union soldiers sank another notch. She made her way back up the street to the front of the newspaper office to study the lists of casualties. "Lee Defeated At Antietam" read one headline, "Lincoln Declares Slaves Will Go Free," another. Her heart nearly stopped when she read the name Zachary on the dead list but started again when the last name was Arches.

She continued her stroll through the town, past the stores, looking in the windows at the ladies' apparel shop, then hurrying on. No boy her size would be caught dead looking at ladies' garments. When she passed a saloon the temptation to go on in and look for Dunlivey slowed her steps. *What if he's here?*

"Hey you, boy!" She glanced around to see whom the soldier was talking to and started to walk on when he yelled again. She flinched. *Is he yelling at me?*

She turned, keeping her chin low. "Yes, suh?"

"How old are you? I kin sign you up for the army."

"S-sixteen, suh."

"Ah, the rebels might take boys like you, but you have to be a man to join the Union army."

"Yes, suh." *Like there's any chance I'd join either army, least of all yours.* She bobbed her head, backing away at the same time. About the time she could turn and walk away, she bumped into something soft that emitted a feminine "oof."

"Young man, where in the world did you leave your manners?" The matron staring at her looked so much like her Aunt Sylvania that she almost blurted out the name.

"Ah, sorry, ma'am. Please, I'm sorry." She backed away, touching the brim of her cap and half bowing at the same time.

"You might look where you are goin' next time."

"I will. I surely am sorry." At the corner she turned and jogged down the alley. No way was she staying in this town another minute. But when she rounded the next corner, Union soldiers marched three abreast down the street, gold buttons flashing in the sun, sabers clanking all in perfect cadence. The line appeared to go on forever.

No wonder we're losing the war. They even all have rifles. Her father had been right, the Union army would be much better supplied, and no matter how dashing and chivalrous the southern soldier might be, guns were superior to sabers and rebel yells any day.

Instead of turning around and going the other way, she leaned against the wall, hands in her pockets as if she had all the time in the world. Overhearing the word "bluebellies," she stepped closer to the corner of the building to listen. Maybe she could learn where the fighting was so they could go around it.

"With Grant at Cairo, we got them all over the place."

"If we could get Shelby over here, we might see some changes made."

Shelby? Who's Shelby? Jesselynn tried to appear totally uninterested, taking out her knife to dig under her fingernails. She'd seen her brothers use the tactic all the time. In the same instant, she took one step closer.

"He's too busy in Missouri, and ferrying all those troops across ol' Miss, Grant would have 'em before the hounds could howl."

"I know. If'n only General Lee would send someone here to help out. 'Course they got him all tied up in Virginia."

The bugler passed, along with three drummers, and a platoon of prancing horses kept pace behind them.

Someone shouted an obscenity that brought a laugh from the crowd. The marching soldiers kept their faces straight ahead.

"God protect us," a woman's voice murmured.

God doesn't seem to care much. I think He's ashamed of this whole mess. Young men, old men, all killing each other for what? Sometimes even brother against brother. While she hadn't agreed with her brothers, believing her father might be more right, she was grateful they hadn't been fighting each other. Two brothers of one of the neighbors back home about broke their mother's heart when one went to fight for the North.

Jesselynn snagged her wandering attention and brought it back to the scene before her. And listened to the gossip.

When nothing more was forthcoming, she peeked around the corner to find the bench vacant, the two men gone.

Two young women were taking over the bench. "Ain't he just the handsomest man you ever saw?" They settled their skirts around them and tipped back their parasols.

Jesselynn looked out to see an officer riding by. Not that any man wearing blue could be handsome as far as she was concerned, but he did cut a fine figure. So did his horse. Must be one of the Thoroughbreds from Kentucky—not a Twin Oaks animal but a fine Thoroughbred nevertheless.

When he tipped his hat to the two women on the bench, they both giggled and tittered.

Jesselynn wanted to whack them with their parasols. Instead she pushed off from the wall and strolled on back to where her mule was tied. Slipping the knot on the reins, she swung aboard and turned him toward the back streets. She'd learned what she needed. The Union army was everywhere.

When she told her people the news, Ophelia whimpered, Meshach frowned at her, and the others simply shrugged.

"How we keep away from dem bluebellies if dey's so many of dem?" Ophelia finally asked what everyone was thinking.

"Go further south. They can't control the entire river." Jesselynn spoke with far more certainty than she felt.

They spent the next two nights threading their way between Union camps and scouts. By the time they reached a ferry without a cordon of blue-uniformed guards, they'd about been caught three times. Sometimes Jesselynn thought it might be easier to just head on home and only have the horses to hide. They hadn't had any hot food for three days, not taking a chance on building a fire.

They drove on down south of the ferry and stood looking across the muddy, roiling river.

"I cain't cross over dat." Ophelia sniffed back the tears and clung to Meshach's arm. "Please don' make me go dere."

"Oh hush, 'Phelia. 'Course you can. We all be on a ferryboat just like before. It's not like you have to swim."

"I cain't swim." Now she really was crying. Sammy picked up on her fear and began to wail. Thaddeus clung to Jesselynn's arm, his chin quivering and a whimper in his voice.

"We go home, Jesselynn. Please, we go home."

"Thaddeus Joshua Highwood, my name is Jesse! Jesse, remember that!" She wanted to shake Ophelia but knew it would do no good.

Surely after all we've been through, we won't be stopped now. She looked up at Meshach for reassurance, only to see stark fear on his strong features too.

Chapter Twenty

Louisa felt like saluting.

"So, Miz Highwood, what is it I can do for you today?" The general in charge of the hospital folded his hands on his walnut desk top and gazed at her through eyes that seemed to have forgotten how to smile. His clipped voice made her sit straighter, wishing she had remained standing in spite of his invitation to sit. If she sat any closer to the edge of the chair, she'd be on the floor.

"Ah, well, General, sir, I . . ." *Oh, Lord, please give me the right words to say. I feel like a featherbrain whose feathers were blown away on the wind.* She took in a deep breath, locked her questing fingers together, and started again. "You know that I help out on Ward B." Was that a twinkle she saw peeking out of the wintry blue?

"Ma'am, from what I hear, your helpin' out is savin' some of our men's lives. They call you the 'angel in aprons.' Did you know that?"

She shook her head, the heat racing to her cheekbones and above. "I-I'm glad to be of service."

"And to find your husband wrapped in bandages. Now that is a true miracle."

The heat turned from flaming to full-fledged roaring.

Oh, God, I hate this deceit. How long will this have to continue? If I tell the truth, will he throw me out? Her inner battle must have shown on her face.

"Is there something wrong, ma'am?"

"N-no, of course not. I . . ." She kept her eyes on his and forced a smile to lips that would rather tremble. "My . . . my h-husband, um, will it be possible for him to leave the hospital soon and join us at my aunt's house? We can take good care of him there, and that will free up another bed—on the ward, that is." *You ninny, any fool could tell you are lyin', and this man is about as far from being a fool as . . . as . . .* She wished she could just sink through the floor.

"Why, as soon as the doctor says he can be moved, I reckon he would be much more comfortable there. So good to have a chance to see firsthand a husband and wife reunited." He shuffled a paper in front of him, then looked right at her again. "Is there somethin' else you needed to ask me?"

"Why, yes, sir, there is. You know of Private Rumford, one of the men on my . . . ah, Ward B, sir. He's the one who seems to have lost his grip on reality."

"Like many others, I'm afraid, but yes, I know to whom you are referrin'." The general clasped his hands on the desk in front of him and leaned forward. "What about the private?"

"Well, I thought, I mean, the garden at my aunt's house helped me so much when I first came to Richmond."

He nodded, but one raised eyebrow let her know he wondered what she could be leading up to now.

She rushed full tilt into her request. "You know the gardens out behind the hospital—they've gone to terrible wrack and ruin, and I . . ."

The other eyebrow joined the first.

Oh, now I've offended him. Mama, you told me to always watch my tongue, and now it is giving me nothing but difficulty. "Sorry, sir, I don't mean to be critical but . . ." She took in a deep breath to try to forestall the feeling of a featherbrain bereft of feathers. "Oh, bother!" She scooted forward and leaned against her hands on the edge of his desk. "I believe workin' in the garden would help bring Private Rumford back to reality and perhaps give some of the others who have lost so much a place to heal. Diggin' in the dirt is good for the soul, my mama always said, and I know firsthand that she was right. Helpin' things grow reminds us how God grows us, you see, I mean . . ." She shook her head. She should have stopped while she was ahead, whenever that was.

The general nodded. "I see." He steepled his fingers and studied her over the tips. "And who will oversee this project of yours?"

Up to that point, flummoxed had been just a word in the dictionary. Now she knew how it felt. Featherbrained and flummoxed. She sucked in a deep breath and let it out, praying for any kind of inspiration to answer his question. Would he let *her* supervise? She gave an inward shake of her head. Reuben could do so very handily, but some of the soldiers might resent being governed by a black man, no matter how gentle his orders.

The sun sprang from the horizon, in her mind, that is. "Why, Lieutenant Lessling could do that. Though he can't get down on his knees yet to dig and plant, he could supervise." She nodded and clasped her bottom lip between her teeth. "Why, yes, that's the perfect answer. It might help him with his moroseness too, just like the private."

"Are you suggesting that Lieutenant Lessling is out of his mind?"

"No, sir, of course not. I just thought that . . ." She looked up in time to be sure there was a twinkle in his blue eyes, which were no longer frosty.

"Miz Highwood, forgive me. I couldn't resist teasin' you. It's been far too long since I saw a comely young woman blush. I will give the order for the beds to be dug up this afternoon, and by tomorrow you can have your garden brigade busy out back. Do you have any seeds?"

"I'll find some." Louisa got to her feet. "Thank you, sir. Reuben will bring some extra tools with him in the morning."

"Thank you, ma'am. I'm sure the men will be fightin' over who gets to help you first."

"Sir!" It would be a miracle if her bonnet didn't catch fire from the heat flaming up her face.

"Let me know if there is anything else I can do to be of service. Aide, show Miz Highwood out."

Louisa nodded once more and turned to follow the stiff-backed aide from the room. At the door she paused and looked back. "God bless you, General."

"And you." He cleared his throat and nodded one more time before taking his seat again. The picture she carried with her up to the ward was of a man so burdened he could barely keep his head up. *Think I'll ask the ladies to pray for this man especially,* she thought as she mounted the steps. *Sometimes prayers mean more when there is a face attached to the prayer.*

Keeping her wonderful news to herself took more skill than she imagined. Every time she passed a window, she glanced back at the decrepit roses and the overgrown vines. An arbor sagged to one side, a victim of decay more insidious than the battle wounds suffered by her men.

Zachary lay sleeping again, but one look at the unbandaged side of his face let her know it was the sleep of healing. The man two beds over was a different matter. He flayed at the mattress with both hands and feet until one of the nurses came with strips of old sheet and tied his limbs down so that he wouldn't reopen the wounds so recently stitched closed.

Louisa pulled a chair over beside him and, with a cloth and basin of cool water, began bathing his face. Ever present at her side when she was on the ward, Rumford stared at her hands as if fascinated. But when she turned to say something to him, he wore the same vacant stare as ever.

"Would you like to help me?" She kept her voice gentle and soft so as to let the man in the bed behind her sleep. She extended the dampened cloth to the hovering man, but he never said a word nor showed that he heard her.

But he has to be aware. Why else would he follow me around so? This question, like many of her others, had no answer.

"W-will you read today?" one of the men asked from across the aisle.

"Yes, of course." She flashed him a smile and caught some movement from the corner of her eye. The *shuffle-clunk* of a man on crutches let her know who it was before her eyes did. The lieutenant stopped at the foot of the bed.

"You want I should get the books?"

"Yes, please." *What I really want you to do is read in my place.* But she kept the words inside, not wanting to embarrass him. After all, not everyone loved reading aloud as she did. She took the basin over to her brother's bed and set it on the floor underneath, out of the way of anyone's feet. She'd help him wash as soon as he woke up. Glancing up, she saw her stool set in place and the two books on top of it, her Bible and Shakespeare. She'd thought of bringing Dickens but knew she'd get in trouble if she didn't finish *The Taming of the Shrew*. By sticking to the comedies, she could bring a smile to some of the men and even raise laughter from some of the others. She'd already finished *A Midsummer Night's Dream* and *The Merchant of Venice*.

There was far too little laughter on the ward.

She smiled her thanks to the lieutenant and settled herself on the high stool. "Today we will begin with Psalm 91, for I think we all need to be reminded how closely God holds us." She found her place and began. " 'He that dwelleth in the secret place of the most High shall abide under the shadow of the Almighty. I will say of the Lord, he is my refuge and my fortress: my God; in him will I trust.' " Louisa continued reading to the end of the psalm. From there she went on to Psalm 139, and then to Paul's prayer to the Ephesians: " 'That he would grant you, according to the riches of his glory, to be strengthened with might by his Spirit in the inner man; that Christ may dwell in your hearts by faith; that ye, being rooted and grounded in love, may be able to comprehend with all saints what is the breadth, and length, and depth, and height.'

"And that is my prayer for each of you." She kept her finger in the place and read the passage again, finishing with, " 'And to know the love of Christ, which passeth knowledge, that ye might be filled with all the fulness of God.' "

"Amen." Another man echoed the first.

"You read so purty."

"Thank you. God's words make me want to keep reading them over and over. We need to hear again and again how much He loves us." She glanced around at all her men. "In spite of all this."

The lieutenant had returned to his window vigil while she read and now kept his back to her. The urge to go to him almost made her slide off the stool, but she righted herself and set her Bible on the bed nearest her.

"Read some more—please."

"Which, the Bible or Shakespeare?"

"Don't matter. I jus' like to hear the words."

"Shakespeare."

The men called their preferences in voices tired and hoarse and pleading.

She found her place and began again, sneaking occasional peeks to the still, lean form propped on crutches. He never turned when she finished, not even when she gathered her things to leave a while later.

"Good-bye, dear wife," her brother whispered, holding her hand for a long moment.

"The general says we can bring you home as soon as the doctor releases you."

"Is Aunt Sylvania in agreement?"

"Of course, dear boy."

"You sound just like her."

"I meant to."

He flinched as he shifted on the bed. "I'll see you tomorrow, then?"

"Yes. But I won't wake you." He'd already scolded her for letting him sleep so long.

"As you wish." He paused for a moment. "Are the peaches ripe?"

"All gone, I'm afraid. I'll bring some preserves tomorrow." Her gaze strayed back to the form at the window.

"Well, will ya lookee that." One of the other men who watched out a window turned to the others. "There's someone diggin' up the rose bed."

"You promise." Zachary still clutched her fingers. "Maybe tomorrow I'll be able to see better if they take some of the bandages off."

Please, God, that he'll be able to see out of both eyes. She gently withdrew her fingers and stepped back. "Peach preserves, I promise. And biscuits."

As she and Reuben walked the streets to home, she could hear a train whistle in the distance. That meant new wounded in the morning. Perhaps Zach would be released sooner than they expected.

"Louisa, it came." Carrie Mae waved an envelope in the air when Louisa reached the front portico.

"Who is it from?"

"Jesselynn—our sister—you won't believe it. She left Twin Oaks to go to Uncle Hiram's in Missouri."

Louisa snatched the letter and sank down on the wooden glider, barely able to open the envelope her fingers shook so badly. She withdrew the paper, tears burning at the sight of the dear handwriting. She read it once, glanced up at some children running by, laughing and calling as they went, and then read the letter again. Jesselynn was somewhere between Midway, Kentucky, and Springfield, Missouri, with horses, and no one was taking care of Twin Oaks.

"She had to keep her promise."

"I know." Carrie Mae studied the toe of her black slipper. "Daddy wasn't in his right mind, or he would never have asked that of her."

"But without the horses . . ."

"The land will always be there. Zachary can go home and plant the land."

Louisa set the glider to moving, the squeak of it comforting in the twilight.

"At least we know God is watching out for her when we can't."

"Thank the Lord for that." Carrie Mae let her head fall against the glider back. "Wait until I tell Jefferson this latest news. He won't believe it."

"Won't believe what?" Louisa recognized a look of concern when she saw it.

"That a woman of our family would do such a crazy thing."

"Then he doesn't understand the value of Twin Oaks horseflesh and the burden of a vow." Louisa rose and headed for the door. "I need to wash up before supper." She opened the door and turned back to her sister. "How does Aunt Sylvania seem today?"

"Better. I think the good news helped. She worries more than she lets on — the wedding and all."

"Really." Mounting the stairs to her room, Louisa trailed a hand on the banister. *Glad it's her marryin' Jefferson and not me.*

———

The lieutenant met her at the door in the morning, his jaw clenched so tight the outline of the bone showed through his skin. "And just what is it you think you're doin', Miz Highwood?"

Chapter Twenty-One

❧❧

"Hush now!" Jesselynn knew her voice sounded sharp, but she was past caring.

"Big river," Meshach said from slightly behind her.

"It's not like we have to swim it. Back aways they said there were ferries, depending on where we want to cross. They say General Grant owns this stretch, so we're safe from the Confederates."

"Bluebellies want horses worse."

She wished he wouldn't say such things. She'd just about get her confidence up, and he'd douse it with a few words of common sense. "So we stay away from Grant too. Let's find us a hiding place, and I'll go looking for ferry owners in the morning." She didn't mention the possibility of a guard on the ferry, nor the fact that she was hoping to get them ferried over after dark. Once on the other side, they could disappear into the Missouri woods and rest a bit. She studied the river, the currents changing the face of the water even in the starlight. With only a sliver moon, they would be even less visible.

Ignoring the whimpering of Ophelia and the little boys, she fingered the dwindling supply of coins in her pocket. She *had* to save what she could to get them to Springfield and Uncle Hiram's. At their last stop she'd heard of fighting going on in Missouri too, fierce fighting. Only by refusing to let herself think about what lay ahead could she keep from turning tail and heading back to Twin Oaks. If her father had known what the trip would entail, would he have exacted her promise anyway?

For one brief moment she allowed herself to remember life as it had been before the war. Twin Oaks had sheltered them through all the seasons. She could picture winter and the mares dropping their foals; sowing tobacco seed in special beds; starting other plants; then pegging tobacco; setting out tomatoes and petunias, grateful for the rains that came when needed. She closed her eyes to see the kitchen, separate from the house, but full of harvest smells.

Her stomach grumbled her back to the present. Would they be able to be home in time to plant tobacco seeds? She'd instructed Joseph to save seed from the best plants in case there were none available to purchase, or they had no money. Since there'd be no yearlings to sell this year, the tobacco had to do well.

Surely by now all the stalks were hanging in the drying barn, each hooked over the rods and spread apart just enough to allow air to circulate freely. Drying tobacco had its own pungent aroma, nothing like that of pipe or smoke. To her it smelled like hard money. How many hogsheads could they fill?

"Marse Jesse." Benjamin's soft voice interrupted her reverie, cutting off the ache to be at home tending to the tobacco and putting food by for the winter. "I found us a place."

"Good." The sigh caught her by surprise. "Let's go." *You better toughen up, or you'll be squalling like Ophelia and the babies. If you're going to wear the britches of a man, you'd better act like one.* She spun on her heel, then back at the wagon untied Sunshine's reins and swung aboard.

————

She woke to the sun warming her and two yellow butterflies dancing above her pallet. She lay and watched as they came together and fluttered apart again, one leading up a sunbeam toward the oak tree and the other first following, then tagging and flitting away. They were playing hide-and-seek in the oak leaves when she threw back the quilt and dug under the pallet for her boots. The smell of boiling coffee drove everything but food from her mind.

An hour later, hat pulled low on her forehead, she rode the mule back toward the shoreline. Belatedly, she realized it was market day. Teams of horses, oxen, and mules with their wagons lined the streets in front of brick stores and businesses. Laughter drifted from the saloon, and a dog barked at a cat that ran under the porch of the millinery store. Farmers leaned against posts to discuss their crops and the latest war news while their wives chatted on the benches. Small children played under the benches and around their mothers' feet.

Jesselynn noted several blue-clad soldiers, but they were busy shopping, not guarding or searching for anything—or anyone. At least it appeared that way.

She nudged the mule off Main Street and rode down an alley where a man was chopping firewood. He nodded as she passed by and, wiping the sweat from his brow, set another chunk of wood up on the chopping block. A boy called "hey" to her from where he was swatting a rug with a rug beater and sneezing at the dust he raised.

"Hey, yourself." Jesselynn kept her voice in the low register and nudged the mule to keep on going no matter how inviting a hank of grass appeared.

When she reached the shoreline, she could see the ferry halfway out in the river taking a cargo across. She watched as the three oarsmen on either side pulled to keep the bow straight and the boat on course. A man with a long oar guided from the stern, if the flat ends could be called that. From what Jesselynn could see, they would load and unload from either end. The ferry didn't look big enough to hold a wagon, let alone the team and the others, but the team aboard stayed hitched to their wagon. When the ferry grounded itself on the slope of the bank, planks slid off, and the team pulled the wagon off the ferry and up to the road.

It looked easy.

But would it be so simple at night?

Several horses and riders walked up the planks and the return trip began. As they neared the shore, one of the horses shifted restlessly and the rider standing holding the bridle flipped off his handkerchief and drew it over his quivering mount's eyes.

Jesselynn resolved to take enough handkerchiefs for all the horses. *And maybe my hands too.* If the hands of her men shook as bad holding the horses as they had looking at the river, she knew they were in for a rough crossing. The men knew how to swim, but Ophelia's shrieking was enough to scare Saint Peter. She'd just have to tell Meshach to keep her quiet. Ophelia listened to him as if he were Moses coming down from Mount Sinai.

Dismounting, she tied the mule to a tree and, hands in her pockets, ambled on over to the road when the ferry was still a few yards offshore. Another wagon waited with a farm family, heading home after a day in town, empty tow sacks folded in the back of the wagon bed and held in place by full ones that appeared to hold flour and beans and such. One of the barefooted boys sucked on a red-and-white peppermint stick, and a little girl perched on her mother's hip, arms clasped around her neck.

Jesselynn stopped near the whiskered man. "You use the ferry often?" she asked after exchanging greetings.

"Mostly on market day. We bring over some and take some home."

"Umm. Always this busy?"

"Nope, only market days or when the troops are movin'." He laid his hand on his son's head, and the boy stilled.

"How much for one way?"

"Depends. Jed charges more for someone he don't like or if'n he's in a foul mood. Drink'll do that to a man."

"Ah." *Does he ever run at night?* She knew she'd better keep that question between her and Jed. When the horses and riders walked off the ramp, she saw the broad-shouldered man who manned the sweep oar used as a tiller pull a flat bottle from his back pocket and take a long swallow. Wiping his mouth with the back of his hand, he hollered something at one of his oarsmen, then stepped ashore and climbed the slope with long strides.

"Be back soon." He waved to those waiting and strode on up the street.

Jesselynn watched him push open the doors to the saloon and disappear inside.

Did she dare go in after him? The family pulled their mules over to the shade of an ancient oak tree, and they all sat down, the boy pillowing his head in his mother's lap.

"Might just as well make yourself comfortable." The man indicated the cool of the shade with a sweep of his hand. "Might be a while. They's no hurryin' Jed."

Jesselynn debated. If she waited by the saloon door, perhaps she could talk with Jed alone on his way back to the ferry. She glanced at the six black men over on the plank ferry, which was built on floating logs. Several had curled up by their benches and fallen asleep. One, who appeared to be the leader, paced on the shore, carefully inspecting the rigging of the logs. Another played a Jew's harp, its plaintive notes drifting on the still air.

Laughter floated down the street from a group of children playing tag.

Jesselynn glanced again at the waiting family. All appeared to be asleep except the mother, who sat knitting. In between stitches, she brushed the flies from the faces of her children.

A memory of her mother doing much the same flashed into Jesselynn's mind. They'd been on a picnic by the river and Louisa had fallen asleep just like the boy. *Ah, Louisa, if only I dared write and tell you where I am.* Surely Dunlivey wouldn't go all the way to Richmond to ask his questions. How could he? He was in the army, wasn't he? No longer free to go where he willed?

She tried to bring up a picture of her two sisters sitting in the garden at Aunt Sylvania's house and sipping afternoon lemonade under the magnolia tree. And what of Zachary? Had anyone heard anything of him?

Nodding to the knitting woman, Jesselynn strode up the street in search of Jed. They *had* to cross tonight. She'd just reached the steps to the saloon when the swinging doors blew open, and Jed, another flat bottle in his hand, roared in laughter at something someone behind him called. If Jesselynn hadn't stepped back, he would have barreled right over her.

"Ah, sir. Mister Jed."

"Who's callin' me?"

"I am." Jesselynn stepped in front of him, her gaze traveling up an unbuttoned dirty shirt worn over a filthier woolen union suit. A small stick lodged in his beard, and dark eyes flashed under bushy caterpillar brows. She swallowed, then cocked her head at an angle and started again. "Ma daddy sent me to ask how much you'd charge to take over a wagon and team, along with a couple other horses."

"How many folk?"

"Five grown and two little'uns." She spat off to the side of her boot after he did it first.

"When?"

"After dark."

"You runnin' from the law?"

"No, sir."

"The army?"

"No, sir. Just got to get to a funeral. Grandpappy died unexpected like." The story came out before she even had time to think on it.

"You wouldn't lie to ol' Jed, now, wouldja?" He took another slug from the bottle and held it out to Jesselynn, who shook her head.

"Ma daddy would tan me good if'n I came home with liquor on my breath."

Jed nodded and swigged again. He named his price.

Jesselynn kept herself from flinching with the most supreme effort. After talking with the man at the ferry, she knew the price was doubled. But there would be more dangers at night, so she nodded. "I'll tell him. You need to know what time f'sure?"

"Jus' come." Jed clapped her on the shoulder and strode off down to the ferry, leaving her with both a smarting shoulder and the desire to jig her way back to the camp. She had found a way across the river. Now to get her people ready for it.

Back in camp, the boys, both big and little, were sleeping soundly. Meshach sat under a tree with his Bible on his knees reading to Ophelia, who still rocked back and forth in her distress. Jesselynn stripped the saddle from the mule and, tying him to the long line, took off the bridle as well. She studied the horses grazing so peacefully. They looked too good, even though they had matted manes and tails and hadn't seen a grooming brush since they left home.

"Is there some way you can make Ahab limp?" she asked after sitting down by Meshach.

"I 'spects so. Why?"

"I don't know, just got me a feelin'." Jesselynn turned to study the horses. Domino, the younger stallion, stood looking off to the west, ears pricked, the breeze blowing his tail. No matter how filthy, he showed Thoroughbred through and through.

"We're takin' the ferry tonight and . . . and if he was limping with head down, maybe . . . maybe he wouldn't be so . . ."

"I kin make 'im limp."

"But it won't hurt him permanently?" She could hear the anxiousness in her own voice. She sucked in a breath. "What about the others?"

"If we harness the mare with the mule, get ol' Ahab to limpin' so I'm leadin' 'im and Chess . . ." He thought a long moment. "I got some stuff to set Domino to coughing, so Benjamin can lead him. Then you drive the wagon, and Daniel can ride Sunshine and lead the filly. Shouldn't nobody look twice at 'em dat away."

"Don' wanna go over dat der river." Ophelia's hoarse whisper made Jesselynn flinch.

"Won't be any different than crossing the Tennessee. We took the ferry there too, remember? And others before that."

"I 'member." She shook her head slowly. "Not big like dis here one."

"Okay, you stay in the back of the wagon with the babies, and all of you can cry all you want. I'll tell the man you got the vapors or something. But we are crossing the Mississippi River tonight, and that's that!" Jesselynn stood and glared down at the wide-eyed woman. "I told him we are goin' to a funeral, so your weepin' and wailin' should be right appropriate."

"Now, 'Phelia, God done took care of us till now. He can float us 'cross dat river jus' like de Jordan."

A sniffle was her only answer, but Jesselynn could tell the woman was calmer. Meshach's gentle words put her in mind of the song she'd heard sung so often from the slave quarters. *". . . my home is over Jordan. Deep river, Lord, I want to cross over into campground."* She sighed. "Let's get on with it. Meshach, you better say an extra prayer or two for all of us." Turning away, she headed for the wagon. Sometimes the burden seemed beyond her strength to bear. Maybe letting the army have the horses so she could head on back home would be the best choice after all.

———

Stars provided enough light for them to make their way through the town and down to the ferry. The water lapping against the bulky craft sent the timbers to creaking and, along with the creak of the wagon, sounded loud in the stillness.

"Marse Jed?" Jesselynn kept her voice low but insistent. She waited, hearing a scuffling on the boat.

A light flared and lit the lantern. Jed seemed even bigger, if that were possible, in the glow of the lamp as he staggered down the plank to the riverbank. "You ready?"

"Yes, suh."

"You got the money?" Jed swung the lamp up to look her in the face.

"Yes, suh." Jesselynn ducked her head and dug in her pocket for the coins needed. She counted them into the shovel-sized palm. "That's what you said."

"I know." He spun around and picking up the end of the plank, thudded it against the ferry planking. "Let's go, boys. We got us a load."

Men scrambled up from where they slept and took their oars. Several more planks were slid into place, and Jed gave orders from the ferry.

"Lead your horse on up here real easylike. They ever been ferried before?"

"Yes, suh." Jesselynn climbed down from the wagon, hearing Ophelia moaning "Jesus" over and over. She took the mule's reins under his chin and, clucking him forward, led the team up the ramp and forward on the low craft. With horses on either side, all facing forward, the men pulled in the planks, and Jed pushed off with his long pole. The stroke of six oars slicing the water in tandem and the sweep of the stern oar brought them out into the current. The prow of the ferry swung downstream with the current before righting and plowing forward.

Jesselynn felt the planking shuddering under her feet. The mule laid back his ears and stamped one front foot. Domino coughed until he broke wind, and the sailor nearest him made a rude remark that brought laughter from another.

Short chop broke over the prow, soaking Jesselynn's boots. Ophelia moaned again, and Sammy set up a wail.

"Ohh." Even Meshach groaned.

"Enough!" Jesselynn forced out the word in spite of the shaking that she attributed to the creaking craft. The far shore seemed to get farther away instead of closer.

Was the current carrying them downriver? She turned to look at Jed, who appeared more shadow than man at the stern. Was crossing at night against the law? Why had he blown out the lamp?

"Heave on, boys," the order came, calm as a summer day.

"Oh, Jesus, sweet Jesus, we comin' home," Ophelia sobbed.

Jesselynn wished she had put a rag in Ophelia's mouth before they'd left camp. Sammy hiccuped after crying. Must be hours that passed, the ferry held prisoner by the river.

"Pull, you worthless scum. You want a glug of rotgut at the shore, you pull now."

"Oh, Lord, bring us safe to shore, please, precious Jesus." Like Ophelia, Meshach murmured his prayer over and over.

The young stallion coughed again, pounding his front hooves on the planks.

"Whoa, son." Benjamin could be heard above the creaking.

An expletive choked.

The raft shuddered from the impact and spun to face downriver.

"Easy! No!" A mighty splash drenched those nearest and then another.

Chapter Twenty-Two

RICHMOND, VIRGINIA

If looks were spears, she'd have been run through more times than she could count.

Louisa focused her attention on the men kneeling in the dirt and those missing a limb who were learning to use shovels and rakes to clear out the dead wood of the rosebushes and encroaching vines. In spite of herself, her gaze repeatedly drifted toward the lieutenant. His orders had been to supervise, as if leaning on his crutches and glaring provided good supervision.

As the hours passed, she surreptitiously wiped the perspiration from her forehead and neck. When she caught him staring at her, she dropped the corner of her apron at the same instant she raised her chin. After all, she'd suggested working in the garden for the good of *his* men. As if all these were under *his* orders, anyway. They were from all different regiments, not just *his*. She nodded an answer to a question from one of the others.

As she was just about to stalk over and confront her nemesis, a shadow gave her shade. She turned enough to realize he stood right behind her, so close that if she took in a deep breath, she might touch him. While taking a step back might indicate defeat, she did so anyway. Sometimes retreating was the better part of valor.

At least she could breathe then.

"Goodness, do you always sneak up on a body that way?" She clenched her fists to keep them from offering calming pats to her tripping heart.

"I *was not* sneaking." His lips barely moved, his jaw clamped so tight. Even so, he kept his voice low so that the others might not hear.

Feeling loomed over, she took another step back. "Well, *sir,* since I am not one of *your* soldiers, I would appreciate a more civil tone." *Oh, fine, now you've gone and done it. He finally talks to you, and you scold like his mother.*

She watched as he forcibly gathered himself together, stood straighter, and adopted a polite expression that wouldn't fool a year-old baby.

"Pardon me, ma'am. I believe I have a right to know why you asked the surgeon to assign me to garden duty."

She straightened as he had, if it were possible for her to get any taller and straighter. Totally ignoring the memory she had of suggesting to the surgeon general that garden duty might be good for the lieutenant, she matched him glare for glare. "I asked if I could bring Private Rumford and some of the others out here because I thought that working in the soil might help them. My aunt says gardening is one of the best medicines God has given us, and I concur." She didn't add that such had been her salvation when her sister exiled her from Twin Oaks to Richmond. Before she took time to think, she stepped forward and pointed a soil-crusted finger at his chest. "And if *you,* Lieutenant Lessling, would unbend even a smidgen, it might help you too."

She caught her breath at the narrowing of his eyes. For sure she had gone too far. *Oh, Lord, why can I no longer control my tongue? What is happening with me? My mother would turn over in her grave to hear her daughter attacking any person, let alone a young man like this.* And a wounded man, at that.

"I . . . I'm sorry. That was unbelievably rude of me. Please . . ." She looked down at her dirt-crusted hands and even dirtier apron. Shame can cause as much heat as pure embarrassment. She felt it flaming her face. "Please forgive me?" She glanced up from under her eyelashes in time to catch a hint of something in his eyes. Was it compassion she saw? By the time she named it, the look had fled, and one of such bleakness that it made her heart cry out for him took up residence instead.

"Forgiveness needs to go both ways, Mrs. Highwood. I'm sorry for the way I've been actin'. Such conduct befits neither an officer nor a gentleman."

Could one drown in eyes so sad?

She gathered her ruffled feelings around her like a hen gathering chicks and allowed her lips to smile in what she hoped was a motherly fashion. Why could she treat all the other men like her brothers or cousins, but this man refused to be treated as such?

"Then may we be friends?" The words crept out before she had time to cut them off.

"Friends, yes." He touched one finger to the fading scar on his forehead. "If your husband won't mind."

"But I—" This time she caught herself. "No, I reckon he won't mind at all."

"Miz Highwood, you think this here is dug deep enough?" one of her workers called out.

She turned to answer the soldier's question and, throwing a smile over her shoulder to the lieutenant, made her way to inspect the holes being dug to transplant some of the overcrowded rosebushes.

"That will be fine." She glanced over to where Rumford and Reuben had dug around the well-watered bushes to prepare them for lifting. As long as Reuben indicated exactly where to place the shovel and when to step on it, the young man leaning on the handle and staring into the distance was able to dig.

At further instructions he lifted the roses out of their holes as carefully as if he were lifting a baby. By the time they'd moved four bushes, watered them in, and pruned off a couple of broken branches, the orderly announced the noon meal.

"Now, doesn't that look much better?" She stood with her crew gathered around her and surveyed the results of their labors. While there was still a lot to do, the newly planted roses gleamed against the rich soil, and the weeds were now piled off to the side instead of choking life from the bushes. A mass of tangled vines topped the weed pile.

"As my mother always said, 'Termorrer is another day.'" Corporal Shaddock wiped sweat from his brow with the back of his good hand.

"So true, and thank y'all for helpin' me out here."

The snort from behind her could have come from only one voice. She ignored him, and together she and her crew made their way back to the ward, those on crutches hopping up the marble stairs, the seat of their pants mute evidence as to how they'd managed to work in the garden. Only the lieutenant bore no badges of honorable work, but he had been there, and he had asked her forgiveness. He'd even smiled at a joke one of the men made.

When she brought around the bowls of stew, she nearly dropped one when she reached her brother's bed.

"You're sitting up, and I can see part of your face."

"Now, aren't you the observant one?" His drawl sounded more familiar now that more bandages had been removed, and the teasing sparkle in his eye had not dimmed. "Looks like they'll be calling me One-Eyed Jack, though." He touched the bandaged side of his face with his fingertips. "Guess my right side took quite a beatin'." Talking was still difficult with the jaw healing.

His teasing tone dropped on the last words as the sparkle flickered from his eye.

"But you're alive."

"Half of me anyway."

"Soon as we get you out of here, I reckon you'll be feelin' some better with Aunt Sylvania fussin' over you."

He studied the bowl of stew she set beside him. "The food'll be better. That I know." He took the spoon she handed him and dug in, slopping some of the colorless liquid over the edge. "Shame I didn't work on becoming ambidextrous like Adam did."

"Learnin' to use the other hand is never easy." She kept herself from reminding him he was fortunate to have one good hand. Some didn't.

————

"I think you should be able to take him home in two or three days," the doctor said when he made his late afternoon rounds. "Unless we get another battery of wounded, that is, and need his bed. How did"—he nodded toward Rumford—"do outside?"

"I set him to working with Reuben, my aunt's gardener, and he followed all Reuben's orders without a grumble."

"With no visible response, you mean?"

"Well, he did do as asked."

The doctor nodded. "You're right. Thank you, my dear, for all your efforts on behalf of these men. If I had ten more like you, the care here would improve dramatically."

"Doctor?" one of the orderlies called from the door.

"Yes?"

"Train just pulled in full of wounded."

"So much for two or three days. I hate to ask this, but can your aunt or anyone else take in some of these men?"

"I'm sure, but I'll ask." Louisa untied her apron as she headed for the doorway. "We'll be back with a wagon as soon as we can."

She nearly tripped over her skirts in the rush up the front steps to Aunt Sylvania's house. She paused only long enough to catch her breath, knowing that a scolding about propriety would set her aunt in a less-than-generous fashion. But then, she had asked what more she could do for the "dear boys," as she referred to the soldiers. Only, up until now, the dear boys had not been needing one of her lovely rooms.

"Aunt, where are you?" Louisa paused for a moment to know where to search.

"In here." The answer came from the back of the house.

Louisa found her aunt watching Abby arrange flowers in the pantry.

"You're home early." Weariness rode Sylvania's face and left her hands shaking.

"I know. I need to get back. The doctor said we could bring Zachary home if we had a place for him." Louisa breathed another calming breath. "But we couldn't take him upstairs very easily."

"Then we will have to move a bed into the parlor." Sylvania rose from her chair. "Come, Abby, call Prissy to help you."

"Ah, while we are moving one bed, could we do two—or maybe three?"

Sylvania studied her niece over her glasses rims. "What did you have in mind? Bringing in the whole hospital?"

Louisa ignored the sarcasm and shook her head. "A train pulled in with a load of wounded. The doctor asked if I knew anyone who would be willing to help with the men who are so much better, that's all." *Please, God, let her decide to help.*

"I see." Sylvania turned to Reuben. "Go next door and ask for Miss Julie's Sady. She can run notes around while you and the girls get the parlor ready. We can lay a pallet or two in the dining room if need be."

Louisa breathed a sigh of relief. Why had she been so afraid to ask this of her aunt? It wasn't as if she hadn't been knitting socks and sewing uniforms for their soldiers like the rest of the women. She just hadn't approved of her niece working at the hospital. After all, women nurses were considered little above the prostitutes, of whose existence Louisa was not supposed to even know. Her brothers had called them various other names, but she had eavesdropped often enough to learn things not discussed around womenfolk.

Thanks to her brothers, both she and Jesselynn knew many things young women were not supposed to know. Carrie Mae, however, had never cared to follow her sisters. Instead, she had become an expert musician, and her singing, as well as her piano playing, had entertained them all, including the surrounding neighbors.

Suddenly, homesickness for Twin Oaks bathed her like a pouring rain. *Please, God, let the war end soon. I want to go home.* Taking time to count the numerous pleas of this sort she'd sent heavenward would be a waste of precious seconds.

They had two beds set up by the time Sylvania's notes were ready to be carried around. Reuben listened to his instructions, nodded, and slipped out the door as Abby and Louisa smoothed the clean sheets into place and folded a blanket at the end of each bed. The weather was still far too warm to put two blankets on, let alone winter quilts. By the time they'd folded the quilts up for pallets and made up two in the parlor, Reuben returned.

"We's got two yeses, two maybes, and one not to home." He handed the papers back to Sylvania. "Asked Widow Penrod if we could borry her horse and wagon, so soon's I git dat, we be off." He smiled at Louisa. "Dat brudder of yours be home before supper."

"I already told Cook to make enough supper for four more." Aunt Sylvania sat in her chair and picked up her fan. "Lawsy, this is unseasonable weather. No wonder those men in the hospital are so miserable."

Louisa didn't tell her about the garden efforts, figuring that the borrowed garden tools would be back before they were missed. At the same time she wondered who their guests would be. The thought of the lieutenant flitted through her mind, but as if it were a yellow jacket, she brushed the thought away.

She'd just started out the door toward the wagon when another thought buzzed by her. This one made her stop and blink. How would she keep these men from realizing she was not the wife of Zachary Highwood but his little sister instead?

Oh, Lord, now what have I gotten myself into?

Chapter Twenty-Three

ON THE MISSISSIPPI RIVER

"Benjamin and Domino fell in!"

The oars stopped. Shouts filled the air. Ahab whinnied, just about breaking Jesselynn's eardrums. The ferry drifted downriver.

"Can you see him?" Jesselynn didn't dare leave her post at Ahab's head to go see for herself, or everything might end up in the river.

"Lawd, Lawd, we's comin' home," Ophelia added to the din. The boys' cries could be heard from the back of the wagon.

A string of expletives came from the ferry owner at the rear. "Pull, you fools, or we'll end up on a sandbar. Row!"

Oh, God, not Benjamin. Let him live. The shore isn't that far, Jesselynn pleaded over and over in her mind while she kept up a steady murmur that calmed both herself and the horses.

" 'Phelia, enough!" Meshach's command cut off the blubbering like blowin' out a candle. "Good. Now take care of de boys."

"I is."

Benjamin, where are you, Benjamin? Jesselynn and Benjamin had grown up together, playing games in the orchard and snitching cookies from Lucinda's baking only to run off laughing when scolded. He couldn't be gone, not after living through the war and bringing her daddy home to die. He'd saved her father, and right now she could do nothing to save him.

The ferry moved ahead again and within minutes bumped into the packed sand of the shoreline.

Ahab shifted at the jolt, and Jesselynn clamped the reins under his bit even tighter. "Easy, son." She resumed her reassuring murmur as two of the oarsmen slid planks in place for them to disembark. Meshach led his horses off first, then Sunshine, before coming back to lead the team down the incline. Once they were all on the ground, Ahab shook himself, setting harness and chains to rattling.

"Sorry as I kin be 'bout that other horse and your boy. I wouldn't give up hope, though. They mighta swum in." Mister Jed shook Jesselynn's hand and motioned his hands to ready the ferry for the return. "Floatin' logs and such are the hazards of night crossin'."

"I understand. Thank you for the service." Jesselynn climbed up on the wagon seat and clucked the team forward. "Meshach, you go look that way, and Daniel, you go downriver." When the two riders took off, she turned to the woman still whimpering in the back of the wagon. "Ophelia, if you don't stop that, I'll send you back across the river."

"There's a road back up thata way," Jed called as he poled the ferry back out into the current.

Once on firmer ground, Jesselynn stopped the wagon and got out again, this time to remove the stone that Meshach had wedged in Ahab's hoof to make him limp. Last thing they needed now was a truly lame horse. Once moving again, the horse and mule leaned into their collars as the wheels rolled through shallow sand. She slapped the reins to keep them pulling forward, sure that if they stopped, the wheels would sink. Between Ophelia's continued sniffling, the boys' whimpering, Benjamin's getting lost, and not knowing where the road was, Jesselynn wanted to do nothing more than run screaming down the road or hide her head under a blanket and sleep until life improved.

Where was the road? Surely they hadn't drifted that far off course.

Just as she recognized a lighter spot in the woods as the break for the road, she heard a horse cough, the kind of cough induced by the herb that Meshach had given Domino.

"Benjamin?" She raised her voice and called again. "Benjamin?"

Ahab nickered, and a horse answered, then trotted out of the darkness to meet them. The filly tied to the tailgate joined in the welcome, and Jesselynn tightened the reins enough to stop the team. Flipping the reins around the brake pole, she vaulted to the ground and dashed to the end of the wagon before slowing and picking up the cadence of her soothing murmur. Domino flung his head up, then at her familiar song, nosed her outstretched hand and let her grab his reins.

"Oh, Lawd, you took Benjamin down to de depths of de river, and now he's home wid you. Lawsy, lawsy." Ophelia's crying and moaning renewed the wailing of the two boys, who might have dozed off again had she not started anew.

Jesselynn felt around in the wagon bed until she located a lead shank. She snapped it to the horse's halter, then removed the water-soaked bridle. As long as her hands kept busy, she could keep at bay the thought of Benjamin drowning.

If Ophelia didn't shut up, she was going to scream.

"Ophelia, stop! I can't hear myself think." In the ensuing quiet, she listened hard. Was that a horse she heard coming from the river? Scant seconds later, she heard Meshach call her name.

"Marse Jesse, I found 'im. Benjamin be alive."

"Oh, thank you, blessed Lawd."

This time Jesselynn didn't try to quiet Ophelia; rather she wanted to join in, but instead, she ran back on the road to meet Meshach.

"Praise de Lawd, Marse Jesse, our boy done be saved."

Benjamin slid off the back of the horse and right into her arms.

He raised his head enough to ask, "Is . . . D-Domino all right?"

"Yes."

At her answer he straightened, then bent over coughing until he vomited up half the river.

Jesselynn put her arm around his waist and half dragged him back to the wagon, where Meshach had his horse tied by this time. The big man lifted the smaller and, gentle as a mother with her baby, laid him on the quilts Ophelia spread out.

"I get dem wet." Benjamin tried to rise, but Jesselynn put her hands on his shoulders and pushed him back down. "Just rest for now. Soon as Daniel catches up, we'll see where this road goes."

Meshach dried off the younger stallion while Ophelia and Jesselynn rubbed Benjamin until he no longer shook from cold and exhaustion. With him and the boys asleep in the wagon bed, Jesselynn leaned against a wheel, growing more restless by the moment. They were right out in the middle of a road with land flatter than Lucinda's hot cakes stretching on either side of them. While the moon didn't show much light, other than the willows and cottonwoods along the river, the land looked bare.

Ahab whinnied, and a horse answered. At the same moment, she heard a horse trotting toward them from the river. Ahab whinnied again.

"You're better'n a watchdog." Jesselynn joined Meshach at the back of the wagon. "Think it's him?"

"A'course. Ahab done say so."

"Sorry, Marse, I din't find nary horse nor—"

"I found 'im," Meshach interrupted the rush of words.

"Thank de Lawd."

"Benjamin's sleepin' in the wagon. Domino here is all right too. We're glad you're back. Now we can go on." Jesselynn patted Daniel on the knee and swung up onto the wagon seat. "Now, let's find us a place to camp."

———

Jesselynn woke that afternoon when the sun had crept past the high point. The willow branches had shielded her up to then, but the sun in her eyes made further sleep impossible. She stretched and tossed her quilt aside. Today she would write home and tell them that she and her band were now safe in Missouri. Surely Dunlivey would not track them there, and even if he could, they would soon disappear in the oak and hickory forests her uncle had written about those years ago. He'd passed through them and broke land on the prairie for his horse farm. She'd read his letters before she left home, not that there were too many of them.

Taking paper and the ink bottle, then sharpening a quill, she accepted the coffee Ophelia brought her and began to write. She covered two sheets before signing Jesse Highwood and blowing on the still-damp signature. She stared at it, shaking her head. Seemed like she'd been a male now for longer than three weeks, as if her life had begun the night they fled Twin Oaks.

While folding the letter, her thoughts roamed to the homeplace. Surely all the Burley was cut by now and hanging to dry in the barn. It shouldn't be long before it could be stripped and packed in the hogsheads for transporting to Frankfort.

They'd always held a celebration when the tobacco was sold. All the neighbors joined in too. There was dancing and tables groaning with delicious food. Her stomach rumbled at the thought of all the spicy boiled shrimp, the sweet potato pie that Lucinda was known for, biscuits lighter than a cloud. Her stomach rumbled louder.

She finished addressing the envelope and went in search of a dab of flour and water to paste the flap shut. While she'd brought her father's sealing ring, she'd neglected to bring the sealing wax.

"You want to go into Charleston with me?" She paused by where Meshach was cleaning the harnesses and bridles.

He shook his head. "I needs to grease de axles and tighten up de shaft. 'Sides, no one recognize Daniel."

"You don't think . . ."

"No sense takin' chances. We come too far for dat."

The hairs up the back of her neck stood at attention. And here she'd just been congratulating herself on getting away and was beginning to feel safe.

"Take de mule. De horses need more grazin' time and a rest."

Jesselynn sighed. When would they really be free?

A short time later they trotted into town double mounted, both of them leaning back to keep from being jostled to bits by the mule's sledgehammer trot. The bony ridge of his back didn't help either. They both sighed when they slid off behind some buildings.

Daniel rubbed his seat. "I think he do dat on purpose."

"What? Trot harder?" Jesselynn grinned. "Might be. You go that way, and I'll try this way. Just stop and listen to people talkin'. Like you used to do at home."

Daniel tried to look affronted but laughed instead. "Don' you go leavin' me behind now."

"Then be back when the sun goes behind that willow tree over there." She nodded to a tree that had obviously outlived many a flood.

Jesselynn located the post office first thing, mailed her letter, then strolled across the dirt street to the store where several men had gathered.

She dug in her pocket and pulled out a jackknife to begin cleaning the dirt from under her fingernails. With her rear tight against the porch floor, she hoped she was as invisible as she felt.

The more they talked, the more her stomach churned. There were more skirmishes going on in Missouri than in Kentucky, and the fighting had started earlier. Why hadn't she known that? She could answer that question before thinking. They'd been so isolated at Twin Oaks that until the army took the horses away they'd not been much bothered by the war.

One thing for sure, they'd not be going north to try to hook up with the Wire Road. Whyever they called it that was beyond her. When the talk turned to the bands of deserters who were terrorizing the countryside under the guise of Confederate soldiers, her throat went dry. She'd heard about Quantrill's Raiders in the last town, but they were said to be more in the Kansas City area. Springfield was a far cry from Kansas City.

At least Dunlivey was on the other side of the river. If she'd reminded herself of that once, it had been ten times. It wasn't hard to picture him as the head of a band of raiders. But he'd been an officer in the Confederate army the last time she'd seen him. Then what had he been doing in that tavern? Of course the army did move their forces around.

The argument kept up in her mind apace with the cussing and discussing on the porch. When they began in on "that nigger lover in the White House," she sidled away. Her father had a great deal of respect for President Lincoln, and therefore she did too. *"One nation under God, the way the United States had been founded, and the way it should stay."* She could hear her father's words as plainly as if he were walking beside her.

Checking the angle of the sun, she moseyed back to where they'd tied the mule. Daniel sat with his back against the wall, chewing on the end of a stalk of grass. Jesselynn swung aboard and braced her foot for him to use as a step to swing up. Once he'd settled behind her, she turned the mule back the way they'd come and headed out.

"What'd you hear?" she asked when they were out in the country again.

"Dem folks sure don' like Marse Lincum."

"I heard that too. What else?"

"Bad sojers about. Man in tavern laughin' him head off 'bout dem hangin' a runaway slave."

"Where?"

"Don' know."

"This side of the river?"

"I guess. Dey talkin' 'bout Missouri."

Jesselynn looked up to see if the despair settling over her wasn't a cloud in the sky instead, but the sun still shone as it sank closer to the horizon.

What if someone found their camp and wouldn't believe Meshach when he said they were free blacks?

Chapter Twenty-Four

❧

RICHMOND, VIRGINIA

"I can't believe I'm in a real house."

Louisa folded back the sheet over her brother and smoothed it into place. Her eyes burned at the relief she heard in his voice and the way his hand repeatedly smoothed the sheets.

"Where's Aunt Sylvania?"

"Helpin' the neighbors get their boys settled in. She'll be home soon for supper." She turned to see Private Rumford, dark hair falling in his eyes, sitting in the chair by the window where they had put him. Not looking out—just not looking. *Tomorrow,* she promised herself, *tomorrow he will be out in the garden here, and I know that will make a difference.* The thought of the lieutenant living in the house next door set her pulse to tripping.

"And Carrie Mae, where is she?"

"Off with her betrothed, I believe." *As if she were ever anywhere else. You'd think they were already married.*

"When's the wedding to be?"

Louisa thought for a moment. "Why, it's only two weeks away. Where has the time gone?"

Zach studied her for a long moment.

She could feel it even though she resisted looking into his one good eye. Somehow she knew he was going to ask a question that either she wouldn't like or would have no idea how to answer. She heard the front door opening and gave a sigh of relief. Saved by Aunt Sylvania. When she started to rise, Zach laid his hand on hers.

"What are you going to do about tomorrow?"

"Tomorrow?"

"The hospital. I don't like the idea of you workin' there."

"I don't *work* there. I volunteer there." She could feel her face begin to heat up, let alone her temper. "What difference does it make to you?"

"Well, you . . ." He glanced over at the corporal and shook his head. "We'll talk about this later." Like hers, his accent broadened when he grew agitated.

"Private, would you like to join us at the supper table?" Aunt Sylvania appeared in the doorway, smiling her welcome to their guest. "Cook is fixin' plates for the others." She crossed to Zachary's bed. "Do you need help, nephew, or can you manage on your own?"

"He needs . . ."

"I can manage." Zachary and Louisa spoke at the same time.

"Well, which is it?"

"If someone will help prop me up, I imagine it is time I continue learning to use my other hand." He lifted his left hand. "Shame I didn't learn to shoot with either hand like Adam did."

"Lot of good it did him." Louisa was as surprised at her comment as the other two. Surely shooting with either or both hands hadn't been instrumental in getting her older brother killed in action, but then it hadn't saved him either. To carry the thought to a logical conclusion, cannonballs and artillery shells didn't discriminate. She spun on her heel, her skirts swishing in the speed with which she left the room.

More and more she was learning how much she resented the war—and the men who'd been so vainglorious about whipping the Yankees in two weeks. No wonder Jesselynn had taken the horses away from home. They'd need something to rebuild with when this massacre was over.

Maybe she'd read the letters to Zachary after supper so he could know what all had transpired since he'd left home. Come to think of it, strange that he'd not questioned her about Twin Oaks. Of course, she'd told him about their daddy dying, so maybe that was all he wanted to know for now.

Soon though, soon they could go home. Even if Zachary was badly crippled, he would find things to do at Twin Oaks. Surely he'd be able to manage getting around with crutches or maybe just one. And anyone could learn to use the opposite hand.

Curious, she assigned herself the task at the supper table.

"Whatever is the matter, child?" Aunt Sylvania stared at the gravy blob staining the white linen tablecloth.

"I . . . I was trying to cut my meat with my left hand. The knife slipped." Using her napkin, Louisa dabbed at the spreading blob.

"Whyever for?" Sylvania sent Private Rumford a questioning glance, but he never looked her way. He did clean up his plate, however, without anyone prompting him. Since sometimes at the hospital she'd hand-fed him when he paid no attention to his food, Louisa felt a stir of pleasure.

"Well, since Zach will have to learn to use his other hand, I . . . I wanted to see how difficult it would be. But I have two hands, so really it isn't the same after all." Her words came in a rush.

Her aunt's "tsk-tsk" sent a shot of stiffener up Louisa's spine.

"We can't wait on him forever. Like he said, it's time he began to try things on his own."

"We shall see."

Louisa studied her aunt. Instead of looking worn-out as she'd been the few days before, the new responsibility seemed to be bringing the older woman back to her earlier energy. She, too, had cleaned up her plate, rather than picking at her food, which had become the norm. Pink had reclaimed its place on her cheeks, and the pallor of the past weeks seemed in retreat.

"Perhaps you would like to read to the men tonight? They missed out on their chapters of Shakespeare since we were moving them at the time I usually read. I always read a psalm or two and a chapter from one of Paul's letters."

"Why, I reckon I might just do that." Sylvania nodded her approval at the tray of desserts Abby showed her. "See how my nephew is doing too, will you, please? Peach cobbler has always been his favorite dessert."

"I thought the peaches were gone." Louisa shrugged at her aunt's innocent look. Life had always been like that. Her brothers were treated like royalty by Aunt Sylvania, and the girls were made to mind. Surely that wasn't fair, but then, as her mother had always said, *"God didn't promise life would be fair."*

After supper, when she had Sylvania set up in the hallway to read so she could be heard in both rooms, Louisa wandered out on the front porch to catch any breeze that had come up. Not sure why she didn't head for the garden as was her wont, she settled into the rocker, setting it into motion with the push of her foot.

A young boy and a girl ran by laughing, the pong of their sticks on the hoops rolling in front of them adding to their merriment. A flycatcher called from swooping about the trees. A squirrel chattered in the elm directly in front of the house. She caught sight of him descending the tree in quick bursts of speed.

The chair creaked its own song. Louisa sighed and leaned her head back against the cushion, remembering home . . . the slaves singing down in the quarters, and Jesselynn sitting on the veranda, busy with some kind of needlework.

As you should be doing.

The thought brought her foot to the floor. Wasting time like this! What in the world was the matter with her? And how come she kept thinking of home so much today anyway? But with Jesselynn gone, someone should be there to keep things running. After all, could the slaves—she had to remind herself that their people weren't slaves any longer, thanks to the papers Jesselynn had given them—could their *workers* keep the place running without someone overseeing them?

"Good evenin'."

The male voice so near brought her hand to her throat.

"Why, land sakes, you need to sneak up on a body that way?"

"I didn't sneak up on you. I came to check on my men." The lieutenant straightened his shoulders in spite of the crutches.

"Oh." Bringing her mind back from Twin Oaks took some doing. Now, if a man like this came calling there, he would be treated—Louisa cut off her thought. She was getting tired of her face flaming at the slightest provocation. The man in front of her was the lieutenant, coming to check on his men, not a potential suitor.

A buggy pulled up at the street and the two laughing occupants stepped down, or rather, her sister was handed down by her adoring fiancé, who had learned to use his one arm to an advantage. No morose scarecrow he. As the two of them came up the walk, the lieutenant glanced their way, then gave Louisa one of his formal stares.

"My men?"

"Ah yes." Louisa started for the door when Carrie Mae, who had taken her eyes off her escort long enough to see her sister and the lieutenant, spoke.

"Why, Louisa, I see you have comp'ny." Carrie Mae's soft Kentucky accent had turned entirely Virginian since their arrival.

"Ah, n-no. The lieutenant is j-just here on business." Since when had she taken up stuttering?

Carrie Mae paused at the bottom of the steps. "Are you not going to introduce us?"

Oh, sugarcane and cotton combined. Louisa thought two of her most vitriolic incantations, all the while keeping what she hoped was a smile on her face. She turned to Jefferson Steadly, Carrie Mae's fiancé. "Pardon my manners, Mr. Steadly."

"Since we are about to become related, surely you could call me by my given name by now."

"All right." *Let's just get this over with.* "Jefferson, this is Lieutenant . . ." For the life of her, she couldn't remember his last name. Had she ever heard him called anything but the lieutenant?

The lieutenant straightened and extended his right hand. "I'm Gilbert Lessling, First Lieutenant of the Second North Carolina Rifles." He nodded. "Pleased to meet you, Miss Highwood. Miz Highwood here has spoken of you often."

The floor couldn't open and swallow her soon enough.

Chapter Twenty-Five

SOUTHEASTERN MISSOURI
OCTOBER 6, 1862

So far, so good.

Jesselynn looked back over the marshy river delta and shook her head. Thanks to Benjamin's careful scouting, they'd missed burying the wagon in swamps and ponds more than once. The one digging-out they'd had to do was bad enough. But they were still safe, and considering the possibilities, that was a miracle in itself.

"Found de Indian trace dat man tol' me 'bout." Meshach rode beside her as she guided the horses up the faint road.

"Where?"

"South of here. Not better'n dis but no worse."

"If only we dared go on up to the Wire Road. Heard tell there are even bridges across some creeks." Jesselynn rubbed her forehead with one hand, wishing the headache that came with her monthlies would disappear, the cramps too. Maybe she should let Ophelia drive the wagon and she could sleep in the back with the boys.

Thoughts of her mother handing her a hot brick wrapped in flannel and tucking her back in bed for a nap crossed her mind. A breeze fluttering the curtains at the window, clean crisp white sheets, a pillow, and when she woke up, she could curl up with a book if she wanted. The work of the plantation would go on around her, and . . .

"Marse Jesse, you all right?"

Jesselynn sighed. "I reckon. Show us the way to the trace. I can't wait to get to Uncle Hiram's, and if that way is faster and safer than this, I'm all for it."

———

Since they hadn't seen any sign of habitation for the last two days, they had decided to travel in the daylight, hoping to make better time. With Meshach clearing brush with his machete at times, they still were able to keep moving. A campfire at the end of the day, hot food and coffee, and the dreams of home didn't cause quite so much pain. She sat on a log and opened her journal, using the light from the fire to guide her.

> *We made a good twenty miles today, the best in some time, but now the trail is thickening in again, the brush trying to reclaim the space. Finally Sammy is feeling good and he and Thaddy, or Joshwa, as he insists on being called, are near close as brothers. To think I even considered leaving him. If Mama knew the thoughts I've had, she would be so disappointed in me that I couldn't bear the sorrow in her eyes. She would tell me to get down on my knees and ask the Lord's forgiveness, but I cannot tell her that I have begun to wonder if there really is a God who would allow such terrible things to go on. She would say "God is love," but all I seem to see and hear lately is pure hatred.*

She glanced up to see Ophelia scoop the two boys up and whirl them around, making their giggles bring a smile to her face. No, not all was hatred, at least not here in the safety of their camp.

Ahab stopped grazing and, lifting his head, nickered, his ears pointing into the scrub oak. Meshach slapped his Bible closed and in one smooth motion stood with his rifle in hand. Jesselynn reached for the pistol she kept at her side.

"Don't shoot." The voice sounded like a child's cry.

Jesselynn capped her ink bottle and set her journal down on the log, easing to her feet at the same time.

"Come, show yo'self." Meshach held the rifle at the ready.

"We'uns was jus' hopin' fer some supper." Only her tattered skirts let them know she was a girl. She clutched the hand of a stick-figure boy. They were both barefoot and shivering in the evening chill. While the days had stayed warm, the nights were a different matter.

Ophelia set the boys down and swung the kettle back over the low flames. "Come on over here and git warmed up."

The two moved toward the fire as if walking on coals, so hesitant were they.

"We don' mean no harm." The girl held out her empty hands. "Don' got no gun nor nothin'." The boy clung to her skirt, staring at the kettle as if he'd never seen anything so fine in his life.

"My name is Jane Ellen, and this here is John Mark."

"Where are your folks?"

"Daid. Shot by some soldiers in butternut uniforms. We was hidin' in de cave where Mama kept food cool. We'uns went back too fur for anyone to find us. They took all our food and the cows and chickens."

Ophelia handed them each a bowl and spoon and stepped back. Before she could turn around, they'd scraped the bowls clean.

"Dey need more." Meshach filled the bowls again. "Y'all better slow down or you be sick." He glanced over his shoulder. "Dey might like hot water to wash."

Benjamin threw more wood on the fire, poured water into another pan, and set it in the coals. "I git some more."

"We ain't had hot food for I don' know how long. I caught us a squirrel in a snare, but it weren't easy to eat without cookin'." When Ophelia handed her a cup of hot coffee, the girl cupped her hands around the heat and sniffed the aroma, her eyes closed in delight.

Sammy and Thaddeus edged closer to the boy, who used his fingers to scrape the bowl clean. They stared at each other, then back at the boy.

John Mark looked up at them, then edged closer to his sister, if that were possible, clutching the bowl to his chest as if they would snatch it away. Just as Ophelia reached for the two little boys, the shivering boy on the ground vomited his supper all over both himself and his sister.

"Pew." Thaddeus stepped back, Sammy with him. "Stinky."

"Don't you no nevermind," Jane Ellen said, comforting her little brother, while trying to shake the gluey mess off her already filthy skirt. "You got any bread or biscuit he might have?"

Ophelia dug in the box where she kept leftovers and handed a biscuit to the boy. "Now you eat dat nice an' slow, you hear?"

At the same time, Meshach poured a cup of warm water and gave that to the child. "Here you go, easy now. Maybe soak yo' biscuit in de water and chew real slow."

The boy flinched away when Meshach extended a hand to help brush him off. " 'Phelia, surely you got some soap and water fo' dese two young'uns."

His gentle voice and warm smile did more to stop the two from shivering than anything else.

"We don' gots no other clothes." Jane Ellen stiffened her back and raised her chin, daring them to clean her up.

"No, I 'spose not. But we do." Meshach rocked back on his heels. "Y'all go behind de wagon and strip off dem things, and 'Phelia bring you hot water and soap to wash in. You feel better den."

"I'll get them something to wear." Jesselynn tucked her pistol in the back of her pants and headed for the wagon. Sure enough, here they hardly had enough to keep body and soul together for those she had with her and now they had two more. Three more mouths to feed than she had counted on, plus one more horse. And only one five-dollar gold piece left along with two nickels. How could they earn some money to augment what they had?

How long would it take them to get to Uncle Hiram's anyway?

She paused with one foot in the wagon. Was that gunfire?

"Douse the fire! Now!"

But Meshach was ahead of her. Steam billowed up from the soaking ashes.

Within moments, the men brought in the horses and hid them in a thicket with the others standing to clamp a hand over a horse's muzzle in case they started to whinny. Ophelia had the boys tucked down in the wagon, the two guests hunkering under the wagon bed.

Jesselynn stroked Ahab's shoulder and kept a hand on his muzzle. "Easy, old son," she whispered. "You gotta keep quiet. Easy." All the while she strained to hear anything else. Surely there hadn't been enough shots fired to show an ambush or an attack. Wouldn't they have heard something earlier if there was a military patrol around?

But they had gotten lax. No one had been on guard or scouting. *Never again,* she promised herself. *No matter how safe we feel, someone stands guard.*

Rifle fire crackled again, sounding farther away. How many shots? She tried to count them so she'd know how many men. Were they regular troops or the marauder they'd been hearing about?

But according to what I heard in town, there are no regular troops this far south. Unless the Confederates have come up from Arkansas.

But no matter how hard they listened, they heard only the night sounds that had come up again in the forest around them. An owl hooted. A coyote yipped and was answered by another. If the wild animals felt safe enough to resume their hunting and foraging, there could be no better alarm system.

She let out the breath she didn't realize she'd been holding and led Ahab out of the thicket. Moonlight washed the wagon in silver and glistened white on the pairs of eyes peeking over the wagon sides.

"Dey's gone?" Ophelia's whisper carried on the gentle breeze.

"I guess." Ahab nudged her in the back, so Jesselynn handed his lead rope to Meshach to tie them out again. "I'll take first watch. The rest of you get to sleep."

With the two guests cleaned up and their clothes washed in water from the stream, Ophelia tucked them into the blankets with the boys in the wagon bed and crawled in beside them all. The men rolled in quilts under the wagon, and the only sound was the horses grazing.

Jesselynn hunkered against the base of a tree overlooking the trail back the way they'd come. Because of the moonlight, the shadows seemed even deeper and darker. But the forest critters went about their business, so she felt about as secure as possible in spite of the shots fired.

In the morning she'd send Benjamin out to scout, but for now they all needed their rest.

She stretched and hunkered down again several times, yawning to keep awake, even resorting to pinching herself. While walking around helped, the forest noises quit at her movements, and she would feel the hair stand up on the back of her neck. Surely there was someone behind that big oak, the hickory, in the brush.

When Meshach spoke her name, she bit off a shriek, leaving the taste of blood in her mouth.

"Sorry, thought you heard me comin'."

"How could I when you don't make a sound?" Jesselynn whispered back, her heart still racing as if she'd been jumping logs.

"Heard anythin'?"

"Nope. One of the horses grunted and rolled—that 'bout gave me the shakes—but other than wild critters, nothing."

"I'm goin' take a look around. You stay here."

"Good." How could she tell him that the thought of tramping around in the dark like that scared her spitless? Maybe because her brothers used to jump out at her from dark places and scare her witless, she'd never been comfortable without a lantern or candle in the dark. Now driving the wagon, or riding, that wasn't so bad, but walking? Uh-uh. She settled back against the tree trunk, every sense on full alert.

When Meshach returned, he cleared his throat a distance away, then whistled a whippoorwill's song to let her know it was he. "All's good."

"I thought so." Jesselynn stretched and handed him the rifle. "Call me if you need me."

"I will."

She was asleep before she had the quilt wrapped clear around her.

———

She opened her eyes when Benjamin rode back into camp. Throwing back the quilt and pulling on her boots all in one motion, she dug her jacket out from under the quilt where she kept it so the dew wouldn't be able to soak it in the dark hours before dawn. By now she'd learned to never stand up until she crawled out from under the wagon. One crack on the head had taught her the lesson well.

She headed to where the two men stood talking. "What did you see?"

"Nothin' much. Someone camped but left in a hurry." He handed her a tow sack. "Couple men, I think."

She opened the mouth of the sack and saw dried beans, a side of bacon, and two small bags she assumed to be salt and coffee. "But what if they come back for their supplies?"

Benjamin shrugged. "One never come back. He daid. Confederate sojer. Found 'im in de woods some ways from camp."

Sure, nothin' much. Has death gotten so normal we think nothing of it?

She kept the thought to herself. "See any tracks?"

"Spent shells. Horses leave fast."

"How many?" Getting information from Benjamin was like pulling pokeweed.

He shrugged. "Din' count but dey gone."

"Which direction?" Meshach looked up to study the clouds coming in from the west.

"Dat way." Benjamin pointed south.

"And we're going west." She looked up at the man beside her. "Stay or go?"

"We go, but dere's rain in dose clouds. Rain soon."

———

The man could be a prophet. Jesselynn hunkered under her canvas, the pouring rain splattering on the rumps of the team. They were climbing again, the horses straining against their collars. Wet leaves plastered their hides, yellowed by an earlier frost now that they were climbing higher. She braced her feet against the floor of the wagon and tried to keep the tent over her head from slipping.

They breached the crest and let the horses stop under a tree to catch their breath. Jesselynn rubbed her wet hands together and studied the sodden world. Nothing looked drearier than oak trees losing their leaves to a pounding rain and horses hanging their heads, rivulets running down their manes.

After a short rest Meshach waved, signaling it was time to move forward.

Jesselynn slapped the reins and clucked to the team. They leaned into their collars, and the wagon groaned but began to move. The sound of a galloping horse could be heard above the rain.

"Hey, I found us a cave." Benjamin pulled the mare to a stop. "Right near."

Jesselynn didn't wait for her heart to stop pounding, she just turned the horses in the direction he pointed. Within minutes she saw the hole in the limestone cliff face. While it wasn't big enough to drive the wagon in, the horses would make it. And they could build a fire.

"Get inside," she ordered the passengers in her wagon as she leaped to the ground to unharness the team. "Take what you can with you."

Benjamin came out of the cave, his hands raised to stop them. "Someone in dere."

"Someone who?" Meshach strode into the opening.

Jesselynn finished unhooking the traces and hooked the ends up on the rump pad. She was already soaked from the driving rain. Who cared if there was someone else there? Surely there was room for all. Unless of course that somebody didn't want to share or would steal some of their precious supplies.

Meshach waved her in. "Leave de horses for now."

Jesselynn knotted a tie rope around a tree trunk and entered the cave. A man lay on the cave floor; another was propped against the wall. Dressed in the butternut uniform of the Confederacy, both wore the bloodstains of terrible wounds.

"Dey alive?" Benjamin squatted down to check.

"They won't be arguing over the cave, the condition they're in." Jesselynn couldn't believe she'd said anything so uncaring. Whatever happened to her mother's training? She froze. Was that a gun cocking she heard?

Chapter Twenty-Six

❧❧

RICHMOND, VIRGINIA

"Miz Highwood? What kind of game are you playin'?" the lieutenant asked.

Louisa shot her sister a look that should have fried the flowers on her bonnet. *Please, Carrie Mae, don't say anything more.*

"Oh, did I say somethin' I shouldn't?"

If she'd been closer, she would have stamped on her blabbermouth sister's foot. Instead Louisa made the mistake of looking up at the lieutenant. If he'd looked sober before, he did so no longer. Thunderclouds now rode his brow like a cavalry unit set to charge.

Jefferson Steadly gave Louisa a pitying look, took his betrothed's hand, and tucked it back under his arm. "Come, my dear, let us go in and speak with your aunt as we had planned." The wink he sent Louisa as he passed her made her face flame anew.

"Would you like to tell me what is going on?" The lieutenant's tone had softened but only enough that an ear tuned to his voice would pick it up.

Louisa had learned it well, even with the few words he spoke so seldom. Could she brazen it out? She felt her shoulders sag. Now, if it had been Jesselynn caught in a lie of this magnitude, she might have breezed right through it, but not Louisa. Living this lie had been one of the hardest things she had ever done in her life.

"Would you like to sit down?" She motioned toward the chairs on the portico. "This will take a bit of time."

"Seems I have all the time in the world at this point." The lieutenant put both crutches under one arm and, using the handrail to pull on, hopped one-legged up the three steps. When he took the chair she indicated, he sat down with a sigh.

Louisa sat in the other chair. "Does your leg still hurt awfully?"

"Not always. But I banged it in the move, and now I'll pay for that for a time."

Louisa leaned forward and pushed the hassock next to him. "Put it up on that."

"Thank you." The lieutenant settled his leg and tried to cover the sigh. He leaned his head against the high back of the rocker and closed his eyes.

Louisa studied his profile in the dimming light. Surely the bones in his face were no longer so prominent, and his color had most definitely improved. The scar on his forehead had receded until now it only made him look more interesting. When he went home, the girls would comment that it made him look more dashing.

Why did that thought not make her chuckle as she'd hoped?

A whippoorwill called, his song gentle on the ears, almost melancholy in tone.

The lieutenant would be going home—soon. All he needed was a mode of travel.

"So, Miz Highwood." His accent on the *Miz* told her what he thought about the whole thing. "Maybe you'd like to explain now."

"No, I would not *like* to explain, but if you can keep from informing the surgeon general, I might *choose* to explain. You see, I am not one of your men to be ordered around, and . . ." Her words came faster as she got up a head of steam, much like a locomotive leaving the station.

"I'm aware of that. Let me rephrase my question. Would you please explain? And I cannot promise not to tell the surgeon general. I will have to do what I believe best."

Louisa nodded. And sighed. This seemed to be an evening for sighing. "I have to go back a ways."

It was his turn to nod.

"When my sister Jesselynn decided it was no longer safe for us at Twin Oaks, she took it upon herself to send her two younger sisters here to Aunt Sylvania's. Since her fiancé had been killed in battle, I think she was hoping we would find—" Louisa clapped a hand over her mouth. *Oh, Lord, what am I saying?* She took in a deep breath and began again. "Safety. Yes, she hoped we would find safety here in Richmond. Right from the first we attended the meetings with Aunt Sylvania where the women knitted, sewed uniforms, and wound bandages for our men in the war. But I wanted to do something more. It was like . . . like all our fine men were without faces, and while I stitched the best and fastest that I could, I . . . I wanted to be where it mattered."

"You think socks and uniforms and bandages don't matter?" One eyebrow arched.

"No. No, that isn't what I meant at all." Louisa stopped her hands from wringing together. What kind of a ninny was she becoming? Sighing, hand wringing? She let out a huff of air and gritted her teeth.

"You are deliberately misunderstanding me, sir, and I resent that. You asked for my explanation, and I am doing the very best that I can."

"Yes, forgive me. I'm sorry."

Her eyes flew wide open, and she closed her mouth before it gaped. He, Lieutenant Lessling, had asked for her forgiveness.

"You're forgiven." She clasped her hands primly in her lap, but even so, one forefinger insisted on smoothing the one beneath. "One day I heard one of the women talking about volunteering at the hospital. She said they needed widows to come in and help on the wards, but that young unmarried women would not do since we, since . . . ah . . ."

She knew they would need no lamp on the veranda. Her face would light them better than ten lamps—with reflectors.

"So I appropriated my mother's ring and introduced myself as Widow Highwood, telling everyone my husband Zachary had died in battle. We were so afraid he had, you see."

"And no one questioned you?"

"Some." She remembered how she had feigned tears when they did, wiping her eyes with a handkerchief she kept in her sleeve. The interrogator then had gotten flustered and withdrew. Worked every time. *That* she would not tell the lieutenant.

"And?"

"And so I began working in the ward, bringing water, reading, writing letters. I've never done any nursing chores. I'm not trained for that." When she thought about it, that was not entirely true. Her mother had trained all three of her daughters in the healing arts, how to use herbs and unguents she'd created, how to apply poultices, dress wounds, even set broken bones. All manner of accidents happened on a plantation like Twin Oaks.

She sighed. Lying was so difficult. Why had they forced her into it?

"I know I have been a help." The silence lay between them, soft like the air that kissed one's skin like a lover. "You'll keep my secret, won't you?"

It was the lieutenant's turn to sigh. "You put me in a difficult position."

"But isn't your job to look out for the good of your men? And I have been part of that good. I know their lives in the hospital are easier when I am there."

"Granted, but there are rules."

"I'm not hurting anyone."

"Does your brother have anything to say on this?" The question came after another companionable silence.

Oh, cotton bolls. She straightened and lifted her chin a fraction. "He said he doesn't want me going back there."

"And you would defy him?"

"He is being well cared for. Why would he deny that care to others? If I were not his sister . . ."

"Ah, but you are."

"I can run faster than he can."

For a minute she thought he was choking, then realized he was laughing, a rusty sound as if it hadn't been used in far too long. She'd actually made the dour lieutenant laugh.

"Could when we were younger too, but don't you dare tell him that. Then he'd have to tell a lie."

The man beside her snorted again.

"Won't you have enough to do caring for the men at your aunt's house?"

"Her servants can do most of the work here, and I will read to them as I do at the hospital, unless Aunt wants to do that. I plan to set Private Rumford to work in the garden with Reuben overseeing him." She grabbed her audacity with both hands. "You could help if you'd like."

"I will if you are there."

Oh, cotton and tarnation tripled. He had her there. How could she be in both places at once?

"Is it a bargain?" He extended his hand, obviously expecting her to shake on an agreement.

"For the mornings." She put her hand in his. Heat shot up her arm and suffused her neck, flaming up her face. "I . . . I think I hear someone calling me." She leaped to her feet and disappeared into the house as if an entire cavalry unit were charging behind her.

"Oh, Lord, help!"

Chapter Twenty-Seven

A MISSOURI CAVE

"How bad is he?"

"Alive, but not for long 'less we help 'im." Meshach looked up at her from his kneeling position by the wounded soldier. As he spoke he removed his handkerchief and tied it above the man's knee, then examined the wound in his side. "He in bad shape."

"Put the horses back there." Jesselynn pointed to the rear of the cave before it shrank down to a small tunnel. "Get wood and let's get a fire going. Get him warmed up and us dried out. Thaddeus, you and Sammy sit over there and don't you move. Jane Ellen, keep your brother close beside you."

"I kin git wood."

"I know you can. Thank you, but I think your brother needs you more right now."

John Mark shuddered and coughed, a deep, gagging cough that made Jesselynn shiver. She'd heard that kind of coughing before, and a damp cave with wet clothes was not a place to start coughing like that.

"Don' worry, Marse, John Mark cough like that alla time." Jane Ellen patted her brother's shoulder, clutching him close in front of her. "He been puny since the day he was borned." Her declaration seemed a banner of pride. "I allus takes keer of 'im."

Jesselynn nodded and headed back out in the rain to help find wood. Wet as she was already, what could a few drips more matter? Finding dry wood in the downpour was no easy task. She broke dead branches off the underside of pine trees and, carrying an armload, dragged a larger branch behind her. She hoped the men would fare better. How far away was water? They needed plenty of hot water to clean the soldier up. What could they use for a poultice? If those wounds were infected . . . She shook her head. *Mother, what would you do?*

No sense in waiting for an answer. If there were to be any answers, they would have to come from her, and right now she felt cold, wet, and long out of answers. She stumbled over a rock just inside the cave entrance and tossed the wood into a pile before stopping to rub her toe. Felt like a horse just stepped on it. No, stood on it.

She headed back out to the wagon for an ax to chop the bigger pieces. Where were the men?

By the time she returned, Ophelia had shaved off curls of wood to lay over the smoldering coals they kept in a lidded pan for fire starter. Within moments tendrils of smoke arose and then flames as soon as she blew on it. Thaddeus squatted beside her, breaking twigs into smaller pieces to add a bit at a time. Sammy sat in the dirt behind them, picking up handfuls of sand and watching them drizzle back to the floor.

"Jane Ellen, take one of those quilts and wrap it around your brother. Then you can help with the fire while Ophelia and I get a pallet made for the wounded man." Talking was difficult with your teeth chattering.

Benjamin and Daniel dragged in a tree trunk that would burn for long hours, but no one had seen Meshach.

Once a canvas had been folded into a pallet, they each took a limb and hoisted the still-unconscious man into place next to the fire. As soon as a bucket of water from their barrel on the wagon was hot, she knelt down to inspect the wounds. The hole in his side had both an entrance and an exit, so she knew there was no bullet to dig out. Dirt mixed with blood crusted the wound, setting her to shaking her head. How could she clean it?

She rocked back on her heels, wishing she were anywhere but in a cave—in Missouri—tending an injured man she'd never before laid eyes on. She glanced up and caught sight of the dead man propped against the cave wall. If she dragged him outside, the wild animals would get the body during the night. There was no way she was sending her people out in the pouring rain to bury a man. So he had to stay, gruesome or not.

Where was Meshach?

She shifted her inspection to the leg. Cutting away the remains of the man's pant leg, she kept herself from gagging only with the greatest effort. She closed her eyes and took several deep breaths to calm the need to faint. If there was to be any chance for the man to live, the leg would have to go. With all the dirt and shredded flesh and bone, the wound would putrefy before morning.

Whatever had kept this man alive this long?

"Well, sir, if you want to live this bad, we'll sure do all we can to help you." She got to her feet. "Benjamin, bring in our saw. Ophelia, get your sewing kit. We got work to do."

"My ma allus said, you cut off a limb, you gotta burn it with a knife or somethin'." Jane Ellen had the three boys huddled under a quilt with her, so only their faces showed in the flickering firelight. "Might help that hole in his side too."

"Thank you. My daddy said pouring enough whisky over any wound would clean it right up, but we don't have any whisky, and we do have a big knife or two." Jesselynn dug into her box of simples that was becoming sadly in need of replenishing. What could she use to help keep away the poison? If only she had some onions, or mustard, or even bread and milk—all things they had taken for granted at Twin Oaks. And whisky . . . there had been plenty of that too.

Where was Meshach? Good thing the soldier had yet to regain consciousness, but even so, she wanted Meshach there not only to help hold him down but to saw off the leg. Should they try to save the knee?

She took soap and water and started scrubbing, then rinsed and went back to studying the wound. Looked like good bone below the knee for a couple of inches anyway. Unless the infection had already set in and traveled upward. She sniffed the wound. Nope, it didn't smell like the one that killed her daddy. Putridity had a stench all its own.

"Any of you know where Meshach went?"

Benjamin and Daniel shook their heads.

Ophelia said, "He took the rifle."

So that was the rifle cocking she heard. He must have gone hunting, whether for man or beast she wasn't sure.

One of the horses stamped and snorted. Firelight flickered on the walls, setting shadows to moving in a macabre dance that sent shivers up and down Jesselynn's back. She glanced over at the children and saw they were all asleep, piled like puppies in a heap.

Dumping the bloody water, she poured more from the kettle and went back to work, not even bothering to clean the lower leg. His foot was cold to the touch, as if it had already died. The wound in his side started to bleed again as she cleaned out bits of shirt fabric and removed the handkerchief he must have packed in the wound to staunch the bleeding.

She listened to his breathing. Sounded pretty strong for a man in his condition. Could she touch the hot knife to his flesh and hold it there long enough to do its job? She eyed the broad-bladed knife that Ophelia had set in the flames. Meshach could do this better than she, but since he wasn't here, she'd better do it.

She called Benjamin and Daniel to help. "All right, hold him down," she ordered. The eyes of the two men and Ophelia glistened in the firelight, but they took their places and leaned on the still form. Jesselynn closed her eyes for a moment, then taking the bone handle of the knife, she applied the blade to the front of the wound.

The man bucked and groaned. The stench of burning flesh made Jesselynn gag. None of her helpers watched the knife, but Benjamin threw his body across the man's upper legs to hold him down.

Jesselynn put the knife back in the fire. "We got the back to do too. Roll him over real careful-like, so the bleeding doesn't commence again."

By the time they were finished, sweat ran down their faces, but the wounds were clean. The leg would have to wait for Meshach. Jesselynn could hardly grip the handle of the knife she was shaking so. Sammy and Thaddeus now whimpered from under their quilt, but Jane Ellen held her ground, her arms securely around all three boys, murmuring a soft singsong, trying to calm them.

"What do we have for bandages?" Jesselynn asked.

"I gits dem." Ophelia dug in her box and came up with several rolls of old sheeting. "Lucinda packed dis. Thought we might need 'em."

"Looks like we do." Jesselynn took the rolls and folded some into pads to apply back and front, then wound more around the man's midsection to hold the pads in place. They'd just have to wash the bandages in between. There were not enough to throw away. "We'll let him sleep now. Ophelia, we need to make a tea of this willow bark. Get him to drink it soon as he wakes up. If only we had some meat to make a broth. Mother always said to give a wounded man beef broth to build the blood back up."

"Will venison do?" Meshach and the deer he had tied over his shoulders filled the mouth of the cave.

No need to ask where he'd been. He laid the carcass down on the other side of the fire and untied three rabbits from his belt to hand to Ophelia. "We can skin dese de quickest and get dem to boilin'. I spotted some wild onion and Jerusalem artichoke for diggin'. I gits dem next." He stepped around the fire and knelt down by their patient. Nodding, he smiled up at Jesselynn.

"You done fine, Marse Jesse."

"I thought to wait a bit on the leg, let him gain some strength." *Liar. You just couldn't bring yourself to do it.*

"No, poison get 'im. We do it now. Got to come off?"

Jesselynn nodded. "All I can see. Good flesh and bone just below the knee, so maybe we can save that."

"We try."

Within minutes, they were ready. Even with four of them holding the man down, he bucked at the first bite of the saw. Jesselynn nearly screamed herself. Instead she hummed a song under her breath, anything to blot out the horrible noise.

"Done. Hand me de knife." Again the stench of burning flesh filled the cave.

Jesselynn sewed the flap of flesh over the stump and applied the bandages. Very carefully, she released the knot on the tourniquet above the knee and watched to see if blood would soak the white cloth. When it didn't, she finally let out the breath she'd been holding, surged to her feet, and dashed outside. After throwing up in the bushes, she tilted her face to the sky to let the rain wash her clean again.

She looked heavenward and raised her fist in the air. "God, if you are indeed God, how can you let this war go on? I don't want any part of you ever again. You hear me?" Tears and rain flowed over her cheeks and down her neck.

Shuddering both from cold and wet, she strode back into the cave to find the soldier covered, the dead man gone, and the rest of the group eating warmed-up beans and biscuits. One rabbit simmered in the cooking pot, and cut-up pieces of another sizzled in the frying pan. The stench of blood and burnt flesh had been replaced by supper cooking, and the cave now seemed more like a home than a hospital.

"Jesse, sit here." Thaddeus patted the empty space on the log beside him.

Ophelia handed her a steaming bowl and, while Jesselynn had thought it would be a long while before she could force food down, she shoveled the beans and biscuits in, grateful for the warmth and the flavor.

"I'll be gettin' the onion and chokes," Meshah said. "Benjamin, you rope up de horses, and I show you a clearin' I found. Wet or not, dey need grazin'. We can skin de deer after dark, dry some of it all night. Ophelia, you kin scrape de hide."

"I knows how to do that," Jane Ellen volunteered.

"When de sun come out, de hide kin dry on de wagon."

"My ma used de brains, lye from fire ashes, and water fer tannin' de hide."

"Good. That be your job den, girl."

"No rush, we won't be leavin' here anytime soon," Jesselynn said, shaking her head. "Can't leave him and can't take him with us yet, so looks like here we stay." She glanced over at John Mark, who was doubled over with coughing. Another reason they wouldn't be going anywhere fast. Her mother always made cough syrup out of honey, whisky, and lemon juice in hot water. What could she use instead?

By the time they settled into their quilts that night, thin strips of deer meat draped on racks of green sticks hung over a low fire. They'd gotten some broth down the wounded man, and the deer hide was scraped and ready for tanning in the morning. Best of all, Daniel had found a bee tree, so they had honey on the biscuits that went along with fried rabbit, boiled artichoke roots with wild onion, and carrots. Quite a feast, and to top that off, they were warm and dry.

Stars shone overhead when Jesselynn made her final trip outside. Snuggling down in her quilt later, she listened for their patient's steady breathing. The odor of fresh horse manure overlaid the sizzle of drying deer meat. Things seemed as right as possible, but she'd closed her ears when Meshach read the nightly Scripture. While she wasn't about to tell him to quit reading, she knew she'd been living a lie. No longer did she believe there was a God, let alone a good one.

Somewhere in the wee hours, she got the soldier to take some more broth, and while his mumbling didn't make sense, the fever seemed only mild, so far.

She fell back asleep without waking anyone else. They needed their rest as much as she.

Screams brought her straight up and out of sleep. Tiny furry feet crawling all over her made her scream too. She flung one of the creatures off and saw an arched tail in the dim firelight.

Only one critter looked like that! Scorpions!

Chapter Twenty-Eight

❧

RICHMOND, VIRGINIA

The dour look returned with the lieutenant in the morning.

"I'm happy to see you decided to join us." Louisa, resolving to ignore the dark cloud on his countenance, gave him the same smile she gave the others. Last night was as though it had never been. She hid the sigh behind a flurry of pointing, assigning jobs, and identifying plants for Corporal Shaddock so he would know which were weeds and which were perennials gone dormant. She hoped to divide the irises today and the butter lilies.

"If we dig up the clumps, do you suppose you could stand at the bench, or sit if you prefer, and divide them?" She motioned toward the potting bench along the brick wall, glancing up at the lieutenant at the same time.

"I reckon."

So much for conversation.

"Have you ever divided irises before?"

"No, can't say that I have."

"Fine, I'll be right with you, then." She trotted over to where one of the other men was digging with a fork. "Sergeant Andrews, over here, please." Within moments she had several washtub-sized clumps of iris covering the potting bench and Andrews back to digging up the iris bed. "We need to dig in manure and compost. That's behind the shed."

While Sergeant Andrews had only one eye and still wore a bandage around one thigh, the smile he gave her lacked for nothing in the male-appeal department. "I'll get right to it, ma'am."

Louisa could feel her face heat up in spite of the broad-brimmed straw hat she wore. Maybe it was more important to get these men back out in society than to improve their attitudes through digging in the dirt. If only she could discuss such things with the lieutenant.

She checked on Private Rumford and, laying a hand on his shoulder to get his attention, smiled and nodded. "Very good. It looks so much better." Was that life she saw in his eyes or a trick of the shadow? But when she smiled again, the corner of his mouth lifted ever so little. He had responded. Her heart sent joy spiraling upward and blooming on her face, such joy she could scarcely contain it. If she ran and danced as she ached to, all the men would be appalled. One just didn't do such things. "Thank you, Private. Thank you so very much."

He returned to his digging and she to the lieutenant.

"Did you see?" she whispered.

"See what?" The man stared from the knife in his hands to the tangle of rhizomes, roots, soil, and long slender leaves.

"Private Rumford started to smile, barely, but it's a step in the right direction. Now." She rolled the clump over so the leaves and rhizomes were on top. Pointing as she talked, she identified the old wood for him, the new growth, and where to cut. "Now, iris are really hardy, so you needn't be too careful, but keep the new plants from each clump together and separate from the others, as they are of different colors." She glanced up to see that he was following her instructions but caught him staring at her instead.

"What? Do I have dirt on my nose or something?"

He shook his head and transferred his attention to the iris. "I cut here and here and—"

She leaned forward and her shoulder accidentally bumped his. They both leaped back as if they'd been burnt.

"Sorry." Their apologies even came at the same instant.

Why had she never noticed how long and fine his eyelashes were? And the gold that flecked his eyes. *Louisa Marie Highwood, quit acting like a . . . like a—*

"Miz Highwood, this somethin' you want dug out or left?" Andrews called out, breaking the spell of the moment.

"I . . . ah . . . I'll be right there." She drew back, wishing she had a fan. A big fan that would create a big breeze and hide her face.

Lord, I feel like I can drown in his eyes. I want to smooth that frown from his forehead, and . . . and . . . I've never felt like this. Do you think he feels the same way? Is this the beginning of love? And if so, what do I do next? She hustled over to Andrews and bent down to study the clump of leaves. "No, that stays, but you can dig around it. I forget what Aunt called it, though."

On her way to fetch the wheelbarrow, the thought hit her. *What if he doesn't feel the same way?* Trundling the wheelbarrow back, she let the posts down with a thunk. Tonight she'd ask Carrie Mae about it. Surely she would know.

By the time Abby came out with glasses of lemonade and fresh lemon cookies, the iris were all replanted in the re-dug bed with a thick layer of compost on top, the peonies were weeded, and another bed was prepared for winter vegetables. The men were wiping sweat from their brows in the full heat of the sun, and Louisa's nose felt pink, since she'd given up trying to keep her hat on hours ago.

"Dinner be ready 'bout an hour." The slender woman with skin like creamed coffee handed 'round the glasses. "Looks like you been diggin' up a storm."

"Miz Highwood here, she keeps us right busy." Corporal Shaddock grinned up at the serving woman from his seat on the grass. "But we make her pay back by readin' to us. Out here would be a fine place to lay back and be read to. Right after dinner."

"But I . . ." One look from the lieutenant and she clamped her lips shut. "What about the others?"

"We bring 'em out too. Be better out here in the sun and breeze than inside."

Louisa stared at the young man in astonishment. He'd never said so much at one time since she handed him his first drink of water three weeks earlier.

"Bring 'em out here to eat, right, Lieutenant?"

Louisa looked at the man leaning back in the recliner with his eyes closed.

"Now, how you goin' to bring them out? Gettin' 'em here yesterday was hard enough." He brushed at a fly that insisted on buzzing around him.

Abby had the answer to that. "Reuben fix dat last night. He make up a two-wheel chair. We bring dem out."

Abby was as good as her word. Zachary came out first and settled onto the lounger the lieutenant vacated. The two young men from the parlor followed.

"Now if we could fashion a gate through that wall." Louisa stared at the brick wall, daring it to form a gate so the men in the other house could join them.

"Gettin' over here will be a good incentive for those two to walk again," the lieutenant said from beside her.

"Gardens have a way like that."

"It's not the garden, Miz Highwood, it's you." He spoke so only she could hear, but she jumped anyway.

"What a thing to say," she hissed. "I never—"

"Dinner is served."

She spent her time helping the men eat, cutting meat for those missing a hand and adjusting pillows so they could sit straight enough. When she sat down to her own meal, she found herself between Zachary and the lieutenant. Her brother started the storytelling, and soon the others took part, stories of home and growing up and families that wrote more often now that they knew where their boys were.

Surely she could go over to the hospital while everyone napped in the afternoon.

As soon as silence fell, she left her place and sneaked back in the house. Aunt Sylvania had returned from her morning with the sewing group, and now she too was taking a lie-down.

"I'll be back in an hour or two," she whispered to Reuben as she packed some leftover biscuits and honey in her basket. She added cookies and contemplated the jug of lemonade.

"I carries dat for you." Reuben hoisted the gallon jug, sweating in the warm kitchen.

"Surgeon general wants to see you," the orderly said when she walked into the ward a few minutes later.

"Oh." Her heart set to triple timing. Had the lieutenant broken his word, then? The thought made her stand two inches taller and march out of the room and down the hall to his office. The subaltern showed her in.

"Why, Miz Highwood, I'm surprised to see you here." The surgeon general rose from behind his desk and motioned her to the chair.

"And why is that, sir? I am sorry to be late, but—"

"But you have men to care for over home, and your husband sent me a message saying you would no longer be helping us here."

"He . . . he what?" She felt like scrubbing at her ears. Surely she had heard wrong.

"So I want to thank you for all you've done for our men and for taking soldiers into your home."

"General, sir, more wounded coming in." The young officer made the announcement from the doorway.

"I'll be right there." The surgeon general came around the desk and extended his hand. "Thank you, indeed, Miz Highwood."

Rising, she placed hers in his and nodded. "I will go back home then and care for my own men." She fought to keep a smile on her face when all she wanted to do was scream.

Chapter Twenty-Nine

A MISSOURI CAVE
OCTOBER 10, 1862

"Get 'em off! Get outside."

"Oh, Lawdy, save us!"

"Come on, run!"

"It's in my hair!"

Screams echoed around the cave. The horses snorted and shifted restlessly. People ran for the cave mouth, brushing at the crawling things and screaming all the while.

"Thaddy, are you stung?" Jesselynn scooped her baby brother up in her arms, checking for the telltale red spot of a bite.

"No." He reached up and brushed one off her hair. "Gone now."

Ophelia shook out her clothes, her eyes rolling white, gibbering and crying all the while, screaming again when she saw one of the black bugs on Meshach's shoulder.

"Stop!" Meshach caught one of the bugs that was trying to burrow under the leaves. He knelt down and studied the insect, then began to chuckle. His great belly laugh grew while the others stared at him. Surely the big black man had lost his senses.

"Dey's no scorpions. Dey's vinegaroons. Lookee here, dey no hurt no one. De fire musta brung 'em out."

Ophelia shuddered, and it was all Jesselynn could do to keep from it. Jane Ellen tittered, the first smile to decorate her face since her arrival.

Benjamin slapped his knee and joined in the guffaws.

"Hey?" The voice came from the cave, and if Jesselynn hadn't been leaning against the entrance wall, she'd not have heard it. She returned and crossed to the sick man's pallet. Kneeling, she studied his gray face.

"Good mornin'. I reckon you might be thirsty about now."

"I didn't die, then?" His voice rasped like a file on wood.

"Not yet, and if we can help it, you won't." She didn't add, *You might wish you had*, but she thought it awful hard. "I'll get you some water. Broth'll be hot as soon as we get the fire goin' again." She brushed a vinegaroon off his shoulder. "Don't worry 'bout these bugs bein' scorpions. They aren't. Meshach says they're vinegaroons."

"Oh." His eyes drifted shut. She laid a hand on his forehead. Hot but not blazing. He might not be minding the cold like the rest of them. But then she wouldn't ask for a fever to keep warm by.

The others wandered back in the cave, and while Jesselynn and Ophelia started the fire, the men took the horses out to water and graze.

"You want I should git some wood?" Jane Ellen offered.

"Would be a right good help. Thanks." Jesselynn blew again on the curls of wood and small twigs she had laid over the coals left from the night. They had almost let it go out. Whose watch had it been? Daniel, that's who. She'd have to have a talk with him when he came back. Just because they were relatively safe in the cave, they still needed a lookout, at least to keep the fire going.

Sure, and a good fire will bring out our marauding insects again. The thought made her chuckle. What a sight they must have been running around and screaming like that. Scare any self-respecting critter back into its hiding place. No wonder the poor things were scurrying so fast under leaves and whatever they could find for cover. One crawled out from under the wood stack when she took off a larger piece for the fire, then scuttled away, tail raised, mimicking the dangerous scorpion. All their patient needed was a few scorpion bites to push him right over the edge.

She glanced over at the man on the pallet. Between the now flickering flames and the fever, he had some color in his face, what you could see above the beard.

Meshach came back into the cave and retrieved his Bible. "Buried de other man. Got to read over 'im."

Jesselynn set the stew kettle over the flames. "If you want." She could feel the look he gave her but kept her attention on the fixings. He wanted to believe in the God that wasn't, fine, but no more for her. Not until she heard him leave did she look up to find Ophelia giving her a quizzical stare. Thaddeus came and leaned against her shoulder.

"Hungry, Jesse."

"I know. This will be hot pretty soon." She put her arm around him and hugged him close. So much to endure for such a little guy. He should be home safe in the kitchen of Twin Oaks, chewing a piece of bacon and giggling with the slave children. They would be chasing each other around the room and out the door and back in until Lucinda would shake her spoon at them and threaten their eternal banishment if they didn't stay out of her way. There would be corn bread hot from the oven, eggs splattering in the frying pan, and redeye gravy set off to the side.

She could almost smell the ham slices and the rich aroma of good coffee, along with the corn bread.

Instead, she stirred the rabbit stew, making certain it was heated through and didn't burn. If it hadn't been for the lid on the three-legged pot, they'd most likely been having stewed vinegaroons for breakfast.

Ophelia set the biscuits to baking in the frying pan, the tight lid almost making an oven. After they ate, they'd bake up a bunch more and let them dry hard. That way they would travel well.

As if they needed to worry about that for the next few days. Moving this man would kill him for sure. When he woke, she planned to ask him his name. Going through his pockets hadn't been even a thought yesterday. Just keeping him alive was enough.

Jesselynn checked the strips of venison. They needed longer for drying too. That lazy Daniel. She'd tear a strip off his hide if he didn't watch out.

Jane Ellen, along with the help of Thaddeus and her brother, dragged in more branches and began breaking up the ones small enough. With the cracking of the branches and the ensuing giggles, the cave took on an even cozier feeling.

Only Daniel didn't come in to eat with the rest of them.

"He with de horses," Meshach said. He nodded to the again-drying venison. "He let de fire go out."

Jesselynn breathed a small sigh of relief. Thanks to Meshach, she wouldn't have to get after the boy, for that's what he was at sixteen, no matter how hard he tried to be a man.

In wartime, we all grow up fast. Jesselynn's mind flicked back to Twin Oaks, back to the games she played with her sisters and brothers on the lawn. Croquet had been their favorite even after the boys thought they were men and went away to school at Transylvania College in Lexington. How often she'd made Carrie Mae angry for whacking her ball off into the rose garden, and once into the pond. Now that had brought a shout of laughter from the boys and reprimands from their mother.

Had the letters she'd written gotten to them, so they knew where she was? If only she could hear from home or from Richmond, this journey might not seem so . . . so arduous. How long it had been since she'd learned a new word and found ways to use it that day. It seemed like centuries, like another lifetime that happened to someone else.

"Water." Their patient was awake.

Jesselynn spooned broth into a cup and, lifting his head with one hand, held the cup to his lips with the other. After only a few swallows, he gagged and shook his head, his groan rising to a near shriek. "God, it hurts."

"Would a spoon work better?" At his nod, she spooned the liquid to his mouth and watched him swallow. By the time the cup was empty, he'd drifted off again, but even in sleep, his moans persisted.

He has nice eyes, gray, I think, but it's hard to tell in here. If only they had more bandages. She glanced around the cave. What could they tear up? Short of Ophelia's spare skirt, nothing had the length. She studied the bandages around the stump of his leg. No blood had seeped through there. Perhaps the stitching was enough to hold it as long as he didn't move around, then she could wash those and change the ones around his belly. How the bullet had gone clean through like that and not hit any organs was nothing short of a miracle.

But it had seemed only a flesh wound. She felt his forehead again. Cooling. Maybe they'd be able to travel sooner than she thought.

Meshach stopped right behind her, studying the sleeping man. "He lookin' better."

"I know. Yesterday I wouldn't have given two bits for his chances, but today . . ." She paused and looked up. "He might just make it."

Meshach nodded. "We been prayin' for him too."

Jesselynn had no answer to that.

Jane Ellen stumbled into the cave carrying her brother. "He coughed so bad, blood came." The terror in her eyes told Jesselynn that had never happened before.

"Quick, put him down." Jesselynn saw the trickle of blood from John Mark's mouth streaking down his chin. His skin looked clear enough to see right through.

Jane Ellen mopped at the trickle of blood. "What we gonna do?"

Jesselynn tried to think back to what her mother had taught her. Coughing like that meant lung sickness. And most people didn't get better from it, especially those who'd gone without good food and lived in the cold and damp.

She chafed his cold hands and watched his chest rise so slightly that each breath could be his last.

"Did he fall or anything, hurt himself?"

"No, just coughed till I thought his insides come out." Jane Ellen stroked the stringy hair back from his forehead. "Come on, John Mark, wake up. Please wake up."

His eyelids fluttered. Jane Ellen pulled him close and rocked him in her arms, crooning a song only she knew.

Jesselynn stood up and walked to the front of the cave, her eyes burning and her nose running, but not from any smoke coming from the fire.

The coughing sounded more like a retch.

Jane Ellen squeaked like a mouse caught by a cat, then resumed her crooning and rocking.

Jesselynn returned to see a froth of pink bubbling from the side of the boy's mouth.

"Here, chile." Meshach knelt and tried to take the boy, but Jane Ellen hung on with a fierceness stoked by terror.

"I takes keer o' him."

"Let us help you." Jesselynn took one of the quilts and laid it in front of the log for a pallet. "You sit here where you can hold him more easily, and the quilt will help keep him warm." Together Meshach and Jesselynn moved the two and added another quilt to cover John Mark.

Jesselynn and Ophelia cut more strips of the venison and hung it in places where the others had dried. They rubbed salt into a haunch and hung it above the fire to absorb the smoke. Thaddy and Sammy eventually quit playing in the dirt and fell asleep. Benjamin took one of the horses and went off scouting while Meshach chopped the deer brains, mixing them with ashes and water and working them into the inside of the stretched-out hide.

The afternoon passed to the rhythm of breathing, coughing, and moaning from the man and the boy. And while the man accepted the offers of water and broth, the boy refused everything.

"Help him, Marse Jesse." Jane Ellen raised eyes so darkened by fear they looked black.

"Here, see if you can spoon some of this into him." She took Jane Ellen a cup of broth and held it for the girl to dip from. Every drop drained out the side of his mouth. "Stroke his throat while I try."

Jane Ellen stroked her brother's throat with fingers of pure love, her eyes never leaving his face.

Jesselynn tipped a spoonful of broth between the boy's lips, and this time they watched as, with a convulsive swallow, the liquid went down.

"Oh, another." Jane Ellen resumed the stroking, and Jesselynn tipped the spoon again.

A swallow, a gag, a retching cough, and blood drenched the front of his shirt.

"Oh, John Mark. John Mark. Please, please." The girl rocked and hugged, her hands gripping the skinny child as though someone were pulling him away.

"He's bad, isn't he?"

Jesselynn looked over her shoulder to see their soldier gazing at her with eyes clear and as full of sadness as she knew her own must be. All she could do was nod.

"If you could . . . find my pack." He paused to catch a breath. "I had some . . . laudanum in it."

"Any idea where it might be?"

"Find where we were . . . ambushed. Could be . . . there. Black leather."

"You know how you got here?"

"Partner . . . carried me. How is he?"

"Gone. Meshach buried him this morning. He was sittin' against that wall there, with you lyin' on the floor."

The man closed his eyes. "How come . . . I'm alive and he's dead?" A pause stretched. "Makes no sense."

"I know." Jesselynn glanced at the girl still rocking her brother. "Makes no sense a'tall."

She added more wood to the fire, keeping it low so the strips of venison wouldn't burn.

"How bad is my leg? Hurts like fire."

How to tell him. "Ah, we . . ." Jesselynn sighed. No sense beating around the tree. "We had to take it off below your knee. Wasn't much left of it, and the gangrene would've set in and killed you for sure."

He closed his eyes tighter and swallowed hard enough for her to see the reflex in the firelight.

"I'm sorry." Such a meager word for such a loss as his. But at least he was getting stronger. Her gaze strayed back to Jane Ellen. While she kept wiping her tears away, sometimes she had to wipe them from her brother's face too.

Her brother was all she had. She said so. She hugged him as if her very strength could heal his chest, could stop the trickle of blood from every cough. Coughs that had grown weaker.

"I'll send Meshach lookin' for your pack." Jesselynn got to her feet, her knees creaking, stiff from sitting so long. She stepped outside the cave into sunshine a mite watery but still offering heat and light. From inside the cave, it had seemed dark outside, as if it still must be pouring rain like the day before.

When she told Meshach, he nodded. "Me an' de boys all go look." He got to his feet, laying a hand on Ophelia's shoulder and squeezing gently. "You go on in der. I be back."

Dusk dimmed the trees by the time the horsemen rode back to the cave. Daniel swung the pack down into Jesselynn's arms.

"I found it."

Jesselynn nodded. "Thank you." She knew he'd offered the pack as penance for letting the fire go out. She also knew he'd be more alert the next time he stood watch—Meshach would make sure of it. Now if only the laudanum could help relieve the pain for both of the sick ones.

Chapter Thirty

RICHMOND, VIRGINIA

"Men!"

"What dat, Missy Louisa?" Reuben hurried to keep up with her.

"I said *men* and my brother in particular!"

"Oh." He wisely let a pace or two widen between them.

"If he thinks he can waltz right in here and mess up my life, he has another think coming." She flung open the gate before the older man could get there and stomped her way up the walk, her thudding steps echoing on the stairs. She let wisdom and caution gain a mite of control so she didn't slam the door open or closed.

"Where is he?" Her words came more as growl than question. But her glances into the sickrooms yielded only more frustration. No one was in bed.

She stopped at the open French doors leading to the gardens. Aunt Sylvania sat like a queen in the middle of the group, holding the book up to get the best light. Reading from *The Taming of the Shrew,* she went on, "And Petruchio says,

" 'I pray you do; and I will attend her here, —
and woo her with some spirit when she comes.
Say that she rail; why, then, I'll tell her plain,
She sings as sweetly as a nightingale.' "

"Here, here," applauded Andrews. "You read right well, Miss S."

Miss S.? What is this world coming to? Her aunt was actually smiling and batting her eyelashes at the compliment. Louisa located her brother and shot daggers his way at twenty paces. The volley didn't phase him. In fact, he spoke the next lines from memory.

" 'Say that she frown; I'll say, she looks as clear
As morning roses early washt with dew.' "

They don't need me here, but the men at the hospital do. Why is he being such a selfish prig when I can be doing some good? She started to step back into the house, but the lieutenant turned and beckoned her with a smile.

Even he is smiling. What magic does Aunt Sylvania possess?

Louisa walked forward as if she were dragging a heavy chain. She couldn't talk to her brother now, and when she saw the devil dancing in his one good eye, she knew he realized he was safe. *Cotton and conniptions, I swear I'm going to get even with him if it's the last thing I do. Two can play at this game.* She dredged a smile up from somewhere and sprinkled it with sugar.

"The surgeon general sends his greetings, Mister Highwood, and hopes that all of you are settled in and on the fast road to recovery." She took the seat vacated by the lieutenant and leaned forward. "Keep reading, Aunt. That is most entertaining."

Zachary rolled his eyes.

Good! He knows he's in for it in a big way.

———

The lieutenant had taken Private Rumford for a walk, so they had the room to themselves. With both doors closed, Louisa felt reasonably certain they wouldn't be interrupted.

"Why did you do that?"

"I told you, I don't want you working over there." He held up a hand. "Yes, I understand the difference between paid work and volunteering, but that ward is no place for a young woman of your sensibilities."

"Meaning I'm too good to give the cup of water our Savior spoke of or to help a suffering neighbor?"

"Louisa, don't go twisting my words."

"I am not twisting your words, brother dear, I am merely trying to understand your motives."

"I have no *motives*, as you say. I just want you safe."

"Safe? Safe? As if anyone would harm me there!" She leaped to her feet, her needlework going one way, her scissors another, and paced the room from one end to the other. "I brought succor to the dying and comfort to the living. Now what on God's earth can be wrong with that? Mother and I did so at Twin Oaks, and I feel called to do so now."

"As the oldest Highwood man, I forbid you to work in the hospital." His eye narrowed and his words lashed.

A soft word turneth away wrath. Her mother's voice floated in her mind so clearly she was sure Zachary could hear it too.

Soft word, my right foot. She took in a deep breath and sniffed back any inclination to tears. Never in her life had she been so close to bludgeoning someone with her soft shoe or whatever else she could pick up.

"Zachary Highwood, you are being utterly cruel, both to me and those I can help."

Zachary shook his head and slumped against his pillows. "Ah, Louisa, I have seen such carnage and waste of good men that I cannot and will not ever try to tell you, but please, I just want to keep you from experiencing even a small part of that. Is it so wrong to try to keep the ones you love from harm?"

Louisa felt the starch go out of her spine. She knelt on the floor and took his hand in hers. "Wrong, my dear brother, no, I suppose not, but perhaps more than a bit selfish." She laid her cheek on his shoulder, where she could hear his heart beat. It would have been so easy for him to have died on the field and never returned to them.

Silence, but for their beating hearts, quieted the striving in the room and let peace tiptoe in and make itself comfortable.

"When we go home, things will be all right again." She whispered the words she prayed so fervently. "Soon, soon we'll go home, home to Twin Oaks."

A harsh sound, more groan or laugh she wasn't sure, ripped from his chest. "Home to Twin Oaks! Don't you know I cannot go home until the war is over?"

She raised her head and looked at him, his face suffused with red heat. "Whyever not? Look at you. You cannot fight again."

"If a Confederate soldier crosses into Kentucky, no matter how severely wounded, he will be shot or hung as a spy. On sight."

Oh no, God, please, I want to go home, please. Her tears dripped silently down on the back of his hand.

Chapter Thirty-One

ॐ

A MISSOURI CAVE
OCTOBER 11, 1862

Back and forth Jane Ellen rocked as dawn sent tentative fingers trembling into the cave.

Jesselynn heard her crooning the same song she'd fallen asleep to, only now the girl's voice was so hoarse the words were nearly unintelligible. All she wanted to do was pull the quilt over her head and go back to sleep, but something made her look over to Meshach as he stoked the fire. Sparks lit the air above him and the snapping wood sounded friendly. But the sorrow on his face and the way he looked at Jane Ellen answered questions before they were asked.

"Ah no." Jesselynn's eyes and nose ran at the same time, and her heart felt like a giant hand was squeezing the life out of it. She glanced over at Ophelia to see her wiping her eyes with the corner of her apron. The cave vibrated with the absence of coughing or gurgling, the last sounds she'd heard before she finally fell asleep.

Ophelia took a gourd of water to Barnabas White, as they'd learned was the soldier's name. Sergeant Barnabas White of Pine Bluff, Arkansas, serving in the Sixteenth Arkansas. He'd said the words with pride, whatever pride one can have flat on his back with a hole in his side and missing part of a leg.

Both wounds were still clear of putridity, and that alone made Jesselynn hopeful. They all needed a big dose of hope with the girl rocking her dead brother. How could they help her?

But the question deviling Jesselynn as she threw back the quilt and pulled on her boots was more basic than that. *Why do I keep gettin' more people to take care of? First Sammy, then Jane Ellen and John Mark, now the sergeant. Here we are somewhere in Missouri, where the fightin' is worse than at home, and I get more people and a Union horse to feed and keep safe.* She slammed her booted heel against the sand-covered rock beneath her and pulled on the other. Clapping her hat on her head, she headed for the cave entrance. At least she could be alone when nature called.

"Jesse, I got to go."

When she looked over her shoulder, Thaddeus was sitting up, rubbing his eyes. As always, he had to go first thing. She wished she'd gotten away sooner; the crooning was digging into her like a drill into wood. And she didn't want to wait a moment longer. That meant she'd have to carry her baby brother.

Well, why not? She was carrying everyone else. She stomped across the cave, swung him up to sit on her hip, and again headed for the outside. *Death and tarnation.* Only her mother's training kept her from using some of the words her brothers had taught her. They'd had their mouths washed out with soap for using such language.

"You mad?" Thaddeus patted her cheek.

Jesselynn stopped in midstride. Mad? No, yes. Disappointed? For certain sure. Scared? More so than she wanted to admit. She looked at her little brother only to see a tear trickle down his cheek.

"Ah, Thaddeus, it's not your fault." She hugged him and nuzzled his soft cheek, kissing away the tear at the same time. "Come on, Joshwa, let's get this over with so we can eat, all right?"

His smile beamed in spite of wet eyelashes. Throwing both arms around her neck, he whispered in her ear, "Joshwa loves Jesse."

Frost stenciled a spider's web across their path and glittered the grasses. Jesselynn sucked in lungfuls of crisp air. For right now she could ignore the ordeal ahead in the cave and make her little brother laugh. The tears would come soon enough. How would she be acting if the dead boy were Thaddeus?

Tears choked her throat and made her stumble. She swung him to the ground, but only after another hard squeeze. As soon as he finished, she pointed him back toward the cave.

When she returned, Jane Ellen was still crooning and rocking. Jesselynn glanced at their patient, only to catch his gaze, as sorrowful as she knew was her own. Meshach and the others had taken the horses out to graze and water, and Ophelia moved like a puppet with tangled strings, trying so hard not to look at the misery to come.

Meshach, you take care of this. You'll have the right words. I have none. I'll take care of the horses.

Sammy fussed and demanded to be carried, so Ophelia held him on her hip while she stirred the pot of cornmeal mush. Thaddeus clutched his sister's pant leg, his thumb in his mouth, sending surreptitious glances over at Jane Ellen.

Jesselynn mixed some of the cornmeal into a gruel with the broth from the stewing venison and took it to Barnabas, as she referred to him in her mind. Sergeant White seemed so formal when caring for him.

"You up for some real food?"

"I think so." He flinched when he moved, and sweat broke out on his forehead. "If you'd help me sit up a bit?"

"You sure? Why don't I just prop a saddle behind you or another quilt? The less you move around, the less chance you'll start bleeding again."

"All right." Taking a deep breath brought his hand to his side. "Whew, guess I dreamed I was all better or somethin'."

"You want a dose of that laudanum first?"

"A bit in water I guess." He held out a hand, shaking as though he had the palsy. "Sorry to be so helpless like this."

Jesselynn didn't answer, just prepared the drink for him and held his head up so he could drink it. She too took great care to not look at Jane Ellen. *Meshach, get on back here.*

After about half a cup of the gruel, the sergeant shook his head and collapsed back against the padded saddle Jesselynn had fixed and propped behind him. "Thank you." His soft drawl made "you" into two syllables. Before she could turn around, he was asleep again.

She studied the flat glass bottle she'd corked again so carefully. Maybe a swig of that would let her sleep through the hours ahead, and when she woke, everything would be fine again. Instead, she nestled the precious stuff down into Ophelia's cooking box, where it was well padded.

Who knew when they might need it once more?

Jane Ellen coughed once, then picked up her singsong again, eyes closed, rocking and rocking.

When they'd finished eating, Meshach looked at Jesselynn with one raised eyebrow and a glance at the rocking girl. Jesselynn shrugged and nodded in that same direction.

Meshach closed his eyes.

She knew he was praying, and the thought sent a bolt of anger from head to foot. *Don't you know, man, that you're wasting your time praying? There is no God!* She clamped her fingers so tight her nails bit into her palms. She looked down and opened her hands to see red crescents where her nails had been. *Or if there is, He doesn't care. He lied.*

Then why did you wait for Meshach to come? The thought sent her on a headlong flight out of the cave. She ran through the brush with hands in front of her face, shoving away the branches that snagged at her clothing, tried to trip her, and ripped off her hat. Then, breath heaving, the cold air burning her lungs, she finally leaned against the trunk of an ancient oak. "I will not cry!" She shouted the vow to the few dried leaves that clung to the branches, stark fingers pointing to a sky feathered with strings of clouds. It should be raining.

They had to bury the body. Would Meshach be able to take the boy from his sister's arms?

The unearthly scream that rent the air sent the chills racing from her heels to her hair and raising those on the back of her neck. Taking in a deep breath she started back the way she had come.

Her hat waited for her, still snagged on the branch that had poked a hole in the crown. She crammed it back on her head, using it to push the hair back out of her eyes. She needed to cut her hair again. Concentrating on putting one foot in front of the other, on brushing the branches from her face, on wiping the tears from her cheeks kept her from thinking about the cave and what was happening there.

Meshach met her at the entrance. "De boys diggin' de grave."

Don't think. Don't feel. She nodded.

Thaddeus ran out of the cave and threw himself against her legs. "John Mark dead." He raised a tearstained face to look at her. "No play no more." He raised his arms to be picked up.

Jesselynn started to tell him no but instead reached down and hoisted him to her hip. "I know." *Get in there and hold Jane Ellen.* But no matter how hard she told herself to go, she could not take one step inside the cave. She could not look upon that poor girl, see that still face.

"We's done." Benjamin joined them in the sunshine.

"You want to read?" Meshach held the Bible out to her.

Jesselynn shook her head. "You do it."

Meshach studied her face for a long moment; she could feel it without looking up.

"Yessuh."

Ophelia brought Sammy out first and handed him to Benjamin, then went back in the cave to return with the body, now wrapped in one of their quilts.

Don't throw away the quilt like that, we're going to be needing it worse than he.

Ophelia handed the bundle to Meshach and returned to the cave, this time leading out Jane Ellen. The girl walked stifflike, as if she'd been dunked in a vat of heavy starch and it froze up her joints. Her blue eyes were washed of all life and feeling.

All through the simple service, she never said a word nor wept a tear.

Jesselynn studied the tree branches that shaded the grave. When Meshach finished his prayer, the final leaf broke off and drifted down to settle on the quilt. Even the birds kept silence. Ophelia took Jane Ellen by the hand and led her back to the cave, Sammy resting on her hip. Jesselynn set Thaddeus down.

"You walk now. You're gettin' too heavy to carry."

He clutched her hand and, instead of walking with his sister, turned back. " 'Bye, John Mark."

Jesselynn rolled her eyes upward to give the tears no place to form. She sniffed once and tugged on her brother's hand. Thaddeus walked with her as far as the cave entrance, then plunked himself down.

"Play here. Bring Sammy."

"You stay right here, then."

He nodded, searching for a stick to dig with, crackling the leaves as he dug around.

Jesselynn knew she should go in and help care for Barnabas. She could hear the plunk of dirt clods back at the grave. From inside the cave, the only sound was Sammy telling Ophelia something only he could understand.

"I'm goin' ridin'."

Thaddeus looked up at that. "Me go?"

"No, you stay here." She caught a glimpse of the hurt in his eyes as she swung away. "Benjamin, when you're done there, make sure Thaddeus stays put. You can help work that hide, and Daniel, slice off more of that venison so we can get it all dried before it spoils." She knew she sounded gruff. At the moment she didn't care. If she didn't get out of there, she was afraid she'd be wailing against the tree.

She reentered the cave only long enough to get a bridle and dashed out before Ophelia's song could bring her down. Deep river all right and there was nothing on the other side, no matter what the song said. No home, no Father God waiting, no joyous day.

She bridled and swung aboard Ahab, setting him into an even canter in spite of the trees. Only some small semblance of good sense kept her from urging him to a dead run, as she could have on the track at home.

———

Each day they stayed at the cave made life together worse. Jane Ellen crumbled into the corner, never speaking, never eating unless someone fed her. If she slept, it was with her eyes open, for every time Jesselynn looked at her, she was staring into nothing.

"Give her time," Meshach said.

Sammy burned his finger on a stick in the fire. Thaddeus whined from morning until he fell asleep at night. He even whimpered in his dreams, setting Jesselynn's teeth on edge even more than they already were.

The only good thing was that Sergeant White grew stronger each day.

"Thanks to all of you," he said in response to her morning question of "How you doin'?"

Meshach brought him a crutch carved out of a slender maple trunk and padded with part of the deer hide. "You wants another?"

"No, thank you." Barnabas sat leaning against the quilt-padded log. He fingered the stout piece of wood. "One of these days I'll carve me a peg, when the stump is all healed. Saw one one day attached with a leather harness. Maybe if I start on it now, I'll have it ready."

"Den I'll find you a good piece of hickory. Coulda made the crutch outa hickory too, but dis little tree looked so perfect-like."

"It is perfect, and I thank you. Perhaps we can get me standing up tomorrow and see how I do."

Two days later he hobbled out to the already loaded wagon, Meshach and Jesselynn on either side of him ready to grab him if he started to fall. When they boosted him up in the wagon bed, he fell back against the box they'd padded for his backrest. Sweat dripped down his cheeks and ran off the end of his nose. Two red spots stood out like brush fires on his face gone stark white at the effort.

Lastly they led out Jane Ellen and settled her in beside the sergeant. If they stood her up, she stood. If they set her down, she sat. Even the two boys tumbling about her lap brought no reaction.

———

Two weeks later they arrived in the Springfield area. Leaving the rest of them down in a hollow, Jesselynn rode the mule into town and up to a store. Fingering her remaining coins, she approached the counter.

"Help you, son?" The aproned man behind the counter turned from filling a bag with coffee beans.

"Yes, suh, I's lookin' for the farm of Hiram Highwood. He's my uncle."

"Oh, that's too bad." The man shook his head. "I knowed Hiram for a long time. Good man. Hope you ain't come too far. Hiram was one of the early casualties of the war."

Jesselynn kept from stepping back with a superhuman effort. "And Aunt Agatha?"

"Not sure where she went to. Farm got burnt to the ground, long about a year ago now." He leaned forward.

"You all right, young man? You look whiter'n a sheet on washday."

Chapter Thirty-Two

ᏭᎯᏗ

RICHMOND, VIRGINIA

Her sister's wedding day dawned, and all she wanted to do was stay in bed.

"Louisa, are you up yet?" The knock came softly on her door.

"No, and neither are the birds."

"I couldn't sleep any longer." Carrie Mae peeked around the slowly opening door. "Can I come in?"

"Of course." Louisa patted the bed beside her. "Just don't expect any brilliant conversation." When Carrie Mae drew closer, Louisa sat up. "You've been crying."

Carrie Mae sniffed. "I know. All I can think is that I want Mama and Daddy here for my wedding. It's not fair." She flung herself on the covers and great sobs heaved her shoulders. "And . . . and it . . . sh-should be at . . . at T-Twin Oaks."

"I know." Louisa patted her sister's shoulder, tears now streaming down her own face. And here she'd wondered at times if Carrie Mae even thought of home. "We can be grateful that Aunt Sylvania didn't say you had to wait a whole year for proper mourning."

"I . . . I know." Carrie Mae used the bed sheet to mop her eyes. "I don't think I could have borne it."

The silence stretched, punctuated by occasional sniffs on both their parts.

This is the last time we share a bed like this, the last time for all the girl talks we've had through the years. Since the two of them were closer in age than the others, only a year apart, often they had banded together, playing tricks on Jesselynn and tormenting their older brothers. Until the brothers grew up and went away to school and the tutor remained for the girls. Until the war.

Louisa sighed. Should she? "I have a question to ask you."

Carrie Mae rolled up on her side, head propped on one hand. "What?"

"Well, this is kind of personal."

"So?"

"How . . . how did you know when you were in love with Jefferson?" She couldn't look her sister in the eyes.

Carrie Mae flopped onto her back. "Ah, Louisa, when love strikes, you know. I wanted to be with him all the time. When he came near, sparks seemed to fly—even off our clothing." She propped her head up again. "You know how I love chocolate mints?"

"Of course, how many times did I have to beat you away from mine."

"I gave mine to Jefferson because he said he really likes them."

"You didn't."

"Did so. And that isn't all. You know how we prayed for the perfect men to be our mates, how mother had prayed for us that way for years?" Louisa nodded. "Jefferson is that man. He is kind, intelligent, works hard—Daddy would want those traits—makes me laugh—and you know how I love to laugh—will be able to support a family, and"—she paused and her eyes grew dreamy—"he thinks I am the most wonderful woman God ever created, and I plan to make sure he keeps on thinking that. We believe the same and come from the same backgrounds."

"Sounds like a marriage made in heaven. Surely there is something you want to change."

"I wish . . . I wish I could give him his arm back." Tears cushioned the simple words.

"Anythin' else?" Louisa forced her words past the tears clogging her throat.

"Would that we could live at, or at least near, Twin Oaks."

"You'll have to visit often. There's plenty of room, you know." Louisa closed her eyes and pictured the stately columns, the front portico, brick walls warmed by the Kentucky sun, green lawns, and honeysuckle growing up past some of the bedroom windows.

A cardinal sang and another echoed.

"We better get to movin' if you're to be at the church at eleven."

"I know." Carrie Mae turned on her side again. "It's the lieutenant, isn't it?"

"Um-hm." Louisa lay on her side facing her sister. "But . . . but I have no idea if he . . . he . . ." She drew circles on the sheet with her fingertip.

"If he cares for you like you do him?" Carrie Mae sounded older and wiser instead of like the younger sister.

"But I'm not really sure how I feel. I mean like . . ." Louisa drew circles on the bedspread with her finger. "Guess I just better keep on praying, right?"

"And I will too. Oh, Louisa, I want you and Jesselynn to be as happy as I am right now. And Zachary too, though I'm not sure men always know when they are happy."

Louisa nodded again. How seldom she had seen a glimmer of laughter or joy in the lieutenant, but then his situation wasn't of the kind to be laughing a lot over.

But other men find things to laugh about, even in the hospital. Joy is everywhere. You just have to recognize it.

She reached over and hugged her sister. "You grab all the joy you can and spread it around. 'Cause sometimes it's shy and needs invitin' in. Mama and Daddy had it, and I wish it for you. Lord, bless my sister with joy unending, no matter what happens in her life."

Carrie Mae wiped her eyes again, this time with the tips of her fingers. "Thank you. I'll ring for coffee, and we can begin getting ready."

———

Hours later, standing beside Carrie Mae in front of the altar, Louisa looked up at the Shepherd in the window above them. It seemed He looked right down and smiled at her, a smile so full of love and warmth that she wanted to squeeze her sister's hand and point upward. *Thank you for the blessing. Oh, Lord, fill this marriage with such love that everyone sees it and knows where it comes from.*

"I do." Carrie Mae responded in a clear voice that left no doubt as to her commitment.

"Therefore what God has joined together, let no man put asunder. I now pronounce you husband and wife."

The minister gave the benediction and the organ swelled in a song of joy as the newlyweds made their way up the aisle. When Louisa took the arm of Jefferson's brother, she glanced up to catch the gaze of a tall, no longer quite so thin, man who seemed to have eyes only for her.

She smiled at him as she passed and waited in the vestibule until he could join her. "You will be coming back to Aunt Sylvania's for cake and punch?"

"An army couldn't keep me away."

Shivers ran up and down her back. Did this mean what she hoped it meant?

Though the wedding had been small due to the recent losses of so many, still the house and garden thronged with people. Louisa helped with the serving since they had such a small staff and wished she could have time to talk with the lieutenant—alone. Once she had even slipped and thought *my* lieutenant. When she passed him a cup of punch, their fingers brushed, and she nearly dropped the cup.

"Can we talk a bit after . . ." He sidestepped as a young boy chased after another and nearly took out his crutches.

Louisa smiled, fighting to keep from breaking out in song. "Of course."

She helped her sister change into a gray silk traveling dress, since the two would be going to Williamsburg for a week before they returned to Richmond and he to his law practice. They would be living in a little house not far from his office.

"Well, Mrs. Jefferson Steadly, you behave yourself now, you hear?" Louisa tried to sound like their mother at her sternest.

"Oh, I will." Carrie Mae adjusted the brim of her hat and tucked a strand of hair back into her chignon. "There, now, how do I look?"

"Blissfully happy and enchantingly lovely." Louisa dabbed at the corner of her eye and sniffed. "God be with you, my dear sweet sister." The two wrapped their arms around each other and hugged as if they were saying final good-byes.

"Now, off with you. I heard Jefferson is waiting at the bottom of the stairs."

Louisa watched as her baby sister descended the stairs, the plume on her hat bobbing gaily. *Lord bless them, take care of them, and please bring them back home safely.*

Carrie Mae turned at the door and blew her a kiss. Louisa caught it like a treasure.

The company couldn't leave quickly enough. Dusk came and still some lingered on the veranda. Short of pushing them out the door, Louisa joined in the conversation, making sure her brother and the other invalids were comfortable. When finally the last guest wandered down the front walk, she turned to find the lieutenant sitting in the glider, his crutches balanced against the front railing. He patted the seat beside him.

Louisa sat as close to her end of the swing as her skirts permitted, but still she could feel the heat from his body. "Ah, such a lovely wedding, don't you agree, sir?" She glanced over at him. Where had the smile gone? "Is something wrong, Lieutenant?"

"Do you think you could call me Gilbert?"

The deep timbre of his voice sent a tingle clear to the end of her fingertips.

"All right, Gilbert." She whispered his name as if they were sitting in church.

"And I may call you Louisa?"

Why did her name sing when he said it?

"Yes." The glider moved back and forth just enough to stir the stillness of the surrounding dusk.

"Miss Louisa, I . . . I'm so grateful you aren't married." His words came out in a rush, as if he'd been choking them back for some time.

"Really? Me too. I mean . . ." Oh, gingersnap, was she going to mess things up again?

"I . . ."

He hardly seemed to notice what she had said, concentrating on something he needed to say. Her heart settled into a deeper beat.

"I find I am coming to care for you." He turned and took her hand in his. "Do you . . . I mean . . . is there, I'm . . ."

"Yes."

"Yes, what?" He blinked and rubbed his thumb over the back of her hand.

"Yes, I too think I am coming to care, for you, I mean."

"Ah." He closed his eyes. "The foot, it doesn't matter?"

"Why should it?"

"I'll never walk properly, and riding a horse will be difficult. At least that's what they tell me."

Louisa longed to lay her hand along his cheek, to smooth the lines from his eyes and the deep gashes from the sides of his well-etched lips. "I pray there will be no lingering pain, that is all."

"I . . . I would like to court you. I've already talked with your brother."

Leave it to the lieutenant, right to the point. "I'd like that."

"But I have a bit of a problem."

"Oh?"

"I have to leave for my home in North Carolina tomorrow, and I'm not sure when I will be back. The army discharged me this morning."

"But you *will* be back?" Where did the tears come from so quickly?

"Ah yes, I will be back, and in the meantime we can write?"

"Of course." *At least he isn't going off to war again.*

Chapter Thirty-Three

❧

SPRINGFIELD, MISSOURI
LATE OCTOBER 1862

Where can we go?

Jesselynn slumped against the counter, the edge of it cutting into her hip. The candy jars in front of her grew smaller, then larger. Her head felt as if it would float right off. She blinked and sucked in a deep breath.

"I say, boy, are you all right?" The man reached a hand across the counter and clamped on Jesselynn's wrist. "Lizzie, come here and help me." His raised voice penetrated the buzzing in her ears.

If this was what fainting felt like, Jesselynn knew she was right close to the edge. She bit down on her tongue until she wanted to yelp and blinked again. This time the jars settled back into place, their red-and-white-striped sticks no longer dancing.

"What?" She shook her head. "Did you say something?"

"I asked if you was all right. You looked some dreadful."

"What is it, Lawrence?" A woman slender as her man was portly bustled into the room, took one look at Jesselynn, and changed direction. She pulled a chair from near the potbellied stove that reigned in the middle of the room and, setting it behind Jesselynn, pushed her down onto it. "Now put your head down, young man, and in a couple of minutes you'll be right as rain." Since the woman had hold of the back of Jesselynn's neck and was pushing downward, there wasn't much else she could do.

She shut her eyes and sucked in a couple of deep breaths. "I . . . I'm fine now, ma'am." As the patting hand released, Jesselynn sat back up to hear Lawrence telling his wife the story. It didn't sound any better the second time, worse in fact. Some of the slaves had been burned with the barns.

"You know where Miz Highwood is livin'?" Lawrence asked his wife as he leaned on his hands, arms stiff to prop him up.

"I might kin find out." The hesitancy in her voice gave Jesselynn an idea the woman knew more than she was letting on. "If I kin find her, where can she find you?"

"Ah, I'm not sure. You see, we just arrived here from Kentucky, and I was plannin' on stayin' with my kinfolk." Jesselynn knew her accent was going in and out but didn't seem to be able to do much about it. The shock had her stomach so tied in knots she could hardly swallow.

What will I do with the horses? Where can we stay? Can't go home until spring, and spring is a long way off from now.

Her legs gave way, and she plunked back down in the chair. *How can I feed all those people and the horses through the winter?* She didn't have to jingle her pockets to know how little money they had left.

Not near enough.

She got back to her feet. "I thank you for the information, and now I'd better get the other I came for and head on back." Mentally she rewrote the list. "I need five pounds of beans, same of flour and cornmeal, half a pound of salt . . ." She crossed off coffee and sugar. "And a sack of oats." The two mares would need extra feed for the next couple of months, since they were due to foal in early February.

"You want those oats rolled or—"

"No, regular is fine." She eyed the candy jars. Thaddeus and Sammy hadn't had any candy since halfway across Kentucky. She gritted her teeth. "And two sticks of that peppermint there." She watched as the two went about filling her order. *Eggs, I want an egg, and milk.*

"You know anyone could use a good blacksmith who can fix about anything, set wheels, shoe horses—?"

"You could check over at the livery down the street and to your right. There's a foundry in town too. He might want some help. Things been right busy since the army been in and out."

"Union or Confederate?"

"Union." He studied Jesselynn over his half glasses. "Why?"

"Just curious."

"You got slaves?"

Jesselynn shook her head.

" 'Cause some don't hold too highly with that. Could cause all kinds of trouble."

Jesselynn picked up the warning note in his voice. Did that mean her people were safe from slave traders here? Did she dare ask?

Like her daddy always said, "You learn more with a closed mouth and open ears."

"That'll be one dollar and seventy-five cents."

She brought out her five-dollar gold piece and laid it on the counter. "Know anyone wantin' the services of a good stud horse?"

"What's his breedin'?"

"Oh, this 'n that, but he throws mighty fine colts."

"I'm certain the military would be interested." He counted the change back into her hand.

"Most likely, but not for stud." Jesselynn gathered up her purchases and stuffed them into the tow sack she had with her. "We'll have to tie the oats on behind the saddle. That's my mule right out there." She nodded over her shoulder. Turning to the woman, she finished, "If you happen to see my aunt Agatha, tell her Zachary Highwood is lookin' for her. She kin write me a letter to the post office, and I'll pick it up there."

"Of course, young man, we'll do just that." She came around the corner of the counter as her husband left to get the grain. "Any message you want me to give her—if I find her, that is?"

Jesselynn nodded. "Tell her my daddy came home to die from the war and said we—I—was to come stay with her."

"All right. I'll do that. You know where the post office is?"

"No, ma'am."

She gave Jesselynn the instructions and closed the door after her. The bell tinkling overhead sounded as friendly as it had when she went in, but now the whole world was changed.

Clouds had covered the sun, and a chill wind picked at the edge of her coat and the brim of her hat, making her body feel as cold as her spirit.

Had Aunt Agatha even gotten the letter she'd written, the one that said Major Joshua Highwood had died and she was bringing the horses to stay at Hiram's? For a moment she wished she'd stayed out of sight and waited to see if the woman at the store had left to go find Aunt Agatha. She was certain she knew where Aunt Agatha was staying. Why would that be a secret?

Jesselynn kept watch over her shoulder as she crossed the prairie, meandering between farms and back to the willow-lined hollow where they'd sheltered the night before. The banks had been knee-deep in grass, so the horses were having a good feed. Maybe Daniel had even caught some fish in the creek. Now wouldn't that be a treat after their weeks of venison, rabbit, and more venison? The wild turkey that Benjamin brought in one day had disappeared faster than water on a hot stove. She'd kept a couple of the primary wing feathers for quills to write with and let Thaddeus play Indian with the others.

She whistled the three-tone greeting they'd agreed upon long before and waited for an answer before riding down the bank.

"What wrong?" Meshach stood at the mule's shoulder, staring up into her face.

"Hiram, the farm, all gone." Jesselynn shrugged and her shoulders sagged. "They said Aunt Agatha might be around. I'm sure she is, but the folks at the store weren't givin' her away."

"The farm?"

"Burned to the ground over a year ago. Why did no one write to us? I wondered why we didn't hear at Christmas, but . . ." She pleated the mule's brushy mane with her fingers. "Lots of times letters get lost during a war."

Like hers might have been. Maybe Agatha had no idea they were coming. She shook her head again and slid to the ground. "That's oats for the mares in the big sack. Ration it." She untied the tow sack from the saddle and slung it over her shoulder. Cursing the war and the men who started it, she plunked the sack of food in the wagon and looked around for Ophelia and the boys.

"Daniel got a mess of fish."

"Good thing. And we better be finding us a hidin' place. Most likely another cave."

"I take it you didn't have good news?" Sergeant White sat on the wagon tongue, rewrapping the bandage on his stump of a leg, his crutch at the ready beside him.

Jesselynn shook her head. " 'Fraid not."

"How are you for money?"

Jesselynn stopped and turned to stare at him. "Why?"

"I got me some cash and I'd like to share it with you, since you been carin' for me and all."

Jesselynn stuffed her pride in her back pocket. "Paper or hard money?"

"Both."

"If it's Confederate script, it's not worth the paper it's printed on. Might as well start a fire with it, but the other, well . . ."

"Good thing you didn't have to cut this boot off." He pointed to his boot. "If you would do the honors."

Giving him a disbelieving glance, she did as he asked and handed him the boot.

He reached inside, dug in a slit, and brought out two gold coins. "The paper is in my pack."

"No, it's not."

"You didn't know where to look, and if the Confederates take over this area, the script might be worth something again. We can hang on to it." He reached toward her with the coins. "Here."

Jesselynn shook her head. "How will you get home without it?"

"How will I get home with it?" He pulled his hand back and stuffed one coin back in the boot, then handed her the other. "We'll split it, but if you need this, you tell me. Promise?"

Jesselynn took the ten-dollar gold piece and, hefting it once, dropped it into her pocket to mingle with the change there. That would help them for a while, but the winter stretched ahead like a painter about to pounce.

Barnabas set his boot on the ground and tried to stuff his foot in it, but the force sent him nearly tumbling over the side of the wagon tongue. Jesselynn jumped just in time to brace him. His head rested against her chest until between them, they got him upright again.

The look he gave her made her step back. "What?"

"Marse Jesse?" His voice came thick and hoarse.

"Yes." She took another step back.

"Okay, if that is what you say."

He knows. No, he doesn't. He can't. He knows.

But his gray eyes twinkled just the tiniest bit, and a smile quirked the side of his mouth, barely discernible with his beard but there nevertheless.

That night around the fire, Jesselynn clasped her hands, her elbows resting on her knees. She'd already told everyone what had happened in town, so continued. "Now the way I see it, we need to find a good warm cave to hole up in until we can go back home in the spring. Surely the war will be done by then." *Dreamer.* She ignored the accusing voice in her head to add, "Maybe Meshach can find work in town. Places are always in need of a good blacksmith." She studied the calluses on her hands. "We'll just have to live off the land." Glancing over at Jane Ellen, who sat wherever Ophelia put her, and down at the two boys, one sleeping on Ophelia's lap and Thaddeus leaning against her own side, she sighed. So many mouths to feed.

"I kin watch the young'uns." Sergeant White smiled at her across the camp-fire. "And I was a right good cook. So I'm sure losin' part of my leg won't change that once I learn to hobble better so's I don't tip over in the fire."

Meshach and Benjamin chuckled at that. "We save his hide mor'n once."

"So, tomorrow we're off to the hills to spy out a cave."

They all nodded.

"I kin still shoot, you know. If y'all want to leave me here with Ophelia and the young'uns."

Meshach and Jesselynn exchanged glances, then both nodded.

It took the four of them searching for two days to find a cave sufficiently large for them all and far enough away from any farms or main roads. It lay on the south face of a steep hollow several hours south and west of Springfield.

There was plenty of pasture close by and not many farms, due to the roughness of the terrain.

Once they were settled in, Jesselynn took time to write letters, one to those at Twin Oaks, the other to her sisters in Richmond. After describing their journey so far, she asked if they had heard anything from Twin Oaks. She had really expected a letter from Lucinda to be waiting at the post office, but when Benjamin went in to check, there had been nothing for them.

> *Please write soon. I must know how you are. Have you heard anything from Zachary? I keep telling myself that no news is good news, and I am grateful every time I read a casualty list and his name is not on it.*
>
> *Louisa, with all your gifts for healing broken creatures, I wish you were here to help us with Jane Ellen. She has not made a peep since that terrible scream when Meshach took her brother away to be buried. Sergeant White is healing up fine, getting around better on his crutch every day. I am as ever. Someday you'll have to try wearing britches. It's hard to think that I will ever have to go back to skirts and dresses.*

She thought of telling Louisa of her suspicions that the sergeant realized she is a woman, but the possibility of even a long-distance diatribe from Aunt Sylvania made her wish she hadn't said the latter.

She signed her name and, after waiting for the ink to dry, folded the letter and addressed the envelope. Daniel could take it into town in the morning. On a whim, she took her writing folder out to where Sergeant White was whittling on something and keeping an eye on Sammy and Thaddeus as they played in the sunshine.

"You want to write a letter home?" She extended the leather-bound case. "Perhaps your girl would like to know if you're alive or not too."

He took the case. "Don't have no girl." He paused and stared up into her eyes. "Yet."

Jesselynn felt a flash of heat from her heels to her head. *He knows.* She thought of challenging him on it but decided letting sleeping dogs lie might be wiser. He was comely, not handsome in the truest sense, but a fine figure of a man in spite of the crutch. Surely there was some young woman down in Arkansas who would be glad to hear from him.

The thought of his leaving gave her a curious hollow feeling. So many people came into her life and then left, one way or another. Each seemed to take a bit of her with them, till pretty soon there might not be anything left. And besides, Sergeant White was right nice to have around.

"Now, remember, you get the mail, and you be lookin' out to see if anyone's watchin' you."

"Then you make sure to lose dem befo' you come home." Meshach finished giving Daniel the instructions for her. "An' you be watchin' out for bluebellies or sojers of any kind."

"Don't you go gettin' lost in Springfield either, hear?" After most of the hamlets they'd stopped at on their journey, Springfield seemed about as big as Lexington back home. Not that they'd ever gone there much, but still.

Jesselynn watched Daniel ride off whistling a tune and wished she were going instead. Surely they would at least hear from Aunt Agatha soon. With Meshach and Benjamin leaving to go hunting, the cave seemed huge. "I'll take the horses to graze." She glanced down to see the imploring look Thaddeus gave her. Her heart melted right then, even though time alone had been a prize. "And take Thaddeus along with me. High time he had a riding lesson, I'm thinking."

Thaddeus let out a squeal and threw his arms around her leg. "Me ride Ahab."

Ophelia giggled behind her hand, and Sergeant White had a hard time keeping a straight face.

"Thataway, boy. Start right at the top."

"You'll ride Dulcie." She took his hand. "Now, let's go."

"Bye, Sammy. Bye, Jane Ellen. Bye, 'Phelia. Bye, Sarge White."

Once outside the cave, Jesselynn scooped him up and set him astride the oldest mare. "Now you hang on to her mane, and I'll lead her real slow-like. All right?"

Thaddeus nodded, his grin so wide, his eyes barely showed.

Like all of the Highwood children, he seemed to be born to ride, his balance already good and his eyes dancing with delight. Even when the mare put her head down to graze, he stayed on her back, petting her neck and crooning his own version of the language between rider and horse. Dulcie twitched her ears, keeping track of everything going on around her. She raised her head at what sounded like a gunshot. When a second one followed close on the heels of the first, Jesselynn hoped it was Meshach and Benjamin and they'd gotten a deer.

After a while she lifted Thaddy down and gave him one of the biscuits she'd stuck in her pocket. A third shot some later and farther away sent chills up and down her spine. Was something going on that she wanted no part of? She hustled Thaddeus back up on the mare and, gathering the lead lines, took her charges back to the cave. She'd take them out later when she knew if she should be worried about the shots or not.

Sergeant White stood at the mouth of the cave, staring off to the southern hills.

"You heard them too?" Jesselynn lifted Thaddeus down and sent him into the cave.

"The first one was Meshach with the rifle, and the second was Benjamin with the repeater. Not sure about the third."

"It was farther away."

"I know."

Jesselynn hated playing the waiting game. She'd waited for her father and brothers more times than she liked to count. She'd waited for John and he'd never returned. She'd waited for her father to come home, and he'd died in her arms. Why were women the ones who waited?

The sun crept farther down the sky and still they waited.

Wouldn't it be easier to be like Jane Ellen and have no idea of time?

Chapter Thirty-Four

RICHMOND, VIRGINIA

Dear Jesselynn and Thaddeus,

I suppose I should address you as Marse Jesse, but I cannot seem to do that. I will address the envelope that way as you are already aware I did. First I will bring you up-to-date on the events here. The wedding was beautiful, and our sister was a lovely bride. She and Jefferson are so much in love that one can do nothing but be thrilled for them. Even Aunt Sylvania approves, and you know what a miracle that is. While the wedding wasn't the social event of the season, which it might have been had not there been deaths in the family, all the family and friends who attended did indeed wish them many blessings. Strange that even though Carrie Mae wasn't here much of the time, I miss her and know that our lives will never be the same again.

Not that there has been much sameness lately. Oh, sister, I long so for Twin Oaks and for our family to be together again. Thaddeus is growing up without us all to pet and tease and hug him as we were. Will this wretched war never cease?

I hope you are all settled at Uncle Hiram's by now and safe from the marauders I hear so much about. As if regular soldiers weren't enough.

Speaking of soldiers, we have several of the wounded from the hospital living here with us. Zachary is ready to use crutches, but without the right hand, this will take some thinking. We are trying so hard to keep him from slipping into a morose state like some of the others who have lost limbs. Like me, he feels he will be so much better when he returns to Twin Oaks. Did you know that until the war is over, he cannot even do that, or he will be shot? I pray daily for an end to the battles, that we might all go home.

I have news of my own. You remember the Lieutenant Lessling that I wrote about? He was one of the patients on my ward. He has asked if he might court me and had talked it over with Zachary before informing me. And here I was wondering if he felt the same as I do. Not that I always know what I am feeling, this is all so new and, at times, frightening. I can't wait for you to meet him. The sad thing is that he announced, nearly in the same breath, that he had been discharged and would be leaving for home in the morning and would return within a fortnight. A fortnight isn't really that long, I keep telling myself.

Aunt Sylvania is much improved now that the weather is cooler and she has "her boys" here to mother. She has taken over the reading in the afternoons, and some of the boys tease her until her cheeks are pink.

That is all from here. Your letters, few though they have been, bring such joy to us all. I commend you to our sovereign Lord's gracious care.

Love,

Louisa

P.S. Zachary told the surgeon general he didn't want his "wife" working in the hospital any longer, so I must find something else to do for the war effort.

———

My dear Louisa,

I miss your sweet face already, and I have been on the train for barely more than an hour. I was not able to take the one I had intended, as it was full of troops off to another front. Would that I could go with them, but the army says I am no longer of value. All that training at West Point gone to waste, thanks to an enemy shell. But I keep reminding myself that through the grace of God I am alive, and He has given me something to live for, after all—you. So many things I've wanted to say to you, but the time never seemed right, and I still cannot believe you return my feelings.

As soon as I straighten out things at home, I will return on the earliest train. Please write to me so that I may continue to have smiles in my life, the joy you so willingly share. I will mail this at the next stop, so it doesn't take so long to get to you.

Yours truly,

Lieutenant Gilbert Lessling

———

Dear Gilbert,

As the fortnight has come and gone and there has been no further word from you, I am praying that you are well and only so buried in business that you have no time to write. I treasure your letter and have read it so many times that the creases are working their way through the paper. I do hope you have received my other letters and that you are in better health each day. I ask our God to watch over you and bring you back safely.

Yours,

Louisa

———

"Can I bring you anything else?" Louisa stopped at the door to the parlor where Zachary and several other officers were visiting amid a cloud of cigar smoke.

"Nothing, thanks." Zachary waved his cigar, obviously waiting for her to leave before the conversation could continue.

What is he up to now? Louisa glanced back at the door that was now closed. "I know they are hatching something," she said aloud.

"What dat you say?" Abby stopped to ask on her way to take refreshments out to the men gathered around Aunt Sylvania and her open Shakespeare book.

"Just grumbling." Louisa set the tray down on the kitchen table and picked up a cookie to nibble on. While every morning on waking she promised she would leave the lieutenant in God's strong hands, by afternoon she felt ready to fly apart. Why hadn't she heard from him again?

"You know that mail can't get through much of the time, and you know what God says about worry, so go knit socks or do something helpful." She took her own advice and her knitting out to the front glider. If only Zachary would let her go back to the hospital where she felt useful.

After the three men left, tipping their hats to her as they filed past, Zachary called to her from the parlor.

Sure, he needs me to help him back to bed but sends me off with a wave of his hand when . . . Oh, stop feeling sorry for yourself, Louisa Marie Highwood. Others have things so much worse than you do. Put a smile on your face and kill that rapscallion brother of yours with a hearty dose of kindness. She set her knitting back in the basket and stood, smoothing her skirts before she entered the house.

Zachary didn't look up when she entered the room; instead he stared out the window. From the look of him he wasn't seeing the jasmine vine that created a fragrant frame of white blossoms and green leaves beyond the curtains.

She crossed and opened the window to let the flowers' fragrance take away that of the cigar smoke.

"Come, sit here." He patted the horsehair seat beside him.

Louisa felt a catch in her heart. She crossed the room, never taking her eyes from his face. "What is it, brother?"

"I . . . I'm afraid I have bad news for you." He took her hand in his and finally looked in her eyes. "We have reason to believe that the train Lieutenant Lessling was riding on was the one blown to smithereens by the Yankees."

"Reason to believe? That means you have no proof." She hung on to his hand with all the power in her.

"No. No proof, but a certainty."

"Without proof, I will not believe it. The lieutenant gave me his word he would come back." *Lord, I cannot bear this. Unless you tell me, I will not believe.*

"Trust me."

Louisa got to her feet. "I . . . I think I need to be alone."

Dragging her feet up the stairs, she entered her bedroom and dropped down on the side of the bed. "He can't be dead, Lord. Wouldn't I have some sense if he were dead?"

"Trust me." The lace curtains moved gently in the air, as if puffed by a whisper.

"I've trusted you with everything, with everyone, but you take them away." Her eyes burned, the tears refusing to fall to cleanse this mighty trauma from her soul. "What else can I do?"

"Trust me."

The words seemed to hang in the stillness.

Louisa gritted her teeth and clamped her fingers into a fist until the skin broke. "I will trust you." Each word was ripped from her heart. "I will trust you, God, Father, S-Savior." A tear overflowed her now wet eyes and ambled down her cheek. "I will trust you, Jesus, my Lord."

The curtains moved again, and this time peace flooded her soul.

Chapter Thirty-Five

The closer the sun slid to the horizon, the dryer Jesselynn's mouth grew.

Meshach arrived first, a deer carcass slung over his shoulders. Benjamin trailed him by several hundred yards, the deer on his shoulders heavy enough to make his slighter frame stagger with the weight.

When she shot Meshach a questioning look, he winked at her and whispered, "I offered to help, but . . ." His shrug said it all. He swung his burden to the ground.

Benjamin dropped his next to it with a *thwump*. The rise to the cave had him panting like a hound after a hunt. His deer sported two-prong antlers.

"Good, those horns can come in handy." Sergeant White's comment brought a wide smile, and Benjamin stood straighter. "And two hides. I see you brought me somethin' I kin do."

"Happy to help you, suh." Benjamin's beaming smile had pride written all over it. "Biggest deer I ever shot."

"Onliest deer you ever shot." Meshach clapped the younger man on the shoulder. "Let's get dem hung, and you can skin 'em." He looked around. "Where's Daniel?"

"Not back yet." Jesselynn hated saying words that immediately sucked the joy out of the moment.

"We better go lookin' for 'im."

"I was about to."

Meshach saddled one of the mares and Ahab. He slammed his rifle into the scabbard laced to the saddle and swung aboard, the look on his face grim enough to scare Sammy, who clung to Thaddeus. Meshach held an impatient Ahab steady while looking at Sergeant White. "Keep watch." He nodded to Benjamin. "Give him the rifle while you skin the deer."

Jesselynn mounted the mare and followed Meshach up the hill, then once out of the hollow, they nudged the horses into an easy canter that ate up the miles. They rode halfway to Springfield before they saw Daniel limping toward them.

"What happened," Jesselynn called, "the mule dump you?"

Daniel shook his head.

As they rode closer, they could see one eye was swollen shut, the cut on his head left a trail of dried blood down the side of his face, and he clutched one elbow to his side. One shirt sleeve hung by a thread.

"What? Who?" Jesselynn could feel rage bubbling and snapping in her midsection.

"Dey took de mule." He swiped blood and dirt from under his nose with his good hand and looked down at his bare feet. "An' my boots."

"They who?" Jesselynn dismounted and flinched at the close-up sight of his beaten body.

"Dey was fixin' to hang me for stealin' de mule, but some other men come along, and dey run dem off." He leaned against Meshach when he dismounted, and Meshach put his arm around the boy. "I tried to fight dem off, but one against three . . ." His voice trailed off, and he shook his head. "I'se sorry."

"I reckon you're more important than the mule anytime." Jesselynn gently pulled his arm away from his body, her lips tightening at the bruise on his side.

"Dey kick me. I never hurt so bad in my life." He dug in his pocket. "But dey din't take de letter." He thrust it into Jesselynn's hand and swayed on his feet. "Sorry, I'se gonna be sick."

Meshach held the boy's head with one hand and clamped the other around his waist until the retching finished.

"Ah, dat hurts." Daniel gasped.

"Broken ribs?"

"Cracked anyway." Meshach led Daniel over to Ahab, who, nostrils flared wide, skittered away at the smell of blood.

"Easy, son." Jesselynn held the stallion steady while Meshach boosted Daniel up into the saddle, then mounted behind him. She patted Daniel on the knee. "We'll get you right fixed up back at camp. Guess we better use some of that deer hide and make you a pair of moccasins to keep your feet warm."

"Thank you, Marse Jesse. You mighty good to dis black boy."

Jesselynn felt rage hot and sweet course through her as she followed the pair ahead. Who had taken the mule, and why did they beat Daniel so viciously? Pure meanness was all she could think of. Now, stealing the mule, that made sense, but beating someone half to death? And then stringing him up.

A picture of Cavendar Dunlivey beating one of the slaves sprang into her mind. That was when her father ordered him off the place. But she could still see the look in Dunlivey's eyes. He had enjoyed giving the whipping. Thinking back like that made her keep looking over her shoulder, her pistol at the ready.

———

"We kin track dat mule." Benjamin repeated his comment again. Supper finished, they were sitting around the fire before going to bed. "You know him hooves, Meshach. You shod 'im, after all. De right front, how it curve in? We go find dem and bring 'im back."

"No! There'll be no talk of trackin' the mule. Those men are killers. You want to end up like Daniel or worse?" Jesselynn nodded to the young man huddled under a quilt and whimpering in his sleep.

"What de letter say?" Meshach used the deerhorn to smooth the piece of wood he'd been working on.

"I forgot all about it." Jesselynn dug in her pocket and pulled out the envelope. Slitting it open with her finger, she extracted the paper and, tipping it, leaned closer to the light.

" 'Dear Zachary,

"Welcome to Springfield, although I am sorry I was not at home to greet you. The sad news is that Hiram died early on in the war, and some worthless scalawag burned us out. They do that a lot around here. All our horses were already gone, and several slaves died in the fire. I am living with a friend here in town, but since neither one of us has a husband for support, I have not even a room for you to stay in. Please come to visit me when you can.'

"She gives the directions and signed the letter, 'Sincerely, Mrs. Hiram Highwood.' "

Jesselynn looked up to find Sergeant White studying her across the fire. "Zachary is my older brother." She could feel her cheeks growing hot, surely from the fire.

He nodded and went back to his whittling. "When you goin'?"

"First thing in the mornin'." *Surely Aunt Agatha knows somewhere we can keep the horses over the winter. And maybe she's heard from the girls.*

"I go wid you." Meshach never looked up from his scraping.

"No, I'll be—" Jesselynn stopped when Meshach glanced over at the sleeper who came so close to leaving this life. "Thank you."

———

They had no trouble finding the house in the morning, but Jesselynn about choked when she saw the place. Disrepair hung over the house like a rent and rotten garment. Windows, doors, and porch all sagged, as did the gate to what used to be a picket fence. By the steps, one lone pink rose struggled to reach the sun. The nearby houses didn't look any better.

Meshach held the horses while Jesselynn went up to knock on the door. She waited and knocked again before she heard someone coming. The person fumbled with a lock on the inside, then peered around the barely open door.

"What do you want?"

The voice Jesselynn recognized, but the face bore only faint resemblance to the one she remembered. Once round with a habitual smile, this face had skin hanging off prominent bones and blue eyes that pierced rather than sparkled.

"Aunt Agatha?"

The door would have closed but for Jesselynn's quick thinking to put her foot into the opening. "Aunt Agatha, I know you were expectin' Zachary, but I'm Jesse, er, Jesselynn."

The woman behind the door gave her a once up-and-down look. "Young man, this is not funny."

"I'm not trying to be funny. I had to become Jesse to get us here safely. I promised my father—"

"And who is your father?" She might be living in dismal surroundings, but the starch had never left her tone.

"Major Joshua Highwood, deceased. My oldest brother, Adam, died in the war, and we have not heard a thing about Zachary. Mother Miriam died in childbirth, and I have little Thaddeus with me—er, back at the camp. I sent Louisa and Carrie Mae back to Richmond, where I thought they would be safe. Twin Oaks is—"

"Well, I'll be switched." The caricature opened the door a mite farther. "When and where was your daddy born?"

"Born in 1815 in the same bed he died in at Twin Oaks in Midway, Kentucky."

"Well, I'll be a—come right on in, child." A surprisingly strong hand reached out and yanked her inside to a hall that looked about even with the outside. She peered closely into Jesselynn's eyes. "Well, you certainly have the look of the Highwoods, but with those clothes . . ." Her nose wrinkled on the last word. "We'd better look through things and see if we can find something more appropriate to a young woman of what? Nineteen, or is it twenty by now?" All the while she talked, she dragged Jesselynn down the hall by the arm. "Leastwise you can have a bath."

Trying to stop her was like trying to harness a hurricane.

"Aunt Agatha, Aunt Agatha, wait." Jesselynn clamped a hand on the doorframe to bring the procession to a halt.

"Now what?" Agatha turned to look at her niece, only to shudder. "Britches! I can't believe a niece of mine is wearin' britches!"

At the moment, *that* niece was wishing she'd never come.

Jesselynn disengaged her aunt's stranglehold on her arm. "I have to stay dressed like this to keep me and the horses and my people safe. A woman in skirts would be fair game to any polecat out lookin' for sport. You know that."

"I declare, such talk. What would your dear mother say?"

My dear mother would be right glad her daughter was alive and in one piece. "And, Aunt Agatha, you must not breathe a word about who I am to anyone. You understand that? Not anyone."

"Why, land sakes, child, who would put two and two together anyway? I—"

"You have to promise me or I'll take my people and just fade into the backwoods where no one would know or care who I was." Jesselynn stood straight and leaned forward just the least bit. "It could mean life or death."

Agatha sagged, both inside and out. "Yes, I promise."

"Good. Let me go get Meshach. Is there somewhere we can tie the horses out of sight?"

"Why, why I guess in the shed out back. But isn't he one of your slaves?"

Jesselynn stopped in midstride. "No longer. I set him and the others free."

"Oh, why . . . ah . . . um."

Jesselynn turned back around so she could watch her aunt's face. "What happened to all your slaves, Aunt Agatha?"

"I sold them that didn't die in the fire. Other than the land, which will most likely go for taxes, that's all I had left. After all . . ."

Jesselynn held up a hand to stop the flow. "I'll go put the horses away."

"I mean, he can sit out on the back stoop, and . . ."

Jesselynn closed the door behind her. Obviously she and Aunt Agatha were about half a continent apart on the slavery issue. Maybe it was a good thing that they wouldn't be staying with her. *What about the woman she lives with? Where does she stand? And more importantly, who does she know?*

Right there she resolved to tell her aunt as little as possible. Their safety might depend on that.

"Have you received any letters from home or from Richmond?" Jesselynn and her aunt were now sitting in the parlor drinking tea. Meshach had gone off to the livery to see about a job as a blacksmith.

"Forgive me, child, I have. They went right out of my mind." She set her teacup down and pushed herself up with both hands on the arms of the chair.

The sound of her knees popping and creaking could be heard clear across the room, let alone to the next chair.

"Aunt Agatha, let me. Just tell me where to find them."

"I should say not. I'm not too decrepit to do for myself. Got to keep moving after all. Why, that's what's wrong with Lettie, poor dear. She just gives up at times."

Jesselynn had learned about Lettie Copsewald while they were making the tea. She'd been having one of her bad spells and, after retreating to her bed, asked to not be disturbed lest the headache return.

"After she takes her bit of laudanum," Aunt Agatha confided, "she sleeps like a baby and wakes up the next morning feelin' more like herself again."

Aunt Agatha returned to the dim and dusty parlor where she had insisted they take tea and handed Jesselynn two letters, both from Richmond.

"Thank you." She kept her sigh to herself. What was happening at Twin Oaks? Lucinda had promised to write. Taking the sheet of paper from the envelope, she started to read, only to look up in guilt. "I'm sorry. Where are my manners?"

"You go right ahead. I'll just enjoy my tea while you catch up on the news. Oh, and that one on the top just came yesterday."

By the end of the few minutes it took, Jesselynn knew that Carrie Mae was engaged to be married, Louisa volunteered at the hospital, and Zachary was alive. That last she learned in the more recent letter. She put the letters down in her lap and fought the tears that threatened to break loose.

Zachary is alive. She wanted to dance and shout, but a glance at her aunt with her chin on her chest helped calm her to only a quick squeezing of her fists. *No matter how badly he is wounded, he can go home to Twin Oaks and start over. I'll take the horses home in the spring, and life will begin again.*

She ignored the voice that reminded her the war might not be over by then.

She read the letters again to savor every word and nuance. What had Louisa meant about her work in the hospital? Surely they didn't let young unmarried women take care of the wounded men. She read the paragraphs again. Certainly sounded like that was just what she was doing.

Whatever was Aunt Sylvania thinking of to let Louisa do such a thing?

The thought "let Louisa" made her eyebrows rise. How could she expect Aunt Sylvania to do what she had been unable to accomplish herself? She folded the letters and slid them back into their envelopes. The clink of her cup in the saucer brought Aunt Agatha upright.

"Isn't that good news?" She picked up her cup and wrinkled her nose when the tea she sipped was cold. "I must have slept a bit. Forgive my bad manners, please. When Lettie is unwell, I have a difficult time sleeping."

Jesselynn refrained from asking why and handed the letters back to her aunt. "Thank you for sharing them with me. I wrote the other day to tell them we were here safely." She heard a discreet rap at the back door. "I'd better be going. That is sure to be Meshach." She paused. "Is there anyone you know of, Aunt, who would let me keep the horses hidden on their farm until we can go home again?"

Agatha shook her head. "No one I would trust. I'm sorry, my dear."

Jesselynn said her good-byes, promising to return often, but not telling her aunt where they were camped. "If you need me, leave a letter at the post office, and whoever comes in to town will get it."

"Go with God, child. I just wish I could do more."

Jesselynn ignored the first part of the sentence and shook her head over the last. "I wish I could help *you* more." She looked around at the dilapidated house. "Perhaps we could come in one day and do some fixin' up, though. If it wouldn't offend Miss Lettie?"

"We shall see." Aunt Agatha stepped back from the horses and stared up at Meshach. "You take good care of her now, you hear?"

"Yessum, I hears." Meshach gentled Ahab and grinned when Agatha *tsked* at Jesselynn mounted astride.

Jesselynn waved one last time as they trotted down the rutted street. "Let's stop at the post office. Might be a letter from home."

All the way there she told him the news from Richmond and got a lump in her throat again at the sheen of tears in the big man's eyes at the good news.

"I'm right glad to hear that," he said. "Thank you, Lord above, for takin' keer of our boy."

Jesselynn rolled her eyes. Leave it to Meshach; he just didn't understand. Zachary making it through was luck, pure and simple.

"I have a letter here for Miss Jesselynn Highwood. Would she be any relation to you?" the woman behind the counter asked.

"Ah yes. That's my sister. I'll take it to her." Jesselynn took the envelope and studied the unfamiliar handwriting. "Thank you." She stuffed the envelope into her pocket and followed an elderly lady out the door. As she'd made the men promise to do, she glanced around but saw no one that seemed interested in her or what she was doing.

But once on the horses, she felt shivers run up her spine. Lucinda used to call it "someone walkin' on mah grave."

Before mounting she looked again, but everything around them seemed to fit.

"What wrong?" Meshach asked in an undertone.

"I don't know. Just feels like someone is watchin' me."

"Don' see nobody."

"I know. Me neither. Let's get outa here."

Once out of town, she opened the letter. A blank page stared back at her.

Chapter Thirty-Six

MISSOURI CAVE

"Why would someone send a blank page?"

"I don' know."

If Jesselynn had asked the question once in the last three days, she'd asked it a hundred times. While they had posted lookouts around the clock, no one had seen anything or anyone suspicious. They grazed the horses both morning and afternoon, and Meshach went hunting early every morning, returning with rabbits from the snares he set, another deer, and a couple of ducks. Those at the cave kept the fire going to cure the meat and worked at tanning the hides. Daniel wore his new moccasins, a gift from Sergeant White, with pride.

Barnabas, as he asked to be called, took one of the tanned rabbit pelts and created a pad for the stump of his leg, so he could begin to wear the peg that he and Meshach designed. While he couldn't wear it long or put all of his weight on it, the peg leg helped his balance.

"What if we carved me a foot and put a boot on it, then it would look more like a real leg."

"We kin try." Meshach studied the piece of wood in his hand. "Carvin' it ain't the problem. It'd be mighty stiff." With two fingers, he hung on to one end of the foot-long piece and bobbed it up and down. "Look, see how a foot walks. Needs to bend at de ankle." He leaned over and stroked the hair back from Jane Ellen's forehead.

Jesselynn often wondered how a man's hand so big and strong enough to shoe horses and all the other chores Meshach accomplished with such ease could still be so gentle with their silent girl. Walking Jane Ellen had become Jesse-lynn's job, and as long as she held the hand that was becoming more clawlike daily and led her around, Jane Ellen walked. Otherwise she sat—and stared into nothing. They took turns feeding her, the boys chattered to her as if she were indeed listening, and Ophelia combed her hair and sang to her.

If Jesselynn allowed herself to think beyond the moment, she wondered if the young girl would just fade away and one morning they would wake up to find her cold and stiff, instead of warm and silent.

"What about a wire hinge or even a wooden one?" Barnabas took the wood from Meshach and outlined a hinge on the end of the wood. "Then notch up into the wooden leg."

"So, how you keep it from floppin' down when you walk?"

"Oh." The two went back to their carving and pondering.

Jesselynn took her sewing outside to sit in the sunshine. Sammy needed clothes for the winter, so she cut up one of her father's shirts and fashioned a shift for the black baby. She figured to make him a vest out of the rabbit pelts as soon as they were ready. The way Thaddeus was growing, she'd need material, or hides, to sew new pants for him too.

Ophelia had been down to the swamp and brought back cattail leaves for making baskets, along with stalks and roots for cooking. When she had a few minutes, she would sit down to weave again. "Babies sleepin'." She brought her work out into the sun to sit near Jesselynn.

A crow flew overhead, his raucous call causing Jesselynn to look up. A blue jay joined in the warning announcement.

Jesselynn's heart picked up the pace. She scanned the area she could see, set down her sewing, and stood to look up the hill above the cave. Nothing. She listened, but other than the breeze rattling the few remaining leaves, she could see or hear nothing. Nevertheless that feeling of being watched returned. Could someone be watching them and stay hidden? She examined the oak trees around them, one by one. Many had trunks large enough to hide a man, but who would dare come so close? They kept the rifles in plain view.

"What is it?" Barnabas stumped his way out to stand beside her.

"I don't know. It's just a feelin'." Jesselynn rubbed the back of her neck. "Guess I'm just spooked ever since that letter."

"Know anyone who could be lookin' for you?"

"Yes." *Should I tell him or not? And how can I without telling him who I really am?*

She continued scanning the trees, lingering over a broad trunk made even wider with a burl the size of a washtub. Now where would she hide if she were watching the camp?

"We need more wood. I'm thinkin' of tryin' to chop down one of those smaller trees."

"Choppin' wood puts lots of pressure on the knees."

"I know." He stood beside her, giving the trees the same once-over she did. He stumped along with her as she walked to the edge of the clearing where the bank sloped off down to the creek that threaded its way between the hills. Ridges and hollers, according to the locals.

"Jesse, mayhap I could be more of a help if I knew the whole story."

Jesselynn heard the caring in his voice. She knew if she turned around his eyes would be warm and his mouth curved in that gentle smile he had. Once or twice she'd even thought on what kissing him would be like. She straightened just enough to put a bit of distance between them.

"I know you're no lad."

"Umm." What could she say? Did she dare tell him?

"But I know too, you got yourself a mighty good reason to keep up the masquerade."

"I reckon what you don't know can't hurt you." *Or me either.*

"That's not always true."

"Maybe not, but I got to do what's best for everybody here."

"What about what's best for Jesse?"

"Jesselynn." *There, I did it.* "And the man who can do us the most harm is Cavendar Dunlivey. When my daddy kicked him off Twin Oaks and I turned down his proposal, he swore to get us all, including the slaves and the horses. While I've emancipated my people, he could sell 'em down the river if he caught them."

She shuddered inside at what he would do to her. "I'd kill him myself before I let him touch any one of us." All the while they talked, they both studied the surrounding area, rather than each other. But every particle of skin and clothing seemed charged, and she was sure sparks would snap if they touched.

Telling him let her stand a little straighter as he shared her burden.

"So, what will you do?"

"Hide the horses here through the winter. Then when the war is over in the spring, we'll go home again." The thought of seeing Twin Oaks when the infant oak leaves were pinking on the stems made her eyes water.

"What makes you think the war will be over by spring?"

"It has to be." She turned at the sound of the whistle that announced Benjamin was back with the horses. She whistled back and bumped into the broad chest of the man who'd been standing with her. The thought of leaning on that chest and letting him put his arms around her made her catch her breath. Not since John rode off so gallantly had she stood in the stronghold of a man's embrace.

She swallowed and stared at the button midway up his shirt. "I . . . I'd better go." Her hands itched to touch him.

"Jesselynn."

Ah, the sound of her name. So long since she'd been Jesselynn, it seemed a lifetime ago.

"Jesse." She stepped back. "Please remember that." When he reached to touch her hand, she sidestepped the contact. "I'd better get back to sewing if Sammy is to have something warmer to wear."

"We'll talk again."

"Oh, I'm sure we will." She swallowed the catch in her throat. *Could she love this man in the same way she had loved John? Did she really know what loving a man was like, since all she'd shared were a few kisses and dreams?* She stepped around him and returned to her sewing, stitching as fast as her thoughts swirled until she pricked her finger and a dot of blood glowed on the white cloth. The word she thought was not the one she uttered, which was a good thing because just then Thaddeus ambled out of the cave, rubbing the sleep from his eyes as she rubbed the blood from her fingertip.

That night before going to bed, Jesselynn stopped Barnabas at the mouth of the cave. "If you figured out that I'm . . . I'm not a man, is it that I am such a poor actor?"

White shook his head. "No. Don't worry yourself about that. One would need to be around awhile to figure it out."

"What then?"

"Little things, like your sewing. No man sews such a fine seam, and most men, especially young ones, aren't as tender as you with children or as gentle with the ill, like the way you care for Jane Ellen."

"Anything else?" She knew her tone was clipped, but the worry of it all sharpened her every which way.

"Well, ah . . ." His hesitation brought the memory back to her of when she'd helped him eat and drink, and the look on his face the one time he'd fallen against her chest.

"Good night, Sergeant White." She brushed past him and darted off into the trees, her cheeks flaming as much as she suspected his were, but he had a beard to disguise the condition.

————

"We'd better make another trip to town," Jesselynn said several days later, days she'd spent making sure she was always on the other side of the fire from Barnabas White. Being near him made it more difficult to think, and she couldn't afford herself that luxury. Even thinking his name made her feel soft inside.

"Kin we git some sugar or molasses an' maybe milk?" Ophelia looked up from hanging more venison over the drying fire. "De babies, dey need milk."

"I know." Jesselynn heaved a sigh. They all needed so many things, things she had taken for granted at home, like cloth and thread, flour and cornmeal, horseshoes and cowhide or pigskin to repair harnesses and bridles. One of the reins had broken the day before on the bridle Ahab wore. "Maybe if we get to Aunt Agatha's before dawn, the horses won't cause a stir." Oh, how she missed that mule right about now. No matter how they tried to disguise them, Thoroughbreds were Thoroughbreds, and anyone with a decent eye for horseflesh would spot them. If only they knew of a place outside of town where they could leave the horses and walk on in. And if Meshach got work at the livery, how would he get back and forth, or if he stayed in town, where?

Too many questions and no answers.

Instead of worrying about the possibilities, she took out paper and pen to write to her sisters. While she had as many questions for them as they'd had for her, none of them made a life-or-death difference. Now if only there'd be a letter from Twin Oaks at the post office, she would have one less thing to worry about.

————

The next morning after an uneventful daybreak ride, they tied the horses in the shed at Aunt Agatha's and rapped gently at the back door. Agatha answered the door, mopping her eyes at the same time.

"What is it, Aunt?" Jesselynn took her aunt's icy hands in her own.

"Lettie is so sick. I've been nursing her, but last night she took a turn for the worse. Please." She gave Meshach an imploring look. "Could you go for the doctor?"

"Of course he will. Where is the doctor's house?"

While Agatha gave Meshach instructions, Jesselynn crossed to the stove and checked the firebox. The fire was nearly out and the woodbox empty, but when she stepped outside, the woodpile was down to a few sticks. Checking the back side of the shed, she had to admit there was another problem: the two old women were about out of wood. If the temperature of the day was any indication, winter was shoving fall out of the way and taking over.

She'd have to set the men to cutting wood and bring in a wagonload, but that wouldn't help today. What could she do? Wasn't there anyone in this town who watched out for widow ladies? She picked up her load and headed back for the house.

Agatha met her at the door again. "I just don't know what more to do for her."

"I know. You've done the best you could." Jesselynn shaved a few slivers off the wood with the butcher knife on top of the stove and laid them over the few remaining coals. If she'd seen the ax, she'd have split a piece or two for fire starter. Opening the draft wide, she blew on the coals until a tendril of smoke rose, then another. She set the lid divider in place and then the back lid so the draft would work when she added the two smallest pieces. By the time the burners were hot enough to heat water, she could hear Meshach's boots on the back step.

"Doctor say he be right over." He caught his breath, then added, "Also ask why you not call for 'im sooner."

Agatha straightened as though she was about to fight, then slumped. "We have no money to pay a doctor, so we do what we can."

Jesselynn felt like crying for her, but more tears would only water the soup, as Lucinda was wont to say. "A cup of tea will help, I know."

"No tea."

"Coffee?"

A shake of her head. "And there's nothin' left to sell, neither. We already did that."

"What have you been livin' on?"

"The fruit and vegetables from our garden. The two hens left give us eggs. We manage."

"Good." The thought of an egg made her mouth get all set for the taste.

"But I've been thinkin' maybe some chicken soup would help—"

A rap at the front door stopped her in midsentence. "The doctor." Her slippers *flap-flapped* down the hall as she hurried to let him in.

"I'm goin' to de livery now, if you don' need me anymore."

"Not unless you can find something to cut up for firewood."

"Kin do dat tomorrer and bring it here in de wagon."

"I know." Jesselynn rubbed her forehead with the fingers of one hand. "You go on." She jingled the coins in her pocket. Should she buy wood for the women or scrape by on what was out there? The money in her pocket was all that stood between them all and . . . the thought didn't bear thinking about. She could at least have brought in some dried meat, if she'd known things were so bad here.

The doctor came out of the sickroom shaking his head. "Not much we can do but keep her comfortable. When a body don't want to live anymore, hard to keep 'em here." He shivered and came to the stove to rub his hands over the heat. "They let the fire go out?" he said under his breath to Jesselynn.

"About out of wood."

"Long on pride, these two, and short on sense." The doctor shook his head. "I'll get some wood over here sometime today."

"We can bring in a load tomorrow."

The doctor nodded. "You a relative?"

"Agatha's nephew from Kentucky. Thought to be safe here."

The doctor barked a laugh. "It's bad now but goin' to be worse, you mark my words."

"Worse?"

"Those hotheads down in Arkansas . . ."

Jesselynn didn't even want to ask him what he meant. Bluebellies, gray-coats, no matter, she just wanted the war over so she could go home. She saw the doctor to the door, refusing to dip into their meager cash store to pay him, then returned to the backyard to see what she could turn into firewood to keep these two old ladies warm until the morrow. Since there were no animals, she tore off the manger and hacked it into stove-size lengths, likewise the posts and sides of the stall divider. That along with the remaining chunks of wood should serve them. The two hens eyed her, then went back to scratching in their pen. Since the grain bin was empty, Jesselynn brought in some garden refuse and threw it down for them.

Now she had all the old biddies cared for. The thought brought an almost smile. She went back in the house and set a pot of water to boiling to make soup out of dried beans, dried corn, fresh carrots, turnips, rutabagas, and potatoes, all from the cellar, along with a bit of cabbage. Again she wished she'd brought some of the dried venison along.

Agatha came out of the sickroom some time later and sank down onto a chair at the kitchen table. "She's sleeping, poor thing." She eyed the bottle of laudanum the doctor had left on the table. "At least she's not so restless. I could tell she was in pain, and at least now that can be helped."

Jesselynn watched her aunt straighten the saltcellar and smooth out the crocheted doily. She moved the medicine closer, then set it farther off again. Had the doctor told Agatha what he believed?

"You want me to spend the night?" She waited until she heard Meshach's boots on the steps to ask.

"No, no. You've done plenty, what with the wood and the soup and all. We'll be fine. Perhaps by tomorrow Lettie will be feeling much better."

She doesn't know. Good grief, what am I to do?

"You go on now. Your people need you worse than I do." Agatha made shooing motions with her hands. The vigor had returned to her voice, giving her almost as much a commanding presence as in earlier days.

"We'll be back with wood tomorrow, then." Jesselynn gave her aunt a hug and let herself be ushered out the door.

"No work here 'less I go to de army. But got a letter here for Sergeant White. Make him right happy." Meshach patted his pocket.

As they left town, that old feeling of being watched kept Jesselynn looking over her shoulder. *You'd think I'd be used to it by now.* But her interior muttering did nothing to dispel the feeling, so they returned to their cave a different way.

"Letter for you," Meshach said, handing Barnabas the envelope as soon as they got to the cave.

"Ah, from home." His smile widened. "A letter from home." He opened it carefully to save the paper and pulled out a single sheet. Only moments after beginning to read, he raised stricken eyes to meet Jesselynn's. "I've got to go home as soon as possible. My mother is desperately ill, and there is no one else to care for her. May I use one of the horses to ride to Springfield? I can catch the stagecoach to Fort Smith from there."

Chapter Thirty-Seven

❧

MISSOURI

"I'll be back," Sergeant White assured Jesselynn.

Why did those words seem so familiar? Jesselynn nodded. "Maybe you'll have to come all the way to Kentucky."

"No matter where, I'll find you."

She nodded again. "You just get your family taken care of." She stepped back when he reached for her. Two men hugging in public would cause all sorts of raised eyebrows, and she didn't want to draw any more attention to herself than necessary.

"I left you my address. You'll write?" The plea in his eyes tugged at her heart.

"And you? We'll miss you." *I'll miss you.* She didn't want to admit that to anyone, let alone herself.

As soon as he boarded the stage, she turned and headed back for Aunt Agatha's, where Meshach would be unloading the wood. *You will not cry!* She kept the order pounding out the same rhythm as her marching feet.

As soon as she'd checked with her aunt, who said Lettie was about the same as yesterday, she climbed up on the wagon seat and, taking the reins, headed the team out of town.

"De neighbors want to buy a load of wood," Meshach said after they were halfway back to the cave.

"Really? For how much?"

He named a price, and she smacked her lips together. "That will buy flour and beans."

"Miss Agatha, she send home some veg'bles." He motioned to a tow sack behind the seat. "An' three eggs."

Amazing, we actually think of the cave as home. She had realized that the day before when thinking the same thing herself. But this time there was no Sergeant Barnabas White to look forward to talking with. She stopped the next sigh in mid-exhale. Sighing could become a habit, a bad habit. If she let herself think of all the people who'd gone out of her life the last couple of years, the sighing would lead to crying, and no way was she going to let *that* happen.

"Maybe someone else would buy wood too." *If only they didn't have to use the horses as a team.* She wished they could have caught whoever stole their mule.

"Marse Jesse, I gots sumpin' to ask you."

Jesselynn glanced at the man sitting beside her. "So ask."

"Well, you heard Sergeant White talkin' wid us 'bout goin' west? Go on to Oregon for free land."

"Mmm. Guess I didn't pay much attention."

"I wants to do dat. Dey no niggers dere. Only black men free on their own free land. 'Phelia an' me, we wants ta be married, then up and go west." The final words came in a rush. "Sammy too."

"Oh." His words hit her like a dozen knife slashes. "You don't want to go home to Twin Oaks?"

"No'm. I wants land of my own."

She could hear the pride in his voice, the kind of pride she'd been nursing along so that he could become the man she knew he was.

"Would you wait until I get the horses home? Then I'd send you with my blessing."

"Yessuh, we would wait. Planned it thataway anyhow. I'd never leave you alone in dat cave."

"Good, that's settled, then. But if you and Ophelia want to get married sooner than that, I see no reason to wait. You could go to a minister in Springfield."

"I'll think on dat."

A scream from up ahead made her slap the horses into a trot. She pulled them to a stop near the top of the ridge and slung the reins around the brake post. Meshach was halfway down the hill before she crowned the ridge.

"Don't come any further!" The voice came from her worst nightmare.

"Now drop your gun or this nigger here won't have no head." Meshach did as ordered.

Jesselynn hid behind the tree with the huge burl and surveyed the scene below. She counted five of the roughest-looking men she'd ever seen, and Cavendar Dunlivey was the ugliest. How had she ever thought him handsome in those long-ago days at Twin Oaks? He wore a coat that once had been gray and cut for an officer, but now dirt warred with holes as to who owned it. His hat slouched over one eye, but the pistol he held against Ophelia's head glinted in the sunlight.

One man held a gun on Benjamin and Daniel, while two others were leading the horses out of the cave.

For an instant, Jesselynn was grateful they'd hooked Ahab up in the team, but that made no difference now. How could she get them out of this? She fingered the pistol she'd taken to wearing in her waistband and had drawn when she ducked behind the tree. She could get Dunlivey, but what about the others?

Jane Ellen sat where they must have dumped her, face slack, focusing on nothing. Sammy and Thaddeus huddled with Benjamin and Daniel. Looked like both the young'uns had been crying.

"Now, whar is she?" Dunlivey roared, nudging the mouth of the pistol under Ophelia's chin. Her eyes rolled white, and she whimpered, the sound such pure terror that Jesselynn drew back on the trigger. One shot and he would be gone.

"Who?" Meshach burned with a fire of his own, leashed only by a will that knew he'd be dead, and then what would happen to the rest?

"Miss Jesselynn Highwood, that's who."

"Don't never seen another woman here, boss." The man guarding the others called.

"She done gone back home." Meshach stood taller.

"And left that brat here. Naw, she's around." He poked the gun again. "Now whar?"

"Gone to her aunt's house." Benjamin drew back from the gun aimed at his head.

"Ah, then we wait. She's comin' back." Dunlivey lowered his gun, and Ophelia collapsed in a heap at his feet. He kicked her aside and strolled over to Meshach. "You 'member that beating I owed ya?" He walked around the statue of ebony. "Answer me, niggah!"

The gun now dug into Meshach's neck.

"Yessuh."

One of the men who'd tied the mare to a nearby tree now reached down and picked up Ophelia, dangling her as one would a doll. "Now this here might be a fun plaything."

Meshach growled like an animal at bay.

Oh, don't move, Meshach. Wait, please wait. You remember Dunlivey. He likes to tease and torture. Hang on.

The man reached out and ripped Ophelia's dress down the front. She screamed and tried to cover herself. Meshach made a slight motion to go to her, and Dunlivey clubbed him over the head with his pistol. Meshach dropped like a steel weight.

"Watch 'im!"

One of the men shifted over to rest the tip of his rifle on Meshach's cheek.

Oh, God, what do I do?

"Let them all go, Dunlivey, and I'll come in!" Her voice rang with authority.

"Ha! I got them, and now you too."

Jesselynn aimed at the side of his boot. The shot rang out, and he jumped as if he'd been stung. "That wasn't a miss."

A string of curses heated the air.

"You want me to try again? Closer maybe?"

More curses. A snicker from one of his men.

"Let my people go!" Where had she heard those words before? The shot took off his hat.

Dunlivey nodded to his men. "Let 'em go. But we keep the guns. They won't go nowhere."

His men stepped back.

"Benjamin, get them outa there."

Like an adder striking, Dunlivey snatched up Thaddeus. "Now show yourself."

"Put him down. I told you I'd come in." Her heart pounded so hard she thought it might leap from her chest. *Not Thaddeus!*

"Let them all go, Dunlivey, or my next shot is through your heart." Her hand clutching the pistol shook so hard she couldn't have hit the cave wall.

"Show yerself!"

Thaddeus screamed. Jesselynn stepped out from behind the tree.

A shot rang out. Dunlivey dropped Thaddeus and clutched his belly that blossomed red with blood.

One of his men raised his gun, but before he could fire, Jesselynn's shot caught him in the shoulder and spun him around. The other three grabbed him and all disappeared into the trees.

Jane Ellen stood, feet spread, the gun in her hand now pointing at the ground.

"I'm gut shot." Dunlivey sagged to the ground, trying to hold his lifeblood in with spread fingers. "Don't leave me! You filthy scum, get back here!"

By the time Jesselynn got down to the clearing, Benjamin had an arm around Jane Ellen and held her as sobs rocked her skeleton body. Ophelia held Meshach in her arms, his head cradled in her lap. Sammy, tears streaming over his cheeks, toddled over to them, and Thaddeus drove straight for Jesselynn.

She scooped him up in her arms and rocked him, raining kisses on his cheeks.

"Someone, help me."

Jesselynn strode over to the clothesline she and Ophelia had hung and ripped a cloth off the rope. Tossing it to Dunlivey, she said calmly, as if she did this every day, "Fold that up and pack it in the wound. Might stop the bleedin'."

"The rest of you, let's get the things out of the cave. We can't stay here any longer."

Within half an hour, they were ready to load the wagon. As they went about their chores, no one looked at Dunlivey.

When they trudged up the hill with the supplies, he cried, "Give me a drink at least. Please give me a drink."

Meshach looked at Jesselynn, ignored her when she shook her head, and took a cup of water to the wounded man, who'd now managed to get himself backed up against a tree trunk.

"Dis only make it worse."

"You aren't goin' to leave me here?"

"Surely your men will come back for you." Jesselynn knew they wouldn't. Not the way they hightailed it. Knowing Dunlivey, he'd probably beaten each of them at one time or another.

He coughed. "You got any whisky?"

" 'Fraid not." She went back in the cave to see if they'd forgotten anything.

"All ready up here," Benjamin called from the lip of the ridge.

"Be right there." She took one more look around. *"Take him into town and leave him at the doctor's. Surely you can do that."* Her mother's voice rang clear as if she stood right there. Jesselynn sighed. Yes, she could do that, even though he'd need a miracle.

"Ya can't go back, ya know."

She stopped and stared at him.

"I burnt it." His eyes slitted, and what might have been a laugh choked from his mouth. "I burnt Twin Oaks to the ground the night you left. You got nothin'."

"What about Lucinda, the others?" *He's lyin'. He's got to be lyin'.*

"Slaver got 'em."

"But they had their papers."

"Not after the burnin'." He coughed, and pink spittle bubbled from his mouth.

Jesselynn staggered. Twin Oaks burned to the ground. "You're lyin'!"

He dug in his breast pocket and tossed her something. She bent down and picked up her silver comb, half melted but still recognizable.

"Found that in the ashes."

She looked him in the eyes. His glee could mean only one thing. She rubbed the ashes off the comb, spun, and strode off.

"Shoot me, then. Put me out of this misery."

She looked back. "I've never shot a man and I won't start now." With that she strode up the hill to where the others waited. *Where do we go? What do I do? No matter what I—oh, God—what do I do?*

She stopped at the oak with the big burl and, taking a deep breath, turned around. "I'll send a doctor back for you." *There, Mama. I tried.* Each foot felt shod in granite. *Where, God, where do we go?*

She topped the rise as the fiery gold disc slipped behind the horizon. Oranges, pinks, purples, and magenta bled across the sky and burned the clouds to silver. Then the answer came.

"Where we goin'?" Benjamin handed her the reins.

"West. Soon as we can. West, where there's no 'niggers,' only black men as free as the land."

SISTERS of the CONFEDERACY

DEDICATION

To the Sharons in my life.
You encourage me, push me, love me,
make me laugh, make my life richer as my friends.
Thanks, and may God bless you
even more richly than you bless me.

Chapter One

SPRINGFIELD, MISSOURI
EARLY JANUARY 1863

"Hey, boy, lemme see that horse of yours."

Marse Jesse Highwood, in reality Jesselynn, turned at the shout. A blue-clad soldier, his belly protruding between dark suspenders and hanging over the waistband of his blue britches, waved at her, letting her know whom he was accosting. As she turned her mare and drew closer, she could see a scar starting below his left eye and disappearing into a fox red beard. His eyes, the faded blue of a Yankee shirt washed too many times, glittered beneath bushy eyebrows. Sergeant stripes on the shirt sleeve made Jesse sit straighter.

"Yes, suh?" She kept her gaze below his chin.

"What you doin' with such a fine horse? Don't you know we need every horse we can git for the Union army?"

"Old Sunny here, suh, why she just near to foal and might would die with heavy ridin'. My daddy rode her home from the war so he could get well again and go back to fight. He say she need rest, jus' like him."

"What army was he with?"

Oh, drat, my mouth's got me in trouble again. Who would he have fought with on the Union side? As if he would have fought for the Union, but . . . She wracked her mind for the name of a Union general, all the while knowing her daddy fought in the legislature to keep the Union before he was forced to put on a Confederate uniform and go off to be killed. "With Kirby Smith, suh." She knew this man couldn't be from Tennessee, his accent was more mountain than Northern. Even so, her answer was a gamble. At least he had called her "boy."

"Good outfit." He walked around the mare, who was obviously heavy with foal. The only reason Jesselynn rode her instead of one of the stallions was because of the influx of blue army men in Springfield. She should have tied her outside of town and walked in.

But then, leaving a horse in the care of a young black man left them both open for thievery. Slave traders or horse traders—neither much cared if their new possession was free before they caught them. If only she hadn't felt the need to check on Aunt Agatha, who'd been living in Springfield since her husband, Hiram, was killed in the early days of the war. But with the death of her housemate, Agatha needed family.

"Be on your way, then. And greet your daddy for me. He musta took a lot of abuse from his neighbors if he went north to fight."

"Yes, suh, he surely did. Why they nigh to burned our barn one night, they was so fired up." *Shut your mouth and get on out of here.* Jesselynn touched one finger to the brim of her droopy felt hat and nudged Sunshine on up the street.

"You got any other horses out to home?"

His call sent shivers up her back. "No, suh, you done took them all." That part at least was true. There were no more horses at home in Kentucky. She had the remaining stallions and mares with her in a cave southwest of town.

One good thing, she'd sure enough learned to lie well. Just tripped right off her tongue, they did. Dealing with the guilt was something else. All those years hearing the Scriptures at her mother's knee made her detest lying. But keeping everyone alive was more important. Why in the world was a Union sergeant lurking on the back streets like this? Their encampment was north of town. An area she wisely stayed away from—far away from.

When her heartbeat returned to normal, she patted the mare's shoulder and straightened her own. "That was one close call, old girl. This is the last time I bring you to town." *Or any of our other horses.* But Aunt Agatha most likely needed more wood by now. In the saddlebags she carried a rabbit Benjamin had snared. She hoped her aunt would volunteer to repay her with some of the vegetables stored in her root cellar. The two old ladies had raised a fine garden and kept enough hens to sell a few eggs.

Now, with Lettie gone, Agatha lived alone in a borrowed house.

A house that looked as if it would fall down if one kicked a porch post. Jesselynn rode on past the hingeless gate, now tied in place with hemp rope, and into the shed-roofed barn. The barn had been built with stalls for horses and a bay to store a buggy. The stalls had gone the way of firewood, and who knew what happened to the buggy. Most likely it was sold early on for supplies. Now only a few laying hens clucked and scratched in the dusty corners.

Jesselynn tied the mare to one of the posts and, after loosening the saddle girth, swung the saddlebags over her shoulder and headed for the house. Off to her left the remains of a garden long ago harvested appeared to be sprouting new cabbage from the stalks. A row of greens had shot up new growth too. Jesselynn ducked under the clothesline and crossed the muddy soil to check on the green leaves that looked so bright against the bleached cornstalks. Each time she came, she'd been cutting more of the garden refuse for the hens. If they had some fencing, they could build a run from the barn to the garden and let the hens help themselves.

Had her aunt even been outside to see this bit of bounty?

Back at the door she dragged her boots across the scraper set into the step, trying to remove the mud from the garden. Not hearing anyone moving around, she knocked and waited.

No answer. Had Aunt Agatha gone somewhere? If so, where?

She pounded on the door, rattling the frame as she did so. She should have brought Meshach along to make necessary repairs.

Still no answer. She turned the knob and pushed open the door, sticking her head in to call for her aunt again before she entered. Removing a hat that looked as if some rodent had been nibbling the brim, she ran her fingers through hair that had recently been darkened by walnut-husk dye and shorn by Ophelia, formerly one of her father's slaves and now freed along with the rest of them. Ophelia had cut only men's hair before, but since Jesselynn was acting that part, short was best, and ragged didn't hurt.

Since the shearing had happened the night before, Jesse was still trying to get used to it. Would she ever be able to have long hair again and regain her place in the world of women? Did she even want to?

She brushed mud and horsehair off her britches. Her apparel was always a bone of contention between her and her aunt. At least if her clothes were clean, maybe the old lady wouldn't huff so stridently.

"Aunt Agatha?" Jesselynn laid the rabbit carcass that she had skinned and wrapped in brown paper on the table and traipsed through the house, checking every room in case her aunt had fallen or something. No one was about.

Surely she hadn't left that long ago and would be back soon. The stove was still warm, and embers glowed in the firebox. Jesselynn added a few more sticks of wood and filled a pot with water from the reservoir. Taking a knife from the drawer, she cut up the rabbit and put the pieces in the heating water. She found an onion in the pantry, chopped and added it, along with salt and pepper, and set the lid on the kettle.

Now, how else could she make herself useful?

Nothing was out of place. Each tabletop was dust free. Her aunt's Bible lay on the whatnot table by her chair, the bookmark set in the New Testament. Jesselynn flipped open the pages and read the words of 2 Corinthians 1, shaking her head. The Lord of comfort had been remarkably absent from her life in the last months. Of course her saying—nay, screaming—"I want nothing to do with you. You don't bother me, and I won't come sniveling to you" might have something to do with that. She shivered in the chilly house, though it wasn't cold. Life just wasn't what she had dreamed it to be, all because of that wicked war.

She gritted her teeth and returned to the kitchen. Perhaps she should start bread.

She combed the pantry, but the empty shelves told their own story. Her aunt had not had money to put in supplies. And Jesselynn had nothing to give to her. She and her band were living hand to mouth as it was. Surely she could put flour and sugar and such on the account at the store.

Hearing feet scraping at the back door, she returned to the kitchen to check on the stewing rabbit and moved the kettle to the back to slow down the boiling.

"Ah, Jesselynn, how good to see you."

The humph at the end had to do with Jesselynn's clothing, but as Jesse had no intention of donning the petticoats and skirts her aunt had dragged out of the clothes press, she ignored it. "Brought you a rabbit snared just this morning," she said, greeting her aunt. At five foot seven, Jesselynn was tall for a young woman, and when she hugged her diminutive aunt, shock bolted from mind to heart. Her aunt had lost more weight. Pleasantly rounded when Jesselynn first arrived in Springfield back in November, Aunt Agatha no longer filled out her waist, and the skirt had been taken in. Bones poked through the shawl she wore around her shoulders, and the skin of her face hung in folds under her chin.

"How long since you've eaten?" Nothing like getting directly to the point.

Agatha pulled herself upright, and starch returned to her backbone. "I had an egg for breakfast, thank you."

"And bread?"

Agatha turned away to lift the pot lid and stir the cooking rabbit. "Never you mind, young lady. I have my fruits and vegetables in the cellar, and—"

"What if you traded some of your stores for the things you can't grow? Surely there must be a merchant willing to trade."

"There might be."

Jesselynn waited, but her aunt continued stirring the pot. *How can I help you if I don't know what's wrong?* Like a whop up the side of her head, she suddenly realized the problem. Agatha couldn't get them there. Had even a basket become too heavy for her to carry? Of course, she wouldn't ask for help. But surely someone going by in a wagon could take her few tradable things to the store.

As her mother had always quoted, "Pride goeth before a fall." And her aunt was certainly long on pride. Somehow Jesse wasn't surprised. *Must be a family trait.*

How could she phrase her question so she wouldn't get lambasted for interfering? "If . . . if you'd like me to, I could carry some cabbages and carrots to the store for you, on my horse, that is."

"That would be right nice. I reckon I can spare a few of each."

"What about one of those barrels of apples I saw down there?"

"Need a wagon for that."

"True, but the next time Meshach comes in, we could manage it."

"All right, but you must take some of the things with you too. I'm sure you could use them."

"I will. Now, what would you like me to bring back?"

"Oh, flour, sugar, lard—"

"Beans?"

"No. Got plenty of them. How I would dearly love a cup of tea."

"You have dried beans?"

"Of course. Leather britches and dried shelled. You take a basket on down to the cellar and bring us up a potato or two and a mess of leather britches along with carrots and a turnip. Then fill a gunnysack to take to the store." With every word, Agatha's energy returned and her voice resumed more of its normal commanding air.

With all that food in store, why was the old lady fading away as she appeared to be? Was she ailing and not mentioning it?

"Oh, and go by the post office too, if you would. Just think how pleasant dinner would be if we heard from Richmond."

Jesselynn hadn't planned on staying for dinner, but what could she say? She took a gunnysack from a hook by the back door and went out around the house to the cellar doors. She shoved up the rusty hatch and, bending over, pulled one of the angled doors upright to lean it against the post set for that express purpose. "I bet she can't even open these doors. I should have thought of that and brought more into the house for her. Can't believe she's growing weak so quickly." Jesselynn continued muttering as she made her way down the six rock steps onto the dirt floor of the cellar. While the flat rocks laid a path to the bins, water from the winter rains had been seeping in already and turned most of the floor to mush. Someone at least had had the foresight to build the bins on raised dirt and put logs beneath the apple barrels. The bags of snap beans dried whole with two on a stem to resemble britches and the other dried vegetables hung from nails pounded into the floor joists above.

Aunt Agatha might be frail looking now, but she and her friend Lettie Copsewald had worked like Trojans during the summer and fall to get all this set by. Jesselynn chose an assortment of carrots, turnips, parsnips, and ruta-bagas, plus some potatoes and two heads of cabbage for her bag for the store, then placed some of each in the basket for upstairs. She'd get more to take out to the cave when she returned from her errands.

The clouds hung sullen gray as she mounted Sunshine for the ride to the store. She might be better walking, but time was running out if she was to be back to camp by dark. The new cave they had located after leaving the one where Dunlivey found them was south and west of Springfield, several miles farther from town. Not anywhere near as convenient as the first had been, especially if they needed to walk in all the time now.

The mule had been more of a loss than she'd anticipated.

With thoughts chasing through her mind like dogs after cats, she still remem-bered to stay off the main streets. No sense letting herself in for more trouble, although that hadn't helped earlier. *"Greet your father for me."* Not likely. Her snort made Sunshine flick her ears and pick up the pace.

Once at the store, she wasted a couple of minutes talking with Lawrence Dummont, the proprietor. "Just as I thought," Jesselynn said, expelling a sigh that had been building for some time. "So you're saying my aunt could put it on account if she wanted to?"

"I wouldn't let that dear old lady starve. What kind of a man do you think I am?"

Jesselynn blinked at the "dear old lady."

" 'Specially after all she's been through. But without her or someone telling me, how was I to know?"

"You have a point there, Mr. Dummont." Jesselynn set her sack of produce on the counter. "So you would be willing to trade, then?"

"Of course." He opened the bag, peered in, and set it to the side, nodding at Jesselynn. "Now, what can I git you?"

Jesselynn gave him her list and waited while he measured things out. She ambled around the store looking longingly at the boots, the bolts of cloth, the ready-made pants and shirts for the two little boys in camp, her brother Thaddeus Joshua—or Joshwa, as he said it—and Sammy, the baby they'd found beside a dead slave woman. Wouldn't Ophelia love that bolt of red-and-white check cotton? But they'd have to get by. She fingered the money in her pocket.

At the counter as she was putting her supplies back in the tow sack, she remembered to ask, "Could you use a barrel of apples?"

"Sure enough. Those soldiers love to come buy apples, or anything fresh for that matter. According to them, army food gets pretty monotonous."

"Well, at least they get enough to fill their bellies. You wouldn't know anyone who had a gallon or so of milk for sale?"

"Not right offhand. You might ask at the farms outside of town." He wrote some numbers in his ledger. "Now you tell Miz Highwood to come in anytime. She has all the credit she needs right here on the books."

"Thank you kindly, Mr. Dummont. I'll find a way to pay you somehow."

"Don't make you no nevermind. Between God and Miz Dummont, I'd suffer in both lives if I didn't help out where I could."

Jesselynn debated leaving her horse tied beside the store but decided that was more dangerous than riding her the two blocks to the post office.

The city bustled with what looked to Jesselynn like twice as much wagon traffic as usual, army personnel and the civilians who accompanied their men-folk in the army. If nothing else, the war was a boon to places like Springfield, bringing increased business on all sides. Unless, of course, a battle was fought over it.

Jesselynn trotted up the steps and inside the brick building with a sign reading *United States Post Office.* She crossed to the counter, her heels clicking on the marble floor. "Good day. Do you have any mail for Mrs. Hiram Highwood or Master Jesse Highwood?"

"Let me see." The man with the green eyeshade and arm bands holding back the sleeves of his white shirt turned and sorted through the boxes along the wall. He returned with three envelopes. "One for Miz Highwood and two for you. You are Jesse Highwood, right?"

"Yes, sir. Thank you, sir." Jesselynn looked at the handwriting on her two letters and could have jumped for joy. One from her sister Louisa in Richmond and one from Lucinda, the head of the household help at Twin Oaks. Cavendar Dunlivey had lied when he said slavers got all those left at Twin Oaks. No longer could she call her people slaves, since she herself had signed the manumission papers in her father's name, but what other title could she give them? Perhaps if Lucinda and the others were still on the home place, Dunlivey had also lied about burning the farm to the ground. Letters from home! No longer did she notice the lowering gray clouds.

Not even attempting to hide her smile, she tucked the letters in her shirt pocket and mounted her horse. No sense loitering here in plain view while she read the letters. She could do that at the house. "Come on, Sunshine, let's hustle on back."

―――――

"A letter for you," Jesse called to Aunt Agatha when she entered the kitchen.

"Coming." The answer floated down from upstairs.

Jesselynn moved the teakettle to the hottest part of the stove. She picked up the lid on the stewpot and savored the fragrance of rabbit stew. The wild roots and herbs they'd been using at the cave in no way measured up to good garden fare.

"Where's your teapot?" she asked as Agatha entered the kitchen, several pieces of clothing slung over her arm.

Agatha pointed to a high shelf in the cupboard and laid the garments across the back of a chair. Bright pink spots on her cheeks, most likely from the exertion of bending over trunks or boxes, made her look more like herself. "Why?"

"Because Mr. Dummont included a packet of tea with the groceries. He said you must be in terrible need of a cup of tea by now." A little fib to make her aunt feel better paled against the lies she was forced to tell on a regular basis.

"Oh, he is such a good man." Agatha gazed at the brown paper packet with shining eyes.

Then why are you so tied in knots about asking for flour and other things you can't live without? But Jesselynn kept the thought to herself and slit open the letter from Lucinda.

Dear Marse Jesse,

I am sorry I did not write before, but things have been very bad here. Dey burned de house and barns right after you left and cotched many of de field hands to sell to de slavers. Some of us got out and hid in de woods for weeks, too 'fraid to come out. Dere no place to dry de t'bacca, but we go ask Marse Marsh if we can use his barn. He say yes, so if dere be some crop, he sell it for us. When you come home, Marse Jesse? We made a shack out of logs so we be out of de rain. Joseph hurt him back. You write us by Marse Marsh. He bring it here. God bless you. Come home soon.

Lucinda

Jesselynn closed her eyes. So Dunlivey *had* burned Twin Oaks and sold most of the freed slaves. Her gorge rose, threatening to choke her.

She opened her eyes to see her aunt staring at the sheet of paper she held, her face as stark white as the letter.

Chapter Two

"*Aunt, what is it?* What is wrong?"

Agatha waved the paper and blinked her eyes as if she were having trouble seeing.

Jesselynn dropped to her knees beside her aunt and took the lady's shaking hands in her own. They were icy and quivering like cottonwood leaves in the breeze. "Please tell me. What is wrong?"

The old woman seemed to shrink within herself right before Jesselynn's eyes, aging years in moments. She handed Jesselynn the letter, mouthing words but unable to speak.

Was she having a fit? Jesselynn had once seen an old man sink to the ground and start twitching, then go slack, one side of his face looking like candle wax in the heat as it melted to one side.

Agatha pointed to the paper. "Read it," she croaked.

Jesselynn scanned the precise legal writing, then went back to read the entire letter. Her heart took up a staccato beat. "They can't just throw you out!"

"But of course they can. I thought dear Lettie had paid the taxes last year, but obviously she didn't. I hold no title to the house since she died. I just lived here at the gracious invitation from a friend to a widow in dire straits. And even if I did have the title, I have no money for taxes. Appears to me I shall be homeless before the robins nest."

Jesselynn studied her aunt. The woman was not complaining, just stating facts as she saw them, and at the moment, Jesse saw no other alternative either. "Is there someone else you can live with?"

Aunt Agatha shrugged, a brief motion that barely raised her thin shoulders. "I shall ask around. I am strong. I can be a good companion to someone who is more advanced in years than I."

Strong? It wouldn't need a brisk breeze to blow you over. Had her aunt no idea that she had slipped so far downhill in the last few weeks? Did she never look in a mirror? What had she done with a disposition more than slightly verging on that of a sergeant or a general, a woman sure of her place in Southern semi-aristocracy? Had it slid away with the disappearing flesh?

War! And man's ego! They are responsible for this. Both Father and Uncle Hiram thought they could help save the South. Now their families have to pay for their gallantry by being left with nothing. Aunt Agatha should be able to go to Twin Oaks, where relatives would take her in. But her relatives are no longer there. They're now hoping to be taken in themselves. It's always the war! The horrid war! She had to clamp her teeth together to keep the anger from spewing forth.

Jesselynn folded the paper and inserted it back in the envelope. "Perhaps the new owner would let you continue to live here."

"Perhaps. If I were able to pay for the privilege. But look around. This place is falling down around its posts. The roof leaks. The walls are riddled with vermin and dry rot. The best thing to do is burn or bury it." Her face sagged, sorrow seeping out of her pores. "Not like our home place. Ah, Jesselynn, Oakfield was beautiful. Much like Twin Oaks, since Hiram always thought of that as home." Her eyes sharpened. "But the dirty deserters stole what horses we had left, burned our farm, and even knocked over Hiram's gravestone. There was nothin' left."

Except the slaves you sold like they were cattle. Jesselynn still couldn't understand her aunt doing such a thing. Why, she could no more have sold Twin Oaks's slaves than cut off her right hand. That was why she had freed them all before she left home, not that it saved those Dunlivey had caught after burning Twin Oaks. Burning seemed to be a favorite tool of ruffians, deserters, and Yankee soldiers. That and lynching.

The thought made her shudder. Benjamin had come so close to being hanged. The freed slaves she had with her were more her family now than her two sisters whom she'd sent to Richmond to keep safe. Danger and hardship had a tendency to draw folks close together no matter what color their skin.

You'll have to invite Aunt Agatha to come west with you. The thought, more like her mother speaking across the reaches between heaven and earth, made her catch her breath. No. No way would she take this weak and trembling woman with them, nor the whaleboned one she'd known when they arrived in Springfield in November. Either way, there was no room in the wagon for Aunt Agatha.

"I need to be going so I can get back to the cave before dark."

Agatha nodded. "Make sure you get yourself plenty of the store from the cellar. Hate to see any of it go to waste." She motioned toward the stove. "I wouldn't turn down any meat you might want to bring in. And wood."

"I'll see to it, Aunt Agatha. But with all the soldiers in town, using the horses to pull the wagon is taking a big chance. Since the mule was stolen . . ." She shrugged. "After coming all this way, I sure don't want to lose them now."

"No, no. Of course not." The older woman traced the outline of the envelope lying on the table. "Think I'll ask Mr. Dummont at the store if he would like to come by and help himself. That would allow me to purchase more of the things I need. Unless I find another place to live, of course. I would want to take some with me."

"I reckon." Jesselynn lifted her coat from the hook on the wall. "I'll be back when I can. You take care now, you hear?"

"Oh, I will. Give that little Thaddeus a kiss for me. I sure do want to see that baby before he's a grown man." Agatha tipped her head sideways to make it easy for Jesselynn to drop a kiss on her cheek.

"I'll try to bring him in. One day Meshach may come and bring you back to our camp. If you would like to visit, that is." Jesselynn could hear her mother extending an invitation in the same tone of voice. What on earth was the matter with her for even suggesting such a thing?

"We'll see." The arch of her eyebrow was more reminiscent of the *real* Aunt Agatha than anything else Jesselynn had seen since she arrived.

With two tow sacks full of vegetables, both dried and fresh, and apples on top for the pure joy of eating, she headed on out of town, keeping a sharp lookout for any more soldiers. Perhaps they were all back at camp by now. If that were the case, then she or Meshach should come and go just about twilight. She'd heard from home. Remembering made the ride seem like minutes. Carrie married. Zachary still alive. Life went on even here.

Darkness hid the land by the time she drew near to the cave. She whistled the three notes they'd agreed upon for a signal, and when one answered, she rode down the bank to where the mouth of the cave was fairly well hidden by a trio of maple trees and brush. They had stumbled on it quite by accident. Of course Meshach said God had led them to their new home, but she had only nodded. Benjamin found it when he'd skidded down the bank on the way to the creek that meandered along the bottom of the hollow. Ridges and hollows, as the locals called the terrain, the Ozark Mountains without any peaks.

"What take you so long?" Meshach met her at the cave entrance. A big man in every way, long legs, broad shoulders, hands big enough to hoist a tobacco hogshead yet gentle enough to comfort little Sammy who clung to his leg like a bloodsucker. Meshach bent down and swung the toddler up to his shoulder. Since they'd found Sammy, he had learned to walk. He was perhaps too weak before, but it didn't take him long to totter after Thaddeus once his legs grew strong enough. Sammy tangled his little fingers in Meshach's kinky black hair, the better to hold on. Meshach had the little one's leg in a firm grip should he start to topple off.

Jesselynn swung to the ground and untied the tow sacks, so heavy that one was beginning to fray at the bottom. "Here. This should help our larder, and we each get a big red apple for dessert."

"Good. Daniel done brung in another deer. 'Phelia settin' strips to dry already. Fried liver for supper." He flinched as the little one on his shoulder yanked on a handful of hair.

"Where's Thaddeus?"

"Down de creek with Daniel, fishin'. Benjamin still grazin' de horses."

"Good." They each picked up a sack and started for the cave. At the same time Meshach swung Sammy down from his shoulder and under his arm like a tied-off sack of grain. Meshach's hair grazed the roof within the cave, but he had to duck to enter. With the horses roped off at the back where the ceiling was higher and the fire kept burning near the front, they were safe from wild animals as well as the elements. Curious humans were another matter; thus, they took great care not to make visible trails to the cave and the surrounding area.

"Oh, Meshach, Ophelia, I got so excited about the apples I almost forgot to tell you. We have a letter from Lucinda and one from Louisa, which I forgot to read to Aunt Agatha. For shame."

"Glory be to God. Dey's safe." Meshach spoke as reverently as if they were in front of the altar in church.

Ophelia clasped her hands to her chest and rocked back and forth. "Thank you, Jesus. Thank you, Jesus." She opened her eyes again and shook her head. "You read to us right now?"

"You don't want to wait for the others?"

"Kin read it again. Dat man lied to us."

"If you mean Dunlivey, not quite." Even the mention of his name made her stomach churn. Cavendar Dunlivey had been pure evil wearing men's britches. At least she hoped and prayed he was gone. When they left him gutshot in the clearing, she'd promised to send a doctor back, and Meshach had done so, but there had been no word of his demise. But no one lived being gutshot.

Without a miracle.

The vivid memory brought burning anger. She hoped he'd died a very slow and extremely painful death. A quick death was far too merciful for the likes of him. Her mother would say she had to forgive Dunlivey in spite of the atrocities he had committed. But she wasn't ready to grant forgiveness to a man who could do such awful things. Would she ever?

As she read the letters in the light of the fire, she kept one ear tuned for the jabbering of one little boy and the teasing of the two young black men who cared for the "young marse."

"Praise de Lawd, Marse Zachary still alive and gettin' well. And Missy Carrie Mae done got married." Tears coursing down her cheeks, Ophelia used Meshach's broad chest for a towel.

Tell me these people don't care for us as much as we care for them. They are not my slaves, but my family. Jesselynn wiped the tears from her own eyes and sniffed. She still had a brother—not a whole one, but a live one nevertheless. Restoring Twin Oaks would be up to him. Saving the Thoroughbreds was even more important to her now. They had to have something left to start over with.

Hearing the fluted call of a mockingbird, Meshach loosened his hold on Ophelia and stepped to the mouth of the cave to answer. Within moments Thaddeus tore into the cave, a string of two small fish hanging from one hand. "I catch fish. See, Jesse, my fish."

Jesselynn held them up and glanced over to see a look of delight on Benjamin's face.

"He done caught dem hisself." He laid a hand on Thaddeus's curly head. "He be good fisherman."

"Those are some fish." She reached over, grabbed Thaddeus around his middle, and pulled him right into her arms so she could hug and kiss him. He made a face and wriggled to escape.

"Show 'Phelia."

"Good fish. Good boy." Ophelia admired his two fish and glanced up to see the string that Daniel held. "Oh, hallelujah days! We have fish and fried potatoes for supper."

"And cooked cabbage with onion and a bit of dried venison." Jesselynn wrapped her arms around her middle. "My belly is dancing up and down."

"Read to dem." Meshach had to shout to be heard above the chatter.

"We got two letters today, finally one from Lucinda and one from Louisa. Which do you want first?"

"Lucinda," the two said in unison.

Jesselynn read the letter again amid tears and cries of "praise de Lawd" and "thank you, Jesus" as if no one had heard it before.

"Dey's alive." Benjamin cleared his throat and turned away to wipe his eyes. "Smoke bad in here."

"I know." Jesselynn ducked to hide her smile. Why shouldn't he cry? The rest of them surely had been.

"Someone still live at Twin Oaks." Daniel spoke reverently, much like Meshach had. While the buildings were gone, their family was still there, at least part of them.

"Read de next one—please."

Jesselynn did so, receiving many of the same reactions. Who could accept it all? Such wonderful news in both missives!

"De Lawd giveth and de Lawd taketh away, blessed be de name of de Lawd." Meshach's deep, rich voice rolled around the cave almost like music.

As the others agreed, Jesselynn wanted to cover her ears. The Lord did too much taking, far as she was concerned. "To think Louisa had been caring for this poor soldier, not knowing that he was really her brother, and now he's back at Aunt Sylvania's along with other wounded." She shook her head. "Amazing."

"De Lawd's doing." Meshach managed to have the last word.

Supper that night was a grand affair, and when she brought out the apples for dessert, the only sound to be heard in the cave was the crunch of teeth into crisp apples and the slurping of juice.

"Ah, me. That some supper. We save de liver for tomorrow."

"With more potatoes." Jesselynn never would have dreamed she could be so ecstatic over apples and potatoes.

Jane Ellen, another one of the additions to her family since the trip began, started getting the boys ready for bed. While she still spoke little, she no longer had to be fed and walked, as she had after her brother's death. Now she took on her share, helping Ophelia with the cooking and the smoking of meat. She had volunteered to take over tanning the hides so they would have one hide for a blanket and the other to make moccasins for Daniel and the two little ones. Thaddeus had outgrown his boots and now wore thong-laced foot coverings, more makeshift than moccasin. She'd make his with the hair side in and an extra pad for the sole. That should keep Thaddeus's feet warm. They were fortunate the winter had been mild so far.

They all heard the noise at the same time and froze to listen better. Benjamin faded out the opening of the cave like a wisp of smoke.

Chapter Three

❧❧

The men were arguing again.

To keep from eavesdropping, Louisa Highwood strolled between the rose-bushes in her aunt Sylvania's garden, the garden she and her wounded men from the army hospital had brought back into its former beauty. Golden daffodils nodded a greeting, and primroses glowed under the magnolia as though an artist had dabbed his brush in bright yellows, reds, and pinks, then spattered the colors in happy profusion. Red and pink azaleas bordered the fence and the house, inviting her to cut a bouquet or two for the rooms inside, which she did, filling the flat basket she carried for just that purpose.

Cutting and arranging flowers always brought her a time of peace. As usual, the Lord met her there too.

I know you know where he is. I just wish you would give me some indication. If my lieutenant is alive, please bring him back. If he's already gone home to be with you . . . The tears blurred the branch of azalea, so she snipped thin air, grazing her finger enough she was sure she'd see blood. "That was close." She blinked and sniffed, settling her clippers in the basket in order to blow her nose on the hanky she always carried in her apron pocket.

The crinkle of paper reminded her that Lieutenant Gilbert Lessling's last letter lay hidden close at hand. Reading the letter brought his face vividly to her and made praying for him easier. If she could see him so clearly, he surely must still be on this earth.

At least that's what she told herself. She sniffed again and, putting the hanky back in her pocket, smoothed the white apron over her sky blue dimity dress. Gilbert had said he liked her in blue. It brought out the blue of her eyes and made her hair look even more golden. Since Gilbert rarely spent a portion of his few words on compliments, she hoarded every one of them.

"Miss Louisa, breakfast ready."

"I'm coming." She cut a couple more branches and with a last sigh turned back to the house. Since her brother Zachary had come home, he forbade her volunteering on the ward at the hospital, so her day stretched long in front of her. Thinking of his stubbornness tightened her jaw. "I'll have it out with him again. Just because we have three extra men here doesn't mean I don't have time for those poor miserable men at the hospital. Such selfishness. Mama would take a willow switch to him if she were here."

"You say sumpin', Miss Louisa?" Abby looked up from forking ham slices onto a platter.

"Just muttering." Louisa set her basket on the bench and, picking up the full bucket of water, poured some into another. Then sticking the branches in water, she wiped her hands on her apron. "There, that'll hold them until I get back to fill the vases. Let me take that in, and you bring the rest of the food."

She bumped the swinging door to the dining room open with her backside and entered the room where four recovering Confederate soldiers cut off their discussion as if blowing out a candle, even to the smoke still rising on the air.

One more reason to want to tear into her brother. Before he came home, she'd been privy to whatever discussions had gone on in this house, and there'd been plenty. "Carry on, gentlemen. My ears aren't that tender." Instead of slamming the platter down, which was what she felt like doing, she set it gently and with a pleasant smile. The fury she would reserve for Zachary. Holy fury seemed appropriate at the moment.

"And a fine good morning to you too, dear Louisa." Zachary Highwood winked at her with his remaining eye, an act made even more a caricature by the scar that ran from above his eyebrow, under the black patch worn to cover the missing eye, and down to his jaw. Only a man made of pure dash could carry off such an act—and Zachary did. While she wanted to rant and rave, as usual he made her laugh.

The sound released the other men from their frozen stances, and chuckles made their way around the table.

"Now, that's much better." Aunt Sylvania, in a gray morning dress and a lace cap on her head, set the silver coffeepot in front of her place and took her seat. "Who would like to say the grace this morning?" She smiled at each of the men. "Sergeant Blackstone, it must be about your turn."

Louisa bowed her head, the desire to see the flush running up the good sergeant's neck nearly irresistible. He had come so far in the last weeks that soon he would be ready for discharge. To this point at least, none of those missing a limb had been sent back to battle, not that they weren't willing, if not ready.

"Bless us oh Lord for these gifts we are about to receive, in thy precious name amen." The words ran together in his mumbled haste.

The amen echoed around the table, and they each reached for the platter nearest them to pass on to the next.

Louisa, sitting next to her brother, who still liked to tease her about calling herself *Missus* Zachary Highwood, since that was the only way she could work at the hospital, delivered a quick kick to his ankle. *That ought to get his attention.* She'd learned the practice years earlier at the family table at Twin Oaks.

If she hadn't been watching, she would have missed his flinch. His chuckle said he knew what was bothering her.

"No, you cannot return to work at the hospital." He hid his remark behind the biscuit basket.

"Whyever not?" She kept her smile in place and spoke through her teeth, another skill from long ago when they didn't want their mother to know what was going on.

"You know why not." He did the same.

"Zachary, dear, would you please pass the ham?" Aunt Sylvania arched an eyebrow.

Had she figured out their little trick? Louisa turned to the silent man on her other side. "Would you like me to cut your meat? Just this time, of course." Trying to save face for those missing a hand until they got the hang of it had become her specialty. She kept her whisper low.

His brief nod was her only answer. She had yet to get him to converse with her, but she didn't let a tide of silence stop her.

"The garden is beautiful this morning, Lieutenant Jones. Those pansies you transplanted yesterday were all smiling up at me." While she chatted, she buttered a biscuit, spread honey on it, and cut up the slice of ham. "I surely do appreciate all the work you fellows are doing out there. Miss Julie next door is hoping y'all will come on over to her house and get at the weeds there. Shame how our gardens have nearly gone wild since the war. I'm hoping to get the potatoes and peas in the ground today. Wouldn't fresh peas be the perfect thing?"

She felt like a ninny running on like that, but she had learned that the tone of her voice and her ready smile accomplished far more than silences and frowns. These men needed a taste of home, and she aimed to supply it.

With breakfast finished, they spent the next hour exercising injured muscles, retraining the remaining limbs, or applying new dressings, all the while listening to *The Merchant of Venice* being read by none other than Aunt Sylvania herself.

"I have work to do here today, so I'll not join you in the garden." Zachary stopped at her shoulder as she gathered up her supplies. He'd grown adept at using one crutch now that he had fashioned a short peg to strap to the remaining stump of his right leg. Even though the stump came up raw at times, he refused to hop and hobble any longer.

"I'll be back." She smiled brightly for the benefit of the others.

"I'm sure you will."

Once she had the men teaming up to plant or dig, she headed back to the house, smiling at Reuben, who had set one of the men to stirring the sheets boiling over the outside fire. The laundry was never ending, just like the cooking and cleaning.

"I'm on my way to church," Aunt Sylvania said, pulling on her much-darned gloves. "I do wish you would come. There are never enough hands to roll bandages or sew uniforms." She set her hat at the proper angle and picked up her basket.

"Perhaps later." They both knew those words were a fabrication. Louisa had chosen to attend the Friends Church, much to her aunt's consternation. "Where is Zachary?"

"At his desk."

"Have a good gossip while you work." She kissed her aunt's cheek, closing the front door behind her. As if caring for the men the way they did wasn't enough. She stopped in the arched doorway to watch her brother laboriously writing a letter with his left hand. While his penmanship was at least legible now, she knew how he hated the ink blots that at times disfigured the pages. Who could he be writing to with such intensity?

"The answer is no," Zachary said before Louisa could even ask the question.

"But, Zachary . . ." She clenched both hands and teeth.

"It is bad enough that you are working like a fishwife here." He set the quill down and capped the ink.

"Who are you writing to?" Changing the subject might help.

"A friend."

His short answer did more to arouse her curiosity than anything else.

"Oh? Male or female?" She stopped behind him, trying to get a peek at the salutation. He covered it with his arm, leaning back nonchalantly as if the covering was not intentional.

She knew differently.

"Actually, dear wife, it's none of your business." The emphasis on *wife* warned her someone was behind her. She dropped a kiss on the top of his head for good measure.

"I'd write it for you if you asked nicely." Keeping a hand on his shoulder, she turned enough to see a strange man standing in the archway she'd so recently vacated. "Can I help you, sir?"

"No." Zachary answered for the man. "He came to see me. Could you bring us some lemonade, please, dear?" At the same time Zachary gestured to the chair by the desk. "Have a seat, soldier."

"Of course, *darling.* I'll be right back." He'd already drunk enough lemonade to float a ship was her thought as she left the room. Once out of sight, she paused long enough to hear one word—morphine.

Chapter Four

Springfield, Missouri

"Sojers on de road."

"Blue or gray?" Jesselynn knew when they took this cave so near the Wire Road that there could be problems, but no other caves they'd seen had been so perfectly fitted for their needs.

"Confederate."

Benjamin, at twenty years old, had seen war before when he'd accompanied Jesselynn's father, Major Joshua Highwood, off to battle. Thanks to Benjamin's fortitude, he had brought the major home to die. He'd become their scout, since he could move through a thicket like a puff of smoke and run for miles without dropping.

"Many sojers. All on horses. With light cannon."

"Oh, Lord, if they attack the garrison at Springfield, what will happen to Aunt Agatha? Her house isn't four blocks from the camp, since they took over the middle of the town."

"Plenty bluebellies dere. Many guns." Meshach had often been looking for work and gotten to know the town pretty well. "Dey marchin' all de time."

"Dey ask we want to join up." Benjamin shook his head, the light of laughter in his eyes caught by the firelight. "I'se done wid de war."

"I wish we *all* were done 'wid de war.' " Jesselynn couldn't resist teasing him. She and Benjamin had grown up together. He had been a member of the household staff. When he went off to war with her father, sorrow struck her almost as badly as when her brothers had gone. The stories she'd heard of the ways some Southern planters mistreated their slaves bore no relation to the way her father had run Twin Oaks.

So what do I do about Aunt Agatha? Jesselynn looked around the cave. The boys and Jane Ellen were sound asleep against the wall nearest the fire. The six horses were roped off in the rear of the cave. A long, low fire lay between a tunnel of racks full of drying venison, and a salted haunch hung just above the racks to smoke as a ham. Meshach had used vines to tie cut saplings and branches together into shelves for their few household things, and their foodstuffs were stored in the wooden boxes they'd brought from Twin Oaks. The wagon was hidden in a thicket up on the edge of the ridge. Pegs driven into cracks in the limestone walls held the harnesses and other tack.

There was just no more room.

And Aunt Agatha was an old woman, an opinionated old woman.

"You want I should go see to the road again?" Benjamin hunkered down beside her.

Jesselynn shook her head. "No sense to it. Since the mouth of our cave faces east, there's no chance of someone seeing our light. Least not from the road. And a scout might just happen upon you. They'd shoot you for spyin'."

"Dey not catch me." His tone carried no hint of bravado, just stated a simple fact.

While Jesselynn believed him, she wasn't about to take a chance. "Someone will have to go check on Aunt Agatha in the morning." She had a pretty good idea who that *someone* was going to be.

———

A snort from one of the horses woke her from a dream-riddled sleep that had caused her to miss out on any rest. She sat up, listening so hard her breathing seemed louder than a windstorm. Nothing. One of the men mumbled in his sleep. Someone else snored gently. Normal night sounds. Soundlessly she laid aside her quilt, picked up her boots from under the edge of her bedding, and, carrying them, made her way to the mouth of the cave. Overhead the stars hung close in an azure velvet sky, but off to the east, the sky had lightened only enough to be noticeable.

She sucked in a breath of air not redolent with drying meat and horse dung and sat down on a rock to pull on her boots. Even the birds had yet to realize the new day was almost upon them. Quiet and solitude, two things that had been seriously lacking from her life for some time. She struck off to relieve herself and gather wood on the way back. They were having to range farther and farther for wood for the fires, since they'd now been in this cave nigh onto two months.

Time they looked for another. They had to take the horses farther to pasture too. If only she dared start for Independence now while the roads were still firm. Once the spring rains began, they wouldn't make anywhere near ten miles a day. But if they left now, they'd have to find someplace to live out there until the wagon trains heading west started forming up. From what she'd heard, caves like those around this area were next to nonexistent. About like their money.

Besides, she couldn't start until after the mares foaled and the babies grew strong enough to handle the trip.

As the sky lightened, the birds took up their chorus. A cardinal sang his lovely aria, and a jay scolded her for trespassing. Off in the distance a dog barked. If an army the size Benjamin saw had passed through, the morning woods had little to say about it. Surely if Springfield was under attack, they would hear the guns, at least from up on the ridge.

She checked Daniel's snare line, tied two dead rabbits to her belt, and kept on walking. How were they to get enough money for the journey? Selling Chess would break Thaddy's heart, but the horse was fully recovered now from his gunshot wound and would bring them over a hundred dollars, maybe even as much as a hundred fifty. She'd hoped to use him to help pull the wagon and ease up on the mares awhile, then sell him in Independence.

Picking up wood as she went, she circled back to the cave, dragging a couple of big branches she'd lashed together and overlaid with other wood on the top. The downed tree she'd located would make up quite a stack of firewood.

Meshach met her at the cave's entrance. "You all right?"

"Just woke up and couldn't go back to sleep." She dropped her load. "I found a downed tree that looks to be good and dry but not yet rotted." She pointed to the southeast. "Over there. I can locate it again."

Not that the woods were impenetrable. Up on the ridges lay prairie with the trees in the hollows and along the creeks and lakes. At this time of year, instead of green, the land wore an orange garment of grasses, dead clinging leaves, and underbrush. The rising sun gilded the edges and lightened the tree trunks on the eastern face, darkening the bark on the other. Staring south she thought about Sergeant Barnabas White, the Confederate soldier they'd nursed back to health so he could return to his home in Arkansas. He was minus part of a leg but hale otherwise.

He'd promised to write. But there'd been no letters from Arkansas, so it was a good thing she'd not given her heart away a second time. The first time seemed so long ago, in another lifetime, another world. Now thoughts of John Follett were more a friendly haze than a heart-tearing ache.

The morning seemed ripe for reflection.

"I take de horses for to drink and to graze." Meshach stretched, the muscles bulging under the fabric of his shirt. "Den go to town. Check on work and Miss Agatha?"

"Have you eaten?"

"Got me biscuits and dried deer. Be enough." He patted his pocket.

Jesselynn untied the two rabbits from her belt. "I checked the snares." She held them up by their ears. "You take these in to Aunt Agatha. I'll gut them first. Bring back the skins." Relief that Meshach had volunteered to go to town made her want to tap her feet and whistle a tune. While she set about dressing the rabbits, Meshach went into the cave and returned with two horses. Ahab, their oldest Thoroughbred stallion, snorted and pranced in the brisk air. No matter how matted and dirty they kept him, when he stood at attention like this, there was no doubt of his lineage.

Jesselynn sighed. Good breeding showed no matter what. Within moments Meshach had all six horses attached to a long line so that one man could lead them and set off down the hill to the creek.

Silence settled around Jesselynn again. She swiftly gutted the two rabbits and, tying their back feet together, hung them over a tree limb to keep them out of the dirt. The entrails she threw off into a thicket for the wild critters to eat. No sense wasting them.

The children were still sleeping, but Ophelia had cornmeal sizzling in a skillet over the coals. She'd made up the mush the night before and set it to cool in a pan, then sliced it for frying. From the looks of it, she'd mixed in meat of some kind. The other pan held the four smaller fish. Daniel and Benjamin were just cleaning their plates.

"Looks good. We haven't had fried mush for too long."

"Din't have no cornmeal." Ophelia used her apron as a potholder and pulled one of the frying pans back to cooler coals. "You ready for eatin'?"

"Yes, thank you."

Benjamin and Daniel cuffed each other on the way out of the cave, their laughter echoing a friendly sound, like home.

"Jesse?" The sleepy voice came from the pallets. "I got to go."

"I'll take you." Jane Ellen rolled to her feet, shook out her shift, and reached down for Thaddeus's hand. Since her brother had died from bad lungs and she'd finally returned to the real world from wandering lost somewhere in her mind, she pretty much took care of the two boys. Their antics seemed to help her through her grieving.

"I want Jesse."

"Come here, baby, and give me a hug, then you go on with Jane Ellen. I've already been outside, and I'm fixin' to eat right about now."

"Not baby. Sammy baby." Thaddeus rubbed his eyes with his fists as barefooted he crossed the sandy floor of the cave. Jesselynn gave him a quick hug and a peck on the cheek because his squirming meant he needed to go *now*. Jane Ellen swooped him up in her arms and trotted with him, giggles and all, out the entrance.

The quiet of the cave let Jesse's thoughts take over again. *What do I do about Aunt Agatha?* She took her plate and wandered to the cave mouth, listening for gunfire. She heard only normal sounds. While her mind said that was good, her heart cautioned that something was going to happen. Not if, but *when*.

As soon as she finished eating and Daniel and Benjamin had brought in a stockpile of cut wood, Jesselynn sent Benjamin off to scout Wire Road and on north toward the town of Springfield. Ozark lay closer, but the post office and her aunt were in Springfield.

"Now, you be careful. Don't take any chances, you hear?"

He nodded. "You wants me to see 'bout Miz Highwood?"

"No, just find out what you can. Meshach will go in later." But it all depended on whether or not there had been a battle. Not knowing kept her stomach roiling.

Daniel went fishing and setting a trotline, Jane Ellen entertained the little ones, and Jesselynn and Ophelia sliced more strips of the venison and hung them to dry. While she sharpened her knife, Jesselynn tried to figure out when and where the troops would attack. And why now? Did the Confederates hope to take over Missouri? Why couldn't they just stay down in Arkansas?

But when Benjamin returned with reports of seeing nothing but that plenty of soldiers had passed, she took in a deep breath and decided everyone should stay at the cave. If only she knew what was happening!

As the next day passed, they could feel the temperature dropping by the hour. Everyone pitched in to sew rabbit skins together for warm shirts, mittens, and moccasins for the two little boys. Jane Ellen was another matter. Taking the softest deerskins, Jesselynn fashioned them into a jerkin that reached her knees. Meshach and Ophelia stitched more skins into over-the-knee moccasins, wrapped with a thong for the young woman.

Jane Ellen put on her new clothes and turned in place, running her hands down the soft leather. "I never had nothin' so purty in all my life. You sure this is for me?" Her eyes and face shone like a mirror reflecting the sun.

"Doesn't look like it would fit anyone else." Jesselynn pulled a rabbit-skin shirt over Thaddeus's head. "Okay, little man, how does that feel?"

"Warm." He rubbed his cheek on the fur-side-up collar. "Soft." He flung his arms around Jesselynn's neck. "Thank you."

"Why, you are most welcome. And who's been teaching you to say thank you?" *You should have been, you ninny. What kind of manners is he growing up with? Mother would be so ashamed.*

Thaddy pointed at Jane Ellen, who stood clenching her hands together.

"I don' mean to be fo'ard or nothin'."

"Jane Ellen, I am so truly grateful for all the things you do around here. Why, child, what would we do without you?" Jesselynn knew she sounded exactly like her mother. Not that that was a bad thing, but it caught her by surprise nonetheless.

Two days later they heard cannon fire to the north of them.

Chapter Five

"Where you goin'?" Meshach gripped the reins under Chess's bit.

"I've got to see if Aunt Agatha is all right."

"You can't go now. Dey's still shootin'."

Jesselynn slumped forward in her saddle. She couldn't help but recognize the wisdom of his words, but she had the terrible feeling her aunt was in trouble and needed her.

"We go together on toward dark so we can sneak into de town."

But what if she is wounded and there's no one to help her? Jesselynn dismounted, feeling guilt like the weight of the heavens pressing her down. So many to take care of. How would she stand it if Aunt Agatha was forced to join them in the cave earlier than either dreamed?

Within herself she cursed the war and the men who thought war so glorious, including her brothers. Her father had done everything he could to keep Kentucky out of it, but hotter heads than his had prevailed.

The thought of the western prairies and Oregon was becoming more practical all the time. And more real. What started as Meshach's dream was rapidly becoming hers. Anything to get away from battles and skirmishes and soldiers of either gray or blue. If she never saw another uniform, it would be far too soon.

"Is Chess trained to harness yet?"

"Some. You want we take him and Dulcie to pull de wagon?"

"I think so." Jesselynn rubbed her forehead. "I don't know what I want." With her monthlies upon her again, she felt like crawling under her quilt and pulling it over her head. None of this thinking and worrying. She shivered in a blast of cold air blown from the north through the hollow, turning it into a wind tunnel.

The wind also brought the sound of artillery fire. She flinched every time a cannon fired. If they could hear the reports this far away, what was it like in town? One of the four small forts built throughout the city was only a few blocks from Agatha's home. Who was firing? Union or Confederate howitzers or both? While she'd never been in an area under siege, she'd seen the aftermath.

"Jesse. Up." Thaddeus reached his arms high as he begged. When she paid him no nevermind, distracted by another volley, he tugged on her pants leg.

Acting on habit and paying no attention to her actions, she swung him up into her arms and rocked from side to side. "Can anyone live through all that?"

"Jesse." Thaddeus swung to the side to look directly in her face, and when that didn't work, he put his hands on both her cheeks and turned her face his way.

"Stop that." She jerked away but melted instantly when his round blue eyes swam with tears. "Sorry, baby. Jesse is thinking of something else."

"Guns go boom."

"Yes, that they do." *And people die, and houses and stores are destroyed. Why can't they go fight out in the woods instead of in a town?* She had heard stories of how the fashionable people from Washington and other cities had taken picnic baskets out to sit on the bluffs and watch the fighting down below. In some cases retreating soldiers ran right over the spectators.

Sometime later Benjamin returned from a scouting trip, and after standing by the fire to warm himself for a bit, he turned to Meshach. "I found somethin' real interestin'."

"What you find?" Meshach kept working the deer hide, softening it so they could make clothing from it.

"Tracks of our mule."

Jesselynn looked up from her stitching. "Where?"

" 'Bout three miles south. I follow, cotch up, and watch. Dey got five niggers in chains."

"Slave traders!" Jesselynn hissed the word with pure venom. "The ones who beat Daniel."

"But why dey beat 'im and den try to lynch 'im?"

"Pure stupid mean, like Dunlivey. That's why." *What if these are Dunlivey's men? The ones who deserted him?* Jesselynn let her thoughts take off on this trail. Having the mule back would be a godsend. But having five extra mouths to feed would be tantamount to disaster.

"We get dem. I takes care of movin' dem on." Meshach looked up from studying his clasped hands. Sitting on the other side of the fire, his eyes shone white in the gloom.

"But they'll come lookin' for them."

"Maybe not."

"You'd . . ." Jesselynn gulped. Shooting in self-defense was one thing. Looking to murder was another. Yet how many people had this band murdered, lynched, or burned out? "But the Bible says, 'Thou shalt not kill.' "

"Bible also say, 'eye for an eye.' "

Here she was arguing with Meshach, using the Bible, all the while trying to convince herself that God didn't really matter. Or at least that He didn't care what happened in this brutal mess of man's own making. She shook her head. "I'll go with you."

"No." Meshach motioned to the two sleeping boys, to Jane Ellen and Ophelia. "Someone need take care of dem."

Jesselynn knew he meant if the three men didn't come back. The thought gave her a raging case of dry mouth. She set her sewing aside, rose, and got a drink out of the bucket of water. Standing, sipping the cold water, she studied the big black man across the cave. Gentle was always her first thought of him. She thought she knew him through and through.

"When?"

"Tonight."

"But you said we would go for Aunt Agatha." She was the mistress. She had to take control here.

"Yes. First town, den we go."

Five fugitive slaves and Aunt Agatha? But then, Aunt Agatha might be just fine, mostly frightened out of her wits by the shelling but cooking meals and reading her Bible, and . . . Jesselynn thought longingly of that quilt again. And her silent surrender to its comfort.

What if they didn't come back? What would she do?

"We come back, Marse Jesse. Don' you fear."

She shoved her hands in her pockets. "That's what Father said too, and Zachary and Adam and John and every other man I know. Meshach, they will do their living best to kill you. Don't doubt that for a minute."

"Not if dey don' hear us comin'." His words fell in a silence punctuated by Ophelia's sniffling and a log breaking in the fire. Sparks flew upward. Meshach stood. "I get de wagon ready. We start soon."

With cut firewood loaded in the wagon bed, they set off for town under gray skies and a chilling wind. They would either leave the firewood off for Aunt Agatha or take it to Mr. Dummont at the store in exchange for grain for the two mares. The closer the time for foaling, the better feeding they needed.

Jesselynn pulled her wool coat tighter around her shoulders. Now if she'd only made herself a cap of the deerskin, the wind wouldn't penetrate clear to her bones. They could see smoke on the horizon as soon as they topped the last ridge to the prairie.

As they drew closer, Jesselynn shuddered. From here it looked as if the entire town was afire. Surely they wouldn't torch Springfield. But within a mile or so, they could see the fires were separate, not a massive conflagration.

When Meshach drove into a yard that had a large open barn, she looked at him with questions jumping faster than her words.

"What . . ."

He held up a hand. "We be safe here. We walk rest of de way."

"Oh. How do you know—?" Again her question was cut off by that same hand now guiding the horses into the dark barn. He wrapped the reins around the brake handle and stepped to the ground. While he tied the horses to a post, Jesselynn stood and stamped her feet, willing feeling back into them before she tried the descent.

"Don't we need to ask, to tell . . ."

He shook his head and strode on ahead of her. She dogtrotted to catch up to his long strides.

"Meshach, wait!"

"Sorry, Marse Jesse. I got to thinkin' 'bout dem slavers, and I get so mad I want to go after dem now."

He slowed to her speed, even though she knew she walked fast. And thinking of Aunt Agatha leant wings to her feet anyway. They walked around a hole in the street caused by an exploding cannonball. One of the houses a block from her aunt's was burned to the ground and still smoldering. A dog lay dead in the street. An old man and a woman stood crying in front of a house now minus half a roof.

Jesselynn broke into a jog. "Please, God, please, God." She had no idea what she was saying. All she could think about was Aunt Agatha. Agatha lying dead under a tumble of rafters. Agatha bleeding with no one to bandage her.

They stopped in front of the house. Several windows had been shot out, and the brick chimney now lay in a pile of bricks. And while other homes were starting to light lamps and candles against the graying dusk, not a glimmer showed in the black eyes of the sagging house.

"Aunt Agatha?" Jesselynn pushed open the back door. "Agatha, where are you?" She listened for an answer that never came. She rushed through the house, checking the rooms downstairs while Meshach took the second floor.

"Nothin'." They met at the foot of the staircase.

"Me either. Where could she be?"

"Someone take her in? Big hole in de roof. Cannonball go through de wall too. Bad time when rain or storm come."

"You check that way, and I'll go this way." Jesselynn pointed up the street. "And we meet back here in just a few minutes."

She pounded on doors, but no one would or could answer. Where were all the people who lived on this street? Were they in hiding, afraid to answer? Had the soldiers rounded up all the citizens of Springfield? She darted out of one picket gate and ran to the next house. Looking over her shoulder, she saw Meshach heading back for Aunt Agatha's, so she turned and ran back.

"Dey's in de church two blocks dat way." He pointed toward the west.

As they jogged down a side street, he added, "De reverend put out a call for all who were hurt or dere houses shelled to come to de church. De people bring food and keep warm dere."

But Agatha wasn't at the church. And no one claimed to have seen her.

"I'm sorry," the pastor said. "If she arrives, I will tell her you are looking for her. Ah, did you check the cellar? Many of the older people around here hid in the cellar and barricaded the door."

"Thank you, no, I didn't think of the cellar, but we hollered loud enough to wake the dead."

Jesselynn and Meshach trotted back to the house. "I'll get a candle, and you see if you can open that door."

Jesselynn found a candle but not a spill to light it, and the fire had long since gone out. She dropped the candle on the table in disgust and hurried back outside.

"De door locked from inside." Meshach stood and, puffing slightly, put his hands on his hips. "Call her. Say who you are."

What if she hid in the cellar like a cat that crawls away to die? Father would never forgive me for not taking better care of his sister. Jesselynn leaned over the door. "Aunt Agatha, it's me, Marse Jesse, your nephew." She knew those words, if anything, would bring her aunt out of hiding, if she were able. "Aunt Agatha, can you hear me? Are you hurt?"

"Jesselynn?" The weak voice brought tears of gratitude flowing down Jesselynn's cheeks.

"Yes, Aunt, it's me. Can you unlock the door?"

"Who's with you?"

"Meshach has come to help. Just open the door now, hear?"

They listened to the scratch and thud of a board being removed from the brackets on the underside of the doors.

"There."

Meshach pulled up on the edge of the door and laid it back, then the other one.

Aunt Agatha's face glowed white in the dimness. Jesselynn clattered down the stone steps and took her aunt in her arms. "Come, let's get you out of here. You must be freezing. You are shivering."

"I carry her?"

"I can walk, thank you." The spice back in her voice made Jesselynn smile at Meshach and receive one in return. Spice was good.

A silence lay over the town, the sound of no shooting or yelling almost as loud as the battle. Smoke hung in the air, smelling both of burning wood and gunpowder. The wind of earlier had died with the falling of the sun, even though the cloud cover prevented them from seeing a sunset. A child wailed in a house somewhere near them.

Agatha used the railing to pull herself up the remaining steps. "How bad is the damage to the house? I heard a terrible crash some hours ago."

"Cannonball knock over de chimbley. Big hole in roof and one wall. Rain come in some bad."

They entered the dark house, following Agatha, who had no need to feel her way.

"Then I shall have to sleep in the parlor." She crossed to the stove and rattled the grate. "If you would light the stove, Jesselynn, I will put supper on to heat."

"But you have no chimney."

"Surely the stovepipe works. Start it and we shall see how it draws."

"Aunt Agatha, I think you should come with us. We have the wagon near here, and you can bring a few of your things."

"Pshaw. Reckon I will remain here until they force me to leave." She returned from the pantry with the pot Jesselynn had started the rabbit stew in. "Not a lot here, but we can make do."

"Aunt, you aren't listenin' to me. You would be safe with us in the cave."

"Ain't never lived in a cave and don't intend to start now." She glared at Jesselynn. "Now you goin' to start that stove, or am I goin' to have to do it myself?"

"The army may come through here and force everyone to evacuate tomorrow." Jesselynn found a live coal in the ashes and shaved small curls off a pitch-pine log from the woodbox. When that began to smolder, she blew on it gently until a tiny flame flared bright. Adding more bits, she had the fire burning merrily within a matter of minutes. She added a couple of pieces of split wood and set the lids back in place, adjusting the damper for maximum draw.

Meshach cleared his throat from his place by the door. While it wasn't full dark yet, it was getting close.

What could she do, short of manhandling the old woman out to the wagon and tying her down?

Chapter Six

RICHMOND, VIRGINIA

"Where you goin'?"

"Out." Louisa adjusted her hat in the hall mirror. A glance at her brother lounging against the newel post made her clamp her teeth against further information. Two could play the secrecy game.

"When you comin' back?"

She turned, blew him a kiss, and patted his cheek. "When I get here." She could hear him fuming as she sailed out the front door and knew he watched her, so after latching the gate, she turned right instead of left. She'd have to make a detour around the blocks to get back to the hospital, but if the men needed morphine, she would get it for them. She'd go right to the top and ask the general where she could obtain some. The last time she'd been to the apothecary, he'd shaken his head. Laudanum would have to do. All the morphine was going to the troops.

A breeze kicked up as she neared the hospital from the opposite direction. She looked up to see the high clouds of a few minutes earlier lowering and threading together. Rain might be in the offing. She hurried up the brick steps and pulled open the heavy front door. The miasma of pain and stench greeted her before she could take one step over the threshold. She'd been away from it just long enough to have forgotten how terrible it really was.

"Why, Miz Highwood, how good to see you." One of the doctors stopped on his way down the stairs. "We surely do miss you around here, but perhaps you are doing more good with the men you are caring for. I, for one, am grateful for the efforts of your family and friends, let me tell you."

"Thank you, Doctor. We'll have room for two new ones in the next couple of weeks, I think." No matter how she wanted to return to her mission here, she would not whine and whimper. They expected her to be home caring for her husband and the others. "Is the general in?"

"Up in his office." The doctor indicated the third floor.

"Thank you." She felt like gagging as she mounted the steps. Someone screamed; others moaned. Things hadn't changed a bit.

The general's adjutant sat at the desk in the hall. That hadn't changed either, except that the young man in the uniform wasn't someone she recognized. *Bother. How long had the other been gone?*

"Good afternoon, ma'am. How can I be of service?"

She glanced down to see a newly lettered nameplate. "Ah, yes, Mr. Bromley. My name is Louisa Highwood, and I would like to see the general for a few moments."

"And your business, ma'am?" He halted in a brief motion to stand.

"I . . . ah . . . I need to see him on a matter of medications, for some of his men, those staying with us at my aunt's house." At the confused look he sent her, she knew he had no idea what she was talking about. "Just tell him Mrs. Highwood is here." *Surely he'll see me. He can't have forgotten.*

The young man returned instantly and held the door open for her. "The general will see you now."

Louisa walked through the door as the general came around the end of his desk, hand outstretched. "Good of you to see me, sir."

"Ah, child, if you only knew what delight your smiling face brings to this old heart of mine. We do miss you around here. We most certainly do." While he spoke he pulled out a chair and ushered her to it. "Sit and let me just look at you."

She sat as he'd asked and folded her hands in her lap. Dust motes danced in the sun streaming in from the window, making her wonder if the storm had blown the other way or just held off. Finally, in place of squirming, she smiled and leaned slightly forward. "I have come to ask a favor of you."

"Anything I can do for you, just ask. I owe you so much for all your service here. But before you continue, first tell me how that husband of yours is doing."

"Just fine, General. He is able to get around well with one crutch and makes a joke out of stumping around on the peg he fashioned for his missing foot." She didn't tell him of the dark times when Zachary withdrew and refused to come out until he had "his demons under control," as he put it. "He helps the others when he can and makes sure they all realize they are still in the army."

"We now have other homes opened up to us, thanks to your willingness to start the ball rolling. The men who convalesce in private homes do much better than those here. If only we had a hundred women like you."

Louisa could feel the heat surge up to her hairline. "Thank you, sir." She took a deep breath and leaped in before he could say something else to embarrass her. "I heard my br—er—husband mention . . ." She looked up to catch a twinkle in his eye. *Had he caught her gaffe?*

The surgeon general leaned forward, hands clasped on the desk in front of him. "That is all right, Miss Highwood." The emphasis on the *Miss* let her know that he knew.

"When did you figure out my little charade?"

"Not long after you took your brother home with you. Someone, I don't remember who, had known him from before. When we bragged about our Missus Louisa Highwood, he set us straight." His face sobered. "You know I never would have let an unmarried young woman work here like you did."

"I know that. Living that lie was one of the hardest things I've ever done." Louisa took her turn to lean forward. "But I had to do something more than sew and knit. I just had to."

"I understand. But if the favor is to come back here to help us, I would have to say no."

"I realize that, but that's not it. Zachary mentioned morphine, and while I tried to get some at the apothecary, he said none was available. If one of my men needs morphine, I knew to come straight here for it."

The general shook his head. "I'm sorry, my dear, but I'd give my right arm for it myself. What little bit comes in is used on the frontlines. We resort to whiskey here—get the men as drunk as possible before surgery. There's no morphine to be had south of the Mason and Dixon Line."

"I see."

"I wish I could help you. I wish I could help my men." He shook his head. "Short of hijacking a Northern train, I fear . . ." He stared into her eyes. "Now, don't you go getting any wild-headed ideas, young lady."

Louisa stared down at her lap. *Calm down, heart. We must think this through before going off half-cocked.* She raised her gaze back to the man behind the desk, using her eyelashes to their best advantage. Appearing young and innocent was not difficult. "No, sir, but I do have one more question."

"Yes?"

"Ah . . ." She tried to cut off the dream. "Have you heard anything more about Lieutenant Lessling? Was his body found in that train wreck?"

The general sighed and shook his head. "No, but then many were beyond identifying."

"And you are sure he was on that train?" *Dare I even hope?*

"No, I cannot say for absolute truth he was on that train. But he never reached home. His sister wrote and asked about him, and we've not found him in any of our hospitals."

"Could he be a prisoner of war?" She could scarcely get the words out, the thought was so terrible. But better that than dead. At least that way there was a chance of seeing him again someday.

The general came around the desk to take her hand. "My dear Miss Louisa, I cannot hold out false hope for you. Gilbert was a fine young man and an outstanding soldier. I'm sure that if he were alive, we would hear. Somehow, we would have heard."

Louisa turned from the compassion in his gaze to stare out the window. Sunbeams no longer danced. Instead, deepening gray filled the window. Was that thunder she heard?

"I . . . I better go before I get soaked. Thank you for your time."

"You're welcome. Greet your brother for me." He walked her to the door.

She stopped before leaving. "But there is morphine available in the North, correct?"

"I imagine. For those who have the money. Anything can be bought if one has the money and the resources." He laid a hand on her shoulder. "But don't you go getting any farfetched ideas, young lady. You are too valuable for the Southern cause right where you are, helping our men to heal."

"Yes, sir. Good day." She fetched a half curtsey and, after flashing him a smile, added, "You come on over for dinner one day and visit with your men. It would do them a world of good."

"Thank you. I'll do that."

She kept her feet to the ladylike walk her aunt would be so proud of and made her way down the stairs, out into the blustery wind.

"If there is morphine to be found, I will find it." Her vow met with a thunder roll. Lightning flashed a few seconds later as she bent against the wind to hurry home.

"Dere's mail." Abby, nearly dancing with anticipation, met Louisa at the door.

"From Jesselynn. Oh, praise be to God." Louisa sat down on the stairs without even shedding her shawl. Opening the envelope, she unfolded the thin sheet of paper and read swiftly.

"Oh my, things aren't what she'd planned. They are still living in a cave near Springfield, but they are all well. Here, let me read this part.

'Christmas made me so homesick for Twin Oaks I thought I might fall weeping and melt into a puddle, nevermore to suffer like this. We fashioned gifts for Thaddeus and Sammy, but all I could think of was the festivities of home: the house decorated with cedar boughs; the tree lit with candles; our singing at the church and at home; Lucinda carrying in the Christmas goose, all roasted to crackling brown; and pecan pie. My mouth waters at the thought. But worst of all, no mother or father to wish us Merry Christmas.' "

Louisa stopped reading to wipe the tears from her eyes with one finger. "Ah, me. We had such a merrier Christmas here." She glanced up to the ceiling. "And at least we were warm and dry with enough to eat and a roof over our heads. Lord, forgive me for taking so many things for granted."

"Me too." Abby used her apron to wipe her eyes. "Dem poor chilluns." Louisa sniffed and returned to the letter.

" 'Forgive me, dearest sister, for sounding so gloomy, but I have one more thing to say, and then I shall write of livelier things. I have decided that if God does indeed exist, He no longer can stomach what men are doing to one another and has withdrawn from the affairs of men. I will no longer pray or read that book of His, because doing so is a waste of precious time.' "

Louisa shut her eyes. "Ah, Abby, we must pray for her. Pray without ceasing. One thing that has always been a comfort to me is that my brothers and sisters have all accepted Jesus Christ as their Savior, and no matter how far apart we are in this life, we shall be together again in heaven. I know Mama and Daddy are waiting for us, and that one day we shall all go home."

"And in heaven, dere is no white nor black, no slave nor free, but we shall stand before de Lawd, all his chilluns together." Abby blew her nose. "Is dere more?"

"A little." Louisa took up the paper again.

" 'Greet my dear brother and sister. I am grateful to know you are all safe. Thaddeus is growing faster than we can keep him in clothes, and Sammy too. Jane Ellen has taken over the care of those two, and I believe caring for someone else is bringing her back to herself. We all send our love. I am sorry this letter has been so dreary, but I cannot talk of these things with the others. Please forgive me.

Your loving sister,
Jesselynn

P.S. I almost signed this Jesse, but I have to have one place where I can be Jesselynn, a woman, daughter, sister, and friend. JH

P.P.S. I should just tear this up and not mail it, but paper is too precious for such waste. JH' "

Louisa folded the letter and slid it back into the envelope. "The war. Always the war."

"I best get to fixin' de supper. Reuben done bought a chicken at de market. He say meat gettin' scarcer ever day."

Louisa knew that feeding the extra men was causing distress with her aunt's finances, but what else could they do? "Then we'll have to make it stretch for two meals. Add lots of vegetables and extra dumplin's. That bread I smell will have to fill up any holes." She pushed herself to her feet and hung her shawl on the coat-tree by the newel post. "Let me change my clothes, and I'll be down to help."

As she climbed the stairs, her mind roamed back to her discussion with the general at the hospital. *Lord, what do we do? Oh, Father, please take care of my dear confused sister. Bring her back to you so she can be comforted. Please, Lord, let us all make it through this terrible war and get back together.* God had done miracles before, but would He do this one?

Chapter Seven

SPRINGFIELD, MISSOURI

"I should have made *her come."*

"How? Tie her up?" Meshach clucked the horses to a faster pace. Darkness hugged them round about.

Jesselynn felt at any turn they might meet something terrible, like those three renegades with the chained slaves. *People kill for horses, to protect themselves, or to avenge another. Some kill for pure pleasure, like Dunlivey.* Everything evil she measured against the Dunlivey scale. Would killing the slave runners make Meshach and the others murderers? How would they live with that? Or was killing different for men? She knew now that she would kill to protect her family. And she would have killed to protect Twin Oaks. She knew that for certain. She withdrew into the hood created by the blanket Aunt Agatha had pressed upon her. In payment for her stubbornness perhaps? So many things to think about. Had the war loosed some evil monster across the land that gave people the right, or the need, or the desire to kill? Or was the monster always buried beneath the surface, waiting for the opportunity to raise its filthy head and be loosed?

Had Meshach ever killed anyone before? That thought made her slant a look his way, but the dark was so profound she saw only a blurred hulk. Yet she was close enough to him on the wagon seat to feel his warmth through the blanket.

Was killing animals for their food and clothing making it possible for him to kill another human being?

Suddenly she thought of the wood they had brought to town. The wagon was light again, the wood gone. "What happened to the wood?"

"Left in de barn."

"Why? Do you know those people well?"

"Good 'nough. Dey need wood."

"Did they pay you?"

"No, suh."

Leave it alone. Jesselynn ignored the voice of reason. "But why them?"

"Dey be Quakers."

"Oh." *And that is my answer? After all, I didn't cut the wood, but . . .* Like the sun coming up right now in the west, the truth hit her. Quakers were often part of the underground for carrying escaped slaves north to freedom. She started to ask another question but clamped her lips before the words passed them. If they freed those captive slaves tonight, they would most likely go to that house. The wood was Meshach's way of helping out.

"Meshach, did you ever think of leaving Twin Oaks, of running away?"

"Thought about it, but dat my home. Marse was good to me. Teached me to read and write, teached me a trade, and let me keep my own money. I owe him."

"But now?"

"Now I make sure him daughter and son be safe. Den I farm my own land, land I homestead so it be free like me."

His voice rang in the darkness, so sure, so proud. Not the Meshach she had known all her life, but a man who understood the difference between slave and free and would never go back.

No wonder he wants to free those poor wretches in irons. "I'll go with you."

"No, someone need take care of de others."

Meshach whistled their signal, and as soon as it was returned, he drove the wagon into the thicket and unhitched the horses to lead them out the other side. Jesselynn gathered up the stores Agatha had pressed upon them and followed him down the steep slope to the cave.

The three black men, none of them smiling now, took one of the rifles and the pistol and the cold chisel to break the chains if they didn't get a key, then disappeared out the mouth of the cave. Ophelia ran after them for one more hug and kiss from Meshach, then returned to the fire to sit rocking with her arms around her middle. With the children already asleep, Jesselynn stoked a small part of the fire higher so she could have light to sew. She didn't try to make conversation.

Ophelia knew as well as she what the men planned to do—and the danger inherent in the scheme. At any word she might shatter into sobbing little bits and slip down onto the sandy floor.

After a while her mutterings penetrated Jesselynn's own chambers of fear and horror.

"Lawd, Lawd. Jesus, Son of God, have mercy. Lawd, Lawd." She repeated the words without seeming to even draw a breath.

Jesselynn gritted her teeth. The singsong seeped into her bones and reverberated there, ringing clear like a crystal glass struck by a spoon. Rising and falling, now intelligible, now not. If they brought her comfort, Jesselynn didn't see it. She wanted to scream at the woman to stop.

She wanted to run after the men and plead with them to come back.

She kept on stitching.

Once she went and stood at the mouth of the cave, listening, straining to hear over hollows and ridges to a camp somewhere south. It was not so far away that they'd taken the horses, but it was out of hearing range. She should have forced Meshach to take the traders in to the law in Springfield. That was the proper thing to do.

But trafficking in slaves wasn't illegal in Missouri. All the scum had to say was they caught these runaways and were taking them back to their masters. They might even have papers to show that they were hunting certain escaped slaves. And besides, how would she *force* Meshach to do anything?

She rubbed her arms to warm them and returned to the fire, trying to ignore Ophelia's haunting song without end.

She caught herself nodding off after stoking the fire more times than she cared to count, so she decided to skin and cut up the rabbits she'd forgotten to take to Aunt Agatha and set them to frying. The fragrance of sizzling meat overlaid the smell of horse droppings. Even though Daniel cleaned the cave floor every day, the smell could still get a bit strong.

One of the horses snorted. Jesselynn leaped to her feet and ducked under the rope to clamp a hand over Ahab's quivering nostrils. If there was someone out there and they heard a horse whinny, sure to heaven they'd come looking. She looked longingly at the rifle leaning against the wall of the cave.

" 'Phelia." She tried again, hissing louder, not wanting her voice to carry beyond the fire. " 'Phelia, hush and get the gun."

Ophelia rocked again, then rose and drifted across the sand to pick up the rifle. She held it barrel down and brought it to Jesselynn.

"Here, you guard the horses. Do not let Ahab whinny. He's heard something." Shifting places, she took the rifle and ran to the mouth of the cave, hugging the shadowed wall. Not that much of the firelight showed beyond the slight bend anyway. But shadows would show with so little light. She stopped just inside the overhang, holding her breath to hear anything untoward.

The two-tone whistle came. She grabbed the wall to keep from falling when her knees started to buckle. Jerking herself upright, she took two steps outside to whistle back. It took her three attempts before she could work up enough spit to wet her lips and whistle.

The rattle of iron chains preceded the arrival. Horses snorted. Meshach led one horse with a scarecrow on its back. Two other horses and Roman, their mule, carried two riders each. Leave it to Meshach to put the others ahead of his own need.

Daniel slid off the back of one of the horses and came to stand in front of Jesselynn. "Dey de mens what beat me up." The narrowing of his eyes as he spoke said more than his words.

"One of dem's Dunlivey's partner." Meshach helped the first of his charges down from the horse, a young woman who clutched Meshach's jacket over her bare breasts. If there were welts on her back to match those on her legs, it was no wonder her eyes wore a wild-animal look.

"You're sure?"

Meshach nodded. "I never forget dat face."

Jesselynn took in a deep breath as she saw the open sores on legs gone stick thin from lack of food and eyes of men too afraid to hope. None of them looked as if they could have gone a step farther.

"Supper is ready." Ophelia was dishing up plates as the new people straggled into the cave and sank down around the fire, holding their hands to the heat. Tears ran down the woman's face.

Looking at them, Jesselynn knew they couldn't send them to that house in town without first getting them stronger. They definitely needed a bigger cave—now! It was a good thing Aunt Agatha hadn't come home with them.

With hardly a word, the newly freed slaves collapsed around the fire as soon as they finished eating. They didn't ask for blankets. They didn't ask for anything. They fell as if a giant puppeteer had cut their strings.

As Jesselynn crawled into her quilt, so exhausted she could barely fold the top over her shoulders, she heard Ophelia crooning, this time a song of praise, and Meshach comforting her with a gentle rumbling voice. Between the two of them, they soothed Jesselynn into a deep sleep.

Daniel and Benjamin took turns standing watch.

———

"How are we going to feed all these mouths?" Jesselynn asked Meshach in the morning as they stood outside the cave. Their guests had yet to stir.

"Go hunting. Cut wood for Marse Dummont for store supplies. Won't be long before dey ready to travel again."

"And clothe them?" Jesselynn had already decided to cut up the blanket from Agatha to make shirts for the men. Their bare feet were crusted with chilblains, and some of the sores looked gangrenous to her. The cruelty of the slavers made her turn cold inside. How could one man treat another this way?

"We share what God gived us." His simple answer made her snap back.

"Looks to me like we work backbreaking hard for every small thing that we have."

"We not like dem slavers." Another simple answer, this one making guilt wash her face white.

"Thank G-G—heavens for that."

"I do."

Jesselynn threw her hands in the air and let them drop. How was she to reason with this man?

"Dey work when dey have de strength. Maybe weak now, but a day or two of belly being full and dey strength come back."

"I surely do hope so."

"Better to pray so."

Jesselynn had started back into the cave but spun around to point a finger in Meshach's direction. "You go too far, Meshach, into what is not your business."

But Meshach only looked at her. With what? Pity? Jesselynn spun away again and strode on into the cave. Daniel had the horses out to water and graze already, and even the horses walking out hadn't awakened the newcomers. Were they still alive, or had they died during the night?

She knew the answer to that, since she'd already watched them breathe to make certain they needn't dig more graves. Ophelia smiled at her, nodded a good morning, and handed her the long-handled wooden spoon to stir the mush laced with chopped bits of dried venison. The rabbit stew last night had disappeared within minutes.

The boys woke up, and Jane Ellen took them outside for their morning duty, both staring openmouthed at the floor crowded with slumbering bodies. They kept quiet only by a strict glare from Jesselynn. Sammy had his thumb in his round mouth and stared back over Jane Ellen's shoulder.

As Jesselynn stirred the pot, she studied the tangled mass of limbs. Three of the men were the same deep black as Meshach, with kinky hair cut so short it appeared to have recently been shaved. The lighter-skinned male still wore signs of boyhood, his shoulders not much wider than his waist and long of leg and arm, as though he had yet to grow into them. His face in repose would be beautiful once the bruises healed. One eye was swollen shut, one ear cut and bloodied, and the side of his face had a long scrape that looked as if he'd been dragged along the ground.

The woman definitely had white blood and, once her lashes healed, would be comely. It looked as if a whip had taken a chunk of flesh from beside her eye. So close she came to losing it. From what appeared to be blood on her shredded skirt, Jesselynn suspected the men had raped her more than once.

If they weren't already dead, I'd kill them myself. The thought made her stop stirring for a moment. She knew it was true. No one should ever be treated as these poor souls had been.

One of the men opened his eyes and looked around. He rolled his head to the side as if he didn't remember coming here during the night. He lifted his shackle-free hands and looked down at his feet. "Thank you, Jesus," he whispered. "And you, Mi-Marse." His brow wrinkled as if not sure which she was. "Kin I go outside?"

"Yes, of course, but stay right near. We have to be cautious so we are not found out."

He pushed himself to his feet and staggered a bit before getting his balance, then limped outside, bracing himself on the wall with one hand. One by one the others followed except for the woman, who had yet to move. The men returned with Meshach herding them.

"Breakfast ready?"

"Yes. Call Jane Ellen and the boys."

"Dey wid 'Phelia down at de creek. Sammy hate him face washed."

"In that cold water, I don't blame him." Jesselynn filled wooden trenchers with the mush and the men dug in with their fingers. When she handed them each a hot biscuit, one stared at it as though he'd seen gold.

"Thankee, suh." The others chorused their appreciation, emptied their trenchers, and eyed the kettle.

"As soon as the others eat, you can have the rest." She chose to chew on a piece of dried venison. The sight of their hunger turned her off mush.

While the family ate, she laid a hand on the sleeping woman's cheek. Sure enough, she had a fever, and her breathing seemed labored. Jesselynn set Ophelia to boiling up some willow bark tea, and taking warm water and a cloth, she washed the woman's face, shoulders, and arms. In one hand she found clenched a bit of meat from supper the night before.

"What is her name?" She looked to the men who now seemed much more lively.

"Sarah. Dey already have her befo' me," the light-skinned youth answered, and the others nodded.

"Has she been sick long?"

"Him kick her in belly. She lose baby."

Jesselynn didn't want to know who *him* was. Once more she was grateful her men had done what they felt necessary.

"When did that happen?"

"Two, three days ago." At least the boy knew that many numbers.

"She too sick to walk, so we stay in one camp," one of the other men added.

Jesselynn and Ophelia exchanged glances and set to making things better for poor beaten Sarah. They fixed a pallet for her, bathed her, and dipped broth from a kettle simmering with the rabbits Daniel had caught in his snares. Her eyes fluttered open one moment, and a smile lit her face. She drank the broth and fell right back to sleep. They set Jane Ellen to tending the sick woman, and Jesselynn took the boys outside to play while the sun shone. The air crackled with cold, and frost still glittered near trees in the shade.

"They bad sick?" Thaddeus shook his head. "Jesse, you fix." He looked up at her with eyes full of trust as he took her hand. "Find catepiwar?"

"Sorry, Thaddy—"

"Joshwa," he corrected her absently as he moved leaves around, looking for fuzzy caterpillars.

"All right, Joshwa. The caterpillars have all gone to sleep for the winter in cocoons so they can become butterflies next summer."

"Butterflies?" He looked all around as if expecting them to flutter by.

"No, not now. Next summer."

"Want butterflies."

"Sorry." She chuckled at the look of intensity with which he glared at her. She shook her head. "I can't help it. Many animals and insects go to sleep for the winter."

He planted his fists on his hips and with legs spread looked so like his dead father that she caught her breath. He was Joshwa all right. They'd named him perfectly.

"Here, let's build a house with these sticks. Help me stack them for the walls, like a cabin." She set the sticks on top of each other to form a log cabin. What she wouldn't give for one right now. But to care for all these, it would have to be huge.

Thaddy had the walls several sticks up when Sammy stepped right in the middle of it. With a howl, Thaddy shoved Sammy smack on his rear. Sammy responded with a louder howl. Meshach scooped both boys up under his arms and strode down the hill with them, threatening to dump them both in the ice-cold creek if they didn't hush.

Jesselynn got to her feet and dusted her hands off on her britches. They'd not heard any more artillery fire, so maybe the battle ended the day before. She could hear the boys still giggling. She'd have to talk with Thaddeus about his temper. Stopping, she counted out the days. Why, he had a birthday in a few weeks. He would be three. "Little Marse," as Meshach called him, should have a present of some sort for his birthday. Her mind flipped back to Twin Oaks. Birthdays had always been important celebrations in their family. Lucinda would bake a three-layer frosted cake. Lighter than air were Lucinda's cakes.

Jesselynn's mouth watered at the memory. Would she ever taste one of Lucinda's lemon cakes again? She dusted her hands and returned to the cave for her writing materials. While everyone was busy elsewhere, now was a good time to answer the precious letters. They could take them to the post office next time she went to Aunt Agatha's.

By the time she finished, the sun rode close to its zenith and Ophelia was calling her name.

"She gettin' weaker not stronger."

Jesselynn knelt by the sick woman. "She lost too much blood, I imagine. Poor thing. Come now, Sarah, you must try to drink more broth." She held a cup to the woman's mouth and propped up her head with the other hand.

Sarah drank three or four swallows, then tipped her head away.

"No will to live." Jane Ellen wrung out another cloth and laid it over the sick woman's forehead.

"I know. Can't say as I blame her."

The men filed into the cave again as if they were still chained together and sat in a row by the fire. They'd given their names, but Jesselynn still had no idea who was who, other than the boy and Sarah.

That night Meshach gathered the fugitives around him and laid out his plan. They would go to the house in Springfield in the night. There, others would take them north to freedom. "But first you get strong enough for de trip."

Jesselynn brought over the two shirts she'd made from the blanket. "Sorry, the other isn't done yet. I have more piecing to do on it."

The biggest man, Moses, brushed the nap of the shirt with a reverent hand. "I neber had such a good shirt."

"Put it on." She mimicked pulling it over her head. "That should help keep you warm. Now if only we had something for your feet."

Ophelia had given them all hot water to wash with and then bandaged the sores that needed it. With the new shirts on, they looked almost human again, instead of like refuse left by the roadside.

———

"Marse Jesse?" The voice woke her in the middle of the night.

"Yes?"

"I think Sarah done gone home to be with the Lord." Jane Ellen's voice was muffled with tears. "I tried to keep her alive, Marse Jesse, I tried."

"I know. You did all you could." After checking to make sure the woman had truly left this world, Jesselynn covered the black woman's face with the blanket. Rage at the cruelty of it all boiled red before her eyes.

Fighting tears herself, Jesselynn gathered Jane Ellen into her arms and rocked her until she slept. Glancing up, she saw one of the men watching her with a puzzled look.

Ah, if you only knew the whole story. What did it matter if they suspected she was Miss instead of Marse?

Chapter Eight

Did they bury those men? The ones they . . . Jesselynn slammed the door of her mind.

"De Lawd giveth and de Lawd taketh away. Blessed be de name of de Lawd." Meshach raised his voice on the last words at the gravesite of Sarah. They didn't even have a last name for the poor woman, only an idea of how terribly she'd been treated during the final days of her life.

Before she came to them.

Jesselynn made herself stay at the service, for politeness if nothing else. While Jane Ellen had tears running down her cheeks, none of the others had had time to much care about the deceased. Was death becoming such a commonplace thing that she couldn't even summon up sadness? All the regret stemmed from not being able to save her.

"We'll go tonight," Meshach said as they walked back up the slope to the cave.

"I'll come too. That way if we are stopped, I can say I'm taking my slaves in to work on my aunt's house. No one can argue with that, and that's what we will do if followed." For a change, Meshach didn't argue with her. She had hoped he would see the reason in her plan.

He'd spent the day breaking two of the new horses to the harness so they could leave the Thoroughbreds safe in the cave. Neither of the mares should be working now, and they surely didn't want to use the stallions. The filly was getting big and heavy enough to train, but Jesselynn hated to break her to harness before the saddle. Chess and Roman had a kicking contest while out to pasture. They'd have to learn to get along, that was all.

"I loaded the wagon with wood too. Best we take some tools along if we be workin' on de house." His raised eyebrow told her he was teasing her.

"Good idea. I reckon we'll look right proper."

By afternoon the temperature was dropping again after two fairly warm days. Jesselynn took the two remaining deer hides and wrapped the men's feet. Daniel had given the younger man his deerskin shirt, saying he could always make another. They shot deer aplenty.

The shirt he now wore of Meshach's looked like a tent on his slender frame.

Thaddeus pointed at Daniel and giggled, setting Sammy off, which made Jane Ellen smile and the freed slaves actually laugh. Never had the cave heard such ringing laughter.

Jesselynn wished she could laugh. Lately it seemed that as tears had dried up, so had her laughter, blowing away like puffs of a dandelion. What if they were caught? Would her story hold up? Of course it would. It sounded perfectly plausible. But what if someone acted suspicious? Could she trust these men to carry out the deception if needed?

She was getting plenty of practice in shutting off disturbing questions. As her mother always said, *"One step at a time."* Of course she had added something like *"God only lights the way ahead one step at a time."* But Jesselynn was trying to ignore that last part.

Frost was already coating the ground when they hitched up the team and started off. The two-hour trip to town seemed to go on forever because they couldn't see the landmarks. A sickle moon hung low in the west by the time the lights of Springfield came into view. Many houses were dark already, either the folks gone to bed or the house damaged too badly in the battle to use.

Since the Quaker house was close to the edge of town, Jesselynn halted the wagon under an oak tree that would have been good shade in the summer. Tonight its naked branches rattled in the rising wind.

"Now follow me like I said." Meshach spoke softly. Within seconds they all disappeared into an alley running along the backs of the houses. Jesselynn gave them a few minutes head start and then drove her wagon on up the street, turning at the corner to pass the Quaker house. As she drew even with the barn, Meshach climbed back aboard the wagon, and they continued on until they reached Dummont's store. Quickly they unloaded the wood, stacking it behind the building. Jesselynn stuck a note into the doorframe telling who left the wood, and they headed back out of town.

They'd driven for some time before Jesselynn said, "Now I feel I can breathe again." She slapped the reins, and the horses picked up a fast trot. If they loped, the wagon might fall apart for sure. By the time they arrived back at the ridge, the moon had set and clouds hid the stars.

"Snow." Meshach shivered as he unhooked the traces. "No one be able to track dem back to here, and dey not know de way."

Jesselynn knew he meant if someone forced the black men to talk, they wouldn't be able to tell where they'd been. For all they knew they'd been north or east of Springfield, from the roundabout way they entered town. And snow would cover any trails that had built up around the camp. Now if only they could figure out what to do with all the extra horses until they could be sold. Even with putting them farther back in the cave, feeding and watering them took more effort.

But selling them would bring in the money they so desperately needed, and the Union army was always looking for horses. Now they could keep Chess longer.

"God do provide," Meshach said with a grin and a pat on her shoulder. Jesselynn tried to ignore him, but his joy was as catching as a yawn. She caught herself whistling under her breath as she went about her chores.

———

They woke in the morning to a drift of snow halfway into the cave and to their own shivering, even though the fire had been kept going all night.

"Now I wish we had those extra deer hides to stretch across that opening." Jesselynn shook her head. "And to keep us warm." To think she'd gone to sleep dreaming of selling the extra horses today and bringing home bacon and lard, even eggs and peppermint candy for the boys of all sizes. And coffee. How wonderful a cup of coffee would taste on a cold morning like this.

The storm settled in and howled around the cave for the next two days. It let up, then returned with a vengeance. Meshach built a partial wall at the cave mouth to keep out the worst of the wind and cold. While they took most of the horses down to the creek to drink, Jesselynn chose to melt snow for the mares. She didn't want them slipping and sliding going down the hill as the others had.

She doled out the oats, wishing she had some for the others when Ahab nickered for a treat too.

"Sorry, old son, but the mamas need this worse than you."

That's something else she would buy—oats for the horses and hay if she could find some.

On the good days, Daniel and Benjamin each brought in a deer, and Meshach stretched the hides over a bar at the top and hung another at the bottom so his swinging door could be pushed aside when they took the horses out.

The cave instantly felt warmer, though darker.

"Good thing we got de horses. Dey help keep us warm."

"I wonder how Aunt Agatha is. With that hole in her roof . . ." Jesselynn shook her head. "Stubborn old woman." *Runs in the family,* giggled her inner voice. But the concern for Aunt Agatha wouldn't leave her alone. She went to sleep with it and woke up with it.

As soon as the snow stopped coming down and started melting, she decided to head for Springfield. They couldn't take the wagon yet, but they could take the horses into the army encampment and offer to sell them to the Union soldiers. If the Confederates were in charge, she'd sell them there if they would pay her in gold.

She gathered some of the dried venison for Aunt Agatha, along with the day's catch of rabbits, but as she got ready, she thought more and more about the Confederates having taken Springfield. They would conscript the horses, pay her in Confederate dollars, and wish her well. She knew that as well as she knew her own name. Only the Yankees had gold.

"Meshach, do you think the folks that own the barn we kept the wagon in would mind if we tied some horses there for a while?"

"Dey not mind. Why?"

"Can't take them in if the Confederates are in power."

He nodded. "I take Roman, you ride Chess?"

She nodded. No sense trying to go alone. "We can stop at Dummont's and pick up supplies too." Knowing they had a credit at the store took another load off her mind. She refused to let her mind play with the money they would get for the horses. Still seemed like blood money to her, but caring for her people was more important to her than mourning three men who took delight in destroying others. She had yet to ask Meshach what had actually happened that night, and most likely she never would.

Sometimes there was safety in not knowing.

White waves crested across the prairie, blown in drifts by a determined wind that even now tugged at their hats and tried to blow holes in their coats. Had it not been for the wind, the day would have been right balmy after the blizzards of the last days. She squinted against sun so bright off the snow, her eyes watered. Even the brim of her hat, pulled down low to shield her face, failed to protect her.

The horses worked up a sweat before they'd gone more than a mile and were blowing hard after plowing through a section of belly-deep snow, too soft to have a crust. By the time they got to town, she and Meshach had to dismount and stamp their feet to get the circulation flowing again. The United States flag snapping in the wind over the fort let them know who was in charge. The Confederate attack had been repulsed, so they could take the horses right in.

Snow had cleaned the town up, hiding the shell holes, trash, and dirt. White roofs with smoke coming from chimneys, capped fences, and a snowman here and there said Springfield had gone back to life as usual. The main streets were fast becoming mudholes as wagons and horses traversed the town.

A sentry stopped them at the edge of the parade grounds.

"Can you tell me where to find the quartermaster?"

"What for?"

"We have some horses for sale." She nodded to the three on lead lines.

"Then you'd want to see Cap'n Maddock. He's in charge." The man pointed to a two-story house that had been commandeered by the army. A platoon of soldiers, rifles on their shoulders, marched back and forth across the field at the command of a hard-voiced officer. Smoke rose from chimneys of sod and wood buildings alike. To the side was a corral and low barn, the stables. And a line of wash flapping in the wind proclaimed the presence of the laundry.

Jesselynn nodded and turned to her right. Trotting up the block, she saw enlisted men shoveling snow from walks, women in heavy wool shawls with market baskets on their arms, and a plethora of horses and riders coming and going, many of them to and from the big house. She handed Meshach the lead rein and flipped Chess's reins over the hitching rail to the side of the iron-fenced yard.

Two enlisted men, buttons gleaming gold in the sunlight, stood on either side of the fan-lighted front door.

"I came to see Captain Maddock. I have some horses to show him."

"Second floor on your right. The private then will see you up."

"Thank you." She entered the interior, dim after the brightness outside, and stood for a moment to let her eyes grow accustomed.

"Your name, boy?" The cherry-cheeked man behind the desk in the entry barked at her. He didn't look old enough to shave yet, let alone wear a uniform.

"Jesse Highwood, suh. I come to see Captain Maddock."

"State your business."

"I have three horses to sell."

"Only three?"

"Yes, suh." She felt like saluting and resisted the temptation to give any further information. Benjamin had reminded her of that before they left the cave.

"Jones, take him up."

She straightened her shoulders and sucked in a breath of courage as he opened the dark walnut door.

"Young man to see you about some horses, sir."

"Show him in."

When Jesselynn stood before the desk, she removed her hat and clutched it in front of her. The officer finished what he was writing and looked up at her. "You have horses for sale?"

"Yes, suh. Three."

"Where'd you get them?"

"Found 'em loose in the woods."

"You didn't rustle them, did you?"

"No, suh!" Again she clamped her lips against embroidering her story. After all, they *had* found them in the woods, hard used like the blacks.

"I'll give you a hundred dollars for each one if they prove up sound."

She shook her head. "No, suh, mah daddy tan mah hide if I sells them so cheap."

"A hundred twenty-five."

Another shake of her head. "Hundred fifty. In gold."

"I can't go that high. Hundred forty, and that's my last offer, unless you'll take a hundred sixty a head, in paper?"

Jesselynn didn't have to debate on that. "Gold."

"In gold it is." He turned to the young man standing just inside the door. "Jones, go out and check to make sure these animals are sound."

"I wouldn't bring you a lame horse."

"Others have tried." He pulled out a drawer, drew out a bag that clanked when he set it on the desk top, and began filling out a requisition form. "Name?"

She gave him the information he asked for—and nothing extra.

"Can you read or write?"

"Yes, suh."

"Good, then sign here."

Jesselynn read quickly through the form and signed her name at the bottom. Jones reentered the room as she finished.

"A bit on the thin side, sir, but no limping, no obvious problems."

"Good. Because if I find out one isn't sound . . ." He let a silence stretch. "Why, then we come after the seller."

"Yes, suh." Oh, how she ached to tell him what to do with his gold, but they needed it too badly. Those three horses were the fare for their journey west and feed for both man and beast in the cave. While the officer didn't look as if he'd ever missed a meal, she now knew what real hunger felt like.

She counted carefully along with him as he set the gold out in stacks of fives. Eight stacks plus two, four hundred and twenty dollars. At least he didn't try to short her. She hadn't seen so much money at one time in far too long.

"If you *find* any more horses loose in the woods, come see me again. You drive a hard bargain, young man. Your daddy should be proud of you."

"Thank you, suh." She took the two leather pouches of gold, wishing she had brought the saddlebags up to hold it.

"Sure you wouldn't just as soon have some of that in paper?"

"No, suh."

Outside at the horses, she handed Meshach one of the bags and put the other in her saddlebag, at the same time looking around to see if anyone was watching them. People had been killed for a lot less than what they now carried.

Stopping at the store, they bought two sacks of oats, coffee, sugar, peppermint sticks, and a dozen eggs to go along with the bacon.

"We'll have to come back with the wagon for the rest we need."

"Be glad to deliver if you'd like." Mr. Dummont gave her the change from one ten-dollar gold piece.

"Thanks, but I need to visit Aunt Agatha." She handed him another gold piece. "Hold this for her account."

"I'll do that."

"We might have to walk partway, with all this load." She swung atop Chess, and they headed for Aunt Agatha's house, twin sacks of coffee and tea, along with cheese and other frivolities she knew were needed. Sharing the bounty was half the fun. "Meshach, do you want to give the Quakers one of these gold pieces, or maybe two?"

"Dat be right good of you." His smile made the snow glitter dim.

She planned on giving each of the men a gold piece but not right now. If someone stopped them and they had a ten-dollar gold piece, they'd be thrown in jail for robbery or worse. When they put the horses in the shed at Aunt Agatha's, she gave Meshach two coins.

The first thing she noticed was that no smoke rose from the chimney. Had Agatha run out of wood? No, the stack by the back door attested to that. Where could she be? After a perfunctory knock, she and Meshach entered a room nearly as cold as the outside.

"Aunt Agatha!" Calling her name, they searched every room. No one there, alive or dead. Where could she be now?

Chapter Nine

RICHMOND, VIRGINIA

"I'm coming. I'm coming."

"I gets it, Miss Louisa." Abby came trotting from the kitchen.

Louisa jumped the last step of the walnut stairs and crossed to the front door. "Thanks, but I'm right here." Who could be calling at this time of the morning? Swinging the door open, she broke into a delighted grin. "Why, Carrie Mae, you don't have to ring the bell. You used to live here."

"I know, but Jefferson likes me to be proper, so I'm practicin' every chance I get." The two sisters exchanged hugs and entered the parlor arm in arm. While Carrie Mae was the youngest of the three sisters, she looked older due to her deep green velvet traveling suit, including her hat with a matching feather that swept over one shoulder.

"Don't you look lovely." Louisa ignored a slight twinge of jealousy and stepped back to admire her sister's outfit. "Jefferson must be doing well."

"Oh, he is the best husband." Carrie Mae clasped her gloved hands to her bosom. "He works so hard but never is too tired to attend a rout or dinner or even a ball. I wish you would come with us sometime." She leaned forward with a wide smile. "Why, we were even invited to Mary Chestnut's for tea. Such stimulatin' conversation."

Louisa smiled and patted her sister's shoulder. "You know things like that have never been my style." *Let alone I have no gowns to wear to formal do's, no shoes, nor . . .* She left off the self-pity and guided her sister to a chair. "Now, which would you like—tea or coffee?"

"Oh, tea, thank you. Where's Aunt Sylvania?"

"Gone to church to help the ladies." Louisa hurried down the hall to the kitchen to order refreshments. On the way, she glanced in a mirror and made a face. Her hair needed pinning up, and she wore one of her older house dresses. Forcing men to move limbs that had near frozen in place didn't take a fashion plate. "Could you make tea, please, Abby, and I do hope there are some of your good molasses cookies left." She'd used them as bribes for the men.

"I fixes somethin'. Lawsy sakes, she sure do look purty."

"That she does. I wonder if she and Jefferson"—Louisa put a twist on her brother-in-law's name—"would take one of our wounded soldiers into their home?" She knew the question was catty. Jefferson believed he was doing his part for the South by helping in the legislature, and he demanded that his wife look and act the part of a successful lawyer's wife.

Carrie Mae had always loved dressing up.

Hurrying back down the hall, Louisa remembered the letter. "Oh, sister, I have a wonderful surprise for you. Be right back."

"What is it?"

Louisa ignored the question and dashed up the stairs to her room. The letter from Jesselynn lay in her writing case, along with a partially written answer. Letter in hand, she danced down the stairs again, waving the envelope gaily.

"A letter? From whom?" Light dawned. "From Jesselynn. Oh, don't tease me. Read it, or better yet, let me read it myself."

Louisa handed her the envelope and took her own chair, the better to watch her sister's expressive face. Just as they had for each one she'd read the letter to, tears sprang instantly to her sister's eyes.

"Oh no. I had no idea things were so bad. I . . . I guess I thought they were safe in town or something." She returned to her reading. "Ah, and I have so much. Louisa, I feel guilty for . . . for . . ."

"For being safe and warm and . . ."

"And our Christmas was wonderful. Jefferson's family spoiled me rotten." She laid the letter in her lap. "Is there nothin' we can do?"

"Pray for her. Oh, Carrie Mae, we must pray for the things she needs but more so for the rescue of her soul."

"God will never let her go."

"I know." But Louisa also knew of soldiers who died cursing the Lord they had worshiped as boys.

Carrie Mae put the letter back in the envelope. "I will write to her tonight." She thought a moment. "No, we have a dinner to attend tonight. But I will pray for her, and I will write tomorrow. Where do we send the letter?"

"To the post office in Springfield. She got our other letters there."

During the silence, Louisa glanced around the room. The pallets for two of their recovering men lay stacked against one wall. Their extra clothing was folded in a neat pile on a chair. A pipe and tobacco pouch resided on a whatnot table. While the men were very neat, still there was always what could be called clutter around.

There had been no clutter at Carrie Mae's home, a flat downtown near the courthouse.

"I see you still have your soldiers here." Carrie Mae pulled off her gloves and laid them in her reticule.

"Yes, as soon as one is ready to go home, we'd have two to take his place, had we room for them. One thing we don't lack is wounded soldiers." Did she dare to tell her of the idea that had been brewing since she saw the general at the hospital?

She didn't. "So tell me the news."

Carrie Mae studied her hands clasped in her lap, then looked up to send her sister a smile of pure joy. "The best news of all, short of the war ending, is that I am in the family way."

"Oh, how wonderful." Louisa fell to her knees at her sister's side, taking her hands. "That truly is the most marvelous news. When will the baby be born?"

"August, near as we can figure."

"Have you seen a doctor?"

"No. Whatever for? I've been askin' some of the other wives about a midwife, though. I always thought when I had a baby, Mama and Lucinda would be there to care for me. And Daddy would be walkin' the floor with my husband."

"Most likely passing the whiskey and telling tall tales in Daddy's office." Louisa sat back on her heels. "Are you feeling all right?"

"So far. Just some queasiness in the mornin'." Carrie Mae took Louisa's hands in hers and rubbed the backs with her thumbs. "Ah, Louisa, I want Jesselynn here. I want to tell her my good news, and the three of us can sew baby things together. She would knit me a sweater. You know her knitting is so much better than mine."

"And a hat and booties. Soakers and a little dress so cunning . . ." Louisa fought the lump that clogged her throat and caused her eyes to burn. She sniffed and blinked. "There could be a miracle, you know, and the war end so she can come home."

"But her last letter said they are headin' west." Carrie Mae shook her head slowly, as though hope had died. "We're never goin' to see them again. I just know it." Tears trembled on her lashes; then one meandered down her cheek. "Some days I miss Mama so bad I could just . . ."

They sniffed together, and Louisa pulled a handkerchief out of her apron pocket. She dried her sister's eyes before wiping her own.

"But we go on."

Carrie Mae looked deep into her sister's eyes, as if searching for something. Louisa knew not what. Carrie Mae clenched her lower lip between her teeth. A whisper came, faint and drenched in fear. "Mama died in childbirth."

"Oh, baby sister." Louisa gathered Carrie Mae into her arms. "You are young and strong and healthy, just right for child bearing. You will do real fine, and then we'll have a baby to fuss over."

"A baby?" Abby set the tea tray down with a rattle. "You gonna have a baby, Miss Carrie Mae?" Her face shone with joy.

Carrie Mae nodded, dashed an errant tear away, and smiled with trembling lips.

"Oh, lawsy me. We gonna have a baby. I better gits to hemmin' diapers. We ain't had no baby in dis family in too many years. Wait till Miss Sylvania hears dis. She be over de moon wi' joy." Abby left the room, chuckling as she went.

"Have you written to Jesselynn yet?"

"No, I wanted to tell you first." She accepted the cup of tea Louisa poured. "Jefferson said we must look for a house now. Our flat is too small for a baby and a mammy. Wouldn't Lucinda love to mother another Highwood baby?"

"That she would." Louisa nibbled a cookie after dunking it in her tea.

"You think she would come if I sent for her?"

Louisa stopped chewing. "Why, Carrie Mae Steadly, that is the most wonderful idea anyone has had in ages. Of course, you might have to send someone for her. Can you think of her taking the train here all by herself?"

"I wish Aunt Sylvania would get home."

"Not till late afternoon. She takes her lunch with her, and they work most of the day." Louisa stopped and let the thoughts flow. "Oh, I have the best idea."

"What?" Carrie Mae leaned forward. "Tell me."

"Well, it has nothin' to do with you, but what if I taught my wounded soldiers to knit and sew? They could help with the war effort that way and would most likely feel like they are doing something useful."

"Men sewing and knitting. Louisa Highwood, have you lost your mind?"

"Wait till Zachary hears *this* idea." The words made her chuckle. *Along with the other one. Things are likely to get pretty lively around here.*

Chapter Ten

SPRINGFIELD, MISSOURI

"I can't leave without knowing where she is!"

"Need be home before dark."

"Meshach, I know that!" She felt like screaming. What could have happened to Agatha? Somewhere from the far reaches of her memory, she heard her father saying, *"That aggravating Agatha, I swain . . ."* Jesselynn now understood why. Couldn't she have at least left a note?

"The post office!" Jesselynn spun on her heel and darted out the door, Meshach right behind her. Sure enough, there was a letter addressed to Master Jesse Highwood from Mrs. Hiram Highwood. Jesselynn tore it open and read swiftly. "She's taken a position with an elderly couple over on Sunshine Street." She looked back to the postmaster. "Could you please tell me where that is?"

He gave her directions, and they left as fast as they'd come.

She literally threw herself off the horse and ran up the walk to a house in much better shape than the one Agatha previously had been in. At least the roof appeared to be in one piece. This area of town didn't seem to have suffered any damage from the battle. Again a two-story house, this one painted white with green shutters. Three shallow steps led up to a porch with heavy pillars that stretched across the entire front of the house.

Jesselynn knocked on the carved oak door with an oval glass center.

Aunt Agatha parted the lace curtain and, peering out, smiled and opened the door. "I knew you would find me." She hugged her niece and patted her shoulder. "When the Reverend said these old folks needed some help, why, I knew it was an answer to prayer. Since none of the things in that house of Lettie's were my own, I just packed my bag and came right on over. I was goin' to sell all the food in the basement to Mr. Dummont, but I knew you could use some of it and perhaps would bring some over here for us, as well."

Jesselynn had never heard her aunt run on so. But then she hadn't known her all that long either.

"Would you like to meet the dears?" Agatha took her arm and pulled her toward the kitchen.

"No, I think not, not today. We have to get on home. I just wanted to make sure you were all right. You've even been haunting my dreams in that drafty, old falling-down house."

"Are you sure? You can't stay even for a cup of tea?"

Jesselynn nodded and extricated herself from her aunt's grasp. She patted the liver-spotted hand. "Do you have any money of your own with you?"

Agatha pulled herself upright and managed somehow to look down her nose at her niece, who was a good four inches taller than she.

"Now, don't go gettin' all het up. We're family, and I feel responsible. I sold some horses today. . . ."

"Not the Thoroughbreds?" Agatha gave "aghast" a new meaning.

"No, no. Some we found after a battle in the woods. We healed them up and sold them to the army." She dug in her pocket and pulled out several silver dollars and a ten-dollar gold piece. "Here, just in case you need it."

"No. I will not take money from you when I don't need it." She stared at the coins on the outstretched palm, picked out two dollars, and closed Jesselynn's fingers back over the rest. "I know you mean well, dear Jesse . . ." At Jesselynn's raised eyebrow she cut off the further syllable. "But I am just fine here."

"All right, but if you need anything, you also have a credit at Dummont's store. Keep that in mind, and if you need to get ahold of me, well, you did it." She kissed her aunt's cheek and opened the door. "Take care now, you hear?"

"That's just what your daddy always said when he left. Bless his heart. And yours too."

Jesselynn stepped back out on the porch, so grateful she didn't have to come in with the wagon and carry her aunt out to the cave that she could have leaped the picket fence.

She filled Meshach in on the news as they rode out of town, both of them keeping an eye out for anyone who might be following them. If the captain suspected they had more horses, he might send someone after them.

"Dat old woman goin' to come west, you just watch."

"She's fine where she is." *Oh, I hope so. I do not need anyone else to cart along.*

Meshach gave her that wise smile he wore when he was absolutely sure about something. Her mother had sometimes said she felt Meshach had a bit of the prophet in him, that it would most likely come out more as he grew older. There had been times when he had foreseen something, but Jesselynn had pooh-poohed his predictions. The thought of Aunt Agatha in a wagon heading west didn't bear thinking about.

They circled round and came to the cave from a different direction, even though their earlier tracks led directly to their entrance. Meshach whistled, received an answer, and down the slope they went. The boys ran to greet them when they led the horse and mule into the cave.

"Gone long time." Thaddeus held his arms high to be picked up. Jesselynn hugged him and settled him in the saddle. Had he been much taller, he wouldn't have fit; the ceiling was that low. "Good Chess." He leaned forward and patted the horse's shoulder.

Jesselynn led him back to the horse corral, as they called it, and swung her brother to the ground so she could unsaddle. "Do you hear that?" She cocked her head as if listening closely.

"What?" Thaddeus looked around.

"That sound?" She pretended to listen again. At the puzzled look he gave her, she said, "That little voice callin' your name. Hear it? Thaddeus." She made her voice soft and whispery.

He wrinkled his brow trying so hard to hear.

Jesselynn glanced up to see the big grin on Meshach's face.

"I hears it." He leaned close to the saddlebag behind the saddle. "From in dere."

Thaddeus clapped his hands. "Me see."

Jesselynn lifted the flap on the leather bag and peered inside. "Sure enough. There he is."

"Me see!"

Jesselynn reached inside her saddlebag and brought out the sack of peppermint sticks. Instead of just two, she'd bought one for every one of them. "Here. You hand them out."

Thaddeus did that, his chest swelling enough to pop his buttons if he'd had any. He went to each person around the cave and gravely gave them a red-and-white peppermint candy stick, accepted their thanks, then plunked himself down by the fire to suck on his own. He patted the rock beside him. "Jesse, you sit here."

"I will." She pulled out the sack of coffee beans and gave them to Ophelia, who inhaled the fragrance and closed her eyes in delight. The rest of the food things she set down on the bench of lashed branches Meshach had made during the days of confinement. "That ought to make things easier for a while."

Sammy, candy stick in mouth, sat down beside Thaddeus and held out his candy in a sandy fist. "Good."

Jesselynn debated where to store the gold coins. She was not concerned that one of her people would steal them, but she wanted them safe in case they were attacked. And so they didn't get scattered. The storage boxes were too obvious a place. Finally she kept out one coin and rolled the two leather bags containing the rest in a scrap of leftover deerskin, then set the packet under a rock in the horse corral, off to the side above the ground by a foot or so. When satisfied, she showed the hidden place to Meshach in case something happened to her.

The snow melted within a week, setting the creek to frothing fury so that Daniel and Benjamin had to be careful when letting the horses drink. No longer could they stand in the shallows and drink contentedly. The bank sometimes gave way, and all they needed was for one of the mares to be injured.

Jesselynn checked them daily as their bags swelled and their bellies sagged. "Make sure you hold them tight so they can't take off somewhere to drop those foals," she admonished the men. Benjamin, who'd worked with the horses since he was a small child, gave her a wide, slow smile.

"Yes, Marse."

Jesselynn rolled her eyes and laughed. "Sorry. But we can't afford to lose a baby. Those two are the foundation for the herd after the war. If only we could do something about foaling stalls. We have to separate the mares out. Ahab could get feisty and hurt one of them."

"If we need stalls, we make stalls." Meshach beckoned to the two younger men. "Now we cut posts." Within a week they had sunk posts as far as the floor of the cave permitted and run rails to the walls. While the stalls weren't airy and roomy like those at Twin Oaks, they would be adequate. Next he chopped down an oak tree and split off withes to make two oaken buckets. When he set Daniel to cutting thin withes for baskets, Ophelia wandered around in a happy daze for hours before she began to weave an oaken basket.

Benjamin bagged two deer, so they stretched the new hides over the doorway and brought the weathered ones in to tan.

The next morning Jesselynn was trying to get ready to leave for town when Jane Ellen asked, "Where's Sammy?"

"I don't know." Jesselynn dropped the harness and glanced around the cave. Since the day had dawned clear, the open door let in some extra light, but not a lot. "Thaddeus, where's Sammy?"

The little boy looked up from his building sticks. "Don't know."

Ophelia ran to the mouth of the cave. "Sammy! You get on in here."

Jesselynn joined her, cupping her hands around her mouth. "Sammy!" She called his name twice and shook her head. "Surely he didn't toddle off. He wouldn't leave Thaddeus."

"Then where he be?" Ophelia dashed away the tears already forming. "He can't be gone. Sammy!"

Jesselynn reentered the cave. Could he have crawled back under the covers? She thought for a moment. No. Jane Ellen had gone hunting for wood and leaves by herself this time. Could Sammy have followed her?

"S-a-m-m-y." Ophelia's voice sounded fainter.

"Here."

Jesselynn spun away from the stores and glanced around the dim room. No little black boy. "Sammy?"

"Here."

"Thaddeus, do you see Sammy?"

Thaddeus looked up from his building and glanced around the area. "Over there." He went back to building his cabin.

Jesselynn swallowed. He'd pointed to the horses. She bent down, and her heart took an extra beat. There sat Sammy under Dulcie.

"Sammy, don't move. Just stay right where you are. Thaddeus, go call Ophelia. Now." She eased her way over to the horses. "Thank God, he's not under Roman," she whispered. "Easy, girl, now don't get restless here." She laid a hand on the mare's shoulder. Sunshine shifted, turning to see if Jesselynn had the feed bucket with her. She bumped Dulcie, and the mare laid her ears back.

"Easy." *One kick and he could be dead. God, hold the animals steady, please.* With one hand on the mare's halter, she reached under with the other and grabbed Sammy's arm. He let out a howl, Dulcie backed up, and Jesselynn had the little boy tucked under her arm. "Sammy, I could paddle your behind till you won't sit down for a week." She slipped under the bar holding the horses back and plunked him down on the rock by the fire. "You know better than to go in with the horses. Shame on you!" The finger she shook in his tear-streaming face moved of its own accord. Her heart had yet to settle to a regular rhythm.

Ophelia ran in and snatched the baby up in her arms, raining kisses on his cheeks and hair.

"He needs a switchin' so's he won't do that again."

"Yes, suh, Marse Jesse, I do dat." She turned the little one end for end and walloped him three times. Sammy screamed, Ophelia sobbed, and Thaddeus came running in.

"No, don't hit Sammy. No." He grabbed around Ophelia's leg and hung on. Sammy clung around her neck.

Jesselynn headed for the cave entrance. If she stayed she might laugh at the scene going on. Leave it to Thaddeus to protect his friend. But if she laughed, she might start crying, and if she did that, she might never stop. Once she'd walked off some of the fear and anger, she remembered what she'd done. *So I prayed. That was only in an emergency, mind you. I don't want anything to do with a God who allows war and guerrilla bands and slave traders and little boys almost getting stomped, and . . .* She sniffed back the tears. *So I'm sorry I said anythin'. I won't do it again, you hear?* She propped herself against a rock, thanks to knees that felt ready to give way, and sighed, the kind of sigh that takes the starch out of shoulders and neck and belly. "But thank you anyway."

Sammy still sniffed occasionally when she returned to the cave. Thaddeus glared at her.

"Thank you for savin' the little scamp." Ophelia had a three-foot rawhide string tied around Sammy's wrist and her ankle. "He don' go nowhere now."

"Good idea. At least until Jane Ellen comes back. I'm taking the wagon to town to clear out Agatha's cellar. Think on what you need while I harness the team." *Where I'll store it all, I have no idea, but I know we'll use it.*

———

Sometime later Jesselynn dusted off her hands after loading the wagon at Aunt Agatha's. Keeping some apples out, she took the barrel over to the store and had Dummont credit it to her account.

"There's wood outside the back door of the house and in the shed. You could get that, too, and put it against her account."

"She ain't used any of what you left last time. I feel strange having all this credit built up like this."

"Don't worry. I need a small keg of molasses and ten sacks of oats, if you have them."

"I do. Anything else?"

Jesselynn pulled out her shopping list. She'd drawn around the little boys' feet and the big ones' too. "We need boots in all these sizes, heavy pants for two men, and some yardage. You selling any knittin' wool? My ma would sure like some wool for knittin' stockings." She breathed a sigh of relief. Almost trapped herself there.

Mr. Dummont's face fairly glowed as he set her order on the counter. "Now, how many yards and what kind of material?"

Jesselynn contemplated her list as if she didn't know what the females of the group rightly wanted. "Ah, black wool for britches and some pretty cotton for my sister." She studied the list again, trying to look confused like a very young man might over women's things. "Hard to read her writing. That's three yards wool and four cotton, I guess. While you finish up getting it all in order, I'm taking some stuff over to Aunt Agatha. Be back soon."

But when she drove up to the new house and knocked on the door, a bent-over old man answered. "They's gone to the church," he said in a weak voice after she introduced herself and her errand. "But you can unload the things in the coach house there. We don't have horses any longer."

"Thank you, sir, and please tell Aunt that I was by."

She unloaded the last of the vegetables, both dried and fresh, although some of it looked a bit shriveled now. By keeping the root crops, other than the potatoes, covered with sand, the vegetables had retained their moisture and flavor. Her mind flashed back to Twin Oaks. All they had put by gone up in flames. And the larder had been massive, though they left all the root crops in the ground and covered the rows with straw to dig out when needed. Surely her people were able to dig those to help keep them going. If only she could figure a way to send some of her gold to them.

Back at the store she helped Dummont load the wagon, then drove off for the cave. They should be set now for the next month or so. On her way home she thought back to her habit of praying in an emergency. She'd gotten over a lot in the last months. She could get over that habit too.

———

Rain brought in the month of February, rain in never-ceasing sheets of silver that turned the hills to mud and the creek to a roaring river. No longer did they water the horses near the cave but took them up the hollow to another calmer place. Finding grazing took much of the day for Daniel or Benjamin. The hay Jesselynn managed to buy from a farmer and bring back in the wagon could only be fed to the mares, since they were being kept inside. Besides finding wood, bringing in dry leaves for bedding the stalls was a major part of Jane Ellen's and Thaddeus's day.

"We've got to find another cave," Jesselynn said one night after supper. "We've stripped the area around here bare."

"But we set up for the foalin' here." Benjamin looked toward the back of the cave where the two mares occupied their own stalls, the others dozing in the corral.

"I know that. But any day now we'll have foals, and we can carry them in the wagon if it is too far. I don't know what else to do."

"Spring come soon," Meshach reminded her.

"Not soon enough." Jesselynn laid aside her knitting and rubbed her upper arms. The cold damp was almost worse than the snow and blizzard. This cold ate right into one's bones and belly.

"You want I should take Roman and go lookin' tomorrow?" Benjamin asked.

"No, you stay here and let Daniel go." She glanced over in time to see the younger man look down at the floor as if studying something of supreme importance. She knew since his beating that he rarely headed far from the cave by himself, but she hadn't brought it up. They'd punished the culprits, but there were others as bad or worse. "How about if I go with you?" She surprised herself with her suggestion. She hadn't left the cave for more than brief forays for days. She hated to be gone from the mares. Too much was riding on their progeny.

Besides, like a cat, she hated to get wet. The look of gratitude he sent her warmed her heart even if her hands were freezing.

"Best we wait till it dry out some." Meshach offered his opinion, not looking up from the wood he was smoothing with a deer antler. "I found more pasture a mile or so across another ridge. Take horses there tomorrow."

Jesselynn nodded. Another reprieve.

She checked the mares one last time before going to bed. Dulcie showed the beginning signs of coming birth. She shifted from one front foot to the other and turned her head to nip at her sides. "Easy girl, you've done this often enough to know what's happening." She laid a hand on the mare's side and again on her flank and waited. Sure enough, a contraction rolled through, not hard yet but beginning.

"You s'pose they remember from time to time like women do?" Strange to be having a conversation with Meshach about something so . . . so natural but not usually discussed between a man and a woman. But then, it was not so strange considering all they had been through. This would hopefully be a peaceful and easy time.

"Don' know. But dis mare, she be one fine mama. You go sleep. I call you."

Jesselynn yawned and leaned her forehead against the mare's neck. "Don't let me sleep through it."

"I won't." He settled himself in the corner of the stall. "You get de scissors and a strip of rawhide to tie off de cord. I catch dis baby"—he held up his cupped hands—"right here."

Jesselynn chuckled softly as she spread her quilt on the warm sand by the fire. One of the horses coughed, another shifted, and one filled the cave with the sharp scent of fresh droppings. All the others slept while the firelight flickered on the cave walls.

If only they could stay here. This cave had become home. The next might not be near as nice. She could hear Dulcie shifting in the crackling leaves of her stall.

Fear sneaked in, in spite of her best efforts. What if Dulcie had trouble birthing? What if the foal was breech? *What ifs* beat against her skull as she fell into a sleep made restless with nightmares.

Chapter Eleven

February 1863

"What a beauty." Jesselynn held up the burning brand so she could see better.

"She is dat." Meshach scrubbed the foal, still wet from the birthing sack, with a handful of clean leaves and a piece of soft deerskin. He'd already cleaned its nostrils and wiped its eyes and ears. The baby pulled her head away and tried to get her twiggy legs underneath her. Dulcie nosed her baby and licked her face. Back on her feet and hardly having broken a sweat, the mare drank some warm water with molasses in it and now was encouraging her daughter to get on her feet.

Both Meshach and Jesselynn stayed back out of the way and watched the age-old process unfold. The baby's legs did more folding than unfolding. Forelegs straight out in front of her, she bobbled from side to side, then pushed with her haunches and dug a trail in the floor with her nose. Shaking her head, she lay panting, then tried again. This time she made it halfway up before getting side heavy and crashing back down with a groan, if the little noise she made could be called that.

Dulcie nosed her again, making soft mother sounds that were easy for even the humans to understand. Her daughter didn't seem to speak the language yet. She lay flat out on her side panting.

"Should we help her?"

"Not yet. Just watch."

Suddenly the filly raised her head, rolled up on her belly, and threw herself to her feet, all four legs outstretched to brace her, nose down as if to get one more point of balance.

Jesselynn gave a sigh of delight and relief. Joseph used to say that the best ones were on their feet within an hour, and surely this one was. She'd need plenty of heart to make it to Oregon Territory. Or back to Twin Oaks if the war happened to be over in the next couple of months.

Step by tottering step, the foal made it to her mother's bag and found a teat to nurse. Her bitty brush of a tail ticked back and forth, marking perfect time like the metronome that used to keep Jesselynn in agony at the piano.

"Glad that's over." She checked on Sunshine, who slept placidly in the corner after having observed the foal's arrival. Then taking her journal out, she wrote the date and approximate time of the baby's birth, along with any other information she could think of. Compared to the foaling stalls at Twin Oaks, this one was mighty rough, but it served the purpose. Now to keep the foal healthy, dry being the first order of need. And getting her dam enough water, hay, and grain—all necessary, but not all available. Closing the book, she recapped her ink bottle and wrapped the journal back in its oilskin cloth. Her father would be proud. Dulcie was one of his favorites. Just a shame she didn't throw a colt.

––––––

Thaddeus was ecstatic in the morning. Filly was his new word for the day, and if he said it once, he said it a thousand times. When he strayed into the stall, Meshach grabbed him by the back of the britches and hauled him out between the railings.

"Stay out of there," he reprimanded.

Thaddeus nodded. From then on, he sat with his elbows on the lower rail and reached in to touch the filly whenever she came near enough. When she lay down for a snooze in the corner near him, he nearly climbed in to sleep with her. Instead, he stroked her neck and sang his own little song to the sleeping baby.

"He a horseman through and through." Meshach and Jesselynn sat nearby too, just in case Dulcie decided she didn't want the boy baby petting *her* baby. But Dulcie slept in her corner, flat out, as hard as her offspring.

"Now look, Thaddeus Joshua Highwood, you stay out of that stall, and I mean it. No reaching so far over the bars that you are more in than out."

His lower lip came out, his eyes slit. Jesselynn could tell she was in for a full-blown Highwood tantrum, so she did the same, including hands on hips. She stuck her face down into his. "And if you let out one scream, I am going to turn you over my knee and give you a walloping like you never had before. Hear me?" She didn't shout, but they could have heard her across two ridges if it weren't raining outside.

Nose to nose, the two stood for a long second before Thaddeus had a remarkable change of mind and smiled sweetly.

"Yes."

"Yes, what?"

"Yes me not go in stall."

"Sammy neither?" She'd already discovered she had a devious small brother when one day she found Sammy getting him a biscuit he'd been told he couldn't have.

Again he shook his head.

"Good. You want to play button, button?" At his nod, she pointed to the pile of small branches that needed breaking and stacking for kindling. "As soon as you finish your chores." He started to stick his lip out, thought better of it, and began breaking sticks. Jesselynn looked up to see Ophelia laughing to herself. She shook her head and went back to her sewing. Jane Ellen sat against a log, drawing one of the deerskins back and forth across a ridged stone to soften the leather. She too hid a chuckle. Thaddeus had tried to boss her around more than once, just as he had the others. Little Highwood banty rooster.

Sunshine foaled two nights later with a little longer on the delivery side but produced a strong colt for the labor. He was on his feet even faster than the filly, some pounds larger and heavier boned.

"He goin' be a fast one. Look at dem legs and chest. He take after him daddy for sure."

"Both of these are by Ahab. Shame we don't have another bloodline."

"We got Domino. You watch. He throw good colts too. Breed him to the filly. That be good match."

Jesselynn watched the colt nursing for the second time. Including Chess, they now had eight horses and one mule. Quite a herd when you thought about it. Also quite a bunch to keep hidden—and fed.

And with the sodden morass of the prairies, they wouldn't be able to leave anytime soon. She'd have to buy more hay but not from the same farmer. What kind of an excuse could she use this time? New to the area worked before. Victim of a barn burning? Now that might be an idea. There had been plenty of fighting going on in the area. The memory of a well-filled, sweet-smelling hayloft in the barn at Twin Oaks stabbed at her.

I've got to quit thinking about the past. True words, but not so easily put into practice. Once the door opened, other memories stepped through. The big house, her mother braiding her hair, her father sitting at his desk with cigar smoke curling around his head. All four of the children playing croquet, riding Ahab for morning workouts, the smell of the cookhouse when Lucinda had supper cooking.

Her eyes misted and she sniffed. "God, I hate the war." Clenching her teeth and feeling the rage that shot clear to her fingertips chased the memories back behind closed doors. She locked those doors in her mind and tried to make wise decisions regarding those in her care. Hay for the mares, pasture for the rest of the horses, a new cave to call home until they could head west. And what to do about Aunt Agatha?

Ophelia gave her a wide berth, sensing that Jesselynn bordered on breaking into rage or tears—she wasn't sure which. Any more than Jesselynn herself was. Even the little boys stayed away from her, Thaddeus standing with his thumb and forefinger in his mouth, staring at her, then averting his eyes when she glanced his way.

She sewed with a vengeance, stabbing the needle into the fabric as if her life depended on finishing the pair of pants in an hour. Jane Ellen alternately sat beside her, her fingers busy with softening the hide, her smile offering comfort, or she took the boys to the mouth of the cave to dig in the dirt.

The problem with sewing was it left her mind free to wander in the maze.

———

Three days later they were no closer to moving.

"Rode ev'ry ridge and holler within five miles of here. Many caves but all too small." Benjamin stood near the fire to dry off. Even his deerskin jacket was soaked clear through.

Jesselynn stared at the jacket. If she oiled it, the rain would run off. Why hadn't she thought of that before? "When your shirt is dry, let's rub some grease in it. You won't get so wet that way."

Benjamin looked at her as if she'd walked off and left her mind behind.

"Dat mean we look farther." Meshach looked up from the rabbit skins he was pulling over the stretchers he'd made from stiff branches. Soon he'd have enough skins tanned for someone to sew another garment. Ophelia needed something warmer, as did Meshach himself.

———

"I'm goin' to town." Jesselynn made the announcement the next morning.

"In de rain?" Meshach dropped an armload of wood on the pile.

"It looks to be lettin' up." She stuck her head out far enough to see lightening in the east and even overhead. Surely the drizzle would let up. At least it wasn't pouring. The feeling that she would explode if she had to spend one more day in the dark cave had only intensified. "I'll ride Chess and take Roman to pack some things home, er back." She hated calling the cave home. She waved a hand to cut off Meshach's offer to go along. "No. This way I can bring back four sacks of grain on Roman. Ophelia, what do you need? Or want?"

Ophelia looked at her, questions wrinkling her broad brow.

"I know. We need to save every cent we have for the trip west, but . . ." Somehow, maybe if she spent some of the hoard, she thought she might feel better. So many things they needed—clothes, lamps, even candles would be a wonderfully welcome addition to the dark cave.

"We gonna need horseshoes before we go to Independence." Meshach held up his knife, the blade so shortened by sharpening it could hardly be called a knife any longer. "And this. Goin' have to tar de wagon too. And grease de wheels. I sets de rims before we go."

"We need the wagon for most of those things, though."

"I know. We just got to think of dem."

So many things they had taken for granted at home. Beeswax for candles or tallow. Even though they'd had fat deer here, all the tallow had been used for frying. Shame they hadn't shot a bear. Bear grease worked wonders for boots and waterproofing things. What she wouldn't give for a cup of steaming tea. The coffee was gone again, even though Ophelia had toasted oats and ground them with the coffee beans to make them last longer.

Sammy had a runny nose and a cough, so maybe horehound syrup could stop that.

"We need salt and cornmeal." Since they'd had molasses, the mush had disappeared more readily. While she'd bought the molasses for the mares, they had all enjoyed it.

Jesselynn strode to push back the deer-hide door and check the weather. Sure enough, there was a patch of blue sky up above, but the sun was still under the clouds.

"I get de horses for you." Meshach headed out to where Daniel was grazing the horses. Benjamin was off hunting.

Jesselynn tucked the fresh rabbit and a bundle of dried venison into her saddlebags. Even if Aunt Agatha lived in a decent house now, they might appreciate fresh meat.

"Me go?" Thaddeus clung to her leg.

"No, not this time. Someday." She looked around, trying to think if they had anything else to trade at the store. She ignored his sad look and sat down to replace her moccasins with boots. Lacing them, she broke a lace. "Ophelia, could you please hand me a rawhide string?" She pulled out the remaining shoelace and, reaching to the side, dropped it in Thaddeus's hand. "Now you can tie something together."

The frown turned to a grin. "Tie Sammy."

"No." But Jesselynn had to smile. How like a little boy. She reached over, took the string, and tied it around his wrist. "Now you go play, or you can stack kindling."

By the time she left, the sun had managed to break through the cloud cover. But if she'd thought it muddy at the cave, when she saw the streets of Springfield, she almost wished for the cave again. Mud-weighted wagon wheels, mud-covered horses. She felt as though gray mud weighed down her shoulders. The burden was getting to be too much.

Chapter Twelve

RICHMOND, VIRGINIA

"Aunt Sylvania, don't we have a relative in Washington?"

"Why, yes, your cousin Arlington Logan, twice removed on my mother's side. Why, I haven't heard about him in years. He was studyin' to be a doctor, as I recall."

Louisa felt her heart pick up the pace. *So which side of the war is he on?* "A doctor?" She set the baby sweater she was knitting in her lap. Fine yellow yarn was such a treat after all the natural wool for men's socks.

"He must be . . . let's see . . ." Sylvania closed her eyes to remember better. "Why, he must be in his early forties by now. I think he married into the

Weintraubs of Washington. I didn't have much contact with him after his mother passed away. Fine woman, his mother."

Louisa kept perfectly still, not wanting to interrupt her aunt's memories. Something in it might be important. She heard the front door open and close. Zachary must be home again. He'd been at a meeting, the likes of which he'd refused to share with her, no matter how hard she had badgered him.

"Good evening, Aunt. Sorry I am so late."

Louisa glared at him, receiving a raised eyebrow in return. He bent and kissed his aunt's cheek.

"Yes, dear boy, I am glad to see you home." Sylvania patted his hand. "You remember talk of your cousin Arlington up in Washington?"

Louisa laid down the baby sweater and picked up a sock to continue her knitting as if she hadn't a care in the world.

"A bit. What brought him to mind?"

"Ah, might you like a cup of tea? Abby baked some of her lemon cookies just for you. Shame you weren't here for supper to make her happy." Louisa hoped the barb might distract him.

Like his father before him, once on a scent, he refused to be distracted. "Arlington, hmm."

"Louisa was asking if we didn't have relatives in Washington. Mercy me, I think we have relatives clear across the South, not that Washington is any longer a part of the South." She shook her head. "This war, such a horror."

Zachary turned toward his sister so he could question her with his good eye.

Louisa watched him from under her lashes, keeping her head down enough that he couldn't see. Her needles sang a tune of speed. "Drat!" She stopped, leaned closer to the lamplight, and took out three stitches to pick up one that had dropped.

"Louisa."

"In a moment. You don't want some soldier to get a blister because of a knot in his stocking heel, do you?"

"No, of course not." Zachary sat in the chair that seemed to have become his in the weeks he'd been ambulatory. He rubbed his leg where the leather straps and buckles sometimes dug into his flesh. "Do we have any more lamb's wool?"

"Not that I know of, dear. I'll ask Abby," Aunt Sylvania replied, returning to her knitting. The cry for warm woolen stockings was great in the damp and cold of the winter, and most women toted their knitting with them to pick up at any free moment.

Louisa could smell the cigar smoke from several of the men gathered out on the back veranda smoking and most likely discussing either the war events or their dreams of home. She wished her brother would go join them. She glanced at him again. He seemed to be settling in for the duration.

When Abby brought a tray with teacups and teapot and a platter of cookies, he thanked her and helped himself. The scent of narcissus wafted in the half-opened window, the breeze billowing the lace curtains. Louisa shivered and got up to close the window. While the day had been mild for February, evening was bringing back the chill.

She crossed the room and kissed her aunt. "Think I'll go finish Jesselynn's letter with our good news. Do you have a message for her?"

"Just tell her I am praying that our Father will keep them all safe and bring us all back together one day."

"I will. Good night, dear." She knew if she could get up the stairs, Zachary most likely wouldn't try to question her tonight.

"So soon? Here, I have something I'd like to show you." He heaved himself to his foot, and short of running away, she was trapped. The thought of stealing his crutch almost made her laugh. Now, wouldn't *that* be a trick?

Waiting for him to get moving forward gave her time to finish her cup of tea and set it back on the tray. Then taking another cookie, she followed his no-longer-stumping gait down the hall. When he wanted to, he could move fairly swiftly. Shutting the door behind them, he turned to her.

"All right. Now what are you up to?"

He knew her too well. *Nothing* would not work. She sent up a *help* prayer and took a seat on the horsehair settee. She could hear her mother's voice, the slow drawl emphasizing her wisdom all the more. *"Honesty is the best policy."*

"So be it."

"Pardon?" He sank down into his chair and with his one hand began unbuckling the straps that held his peg in place.

"You are aware that we are out of morphine?" She waited for an answer but received only a studied glance. Laying the contraption aside, he rubbed the end of his leg encased in a footless stocking knit of the finest wool Louisa could find.

"So?"

"So I propose we go and obtain some."

"You what?" He stared at her openmouthed.

"You heard me. I thought to do this by myself, but I believe the two of us would be a lot more effective."

"And how are you planning to bring this commodity back?" He leaned back in his chair, feigning nonchalance.

She could tell he was acting because of the little finger twitching on his remaining hand. Always some portion of his body moved, especially when he was attempting to make her think otherwise.

"I don't know. I heard of a woman bringing something back tied to the inside of her hoops. I imagine I could do that."

"They shoot spies."

"We wouldn't be spies. We would be visiting our cousin. Perhaps we could call on other Southern sympathizers and seek their aid."

"Louisa, drop it."

His tone set her teeth on edge. She leaned forward. "In a word, my dear brother, no. If you don't want to go with me, I will go alone." She arched an eyebrow. "I know the trip would be very hard on you." Her voice dripped with honey.

"Louisa, as the head of this family, I forbid you to even consider such an action."

"You know, perhaps we could carve out your peg and store morphine in there. And in the handle of your crutch."

"Louisa!"

"I heard tell of a false bottom in a carpetbag, and some people store their jewelry in a book, hollowed out for just that purpose. Why, if we used the family Bible, no one would question—"

"Louisa Marie Highwood, you are beyond the realms of possibility."

"Now, what could we take Cousin Arlington that he might not be able to get in that big city? Something of home?"

"Louisa, I swear I will lock you in your room."

"Zachary James Highwood, those ideas went out with the dark ages. Now, when do you think would be a good time to leave? Are the trains running north, or is there fighting between here and there? If there is, perhaps we should go by sea or head west and come into Washington from the North. Surely you would know the best route, since you traveled up there that summer during college." She waited a moment. "Or, if you won't go, perhaps I'll ask Carrie Mae. Two sisters traveling together . . ."

Zachary groaned.

"If only Jefferson would let her go without him. He is so solicitous of her."

Zachary leaned back and closed his eye.

The new lines on his face made her almost stop her planning, but not quite. She had her brother home safe, albeit much the worse for wear. Other mothers and sisters were far less fortunate.

"We must do this, Zachary. If there is any way to alleviate the suffering of our men, we must."

Chapter Thirteen

SPRINGFIELD, MISSOURI

"Hey, young Highwood, that black of your'n still lookin' for work?"

"Yes, suh. But he's a free man, not mine."

"He works for you, don't he?" Dummont leaned on his arms. "Jules needs a blacksmith. His man took sick and died. The influenza, it be bad this year."

"I'll tell him." *And Meshach can ride Roman in now, so that will be easier. Don't think he'd take it otherwise.* She let her thoughts range as she browsed the aisles of the store that had merchandise up the walls and hanging from the ceiling. So much to do to get ready.

With her horse and mule loaded, she rode over to the house where Aunt Agatha now lived. Knocking at the door, she glanced around. Daffodils were sprouting, their green spears breaking through the leaves blanketing the flower beds. Crocus, purple and white, bloomed around the base of a redbud whose stems bore fat buds, promising blossoms soon.

"Ah, Jesse, how good to see you." Aunt Agatha opened the door wide. "Can you stay for a cup of tea?"

Jesselynn's mouth craved a cup of tea as a drowning victim craved air. "I wish I could, but look how late it is. I need to be back by dark." She handed her gifts to her aunt and gave her a hug. "Are you managing here?"

"Yes, the poor dears. They are so happy to have me here, and I feel at home. This . . ." She paused, indicating with a sweep of her arm the cheery kitchen with blue-and-white plates on a rail below the ceiling and blue-and-white checked curtains at the windows. A black-and-white cat lay curled asleep on a chair cushion. "This is more like my home. I wish you had seen Oakfield." She shook herself and set the packet of food in the dry sink. "Thank you, my dear. You are so thoughtful. We shall have rabbit fricassee for supper."

Jesselynn watched her aunt. She appeared to have gained some of her weight back, and the sparkle had returned to her eyes. Maybe she would do fine here and not need to go west with them. For one so used to ordering her own home, with slaves waiting on her, she didn't seem to mind being the one who cared for the two old people.

"I'll tell cook. She's off to the market right now."

"Ah." That answered many questions. "I'll be on the road, then." She kissed her aunt's papery cheek. She smelled of rose water and happiness.

Jesselynn left town feeling more hopeful than she had for days.

Until the rain started again. Cold, wet, the dark cloud over her soul returned with a vengeance. Would she ever know simple joy again?

MARCH 15, 1863

Three weeks later they were on the road west.

Jesselynn slapped the reins over the backs of Chess and the mule. "Giddyup there." She looked over her shoulder to see Aunt Agatha sitting in her rocking chair, knitting as long as the light lasted. Ophelia had the two boys singing with their feet waving over the tailgate of the wagon. Their sweet voices carried over the undulating grass of the prairie. The sun had just set, so the sky changed from vermilion to cerise and faded to lavender and finally gray. The evening star shone like a crystal against the deepening blue of the heavens.

"Come on, Jesselynn, make a wish upon a star." It was her brother Adam's voice, as familiar as if they were playing on the closely clipped lawns of Twin Oaks. Adam, the first of the Highwood men to fall to enemy fire. But so real. She tried to ignore the star that pulled her gaze like a magnet. *I wish . . . I wish for a safe journey and a home at the end . . . for all of us.* So two wishes. After all, she hadn't wished on that particular star for a very long time.

The jingle of the harness, the *clop, clop* of trotting horses' feet, and the singing reminded her more of a picnic than the long journey ahead. But here there were no rolling, bluegrass-waving hills of Kentucky, only flat prairie, broken by scattered farms like toys tossed out by children at play. They not only had a full wagon but two horses bearing packs and a new member, who sat rocking. Aunt Agatha, without a home since the old people she cared for had died from the flu, came along only out of sheer desperation and Jesselynn's threatening everything but force.

Daddy, you'd better be appreciating this.

Ophelia sat beside Jesselynn on the wagon seat, her stomach barely rounding in the first months of growing a baby. Both mares bred again, hopefully settled, but with their foals cavorting at their sides. Daniel, as the lightest, rode the filly, and Meshach and Benjamin the stallions.

If only they didn't have so far to go. The things she'd heard of the journey ahead made her long to remain in Missouri, or return to Twin Oaks. The last letter from Louisa told of the devastation of their home, according to a letter from the Marshes, their nearest neighbors. But the land was still there. And perhaps the silver and other treasures they'd buried in the rose garden. The land would still grow tobacco and feed Thoroughbred horses.

Meshach pulled back to ride alongside the wagon. The smile he gave Ophelia spoke of love and adoration, two things surely lacking in Jesselynn's life. When the letter came from Barnabas White, she'd waited for her heart to beat a bit faster, but even at his pledge to find them, she could only stir dead embers. Surely there was a man somewhere who would make her heart leap with joy at the sound of his voice—as it had for John's. Surely there was joy—somewhere.

She glanced down at the boots and britches she wore. *Humph.* That is, if anyone could ever get close enough to figure out there was a woman under this garb. Longing to wear a soft cotton dress caught her by surprise. To feel the swish of silk against her legs, soft shoes on her feet, hair falling down her back, inviting the fingers of the man she . . .

"Good grief!"

Her mutter gave Ophelia a start. "What dat?"

"Nothing. Just dreaming, I guess." She hupped the horses again. They had to make good time while they could. Who knew what tomorrow would bring? Right now they had the cover of darkness. All they had to do was get to the safety of Independence, Missouri, and sign on with a wagon train. Before the end of April.

They should have started earlier, but the land just now had dried out enough to travel after an unusually wet winter and spring.

"We got to slow down for de little'uns," Meshach said after they'd been riding several hours. So long about midnight they stopped for a breather. Meshach checked the straps and girths on the pack animals. Both foals started to nurse as soon as the mares stopped; then they collapsed on the grass, stick legs straight out. The horses immediately put their heads down to graze, the new grass already knee-deep.

"Milk. We'll buy milk for breakfast." Jesselynn had dreamed one night of buying a cow and taking her with them. Could they take a crate of chickens clear to Oregon? They had to have livestock if they were going to farm. She caught herself dozing before they started out again.

Benjamin, riding point, returned before the dawn made itself known.

"Good place up ahead." He rode beside Jesselynn. "Dere's a small creek. We can camp over de edge of de ridge, so be out of sight of de road."

"How'd you find it?" Jesselynn covered a yawn with her hand.

"Ahab tell me. Him thirsty." Benjamin slapped the shoulder of his mount. "Him better'n a hound dog for findin' water."

"Good. You tell ol' Ahab thank you for all of us." She pulled the wagon to a stop and staggered to the ground. One foot had gone to sleep and was letting her know about it in no uncertain terms, threatening to collapse at the slightest weight. She wiggled her toes and waited until she could hobble.

By that time Meshach had unhooked the traces and was leading the team out to graze.

They all went about their work silently, hoping those sleeping in the wagon would stay asleep. When Meshach volunteered to take the first watch, Jesselynn only nodded, took her deer hide and her quilt, and crawled underneath the wagon just as she had those months before they sheltered in the caves around Springfield. The thick grass formed a soft pallet, and the songs of peeper frogs composed her lullaby.

A rifle shot yanked her awake.

"Mercy sakes. What was that?" Aunt Agatha didn't sound particularly happy, but then she hadn't ever since she arrived at their cave. If the couple she'd cared for had not succumbed to the influenza, she would still be in their lovely home in Springfield. *If* could be a mighty big word.

"Sounds like Meshach shot somethin—maybe our breakfast." Ophelia passed by Jesselynn's bed without checking to make sure she was awake. Birdsong replaced rifle song, and the fragrance of boiling coffee convinced Jesselynn it was indeed time to get up. This wasn't the first time she'd been awakened by rifle fire, and it most likely wouldn't be the last. Gratitude that it wasn't an enemy rifle flooded her as she pulled on her boots. She could hear the boys jabbering. They had their own language when they played, Thaddeus often translating for Sammy when the little one didn't have words for what he needed.

Jesselynn and the others had gotten used to that.

"Bring me a pan of warm water."

Jesselynn spun around in time to see Ophelia doing just that. The tone of Agatha's voice screamed mistress and slave.

"Put it there."

Jesselynn felt the anger swelling hot in her middle. When Ophelia returned to the fire, Jesselynn went on the attack. Only her mother's voice counseling patience kept her from dragging Agatha off behind the two trees and lambasting her good. Instead, she stopped beside her aunt and said in the calmest voice possible with ricocheting insides, "Please, Aunt Agatha, may I speak with you for a minute?"

Agatha, bending over the washbasin with a wet cloth applied to her face, turned her head with a frown. "Can it not wait? As you see, I am in—"

"No, it cannot!"

Jesselynn's clipped voice and tense jaw must have communicated the message to the older woman, for she straightened and dropped her cloth back in the water.

"Yes, dear, what is it?"

Dear? I am not your dear, and when we finish this tête-à-tête, you will most likely wish you had stayed in Springfield. Jesselynn strode the ten paces to the tree line, her heels digging into the tender grasses. She spun and barely kept from crossing her arms over her chest. *What do I do with her? "Patience is a virtue well worth cultivating."* Her mother's voice again.

Jesselynn sucked in a deep breath and let it all out as she waited for her aunt to approach. Keeping her voice low so that Ophelia wouldn't hear, she began. "I know this trip was not of your making, mine either, but we need to get a couple of things clear."

"Really?" Her aunt's chin rose a fraction, and her shoulders straightened.

"Really. First off, Ophelia is *not* a slave to be ordered around, nor even a servant. She is a free black woman who chooses to go west with us. She and Meshach are married, by a minister, and are doing their part to help us all get safely where we need to go." She could tell her aunt was digesting these words by the expressions that flitted across her face.

"Besides that, in *our* family, we did not order the slaves about but rather asked them, said please and thank you, and treated them as civilly as we treated others."

"But—"

Jesselynn held up a hand. "I understand that is not the way of most slaveholders, but that *will* be the way here." Her words were coming faster and more clipped, if possible. "Also, for us to all be safe, I am Marse Jesse, not dear or Jesselynn."

"I know that."

"Yes, but you slip sometimes, and that very slip could cost someone their life."

"Well, I never!" Agatha drew her huff up around her ears. "If your daddy could hear you now, he would turn right over in his grave." She clenched her hands at her sides and leaned slightly forward. "You say your mama treated the slaves"—she gave the word a twist with a sneer—"so proper, well, she surely failed with her eldest daughter."

"Yes, I am sure she feels she did. But failed or not, whether I wanted this or not, I am in charge, and until we get to Independence, we all have to live with that." She let the silence lengthen, sure at any moment that Agatha was going to stalk off. Maybe even head back to Springfield. It would be easy to follow the road.

The boys' laughing made her want to join the circle around the fire, eat her breakfast in peace, and then do the chores of the day. She did not want to stand nose to nose with her aunt and create an enmity that could last forever.

"We will discuss this again later." Agatha turned on her heel and returned to her washbasin as if nothing had been said.

Jesselynn stared after her. So was this win, lose, or draw? Did it matter?

Chapter Fourteen

Heading West

Jesselynn felt as though a cloud hung over her, no matter how bright the sun.

While the boys laughed at the antics of the foals in the morning before they began to tire, she saw it all but couldn't drum up any joy from it. Even Aunt Agatha chuckled.

Every hoofprint carried them farther from Twin Oaks, her sisters, her brother. *I'll never see them again, nor the rebuilding of the big house.* Morbid thoughts dogged her, burrowed under her skin, and refused to let go. Worse than a tick head sunk under the skin that itched and festered, these thoughts poisoned her spirit and added the crack of a whip to her voice.

She felt Meshach watching her and waiting. Waiting for she knew not what.

Spring broke forth in all its glory, blossoming flowers, leaf buds unfurling, giving a wash of green to dark tree branches. Dogwood bloomed creamy white in the draws, and the redbud lived up to its name. When they stopped in the morning, Sammy and Thaddeus picked dandelions till their hands were milk sticky. Daniel showed them how to roll down a gentle hill, and from then on, every hill, of which there were many, needed a roll down.

"Come." Thaddeus tugged on her hand when she woke one afternoon.

"No, Thaddy."

"Joshwa." He said it as if he was fed up with reminding her. "You come see."

"See what?" All she wanted was a cup of coffee strong enough to hold her upright. Last night she'd fallen asleep on the wagon seat. Good thing she didn't topple over under a wheel. Or was it a good thing? Then there wouldn't be so many people to take care of.

Not that she was doing such a good job of that either. Aunt Agatha still said no more to her than absolutely necessary, but she didn't order the others around either. She and Jane Ellen seemed to have hit it off, or at least Agatha had a new lamb to shepherd now. She brought out one of her skirts and together they ripped the seams, cut it up, and made one for Jane Ellen. Then using some of the white cotton Jesselynn had bought, they made her a full-sleeved waist. Meshach carved buttons for it out of deer antlers and painstakingly drilled the holes.

Jane Ellen glowed. Agatha brushed and braided the girl's hair, and with some meat finally attaching itself to her bones, Jane Ellen was actually pretty.

The transformation made Jesselynn feel like an old worn-out rag. Once she had had long, thick hair that curled about her face when she let it. But she'd cut it off to become Jesse. Most days she wondered if it had all been worth it.

One night Benjamin found a large pond for them to camp by, so when Jesselynn fell asleep she could hear ducks quacking and the piping trill of the redwing blackbirds. When she woke, Ophelia dragged back into camp, her skirt speckled with the same mud that covered her arms and legs. But they had cattail roots boiled with onion for supper, along with a mess of crappies Daniel and Thaddeus caught. Fried fish had never tasted so good.

After they ate, Jesselynn wanted to sneak off for another nap. She just couldn't get enough sleep. Meshach beckoned her to follow him. Thinking something needed doing with the horses, she did as asked. But when they followed a track partway around the pond to a log, he sat down and patted the log beside him.

"You ready to tell me what's wrong?" He pulled a stalk of grass and chewed on the tender inner stem.

"Nothin's wrong." She could hear the growl in her voice, but doing something about it went far beyond her capabilities. *If that's so, why are you crying?* She gritted her teeth and stepped on a black beetle crossing in front of her. The crack of its shell pierced her to the marrow. What a wanton, cruel thing to do. Her insides felt as though they might choke her. Her eyes watered so she could barely discern the outlines of the pond and the cattails pushing up green alongside the winter-withered stalks of the year before. Peepers sang their own song, and somewhere a bullfrog chugged.

Her own misery sang louder, obliterating the spring orchestra.

Meshach spread his feet wide and rested his elbows on his knees. "You can't run. He find you all de time."

"He?" But she'd no sooner asked the question than she knew.

"God himself be after you."

Jesselynn snorted. "Naw, He don't care." She started to rise, but Meshach's gentle hand on her arm kept her in place.

"I know He care. And deep down you know dat too."

Jesselynn spun on him. "If that God of yours cares so much, why did He let this war go on? Why have so many men died? So many families been destroyed?" The weight bore her down, even into the wooden log. "All gone. They're all gone." Her voice rose. "Why, Meshach? You tell me why. I hate your God, and I hate what He's done." She shook her fist in heaven's face and crumpled into a ball of misery, her arms gripping her knees tightly, as if she would shatter into a million pieces if she let go. "Answer me, Meshach."

"Don' got no answers. Just got love. De love of de Father far beyond all dat. He keep us safe. He bring Marse Zachary back from de dead, He keep Lucinda from slave traders, we . . ."

"But Father is dead, the South is destroyed, Adam, John—"

"But dey in heaven wid de Lawd."

Digging out another answer took far more than she could muster. Heaven—her mother dreamed of heaven. Her father saw her and Jesus, or an angel, before he died. The joy that lit his face was beyond anything she'd ever seen.

"Dis here not our home. Our home be in heaven wid de Father and de Son."

Jesselynn sighed. Why would He want her back? All the hateful things she'd said, the terrible anger and hatred, the wicked thoughts.

"He waitin', Him and all de angels waitin' to shout joy and hallelujah over de lamb dat be found."

She looked over to see his eyes closed and his lips moving. She knew he was praying for her. One of her responsibilities as mistress was to instruct her people in the ways of the Lord and to live her life as an example to them. *Oh, Mother, I have failed you so terribly.* The tears she'd been fighting so hard spilled over and trickled down her cheeks.

The boot was on the other foot. Meshach took his Lord very seriously to heart.

"He say to lay your burdens at Him feet. 'Take my yoke,' he say, 'for my yoke is easy and my burden is light.' " Meshach laid a hand on her shoulder. "De burdens too heavy for you. Let dem go."

"I can't." *I can't, God. I can't do this any longer. I'm dying inside. If you really are the God my mother loved and the Bible says, forgive me, deliver me, let me loose.* The tears that washed her eyes now bathed her soul and broke through the barriers to let the light back into her darkest corners.

Sometime later she pulled her shirttail loose to wipe her eyes.

Meshach still sat beside her, staring out over the ripples of the pond where several ducks had just landed. "God's Word say it all. Psalm ninety-one is for us headin' west. We like dat little ducklin' out dere who hide under him mama's wing. Only God's our mama and daddy all to once."

Jesselynn had to smile at the mallard hen, trailed by six bits of yellow, riding the ripples and following where their mother led. She sighed and let her head hang forward, like a sunflower too heavy for the stalk. "I think I owe some apologies."

"Mebbe. Mebbe not. But dey worries 'bout you."

She sighed—a long exhalation that dug up from her toes and the ends of her hair. She coughed, clearing her throat of the leftover tears. "We'd better be gettin' back."

"You ready?"

She nodded, chewing one side of her lower lip. "Thank you—I guess."

His smile warmed clear to her heart. "We thanks God."

"I did, and I do." She stood and stretched, feeling lighter than she had for months. She walked off, glancing over her shoulder to see if an old skin was lying on the ground behind her.

That night when Meshach read Psalm ninety-one, she listened instead of blocking his voice from her mind. " 'He that dwelleth in the secret place of the most high shall abide under the shadow of the Almighty. I will say of the Lord, He is my refuge and my fortress; my God; in him will I trust.' " A refuge is what He promised. A secret refuge in time of trouble. She thought back to the times they'd bypassed towns and army encampments as if they couldn't be seen. *A secret refuge? Have I just been too blind to see?*

———

They neared Carthage on the morning of the third day and stopped in a draw before they could be seen by the townspeople. When Jesselynn woke up after another restorative sleep without the nightmares that had plagued her for so long, she lay under the wagon listening to the private chatter of Sammy and Thaddeus. She heard Meshach reading the Bible to Ophelia and anyone else who wanted to listen. A squirrel scolded from a tree, a crow added to the dressing down, and the other birds ignored them, so she knew the fussing wasn't because of someone coming. Besides, Ahab was better than any watchdog if strangers came near.

She stretched and rolled over to her side to see Aunt Agatha's legs and feet not quite reaching the ground while she sat on the tailgate. *How do I go about making my peace with her?* All previous overtures had been coldly rebuffed. The others had just smiled and nodded when she seemed to be her old self again. Thaddeus and Sammy now came to play about her feet and ask to be put up on the horses. Jane Ellen often watched to see when she woke up and brought her coffee if they had it or brought whatever kind of hot drink Ophelia made when they didn't. She knew she'd been forgiven.

Wasn't it too easy? she wondered, her head propped on her arm. She'd read the verses on forgiveness, needing only a reminder, since she memorized them as a child. All the Scriptures said was to ask, and God did the rest. Repent— now that was a word to get hung up on. Had she repented? She believed so. So now, as Meshach had reminded her, don't let Satan get a foothold by telling you you weren't forgiven. Jesus said it was so.

"Thank you, Father," she whispered. "Now to live it." She threw back the covers and pulled on her boots before folding the quilt and the deerskin that kept the damp from seeping into her quilt.

"Next time we find running water, we have to do the wash." She strolled over to the campfire where Ophelia poured her a cup of coffee. "Where's Jane Ellen this morning?"

"She be lookin' for herbs and such."

"By herself?"

"She say she be in hearing distance." Ophelia used her apron as a hot pad to move the kettle back to the coals. "Turkey for supper." She nodded to where Daniel lay soundly sleeping. "Daniel bag it. Cook on spit."

Jesselynn's mouth watered at the mention of the delicacy. Turkeys were wily birds and hard to find. "We still have potatoes?"

"Um. Carrots and rutabaga too. Have a feast tonight."

"I'm goin' to ride into town to see what I can learn."

Meshach looked up from his reading. "Take Benjamin wid."

"No, he can sleep."

"Jesse?"

Jesselynn turned in surprise. Aunt Agatha was actually initiating a con-versation—amazing. "Yes?"

"If a store has . . ." She lowered her voice and raised her head to glance around the camp.

Jesselynn stepped closer to hear better. "Has what?"

"Some finer cotton. I would like to make Jane Ellen some drawers and a camisole." She dug in a leather purse she kept on a chain at her waist. "Here is the money."

"Aunt Agatha, you keep your money. I'll gladly buy the material. Is there anything else?"

"No." She paused. "Unless you could maybe find some lace or ribbon." She leaned closer. "I don't think that girl has had anythin' nice in her entire life." She shook her head, *tsking*. "And she's such a good-hearted little soul."

"That she is." Jesselynn leaned forward and kissed her aunt on the cheek. "You are too." She left before Agatha could say a word.

Long before she got to Carthage, she remembered why she hated riding Roman. His trot tore loose every muscle in her body, at least it felt like it. She dismounted near what looked like a general store and ambled along the board-walk. Touching the brim of her hat when she met a woman with a market basket, she paused and leaned against a wall to eavesdrop on two elderly men sitting on a bench, one smoking a pipe, the other chewing and spitting.

"Sad, ain't it? That Ben sure was a good man." *Hawk. Spit.*

"How he lived that long, I swain."

"You reckon they hung the guy that did it?"

"One of Quantrill's Raiders? They never hang 'em. Can't catch 'em. Strike and they're gone, just like a water moccasin I see'd down in Arkansas. Now that critter come right up over the gunwale of the boat. Beat him off with m' oar, I did."

Jesselynn wanted to beat them with an oar. What about the dead man? What about the Raiders? They *had* to get out of town. And quickly.

Chapter Fifteen

☙☞

"Are you comfortable, Zachary dear?"

"As well as can be possible." The glare he gave her said more than words could have said about what he thought of her plan. He propped his leg along the crutch he braced on the facing seat of the railroad car.

The engine whistled. The train lurched forward, coal smoke blowing by their window. Louisa dug in her satchel and withdrew her knitting just as if they were sitting in the parlor at Aunt Sylvania's instead of on a train carrying them north to God only knew what peril.

The thought made Zachary clench his teeth. "If we ever get back home, I swear I am goin' to—"

"Yes, dear." Louisa played the wifely roll to the hilt, all sweetness and acquiescence now that she had her own way. But to tell the truth, once Zachary agreed to the outrageous plan of traveling north to get morphine and smuggle it back home, he'd begun preparations with a typical Highwood intensity. Gold for the purchases now filled the cavities hollowed out to hold the precious medicine, including the middle of the Bible she had lying on the seat beside her.

Anyone looking would only see a gallant young couple, she caring for a badly incapacitated husband, he a bit cantankerous, which anyone would hardly blame him for, seeing the residuals of his wounds and all. She waited on him hand and foot, even to fetching a coal to light his cigar and seeking a pillow to put under his leg.

Louisa received approving nods from an elderly couple seated across the aisle from them. While she tried to act as if traveling like this were an everyday occurrence, she wanted to plaster her nose to the window and not miss a single sight. *My land, to be rushing across the country at such speeds. Oh, if only Jesselynn were here. She would be near inebriated with joy.*

When the tracks ended at Fredericksburg, they transferred to a buggy for the ride to the Potomac River. Louisa nearly fell asleep but popped wide awake when the driver stopped. While she had a million questions, the look on Zachary's face warned her that silence was a better plan.

"Easy now," the man in black whispered as he helped them alight, traverse a small dock, and settle into a boat with high gunwales and a slender mast. Two men at the oars leaned into the pull.

At the far shore in Union territory, they entered a carriage for the drive into the capital. A basket of bread, cheese, and boiled eggs stilled the rumblings of their bellies. Louisa fell asleep before folding her napkin away.

————

Gawking was not polite; she knew that. Her mother had made frequent admonishments of such when they were little. But this was the capital of the United States, of which she had heard so much.

"Can we drive by the White House?" she asked once they had secured a hansom cab.

"Whatever for? This is no longer *our* capital, or have you forgotten?"

"You needn't speak cruelly like that. Not all of us believe there will be two separate countries."

The glare he gave her should have melted her bones, let alone her spirit, but she ignored him and turned to watch out the window instead. The streets were a quagmire of conveyances of all types. Blue uniforms, women in finer dress than any she'd seen for a long time strolled the boardwalks or rode at a frantic pace, as if the speed with which they arrived made any eternal difference.

"Do you know where we are going?"

"I gave the driver Cousin Arlington's address, or at least the address we have for him. His family might be there, even if he is off with the army somewhere."

"Oh, I hadn't thought of that. Of course, if he is a physician . . ." Her heart felt as though it had gained ten pounds of pure lead.

"If they do not invite us to stay, we will find a hotel, and you will remain there while I see to the availability of our supplies." He kept his voice so low she had to lean close to hear him.

Louisa devoutly hoped they would be invited to stay with their relatives. Surely the bonds of Southern hospitality still held true, even if . . . she couldn't bring herself to say they were on opposite sides. All she longed for was the end of the war. But then, the war hadn't held the allure for all the Highwood women as it had for the men.

What she really wanted was an end to the injured and the dying. Sometime earlier she had ceased to pray for either side, but only for the war to cease. Never would she entrust her brother with her feelings. He'd think her a traitor.

Deep inside she wished she could talk with President Lincoln and entreat him to stop the war. He seemed like a man with a concern for men dying, unlike the Southern firebrands. Again, unbeknownst to those around her, she prayed for wisdom for the two men in charge—Abraham Lincoln and Jefferson Davis—that they would end the fighting.

The cab stopped in front of a narrow three-story house that fronted directly on the cobblestone street, three polished steps from the sidewalk to the door with a shiny brass knocker. An urn with a boxwood topiary sat to either side of the steps, lending a touch of green to the brick face. A sign that read *Physician* hung from an ornate iron bar attached to the wall.

"Dis de place," the black driver announced as he stepped to the street and reached up for their one small trunk. Louisa handed out her carpetbag and accepted his hand to help her step down, turning to offer her assistance to Zachary. Getting in and out of conveyances had not become much easier, even with practice. With the driver's hand under his right arm and the crutch under his left, Zachary led with his good foot, staggering but for the bracing of his two helpers.

"Thank you." Once steady, he dug in his pocket for the coins, paid the man, and stared up at the windows with green shutters on the sides.

"Yo' trunk, suh?"

"On the steps, if you will." He nodded to Louisa. "You want to ply the knocker?"

Her heart felt as though it might knock its way right out of her chest. The moment of decision. What if they were turned away? She swallowed, glanced over her shoulder at the sound of the departing cab, took in a deep breath, and mounted the stairs. With a shaking hand, she let the knocker fall, then tapped it again.

Chapter Sixteen

HEADING TO INDEPENDENCE

Circumventing Blytheville took some planning.

Jesselynn stared at the map Benjamin had drawn in the dirt with a stick. Carthage lay behind them, Blytheville ahead. If there weren't regular Union army located in the area, the dreaded Quantrill Raiders could show up anywhere, anytime. They specialized in night travel too. Only their purpose wasn't a new life of freedom. Theirs was to bring destruction everywhere and plant fear into every heart within reach. They were supposed to be Confederate cavalry, but most people described them as the devil's cavalry.

"But if we go this way . . ." She pointed to a road that ran northwest from the one they were taking to meet the main road between Kansas City and points south. That road used by the armies and freight haulers, besides ordinary citizens, cut a line through Kansas farmland, rich when enough rain fell. Lakes and swamps dotted the Missouri side of the border, so travel could not be as direct. Jesselynn studied the drawing some more. The war! Always the war. Soldiers to hide from, no matter which side they fought for, since they all needed horses.

"We got dis far. We can make it." Meshach held Sammy up on his shoulders and jiggled him every once in a while, eliciting giggles from above and frowns from below. Thaddeus had yet to have a turn. "De good Lawd see us through."

"Which way do you think we should go?" She looked up in time to see Sammy clamp his little hands over Meshach's eyes.

"I think Benjamin should go on into Blytheville and ask around. Or you, like you done planned before." Meshach removed the hands from his eyes and jiggled his rider. More giggles.

Jesselynn sighed. Instead of getting easier to play the part of a young man, it was getting harder. *I should be used to it by now,* she told herself. *I can be a woman again when we reach Oregon.* In Oregon they would be safely away from the war. Away from slavery, armies, and bushwhackers. Away from traveling at night and worrying that they may be found during the day.

She'd heard the land there was free for homesteading, just as Meshach dreamed of. There were mountains and lush valleys where, folks said, you could stick a fence post in the ground and a tree would sprout. Fruit trees, tall trees to cut for cabins, wheat, cattle—everything seemed to do well in Oregon, just like in the Garden of Eden. Only the lazy would starve in Oregon Territory. Folks could eat off the land, they said, with enough wild things to feed anyone willing to pick, dig, or shoot. If the stories were half true, the land would be worth the trip.

But first they had to get to Independence.

She sighed and, ignoring her dreams of possibilities, turned her attention back to the matter at hand. *Lord, which way do you want us to go? Your Word says you'll guide us and keep us, and we need that now, as much as ever.* Daily she gave thanks that she'd turned back to her Lord. Even though at times the darkness would try to sneak in again, she remembered how she loved the light and wanted—needed it, like she needed air to breathe.

She took in a deep breath and let it out. "All right, much as I hate to, I'll take Roman and go explore a bit of the town. Daniel, you want to come with me?"

The youngest of their group, Daniel, roused from his dozing against a log and leaped to his feet. "Shore do, Marse Jesse. I gets Roman for us."

———

Both riding the mule, they entered the town by the back streets, only to find it full of people, all heading toward the town square. They caught the whispers. A hanging was about to happen. Jesselynn had no desire to see a hanging, but wandering through the crowd could most likely fill her in on all the news and the gossip too. They dismounted and tied the mule to a hitching post behind a store. With a pat on Roman's rump that raised a cloud of dust, she pointed Daniel down one street, and she took the other.

"Be back here before the sun goes past that church spire."

He nodded after following her pointing finger. "I be back."

Jesselynn could see the gallows looming black in the westering sun. A rope dangled from the high beam, but while the crowd continued to gather, no one mounted the stairs yet.

A woman pushed by, dragging a young child by the hand. "Hurry up, now. We want to be there when they put the rope over his head."

Jesselynn felt her stomach turn. She ambled from group to group, pausing now and then to listen. She stopped by a couple of townspeople when she overheard mention of the raiders.

"They come like thieves in the night, take what they want, and burn the rest." The speaker hawked and spit, nearly hitting Jesselynn's boot toe. "Sorry." The man glanced at her and turned back to his companion. "I heard tell that they are recruiting again, but you got to have your own horse to join up. Ya'd think the army would supply the horses."

"Shoot, the army ain't got siccum. They's pulling all the troops back to Virginny, I heard."

"Leavin' Quantrill in charge out here?" His look of shock sent shivers up Jesselynn's back.

"No. An army will remain at Fort Scott. They know the rebs will be right back here if there's no troops. Arkansas is too close for that."

When they started jawing about the local sheriff, Jesselynn slipped on to the next group. Who could she ask about the roads north? Who were they hanging and why? As more people poured into the square, Jesselynn almost resorted to pushing to get by a group of five women. Why was a hanging more like celebrating the Fourth of July?

" 'Scuse me. Pardon me." One well-rounded matron stepped backward, right on Jesselynn's foot.

"Ouch." But her voice drowned in the laughter.

"Here now, son. Up on my shoulders, you'll be able to see everything." The man swung his boy up, barely catching Jesselynn with his elbows.

Drawing a breath of relief at escaping the horde, Jesselynn stepped up onto the porch of the bank building and leaned against the post, scanning the crowd while she drew her knife from her pocket and, opening the blade, began to clean her fingernails. Studying the impacted dirt, she listened to the men behind her.

"Hangin' is too good for 'im."

At that comment, she angled herself so she could see them out the corner of her eye.

"Shoulda just shot him. That's what I say. Anyone who'd rob the store and shoot ol' Avery through the heart deserves shootin'. Why, he gave away more food than he sold when times were really tough. Don't care how desperate the man was." He shook his head, then lifted his hat with one hand and smoothed his hair back with the other before settling the slouch-brimmed thing back securely on his head. "I went on the posse, ya know. If the sheriff hadn't threatened to shoot any man who took matters into his own hands, we'da been saved the work on the scaffold and all."

"But the 'portant thing is, he's goin' to swing."

"I just wished he'd been one of them raiders, that's all. Let me get my hands on those thievin' skunks, and I'd—"

"Just pray they don't come out your way."

"Ain't got nothin' for them anyways."

"You got chickens, 'n hogs 'n such, ain't ya? That's what they're lookin' for. And hay left in your barn or grain in the bin? They gotta eat and feed their horses. They don't offer no pay neither."

When a man shouted for their attention, Jesselynn's attention swung back to the raised platform. A quick glance told her the black-coated man boasted a star, so he must be the sheriff. As the crowd roared and pressed forward, the better to hear, she closed her pocketknife and, sliding it back in her pocket, stepped off the porch. All her listening had done was put the fear of night travel back at the top of her list.

What do I do to keep the horses safe? I'll take regular army, gray or blue, any day over this. At least she knew there was a garrison at Fort Scott. They'd have to swing west to miss that. Her mind made up, she strode on back to the general store and entered through two swinging doors, making her wonder if she'd found the saloon by mistake. A man in an apron nearly ran over her in his rush to get out the door.

"You'll have to come back later, boy. I ain't missin' the show."

"The show?"

"You know. The hangin'."

"Oh, could you cut me some cheese first and maybe weigh out a pound of coffee? I got to be on my way. Some of those peppermint sticks too."

The man rolled his eyes and shook his head. "Cain't it wait?"

"Nope."

The man groaned and stomped his way back to the counter. The way he slapped the cheese on the scale told her of his resentment. But when she paid him with a gold piece, his scowl lightened. He shoved her packets across the counter and almost beat her to the door, flipping the *CLOSED* sign as he left.

Jesselynn paused outside the store and studied those around her. Noticing a man who appeared content to stay where he was leaning against the railing of the store, she stopped beside him. "Mister, can I ask you a question?"

"Sure 'nough, boy. What can I do for you?"

"Well, my daddy sent me into town to ask about the best way to Independence. Ya see, we's goin' on west to Oregon." *Why'd you have to tell him all that?*

"Where's your daddy now?"

"Oh, camped some east of here. He's ailin', or he woulda come hisself."

"From what I hear, it takes a powerful lot of strength to go to Oregon."

"Ah, he'll be on his feet again soon." Jesselynn rammed her hands in her pockets and glanced up at the stranger from under her hat brim. "You been to Independence?"

"Many times. If'n it were me, I'd take the road that runs north of town. Cut off a few miles thataway. Road's good again now that the rain let up."

"Thankee, sir. I'll tell my daddy what you said. We be grateful." She started to back away.

"Where you all from?"

Just then a shout from the area of the platform snagged his attention and let Jesselynn slip away without answering. That was the way of folks, always asking questions. Ignoring the spectacle going on behind her, she made her way back to the mule.

"Why are folks so confounded enamored with watchin' some man die?" But asking Roman anything never had gotten her very far.

Daniel was nowhere in sight.

She checked out the church steeple. Sure enough, the sun had passed it some time earlier.

I should just leave him, let him walk back to camp. As the minutes passed, the thought took on more possibilities. Besides, if she thought about leaving him, the fear that something had happened couldn't take over.

A shout went up from the crowd on the other side of the building. The deed must have been done. Her stomach rolled. People would be disbursing now. "Daniel, you good for nothing young pup, I could—"

"*Psst!*"

She looked around.

"*Psst.* Over here, Marse Jesse."

She turned in time to see a dark brown hand beckoning from the other side of the alley and two doors down. She jerked the knot loose that bound the mule and, flinging herself on his back, had him moving before she sat upright. She slowed to a walk. Like a shadow Daniel leaped from his hiding place and had himself up behind her, scarcely touching her foot and extended hand.

"Hey! Hey, you. Stop!"

The shout propelled them into a canter, and within moments they were beyond accosting.

"What on earth did you do this time?" Jesselynn wanted to turn and look into his eyes so he wouldn't lie to her. *Takes a liar to know a liar.* The thought made her slap the reins on Roman's shoulder.

Chapter Seventeen

BLYTHEVILLE, MISSOURI

"*Who was that?*"

"I don' know. Just ride." The terror in his voice fueled her own fear. She kicked Roman to a dead-out gallop. The clatter of horses' hooves sounded behind them. Was someone following them?

No trees, nothing to lose them in. Nowhere to hide.

"Turn off here," Daniel yelled in her ear, the wind nearly snatching the words and flinging them back before she could hear. She pulled back on the reins, and Roman slowed quickly enough to send her up on his neck. When he turned, they fought to stay mounted, even though they felt as if they were at the wrong end of a catapult.

"How far?"

"Dat barn up ahead."

Ignoring the dog barking at their heels, they veered around behind the gable-roofed barn and plowed to a stop. Roman sounded like a bellows in full operation, and Jesselynn knew she sounded about the same.

"What in heaven's name was that all about?" While she tried to quiet her breathing so she could hear if they were still being followed, the growling dog did nothing to help.

"Who's that out there?" The bellow came from the direction of the house.

The dog upped the volume, as if calling his master to come help.

"Daniel!"

"Some white man said I was with the man they done hanged." Between his terror and the barking dog, Jesselynn wanted to clap her hands over her ears.

"You were with what man? We just got to town."

"I knows dat, but he started comin' after me, and dat's when I hid under dat house to wait for you."

The dog raised the pitch on his bark.

"Shaddup, you mangy cur." The owner of the voice rolled around the corner of the barn, rifle at the ready across his broad chest and broader belly. He pointed the rifle at the two on the mule. "Well, let's y'all jist get on down off'n that there mule and answer me some questions. Me 'n the deputy, that is."

The man coming around the other side of the barn wore a shiny star on the lapel of his leather vest and a smile that sent shivers up and down Jesselynn's back.

"Now, boys, just ease on down to the ground so's we can talk all friendly like."

"Where I come from, we don't call pointin' a rifle at a stranger very friendly."

"Well, now, you might if'n one of the strangers was wanted for murder." The deputy used one finger to tip his felt hat farther back on his head.

Jesselynn shook her head as she slid off the mule, shielding Daniel by taking a step forward right in front of him. "No way could Daniel here be wanted for murder. We just rode into town this afternoon, been on the road from Springfield for three days. We're lookin' for to find the best way to pick up the road to Independence."

"Now, boy, why in the world should I believe what you say? A man back in Blytheville says yer slave was with the man who shot poor ol' Avery. Shot 'im in cold blood, he did."

"I'm right sorry to hear that, but first of all, Daniel is not my slave but a freedman, and according to what I heard, the shooting happened over a week ago. We weren't anywhere near here then." Jesselynn made sure she sounded as Kentucky as possible and educated to boot. While she sounded as self-possessed as she was able to, her teeth had a heart-stopping desire to clack together. She hid her hands in her pockets to disguise their shaking.

"Well, son, I think we'll let the judge decide that." The deputy strode forward and grabbed Daniel by the upper arm. "Come along, boy."

"No!" Jesselynn tried to step between them but got shoved out of the way for her efforts. When she reeled back against the mule's shoulder, the dog growled and bumped her leg with his nose, teeth bared and hair raised along his back and shoulders. The urge to kick him made her foot twitch. "Call off your dog, mister, before I —"

"Before you what?" The man's voice rumbled with laughter.

When Daniel hung back and sent her a terrified look over his shoulder, the deputy jerked him hard enough to make him stumble. For that he got a clout with the rifle stock.

"Marse Jesse! Don' let dem take me!"

His cry nearly broke her heart. She started after the pair, but the dog grabbed hold of her pants leg, taking some skin with it.

Jesselynn turned and gave the dog a vicious chop with the side of her hand, right on his nose. The dog yipped and let go. Ignoring the burning in her calf, she started after the deputy, who was now tying a rope around Daniel's chest, binding his arms straight down to his body.

"Hold 'im there, Jason."

The calm command brought the owner's rifle to hand, and a bullet puffed the dirt a couple of feet in front of her.

"He's done nothing wrong. He wasn't even here." But talking did no good as the deputy shook out a few lengths of rope and mounted his horse.

"Give me any more lip, and I drag 'im to town. Take your pick." He settled his hat down on his head and stared at Jesselynn.

God, help us. What do I do now?

"How 'bout I ride into town with you and straighten this all out?" She fought to keep the tremor out of her voice.

"Suit yourself. Perhaps the judge'll want to talk to you too." The veiled threat worked. Her mouth went dry as a creek bed in August.

She swallowed and cleared her throat. "No more than I want to talk with him." With a glare at the dog owner, she swung aboard Roman and followed the deputy around the barn and back out to the road. By now the sun had dipped appreciably lower, and all Jesselynn wanted to do was hightail it for their camp and get out of the area. But leaving Daniel was not even a thought. He would be with them when they hit the road north.

Two men met them on the road and fell in beside the deputy. Daniel trotted to keep up with the trotting horses, but the men in front of him paid him no more attention than if he'd been a cow. In fact, less.

Jesselynn brought Roman up beside Daniel. "Do you have your manumission papers?"

He shook his head. "Back at de camp. Put de papers in Meshach's Bible."

How many times had she told them they needed the papers on their person at all times? Slave traders wouldn't let them go back to anywhere for their papers. But scolding him would do no good now. Most likely he'd been doing a good enough job of that himself.

"I'm heading back to camp then, but I'll be in town as soon as I can get there. Just do what they tell you so they have no call to whip you."

"Dey don' need no call, Marse. Dey gonna whip dis poor nigger sure as de sun rise."

Lord, let it only be a whipping. Please, God, not a hanging.

"We'll pray that not be so."

"Hey, you, leave that boy alone."

At the jerk on the rope that caused Daniel to stumble and nearly go down, Jesselynn dropped back. When they reached the main road, she turned east as they turned west. Digging her heels into the mule's ribs, she slapped him with the reins too. "Hup, Roman, come on."

A few minutes that seemed like hours later, she tore into camp and threw herself off the mule's back before he came to a skidding stop. "They've got Daniel." She tried to draw a breath and speak at the same time but only succeeded in making herself cough.

"Who got Daniel?" Meshach thumped her on the back to help her breathe.

"A deputy. Someone said Daniel was with a man who shot the owner of the store. They hung that man this afternoon in the center of town." Jesselynn took the cup of water Jane Ellen handed her and guzzled it, water dripping unnoticed down her chin. She wiped her mouth with the back of her hand and handed the cup back. "Thanks." Turning to Meshach, she closed her eyes for a moment to get the facts straight. "They'll hang him for certain if we don't do something and do it fast." She sucked in a deep breath and let it out. If she didn't calm down, she'd be worthless. "He says his papers are in your Bible. You get those, and I'll get Daddy's journal. That should prove who we are."

"We take de wagon? Dey see we be travelin'."

"Lawd, keep our Daniel safe." Ophelia clasped her hands to her bosom and looked heavenward. Sammy, clinging to her skirt, set to whimpering, which brought out a quivering lower lip on Thaddeus.

"Here, let me take them babies." Jane Ellen reached for Sammy and, after settling him on her hip, took Thaddeus's hand. "We'll go look for the ducks."

"You want I should go too?" Aunt Agatha looked over her spectacles. "Might lend a note of propriety. I can show letters and things from Springfield. There are dates and such on them."

Jesselynn wrinkled her brow in thought. "I think not at the moment." The last thing she wanted to do was subject the rest of the family to any fracas in town. "Just pray that most of the folks have already gone home. There surely was a crowd there for the hangin'. You'da thought a circus came to town, such an air of jollity." The thought still made her stomach clench. Even worse, she knew there wouldn't be a trial and a formal hanging for a black boy like Daniel. Some group of men would just take him out to a tree or use the beam at the livery and string him up.

"All right, let's harness up Roman and Chess. Benjamin, you make sure the rest of the horses are well grazed and watered. We might be leavin' in a hurry. Ophelia, have supper ready and everything else packed up." She glanced around the camp. No matter what, they were pushing out as soon as they had Daniel in tow.

She glanced over her shoulder as they left the camp. Aunt Agatha was sitting in her rocker, both boys in her lap while Jane Ellen and Ophelia were making biscuits for supper and some to harden for eating later on the trail. They looked so peaceful, as if no one was worried sick about Daniel, but she knew they were. Ophelia might be singing, but her songs were always prayers for the good Lord's intervention in their lives.

Once in town she directed Meshach to the jail, where they tied up the team in the rear so no one would get too interested in the horse. Stepping down, they heard a *psst*.

"Marse Jesse, over here." Daniel, one eye swollen closed and lower lip thick and split, waved at them from the barred window of the jail.

"How bad off are you?" Jesselynn stepped close so they could whisper.

"Dey ask me 'bout dat man dey hung, and I don know nothin' 'bout him. Dey says I lyin' and den dey hit me. Not too bad. Sheriff come in and make dem stop."

Jesselynn breathed a sigh of relief. While the deputy had already made up his mind, perhaps the sheriff was a man of integrity. And the judge, if they could meet with him.

"I'm sorry, Daniel, I should never have brought you to town with me."

"You don't know 'bout dis here man either."

"I know, but—" Jesselynn stopped. Crying over spilt milk never did anyone any good. "You just sit down and rest. We'll take care of this." She caught a nod from Meshach, and the two of them headed for the front door of the building. A sign above the heavy wooden door read *SHERIFF* in letters large enough to be seen from a distance. When they pushed it open, the deputy she'd encountered earlier sat behind the wooden desk drinking a cup of coffee and smoking a cigar.

"I'd like to speak with the sheriff." Jesselynn kept her voice even and polite, in spite of an urge to have Meshach pick the man up and throw him through the window, bars and all.

"He ain't here."

"I can see that. Where can I find him?"

"At home. He don't like to be disturbed when he's eatin' his supper." He waved the cigar for emphasis.

Jesselynn counted to five. Ten would take too much time and effort. "And where might his home be?"

"He'll be back in an hour or so. Thataway I can go eat."

Meshach shifted from one foot to the other. Jesselynn could feel his anger like something alive in the room.

The deputy could sense it too. Eyes slit, he shifted his gaze from one guest to the other. "I wouldn't want to hurry him meself." Slowly he lowered his boots to the floor and sat up straight, his elbows resting on the desk as if to prove his nonchalance.

"Since I heard the dead man had a trial, is there a judge in town?"

"Left on the stage yesterday."

Jesselynn counted again. Why did everything seem to be against them?

The gleam in the deputy's eye said he was enjoying their frustration. *He's most likely the kind of man who pulled legs off live frogs when he was young. Thinks no more of treating black boys the same.*

"Thank you for your information. Now where did you say the sheriff lived?"

"I din't."

Meshach took a step forward and leaned toward the desk. His fists looked powerful enough to drop a horse with one blow.

"Ah, the sheriff lives two blocks over and three down, on Hawthorne. White house with green shutters." The deputy pointed toward the west.

As they turned to leave, he added, "Don't you go worryin' 'bout that nigger back there. After tomorrow there won't be no more problem."

Meshach pulled the door closed behind him with a thud big enough to shake the boards beneath their feet. "I surely do hopes the sheriff be a better man than that 'un."

"Me too, Meshach, me too. Tryin' to figure out what he meant about no more problem scares me clear to Sunday."

"Dis 'bout as bad as Daniel in de lions' den."

"Worse. Men can be meaner than lions any day." Together they followed the directions to the sheriff's house, then sat down to wait, leaning against the picket fence that fronted the street.

Meshach pulled up a blade of grass and chewed the tender stem.

Jesselynn knew from his quiet that he was praying. While she tried to put the entire mess into the Lord's strong hands, pictures of the deputy dragging Daniel at the end of the rope intruded. And fears of Daniel dangling from the end of a rope made her stomach roil and her blood boil. *Lord, surely you wouldn't let him come so far to be strung up for something he didn't do. We have so far to go, yet we're close to being free too.*

She glanced sideways to see Meshach with his head back against the fence, his eyes closed, and wearing a slight smile as though he was lost in a pleasant dream. Surely he was praying, not sleeping. She watched for any sign of awareness. A bee buzzed over his head and was gone. Children shouted from a yard somewhere nearby. A baby cried and stopped in that instant that said someone had come for him.

Jesselynn wished someone would come for her. All this was just too much. *God, what do you expect of me? I can't keep on taking care of all these people, and short of breaking Daniel out of the jail, I don't know what to do.*

She felt like shaking her fist. "He's innocent," she whispered.

"I know dat, and you know dat. Now we just wait 'till de sheriff know dat too." Meshach's gentle answer smoothed over her restlessness like a loving hand.

Jesselynn sighed. "I sure hope that sheriff is enjoying his supper."

When they heard the front door click closed behind them, they both got to their feet and turned to greet a man, nearly as tall as Meshach, settling his hat over a bald spot pushing up through wisps of gray hair. Furry eyebrows nearly met over the bridge of a nose that had encountered one too many fists.

"Good evening, Sheriff."

"Sorry, I didn't know anyone was waiting. Why didn't you come to the door?"

"Ah, your deputy said you didn't like to be disturbed during supper."

The sheriff shook his head. "That Rudy, I'd soon as fire him as keep him." He stopped at the gate. "So what can I do for you?"

"You can release my friend, Daniel, who looks plenty worse than the last time I saw him. I am Jesse Highwood from Midway, Kentucky, and Daniel used to be one of my father's slaves until he was given his manumission papers before we started west."

"What is bringing you this way?"

"We got burned out, so decided that Oregon might be a good place to start over."

"And your father?"

"Killed in the war. I'm the oldest remaining son, and all I want is to get my people west. Daniel was with us in Springfield up until three days ago when we started out. No way could he have been here."

"You got any papers to back all this up?"

Jesselynn pulled Daniel's manumission papers from her pocket. "This here and more in the wagon."

"Come on, then. Let's go on back and study this situation. We have a man who swears your Daniel was with Gardner when he shot and killed Avery Hopkins."

"When was he killed?"

" 'Bout dusk a week ago Friday."

"And this man has seen Daniel today?"

"Yup. Says he's the one."

Jesselynn walked between the two men back to the jail. Surely he believed her. It certainly seemed so.

After he dismissed the deputy, the sheriff took the chair. "I have one question for you, young man. Why did your boy run today?"

"Because someone shouted at him and came after him. If you were young and black, and the white crowd was in a hangin' mood, wouldn't you run?"

"Guess I'd have to say that I would."

Jesselynn let him think for a moment. The silence hung heavy in the room. "So how about if we take Daniel on back to camp with us and get on the road?"

"Sorry, I can't do that."

She saw Meshach's hands clench at his side. "Why not, sir?"

"Because I'm going to have to defer to the judge on this. I've heard both sides, and while what you say makes good sense, the man who identified Daniel is a highly respected citizen of our town. If I just let this boy go, there'll be all kinds of devil to pay. I have to follow the law, and the law says suspects have to be proven guilty."

"But we weren't anywhere near here a week ago."

"So you say. It don't have to take that long to get here from Springfield." He looked up at her, his gaze penetrating. "Can you prove your boy was in Springfield with you at that time?"

Jesselynn turned to look up at Meshach, who gave a barely perceptible shrug. *How, how can I prove he was there?* The question ricocheted through her mind. She felt like melting into a puddle on the floor. "No, I don't guess that I can. I have three other adults that will swear he was with us, but no concrete proof." She thought of her journal. Had she written Daniel's name in during the Springfield stay? Again a no dragged her down further.

"So what happens now?"

"I keep him here in jail until the judge returns in two days, and then we go before him with all the information. He hears both sides and will make a decision. I abide by whatever decision he makes."

"And if he goes with your man's opinion?"

"Then most likely your boy will hang."

Chapter Eighteen

WASHINGTON

"Yes, suh." The maid standing in the doorway failed to smile.

Do we look that disreputable? Louisa thought about checking her clothing to make sure no rents showed. But she knew that wasn't so. She'd brushed and ironed her blue traveling outfit herself.

"Is my cousin, Dr. Logan, at home?" Zachary's voice carried just the correct amount of arrogance, in spite of the all-too-visible scars.

"Yes, suh. Who shall I say is callin'?" The woman didn't move from her position as doorkeeper.

"Zachary Highwood and Miss Louisa Highwood." He flashed her a smile that made the eye patch look only more dashing.

She started to shut the door, paused, and added. "I be right back."

"And leave us standin' on the street?" The shock in his voice apparently made her rethink her dilemma. With a frown, she stepped back and indicated they should enter.

"I send a man for your trunk." She pointed through a narrow archway. "You may wait in there." With that and a flurry of her skirt, she hastened down a walnut-lined hall.

The room they entered looked more like the waiting room of a doctor's office than a front parlor. Chairs and sofas lined the walls, and creamy camellias dropped petals on a hexagonal table with feet swept up in a curl. Oil paintings of rivers and trees, a house and field, horses and hounds hung on the walls. A closed door bore a gold sign reading *OFFICE.*

They had not been shown to the family quarters.

Louisa picked up a magazine and flipped through it, grimacing at the political cartoons. If this was any indication of their cousin's views on the war, she knew he and Zachary would most likely come to radical disagreement.

The maid returned. "This way."

Louisa and Zachary exchanged a look of raised eyebrows and slight shrugs.

We got beyond the first gatekeeper, she thought. *What will be the next?*

A woman with fashionably styled gray hair greeted them with outstretched hands. "Oh, my dears, please forgive Becca's caution. We've had some unsavory visitors in the last months. I am your cousin Annabelle, and I know Arlington will be so sorry to have missed you. He was required at the hospital again, you see. With all our boys—" She stopped and blinked. "Oh, forgive me, here I go rattling off like some ninny when you must be thirsty, and hungry too, for that matter. Have a seat there. Becca, take his cape and have cook bring us some coffee. Doesn't that sound good on a chill afternoon like today?" She bustled as she spoke, settling her guests in two chairs by the fire and pulling up another for herself. "Now, you must tell me all about yourselves as I only know hearsay about my husband's Southern kin." Even her hands fluttered as she raced on. "You're from where now?"

"Richmond, Virginia." Louisa answered quickly before her cousin's rushing flow of words continued.

"Ah, yes, such a lovely city."

"I'm sure it has changed since you last saw it." Visions of the freedmen's shanties down the streets from stately homes flew through her mind. Even though Richmond was the capital of the South and had never been shelled, the war showed itself in homes falling into disrepair due to the menfolk off fighting and no money to be had for upkeep. The frenzy of government had Richmond by the throat.

"As has Washington. Soldiers everywhere, and if not men, then supplies. Why, we have the hardest time getting tobacco."

Shame we don't still have Twin Oaks. We could have brought you some.

Becca entered and set a silver tray with a silver coffeepot and dainty china cups on the table next to her mistress. A silver salver held a variety of cookies and small cakes.

"Do you take cream or sugar?" Annabelle poured a cup and glanced over at Zachary. At the shake of his head and polite "No thank you," she handed the cup on the saucer to Becca along with the platter of cookies to take to Zachary. "And you, Louisa?"

"Yes, please." Louisa refrained from looking at her brother. She could read his mind. *What a waste. What a total and absolute waste.*

"Do you have any idea when Arlington will be home?" Zachary asked after a sip of coffee.

"Goodness me, no. I never do. We were supposed to attend a ball tonight, but his men always come first." The last was said with just enough twist to let Louisa know the woman would much rather be at the ball with her husband in tow. The nerve of him, putting wounded and dying soldiers before the enjoyment of his wife!

Since they were not part of the society in Richmond, they were not subjected to routs and parties, to balls and afternoons filled with calling on friends and gossiping. Louisa had watched Carrie Mae and Jefferson pursue a place in the Southern political theater, wanting no part of it herself. She'd rather work at the hospital any day. At least there she could be doing some good.

Now she sipped her coffee and listened to her cousin's wife rattle on.

"Have you been to Washington before?" Before Zachary could answer, Annabelle continued. "Our city was so beautiful before all those contraband camps sprang up. All those slaves who run away and come up here expectin' *us* to support them."

Zachary set his cup and saucer on the whatnot table next to his chair. "Thank you so much for the delicious coffee, Cousin Annabelle, but we must be going." He pushed himself erect and tucked his crutch under his arm. "Louisa?"

"Oh, I am so sorry to hear that. Becca, bring their things, please. I'll be sure and tell Arlington that you visited. Is there someplace he can reach you?"

"I'll send a message around in the morning." Zachary stooped to let Becca settle his cape about his shoulders.

Louisa kept a smile on her face while inside she seethed. If cousin Arlington was anything like his wife, the less they saw of him the better. As a Union army doctor, there was no way he would make sure they had access to the supplies they so desperately needed anyway.

"Oh, dear, I must call you a cab. Becca, send Harry out for one." Annabelle turned back to her guests. "Won't take but a moment or two. Wouldn't you rather sit down again?"

"No, thank you. As you can tell, it takes me a little longer than most to—"

"Ah, yes." She turned to Louisa. "Do greet your dear aunt for me. Arlington has spoken so highly of her."

"Oh, you mean Aunt Sophia?"

"Yes, indeed, the dear woman."

Louisa smiled so sweetly her jaw ached. "I shall most certainly do that. Thank you again for the pleasant repast." She nodded and, reaching into her bag, took out her gloves and pulled them on. "If you are ever in Richmond, do come to call." *Dear Cousin Annabelle doesn't even know Aunt Sylvania's name.*

Zachary led the way to the front door, smiled at Becca, who stood without moving, and stepped outside. "I'll have the driver get our trunk. Wouldn't want to be a bother or anything."

If the woman understood his sarcasm, she ignored it.

The arrival of the black hansom cab, even with the same driver, caught their attention.

"You wants yo' trunk, suh?"

"Yes, thank you." Zachary waited for Louisa to settle in the carriage while the driver fetched their trunk and put it up on his seat. Then he handed Zachary in and, with a slight bow, shut the door.

Zachary leaned back against the cushions. "Well, I never."

"Me either. Mother would have had us horsewhipped for treating guests so carelessly. And family, at that." She shook her head. "I do pray that this is not a portend of things to come." If Zachary were as angry as she, he was hiding it well. She mentally counted to ten and then to thirty. Still, the seething in her mind set her stomach to lurching, just like the carriage as it hit a pothole. She took another deep breath.

"Well, we know one thing," Zachary said.

"What's that?" Louisa turned from glaring out the window.

"We can't count on Cousin Arlington for anything."

"Perhaps he is different than his wife."

"You always were one to hope for the good." He rubbed his leg to ease the straps. "But I'll believe it when I see it. I shall send around a message of where we are stayin', but that is as far as I go. After all, I wouldn't want to keep them from a ball, for pity's sake."

I won't let pride get in my way, brother dear. If there's morphine to be had, I'll walk on my knees for it.

Chapter Nineteen

BLYTHEVILLE, MISSOURI

"So where do we go from here?"

Meshach leaned against the wagon wheel. "I don't know, but God knows."

"I'm sure He does, but right now it doesn't look like He's talking."

"You been askin'?"

Jesselynn sighed. "Of sorts. I ask, then I wait." *For nothing. I don't hear anything. Why, right now when we need answers immediately, does God go silent? Father, what are we to do?*

"Psst."

They both turned to see Daniel back at the window. He glanced over his shoulder, then beckoned them closer. When they stood within whispering distance, he gripped the bars and pressed his face against them.

"What he say?"

"We have to wait for the judge to return in two days. He has to hear the evidence."

"But we weren't nowhere near here a week ago."

"I know." If a black face could be gray with fear, Daniel's was. Jesselynn figured she didn't look much better.

"What dey gonna do, Marse Jesse?"

"Don' matter what *dey* gonna do. We's prayin' for de Lawd's deliverance." Meshach spoke with such intensity that Jesselynn felt sure if she turned around, she'd see a heavenly vision right behind them.

"Dat deputy, he say dey gonna hang me like dey done de robber."

"Daniel . . ."

"He say niggers like me good for nothin' but hangin'."

"Easy, boy."

"He say hangin' too good for what I done. I should be shot." Tears streamed down Daniel's cheek from his good eye, leaving tracks in the dirt and blood from the beating. One drop leaked from the eye swollen shut. "Marse Jesse, I din't do nothin'." His voice cracked.

Jesselynn's heart did the same.

"Hey, you, get away from that window!" The deputy's voice came from down the alley.

"We'll be back in the mornin'." Jesselynn pressed Daniel's fingers clamped around the bars. "You eat your supper and sleep well. You're safe in there at least."

"Spend the night on your knees, boy. We all be poundin' the gates of heaven. God says He listen when Him chilluns cry. He say He be our protector, our shield. He never leave us nor forsake us. Think on Him words."

"I try." Daniel rubbed his nose with the back of his hand and flinched.

"I said, git on outa there." The voice was slightly slurred and nearer.

Jesselynn and Meshach climbed up on the wagon, and Meshach backed the team so he could turn around. Jesselynn glanced over her shoulder to see the deputy and two other men making their way toward the jail.

"Just a minute." She leaped to the ground and trotted around the brick building to the front entrance. Stepping inside, she waited for the sheriff to look up from his bookwork. "Sir, I hate to bother you, but I got me a real bad feelin'. You *will* keep Daniel safe tonight, won't you?"

The man stared at her through squinted eyes. "That's my job, boy." The steel in his tone impaled her to the floor.

"I . . . I know that, but anybody could stick a gun in that window, shoot him, and be gone before you could get there."

"You think I didn't know you were out there talkin' with him?"

"No, sir. I mean, yes, sir." *But did you hear your deputy threaten to kill an innocent black man?* Jesselynn wished she were anywhere but trapped in the sheriff's gaze.

"I think you don't quite understand, Mr. Jesse Highwood. This here's a good town. Folks abide by the law here. We won't have any funny business goin' on."

"Thank you, sir. Sorry to have bothered you." She turned for the door but stopped one more time.

"I'll move him to another cell without a window."

With that she touched the brim of her hat and headed back out the door. *Just wish I felt as confident as he does, but that deputy reminds me of Dunlivey—mean ugly as sin clear through.*

Back in camp, they told the others, and for a change Ophelia didn't carry on with her moaning and crying. Instead, she drew herself up to her full height and looked Meshach in the eye.

"You better git on back to town and make sure nothin' happen to dat boy."

"Now, Ophelia . . ." Jesselynn started to interrupt but shut her mouth when she saw the look that passed between husband and wife.

"I takes Roman soon as I eat supper. Benjamin, take him to graze for me, will you?"

"Better take the rifle too." Jesselynn fetched it from under the wagon seat.

Man and mule disappeared into the darkness less than an hour later, the thud of cantering hooves their last contact.

"My land, what is this world comin' to?" Aunt Agatha shook her head and kept on shaking it as she sat back down in her chair by the fire and picked up her sewing. "Lord preserve us, this surely does test my faith. I was so certain the Lord would deliver that boy right into your hands."

"I thought so too." Jesselynn slumped against a tree trunk. "I should have gone with Meshach."

"He hide better at night." Ophelia settled Sammy into the quilt next to Thaddeus, who was already asleep. "Now, you be good boy and go to sleep." She sank down on the tailgate so she could pat his back and picked up the words of her song as if she'd been singing it all along. "Our home is over Jordan. Deep river, Lord, I want to cross over into campground." Her rich voice soothed both ear and soul.

Lord, keep them safe, as it seems there's nothing I can do to help. Hurry the judge back and make him listen to the truth. If you would make the man who says he saw Daniel realize the error of his claim, that would most likely be the best way out.

"*The Lord shall preserve thy going out and thy coming in.*" The words seemed to hover on the air.

Tears sprang instantly to water her eyes. Too long. It had been too long since she had felt His presence, had heard His voice.

Ophelia moved on to another one of her songs, and Benjamin, who had just brought in the horses, hummed along with her. Aunt Agatha leaned forward in her rocker to catch the firelight on her stitching. Thanks to her, Jane Ellen had new undergarments to go with her new skirt and waist, Sammy had two new shifts, and Thaddeus had graduated to pants, leaving his worn shift for Sammy to grow into. Aunt Agatha wanted to sew a skirt for Jesselynn but suggested it only once, since the lecture she received on safety had sent Sammy hiding behind Ophelia's skirt.

Jesselynn laid her cheek against her knees, arms clasped around her shins. The music softened to a murmur, like a summer creek whispering over stones.

A stick burned through in the fire and settled into the ashes with a spray of sparks. The *whoo-whoo* of an owl sounded from somewhere above them, and a dog barked in the distance.

Comforting sounds, if she could think of anything besides town and the jail. One by one the others headed for bed, whispering their good-nights as if afraid to break a spell. Her eyes grew heavier until she stood to keep awake. First watch was always hard, but then so were the others. And tonight with only three of them to share the load, it would be a long night.

Around midnight she woke Benjamin and crawled into her own quilt. One good thing about watch, she had plenty of time to pray, and staring at the star-studded sky continually reminded her that God, who'd created the universe, cared about this ragtag band of sojourners.

It seemed she'd just fallen asleep when her eyes flew open. With one motion she grabbed her boots and rolled out of bed. "I'm going to town," she whispered to Benjamin. "Get Chess for me, please." While he did that, she retrieved the pistol from its box, along with shells to fill her pockets.

Benjamin led Chess up to the fire and fetched the saddle. Within minutes she was cantering down the road, leaving him with reminders that he was in charge and if they didn't return by dawn, he should get everyone up and ready to ride, just in case they needed a quick getaway. The sense she was needed in town spurred her to a gallop.

Coming around the back instead of down Main Street, she could see torches flared and hear shouting voices before she reached the rear of the jail. She stopped several houses away and tied Chess to a fence, then ran, staying in the shadows until she could hide in the corner near the window.

"Daniel!" She hissed his name, trying to keep her voice lost in the shouting.

No answer came. She edged to the window but could see nothing inside. Light outlined a closed door toward the front of the building. Either the sheriff had moved Daniel as he promised or . . .

The *or* didn't bear thinking.

Gun at the ready, she edged closer to the street that ran in front of the building.

"Now, folks, let's calm down and talk about this like the sensible folks that you are." The sheriff sounded as if he were at a church social, his voice so calm and reasonable.

"Just let us have that nigger pup, and you can go on back home to bed." The shout sounded like a half-bottle one.

Someone else cheered. Several shouted their agreement. Others laughed.

The hairs stood up on the back of Jesselynn's neck. Where was Meshach?

"Now, you know I can't do that. The lad is innocent until the judge says he's guilty. You elected me to—"

"And we can un-elect you too. Keep that in mind."

"I'm right aware of that, but y'all go on home now, and we'll discuss this in the mornin'."

Please, God, make them listen to him. Make them go home. She shivered both from the brisk wind picking at her jacket and the menace of the voices.

"Marse Jesse, dat you?" Meshach's voice from behind her sounded as welcome as coffee on a cold day.

"Yes. Is there another way into the building?"

"No, suh. I tried pryin' at the window, but nothin' gave."

"Where is Daniel?"

"In another cell. I asked the sheriff."

"So he knows you're here?"

"He knows I *was* here. He think I go on back to camp."

A shout jerked their attention to the street.

"You ain't goin' in there!" The sheriff sounded harried now.

Meshach tapped Jesselynn on the shoulder. "You go dis way, and I go round de other. Dat man need backup."

Jesselynn edged her way to the front corner of the building, counted to ten, and stepped into the torchlight. With everyone's attention on the sheriff, she stepped up on the stone stair before anyone noticed her. Meshach did the same, both of them with their guns raised.

"Well, I'll be . . ." The sheriff muttered as the mob quieted.

"Just some friendly help, sir." Jesselynn aimed her pistol at the man in front who seemed to be the ringleader. She glanced around in the flickering torchlight, fully expecting to see the deputy leading the charge.

"Now, as I said before, y'all go on home. Your wives are waitin' for you, and if I know the ladies of this town, they're goin' to be a little huffy over the shenanigans out here tonight. And, George, see you in church tomorrow?"

The hefty fellow in front growled something, spun on his heel, and pushed his way through the ranks behind him. Within a minute the crowd had faded away like clouds blown on the wind.

"I could have handled them myself." The sheriff let out a breath and turned to the two behind him.

"I know. But we didn't want anyone hurt." *Least of all Daniel.*

"Thank you." The sheriff shook hands with each of them in turn. "There won't be any more trouble tonight. Too close to daylight. And tomorrow night, the women won't let their men out of the house without a fight. Besides, the saloon is closed on Sunday. These men needed a keg of liquid courage to make them brave enough tonight to cause a ruckus. At heart, this is a good town, like I told you before."

"A good town maybe, but a hangin' brings out the worst in folks. Leastwise that's what I been told." Jesselynn stuck the pistol in her waistband and looked up at the sheriff. "Now, can we take our boy and go?"

"Nope. Like I told them out there. The judge will be sittin' on Monday, and he'll make the decision."

"Was the man who mistook Daniel out in the crowd?"

"I believe so."

Meaning yes. How can we prove Daniel wasn't the one?

Chapter Twenty

❧

"*We're goin' to church,*" Jesselynn announced Sunday morning.

"Now?" Jane Ellen nearly dropped Sammy, grabbing him before he took a head dive off the tailgate. "All of us?"

"We better get on the road pretty quick, or we might be too late." Jesselynn looked down at her britches and shirtfront. Never had she gone to church in such filthy clothes. Of course, she'd never gone in britches either, but that made no difference at the moment. She turned to the wagon and dug in her box for a clean pair of pants and a shirt. The shirt had a rip on the right-side front.

"Here, hand me that. I can stitch it up while we ride in the wagon." Aunt Agatha *tsked* as she studied the tear. " 'Pears to me I should be sewing you a shirt along with the others."

"Thank you." Jesselynn turned to Thaddeus. "Come on, little brother, let's get your face washed. You can wear your new pants."

"What's church?" Thaddeus looked up at her, a wrinkle between his eyebrows.

"Don't you remember goin' to church at home? Where the organ music played, people sang hymns, and a man in a black robe preached the sermon?"

"What's a sermon?"

"The pastor teachin' about God's Word, you know, the Bible?" Jane Ellen looked up from searching for something in the wagon.

"Like Meshach?"

"Like Meshach. Come on, we need to hurry." But hurrying Thaddeus was like trying to hustle snails. The more she prodded, the slower he went. When they were all in the wagon but Benjamin, who needed to stay with the horses, Jesselynn looked them all over and smiled. "We look right presentable."

As the wagon rumbled along and Ophelia took up singing in the back, Meshach leaned closer to Jesselynn on the wagon seat. "Not that I mind goin' to church, but we doin' this to impress the sheriff?"

"Couldn't hurt. You know, I been thinkin'. Benjamin and Daniel are much the same size. What if I ask the sheriff or the judge to let Benjamin take Daniel's place and see if that man still says that's the boy he saw runnin' off. That would prove he didn't really recognize Daniel, wouldn't it?"

"But now Daniel all beat up."

"Hmm." She nodded, thinking so hard the horses picked up their trot, setting the harness to jingling and Thaddeus to giggling.

"More. Go faster."

"You set yourself right down, young man." Aunt Agatha snagged him by the back of his britches and plopped him back to sitting.

"So how do you think we could make it work?"

"Beat up Benjamin?"

Jesselynn jerked around to see if he was serious, then studied the horses' rumps. "Actually that might not be a bad idea. If it could save Daniel's life, I bet Benjamin would take a punch or two."

She let her thoughts roam as they trotted the road to town and on to the white painted church with a steeple and bell in the tower. They'd just tied the horses to a shade tree when the bell began to peal.

"Ah, I ain't heard a churchbell since we left home." Meshach paused in helping the women to the ground. "Sounds mighty pretty."

Jesselynn took Thaddeus's hand and leaned down to whisper. "Now, you have to sit still in church and no talking. You understand?"

His lower lip came out, and Jesselynn sighed. "Thaddeus Joshua Highwood, you don't want to embarrass us, do you?"

He cocked his head, question marks shooting from his eyes.

"What emb'rass mean?"

She swung him up to ride on her hip. "It means make us look bad. You can be such a good boy. Please?" She tickled his ribs with one finger.

"I be good." He squirmed and giggled, then gave her a hug and a kiss.

She hugged him back and set him down to walk up the three stairs. Aunt Agatha led the way, greeting the man at the door.

"We're travelin' through and so appreciate a house of worship. Your church-bell made me think of home." With the quaver on the end of her words, the man patted her hand and gestured toward the doors to the sanctuary. "Here, I think there's room enough for y'all in this back pew."

While some folks turned to see who was coming in, most kept their attention forward, where a man walked to the center and raised his black hymnbook. "Welcome, friends. We'll open this morning with hymn number 265, 'Holy, Holy, Holy.' " He nodded to the woman at the piano, and she commenced to play. "Let us stand."

As the music filled the church, Jesselynn gazed around the congregation, hoping to see the sheriff and wishing she knew what the judge looked like in case he was in attendance. How could she convince them to agree with her scheme?

Lord, you know the desires of our hearts. We don't ask for anything but justice. Please set Daniel free. This is the only plan I could come up with, but if you have something better, so be it.

When the minister stood behind the pulpit, Thaddeus shook her arm. "Sit on your lap?"

Jesselynn helped him up, and he snuggled against her chest. She stroked his back with one hand and tried to concentrate on what the preacher was saying. But all she could think of was Daniel.

Her mother would have been disappointed had she known of Jesselynn's worrying. *"Take it to the Lord, and leave it in His hands."* Jesselynn could hear her dead mother talking more easily than she could the preacher. *"Why, frettin' can't even change the color of one hair on your head. God has big hands and broad shoulders. Let Him carry your burdens."*

You made it sound so easy, Mother, and it's not. Daniel is my responsibility, and he is in jail.

She glanced over at Meshach. He was nodding in agreement with the preacher. Sammy slumbered in Ophelia's lap. Jane Ellen kept her fingers busy, pleating the fabric of her skirt. Aunt Agatha jerked, an obvious reaction to falling asleep.

The minister droned on. When he finally reached the amen, the congregation stirred and stood for the final hymn. Jesselynn saw the sheriff several pews ahead of them and off to the other side of the room, right on the aisle. She handed a sleepy-eyed boy to Jane Ellen, and as soon as the people began to move, she darted out the side aisle and headed for the back. She *had* to talk with the sheriff.

She caught up with him as he stepped down the last step and settled his hat back on his head. "Sheriff." When he didn't respond, she leaped the steps and raised her voice. "Sheriff!" She'd caught up with him by the time he turned. "Can I talk with you a minute?"

"I guess so. What do you need?"

"I need Daniel out of your jailhouse, but I'd like to talk with you about an idea I had."

"Well, son, I need to get over and relieve my deputy." He raised his hand to stop her before she got the words out. "No, it's not Rudy. I wouldn't leave him in charge again, not with your boy in there."

Jesselynn let out the breath she didn't realize she'd been holding. "Can we talk and walk?"

"Let's have it."

Jesselynn told him her idea of switching the two young black men. "It would show that he was mistaken, don't you see?"

"I'm not blind, son."

"Oh, sorry."

He rubbed his chin with one finger. "You know, that might work, but I'd have to talk it over with the judge first. We brought your boy a basin and water so he could wash. His eye is lookin' some better."

Jesselynn wished he would quit referring to Daniel as her "boy," but wisely she kept her mouth shut. She shoved her hands into her pockets and kept pace with the sheriff. "Thank you, sir. Would it be all right if I talked with Daniel some?"

"Don't know why not." He opened the door and led the way in. After dismissing the deputy, he took the keys and, unlocking Daniel's cell, stepped back to let her go in. "Call when you're ready."

Jesselynn stood at the bars watching Daniel, not saying anything. He seemed to be asleep on the cot. His face did look better, but overall he appeared to have lost twenty pounds and shrunk in inches, as if caving in on himself. Even if he hadn't eaten, she figured the look had nothing to do with his body but all with his mind. She'd seen a wild animal caught in a trap look the same back home.

If they didn't lynch him first, Daniel would die in here. He'd never have his freedom.

"Daniel?"

"Marse Jesse, you done come to set me free?" He rolled to his feet in one motion and flew to the bars.

"I wish." She wanted to catch his face before it hit the floor. "Now, Daniel, don't take on so. We got a good idea goin' if the judge will go along with us."

"Is de judge a good man?"

Jesselynn shrugged. "We've been prayin' so. The sheriff seems hopeful."

"Why don' he let me go?" Daniel gripped the bars till the tendons in his arms stood out. "I din't do nothin' wrong."

"I know that." If only she could take him in her arms and hug the life back into him. She touched the side of his face near his eye. "This is lookin' better."

"I can see outa it, leastways. Thought I was a goner for sure last night. I prayed de Lawd take me home, but I's still here."

"I know. But you go ahead and rest up, 'cause when we get you out of here, we'll be hittin' the trail hard. Benjamin said you just wanted a night without guard duty." She hoped this would bring a smile, but Daniel just shook his head. "I takes all de nights if'n I gets outa here. Why God do dis to me?"

"And tribulation worketh patience..." She could hear her mother's voice reciting the verses she'd committed to memory over the years. She repeated the verse for Daniel. "I don't know why God allowed this, but that's what the Word says, so we'll just get through this. And we'll all be more patient because of it."

She kept herself from shuddering at the word *tribulation*. Even the sound of it dragged up bad feelings.

"I tries, Marse Jesse. I tries." A tear seeped from under the swollen eyelid.

"I better go so we can get back to camp. Everyone sends you love." She patted his shoulder. If only she could think of something really heartening to cheer him, but the snores of a drunk in the next cell drove all encouraging words right out of her mind. If she didn't get out of there pretty quick, she'd be crying right along with Daniel.

She sniffed and headed for the door. "I'm ready," she called and threw a smile over her shoulder to the young black man, who stood leaning his forehead against the bars, his hands clamped so tightly they looked as if they could bend iron.

God, please help him. Help us. Please. Her feet seemed to weigh twenty pounds each as she left the jailhouse. Meshach had driven the wagon up to the hitching post, so she had to summon an instant smile. Letting Thaddeus know how bad things were was unnecessary. She didn't need two crying little boys.

"Where's Daniel?" Thaddeus greeted her with a frown. "He go with us."

"Soon, Thaddeus, soon."

"Why not now?"

"Ah . . ." She looked to Meshach for an answer.

"Hey, Thaddeus, look what I got." From the rear of the wagon, Jane Ellen held out her closed fist.

When Thaddeus scrambled back to see what she held, Jesselynn breathed a sigh of relief. "Bless you, girl," she said only loud enough for Meshach's ears. He shot her a smile as he hupped the horses and headed the wagon out of town.

Now all they had to do was get through until tomorrow.

Chapter Twenty-One

Dawn came to eyes bleary from lack of sleep.

"Where's Meshach?" Jesselynn asked, stumbling over a rock on her way to the already leaping fire.

"Grazin' de horses." Ophelia used her apron to lift a boiling pot off the cast-iron tripod.

Jesselynn looked over to see that Benjamin still lay wrapped in his quilt and deerskin. He'd stood the last watch. The boys and Aunt Agatha had yet to make an appearance, for which Jesselynn was grateful. Let those who *could* sleep do so. Nightmares, the first in a while, had ridden her all night.

"Here." Ophelia handed her a cup of steaming coffee.

"Thank you. Reckon I don't know what I'd do without you."

"You make your own coffee, dat's what." Ophelia straightened and kneaded her back with both fists. "Breakfast ready soon as de biscuits done." Gravy bubbled gently in one frying pan, and smoked venison simmered in another.

What Jesselynn wouldn't give for two eggs fried till the centers ran only slightly when stabbed with a piece of toast or biscuit, bacon or ham or sausage fried just right, and syrup to drizzle over pancakes so light they could float right off the plate.

The kind of breakfast Lucinda served nearly every morning during their life at Twin Oaks.

Sometimes Jesselynn thought she'd lived another life back then, one with no connection to the one she was living now.

"Think I'll get a letter written while I wait. Anything you want me to tell Lucinda or the girls?"

Ophelia patted her rounding belly. "You can tell dem 'bout dis little one. Dat make Lucinda pleased as punch." Ophelia looked down, shaking her head ever so slightly. "Lucinda do love de babies. You think maybe when we gets to Oregon, we could write Lucinda to come too?"

"She'd never leave Twin Oaks, not when she stayed on after it burned to the ground."

"You never know."

"You just spoke a mouthful of truth. Who'd ever have thought we'd be in a wagon almost to Kansas on our way to Oregon?" Jesselynn stretched her arms over her head and yawned fit to crack her jaw. Since she didn't really expect an answer, she turned and approached the wagon, treading lightly so as not to wake those still sleeping. Once she had her writing case in hand, she returned to the fire, grateful for its warmth in the wind that teased her hat, the brim so limp it flopped in response. She drew her coat closer around her middle and took a seat on a hunk of oak trunk Meshach had carted along since they left the caves. Later on they might need it for firewood, but in the meantime it made for good sitting.

After sharpening her turkey-quill pen she wrote swiftly, first to Lucinda, then to Sergeant White, and finally to her sisters in Richmond. Once in a while she flipped back through her journal to keep track of what all had happened. She didn't mention to Lucinda that Daniel was in jail. No sense bringing her more worry, especially since the letters might be mailed before they knew the outcome.

Sergeant White would understand her consternation, however. When she thought of the Confederate soldier they'd nursed back to health, his smiling face came to mind. Especially the smile he had reserved for her once he realized she was not the young man she portrayed. He'd seen behind the act, but had he touched her heart more deeply than a friend? While sometimes she thought so, other times she just wondered. Perhaps there would be a letter when they reached Independence. After all, he had said he'd catch up with them.

She sighed as she signed her name with a flourish. The one to her sisters took the longest.

> *Why is it that God seems to allow more trials, in this case an actual one, with judge and all? He promised the Israelites that they would pass through to the Promised Land. I so thought He meant the same for us. While Meshach seems to have no doubt that we will journey on with all of our band intact, I am still struggling with trusting a God who has taken so many from me, and so much. I long for Twin Oaks and life as it used to be. Always and always, the war has destroyed the crops, the land, and the people. Are these the years of the locust? Will He really restore us as though this has never been?*
>
> *My eternal thanks will be raised for Meshach, who took me in hand and made me see that life without our Lord is nothing but a long, dark, miserable existence. I am learning to walk with Him, keeping the picture of our mother always as my example. Sometimes, like now with Daniel in jail, I say with my teeth clenched, I will trust Him. I will praise His holy name. A sacrifice of praise, the psalmist calls it, and for me that truly describes what I must do. The black demon reaches out for me, but when I praise our God's holy name, the sun comes out and warms me again. Thank you, heavenly Father.*

She continued on with the news of how Thaddeus was talking and little Sammy was outgrowing his clothes. She told how Aunt Agatha sewed for one and all as she rocked her way across the countryside.

> *You should see her. We have her rocking chair fitted just so between the boxes and supplies, and her needle flies while her chair rocks the miles away. She tells stories to the young'uns and is teaching Thaddeus his numbers and letters. Jane Ellen has appointed herself as Aunt Agatha's protégée and is learning womanly things as the wagon bumps along.*

The two foals don't seem harmed by the travel, but we have to stop to let them graze and rest more often than we normally would. I long for the day when we can travel during daylight instead of darkness. As long as we make it to Independence without a brush with the Quantrill Raiders, I will—no I must—trust our God for His protection. I must. I must.

Your loving sister,

Jesselynn

P.S. As I said before, send any correspondence to the post office in Independence, Missouri. We will be waiting there to gather our supplies and sign on with a wagon train going west to Oregon. I have a feeling we really have no idea what we will encounter on our journey, but I will make sure we are as prepared as humanly possible. May our God and Father bless and keep thee. JH

"You wants breakfast now?" Ophelia held out a plate of steaming food.

"Thank you." Jesselynn closed her writing case and set it beside her. "That smells heavenly." She sniffed again and smiled at the fragrance. "Your biscuits give Lucinda's a real challenge. I'd hate to have to judge them in a contest."

Ophelia smiled and ducked her head. "Thank you, Marse." The glint in her eyes told far more than her smile. Comparing her biscuits was a compliment akin to the Father's "well done."

While she ate, Jesselynn ruminated on the plan to substitute Benjamin for Daniel and show that the man in town hadn't really seen either one of them. Something about it dug down in her soul like a tick on a feeding frenzy. But short of breaking Daniel out and streaking across the countryside, nothing came to mind. When she closed her eyes, she could remember one of the dreams that had plagued her the last two nights. She saw Daniel swinging at the end of a rope.

The stark fear in his eyes when she had visited him in the jail raised the hairs on the back of her neck.

No matter, she'd have to wait until she could ride into town and talk with the sheriff, hoping he'd been able to speak with the judge.

When Meshach sat down beside her with his full plate, she glanced at him in time to see the same weary look she felt.

"You didn't sleep either?"

He shook his head. "Prayin' more important den sleepin'." He cut into his gravy-laden biscuit with his fork. "I asked de Lawd for a sign, but I ain't seen nothin' yet. Dis here's one of de times we got to walk by faith."

Jesselynn felt a shiver race up her back. Talking about walking by faith and doing it were two entirely different things. Especially when a young man's life hung in the balance.

"Surely you don't believe it is God's will for Daniel to hang for something he didn't do?"

Meshach shook his head. "Not God's will, but sometimes He lets folks do bad things. Daniel know who his Savior be, and heaven be home for us all, 'specially poor black men and women."

"Meshach, don't talk that way. We got to get Daniel out of there."

"I knows, but I cain't say how. Be God's grace for sure."

Jesselynn felt like shaking the big man. *Don't you dare give up! We can't let them hang him.* But she kept the thoughts to herself, knowing that Ophelia might go into one of her rantings if she heard them. Jesselynn stared at the congealed gravy left on her plate. She'd thought of mopping it up with another biscuit, but her stomach rolled over at the notion. Instead, she scraped the remainder into the fire and dropped her utensils into the pot of simmering water and soap.

"I'll go on and wash up." Leastways then she could leave camp and be by herself. Somehow she argued with God better when it was just the two of them. But arguing and pleading seemed to do no good, and when she returned to camp, she was no nearer a solution than before.

"I believe we should all go into town with you for the trial." Aunt Agatha delivered her pronouncement as if she were the judge.

Jesselynn looked toward the two little boys with Jane Ellen as their overseer. She had taken to instructing them on table manners, having recently learned them herself from Aunt Agatha.

"No, Sammy, use your spoon." Thaddeus's command overrode Jesselynn's tangled thoughts. "See, like this." He demonstrated, ushering biscuit and gravy to his mouth without spilling, to the applause of Jane Ellen.

Sammy giggled, squirmed, and stuck his forefinger in his mouth—after swiping it through the gravy.

When Thaddeus rolled his eyes in perfect mimic of Aunt Agatha, Jesselynn choked on her swig of coffee, sending splatters to sizzle in the flames.

Jane Ellen took over ferrying food to Sammy's mouth, which opened and closed obediently. In the months he'd been with them, the grinning black baby had come a long way from a scrawny, squalling orphan found on a Kentucky hillside.

Aunt Agatha poked Jesselynn with the end of a stick. "Did you hear me?"

Jesselynn nodded. "Just trying to figure what is best."

"I, at least, will be going along. My thought was we look more respectable if we are all in attendance. No judge will think we are a gang of ruffians when he sees us."

I wouldn't be too sure of that. Jesselynn kept the thought to herself. But yet she had to admit that her aunt was right. They didn't look any worse than other families moving west and most likely better than a lot of them.

"Shame we don't have a buggy. That would make a better impression than the wagon."

"I don't know about that. People sure look twice when they see you sitting up there in your rocking chair, knitting or sewing as we go along." The few times they'd traveled in daylight, the reaction had been just that.

"Hmm." Agatha gave her a studying look, the kind that elicits fidgets, feet and hands that twitch, the urge to rub her hand across her mouth in case food remained on her face.

Jesselynn kept her gaze on her aunt's hands. If she looked into her eyes, she knew she'd see disapproval of what Jesse was wearing—a man's hat and britches. If she thought that donning women's clothes would save Daniel, she'd do it in an instant, but that might endanger all of the rest of them.

"We'll be ready to leave in a few minutes." Jesselynn turned to Meshach and spoke in a low voice. "Any suggestions?"

"I could stay with de horses in case you wants Benjamin to take Daniel's place. We can't take dem to town."

"I know. I'm beginning to think I should go by myself first and talk with the sheriff, then come back and get the rest."

"Might be de best idea." He stood and stretched. "I get de mule."

―――――

She kept Roman at a canter all the way to town, pulling him up at the hitching post in front of the jailhouse. Few people were out on the streets. The general store had yet to open its doors, but she could hear the school bell ringing the children in for class.

She paused in front of the jail door and took a deep breath, then pushed open the door and entered. "Good morning, Sheriff." Gratitude that the man behind the desk wasn't the deputy widened her smile.

"Mornin'. Your boy is lookin' some better. Hope you brought him some clean clothes for the trial. Judge said he'd commence with the proceedings at ten o'clock. The witness has already been notified."

"What did he say about our substitution idea?"

"Said if he caught any such shenanigans in his court, he'd hang 'em both."

The flat way he delivered his pronouncement made Jesselynn wonder which side the sheriff was on. Earlier he'd seemed sympathetic to Daniel. Now she wasn't so sure. But did it matter? "Okay if I see him?"

"Suit yourself. Just leave that firearm here on my desk."

Jesselynn removed the pistol from her waistband and, laying it on the desk corner, followed the sheriff through the door to the cells. While Daniel still occupied the cell away from the windows, two other men were snoring on the cots in the larger cell with an outside view.

"Hey, boy, you got company," the sheriff called out.

Daniel dropped his hand from over his eyes and rolled to a sitting position. He shook his head as he stood and crossed to the bars. "Dey gonna hang me, Marse Jesse. I jist knows it."

"Now, Daniel, don't talk such a way. They have no proof you were even here." She spoke low, for his ears alone as soon as she caught his horrified glance at the other cell. "Your face looks much better."

"Yes, suh." He rested his forehead against the cold bars.

"Did you have breakfast?"

He nodded. "Marse Jesse, I want to go home."

She knew what he meant. Back to Twin Oaks, back to a time before the war when the family all lived and laughed and the slaves had been as much family as anyone. "I know. I'm going back to the camp for the others and will bring you clean clothes. You wash up good."

"I bin prayin'."

"So have we, Daniel. So have we. Surely God hears and will execute His justice." *Surely He will. Father God, please don't let us down, not at the cost of this child's life.* She knew she sounded like the preacher from home, but did she really believe they worshiped a God of justice? At least justice in the here and now? Eternal justice was much easier to believe in, but the daily kind? The war and the resulting carnage caused faith to waver, especially newly recovered faith like hers.

"I'm going back to get the others."

"Who take care of de horses?"

"Benjamin. Ophelia and Jane Ellen will stay in camp with the little ones." She made that decision as she spoke. The courtroom was no place for children or for a keening black woman if the judgment went against them.

"You hurry back?" The stark fear in his eyes made her wrap her hands around his on the bars.

"Have faith, Daniel." She knew she was saying the words as much for her-self as for him. As she left the jailhouse, she glanced up the street to the town square. The gallows still stood, a mute testimony to man's idea of justice. She swung atop the mule and cantered out of town, not daring to gallop or he would be too winded to hitch to the wagon. There was no way she'd harness up one of the stallions today, and the mares had to stay with their foals.

While it seemed like hours, they were on their way back to town within the hour, bearing a packet for Daniel and all wearing clean clothes. Ophelia waved them off, tears streaming down her cheeks.

"Bring dat boy back here. We needs him." Her words echoed on the breeze and reverberated in Jesselynn's heart.

They stopped at the jail, and Jesselynn took the packet in for the sheriff, but the deputy sat at the desk instead.

"Sheriff's gone over to the courthouse. Left me to bring your boy over."

"I brought some clean clothes for Daniel."

"That rope don't care he got clean clothes."

Jesselynn stepped up to the desk and slammed her palms down on the wood surface. She leaned slightly forward on rigid arms. "Mister Rudy! You will take these into him or I will. The sheriff told me to bring them, and I surely wouldn't want to have to tell him you refused his orders." The thought of her pistol hanging heavy at her side pulled at her stiff arms. But she kept her gaze locked on the deputy in the chair.

He dropped his gaze first. "Go on back." He motioned over his shoulder with his thumb. "But don't say I didn't warn you." His eyes glinted mean like those of a weasel she'd once caught raiding the henhouse. At least she'd been able to shoot it. Her trigger finger twitched. She didn't want to kill him, just wound him a bit. Bullies like that deputy never could tolerate pain of their own, no matter how they tried to inflict it on those less fortunate.

Daniel slipped into the clean pants and shirt while Jesse turned her back, then handed his dirty things through the bars. His hands shook so badly he dropped his shirt and had to pick it up again.

"Don't you go minding that cruel creature out there. Men like him's the reason we need so many judges." She rolled his things and tucked them under her arm. "You look right presentable now, so we'll just go before the judge and tell him the truth, and we can be on our way west." She forced every smidgen of confidence she could dredge up into her voice and tightened the smile that threatened to quiver to death at any moment. If she showed her anxiety, she knew Daniel would melt into a whimpering black puddle on the floor. "The truth will win out." That phrase had been one of her mother's favorites.

She turned at the sound of the opening door to see the sheriff enter the aisle between the cells. He started to say something, saw the gun in her waistband, and strode forward with his hand outstretched.

"Just give me the gun, nice and peaceable-like, and we won't have any trouble."

"That deputy didn't ask for it, so I didn't offer." Jesselynn handed the gun over, butt first.

"Thank you." The sheriff stuck it in his waistband and shook his head.

From the look in his eyes, Jesselynn felt right grateful she wasn't walking in the deputy's shoes. "How long until we head for the courthouse?"

" 'Bout half an hour. If you want to go over and get a place to sit, I'll be bringin' your boy over after I shackle his hands." He looked at Daniel. "You wouldn't be tryin' to run on me, would you, boy?"

Daniel shook his head. "No, suh."

"You mind if Meshach comes in to stay with him until then?"

"No, I guess not."

"Good. Then my aunt and I will go over and reserve our places." Jesselynn touched the back of Daniel's fingers, gripped so tightly around the bars that his knuckles grayed. "Not long now and we'll be on our way back to camp, then on to Independence." She took two steps toward the door, but his whimper, like a pup about dead, stopped her. *Lord, what can I say? What more can I do?*

"Trust me." She turned to see who had spoken. Nothing looked different. No one had said a word. She stepped back to the bars so she and Daniel were about nose to nose. "The Lord says we got to trust Him."

"I know. I do, but . . ." Daniel closed his eyes and shook his head. His sigh nearly ripped her heart out. "I'm tryin', Marse Jesse, I'm tryin'."

"I know. Soon now." This time she hustled out the door as though alligators were snapping at her heels. Sending Meshach back inside with orders to stay with Daniel, she backed the team and drove the two blocks to the courthouse. Tying up in the shade, she helped Aunt Agatha down from the wagon. Agatha kept her own counsel after one look at her niece's face on returning to the wagon. The older woman checked the adjustment of her hat, picked up her knitting bag, and let Jesselynn take her arm on their way into the building.

A line of townspeople barred the door until Jesselynn led Agatha forward and whispered to the man in charge. "I'm Master Jesse Highwood, and it is my . . ." What could she call him? He was no longer a slave, but would being a freedman cause more trouble?

Aunt Agatha took a step forward. "The young man in question is my slave, and I am here to see that he is returned to me at the earliest convenience." Her harrumph made her seem to grow a foot taller.

The man started to say something, then nodded and turned to point to a row of benches just this side of a wooden railing. "Right over there, ma'am. You can be seated at any time."

"I will need room for one more."

"You take as much space as you'd like. I'll be lettin' in these other folks in a few minutes."

Jesselynn could feel the dagger stares slamming into the middle of her back. Ignoring the temptation to glare back at them, she followed her aunt down the aisle. Agatha left enough space on the bench for Jesselynn and Meshach and sat herself down, spreading her skirts and sitting board straight as she picked up her knitting needles and commenced the soft clicking of the ivory as the yarn became the arm of a sweater. She glanced once around the room, ignoring the whispers from all around them as if they were not even there. She could have been ensconced in front of a parlor fire for all the peace that seemed to flow out of her.

When a hiss of "nigger lovers" reached her ears, Jesselynn tried to imitate her aunt. If only she had knitting or mending along. She was wondering how men managed situations like this when more murmurs from behind made the hair tingle on the back of her neck. Couldn't these people understand or at least entertain the notion that Daniel hadn't been anywhere near Blytheville? Had no one told them the truth of the matter? If she'd had any hope they'd listen to her, she would have stood and demanded their attention.

Agatha put her hand on Jesselynn's arm, apparently sensing her agitation, then continued with her knitting. Jesselynn got the point, the silent admonition.

The sheriff entered from a side door, one hand on Daniel's upper arm, nearly dragging him forward. They took two chairs behind a table in front of the railing.

Jesselynn didn't need to turn around to be sure the courtroom was full. The hate rolled against her back like surf against a rock, splashing up and dashing back down, sucking at her as if to pull her under. She wanted to turn and search out Meshach. She needed to. But after a comforting glance at Daniel, she kept her back straight and her eyes forward.

"All rise." The sheriff stood as he spoke, pulling Daniel up with him. "Judge Stuart McCutcheon presiding."

Dressed in black from beaver hat to shiny boots, the man compelled attention. Not that he was good-looking in a conventional way, but his face brought to mind granite, cut square and clean. His eyes, sheltered under wild black brows, seemed those of a man who had seen far and wide, both in country and into men's souls.

"Be seated." His words precise, his voice rang with authority.

Jesselynn felt she should stand and salute. Instead, she sat.

The sheriff read from a paper he held open with both hands. "The state of Missouri accuses Daniel Highwood, here seated, to be the accomplice of James Gardner, already convicted of the murder of Avery Dunbar and hanged."

The judge, now seated, leaned forward. "How do you plead?"

Daniel tried to speak, but the words refused to come.

"He says he is not guilty, Your Honor." The sheriff laid his paper on the table and took his chair.

"They all say that!" The growl from the back of the room snapped the judge's head up.

"Quiet! If you cannot be quiet in my courtroom, you will leave." He stared around the room, nailing everyone to their seats. Someone coughed, then silence reigned. "That's better." He looked at the sheriff. "Tell us, Sheriff, how he came to be in your custody."

The sheriff stood and cleared his throat. As if reciting a grocery list, he told of the accusation, the chase, the capture, and the jailing. "And so, Your Honor, this court has been called to determine the guilt of this man." He gestured to Daniel, who stared at his hands.

"What's this I hear about a near riot at your jail?"

"Just a few of the hotheads attempting their own form of justice."

"I see. Who is it that accused this man?"

"Jason Stillwater. Said he'd seen this young man trail James Gardner into the store when he shot ol' Avery. But he disappeared before we caught the killer."

The judge looked around the room. "Stillwater, you here?"

"Yes, sir." A man who appeared to have seen better days stood with his hat in his hand, his fingers crippling the brim.

"Get on up here where I can talk with you." The judge pointed to a chair off to his right.

The sheriff crossed the room and held out a black Bible. "Lay your hand on it. Now, do you swear to tell the truth?"

"I do."

"Then sit."

The judge waited a moment for the air to settle. "Now, Stillwater, tell me what you saw. Not what you thought you saw and with no addin' to it, you hear?"

"Yes, sir. The night ol' Avery was kilt, I was comin' down the street. I saw a man walk into the store, and this here nigger." He pointed at Daniel.

"Enough! I said to tell only what you saw!"

The bench Jesse sat on shuddered with the thunder.

"Ah, yes, sir. I saw a skinny black man follow Gardner into the store."

"How do you know they were together?"

"He was followin', sneakylike. Both was strangers to Blytheville. Leastways, I din't know them."

"How do you know this young man is the one you thought you saw?"

"Same kinky hair, same kinda clothes, same height. I knows he the same ni—ah—boy."

Where is Meshach? Surely this wasn't evidence enough to hang Daniel.

"I see." The judge glanced around the room. "Anyone else see a stranger in town that night?"

Jesselynn started to rise, but Aunt Agatha put a hand on her arm. Jesselynn settled back in her seat. Daniel glanced her way, his eyes rolling in terror.

God, help us, please. For mercy's sake, help us.

Chapter Twenty-Two

Washington

"Bored, that's what I am." Louisa paced to the window again.

Three days Zachary had been going to his mysterious meetings. Three days she'd been stuck in a hotel room, and now she was out of yarn. Three days and they hadn't heard from Cousin Arlington. She'd written three letters, requested three stamps that her dear brother had yet to provide, and thought of at least thirteen ways she could do away with him.

She'd memorized the newspaper, had found it amazing the different views this paper had, compared to the Richmond Gazette. Why, according to this paper, the North had already won the war, no matter how many battles it lost.

But reading between the lines, she discovered the same illness on this side also—leaders who were afraid to lead. Men who would rather talk and let others do the fighting. "Daddy, it's probably a good thing you died when you did. Succumbing to a broken heart might be even worse."

There, now she was talking out loud to herself on a consistent basis. "Zachary Highwood, where in heaven's name are you?" Her stomach complained at the length of time since she'd fed it, but she was under strict orders not to leave the room until he returned.

She crossed back to the window again and peered down at the street two stories below. Rain and incessant traffic had turned the dirt street into a quagmire. While some streets were brick or cobblestone, the lesser ones weren't, hence the mudhole.

Louisa fetched her bag from the nightstand drawer and counted her meager cash. Enough for yarn, if she could locate a store, and for coffee and a biscuit or something light in the dining room downstairs. Calling her brother every name she could think of, she donned her traveling jacket, pinned her hat firmly in place, arranged the net over her face and threw a cape around her shoulders. Sometimes it was easier to ask forgiveness than permission.

Refreshed by her tea and coffee cake in the dining room, she stopped under the portico that extended beyond the front doors. Rain had turned from sprinkles to sheets. Not even for yarn would she brave that downpour. Sighing, she turned back. Perhaps they had a library, or at least a shelf of books, where she could borrow one.

But when she made her request at the desk, the clerk shook her head. "Sorry, ma'am, but books we ain't got."

"Yarn, then? I've run out."

"I'll ask cook. She always has her needles going for our soldiers who be needing wool stockings all the time."

That too is the same as for the South. But did their yarn come in blue?

The young woman returned in a few minutes with a ball of undyed yarn, the same as Louisa used. "Here you go, ma'am. Good way to spend such a rainy afternoon."

Louisa thanked her and turned to head back up the stairs.

"Oh, ma'am," the clerk called, "I have a message delivered for your husband. Might you take it up with you?"

"Of course." Her curiosity running rampant, Louisa took the envelope and returned to her room. It was good quality paper, no return address or stamp, so someone had dropped it off. Zachary's name stood out in bold script, most likely masculine. She tapped the edge of the sealed envelope on the side of her finger. If it hadn't been sealed with wax, she could have steamed it open. But there was no way to redo wax, at least without having wax at her disposal. A candle might have worked, but all the lights were gas.

With a sigh, she set the envelope on the mantel, took her chair, and resumed her knitting. And here she'd thought the trip would be exciting. Dusk parted the rain curtain and eased onto the stage, welcomed by gas streetlights and people hurrying home so quickly that the streets cleared in a short time.

Still no Zachary. When she dropped two stitches turning the heel, she had to admit it. Fear had become a real presence in the room and in her mind. Something could have happened to him. After all, he was seeking contraband to take back to the South. While he'd warned her more times than she cared to count that there was danger here, she'd put aside his admonitions with a light heart. After all, they were doing the will of the Lord in seeking to care for His hurting children. She had prayed for guidance, and the ease with which they'd traveled seemed to be a confirmation of divine intervention.

But where was Zachary?

If Zachary didn't return, what could she do? Best throw herself on the mercy of Cousin Arlington, she decided.

Her hands fell idle, and she closed her eyes. *Dear Lord, please help us. Bring Zachary back safe and sound and provide the morphine that we came for.* Her prayer degenerated into a succession of pleadings, and throughout she felt as though her petitions went no further than the ceiling. *Oh, Lord, have you forsaken us?* The thought made her stomach flutter and her hands shake. Surely not. Surely Zachary was just busy and forgot the time.

What if I can't get home again until after the war is over?

"You goose! Now stop that." She picked up her knitting again and made a choice. " 'The Lord is my shepherd; I shall not want. He maketh me to lie in green pastures: he leadeth me beside the still waters. He restoreth my soul. . . .' " By the time she'd recited the Twenty-third Psalm, the Ninety-first Psalm, and the Sermon on the Mount, she knew where her help lay. God said He would never leave her but would be her protector, and so He would.

Whether proper or not, she descended the stairs to the dining room again, this time for supper, smiling at the man who showed her to a small table in the corner. "Thank you."

"You were almost too late," the waiter said with a smile. "The beef is gone, but cook made a good chicken pie. And the bread is fresh, as always."

"That sounds delicious."

"Will your husband be joining you?"

"I think not. He must be caught up in business. Could I have a cup of tea now, please?"

"Of course."

Sitting there sipping her tea, she caught the eye of a woman, also alone, at a nearby table. Louisa nodded and smiled politely. At least she wasn't the only one eating by herself. She glanced around the rest of the room, then coming back to the other woman realized she had tears running down her cheeks, in spite of an apparent effort to stem the flow.

Louisa beckoned to the waiter. "Could you please bring my supper to that table?" At his nod, she picked up her cup and crossed the short distance. When the woman nodded, Louisa took the other chair and leaned forward.

"Sometimes telling total strangers is easier than talking with our loved ones. I'm Louisa Highwood." She waited for another sniff.

"Mrs. John Hinklen, Joanna." The woman dabbed at her eyes again. "Forgive me for such blubbering, but you see, I received notice two days ago that my husband, Major Hinklen, died of his wounds while trying to cross the Rappahannock. No matter how prepared I tried to be, I cannot quit crying. I thought perhaps some supper might help."

"How long since you've eaten anything?"

Joanna shrugged.

"Have you family?"

A shake of the head. "Not here. We're from New York, and we have no children."

When the waiter set her supper in front of her, Louisa turned to him. "Have you any soup for Mrs. Hinklen? That might sit better than the chicken pie."

"Yes, surely."

"Oh, and a pot of tea, please. A large pot."

An hour later, Louisa knew all about the Hinklens and hated the war even more—if that were possible.

But Zachary had yet to make an appearance.

Chapter Twenty-Three

❧

Blytheville Courtroom

Jesselynn rose and spoke. "Your Honor, may I—"

"No. You'll get your turn."

Jesselynn sank back down on the bench.

Someone stood up behind them. "Yer Honor, I think I saw what Stillwater saw."

"Were you with Stillwater?"

"Not exactly. I was over by the livery, just bringin' my horse out to head on home."

"And what exactly did you see?"

"Ya know how ya see somethin' out of the corner of yer eye, but when you turn quick, you don't see nothin'? Well, that's kinda the way it was, but right on the front stoop of the store."

"Did you see the killer go in?"

"Not exactly, but I heard the shots."

"Thank you. You may sit down."

The judge stared around the room again. "Anyone else?"

Jesselynn started to raise her hand but found it clamped by Aunt Agatha. She glared at her aunt, but the hand held. With a jerk she freed herself and stood.

"Your Honor, Daniel Highwood was with us and has been with us since we left home in Kentucky. We were still in Springfield." Her words tripped faster as she neared the end.

"And you are . . . ?"

"Jesse Highwood, last remaining son of Captain Thaddeus Highwood of Midway, Kentucky. Ah . . . he instructed me to . . . ah . . . join my aunt in Springfield after . . ." She paused. How to tell the tale and yet not all of the tale?

"Your Honor, may I clarify things for you?"

Jesselynn looked down to see her aunt with one genteel hand raised in the air, her voice rich and smooth like warm molasses.

The judge nodded. But when Agatha started to rise, he raised one hand as if in blessing. "No, you may remain seated."

Jesselynn sat down, closing her gaping mouth with a snap.

"I am a widow, Your Honor. My husband, Hiram Highwood, was one of the early casualties of this terrible war. He believed he was needed by our President Jefferson Davis, and nothing anyone said would keep him from servin' with the Confederate army." She lifted a bit of cambric to her nose and to the edge of her eye, cleared her throat and, at the judge's nod, continued. "Some bushwhackers burned our farm to the ground, and since I had no funds with which to pay our taxes, even our land is gone. But with my dear nephew and our few remainin' slaves, I have determined to start over again in Oregon country. But, Your Honor, I am getting on in years, and I desperately need every hand I can get. I lived in Springfield all my life, and if you want I can send for letters from our pastor, from the doctor, and from anyone else you need, sayin' that I was still in Springfield at that time and all my household with me."

Jesselynn schooled her face to not reveal her surprise. Her household? They'd argued fiercely for her to accompany them. And they'd been living in a cave.

"I would be livin' there still were it not for the passing on of my dear husband." The handkerchief fluttered again. "Surely you would want to come to the aid of an agin' widow, destitute due to the travesty of war."

"And you would swear on the good book that Daniel Highwood was with you all the time?"

"I would, Your Honor." She leaned forward. "I will do so right now if you so decree."

"That will not be necessary." The judge folded his hands on the desk top. He looked to the sheriff and then around the room.

Jesselynn held her breath.

The judge picked up a wooden gavel beside him and slammed it down.

She jumped, her air whooshing out.

"Free him. I find this young man innocent due to lack of sufficient evidence to convict him."

A groan rumbled through the room, and snarling could be heard, nearly covering an expletive or two from the direction of the witness.

"Silence!" The gavel thundered again. The judge was forced to slam wood on wood again, but the room quieted down. "Now, Sheriff, remove those shackles so these folks can be on their way." Glancing around the room, his face a study in stern lines and frown slashes, he continued. "And if I hear of disruption of any kind with the intent to harm anyone in my jurisdiction, I will personally nail that scumbag's hide to the nearest barn. Is that understood?"

Jesselynn felt extremely grateful he wasn't directing his diatribe at her. As soon as the sheriff had unshackled Daniel, she, her aunt, and the young man strode up the aisle, looking neither to the right nor to the left. Meshach met them at the door and closed it behind them.

"Where were you?" She kept up the pace even as she asked the big man. "We saved you a place."

"Didn't you see? No darkies down in the front, only in a bitty little section at de back. I stayed dere. Much better." He pushed open the door and ushered them out to where the sun caught them full in the face.

Daniel stopped and lifted his face to the warmth. "Thank de Lawd, I can feel the sun again."

"We need to thank Him for all He has done." Aunt Agatha stopped at the wagon and waited to be assisted to her chair. "I sure do wish we could leave that camp right now and, as the Lord's Word says, 'shake off the dust' of this place from our feet. You think it might be safe to travel during the day?"

Jesselynn took the reins and backed up the horses, since they were hemmed in on both sides with other teams and wagons, then headed them up the street and toward the camp. "All we need is for someone to see the horses, and then we'll have more trouble than a fox in a henhouse. Stealing them and selling them to the army would net someone better'n a year's wages. I sure do pray the sheriff keeps his deputy under lock and key for the next several days. He didn't look like he took too kindly to the judge's final speech."

"I heard the sheriff say somethin' 'bout one more misstep and he was fired." Daniel huddled right behind the wagon seat, casting fear-filled glances back down the road. "I surely do hope the sheriff keep him busy in town."

"What if you and Daniel take the horses and head out across country? Surely you could stay away from farms and such, and we'll go the roads with Benjamin as lookout. We could meet up the Kansas Road aways. Anything to get out of here safely."

Meshach sat, his elbows propped on his knees, and stared at the rumps of the team. He shook his head slowly, teeth worrying his lower lip. "I don't know. If we get stopped without you, we in bad trouble."

"I know. But if I take the horses, then you'd have Aunt Agatha to ward off any unwanted attention." She turned to her aunt. "You were magnificent in that courtroom."

Agatha looked up from her knitting. "Thank you. If you ask me, I think we need to travel on right now, and if you go with the horses, the rest of us will manage. If need be, I know how to use a firearm too. Hiram—may his soul rest in peace—taught me before he left for the war."

Jesselynn shook her head. "Aunt Agatha, you're just full of surprises today." She could feel the smile stretching cheeks that hadn't found a lot to smile about lately. "What do you think?" She glanced at Meshach.

"Don' seem like no best way. Just hope God's sendin' angels around us, 'cause we might be needin' dem."

"Hope doesn't do anything, young man. Prayer does it all." The word came from over their shoulders.

"Yes'm."

"Yes, ma'am." They spoke at the same time.

Jesselynn felt like whistling. Daniel was free, and so were they.

When they reached camp, Ophelia had a meal waiting and all the boxes packed. As soon as they ate, they loaded the wagon and hitched the team of Chess and Roman back in the traces. Standing in a circle, they bowed their heads while Meshach prayed.

"God in heaven, we thank you for saving Daniel from the hangman today. Thank you for watching over us so wise and good, for keepin' us safe. Thank you dat you are puttin' legions of angels all around us to protect us from de enemy. De Bible say you are our sure defense, and we thank you for dat. Keep us safe, Lawd, so we can praise yo' holy name. Amen."

They echoed his amen and helped Aunt Agatha up into the wagon, tossing the boys in after her. Daniel, with one of the guns at his side, took up a seat on a box in the rear with Meshach and Ophelia on the wagon seat. Every time they loaded, the wagon seemed heavier laden. Jesselynn had already decided they would need two wagons and four teams of oxen to transport all the needed supplies for the long march to Oregon. Nightly she stewed over where the money would come from. The stash from the sale of the horses dwindled every time she went to town.

Benjamin held the lead ropes to the mares and filly while Jesselynn mounted Ahab. *Lord, I sure do hope this is what you want us to do.* Jesselynn took the lead lines and watched the two foals galloping and kicking up their heels. They darted around their dams and then charged off again. "You two better save your energy. You're goin' to need it later."

"Dey feisty all right." Benjamin took one of the lead lines. "We might shoulda broke dem to halter. Keep 'em safer dat way."

"Tonight when we stop." She rode up beside the wagon. "Once we reach the road, we'll find a good place to camp and wait for you. Watch for a white rag on a branch."

Meshach nodded. "Go with God." He flapped the reins, and with a groan and screech the wagon eased forward. Chess and Roman pricked their ears forward and plodded on out of the camp.

"You too." Jesselynn and Benjamin waited for only a moment before heading north to go cross-country. She'd asked one of the shopkeepers where the other roads ran and had drawn Meshach a rough map for the best way to stay away from Blytheville. While it would take longer that way, she knew it was for the best. They should meet up by nightfall, but just in case, she and Benjamin had saddlebags of supplies and their quilts rolled in deer hides tied behind their saddles.

After a mile or two, Jesselynn took all the lead lines and let Benjamin travel a bit ahead to keep them out of some farmer's territory. When they crested one of the many rolling hills, he'd steer them away from the secret valleys where cattle grazed and wheat and hayfields glinted green in the dancing breeze. A dog or two barked at their passing as they bypassed swamps in the lowlands and ponds where blackbirds sang and bullfrogs bellowed their spring love songs.

"Fish taste mighty fine for suppah." Benjamin reined in his stallion and let him drink at a shoreline. Jesselynn let hers have a few mouthfuls before pulling Ahab and the mares back. One of the foals stuck a foot in the water and leaped backward as if he'd been bitten.

"That they would." Jesselynn studied the terrain ahead of them. The land glowed golden in the setting sun. They had yet to come across the Kansas Road, and since they'd been traveling more or less west by northwest, she was beginning to feel niggles of apprehension. Had the shopkeeper been less than honest with them? Or had they not made the time she thought they would?

Most of all, had they made a terrible mistake in splitting the family and going two separate ways?

She dismounted and, removing Ahab's bridle, let him graze along with the mares. Both foals now had turned to nursing, their brush tails flicking from side to side. "If you think you could catch some fish in a half hour or so, give it a try. Surely we'll find the road pretty soon, and we'll get a fire started right away."

Benjamin took his fishing line and hook from his saddlebag and made his way farther up the bank. She could hear him cutting a willow branch for a pole and knew he would look under rocks in the shallows for periwinkles for bait. She trapped a grasshopper with one hand but let it go. True, grasshoppers made good bait, but she dared not leave the grazing horses to go look for Benjamin. Both foals flopped over on their sides, ribs rising and falling with their sleeping breaths. Legs straight out, they looked worn-out, like toys a child dropped when tired of them.

Jesselynn propped her back against the trunk of a willow tree, knowing that if she lay down, she'd be out just like the foals. The contented crunching of the grazing horses worked like a lullaby, the blackbirds' trills drifting on the cooling air.

She jerked awake and forced herself to her feet. What was she doing nodding off when who knew how many miles they had left to go before reaching the Kansas Road? She whistled and waited for Benjamin to answer. When no answer came, she sighed. He'd probably found a good fishing hole beyond earshot. The thought of fried fish for supper made her forgive his carelessness.

She whistled again and listened.

Nothing but a blackbird answered. A swallow swooped by, its open beak catching bugs over the water. Ahab lifted his head, ears pricked to the north. She clamped a hand over his nose just before he whinnied.

Chapter Twenty-Four

"Marse Jesse?"

Jesselynn let her breath out on a sigh, not aware she'd been holding it until her shoulders sagged. "Over here." She stroked Ahab's soft nose and let him return to his grazing. She should have known that he recognized the person arriving even if she couldn't. He hadn't acted as if it were a stranger, come to think of it. *Silly goose,* she scolded herself, *to get in a bother like that.*

Benjamin swung into view, grinning wide as the Missouri sky with a string of perch over his shoulder. "Told you we have fish for supper."

"We should have left a while ago." She tightened the saddle girth and buckled the chin strap to Ahab's bridle.

"Sorry. Dem fishes bitin' so good, I din' want to stop." Benjamin handed her the lead lines and mounted Domino, tying the string of fish to his saddle. "Least de horses had a good rest."

The evening star hung in the western sky when they trotted out on the Kansas Road looking both north and south. No sight of Meshach and the wagon—not that she'd really expected any. Still, she'd been hoping. Could the wagon have gone by this point already? Not likely. While she and Benjamin had made many detours, still they'd followed a fairly straight route—she hoped. At least they found the road, but then any route west would have eventually done just that.

Another thing—how far south of Fort Scott were they, and finally, where should they set up camp? The questions buzzed like angry yellow jackets in her mind.

"You think they've gone by?"

Benjamin, who'd been studying the surface of the road, shook his head. "Roman ain't. Can always tell his prints."

"Could another wagon or wagons have wiped those out?" She wished she'd been paying more attention to tracking, but then since Benjamin was so good at it, why did she have to? Questions, questions.

They could hear a dog barking off to the west. The road ran along the eastern edge of a gently rolling open prairie with a series of hills and draws, the likes of which they'd come through to the east. They'd crossed a creek a mile or so behind, but what could they hang a marker on out here?

Benjamin returned from a jaunt north. "Farms ahead, both sides of de road. We make camp back on de creek?"

"I suppose so."

Benjamin swung down from his horse and, with the reins looped over his arm, set about gathering stones.

"What are you doin'?"

"Makin' dem a marker." He piled the stones on the right-hand side of the road and then, a couple of feet due east, piled a few more. Wiping his hands on his pants, he mounted Domino again and headed east. A willow thicket both signaled the location of water and hid it from sight. Rotting stumps showed where settlers had taken out the larger trees for firewood or lumber.

The horses pushed through the willows to drink, Ahab raising his head and looking back the way they had come. When he dropped to drink again, Jesselynn felt her shoulders relax.

Within a short time, they had hobbled the horses to graze, the foals had nursed, and Jesselynn dug in her saddlebag for the flint to start the fire. She and Benjamin gathered dead branches from the thicket, and after clearing out a patch of grass down to the dirt to keep from starting a prairie fire, they laid the wood and soon had a fire blazing. Jesselynn hunkered down on one of the stumps and studied the flames. She should be scaling fish. She knew that, but the knowing and the doing were two different things.

What if someone had stopped the wagon? What if the deputy had come after them in spite of the sheriff's orders? She about gagged on the *what ifs* and threw herself to her feet. Digging a hunting knife out of her saddlebag, she set about the scaling, using the stump as a table. Work always held worrying at bay.

"How are they goin' to see those stones in the dark?" She turned to Benjamin, scale-covered hands on her hips.

"Dey won't. Meshach pull up someplace to wait till dawn. We wait here till dey find us."

"I wish we'd never split up like this." She dug down in her saddlebag for a tin of grease and dropped some in the frying pan. They'd be eating mush if it weren't for Benjamin and his fishing. She dusted cornmeal over the fish and laid them one by one in the sizzling pan. She had to add wood often, since the branches were so small, but the fire was hot enough to fry supper, and that was all that mattered.

"I'se gonna set me some snares. See what we kin get." Benjamin spoke from directly behind her, making her jump.

"Can't you warn me? You're quieter even than Meshach." She knew she sounded grumpy, but frying fish didn't keep her mind occupied, and the worries crept back in. No wonder Ophelia sang a lot. Kept the mind busy so she couldn't worry.

"Sorry. I'll whistle when I come back so's you don' go and shoot me."

"Thanks." The quiet but for the grazing horses should have been peaceful. Frogs sang in the bulrushes. The fried fish smelled heavenly. She set her mind to thinking of how to keep the fried fish overnight so the others could have some when they arrived in the morning.

Supper seemed extra quiet without Sammy and Thaddeus with all their giggles and Thaddeus's eternal questions. She even missed Meshach's reading from the Bible, and since she'd left her writing case in the wagon, all she could do was stare into the fire until her eyes refused to stay open any longer. Since Benjamin said he'd take first watch, she wrapped herself in her quilt and tried to sleep.

Praying didn't help. She'd asked God's blessing and protection for every person she'd ever known and still she lay awake. Until Benjamin started singing to the horses. His rich voice singing the songs of his people, of glory by and by, overlaid the songs of the frogs and peepers, and she slept.

————

Ahab whinnied halfway through the morning. The answering bray could only come from Roman. Jesselynn whooped and danced a shuffle step around the fire pit. She stirred what ashes remained, added thin twigs, and blew on the few glowing coals. A couple of dry willow leaves, an extra puff, and the embers came to life, sending up a tendril of smoke before bursting into flame. They'd have coffee before long.

"Jesse, we's here." Thaddeus, standing beside Meshach on the wagon seat, waved, his face one big smile.

Meshach stopped the team on the first level spot and set the brake. Thaddeus scrambled over the wheel and hit the ground running, straight into Jesselynn's outstretched arms.

"Why you left us?" He put one hand on either side of her face and stared into her eyes. "You don't do that no more."

She kissed his cheek and stood up with him in her arms. "You know we have to keep the horses hidden, and when the wagon is traveling during the day, what else could I do?"

His frown said he was thinking hard. When he shrugged and squirmed, she set him down and, after greeting the others, looked up at her aunt.

"Everything all right?"

"Right as rain. Help me down, please. I about rocked my legs to sleep." Once on the ground, she settled her skirts and looked around the camp, if it could be called that. "We drove until near dark before we found a good place to stop, but other than a wave from a couple of wagons passing by, we talked to no one. Meshach kept looking for a marker, but I never saw a thing when he pulled off the road. How did he know?"

"Two small piles of rocks off the right side of the road."

"Well, my lands." She reached back in the wagon for the coffeepot. "Is there fresh water here?"

"A small creek. Benjamin dug out a hole so we can dip clear water. I'll get it."

When she returned, Jane Ellen had the boys looking for wood, Benjamin was skinning the three rabbits he'd snared, and Meshach had the team hobbled and grazing. Since they'd eaten the remaining fish for breakfast, Ophelia set one rabbit to simmering and cut up the other two for frying. The fragrance of coffee and frying rabbit soon called to them all. Hard-dried biscuits tasted much better dunked in coffee.

They took turns napping in the afternoon heat and at dusk headed north toward Fort Scott, with Jesselynn wondering how they would circumvent the fort when they got there. Just before dawn Daniel returned from one of his scouting forays to wave them off on a track heading west.

"Onliest way to get by de fort," he reported.

They had to dry camp that night and ration the water barrel, letting only the mares get all they wanted so they would have enough milk for the foals.

"We better get another water barrel," Jesselynn said as they ate dried biscuits and leftover fried rabbit. "I'd hoped to wait until Independence, but . . ."

"What we got, four more days?"

"Maybe six." *I wish I could talk to someone about Independence. Is there a fort near there? How will I get enough money for two wagons and all we need? How long, oh, Lord, how long will I have to make all the decisions?*

She knew the answer to that. Until the war was over. Until she could bring the horses back to Twin Oaks. She'd kept the thought at bay, fighting to keep it from living full blown in her mind. If she made it to Oregon, how would she ever bring the horses back to Twin Oaks?

Three nights later they smelled smoke before they saw the orange glow in the sky.

"Somebody's barn burnin'." Meshach clucked the team into a hard trot. Perhaps they could help. Riding Ahab, Jesselynn leaned forward and let him out. Within three strides, he was running free, for the first time in months. The even beat of his hooves sang to her memory of mornings on the track at home, brought back the laughter of old Joseph when he punched down the stopwatch, the smell of horse sweat and good leather. She slowed her horse, swerving to follow Benjamin into a farmyard. Not only the barn was blazing but the house too, even though the distance between the two should not have set one from the other.

Ahab snorted and tried to turn and leave, but she kept him steady with a firm hand. When Benjamin called to her, she dismounted and led Ahab over to a tree where Benjamin knelt by a woman who appeared to have crawled there for safety. But she hadn't been safe. The blood from the gash on her head and another from a bullet wound in her right shoulder said as much.

"Who did this?" Jesselynn handed her reins to Benjamin and pillowed the woman's head on her knees.

"Quantrill's Raiders. They . . . took . . . our . . . cattle. When . . . John . . . my husband . . . shot one of them . . ." The pause lengthened. "Th-they . . ." Her voice grew fainter.

"Don't try to talk. We'll find a doctor." She'd have missed the shake of the woman's head had she not been watching her so closely.

As if she hadn't heard, the woman continued. "They . . . shot . . . John . . . and . . . fired . . . the . . . house. The . . . children . . ."

Jesselynn knew no one would have survived that blazing inferno. With a crash the beams of the barn collapsed. The woman sagged, gagged, and was gone.

Jesselynn laid her back in the dust. The house, too, fell in on itself. A dog howled, a mournful lament that sent shivers up her spine.

Benjamin went to the wagon that had just arrived. Meshach joined Jesselynn beside the body. "How come no neighbors come to help?"

"Quantrill's Raiders." As she said the words, an idea slugged her in the chest. "They must have left just before we got here. We could have run into them. Oh, Lord, our God." Tears gathered and broke. She wasn't sure if they were tears of sadness for the woman and her family or tears of gratefulness that they'd been spared. Surely the raiders would have killed them all to get such horses as theirs.

"He surround us wid angels, just like we asked." Meshach got to his feet. "You see any other bodies?"

"Ask Benjamin. I've been right here." The howl rose again, eerie. "Do you see the dog?"

"Over by de house." Benjamin joined them. "Onliest thing alive, far as I can see."

"Get de shovel. We bury her, den get outa here."

"No, we just leave. The neighbors will come by when they know it is safe." Jesselynn wiped her eyes with the back of her hand. "Come on, let's get out of here."

"But . . ."

She snatched her reins out of Benjamin's hand and threw herself into the saddle. All they needed was to be caught here and accused of killing the family and starting the fire. They'd all be hanged.

They pulled back to a slow trot after they'd covered enough distance from the burning to be safe. Jesselynn settled into her saddle, fighting to keep her mind from replaying the death scene. No wonder people spoke of *The Raiders* in hushed tones. Fear did that to a body.

When the sun rose, she hated to stop. The closer they were to Independence, the safer they'd be—at least from the Raiders. But as the area became more settled, a new danger arose.

"Hey, Marse Jesse, you see dat dog followin' us?" Benjamin motioned with his head.

Jesselynn looked back to see a black dog, part shepherd from the look of him, with a patch of white around one ear. "How long he been with us?"

"Saw him at first light."

"Where do you think he's from? Someone's goin' to be real sad, missing their dog."

"No, I think they all dead."

"Oh." What more could she say? Looked like another war victim had joined their journey.

Where could they hide the horses until they could purchase their supplies and head out with a wagon train? And for how long? The farther north they traveled, the less the grass had sprouted. For the horses it wasn't a problem; for oxen it would be.

Chapter Twenty-Five

INDEPENDENCE, MISSOURI

Jesselynn rode past camps of staring sojourners before she found Independence proper.

"Hey, Chess, if all of these people are wantin' to go on to Oregon, there might not be room enough left over for us." The horse twitched his ears and trotted on. Riding Chess was immeasurably easier than riding Roman. Cows bellowed, horses whinnied, children ran screaming after one another, two men stood toe to toe slugging at each other while a crowd cheered them on. Wash hung from lines strung between wagons and tent poles. The smell that assaulted her nostrils could have used a stiff wind to blow it clear to the Mississippi. By then it might be bearable.

Two dogs ran in front of her horse, setting him to shying and her to paying better attention. Wouldn't that be wonderful to fall in the slop that Chess's hoofs clopped through?

The recent rain hadn't helped—that she knew for certain—but still, had no one dug latrines? Or if they had, didn't the people gathered here use them?

She stopped at the first store she came to and asked how to find a wagon train to join.

"Sorry, son, but most of the trains are already made up, just waitin' for the grass to grow."

"But surely there must be one that will take on two more wagons. We'll more than carry our own load."

"If'n there is such, you tell yer pa to come on in here and do the dealin'. Nobody's going to talk with a young boy like you." The bearded man behind the counter scratched his belly through a shirt that might once have been white.

"Like I said, my daddy is too sick to leave our camp. He sent me ahead to . . ."

"Sorry, can't help you. Next?"

Jesselynn turned away. It didn't help that this was the third time she'd heard those same words, or close to it. She thought of taking out the gold coins in her bag and dropping them on the counter, but from the looks of the crowd, that didn't seem to be a good idea either.

Besides, from what she could tell, supplies cost about twice what she'd heard before. Or more. Maybe they ought to set up an outfitting business of their own. Surely Meshach could get work here. There were enough wheels to fit and repair to keep a hundred blacksmiths busy.

At the end of the fruitless day, she asked directions for the post office. At least she ought to be able to find that. On the way she noticed another store, this one closed for the day. She'd try there tomorrow. She flipped Chess's reins around the hitching rail and took the two steps to the post office in one stride. The four letters the postman handed her when she said her name made up in part for the futility of the day. Two from Richmond, one from Sergeant White, and the last from Lucinda. She stuck them in her pocket to read back at camp and strode next door to an apothecary. She chose a peppermint stick for each of the boys and a packet of horehound drops and another of lemon drops. They'd all earned a treat. After studying the man's wares, she promised him she'd return to load up her simples box, then headed back to camp.

The heavy feeling persisted, just like the gray skies that hung low enough to snag with a fish pole. In spite of the gray she reminded herself that even though she hadn't found a wagon train, she'd learned plenty about getting ready.

And a possible way to make some money. She nudged Chess into a canter all the way back to the river bottom where they'd made camp.

"No wagon train, but we got letters." She dug them out of her pocket. "Which do you want to hear first? From Richmond or from Lucinda?" She'd keep Barnabas's letter to read by herself later.

"Lucinda." Her black members spoke as one.

Jesselynn opened the envelope and withdrew the ink-dotted sheet. While Lucinda could write well enough, she had a hard time keeping the quill from blobbing ink.

" 'Dear Marse Jesse and everyone,

We miss you so bad here. But thank the Lord we are alive and well. Joseph say to tell you he found some tobacco seeds, so we will have some crop in. Thanks to the garden and Joseph setting snares, we been eating well enough. Many have died of influenza, but we are safe so far. Black wagons carry bodies to the cemetery often. Men come home to die if they can.

I thank the Lord He keeping you safe. Tell Ophelia we are glad she and Meshach will have a baby. When will you come home? I got a letter from Miss Louisa. She working at the hospital. What her mother say about that, hmm? We digging the fields with a man pulling the plow. Goes slow.

Crocus come up, war or no war. Lord keep you in His care.

Lucinda' "

Jesselynn let the silence lengthen. She knew the others were thinking of home just as she was. Somehow she could not erase the picture of the big house. Twin Oaks still lived and flourished in her mind.

The letters from Louisa and Carrie Mae told of Christmas in Richmond, what was happening in the legislature, and the things they'd made for Christmas gifts. Zachary added a note of his own, barely legible with his left hand, but he had cared enough to write.

" 'You take good care of those horses, you hear? We need them to start over, but I know you know that and are doing all you can. If I could sneak back to Twin Oaks I would, but I am pretty hard to disguise, missing a foot and hand, let alone the eye.

Louisa is still grieving for her lieutenant, but I keep telling her he is dead, not just missing. She refuses to believe that, since there is no proof, but she must get on with her life. Carrie Mae tries to introduce her to young men, but you know our Louisa, stubborn to the hilt. I do not know where she gets that trait. Of course, none of the rest of us suffer from that affliction. May our God and Father keep you all safe. I trust that one day we shall see each other again—this side of heaven, I do hope.

Your loving brother,

Zachary' "

By the time she'd finished reading the letters, Sammy and Thaddeus had gone off to play, and the rest of them, other than Jane Ellen, were drying their eyes. Ophelia rocked gently, then hummed, and finally her song bathed the others in comfort. It was a deep river for sure, between them and home. How many more rivers would they cross before they found a new home, a free home, a safe home?

When the song died away, Jesselynn pulled herself back to the moment. "While I'm searching for a wagon master and train, you get Ahab back in condition," she instructed Benjamin.

His eyes rounded, along with his mouth. "For racin'?"

She nodded. "But you have to keep it a secret. No one can know about him."

Now he rolled his eyes, along with shaking his head. "Where we got space for dat?"

Jesselynn turned to Meshach. "I know the chance we're taking, but I can't figure any other way to get enough money to outfit us. We need two wagons and at least eight oxen, along with all the rest." She raised her hands and dropped them again. "Any other suggestions?"

"Like you said the other day, I could find work."

"I know. And you better do so. Daniel and Benjamin will have to guard the camp."

"I can graze the horses." Jane Ellen looked up from the willow basket she was weaving.

"And I can help guard the camp. No one expects an old woman to be able to shoot a gun." Aunt Agatha laid the shirt she was sewing for Jesselynn down in her lap. "Besides, with you off racing Ahab, Patch will let us know if anyone is comin'." They'd named the dog that had insisted on joining up.

The dog, lying beside the rocker, raised one ear, the tip of it flopping forward. For some reason he had adopted Aunt Agatha as his mistress, yet at the same time kept a watchful eye on the boys. If Sammy strayed too far from the fire by himself, Patch would go round him up and herd him back. He'd obviously been a cow or sheep dog.

Jesselynn half smiled and shook her head gently. All of them were learning that they could do things they never thought they could or would have to do.

And the dog, who'd shadowed them when they left the burning farm, adopted them so quickly it felt as if he'd always been part of the family.

When Jesselynn thought about the last week, she had to remind herself that God was in control and had a plan for all the goings-on. They'd rushed to get to Independence, and none of the wagon trains were heading out yet, though one wagon master had said "any day now." She still felt guilty for not burying the woman at the farm, even though she knew that staying there long enough to do the job right could have caused them all sorts of trouble. Ahab's throwing a shoe didn't help much either. Cost them a couple of hours. All the rush, and now they waited. And tried to find a wagon train.

For the next couple of days she rode on into Independence in the early morning, talked to as many people as she could, and came home to shake her head again. She had ordered two wagons, longer and sturdier than the one they were using now, and had brought back heavy canvas to make coverings for the hoops. Aunt Agatha, Jane Ellen, and Ophelia had been stitching on the covers ever since Jesselynn hauled it into camp. Meshach had fashioned leather handpieces like sailors used to help force the needles through the heavy fabric. Jesselynn planned to sell the present wagon when she sold Chess.

Ophelia and Jane Ellen dried fish and rabbit, whatever Daniel could bring in above what they ate every day.

One morning she and Meshach rode in to town together, he bareback on the mule, his sack of tools slung over one shoulder, his quilt rolled in a deerskin over the other.

"I'm not so sure I think this is a good idea." Jesselynn sighed and shook her head. She seemed to be doing a lot of that lately.

"Anythin' I can bring in'll buy more flour and beans. Could be I find us some oak for a barrel too. Wish now I made another back at de cave."

"Pray that I find us a wagon train today. With all the people gathered here, there has to be more trains being organized." She squeezed Chess into a faster trot. "Keep your eyes open for oxen. I heard there were more coming in."

"Got money enough to pay for dem?"

Jesselynn shrugged. "We will soon enough." Checking out the horse racing was another thing to watch and figure how best to win.

She left Meshach at the first blacksmith shop and returned to the store that had been closed the evening before. The proprietor smiled when she entered.

"Name's Robinson. How can I help you, son?"

"My family is here to head out on the trail, and we need supplies. And a wagon train."

"You came to the right place. Just this mornin' I heard of a new train formin' up under a man named Torstead."

"Really?" Her heart leaped at the news. "How can I, what do I—"

"Whoa." He held up both hands. "Got a bargain for ya. Buy what you need here—I got about the best prices around—and I give you a list of suppliers for what else you need. No one on my list cheats my customers, or I don't send them no more." He leaned on the counter, propped up by stiff elbows. "Now, what do ye need? Wagons, oxen, feed, flour—I got a list here that most wagon masters go by." He slapped a piece of paper on the counter.

"Already ordered the wagons. Need most everything else."

"How many folks in your party?"

Jesselynn mentally counted. "Nine. Two little ones." She didn't dare tell him about the horses.

"Hmm." The man scratched out some numbers on a slate and held it out for Jesselynn to read.

"Now, that is the amount for each person, you understand."

Jesselynn nodded and returned to her reading. Two hundred pounds of flour, seventy-five pounds of bacon, five pounds of coffee, two of tea, twenty-five pounds of sugar—brown the best—half a bushel of dried beans, one bushel of dried fruit, two pounds of saleratus, ten pounds of salt, half a bushel of cornmeal.

When she started multiplying by six—she counted Jane Ellen as a child—she felt her jaw begin to drop. A keg of vinegar, rope, tools, kitchen things, clothing, a small stove—where would they store all this? And she hadn't added grain for the mares yet.

"That thar list is mighty complete."

"I can see that." She read a section on taking milk cows. How she wished that were possible. "And you say you can supply all of this?" *And we've got the forge and Meshach's tools. Leastways we got our guns already, but we need more ammunition.*

"Either me or my list of suppliers." Robinson scratched his chin. "Goin' west takes all a man has and then some." He nodded as he spoke. "Better to take extra food and water than trinkets like furniture and things. You can always make your own once you get there."

"Well, sir, thank you for the advice." She rolled her lips together and, chewing on the bottom one, slit her eyes in thought. "Guess I better go find that Mr. Torstead, then."

"Wolf, he goes by Gray Wolf."

Jesselynn left the store with the name Gray Wolf Torstead branded on her mind and no idea where to find the man who owned the name.

He was a half-breed. What would Aunt Agatha have to say to that? And what if he wouldn't take them on? The fears hammered in time with Chess's easy trot. Robinson at the store thought the man was camped southeast of the square. All she had to go on was a name: Gray Wolf Torstead. Even the name intrigued her.

By late afternoon she felt as though she were chasing a will-o'-the-wisp or a swamp light. Many people she asked had seen him, but he'd gone somewhere else and they weren't sure where. When she finally located his simple camp, she dismounted and took up residence on a rock. Better to wait for the mountain to come to her than hightailing it after a mountain that moved around more than a hound hot on a rabbit trail.

———

If frustration had a name, today it was Wolf—Gray Wolf Torstead for a full name, but few called him anything other than Wolf. Instead of snarling as he wished, he stood silent, dark eyes blank, body still as his namesake on a hunt. He wanted to be wagon master of this forming train about as much as he wanted to dig an arrow out of his thigh, something he'd been forced to do some years in the past. The scar reminded him of that whenever he stripped to tribal dress.

He listened to the two men arguing and dreamed of home. Of the land of the Oglala Sioux, where the rivers ran clear, not the muddy brown of the Kansas, and the wind blew clean, not fetid as it did in this morass of an encampment. The smoke of cooking fires and blacksmith coals hung like that of a far-off forest fire, burning both nostrils and eyes.

He waited.

"So what do you think, Mr. Wolf?" The shorter of the two turned to the silent third of their party.

"Just Wolf. No mister."

"Ah, sorry." The man scrubbed a hairy hand across an equally hairy face. He reminded Wolf of a badger, pointed skinny nose, beady eyes, and scrabbling for a toehold where there might be none. When backed into a corner, as he was being now, he would fight to the finish.

"Can they join us or not?"

"Only if they have sufficient supplies and a wagon that will go the distance. I inspect everything. Anything less will slow the entire train." He knew from the glances they exchanged that when he spoke the language of his father, white men were surprised. He looked more Sioux than English. Before he died, his father had taught him well. To read, to write and do sums, to speak the good King's English, as Eviar Torstead called it. He also taught his son smatterings of Norwegian, Eviar's native tongue. His mother's people taught him to walk tall on the land and be one with horse and wind.

This would be his last train. The only reason he took the position of wagon master was for the gold it would bring. Gold that would buy guns for his people to hunt the buffalo, knives to skin them with, and blankets to warm them in the winter. Thanks to his father, he believed that whites and Indians could live in peace, learning from each other and sharing the riches of the land.

Everything always came back to the land.

While keeping his thoughts as his own, he waited for a response.

The taller man spat into the mud. "Ain't no breed goin' to inspect my provisions." He turned the last words into a sneer.

"Then you will not be joining my wagon train." Wolf heard the *my* and wondered when he had accepted responsibility. Up till then it had been *their*.

"You gonna let him talk like that?" The spitter spun on the badger.

"He's the boss. He promised to get us to Oregon, and I aim to follow his good sense. He's made the trip four times as a scout and knows whereof he speaks."

"Well, I ain't lettin' no breed tell me what to do." He spat again, this time within inches of Wolf's boot.

"That's your choice, mister." Badger nodded to Wolf and the two walked away, leaving the spitter sputtering.

"Sorry about that."

"Not your fault. We'll have enough trouble on the trail without someone like him along."

"Trouble? You don't mean Indian trouble—oh, pardon me, but do you?"

Wolf shook his head. "There's plenty else waitin' for the unwary. 'A wise man counts the cost before he begins to build his barn.' " Quoting from Scripture came easily to him. After all, he'd learned to read from that one book his father kept with him always.

"You said that right. I'm hopin' one day to do just that, build me a barn, but out in Oregon Territory. They say the trees are so big you only need one to build a house. That true?"

"Depends on if you saw up lumber or build a log house." Wolf paused, catching sight of a slim young boy sitting in his campsite. "Looks like I have someone waiting for me."

"I'll be goin' on, then. How soon you think we might be ready to head west?"

"When I'm certain everyone is ready."

"Oh, 'course." Badger sketched a nod and turned away, settling his hat more firmly on his head as he went.

Wolf kept track of the man out of the corner of his eye, all the while aware of his visitor. If someone had sent the boy, he had to know Wolf wasn't looking for any single young men to join his train. Singles, either male or female, spelled nothing but trouble on a wagon train.

Chapter Twenty-Six

Washington

"Miss, a box came for you."

Louisa turned at the clerk's call. "Thank you." She turned to Mrs. Hinklen, who appeared to have spent as sleepless a night as had Louisa. "You go on and order us coffee while I take this up to my room."

Surprised at the weight, she took the stairs as quickly as possible, what with trying to keep from stepping on the hem of her skirt and not drop the box. Only her name and room number identified the box tied with brown cord. Once inside with the door closed, she tried untying the knots, but when they didn't yield, she snatched up her scissors and cut them away. A note lay on top of a tightly woven bag of something.

"Dear Louisa, take this and do with it as we discussed. Do not count on seeing me again before you leave for Richmond." The Z told her whom it was from, even though the writing was difficult to read. And the message mind numbing.

"Zachary, where are you?" She covered the box again and slid it under her carpetbag in the chifforobe. "Oh, Lord, protect him, please. I almost lost him once. Don't let this be permanent." Knowing that Joanna waited for her, she tucked the note into her bag and, locking the door, descended to the dining room again.

"I have decided to go to Fredericksburg," Joanna announced as soon as Louisa had sat down. "I will not let them bury my husband in some nameless grave. I will take him home for a decent burial."

"Surely the army would ship his body home."

"I'm not counting on anything from the army any longer. They might have owned my husband, but they do not own me." She sniffed back incipient tears and straightened her spine. "I have cried enough. Would you help me get to Fredericksburg?"

"Ah, how do you . . . I mean . . ." *I've not told her I'm from the South. How does she know?*

"Dear Louisa, my husband and I lived in Kentucky for some years. I recognize your accent, and while you might be living here in Washington, I seriously doubt it." She kept her voice low and leaned forward, her hands clasped on the table. "I will have a pass enabling me to travel to Fredericksburg. Where do you live from there?"

"In . . . in Richmond, with my aunt. My older sister sent my sister and me to live with our aunt in Richmond, thinkin' we might be safer there."

"And you are—so far. No one has been able to take Richmond."

"Not for lack of trying, but you're right." Louisa thought of the box upstairs. Without Zachary's hollow leg and crutch, could she stash all of the powder?

"You could travel as my companion."

"Or, once we are in Southern control, you could travel as mine." The two women looked deep into each other's eyes. "And you could come on to Richmond if you like. We will always have a place for you."

"Thank you, my dear, and likewise. I'll contact those in charge and make the arrangements. Hopefully we can leave in the morning, depending on when the trains are running."

When Louisa returned to her room, she found a note on the floor. The simple message made her sigh in relief. "Do not be worried. Z." She sank down on the bed and clutched the paper to her heart. "Thank you, Lord, for listening and caring, even when I don't feel like you are there. I know faith and feelings aren't the same. I believe. Help, thou, my unbelief."

By the time she went to bed that night, she had neat packets of white powder sewn into the lining of her traveling skirt and jacket, into the false bottom of her reticule, and into the false bottom of the carpetbag. She hadn't needed the pocket in her Bible.

———

While the sun returned the following day, the streets remained a quagmire. Louisa dashed off a note to Cousin Arlington, informing him that she was sorry they were unable to meet, but she was leaving for home within the hour. She kept her tongue firmly planted in her right cheek while she penned the letter and readied it for mailing. Every time she heard footsteps outside in the hall, she paused, hoping the doorknob would turn and Zachary would enter.

But he didn't.

Her carpetbag was packed and ready to go. As she scanned the room for anything she might have missed, her eyes fell on the envelope she had placed on the mantel—the letter that had arrived for Zachary. Should she take it with her or leave it at the hotel desk in case Zachary should return?

She made her way downstairs, thankful that she at least had her return ticket. What if it had been with Zachary too? The more she thought about it, the more she realized their preparations had been woefully inadequate. With her mind made up she walked over to the desk. "Could you please hold this for my husband?" At the clerk's nod she smiled. "Thank you."

Once on the porch, she glanced around, hoping against hope to see Zachary and his peculiar gait come to her. She didn't give up until she and Joanna were seated in their buggy and Union officers had checked their papers.

"I'm sorry you have to make such a trip," the sergeant said, touching a finger to his hat. Not until he left did Louisa dare to relax. As the buggy started, her air released, and she leaned against the buggy window.

Within minutes, they both had their knitting in hand and, between watching the scenery and sharing memories of happier days, the miles sped by.

Once they had crossed the river, a Southern officer gave Mrs. Hinklen stern looks until he read her pass and then saluted. "I'm right sorry, ma'am. You'll find the officers' bodies, those we have anyway, in a warehouse in Fredricksburg. He might already have been buried."

"I sent a telegram."

"I understand, but . . ."

"Whom do I need to see?"

"Captain Jefferson, ma'am." The look he sent Louisa made her increase her prayers. Surely this poor woman would be allowed to take her husband's body home for a decent burial. The wagon ride to Fredericksburg showed a land ravaged by war.

They said their good-byes at the warehouse as dusk rolled in. While Mrs. Hinklen still wore traces of the peculiar shade of green she'd turned when identifying the bloated body of her dead husband, she gave Louisa a hug and promised to write.

"One day, my dear, when this war is over, as it eventually must be, please know that there is a place for you in a lovely little town in the Adirondacks. People come from all over the world for the waters, and I will be greeting them on the steps of our small resort."

"Thank you. I know Aunt Sylvania will be sad you couldn't come farther. As I am."

"We helped each other, and that is the way life is to be lived, war or no war."

Louisa waved good-bye as a buggy carried her to the southbound train. Had she and Gilbert had a chance to marry, would she be a widow now too?

The closer to home she got, the more she wondered if there had been a message from him.

What am I going to tell Aunt Sylvania about Zachary?

Chapter Twenty-Seven

❧

"You lookin' for me?"

Jesselynn got to her feet. "If you're wagon master Gray Wolf Torstead, I am." Finding his eyes took some looking up. Straight gaze, straight mouth, straight dark hair caught back in a thong, cheekbones carved of mahogany, rich like the sideboard at Twin Oaks. His buckskin shirt, fringe missing in places but soft and fitting like glove leather, made broad shoulders look more so.

"I am."

Jesselynn swallowed. "My name is Jesse Highwood and my—" She caught herself. If she lied about her father now, she'd be found out much too soon and branded a liar. This man deserved a straight answer. *But what if he says no if I tell him the truth? If?* She caught herself again. *When?* Perhaps telling as much truth as she dared would be sufficient. "My family is lookin' to join a wagon train to Oregon. I heard you were still takin' on wagons."

"How many?"

"Many?" *Wagons or people?*

"Wagons, and do you have all your supplies yet?"

"I've ordered two wagons. They should be ready any day."

"Who from?"

"Jenkins Wagons. Folks said they were built to last."

A slight tip of the head may have meant he agreed, maybe not. "Where's your folks?"

The gold bullion question. "My aunt is back at our camp, along with our freedmen and women. We all want to start new in Oregon." His eyes, they looked right through her.

"You're from the South." Not a question.

She nodded. "Kentucky."

"Confederate?"

She shrugged. Her political leanings were none of his business.

"How old are you, young Jesse?"

"What difference does it make? I can do the work of any man."

His gaze locked with hers. He waited.

She kept from scuffing her boot in the dust only with a supreme effort. Chess nudged her in the back. "Nineteen, no twenty." She caught herself. Tomorrow was her birthday.

His eyebrows joined. "Which?"

"Does it matter?" Why not just tell him? Cat-and-mouse games had never been her forte.

"No. Either way, you're too young. We need men, strong men."

"I have three black men with me. Meshach is bigger'n you and stronger than two men. Benjamin is an expert horse wrangler, as am I, and Daniel can find fish and rabbits where none exist. We can all shoot straight and keep our mouths shut."

"But can you all follow orders?" His question came soft and pointed.

"When need be." She held his gaze only with an effort, finally blinking and looking to his chest. Her heart fluttered like a bird trapped by a window and throwing itself against the pane, seeing freedom on the other side and not understanding the glass between.

"What are you runnin' from?"

She caught her breath. Raising her chin, she stared back at his obsidian eyes. "The war. What are you runnin' from?"

A tiny flare flickered in the depths of black, then it was doused. He too had secrets to hide.

A long pause before he shook his head again.

"I have the money." She broke in before he could utter the final word. At least she spoke only half a lie. She would have the money as soon as she sold Chess and located a race or two.

"Come back to me when you have your wagons, and we'll see." While he still shook his head as he spoke, he hadn't said no.

Her heart settled back to a steady beat. "I will, but what guarantee do I have that there will be a place remainin' for us?"

"None."

She clamped her teeth on the words that threatened to spill out. Sucking in a deep breath, she spoke through gritted teeth. "I may not be a man full grown, but gentlemen do not do business this way. When I meet all your requirements, I expect to be allowed to join your train, sir."

"I am no gentleman."

"I can tell that, but Mr. Robinson at the store said you are a man of honor, that we could trust you, and you would be fair." She took a step closer.

Wolf kept from stepping back before the onslaught of this young rooster. Schooling his face took little effort, in spite of the grin that tickled his cheeks. And his insides. Grown men took his no for an answer. Why not this Jesse Highwood of Kentucky? He said he had freed black men, meaning he'd had slaves. Why was getting to Oregon so important to him? He looked far too young, hadn't even shaved yet, besides not having filled out. If Jesse Highwood was twenty, he, Wolf, was the south portion of a mule goin' north.

"Come to me when you have your wagons."

I'll see you run over by my wagons! Jesselynn flung herself on Chess's back and glared down at the mountain that refused to move. "I will be back."

Wolf dipped his chin in the briefest of nods and turned to answer a man who'd come up beside him.

Pure rage felt hot, but this time Jesselynn felt determination cold as a three-foot icicle on a January morning. Showing up Mr. Gray Wolf Torstead would be the utmost pleasure. Those wagons would be the toughest and tightest ever built. No way was that insufferably stubborn man going to keep them from going to Oregon.

He'd thrown down the gauntlet. She had picked it up.

———

"Three days? But you said they would be ready today." Jesselynn glared at Jenkins, who seemed oblivious to living up to his word.

"One of my men took off wi' dat last train. Can't build wagons widout good men."

"I will bring you a good man tomorrow." Mounting Chess without using the stirrups was becoming a habit. Anger gave strength to her legs. "In fact, I'll bring you two. You can deduct their wages from the cost of my wagons." *If he thinks he can pull the wool over my eyes just because I'm young, he has another think coming.* The ride to the ironmongers took less time than usual.

"What do you mean no horseshoes? You promised me six boxes, for both horse and oxen."

"Sorry. The barge ain't showed up. Spring slows down the river traffic. Maybe t'morrow."

"What about yokes for the oxen?" If they had any sense, she told herself, Meshach could have carved those back in the oak woods too. So many things they hadn't thought of. She shook her head and, turning, strode out the door, her bootheels clacking on the floorboards in a satisfying enough manner. Stomping would have felt better, along with door slamming. But both would have said what she'd been accused of far too often lately—being young. If they figured out she was female . . . It was bad enough being a *young* man, or boy, as she was so often called. No wonder Meshach wanted to go to Oregon. He was far beyond *boy* status, yet so many referred to him that way, all because of his dark skin. On the way back to where she'd tied Chess, she added to her litany of frustrations. Their money would not stretch near far enough, she had yet to find a race for Ahab, and her curse was upon her.

She'd awakened that morning dreaming of Twin Oaks and her mother cosseting her during that time. Today she had no time for cramps or hot bricks. She had to get her people on the way to Oregon.

The first wagon train left the next morning.

On the way back from checking with Jenkins Wagons again, she saw a crowd gathered to the east of town. When a mass shout went up, she angled her horse in that direction and watched the action from his back.

Two horses, one black and one bay, drove across a makeshift finish line, the black a winner by a head. Easing Chess forward, she made her way through the crowd of shouting men until they stopped just short of two men, one with a slate and chalk, the other handing out money.

The money man stepped up to the rider on the black horse and handed him a leather pouch that clanked when changing hands. The purse, and it had to contain gold.

Jesselynn dismounted and, with her reins looped over her arm, waited until the betters collected their winnings before approaching the man who seemed to be in charge.

"Pardon me, sir, but could I ask you a question?"

Porkpie hat tipped up, he turned. With a quick glance at her, he shifted the cigar in his mouth from one side to the other before speaking. "Yeah, boy, what do you want?"

"I want to know how this racin' is set up."

"Just the way you sees it. Two riders, two horses. One wins, one loses."

"And the others?"

"Others?" The cigar shifted again. This time he removed it between two fingers, spat a quid off to the side, and put the cigar back. He seemed to chew it more than smoke it.

Jesselynn stood her ground. "Those who placed the bets. The odds?"

"No odds. Just divvy up the take." He hawked and spat. "What's it to you? That horse don't look to have no speed."

Five days had not been enough to get Ahab in shape, but if the contenders ran no faster than the ones she'd seen, Ahab didn't need to be in condition. The trick would be getting him to run more slowly. So the bets would be more the second time.

Jesselynn headed for home without badgering the ironmonger again.

"He ain't ready." Benjamin shook his head.

"I know, not ready for a real race, but the horses I saw were just fast, not Thoroughbreds."

"What if someone steal him?"

"We won't let them. You and Meshach go with me. Daniel can stay here to guard the others."

Meshach sighed, shoulders slumping after a full day at Jenkins Wagons. "I don't like the bettin'. The purse be enough."

Jesselynn knew she'd made a mistake in mentioning that she planned to bet—on herself. She refused to entertain the thought that if she lost the sixty dollars, she lost a wagon. But Ahab wouldn't lose. She was sure of that.

"Betting makes perfect sense. We can only race one day, then Ahab has to disappear again. With each day, the danger increases, and we can't take that chance. He runs once, barely wins. . . ." She paused. Shook her head ever so gently, a smile, slight, barely moving her lips. Her head nodding only a bit, thinking, planning.

"I don't like dat look." Meshach studied her through narrowed eyes.

"I lose the first race." She held up a hand to stop their sputtering. "By only a nose."

Benjamin snorted. "You think you can hold him back?"

She nodded. "But then I demand a rematch. Give him an hour, and we run again. This time we bet. We win, and we buy the rest of our supplies."

"And pray de army don't get wind of de fast horse down in Independence."

"Who goin' lay de bets?" Meshach looked up from studying his clasped hands resting on his knees. He hadn't left off sitting on his chunk of wood since the discussion began.

Jesselynn froze. Meshach was right. She couldn't ask him or Benjamin. A black with sixty dollars in gold would be suspect immediately. And she couldn't bet herself.

"I will. Won't be the first time, and most likely not the last." Agatha set Thaddeus off her lap and stood. "Only thing, we'll have to take the wagon, then."

Why can't anything ever be simple? I was just going to go race the horse and get out of there again. But what else can we do?

That left Ophelia and Daniel alone with the horses and the camp and the young'uns, though Jane Ellen considered herself as grown as Daniel, at least. And she could shoot too.

Jesselynn looked to Meshach, who refused to look up at her. But she read disapproval in every line of his weary body.

"When will our wagons be ready?"

"Tomorrow or de next day."

"I heard another train is pullin' out in the mornin'."

"Yes, suh. Where you get de oxen?"

"I talked with a man today. He has nine, but not all are trained yet."

"Buyin' all nine?"

"Depends on the purse."

Before she fell asleep that night, Jesselynn wandered out to where Daniel had put Ahab to grazing on a long line. She leaned against the stallion's shoulder and stroked his neck on up to rub his ears. Ahab lowered his head and sighed, leaning into the ministering fingers.

"You want to run tomorrow, old son?" She ran her fingers through his mane, snagging on a burr. "Daddy would die again if he saw how bad you look." The mane and tail hadn't been combed since they left Twin Oaks, and a brush was used only on the places the harness or saddle might rub. She thought of the racing saddle tucked away in the trunk, underneath the two dresses she had brought along. She almost hadn't put it in.

She rubbed the stallion's nose and wandered back to camp. The men had insisted she not take a turn at watch tonight so she would be fresh for the race. Daniel and Benjamin both wore grins that clearly showed their excitement. Even Thaddeus caught the feeling, though no one told him they would be racing Ahab.

"You go to sleep now like a good boy." Jane Ellen's voice wore that patient tone that said she was repeating herself.

Jesselynn reached in the wagon for her bedroll and gave her little brother a poke. Giggles erupted, and Thaddeus rolled over to grab her hand.

"Kiss, Jesse."

Jesselynn kissed his cheek and stroked back his curly hair. If only his father could see him now. He would be so proud. She laid out her bedroll and glanced heavenward. "Daddy, if'n you're watchin', please do all you can to make sure we win that race tomorrow. Might be the most important race Ahab ever ran."

While she kept her voice to a whisper, she lay back on her bedroll and studied the stars, stars they'd be following west. Good thing the Lord said He'd guide their steps. She hoped and prayed that included both racing and westering the miles.

Chapter Twenty-Eight

"Now, you understand the rules?"

Jesselynn nodded. While she wore her stirrups shorter than usual, she tried to look like any normal rider, not a jockey.

"He's mighty light compared to Erskin there." One of the spectators hawked and spit, then squinted up at Jesselynn. "Might make a big difference."

"Erskin been at this long enough. He knows what that black can do."

Jesselynn fought to keep her concentration on the race, not on the gaping group of humanity that looked like bathing might be against their religion. At the Keeneland Track, where her father raced his Thoroughbreds, the crowd dressed for the day as a social event. Hats were *de rigueur*, and the loveliest of gowns the custom. Not the morass of pressing, stinking men who crowded Ahab, making him lay his ears back. He looked ready to bite the next man who came near.

"Hey, boy, you ready?" The owner and rider of the black spat off to the side of his horse. Did everyone chew tobacco here?

"Anytime, sir." She touched a finger to the brim of her slouch hat. The porkpie had a habit of blowing off in a stiff wind, and she planned on a stiff wind from release to the finish line.

The man in charge pointed to a man waving a red flag and waiting better than a quarter mile away. "You start there when he says, and the first one across this line is the winner. There'll be no striking a horse but your own, no jostling, bumping, or cutting off the other horse. I want a clean race. You hear?"

Jesselynn nodded, having a feeling that experience had necessitated the rules. She glanced at Erskin, who wore a smirk fit to rile the staunchest peacemaker. Wishing she had watched more races to see what kind of shenanigans he pulled, she glanced around the crowd to see Aunt Agatha sitting up in her rocking chair in the wagon bed, knitting away just as if she were back in camp. She caught Jesselynn's eye and winked.

Jesselynn acted as if she didn't know her, but the wink warmed her insides. She wished the race were longer. Lots of horses could go the short distance, but it was in the longer races where the Thoroughbreds excelled.

"Hey, Erskin, you not gonna let a young pup like that beat ya, are you?"

"Just put your money down, and let's get on with this. I got work to do."

At that, half the crowd burst into guffaws. Erskin was well known, obviously.

"Okay, now, easy canter up to the starter. Everyone stand back, clear the track."

Jesselynn glanced down. The mud had dried, but *the track,* as he so euphemistically called it, looked hard as a brick, none of the sand and well-dug surface of a real race track. She did as the man ordered and set Ahab at an easy canter to where they would start.

"Where'd you get that horse, boy?" Erskin pulled up beside her.

"Family horse. Just likes to run. Pulls a good plow too." She leaned forward slightly to stroke Ahab's neck. Not that he'd ever been hitched to a plow, but Erskin wouldn't know that.

"You ever raced 'im before?"

"Me? No. Daddy just thought it might be a fun idea." This at least was no lie. She herself had never ridden Ahab at the track in a real race. She had trained him at home. And her daddy, why, he had thought racing Thoroughbreds one of the chief delights of this life.

He'd be heartbroken to see his pride and joy in the condition he was in.

They reached the starter, who looked about as reputable as the man at the other end. "Y'all ready?" he asked.

Jesselynn wished she had goggles but only nodded after settling herself deeper in the saddle. Ahab shifted from one front foot to the other. "Easy, son."

The man pointed his pistol in the air, paused, and the shot rang out. Ahab leaped as if from a starting gate, but before he hit his stride, the black was three lengths ahead and extending his lead.

"Go, Ahab!" Jesselynn crouched over his withers, making herself as small as possible, urging him on with hands and reins.

They lost by a length, but toward the end they were gaining. If only they'd had more track to cover.

Ahab was blowing hard when she pulled him to a canter, then a trot, and turned back to where Erskin stood, accepting the congratulations of the crowd—and the purse.

"Sorry, boy. Someone shoulda warned ya." He turned and slapped his horse's shoulder. "Yes, sir, this old boy can run."

Losing the twenty-dollar gold piece she'd had to put up galled her hide. Losing the race made her see shades of red—bright red. "That he can." She forced the chosen words past teeth clamped together to keep the flood inside. The flood attacked her instead. Calling herself all kinds of names, none of them complimentary, she led Ahab off to walk him around and cool him down.

How stupid to think she could win so easily. Sure, let the other horse catch up and push ahead at the last moment. What was she thinking of?

She stayed away from Aunt Agatha and the wagon.

Leading his horse, Erskin caught up with her. "No bad feelings now, are there? After all, your horse there has a good heart. He didn't quit on ya."

Jesselynn just nodded and kept on walking.

"Tell ya what I'll do. How about you meet me back here again tomorrow morning, same time, and I'll let ya see if you can win yer money back? How's that?"

"You mean no money up front?"

"Right, that's what I mean. Outa the goodness of my heart." He clapped one hand on his chest, even though it was on the wrong side.

"So, what's the catch?" Jesselynn stopped walking and faced him square on.

"No catch. Just that if I win, I keep both horses. You win, you get 'em both—and the purse."

She kept her mouth closed and her eyes from widening through supreme willpower. All her mother's training on good manners and deportment came to the fore. She eyed the man, rock steady. "On one condition." *Oh, Lord, am I being a fool? Or am I just being my daddy's girl? Zachary wouldn't even hesitate. But I've got all these people to think of.* She sighed. That's what she was thinking of—getting her people to Oregon.

She shook her head, turned away. The stakes were too high.

"I'll throw in an extra hunnerd dollars."

He thinks he's got us whupped and down. "On one condition."

"What's that?"

"We double the length of the track."

He studied her through squinted eyes, looked up at the cotton-bole clouds and back at her. "Done."

While she hesitated to shake his dirt-engraved hand, she knew that gentlemen did so. Not that he was a gentleman, more like a conniving lowlife, but the race was set. She mounted Ahab. "Tomorrow then." And rode off.

She headed up the river in order to fool anyone following her, and when she was certain no one was on her trail, she angled back for their camp. As soon as Aunt Agatha arrived, Jesselynn unhitched Chess, saddled him, and cantered back to town, leaving instructions for Daniel and Jane Ellen on caring for Ahab.

Aunt Agatha had only shaken her head. She'd heard the buzz before she left the crowd.

Jesselynn put money down on the oxen, rode by to check on the wagons, which were promised for the morning, stopped at Robinson's store to finish ordering the supplies, including another oak water barrel, and listened again to the excuses from the ironmonger.

"But, Jehosaphat, he come up de river, say my barge be here tomorrow. Dey got stuck on a sandbar, but all right now."

She nodded and left. At least they hadn't thrown the boxes of shoes overboard.

If she kept busy enough, she couldn't think about the morning.

But back at camp, Daniel and Benjamin didn't even try to hide their fear—or was it sorrow? Meshach shook his head and returned to his Bible reading before it got too dark to decipher the pages. She didn't dare ask what the Good Book had to say about gambling—if anything.

"We're going to win," she promised the stars from her bedroll.

———

Ahab pranced in the coolness of the early morning and ate his oats with ears pricked forward as if he knew what was coming. When Jesselynn lifted his front foot to pick the dirt out, he turned his head to nudge her seat, nearly sending her flying flat out.

"Ahab! Whatever is the matter with you?"

"He like dat racin' again." Meshach started to brush off the mud crusted on the horse's shoulder, then stopped. "One day we get to brush and polish this old son till him look like the granddaddy Thoroughbred he be."

"Did you pray for us to win?"

"Hmm." He nodded. "But more I pray for God to keep you both safe and for us all to get on de road before trouble happen. Just do yo' best. That all you can do."

Jesselynn nodded. Earlier that morning she had decided that none of them would place a bet. Winning the purse would be enough.

They hitched up the wagon and, with Aunt Agatha stitching away in her rocking throne, headed for town. Once she dropped Benjamin and Meshach off at Jenkins, Aunt Agatha would drive the wagon herself over to watch the race. Jesselynn made a detour and came toward the racing ground by another direction. When they won, everyone would be on the lookout for her and her horse. Keeping the camp safe was more important than anything.

The crowd was double the size of the day before, and the man with the slate was doing a brisk business. Erskin and his black were the center of an admiring group; a silver flask along with a long-necked bottle made the rounds, upping the hilarity that greeted every joke and sally.

"Come on over, boy, have a tote." Erskin waved to Jesselynn.

She shook her head but smiled to show she wasn't being uppity.

Suddenly she felt like throwing up. Right there in front of everyone. Right now! She wanted to call the whole thing off, but Erskin had signaled the time had come to mount up. Too late. Whether she felt relief or fear, she didn't know.

She sucked in a deep breath, held it, and nudged Ahab forward toward the starter, who was just a speck but for his red flag. Red flag, pistol shot, race. In that order.

All right, calm down. This is just a race like any other, and this time the distance is on our side.

But how do you know the black can't run distance too? And you can lose Ahab!

That was one of those thoughts she'd been refusing to acknowledge. She didn't know. But she would soon find out.

She squeezed Ahab into a canter and could feel him arch his back to take an extra jump or two—sheer energy. As her daddy always said, *"Poetry in motion. That's a good runnin' horse."*

"Well, Daddy, today our poetry had better sing loud and clear." She swept by the starter with a nod and turned in a gentle half circle to bring Ahab back to the starting line. Erskin trotted up and, with a tip of his head, took his place between her and the starter.

"Now, remember, if'n either of you start before the gun, you get one more chance, and after that it's a forfeit."

"You didn't mention that yesterday."

"What's that you say?" The man cupped his ear to hear better, the red flag dangling behind him.

Jesselynn shook her head to signify it didn't matter. Ahab settled on his haunches and stopped the restless shifting. Ready, like an arrow to be released from a bow.

"Ready."

The black jumped forward, eliciting a curse from his rider. Erskin rode him in a circle and came up from behind.

While he performed his move, Jesselynn stroked Ahab's neck. "That's all right, old son, you be ready now. He'll get off faster than we do, but we'll catch him flyin'." Looking neither to the right nor to the left, she concentrated on the gap between Ahab's pricked ears.

The shot! The leap! And they were pounding the dust one length behind the black. Jesselynn crouched forward. "Okay, now, let's get up about his stirrup." She loosened the reins, and Ahab leaped forward as if she'd been holding him back. They came up even with the black's streaming tail, then with his haunches, and then even with the stirrups.

Erskin went to the whip, and the black surged forward.

Wind sang in her ears, hooves thudded, and Ahab grunted as he pulled up head to neck.

Erskin beat the black, both on rump and shoulders, screaming at him for more.

Ahab surged by him, still picking up speed, and crossed the finish line with half a length to spare.

If she hadn't been the horsewoman her father had trained her to be, Jesselynn might have fallen off from sheer relief. Instead, she let Ahab run a bit before easing him back first to a hand gallop, then to a canter. She turned to trot back to where the crowd stood in silent grief. Jesselynn glanced over at Aunt Agatha, who wore a grin from here to Sunday. A brief sketch of a nod was her only answering motion.

Jesselynn stopped in front of the chalk man and leaned forward to pat Ahab's steaming shoulder.

"Here you go, boy. I never saw a horse run like that 'cept at a real honest-to-God track one time. That horse sure can run." He handed her the leather pouch, which she stuck in her pocket.

Erskin strode up and handed her his horse's reins. "I kept the saddle. That weren't part of the bet."

"I didn't bet. You set up the parameters."

He raised an eyebrow, but she didn't bother to explain. "Thank you. We will treat him well. What is it you call him?"

"Blackie."

Jesselynn looked around to see her aunt standing several feet distance.

"That was a fine race, son." Her eyes twinkled. "Your mother must be right proud of you."

"Thank you, ma'am." Jesselynn ducked her head, as was proper. It helped hide her almost smile. She mounted Ahab again and clucked the other horse to follow them. She trotted a ways and stopped. Clear as if someone sat on her shoulder, she heard a voice tell her to offer Blackie back to his former owner for a hundred dollars.

That's crazy. Why, the army would pay two hundred . . . or more. Ahab sighed and shook his head, setting the reins to flapping. Jesselynn looked around. No one nearby was paying any attention. Shaking her head and giving a heavy sigh, she turned the horses back toward the now thinning crowd. Aunt Agatha and the wagon were heading out the other way. When she found the chalk man, she stopped. "You seen Erskin?"

"Probably in the saloon drowning his sorrows. Losing Blackie hit him hard."

"Thanks. Which saloon?"

"Oh, most likely the Western Belle. Favorite place o' his."

Jesselynn found the place after a bit of searching, tied the horses to the hitching rail, and took the steps two at a time. She paused before the swinging doors. Saloons were no places for young women, but since she was a young man, it should be all right. But it wasn't. She stepped back when someone pushed the doors outward.

Come on. Quit wasting time. Get on in there and find the man so you can get Ahab back under cover. With that as a prod, she pushed the doors and followed them inward, blinking in the dim light. Even at this time of the morning, smoke hung like a shroud over the room. Two tables were set up for cards, but she found Erskin leaning against the bar, a bottle in front of him.

"Mr. Erskin?"

He turned with a snarl on his face that only intensified when he saw her. "What do you want now? You got my horse. Ain't got nothin' else."

She nearly coughed on the fumes flung her way by his words. "I have a proposition for you."

"Yeah?" He hoisted the bottle, his Adam's apple glugging several times before he handed the bottle in her direction. "Have some."

"No, thanks. My daddy don't hold with his son drinkin' liquor yet." She leaned against the bar and waited for him to repeat the chugging noise and smack his lips. "Now, I was wondering if you would like to buy Blackie back."

"Buy him back? Are you outa your ever-lovin' mind? 'Course I want him back."

"Good. How does a hundred and fifty dollars sound?"

"Ain't got that much."

"How much do you have?"

"A hunnerd."

"Gold?"

A nod.

"Sold. Come on out and get him." Jesselynn turned toward the door expecting him to follow, but halfway there she realized no sound of boot steps came behind her. She turned.

Erskin stood as if he'd been turned to salt. He blinked, the only part of his body that seemed to work other than his hand that clenched and relaxed before clenching the bottle again.

"Are you comin'?"

"Aye, boy, that I am."

Jesselynn hoped Blackie knew his way home, because the way Erskin swayed and stumbled, he wouldn't be doing much guiding.

She left with his blubbering thank-yous ringing in her ears. Maybe she could be called all kinds of fool, but right now a peace rode her shoulders, and it failed to evaporate on the roundabout ride back to camp.

———

Two days later she had the new wagons loaded and the oxen pulling them into Wolf's camp. "We're here for your inspection."

His eyes didn't look one mite more accommodating. After he went through all the boxes, bags, and barrels, he stopped next to her.

"All right. Much against my better judgment, you can join us. We leave day after tomorrow."

"Good. That'll give me time to sell my other wagon and the extra horse." She glanced up into his face, hoping for a smile, a nod, something that indicated he was pleased. Nothing.

"Now, you've told me everything else you are bringing, right?"

Everything but seven Thoroughbreds, but they shouldn't cause any problem.

"I don't like surprises."

Jesselynn shrugged. "I better get on back to camp." *God, forgive me, but I don't know what else to do.*

Chapter Twenty-Nine

❧❧

On the Oregon Trail

"Here come the wagons!" Thaddeus threw himself back against Jane Ellen's chest.

Her grunt spoke volumes for the strength the little boy gained daily.

Jesselynn released a deep breath she wasn't aware she'd been holding. Sitting high on the wagon seat, she let her thoughts and fears run rampant. What if Gray Wolf took another route? What if he refused them when he saw the other horses? Of course he wouldn't be seeing the horses until later. With the sun barely out of bed, the wagon train snaked along the trail, already raising a cloud of dust. The western sky, however, looked about ready to take care of the dust problem. A chill wind blew, precursor to the black, moisture-laden clouds.

But to the east, the sun shone, waking the diamonds that slept on the spring grass. Dandelions opened their golden faces to the morning and hid in the growing grass. With thirty wagons, this train was smaller than some of the others, and from what she'd heard, was better prepared.

Wolf had seen to that. He rode now at the head of the train, his spotted horse—she'd heard they were called Appaloosas—dancing with energy.

She wondered how far ahead their horses had gotten. Meshach, Daniel, and Benjamin had taken them south to meet with the wagon train later in the day. If she'd dared, she'd have sent them on ahead to Topeka. Once they were well on the trail, surely he wouldn't send them back. But with all the farmlands and small towns dotting the first leg of the trail, he could send them back anytime. Not like farther north where she'd heard the land was still as free as the grass that rippled like waves in the wind. She'd read that in a circular sent out to encourage western migration.

The bluegrass at home did the same just before haying time. Otherwise the pastures were kept short for the horses to have the succulent new grass to feed on. In her other life the foals would be cavorting under immense walnut trees while their dams grazed. The yearlings would be racing each other up the fence line, practicing for their future. Up at the big house, rugs would be on the lines for the beating, curtains down for washing away the winter dust, and workers singing as they washed the windows, making the house sparkle for Easter.

Meshach had reminded her that Easter would be that Sunday. Celebrating Easter on the wagons west. Somehow it didn't seem proper. No church with snowball bouquets, spiked with purple iris, on the altar. No new hats and gowns, no special Easter feast with as many friends and relatives who could come.

But, of course, that was all before the war—in her other life.

One of the oxen bellowed and was answered by one of the oncoming spans. They plodded along as if they'd been on the trail already for days, but she knew that many of them were still being trained the day before. One of theirs, a brindle that Jane Ellen named Buster, didn't want to settle into the yoke. She had him yoked in her span so she could keep after him to pull his share. Jesselynn thought Blister a more suitable name.

Wolf cantered back to meet her. "Good morning." He touched the brim of his hat and nodded to Aunt Agatha driving the other wagon.

Jesselynn could see him looking around, and she knew for whom. The question didn't surprise her.

"Where are your men?"

"Jenkins begged and pleaded that they stay on one more day to finish out an order. They'll catch up with us." Keep this up and pretty soon she wouldn't know truth from lie or what she told to whom. But this one was partly true. Jenkins had pleaded for them to stay on. They had chosen not to. He'd offered them year-round work at a real fair wage, but Meshach said no. He was going west for the free land.

The look Wolf gave her promised more questions to come, but right now keeping the train moving was more important. "You file in at the end. The wagons will take turns eating dust with a new one in front every morning."

"Mr. Wolf, we goin' to Orgon." Thaddeus stood on the seat beside Jesselynn. One thing for sure, no one would accuse Thaddeus Highwood of being shy. It she hadn't a firm grip on the seat of his pants, he would have been down the wagon wheel and racing over to the horse.

"That we are." Wolf tipped his hat again and reined back to answer a call from one of the drivers.

Thaddeus and Sammy waved to those on the wagons and those walking beside. Some called greetings, some didn't, but all wore a look of expectation, as if they would see Oregon next week.

Five months it would be, and that was if all went well.

A baby cried and was hushed. A dog barked. Patch trotted stiff legged out to inspect another that advanced in the same manner. Tails wagged in the tentative way of dogs. They sniffed each other, one darting away, then back again. Patch stood his ground with hackles raised.

Jesselynn watched the ritual. "Get on back here, Patch." She wasn't in the mood to have to break up a dogfight, although she was sure there would be a number of those, the same with the cows and horses, as all the critters set up their pecking orders. Patch ran back to the wagon, tongue lolling, and gave a quick yip to announce his arrival.

Same with the folks. There was sure to be trouble somewhere along the trail.

When all the wagons passed, she flicked her whip out over the backs of the oxen, getting a satisfying pop without touching a hide. The wagon lurched forward for the second time that morning, but she held back in the line, waiting for Agatha to pull in front of her. With the extra ox tied on the rear, she was indeed last, except for the spare horses and oxen that formed a herd following off to the south where the animals could snatch a mouthful of grass once in a while. Several young men, mounted on horses, were keeping the herd on the move.

Children waved from front porches as the caravan passed by, farmers from out in their fields. Their route took them down the streets of Olathe and Lawrence, heading them southwest until the Oregon Trail left the Santa Fe Trail. Then they'd turn north and cross the Kansas River at Topeka. The noon stop was short—no campfires allowed—but it gave the oxen and horses a rest, as well as those walking alongside the wagons. Since they stopped by a creek, the animals drank their fill, and the children waded in the water.

They were barely on the road again when the threatening storm hit with teacup-size raindrops. All the walkers scurried for the wagons, leaving the drivers and the animals to brave the elements. Jesselynn was soaked within seconds. *I shoulda had Jane Ellen take over for Aunt Agatha.* But it was too late now.

"Leastways the canvas ain't leakin'," Jane Ellen said from behind her shoulder. "That greasin' we did makes the water run off slicker'n off a duck's back." She lifted her face to the rain sheeting down. "Smells good, don'tcha think? All clean and fresh."

Jesselynn had to agree. The world always smelled better after a rain, and it wasn't like this one was so cold. Chilly yes, but not bone-deep freezing like earlier in the year.

"Rain like this makes the grass and flowers just leap outa the ground. I love springtime."

Jesselynn had to smile. Not often did Jane Ellen say this many words at one time without someone having asked her questions.

"Sure do hope Meshach and the boys got a place to stay dry. How soon you think we'll be meetin' up with 'em?"

"Long about sunset." Jesselynn flipped the reins to move the oxen along better. The gap had widened between them and the wagon in front. She touched the right rear oxen with the tip of the whip, and he lunged into the yoke. "You just stay up there too. No room for a lazy ox here."

"He's the purtiest one though, ain't he?"

"Isn't he."

"I think so."

"No. I mean, you don't say 'ain't.' The proper way is 'isn't he.' "

"Oh. That's right. He is right purty, ah . . . isn't he?"

"Guess so. But he's lazy." Jesselynn popped her whip over him again. "Got to keep on him all the time."

The sky lightened, and off to the west a band of light broke through just above the horizon. The rain changed to a drizzle, then stopped.

"You think we'll see a rainbow?"

"Good chance." Jesselynn was hoping she'd see Meshach. But the rider coming toward them was definitely not he. The horse's red chest and white-spotted rump were a surefire giveaway.

"You all right back here?" Wolf sat his horse as if born attached.

"Hey, Mr. Wolf." Jane Ellen leaned across the seat to wave.

"Just Wolf, no mister." He pulled up alongside the wagon.

"Is Wolf your whole name?" Jane Ellen slid one leg across the seat and, with a lithe twist, took up sitting beside Jesselynn.

"Nope. Between my father and my mother, they named me Gray Wolf Torstead."

"So you are Mr. Torstead."

"Guess so, but most folks call me Wolf." He nudged his horse into a trot and waved back at them.

"Ain't he beautiful?" The reverence in the words kept Jesselynn from making a smart retort. When she glanced at Jane Ellen, the thought hit her. Jane Ellen was becoming a young lady. One who showed an interest in the male of the species and whose heart could be trampled by a crush.

"Isn't."

"He is too." Like a fluffy hen defending her chicks, Jane Ellen went on the attack.

"No, I mean, remember I said not to use 'ain't.' Use 'isn't.' You asked me to teach you proper English, and that's what I'm tryin' to do."

"Oh, sorry." But the stars had left her eyes, and she wrapped her arms around her middle, leaning forward to check on the squeaky wagon tongue. "Meshach will want to know about that squeak. He said if it squeaks, grease it."

Thankful for the change in topic, Jesselynn breathed a sigh of relief. Far as she was concerned, Wolf might be a striking man, but all he did for her was make her mad. Overbearing, stubborn—she had a long list of words to describe him, not many of them complimentary.

"Speak of the devil," she muttered under her breath.

Wolf rode back into view, stopping at each wagon to speak to the driver. When he got to her, she waited a tick before looking up.

"We're stoppin' for the night about half a mile up the road. There's water there and plenty of pasture. Your wagon will be the last into the circle, so will be the most difficult. We'll be forming circles every night for safety's sake, even though right now there's nothing to fear."

She wanted to ask more about the circle but refrained. If he thought she couldn't maneuver this wagon, he had another think coming. But what about Aunt Agatha? After a long day on the wagon seat, she might be all stove-up. Besides, she hadn't driven four up before, let alone oxen.

"Thanks. We'll manage."

"I can get someone else to drive your aunt's wagon in."

"I said we'll manage." *Don't go doin' us any favors. We can handle things ourselves.*

The look he gave said clearly what he thought of her bad manners. Which wasn't anywhere close to what she thought about his. *My mother would have an attack of the vapors, and I never once saw her go into a spell like that. She didn't have the vapors.*

Jockeying the final wagon into place took several men giving conflicting advice, oxen more well trained in backing and, as Meshach would say, "a heavy dose of prayer." More than once she wished he were there, beginning to be concerned as the sun set fire to the western sky and gilded the edges of the remaining clouds. They'd just dropped the wagon tongue in place when the horsemen trotted up to the wagon.

"Coulda used you a few minutes ago," Jesselynn said by way of greeting.

"Sorry, thought you be farther up de road." Meshach dismounted, signaling for the others to do the same.

"These are *your* men?" Wolf nudged his horse closer to where she stood.

"Ah, yes."

"And *your* horses?"

"Yes."

He leaned over to say softly, "And why wasn't I informed that we would have seven horses along?"

Jesselynn squared her shoulders. If there was to be a fight, she was ready.

He waited.

So did she.

"I remember askin' if you had any other livestock."

"I know, but I've had to keep the horses hidden. They're all that's left of Twin Oaks breeding farm. We need good blood to start over." She knew she was talking too much and sounding breathy on top of it. But they *had* to be part of the train. Who knew when another would form up?

"They're Thoroughbreds."

"Yes, sir."

With eyes narrowed so his gaze was even more piercing, Wolf stared at her. "Does that big stallion have anything to do with winning a race a day or two ago?"

She couldn't think of a lie quick enough. "Yes, sir." Good. Telling the truth felt good.

"Remember when I said you had to be able to take orders?" At her nod, he continued. "One of my most important orders is that no one will tell me a lie. Only the truth."

And I am living a lie. "Yes, sir."

"I will decide by morning."

"Decide, sir?"

"Whether you and your horses will be continuing on with the wagon train." He turned and rode off before she could sputter an answer.

Chapter Thirty

"You can come on one condition."

Jesselynn stood straighter in the predawn gray light. "What is that?"

"If there is any trouble that can be laid at your door, you wait for another train."

"Trouble?"

"With your horses or your men."

"With *you*" was implied.

While dark eyes can become obsidian, green eyes turn to steel. Her jaw matched. "There will be no trouble."

"No racing."

"Do you take me for a fool? Of course there will be no racing. I wouldn't have done so then if we'd had the money for the supplies." She felt like adding a few well-chosen names but clamped her tongue between her teeth to keep it from further flapping.

"Thoroughbreds are too high-strung for a trip like this. You're going to lose them."

"Over my dead body." *He has no idea what we've gone through to get this far. I will not lose them. Thoroughbreds are far tougher than he thinks.* She refused to think about the foals. She'd carry them in the wagon if she had to.

"Suit yourself. I would recommend turning back now."

"We'll be ready when the others are. Thank you for your concern." She couldn't resist the sarcasm.

The look he gave her, other than finely honed anger, asked a question too. Only for the life of her, she couldn't figure out what it was. She was still puzzling on that when he rode off.

The wagon that had been first the day before fell in behind her as the circle straightened to a long line. Jesselynn waved to the driver, a woman wearing a sunbonnet dangling on a ribbon down her back. A black shawl hugged her shoulders and crossed in front.

"I'm Abigail Brundsford."

"Jesse Highwood. That's my aunt Agatha ahead." In spite of the three men now in attendance, Agatha had asked if she could drive again for a while. Since Jesselynn didn't want her walking, she agreed. She'd rather be riding but knew that after the noon break, Meshach could drive. Right now he kept the mares on lead lines and tied Roman and the spare ox behind the wagon. Once they were out of such civilized territory, Daniel would use Roman for hunting.

Daniel had snared two rabbits during the night, and Ophelia rose early to fry them for breakfast. The folks in the wagon in front of them had sniffed appreciatively as they ate their mush.

Throughout the day, other members of the party wandered back to introduce themselves, so that by noon Jesselynn's head was filled with a mishmash of names, trying to remember which went with what face. One family had enough children to start their own town.

When Wolf signaled the stop, Aunt Agatha's hands were blistered from holding the reins.

"Why didn't you put on gloves?" Jesselynn cupped her aunt's hands in her own.

"I don't have any gloves. That's why."

"Ophelia, please get out some of that salve that I bought in Independence."

Agatha tried to pull her hands away, but Jesselynn didn't release them until the salve was rubbed in and two strips of cloth bound the oozing sores.

"All we need is for this to go putrid on us."

"Pshaw, I've had blisters before. Paid them no nevermind, and they healed up just fine."

"Good. Let's hope these do too."

That night after supper, one of the men brought out a fiddle and another a harmonica. They started with music to sing by but moved on to dance tunes. Jesselynn and Agatha sat together on the wagon tongue, Jesselynn clapping while Meshach and Ophelia danced a jig.

"Hi, my name's Elizabeth." Suddenly appearing in front of Jesselynn, the no-longer-a-girl-but-not-yet-a-woman shifted from one foot to another after introducing herself. Her strawberry hair hung in a thick braid down her back, and the same color eyebrows shadowed her eyes so that the color was hidden. But her flaming cheeks matched the fire that now burned in embers.

Agatha prodded Jesselynn so that she turned to her aunt with a question that drowned in the laughter in her aunt's eyes. Jesselynn looked back to the visitor.

"Pleased to meet you. I'm Jesse Highwood."

"I know."

"She wants you to ask her to dance," Agatha whispered.

Jesselynn felt her face flame. She glanced down at her boots, wishing she were out with the horses where it was safer. "Ah, which wagon is yours?"

Elizabeth looked over her shoulder. "The one with the table and checkered cloth. My mama says even though we are on the way to Oregon, we don't have to give up all the comforts of home."

"Oh."

The fiddler changed to a reel, and all the dancers lined up, partners facing each other with some distance between them.

"Do you know how to dance the reel?" Her hands bunched the folds in her skirt.

"Ah, ah . . ."

"You could learn real fast. I taught my brother."

" 'Scuse me. I better go check on the horses." Jesselynn got up so fast she nearly tripped over the wagon tongue in her hasty departure.

"He's just shy," she heard her aunt say before she was out of earshot. *Agatha Highwood, I swear I'm going to make you pay for this.* She didn't return to the circle until long after the fiddle had been put back in its case and most of the bedrolls been laid out under the wagons.

Dodging Elizabeth over the next few days took some doing. Jesselynn chose to ride Ahab as a line of defense. She didn't dare knit or help too much with the cooking. Even braiding rawhide might be thought of as women's work.

Wolf set up an order for night watches, and the men all took their turns, including Jesselynn.

By the time they turned off at Topeka, the train had fallen into the rhythm of the road. Up before daylight, a quick breakfast, hitch up, and move on out as the sun broke the horizon. Then a short noon stop without fires, stopping for the night where there was water and pasture for the cattle and horses. With the scarcity of wood, it became the job of those who walked along to pick up any wood they found, or dry cow pies. Dried cattle dung burned hot and slow.

They paused only long enough on Easter Sunday for one of the men to read the Easter story and everyone to sing a hymn, closing with the Lord's Prayer. For dinner they ate dry biscuits and dust. For grace at supper Meshach announced, "Christ is risen." The others answered, "He is risen indeed." Jesselynn went to bed murmuring those words again, adding, "Thank you, Jesus."

They'd been on the trail two weeks when they neared Alcove Springs.

"We'll do an extra day or two here," Wolf announced as he rode down the line that afternoon. "This place has a good spring, the folks who live here are friendly, and there's plenty of available pasture. There's even some shade, with the big oak trees they have."

"Ah, we can wash clothes." Aunt Agatha turned to Ophelia, who walked beside her wagon. "We have plenty of soap?"

"Yessum." Ophelia snagged Sammy up and set him on her shoulders. "Come on, baby, we got water ahead."

Thaddeus ran back to her. "Play in the water."

"And take a bath."

His smile disappeared. "No bath."

Jesselynn chuckled. "If that isn't just like a boy." Looping the reins around the brake handle, she leaped to the ground to pace alongside the slow-moving oxen. Even Buster, the lazy one, had learned to lean into the yoke and keep a steady, plodding pace. Since they were midway in the line of wagons, they just kept the pace unless something really unusual spooked the animals. And she could walk along beside. Some of the men used a goad and rarely rode the wagon seats. Anything to make the loads lighter.

With the ease born of practice, they circled the wagons downstream of the farmstead and set up camp. The women gathered all the dirty clothes together and headed for the creek. When Jesselynn started off with an armful, Aunt Agatha touched her arm.

"I don't think that is a good idea."

"What? Washing clothes?"

"No, *you* washing clothes. Do you see any of the other men or older boys helping?" Agatha kept her voice low and glanced around to see if anyone was close enough to listen.

"But . . ." She knew Agatha was right. Ophelia, Jane Ellen, and Agatha could go join the party at the creek, but not Jesselynn.

Meshach set up his forge, Daniel raced off with a fishing line, and Benjamin took the oxen and horses out to graze.

"If I graze the horses and oxen, Benjamin can go hunting."

"That's a fine idea."

Jesselynn retrieved her writing case, along with the rifle and ammunition from the wagon, and dogtrotted after Benjamin. *Ah, hours alone. Out on the prairie with no one but me and the animals.* The thought made her run faster. She stopped when she heard a yip behind her. Patch, tongue lolling, came running after her.

"You should be watching Sammy and Thaddeus."

The dog sat at her knee, white ear flopped forward, head tilted slightly to the side. He whined and looked toward the animals.

"You'd rather herd cattle. Can't say as I blame you." She turned and started after Benjamin again, but when Patch wasn't beside her, she looked back to see him still sitting in the same place. "What do you need, a special invitation?" She slapped her thigh. "Come on, then." The dog bounded across the already grazed grass to her side, running with her stride for stride.

Running yielded a pleasure so deep she felt like shouting. While guilt that she wasn't back helping with the wash tried to inveigle an entrance, she brushed it off like a pesky fly. Today she could be free.

"Benjamin, wait up."

He stopped Roman and turned to look over his shoulder. "What you want, Marse Jesse?"

"I'll do the grazing." She held the gun up. "You get to go hunting."

"Ah, fine idea." He slid to the ground and waited for her to catch up.

"How far out do I need to take them?"

"I keeps dem away from de other animals. Ol' Ahab get all excited around other mares. So maybe down de creek a mile or so, wherever de grass be good."

"You take Roman then, and Patch will help me keep them in line. Think I should hobble the horses?"

He handed her the hide and braided hobbles, took the gun, and, mounting Roman, gave her a grin that she knew matched her own.

"Enjoy yourself."

"I do intend just dat. 'Sides, deer taste mighty good. We could dry some on top de wagon."

"Or share it with the others. If you can, get two."

"Marse Wolf, he say dey goin' form up huntin' parties when we get out more."

"Good. You can show 'em how." She watched him head for the hills to the east, then turned to follow the grazing animals. Once Ahab threw up his head and stared off to the south, but when whatever had gotten his attention left, he went back to grazing.

Jesselynn moved them out farther, hobbled the two stallions, and sat down in the grass to write her letters. Patch lay down beside her but leaped up when one of the oxen got too far away from the others and drove it back to the herd.

"You are one fine dog." She scratched his ears and his back when he lay back down beside her. The foals both stretched flat out on their sides, tired of playing. So far they were holding up well, but then, there had been plenty of water and grazing for the mares. The horror stories she'd heard started after Fort Laramie.

Dear Sergeant White,

She still had trouble calling him by his Christian name, even though he'd kissed her once.

I was so sorry to hear that you will be unable to join us like you had planned. I know how it is when family things get in the way of our own dreams. Camping at Alcove Springs in Kansas wasn't what I thought I would be doing, that is for certain. The only thing I knew about Kansas was John Brown's trying to free the slaves. So far, it seems a good place, with hills and valleys threaded with creeks. Right now the land is green and the sun warm but not hot. I have an idea I am seeing this land at its most idyllic. The farms seem fair prosperous, with many acres sown to wheat that is coming up nicely. Seems there's been enough rain for that. Not that rain is helpful to those of us who are traveling.

She told him the events so far, sharing her rejoicing that Wolf, the wagon master, had found no cause to send them back.

In fact, he hardly says anything to me at all. He is more than polite to Aunt Agatha, who is an excellent drover. Whoever would have thought it? But traveling like this brings out the strengths of an individual—that I know for a fact.

I am having some trouble keeping in the guise of a Jesse with all these people around. No wonder you were able to discern that I am a woman in man's clothes. Today Aunt decreed that I would not help with the washing in the creek, so I am the grazer, along with the dog who adopted us from a farm we saw burning on the way to Independence. He is a fine cattle dog and herds Sammy and Thaddeus just like calves.

She knew he would get a chuckle out of that and planned to tell her sisters the same.

Her stomach rumbled, reminding her that she was missing dinner. Ah, well, too far to go back. She glanced around at her charges. Several of the oxen were lying down, chewing their cuds. One of the foals was up and nursing. The other mare lay down and rolled, scratching her back to get rid of the winter hair.

Jesselynn looked to the east, following Ahab's attention. Easy to recognize because of the spotted rump on his horse, Wolf rode with a fluid grace, he and the horse as one body. Seeing him like that brought up a thought. Why did he seem to ignore their wagon? She saw him visiting with the others as they plodded their way across the land, but other than to tip his hat to Aunt Agatha and give them instructions, he stayed away. Now he'd taken his hat off and untied the thong, letting his hair stream in the breeze, dark and thick. She'd heard two men talking about "the breed," as they called him. Not Wagon Master Torstead, or Mr. Wolf, but the derogatory term that set her teeth on edge. She'd felt like punching them. If all Indians looked like him, they were indeed a noble race.

Patch sat up and looked back toward the wagons, a whine catching her attention. Meshach came striding across the field as if he owned the land himself.

"Go get him." She whispered the command to Patch, and he took off as though someone had set fire to his tail.

Patch reached Meshach, ran around him yipping three times, then charged back to Jesselynn and lay panting at her side. He leaped to his feet, raced out after that same wandering ox, drove him back to the herd, and returned to drop in his place in Jesselynn's shade.

"Brung you some dinner." Meshach swung a sack to the ground and followed it down. "Got to shoe the red ox. Found his shoes loose dis mornin'."

"Did some others come to have any shoeing done?"

"Did two horse, one ox. Fixed a handle on a cast-iron kettle. De folks know I can do all dat."

"Good." Jesselynn watched as another of the oxen lay down with a grunt. "Guess they about had enough."

"Don't take long wid grass good as dis." He pulled a stalk and set to chewing the tender end. "I be gettin' on back. Sammy fell in de water, come up laughin', so Thaddy jump in after him. Jane Ellen haul dem out and take off dere clothes, handed dem soap." He shook his head in gentle laughter. "Dey some boys."

Jesselynn took two biscuits and a piece of fried rabbit out of the sack. Patch watched her every move.

"I be goin'." Meshach stood and removed a rawhide thong from his pocket. "Since tomorrow be Sunday, we goin' have a church service. Mr. Morgan be de preacher."

"They should ask you."

"A black man be de preacher?" He gave a short laugh and shook his head. "You been in de sun too long widout a hat."

"You know your Bible better than any of them."

He just waved and went on to tie the loop around the ox's neck, flipped another loop around the muzzle for a halter, then headed back to camp with the ox. "I bring him back when he done."

Jesselynn tossed the bone and half a biscuit to her watching companion and licked the grease off her fingers.

After finishing a letter to her sisters, she took out the journal and caught up the entries for the last couple of days. Describing the place where they camped made it sound like a bit of heaven. Trees along the creek, grass, cultivated fields, gentle hills bordering the wide flat valley, a creek that serpentined its way to the distant river. Sky so blue that the few puffy clouds looked painted on, and birdsong to thrill one's soul. She glanced down to find a tiny pink flower at her feet. Heaven indeed. But black folk weren't welcome here, and the land had a price, no longer free for the working as in Oregon.

She closed her journal with a clap and set it, along with the ink, back in the leather case. Time to work with the foals. The colt didn't like the idea of being led around at all. Time to get over that.

"Marse Jesse! Marse Jesse!"

Jesselynn looked up to see Jane Ellen running across the field, waving at the same time.

What could be wrong now? Thaddeus? Her heart leaped.

Chapter Thirty-One

❧

RICHMOND, VIRGINIA

"Worryin' sure does keep you on your knees," Louisa said to no one in particular.

"What's that you say, dear?" Aunt Sylvania looked up from her stitching. When no answer was forthcoming, she returned her attention to the wool jacket spread across her lap.

Louisa set her stitching off to the side and rose to wander to the window. Every day she prayed for Zachary to return. Every day for these four weeks she'd gone to bed fighting despair. Not hearing from either of the young men foremost in her life had begun to wear on her.

"Think I'll go work in the garden."

"That's a good idea." Sylvania held the jacket up, studying the sleeve cap.

Louisa wandered out the back door and across the flagstone verandah only to find two men already out there, one edging the pathways, the other tying up the sweet peas that refused to climb the trellis. There wasn't a weed in sight, nor a dying blossom to clip off, nor a bit of mulch to be spread. Short of transplanting something that did not need transplanting, there was nothing for her to do. The garden looked better than it ever had, even when Sylvania had had a gardener with helpers.

If only she could go over to the hospital.

If only she could find Gilbert . . . and Zachary.

Lord, I'm caught in the if only's, *and that's not a good place to be. How am I to be grateful for not knowing if my brother or my fiancé*—well, he wasn't quite, but she'd come to think of Lieutenant Lessling as that—*are alive. And my biggest problem is that I am not busy enough to keep from thinking.* She had to be honest. *From worrying. And I know worrying is a lack of faith. I know that. Lord, give me something to do.*

"Go sew on the jacket."

"Is that all you can think of?" She glanced heavenward as she muttered her rejoinder.

"You need somethin', Miss Louisa?" The taller of the two men stood a couple feet away.

"No. No thank you. Would you and Private Daniels like something cold to drink?"

"Hot maybe. 'Specially if Abby has those molasses cookies I been smellin'. Sure makes me think of home."

"You sit down, and I'll bring them right out."

"No, you don't need to wait on us. 'Less o' course you might want to read while we eat?"

His hopeful look made her smile. At least here was something she could do to make someone else happy.

"Come on into the parlor, then, so the others can hear." Two of the newer men were still bedridden and might be for some time, since her team of herself, Abby, and Reuben were still fighting the putrefaction of their war wounds.

By the time she'd read them several psalms and one act of *The Merchant of Venice*, she'd gone hoarse, and two men in bed were soundly sleeping. Since sleep brought healing, she tiptoed out of the parlor and gently closed the door behind her.

"I don't think Corporal Downs looks very good. The fever must be back." She stopped at her aunt's side. "We don't have any morphine left, do we?"

Sylvania shook her head. "A bit of laudanum is all. I thought sure we had him on the road to recovery."

"When he wakes, I think I'll change the bandage on his stump. No sense waiting on the doctor to tell us what we can find out for ourselves."

But while the stump looked like only healthy healing flesh, the man had slipped into delirium. When they called the doctor, he listened to the man's chest and shook his head. "Pneumonia. I can take him back to the hospital, or you can fight it here."

Louisa knew their soldier had a much better chance at the house. "We'll keep him."

"Reuben, let's move Jacob to Zachary's bed. I'll get a mustard poultice started. Abby, you make up willow-bark tea. We've got to get his fever down."

They all headed for their duties, moving like a well-ordered machine, with each knowing what lay ahead. They'd been through this before—won one and lost one. Louisa hated to lose.

———

By the darkest hour before dawn on the second day, they had to admit defeat. The soldier's tortuous breathing had stilled.

Tears flowed down Louisa's face. "God, why? Didn't you hear our prayers? We tried so hard."

Reuben patted her shoulder. "God hear us, missy. He just say no. Dis boy now dancin' in heaven all whole again. You want him back to dis?" His hand gestured to the world around them. "You go on now. Get some sleep so you don't get sick."

"I should . . ." She could barely hold her head up.

"You should go to bed." Sylvania stood in the doorway, her dressing gown belted, her mobcap in place. "They will take care of the body."

"Yes, Aunt." But as Louisa pulled herself up the walnut stairs, her tired mind went to two other men. Where was Zachary? Was Gilbert still alive, and if so, where was he? *Why, God?* turned to *Where, God?* as she threw herself across the bed. "I'll undress in a few minutes, rest first." She wiped her tears on the pillow slip and knew no more.

Sometime later Abby came up and drew the covers over her, gently closing the door on the way out.

Dusk grayed the window when Louisa came fully awake. She lay cocooned in the warmth of her quilt and thought back to the battle. They'd done their best. She knew that. The enemy had been stronger, or their soldier had been weaker. How could he not be, with the septic wound?

"Oh, Lord, how long? How long must this war go on? Please, I beg of you, bring Zachary home again safe and sound. And if you can find it in your will, bring Gilbert also." A vision of Gilbert in the hospital contrasted to Gilbert admitting his love for her on the front porch made her smile. He had come so far. Loving him now was easy.

Jacob was back in his bed in what used to be the dining room, and the other bed was made ready for another soldier.

She sat down at the desk and wrote a letter to the boy's mother, telling her what a fine son she had and how he had fought hard both for the South and for his life.

> *He said our cook's molasses cookies were good, but not up to those his mother made. He spoke of his home and family and how grateful he was that you raised him to know our living Lord. I know he is dancing with the angels in heaven now and wanting you to remember him strong and fine.*
>
> *In the name of our risen Lord,*
> *Louisa Highwood*

She'd written to this mother before when her son first came to live with them. Return letters had been so appreciated.

She stared at the sheet of paper. If only she had Gilbert's home address so she could write her future mother-in-law and ask if they'd heard of their son. The harder she tried not to think of him, the more he came to mind. Was he suffering somewhere? Or had someone taken him in as they were doing? That is, if he were injured.

When Zachary returned, she would implore him to inquire again about Gilbert. Perhaps someone, somewhere, knew something. *When Zachary returned.* So much seemed to hinge on when Zachary would come back.

She refused to consider the threatening thought that surfaced when she least expected it. What if Zachary never returned?

Chapter Thirty-Two

ON THE OREGON TRAIL
MAY 1863

"Some'uns been shot!"

"Who?"

"That man, Jones, with the big black beard." Jane Ellen put her hand to her side and struggled to catch her breath. " 'Phelia said to get you. You the best healer around."

"You stay with the stock, then. Keep Patch with you." Jesselynn tore off across the field, her writing case clutched in one pumping arm. She hadn't thought to ask how bad, but at least she knew where her medical box was packed.

She shut her mind against any speculating and concentrated on breathing and not tripping on a gopher mound. "Where are they?" she asked as soon as she got to the wagon and could breathe.

Ophelia pointed to the right wagon and handed her the wooden box she'd stocked with supplies in Independence. "Dey got in a fight."

Jesselynn took the box and headed across the inner circle of wagons. She had to keep in mind that Ophelia had been the one to call her, not Wolf or one of the other families. But then, how would they know about her training? After all, healing was woman's work, unless there was a doctor around.

"Fools," muttered one of the men standing near the wagon.

"What happened?" Jesselynn paused beside him to figure out how to handle this.

"Got to drinking and got into an argument over something. Most likely too stupid to matter."

"But drinkin' is against the train's rules."

"I know, but when Wolf rode off, these two hit the bottle. You can bet there'll be a thorough inspection after this."

Jesselynn nodded. "I better see what I can do."

The wife of one of the men dabbed at a shoulder wound that still seeped, tears trickling down her thin cheeks. The other man sat with a makeshift bandage around his upper arm.

"I din't mean to hurt 'im, just scare him a mite." Tears rolled down Rufus Jones's cheeks.

Jesselynn dropped to her knees beside the woman. "Here, why don't you let me see what I can do."

"You a doctor?"

"No, but I've done quite a bit of treatin' wounds and such." She didn't say she'd learned it all from her mother.

The woman relinquished her place but moved back only a pace. Jesselynn examined the wound and felt under his shoulder, hoping for an exit wound. No such luck. That meant the bullet had to come out or he'd die of gangrene, not that he might not anyhow.

"I'm going to have to take the bullet out."

"I'se afeared of that." The woman wrung her hands. "He's not a bad man, but when he starts to drinkin', he . . ." Her voice trailed off.

Jesselynn knew that the Jones brothers had already built themselves a reputation as cantankerous and hard to get along with. But with most of the men out of the camp and the women washing clothes, the two had time to go at it.

"I'm going to need some help holding him down."

A snore from the wounded man released enough fumes to make her lean back. "Whew, maybe not. Go get Meshach. He's workin' at the forge."

"I'se here."

The deep voice from behind her made Jesselynn sigh with relief. Between the two of them—her cutting and Meshach holding and praying—they'd manage.

"Get us some water boiling, Mrs. Jones. We gotta get your husband cleaned up some. And is there any of that liquor left? We can use it to clean out this hole in his shoulder."

"Waste of good liquor," muttered the man she'd spoken with earlier.

"Be that as it may, I'll need you to hold down his legs. Anyone else around?"

"Only the womenfolk." His voice hardened. "And that other piece of worthless trash, his brother."

Jesselynn looked over her shoulder. "You can lie across his legs. That shouldn't hurt your arm any." *And it might be good if it did.* She looked again. The low-down dog was sound asleep. She and Meshach exchanged glances. They didn't need words. Wolf had almost turned *them* down, yet he'd taken on this heap of trouble?

Before Mrs. Jones could get the fire hot to boil the water, someone else brought a steaming kettle over and set it on the tripod. "Mrs. Jones, you found that liquor bottle yet?" She raised her voice to be heard over the snoring.

"Yes, but . . . but Tommy Joe, he might be . . ."

"Get the bottle or Tommy Joe might not live to drink anymore."

Mrs. Jones squeaked like a mouse trapped by a cat's paw, but the bottle showed up at Jesselynn's side.

"Sure would be easier if he was on a table."

"We can use the two planks from their wagon."

Jesselynn didn't need anyone to tell her who said that. Wolf's voice sounded flat, like a sharp piece of shale.

"Meshach, come help me set them up." The two men left, and Jesselynn sat back on her heels. The man she'd been working on stirred and blinked, then returned to snoring. She might have to give him a few more swigs, but, then, she'd seen men die, poisoned by the drink they craved. But other than the gaping hole in his shoulder, Tommy Joe—she shuddered at even the name—was in good shape. His color, what she could see under the matted black beard, looked good, and his breathing was steady. A belch made her blink. Her eyes watered.

When they had Jones on the makeshift table, Meshach handed her a freshly honed knife. Jesselynn washed her hands with soap and hot water, and after closing her eyes for a moment to ask for her Father's guidance, she stepped up to the table. Wolf stood across from her, Meshach beside her, and Jones's brother and another man at the hips.

"Ready?" They all nodded.

She barely flinched as she inserted the point of the knife into the wound to widen the hole for her fingers. Jones groaned.

"Hold him." Using her fingers as a probe, she felt around the tissue, searching for the bullet and any pieces of bone. She felt the sharp point of bone and with thumb and forefinger wiggled it free and dropped it on the ground.

Oh, Lord, please help me. Blood welled around her searching fingers. "Come on, come on." More prayer than mutter, she focused only on the sphere beneath her fingertips. Something hard.

Jones groaned, gagged, and vomited, splattering the wagon. "Turn his head." Meshach kept one hand on the man's arm and turned his head with the other.

"Hold him." Before she could say the words, all four men had thrown their bodies over the thrashing man on the table. In spite of the bucking, she probed and knew for sure she had the bullet. "Got it."

She held up the smashed bit of metal. Blood welled where her fingers had been. Jones gagged and wretched again, spewing foul-smelling vomitus all over Wolf's buckskin shirt.

The look of disgust on Wolf's face made Jesselynn want to smile. Instead, she grabbed the bottle of whiskey and, spreading the wound wider, poured the liquid in.

Jones let out a scream that could be heard for miles. He thrashed and bucked, sending his brother flying.

"Ow, my arm," Rufus cried.

"Pour some of that down his gullet." Wolf gave the order but didn't reach for the bottle. He left that to their other assistant, whose expression said what he thought of the whole thing. When their patient settled down again, Jesselynn looked to Meshach.

"You think we need to heat the knife?"

Meshach shrugged. "Might be de other enough. Him bleed good."

Jesselynn nodded and went ahead with the bandages, wishing she had some of the healing salve her mother used to use. While she had the recipe, she'd not had all the ingredients.

"Let's take him back to his own wagon. His wife can take care of him there." Wolf nodded to the three men, and they did just that.

Jesselynn washed her hands and glanced down at her clothes. "Looks like I been butchering hogs."

"Leastways with hogs, you got something good at the end." Aunt Agatha handed Jesselynn a towel to dry her hands. "You get those clothes off, and I'll wash the blood out before it sets up."

"Thanks." Jesselynn felt the quivering start in her toes and work its way up until she was shaking like she had the ague. Her knees turned to mush, and the world started to revolve.

"Sit and put your head down." Wolf grabbed her shoulder and plunked her down on a wagon tongue.

"Let go of me." She tried to flail at his restraining hand, but the action made her stomach roil. She kept her head down.

"Better?"

"Yes." She'd known what to do. He'd just beat her to it. She breathed in and out, deep breaths that brought her world back to standing still. His hand on her shoulder felt warm and comforting.

"Where did you learn to operate like that?"

"From my mother, but it's all a matter of sense." She slowly sat upright, ready to duck her head if the world tilted. When it stayed in place, so did she.

"Well, if he makes it through without gangrene, he'll owe you a debt."

Jesselynn shook her head. "No, no debt. I'd just as soon no one told him who did it. But the next time he punches his wife, you better do something about it, or I will."

"You take care of your business, and I'll take care of mine." The bite had returned to his voice.

So much for any moment of truce. Why couldn't she learn to keep her mouth shut, as her mother had always recommended? Jesselynn picked up her medical box and headed back to her own wagon, where Meshach had the forge back up hot and the iron ringing on the anvil. Two oxen were lined up waiting for his attention. He glanced up when she passed him, nodded and, after raising one eyebrow, went back to work. Didn't take much to read her thoughts, she knew. The thunder sitting on her forehead would be easy to see. Or maybe it was the lightning bolts shooting from her eyes. Shame the object of her frustration wasn't in reach of one.

Even though Tommy Joe Jones recovered with little problems, he never did come by to say thanks. Jesselynn wasn't surprised, but it sure sent Aunt Agatha off in a huff whenever she saw the man.

To the chagrin of the other hunting party, Benjamin returned with two deer and three prairie chickens, while the others had only a few ducks and a goose. Daniel brought back a string of catfish and bluegill, so they ate the fish and parceled the other out among the wagons.

"How'd you do that, boy?" Ambrose McPhereson, who was camped in front of them this night, asked. "I never saw nothin' out there."

Benjamin looked up from scaling fish with a smile that crinkled his eyes. "Think like a deer."

"Anytime you want to give me lessons in deer thinkin', I'll be ready."

"Thank you, suh."

"Name's Ambrose, not sir. What's your name?"

"Benjamin Highwood, suh."

"Well, Benjamin, how about I call you that and you call me Ambrose? Before this trip is over, we're all goin' to be family or foe, and I sure don't want to be any part of the latter."

Jesselynn watched the look on Benjamin's face as the man walked away. That alone made the trip worthwhile.

———

Just before they left the campsite at Vermilion Creek, a single wagon drawn by two teams of horses pulled into the area. The man who stepped down off the wagon seat appeared to have seen better days. When he lifted his hat, wiry gray hair flew in the breeze and matching brush covered his face. Gimping on one leg, he hitched across the packed dirt until he reached the nearest wagon, the one driven by Aunt Agatha.

"Howdy, ma'am." He touched the brim of a hat that was more slouch than firm. "Where's yer wagon master?" He coughed at the end, as if he hadn't done much talking of late.

Agatha nodded to where Wolf stood talking with two men. "The one in the buckskin shirt."

"Thankee."

Jesselynn looked back at his wagon in time to see an elder boy pop his head out and then retreat. Jane Ellen glanced at Jesselynn. "Bet that's his grandpap."

"You think so?" Jane Ellen had an uncanny way of picking up on things. Jesselynn had come to accept this as a gift, so she pretty much agreed.

"Looks like they come a long way."

"Most likely. All of us have."

"His horses need a good feedin'."

Come on, let's get on the road. Jesselynn felt as if she were all dressed up for a party and nowhere to go. First time in their traveling that Wolf didn't have them on the road by full light. She thumped a tattoo on the boot rest. "Hand me those strips of rawhide. Might as well make myself useful if we're going to be a while."

"They sure do be jawin'."

"They can do their jawing while we drive on, can't they?" Jesselynn knotted one end of the three thongs together and hooked that over a nail driven in the boot brace. Braiding rawhide was almost as good as knitting for keeping one's mouth from running off.

The new man limped back past their wagon and climbed up onto his own. When Wolf signaled the start, the new wagon fell in behind them.

"Well, I'll be."

Crossing the bridge over Vermilion Creek sure beat the fording they'd done on others. The hollow sound of hooves on plank, the creak of the gear and wheels was music to Jesselynn. While the rest had felt good, the need to get going again had returned. Besides, the farmer there had been making eyes at Ahab. And who was the man with the wagon? Would he be friend or trouble? Trouble or troubadour? She shook her head. Where had *that* come from?

Chapter Thirty-Three

ॐ

"Highwood, you're on second watch tonight."

"Yes, sir." Jesselynn fought to keep the snap from her voice. Why couldn't she just nod like most of the others?

The dissecting look she got from Wolf made her feel as if he was studying her, not quite sure how to take her.

"Jones, you too."

Jesselynn coughed to hide the groan she'd almost let slip. Rufus was about the last man she wanted to stand watch with. While the bullet hole in his arm was healing well, it hadn't helped his disposition any. He and his brother were weasel-mean clear through.

"Just you keep that fancy pants away from me," Jones muttered with a sneer in Jesselynn's direction.

Jesselynn could feel her right eyebrow arch. *What in the world is the matter with him? He got it in for me just 'cause I let someone else bandage his arm? We saved his brother after all. Wasn't my fault the two of them were fighting.*

Meshach shifted closer to where she sat on the wagon tongue. They'd had the bad luck to be camped right behind the Joneses in the circle of wagons. Not that anyone wanted to be on either side of them. In spite of Wolf having cautioned them, the language was enough to make a washerwoman blush.

Patch came and sat at her knee.

"That's enough." Like a rifle crack, Wolf's command split the air.

Jesselynn felt more than heard Patch's growl. Meshach cleared his throat. The two sounded much alike.

"Git 'im away from that nigger and then see—"

"I said *enough*." The whisper was far more intimidating than the bark.

Rufus shut up but rose from his seat and ambled off behind the wagon.

Jesselynn still wasn't sure what all the shouting was about, but she knew it had something to do with her.

"I switch wid Marse Jesse." Meshach didn't ask—he stated.

Wolf shrugged. "Suit yourself."

Jesselynn waited until the others had gone before hissing at Meshach. "What was that all about?"

Meshach shook his head. "Better dis way."

Across the circle Henry Bronson was tuning up his fiddle. Jesselynn breathed a sigh of relief. Since she had first watch, she wouldn't have to worry about young lady Elizabeth making doe eyes at her.

————

Wolf knew the urge to kick Rufus Jones out of camp was not to be acted upon. But the thought of knocking the meanness out of him had plenty of appeal. Why hadn't he seen what a passel of trouble those two brothers were? Young Highwood had done nothing but help the two, saved the life of one actually, but they still had it in for him.

Instead of joining the dancers around the fire, he saddled his horse and rode out to where the cattle and horses were grazing. The stars looked low enough that if he stood tall in his stirrups, he might pluck one out of the sky. A thin band of light still outlined the western horizon. Animals were better company than people anyway.

The thought of taking this wagon train clear to Oregon galled worse than a burr under a saddle. Especially after that crack tonight. There'd be more blood let on this train before the end of the trail, of that he was sure. Granted young Mr. Highwood was a trifle on the effeminate side, but he was still a boy, and some took longer to fill out than others. From what he heard and saw, the boy knew his medicine. Knew an awful lot for his age. Whatever his age was.

If he was with my people, he would have gone on his vision quest by now and most likely been on a raid to another tribe's camp. Stealing horses was a step in growing to manhood.

He sat listening to the crunch of animals grazing, the occasional snort of a horse, the stamp of a foot. The fiddle sang of love and loss from behind him, the notes holding on the slight breeze like smoke. He sorted the odors on the wind that carried the pleas of the fiddle. Fresh cow manure, spring grass, dried horse sweat, fire smoke, fried venison, again thanks to that young black of

Highwood's. He'd said Benjamin could find deer and rabbit when others failed, and he'd proven himself repeatedly. But now that they were beyond the dense civilization of eastern Kansas, the game would be more plentiful.

He'd rather throw down his bedroll out here than in camp any day.

———

"That old goat," Agatha grumbled as she stirred the morning mush.

"What are you talkin' about?" Jesselynn stretched her arms above her head and yawned fit to crack her jaw.

"Brushface asked her to dance, and she din't take to it."

"Why not? Mr. Lyons seems like a very nice man." Jesselynn dropped forward to touch her hands to the ground, anything to stretch out her back. "And besides, you shouldn't call him that." She must have slept on a dirt clump or something. By the time she roused Meshach for his watch, she could have slept on solid rock—with thorns in it.

"Speak of the angels—"

"Devil, most likely."

"Aunt Agatha, he'll hear you," Jesselynn hissed under her breath.

"Morn'in." Nathan Lyons tipped his hat in greeting.

"Morning, Mr. Lyons. Fine day." Jesselynn watched her aunt out of the corner of her eye.

Agatha's *harrumph* could be heard several wagons away.

Jesselynn glanced at Ophelia, who rolled her eyes and shrugged. When Agatha turned to fetch something out of the wagon, Jesselynn sidled over to Ophelia. "What is goin' on here?"

"Mr. Lyons, he go out of him way to be nice to her, but she . . . oh, she get all riled up."

"I see." But she didn't see a thing. Life would be so much easier if she could just ride and not have to sort out all the people. Like that pile of worthless bones, Rufus Jones. Whatever had gone on last night was sure to come around and cause trouble again. If only she understood what it was all about.

Halfway to the noon rest stop, Mrs. Brundsford caught up to Jesselynn walking beside her lead ox. "Mr. Jesse, I hate to bother you, but could you come look at Mrs. Smith's littlest boy? He ain't been well for the last couple of days."

"The little guy with red curly hair?"

"That's the one—Roddy."

"What seems to be the trouble?"

"A'fore he was just listless, you know, wanting to be held all the time, whiney. But today he's burning up with fever."

Jesselynn called to Jane Ellen walking some ahead. "Come take my place for a while."

Jane Ellen dropped back and took the goad Meshach had fashioned. "Where you goin'?"

"Going to the Smith wagon."

The little boy lay on a pallet on a box in the rear of the wagon, where the rolled-up canvas side gave him a bit of breeze. His mother put another wet cloth on his forehead as Jesselynn and Mrs. Brundsford came around the end.

"I brung Mr. Jesse."

"Thank you for coming, but I don't see what you can do. He's just doing poorly."

Jesselynn laid a hand on the pale forehead. "He's burning up with fever. Get that blanket off him and soak it in water. Wet, it might do him some good."

"But he's got the shakes one minute—"

"I know, but we need to get that fever down." They'd just removed the blanket when the boy jerked so hard he almost fell off the box. He twitched all over and banged his head on the wood.

"Oh, he's goin' to die."

"Hold him in your arms." While she talked, Jesselynn dipped part of the blanket in the water and laid it on the child's body. Roddy jerked again.

"Has he had anything to eat? To drink?" His mother shook her head at both questions. "Here." Jesselynn handed a cup of water to Mrs. Smith. "See if you can spoon some into him when the fit is over." While she worked with the child, Jesselynn racked her brain trying to think what her mother did in cases like this.

Willow tea. But where could they get willow bark out here? And there was no fire to boil water with anyway. *Would laudanum help? But he's not in pain.* She tried to sort out the conflicting thoughts. *Dear God, help us. Please, you love the little children, and we do too. Help us in the name of Jesus.*

The boy lay limp, his chest rising only slightly with each slow breath. But he was cooler to the touch. And he wasn't shaking.

"Oh, dear God, thank you. Thank you, Mr. Jesse." Mrs. Smith kissed her child's little hand, tears trickling down her cheeks. "I already lost two babes, one born dead and another about this age. I sure do pray the Lord spares little Roddy here."

"We'll do what we can. Get as much water in him as possible. If Benjamin can bag some prairie chickens, we can make a broth tonight and get some nourishment in him." Jesselynn laid her hand on the child's chest, feeling the heartbeat only faintly. "Got any molasses or honey you could stir into the water? That might make him want more."

"That I do." Mabel Smith pointed to a box up behind her. "Get the jug out of there," she told her older daughter.

Jesselynn left them spooning honey water into the little boy. He had that look of death about him, like a blown-out candle.

———

A woman's keening woke the dawn. Jesselynn knew Roddy had died in his sleep. While he'd seemed some better the night before, she wasn't surprised.

The men dug a hole while the women dressed the child in a pair of pants and shirt, both sewn by his mother for his upcoming birthday.

"He looks so nice. At least we had something proper to bury him in." Mabel Smith stroked her child's corn-silk hair. "Now, Roddy, you just play with all those children round Jesus' feet." Eyes streaming, she looked to Jesselynn. "Thank you for tryin' to help us. Guess God just wanted another child back in His kingdom."

" 'The Lord gave, and the Lord hath taken away,' " murmured one of the other women. " 'Blessed be the name of the Lord.' "

Jesselynn nodded and turned away. *Little children shouldn't have to die like that. Why, God, do you spare mean hunks of offal like the Jones brothers and take a child away from his loving mother's arms like this? I just don't understand, and it makes me angry—real angry. Roddy brought joy and delight to everyone. Those others bring nothing but misery.*

She heard the others gathering for the reading and forced herself to join them, standing back on the fringes. Two of the men laid the small body, now wrapped in a quilt, in the hole. Mr. Bronson opened his Bible and read the Twenty-third Psalm. " 'The Lord is my shepherd; I shall not want. . . .' " Other voices joined in, and the ancient words drifted across the prairie. Jesselynn sighed, wiped the moisture from her eyes, and felt someone staring at her. She turned enough to see Rufus Jones snickering behind her and pantomiming wiping his eyes, then pointing at her.

The urge to use the oxen whip on the pair of them rose so strong she rammed her hands in her pockets to keep from attacking. Benjamin and Daniel appeared on either side of her, as if drawn by an unseen force. They kept their gaze straight forward, bowing their heads in prayer with the others. Jesselynn sneaked a peek over her shoulder, but the two lowlifes were gone.

"Dust to dust, ashes to ashes, blessed be the name of the Lord."

"Amen."

The wagon folks paid their respects to Mr. and Mrs. Smith, then all returned to their own wagons and prepared to leave. Mr. Smith pounded a wooden cross into the ground at the head of the small grave.

"I hate to tell you this." Wolf stopped at the Smith wagon. "But that cross won't do any good. We have to drive the wagons over the grave. . . ."

"No, Lord, no. Don't let this happen." Mabel's voice rose on a sob.

"But that's the only way we can keep wild animals from digging it up."

"I see." Mr. Smith nodded and blew his nose. "There now, Mabel, we will do what we must." He patted his wife's hand.

Wolf mounted his horse and trotted to the lead wagon. "Roll 'em."

Since the sun was well up by then, Jesselynn knew they would push hard to make up for lost time. But when her wagon pulled up to the now obliterated grave, it was all she could do to stay in line. Her mind flew back to the grave-yard off from the big house at home. Carved headstones, a winged angel, small stones close together marking the passing of babies, manicured grass, a shelter-ing weeping-willow tree, petals of blooming honeysuckle—all surrounded by a wrought-iron fence. A place to dream, to remember, to feel the love that passed from generation to generation. A gentle plot filled with beauty and birdsong.

No markers here, only dust and sky and a westering vision.

Mother, can you hear me? I want to go home.

The horizon shimmered and danced through the veil of her tears.

———

"How are you, ma'am?" Wolf paused at the Smith campfire that night.

"Tolerable." Mrs. Smith sighed. "He did look mighty peaceful, our Roddy. And so nice in his new clothes. I sewed them up special, just for him. First time he didn't wear hand-me-downs."

Jesselynn paused before stepping over the wagon tongue so she wouldn't interrupt the conversation.

"I just wanted you to know how sorry I am."

"Thank you, Wolf. That means a great deal coming from you."

Since she heard Wolf heading the other direction, Jesselynn continued on her way to her neighbors' camp. If only she could figure out why she worked so hard to stay out of his way, other than the way he had treated her in the beginning, of course. Had his attitude changed?

She paused to think for a moment. Surely since she'd taken to doctoring those in the wagon train, he had shown her a measure of respect. And he appre-ciated the extra meat Benjamin and Daniel brought in. That was for sure.

She set her full water bucket down by the fire. Agatha and Ophelia had biscuits baking, beans cooking, and rabbit frying. "Sure smells good."

"Oh, there you are, Marse Jesse. Dat Missy Elizabeth, she be lookin' for you."

Jesselynn groaned. "Which way did she go?"

Ophelia pointed to the west.

Jesselynn headed east. Surely she was needed out by the horses.

Chapter Thirty-Four

‍ॐ‍

THE PLATTE RIVER

"Talk about flat."

"Mebbe dat why dey calls it de River Road." Meshach stood in his stirrups. "Sure do be flat—and long." He and Jesselynn had ridden Ahab and Domino ahead of the wagon train and stopped at the last rise so they could see both ways. The Platte River stretched as far as they could see both east and west, while the northern view across the river looked about the same. Muddy and wet was about all Jesselynn could think of it. Other than that, Wolf had said the River Road to Fort Laramie was the easiest part of the trail. Knee-high grass waved in the wind, just begging their horses and cattle to eat and drink their fill.

"Some sight, isn't it?" Wolf rode up and stopped beside them. "Not much flooding this year, but I've seen times when this was hill-to-hill water."

"Is that the Indian encampment over there?" Jesselynn pointed to an area where spirals of campfire smoke lazed in the air.

"Could be. But there are settlers taking up land along here too, now that the forts are in place."

"And the Indians leave them alone?"

"For now." Wolf didn't look at her when he answered. He didn't want to tell them of the recent attacks he'd heard about. As the whites settled instead of just passing through, the Indians had become more aggressive. Settlers drove off the game or killed it. The buffalo were getting scarce this far east, so the Indians were losing their hunting grounds.

"We've been fortunate, I hear, in not being attacked." Jesselynn turned to
Wolf for confirmation.

"True." Wolf pointed to the west. "Fort Kearney is a day's journey over
there. We'll be stopping for supplies."

The land shimmered in a haze, the light seeming to dance before their eyes.
Bluebells and daisies dotted the grasslands, and meadowlarks trilled their courtship arias, often on the wing, liquid joy in the morning.

The creak of wagon wheels, voices calling with laughter as they glimpsed
the flatlands, the bellow of a cow, all the sounds of the wagon train on the move
broke into her reverie. She should go back and drive the wagon, but the thought
held no appeal. Daniel was doing just fine. And Aunt Agatha would much rather
drive than walk, so no one had spelled her since the beginning of the trip.

"There's a good place to camp about five miles upriver. We'll stop there
for the night." Wolf turned his horse and squeezed him into a lope, seemingly
without signal of either leg or rein.

Jesselynn turned in her saddle just enough to watch them streaking across
the land. Wolf snatched his hat off and let the wind carry his hair in a dark
banner behind him. She knew she rode well, but whether the difference was
in Thoroughbred versus Appaloosa pony or his growing up on horseback and
she in the big house, there was indeed a difference. A big difference. She patted
Ahab's shoulder. At least her horses were holding up beyond his predictions.
As was she.

Jesselynn sat bareback on Ahab, letting him and the others drink out of
the Platte River. Ankle-deep, the stallion blew in the water and started to paw
with one front foot, splashing water everywhere. "I know, you want a bath or
at least a roll, but not here and not now." Ahab kept on splashing.

"He goin' roll on you." Benjamin shook his head. "You watch it."

"No, he won't. I won't let him." Jesselynn raised her face to the breeze that
kicked up ripples farther out in the sand-colored water. Today had been the
warmest so far, a portent of the heat to come.

Ahab buckled his front legs, tipping her forward, and before she could even
gasp, she lay flat out in the river, sucking water with her snort. She scrambled
away from the stallion so she wouldn't get caught under him and got to her feet,
soaking wet from hat to boot heel.

Benjamin about fell off Domino laughing.

Jesselynn looked from her horse, who wisely kept his nose out of the water,
to Benjamin and then down at herself. A chuckle rose, fluttered past the muddy-
water taste, and burst forth. She looked a sight, she could tell. Taking off her

hat, she slapped it against her thigh and crammed it back on her head, laughing all the while.

"Hey, horse, you sure fooled me."

Ahab surged to his feet—one dripping, muddy-coated mass—and shook. Mud splattered five feet in all directions.

Benjamin buried his face in Domino's mane, laughing fit to burst. "You cotched de black spot disease."

Only the thought of her heavy boots kept Jesselynn from diving in and taking a real swim. As she plodded toward the shore, she glanced up to see Wolf staring at her, his dark eyes slit, likewise his mouth.

"The water feels great, not that I planned to . . . take . . . a—" *What is the matter with him? Looks like he's seen a ghost or something.* She looked down to make sure her shirt was buttoned and knew what he was seeing. The strips of cloth she used to bind her breasts to keep them flat. Sure proof she was not who she said she was.

"*Mister* Jesse Highwood?"

At his sarcastic tone, Jesselynn could feel her water-soaked clothing begin to steam. She raised her chin and stared him in the eyes. "For as long as necessary, yes."

"Hey, Wolf." Young Billy Bronson cantered up to pull to a stop beside the paint. "I'll be a jumpin' bullfrog. Hey, Jesse, how's the water?" He leaned his crossed arms on the saddlehorn and gave her a studying look, then shook his head. "Well, I'll be . . . who'd a-guessed it?"

Jesselynn ignored the teasing and, gathering her reins and a hank of mane, swung atop the stallion, who had not the grace to look ashamed of all the trouble he'd caused. With his mud and her wet clothing, she barely made it but finally was able to sit erect without asking for help. *Ask him not to say anything.* She answered that voice with another. *That will only make the gossip more titillating.*

She's—he's a woman. Not Mr. Jesse at all. Fury warred with joy, and confusion defeated them both. Wolf swung his horse around without a word and headed west on the Great Platte River Road as if savages were screaming on his tail. He shut off all thought and left himself to the rhythm of his horse's pounding feet.

"He goin' ride dat horse right into de ground, he keep up like dat." Benjamin brought Domino to a standstill beside her. The mares had already left the water and were grazing on a patch of green grass. One foal lay flat out, the other had gone back to nursing.

"Did I say somethin' wrong?" Billy looked after the racing Wolf.

Or is he fleeing? Jesselynn wondered. She wasn't sure. As unobtrusively as possible she pulled her heavy shirt away from her body. She couldn't go back to camp like this, and with the setting sun, supper would soon be ready.

"No, just got a burr under his hide." At least that was as good an explanation as any. "Did someone need him?"

"My pa was lookin' for him."

Good thing he didn't come out. The whole wagon train would know by now. Not that they wouldn't anyway if the glint in Billy's eye is any indication. Should she ask him to keep the secret? Was the secret necessary any longer? Sure they'd have to keep the horses away from the fort, but would folks knowing about her being a woman cause a problem?

Other than those who felt they'd been hornswaggled.

Like Wolf.

He could refuse to let them travel with the train. But why would he? They'd proven their worth.

She tried to keep the inner war from showing on her face. "We better get on back. How about you go ask Aunt Agatha for a jacket or vest for me." After Benjamin trotted off, she rounded up their horses and let them graze their way back to camp.

From the looks she received when she rode into camp, she knew Billy had blabbed.

"Well, I never . . ." One of the women muttered just loud enough for Jesselynn to hear.

"So what do we do?" Jesselynn asked Aunt Agatha when they met at the rear of the wagon.

Agatha sighed. "Old busybodies must not have enough to do to find time for all the gossipin'." She arched her back and dug her fists into the middle of it. "Land sakes, but that wagon has a hard seat."

"If it would help to put a back on the seat, Meshach could do that for you." Glad to be thinking of something besides her own britches, Jesselynn studied her aunt. In spite of the sunbonnet Agatha always wore, the sun had found its way to turn her aunt's cheeks and chin the color of soft, tanned deerskin. Her eyes had a brightness formerly lacking, and her mouth no longer looked pinched, as though she'd sucked on a lemon.

No wonder Brushface finds her appealing. She is. She knew she'd better be careful in referring to Mr. Lyons that way, but the name was so fitting.

" 'Pears to me that we can handle this in one of two ways."

Jesselynn waited, knowing there was no hurrying Aunt Agatha when she was pondering.

"One, we can call a meeting and tell the whole group, or two, we can ignore them and go on as though nothing was different." She kneaded her back again. "Personally, it ain't none of their business."

And this from the woman who had a conniption fit the first time she saw me in britches? Jesselynn bit her lip to keep the astonishment from her face. But Agatha didn't know about one important fact—the look on Wolf's face when he discovered her secret.

They reached Fort Kearney late the next afternoon. The United States flag snapped in the breeze, blue uniforms swarmed all over the place, and Jesselynn wanted to run back out on the prairie even though they camped half a mile from the fort itself. Another wagon train pulled in after they did. It also came from the east but on the Nebraska Trail, they learned later. After they'd circled the wagons and set up camp, Wolf and several of the men rode on into the fort proper.

When Wolf assigned the watches for the night, Jesselynn stared at him. Tonight had been her turn, and he'd not called her name. Since they were running the Thoroughbreds with the other horses and livestock much of the time, she tried to take extra duty, she and her men, rather than less.

"What de matter?" Ophelia stopped beside her as she stared after the departing wagon master.

"I'm not sure, but I aim to find out." Jesselynn took off at a dogtrot to catch up with his long-legged stride. Wolf Torstead could cover more ground in less time than any man she knew.

"Wolf!"

He stopped and turned around. They were far enough from camp now for no one to overhear.

"Why did you leave me out of the watch?" No pleasantries, just go for the jugular.

"Women don't stand watch."

"Oh." Of course, how could she be so stupid? What to say? "But—"

"No," he interrupted. His eyes narrowed. "Keeping women and children safe is part of my job, and I will do so."

"But I—"

"You want to wear britches, that is your choice, but who stands watch is mine." He didn't have to finish. The "and you won't be" rang loud and clear.

If she'd thought there was any chance of them becoming friends, the look he gave her disabused her of that thought.

"What are you so mad about? I did what I had to do. Even you could tell that."

His face looked like a slate wiped clean, so devoid of expression was he.

"Is it just because I fooled you? Would you have let me bring my wagons had you known I was—am—a female?" She almost said a woman but changed her mind. He most likely thought her still a young girl. At twenty, she was way past marrying age, according to custom.

He crossed his arms over his chest. "Are you finished?"

Looks like it. "Yes."

"Good." He turned and strode off, leaving her with her teeth clenched and her hands clamped into fists.

The names she called him under her breath had plenty to do with his parentage, or lack thereof, along with a few choice epithets overheard on night watch. Being a woman in men's clothing had offered her a different view of life in general and of women in particular. Her ears had burned at times.

––––––

When she went into the fort to buy supplies, she went as Mr. Jesse Highwood. She'd taken Aunt Agatha's advice and gone on as if nothing had happened. Sooner or later the gossip would die out. If only it could be sooner so she didn't have to put up with the disapproving glances and muttered remonstrances from most of the women in the train, and a few of their husbands too.

She laid her list on the counter and wandered down the aisles, looking at the harnesses, the boots, the woolen blankets. Warm as it was getting, woolen blankets weren't needed for some time. When her turn came, she waited while the proprietor finished with the earlier customer and turned to her.

"Hello, son, what can I get for you?"

Jesselynn pushed her list forward. "All of that."

The man read the list, looked up at her, back down at the list. "Ah, this looks like a lot. You, ah . . ."

Jesselynn dug in her pocket, pulled out her leather pouch, and plunked it down on the counter with a satisfying clink. "That should cover it." *Along with a lot more. What difference does it make if I'm a young man or young woman? If I hear one more time 'Is your daddy here?' I shall personally sock 'em with this rather than be polite.*

"Oh, and add on a dozen peppermint sticks and a packet of horehound drops."

"Yes, sir."

"I'll take two bags of oats on the back of the mule and pick up the other supplies tomorrow, if that would be all right."

"Fine, fine. Anythin' else I can get for you?"

Amazing how the clink of gold changed his attitude.

Walking back to camp would be good for her. She'd let Daniel come in to pick up the rest. "Daniel is one of my range hands. He'll be by tomorrow. He's black. That won't be a problem, will it?"

"None 'tall." He waited while she counted out his money, then tried to give her paper in return.

"No, I pay in gold, I get silver in change." She held out her hand.

With a glare and a grunt, he took the paper back and laid out silver. "Paper's just as good as gold here at the fort."

"But it might not be at the next supply station. I'm sure you understand." She gave him stare for stare and strolled out of the store. "He ups the prices for us anyway, Roman. I hate doing business with thieves." Jesselynn checked to make sure the bags were tied and balanced before setting out for the east gate and camp.

Off to her left a platoon of what must be new recruits was drilling, the sergeant barking orders. An officer watched the proceedings from the shade of a porch, smoking a cigar and blowing smoke rings.

"Hey, boy, you want to join the Union army? You look old enough."

"No, thank you."

"Make a man outa you." The officer waved his cigar and leaned against the porch post.

Not much chance. "I'm goin' to Oregon."

"You're making a big mistake." He blew another smoke ring.

Jesselynn didn't bother to answer. The sooner they left the area, the better.

She didn't rest easy again until they were two days west of the fort. In less than two weeks they'd be at Fort Laramie.

Was it time for her to become a woman again—or not?

———

Twelve days, and we'll be at Fort Laramie. Two days of hard riding, and I could be home. Wolf didn't have to close his eyes to see the pine-covered mountains, the clear running streams, and the tepees of his people. Home in Wyoming Territory. Could he force himself to go on to Oregon from Laramie? Instead of going home?

Visions of a laughing Jesse Highwood, soaking wet, dogged him day and night. What was her *real* name?

Chapter Thirty-Five

RICHMOND, VIRGINIA

Dearest Jesse. Louisa dipped her quill again and continued.

> *How I wish you were here, but even more I wish we were all at Twin Oaks where we belong, not scattered about the country like now. I have strange news. When Zachary and I went to Washington for medical supplies, he disappeared, and we haven't seen him since. That was over four weeks ago. I keep praying God is keeping him safe, but lately God seems to be saying no to my requests.*

She continued with a description of her trip and the happenings at the house, including a description of Aunt Sylvania reading to their soldiers and actually turning pink at their teasing. She told about the high life their sister was living with her lawyer husband in the Richmond capital.

> *I'm just grateful I don't have to be part of that, but Carrie Mae seems to enjoy herself. Who would have ever dreamed growing up that the three of us would be living such different lives? Please, please, I beg of you, write and let us know how you are. Regarding my lieutenant, as you referred to him, we still have no news. I am having a hard time believing the old saw "no news is good news" in this case. Surely if he were able, he would have written by now.*

She stopped and set her pen down, struck by a new thought. What if he just didn't care any longer? What if he had met someone new, or someone he knew before the army?

She stoppered the ink bottle and rose to go look out the window.

Her heart surged, and she let out a shriek. By the time she reached the front door, the others had come running.

"What wrong?" Reuben caught his breath.

"Nothing. Zachary is here!" She flung open the door to see her dear brother negotiating the three front steps.

"Easy. Don't knock me over." He raised a cautious stump, hopped the final riser, and leaned against the porch post. "Now." He spread his arms wide and welcomed her hug.

"Ah, Marse Zachary, you done made it home *again*." The emphasis on the last word made Zachary laugh, the pure joy of it rising to the newly budding leaves of the stately elm trees.

"Yes, old man, I am home again, but this time there was no doubt as to *if* but only *when*. Coming the route I did was considerably slower than the train Louisa took." He gave her a questioning glance, and she nodded.

Yes, she had delivered the morphine to the surgeon general at the hospital and nearly cried at the look of gratitude in his eyes. While he admonished her to never do such a thing again, she knew she would. Her boys needed it.

She hadn't gone back to ask if they were out again; she knew the answer without the asking. Five pounds or so of morphine, even rationed, wouldn't last long.

Aunt Sylvania appeared in the doorway, tears streaming down her cheeks. "Ah, dear boy, you have returned. Thank you, Lord above. I was beginning to think He'd called you home."

"Now, Aunty, I'm too mean to die yet. God doesn't want me till I get old and gray and with no teeth to jaw at Him with." He hugged his aunt, accepting all the pats from the help and the congratulations from the one remaining soldier who'd been in the house when he left.

"Lots of new faces. That's good, right?" He sank down into an easy chair and propped his crutch under his thigh so he could rest his leg on it.

"Mostly." Louisa took the chair nearest him, knowing they wouldn't discuss the trip until they were alone.

"You heard from the lieutenant?" he asked in a moment's silence while Abby handed around the coffee cups and a platter of lemon cookies.

"I musta knowed you was comin' home. Baked dese just today." Abby pushed the plate back at him so he could take more than two.

To please her, Zachary bit into one and smiled wide, shaking his head at the same time. "You make the best lemon cookies in the whole world."

"Go on, now, you say dat to all de cooks."

"No, not at all. Yours are the best." To prove it, he took a handful and set them on the table beside his saucer. "Now, then, tell me all the news."

For the next half hour, that's just what they did. When he was all caught up and the coffeepot empty, Zachary sighed. "If y'all don't mind, I could do with a lie down. You'll wake me in time for supper?" He smiled at Louisa. "Then I reckon I'll be really awake for another of our all hours' chats."

———

Later that night the two of them retired to his room after the others had gone to bed. After telling his own tale at her insistence, Zachary turned to Louisa. "Now, tell me everything, and I mean everything, about your trip home."

Louisa complied, trying to remember every detail. When she finished, he nodded, fingertips templed, his elbows on the arms of the chair.

"We need to go again."

"I know, but they know me there. Pretty hard to disguise limbs and a face like mine. If it hadn't been for the Quakers, I'd be in prison or shot. I do have some good contacts now if we can dream up a way to do this."

"I'll go."

"You and what brigade?"

"Zachary, I made it home by myself."

"Yes, thanks to a Yankee army wife."

"There's that too." Louisa waited for him to continue and, when he didn't, decided to ask her own questions. "Zachary, I have a favor to ask." When he nodded, she continued. "Would you please ask whomever you can about Lieutenant Lessling? I *must* know what happened."

"But, Louisa, you know the report said that he died in that train explosion."

"I know about the report, but he might have lived through it. Others did."

"Yes, and to the best of our knowledge, they are all accounted for. When people are alive, they come forth to say so."

"*Please.*"

He nodded. "If it will make you happy."

———

Two days later he sat her down on the chaise lounge on the verandah and took her hand in his.

"You don't have good news, do you?"

"No. But there was finally proof. A watch bearing his father's name was found at the site."

"So, he could be a—"

"No, dearest Louisa, the watch was attached to . . ."

Louisa covered her face with her hands. "No, don't say it."

"I'm sorry, but you wanted to know for sure."

"Yes." Pain struck, not only her heart but her entire being. Lieutenant Lessling was gone, forever and for sure. There would be no wedding, no life together. Her first love, her only love. She sat stone still, letting the tears flow. Finally she wiped them away, steel returning to jaw and spine.

"When can I leave for another trip? I must do some good with my life." She could hear the reckless tone of her voice. The look Zachary gave her said he had heard it too.

"We'll see, little sister. We'll see."

"Now you sound just like Daddy."

"I'll take that as a compliment." He rubbed his leg, digging under the straps. "If only we had all listened to wisdom such as his, perhaps . . . perhaps . . . but that is water under the bridge. Now we must see it through."

She thought he'd forgotten she was there until he looked up with anguish-filled eyes. "Louisa, I cannot lose you too."

"We shall see. After all, maybe the war will end next week." But both of them knew she was only trying to put on a good face. Maybe the war would go on forever, or at least until every Southern male was dead.

"I will never leave you."

I know that, but, God, you seem so far away. And so many no's. Can I bear it?

Surely it was the breeze that whispered, *Yes.*

Chapter Thirty-Six

❧

THE GREAT PLATTE RIVER ROAD
MAY 1863

Why did the land of the Oglala people have such a pull this time?

Wolf had been pondering that question for miles, days, and weeks. Eyes squinted against the sun that set the land to shimmering, he studied the land ahead of them. Sod houses had sprung up in the last year like dirt boxes tossed out by a fretful child. Would the Oglala tolerate the white man taking over the land? Especially if the railroad cut its way across the prairies, as he'd heard it would.

His thoughts shifted back to the wagon train plodding along behind him. Another fight the night before, this time between two families he'd have never thought would cause trouble. And Jesselynn Highwood again patched up the wounded. No wonder she—hard to remember that he was really a she—was so skilled at stitching up flesh. It still rankled that she'd fooled him for so long. Of course now that he knew Jesse was Jesselynn, he could see all the signs that should have told him that in the beginning—the way she cared for her little brother and her ease with cooking and things of the camp. Now that the word was out, he saw that she'd picked up her knitting and patching.

The image of her with an arm around little Thaddeus, head tipped to listen to his story, ate at him. How could he have been so duped? If this was a day for studying on hindsight, he had plenty of studying to do.

"Mr. Wolf!"

And not enough time to do it.

He turned in his saddle to watch young Billy Bronson come flying across the plain. Wolf waited, something he'd learned to do well.

"Benjamin says there's buffalo over the rise. Should we send out a hunting party?"

"Get Benjamin and Daniel. Did he say how far away?"

"Mile or two."

"Good. Tell your father to come out here. You can come too. I'll lead the party."

Billy galloped off again.

Within minutes they gathered on the north side of the rise. "Now listen to me and listen good. A bull buffalo can be one of God's meanest critters, so don't take any chances." He looked right at Billy. "There will be no shootin' for shootin's sake. Each one will hone in on one buffalo. Shoot it, and get out of the way. Unlike bows and arrows, the sound of the rifle shots will spook the herd and send it into a stampede, hopefully away from the wagon train. We're goin' to ride up nice and easy, as if we were buffalo ourselves." He glanced up to see Daniel and Benjamin swap smiles of pure excitement. "Any questions?"

When they all shook their heads, he added, "Aim for the head. Between the eyes is best—lose less meat that way. Don't shoot a cow with a calf either. But above all, be careful."

They walked the horses over the crest. He heard someone suck in a breath and knew it was awe and delight combined. While the herd was not nearly the size of those he remembered as a boy, the sight of hundreds of buffalo roaming across the plain thrilled a man's heart.

Slowly they eased toward the herd, stopping when the animals grew restless, then proceeding again. When they were close enough for clean shots, Wolf raised his hand and let it fall.

Shots rang out and five animals sank to the ground. The hunters hung back as the rest of the herd broke into a run, heading south away from the hunters as Wolf had hoped.

"You want we should get another?" Benjamin trotted his horse up to Wolf.

"No. This is plenty. Get more and the meat will spoil before we can dry it." He rode up to one of the kills. "Make sure they're dead and then slit the throats so they bleed out. Bronson, go on back to camp and have them circle the wagons for the night, then bring as many as you can to help butcher these beasts. We've not a moment to waste."

Working in pairs, they moved from carcass to carcass, bleeding them out, then gutting. Meshach showed up next, then the others as they could come. Working together, they stripped the hide off one, cut it in quarters, and, laying the meat on the hide, tied the legs together over a pole and slung ropes around it to carry it back to camp between two horses.

A cheer went up when the first load of meat reached camp.

"Bring in the stomachs and intestines too."

Benjamin nodded. The hearts and livers had gone with the first load. Every skillet in camp would be frying fresh liver for supper. By dark the only trace of the hunt left on the prairie was blood-soaked ground and the remains from the stomachs and intestines. Even the hooves and horns had gone to camp to be used however Wolf suggested.

The hunters dragged in with the final load.

Soon every cooking pot was bubbling with fresh meat, and every knife in the train was being used to slice thin strips off haunch and shoulder to hang to dry over the fires to be transferred to the sides of the wagons in the morning. The white canvases reflected the heat of the sun enough to continue the process started over the cook fires. Since Benjamin had been the one to spot the herd, one hide had gone to the Highwood wagons. Wolf gave his to Nate Lyons, and while the Jones brothers shouted they should have the third, he gave it to the Smiths, where he knew the hide would be valued for its warmth and tended carefully. Bronson kept one and gave the other to another family.

"Would you care to join us for supper?" Aunt Agatha, as even he'd taken to calling her, asked Wolf when he walked past their wagon.

He started to say no, thank you, but out of the corner of his eye caught the look of total disgust on Jesselynn's face. "Thank you, it would be a privilege." He glanced down at a tug on his pants leg.

"Buff'lo for supper, Mist Wolf." Thaddeus smiled up at him, blue eyes sparkling. "Me shoot buff'lo too."

"Someday."

"Uh huh, someday. Jesse say when I get big."

"Thaddeus, don't bother Mr. Wolf."

The little boy stepped back at the sharp tone in his sister's voice.

"Oh, he's no bother." Wolf heard a burst of laughter from the school-age children gathered around Nate Lyons. Every evening as soon as they'd made camp, he taught ciphering, spelling, reading, and writing. His storytelling drew children and grown-ups alike. His ongoing story of the Jehosaphats had become a nightly ritual for most of the camp before bedding down. That and the singing led by Bronson, the fiddler, and son Billy on the harmonica.

Wolf leaned down and scooped Thaddeus up to sit on his shoulder. "Can he come with me?" He asked the question of Aunt Agatha while keeping an eye on Jesselynn.

"I don't know why not." Agatha patted Thaddeus's knee. "Now you be a good boy, hear?"

Thaddeus straightened his back. "I always good."

Wolf let out a roar of laughter. Jesselynn's mouth made a string look thick, but did he glimpse a twitch at one corner? Maybe he was seeing things. "Hang on, partner. We've got business to attend to." Off they went, with him fighting the urge to look back.

"Why did you let Thaddeus go like that? He could be in the way." Jesselynn darted another withering look Wolf's way but realized she might as well stop. He wouldn't pay any attention anyway.

"If Wolf asked him, I thought it would be fine. Thaddeus didn't ask." Agatha stuck her threaded needle into the material of her waist, between shoulder and bosom, where hopefully it wouldn't snag on anything—or anyone. She tucked the shirt she'd been working on for Sammy in her voluminous apron pocket and, using the lower portion of her apron for a potholder, lifted the lid on the stewing buffalo.

"My, don't that smell good?"

Jesselynn sliced off another strip with enough force to cut into something else. Or someone else. She draped the pile of strips over the iron rack Meshach had fashioned for just this purpose, crowding those that had been hanging long enough to shrink some. She could hear the anvil ringing as Meshach worked to provide racks for some of the others. Other people dried the meat the old-fashioned way, over green willow branches lashed together.

Patch lay watching her, and if a bit dropped to the ground, it was his, quicker than a striking rattler.

"You're furious because you didn't get to go on the hunt," Agatha said, shaking her head and watching Jesselynn glare at Wolf while he talked to someone at the next wagon. Even Benjamin and Daniel had subdued their high spirits when they saw her. "You're being unfair, you know."

Jesselynn snorted and kept on slicing meat.

"Sorry, my dear, but women just aren't invited on hunts like that, britches or no."

"It's not fair." The words were forced between teeth clamped tight.

"I know, but it's not like we had nothing to do." Agatha filled a bucket partway with water and added a cup of salt to soak more meat. "Jesse, take my advice. Let it go and let the men have their fun. Heaven knows, there ain't been much time for fun on this journey."

Jesselynn let out a pent-up sigh. "You're right, but . . ." *But I wanted to at least see the herd. And I'm a good shot. It's just not fair. I know, Mother; the Bible never promised us fairness.*

When she finished cutting the meat off the haunch, she dropped the bones into another kettle. They'd be making soup out of that. She glanced around at the stacks of bones, hide, and meat to tend to. However would they be ready to travel in the morning? Benjamin had promised to make spoons out of the bone, and Ophelia had asked for a comb to be carved out of one of the ribs. Nothing would be wasted. Soon as she had the rack full of strips, she began chopping the meat in fine pieces to mix with cornmeal and onions to stuff in the stomach. Once boiled, the whole made a savory dish that would keep a day or two at least. Sliced, it fried up well.

"You mad, Jesse?" Thaddeus leaned against her knee.

"No, why?"

"Sad?"

She shook her head and leaned over to touch her nose to his. "What makes you ask?"

"You not smilin'."

Oh, Lord, save this child, who sees so far beyond the usual. She glanced up to see Wolf watching them. He always seemed to be watching her. What had she done now? She knew what she needed to do—ask Daniel and Benjamin to forgive her for being such a mean-spirited woman. She'd surely quenched their joy.

She lifted Thaddeus to her lap and blew kisses on his neck to make him giggle. "You are right, little brother. I've been too serious lately." Laughing would be a lot easier if Wolf didn't thwart her at every turn. Not letting her go on the buffalo shoot had been the final offense.

She needs to laugh more. Wolf watched the play between brother and sister. He knew what the other women were saying, that she shouldn't be wearing britches and acting like a man. Several of them had taken to snubbing her, not that it seemed to bother her much. She'd taught several other women how to dry the meat, shared her box of simples as she called them, and never had a cross word for any of them—except him.

If they'd been through what she'd been through—

He cut off the thoughts and held his coffee cup up for a refill. Jane Ellen smiled at him as she filled it.

"Elizabeth speakin' to you yet?" He kept his voice low, for her ears only.

Jane Ellen shook her head. "She says I lied to her, that I shoulda told her Jesse was . . . is . . ." She pursed her mouth and rolled her eyes. "I couldn't. Not one of us ever told nobody."

"Don't you worry about it. Elizabeth just got her pride hurt a bit. 'Twon't kill her."

"Thank you, Mr. Wolf. You want a hunk of cinnamon cake?"

"I sure do. That Ophelia be one fine cook."

"I made the cake." She ducked her head before he could see the blush.

"Then I'd say you are becoming one fine cook also. This wagon is sure blessed with good cooks."

"Good save there." Agatha sat down beside him and held up her cup for Jane Ellen to fill also. Setting her cup down, she took out her knitting and picked up where she'd left off. "I've been wanting to ask you something."

Wolf nodded, at the same time wishing he were somewhere else. Anywhere else. Agatha had that look in her eye. "What?"

She knit a few stitches. "About Oregon country. Do we dare believe all that hoopla about living off the land and anything and everything growing there?"

Wolf let out a sigh of relief. Why had he thought she was going to be talking about her niece? "You can believe much of it. Like Kentucky, the land is rich, the seasons fairly mild. The Indian tribes live off the land and the water. White men will build towns. There will be shipbuilding on the rivers, farming. When the railroad crosses the country—"

"That's nothin' but a pipe dream."

"No. It will happen. And if you think many people have crossed the country on the Oregon Trail, you wait to see what happens when the trains travel."

"What makes you believe that?"

"I've ridden this trail four times now. I see sod houses sproutin' like weeds in the spring, cattle grazing where the buffalo roamed, wheat fields where the prairie grass reigned."

"And will you farm or—?"

"No, I will . . ." He stopped. The song of the fiddle caught his ear. "Let's go hear the next chapter in the story."

"No, I don't waste my time listening to that old reprobate spouting off like that."

"Why, Aunt Agatha, here Nate has had nothin' but good to say about you."

"He better not be saying nothing 'bout me, that old brushface."

Wolf looked up just in time to see Jesselynn roll her eyes. Had she been listening to the conversation all along? He stood and tossed the dregs of his coffee into the fire. "Thank you for a fine meal and a pleasant evening." He tipped his hat to Agatha, nodded to Jesselynn, and followed the stream of folks congregating in the center of the circle.

The legendary Jehosaphats were in rare form that night, with Nate Lyons playing one part of the family after the other, from the grandfather sitting in the rocking chair to the mother scrubbing clothes on the washboard and the children getting in trouble no matter what they did. The fiddler got into it, playing on the low notes in the dark parts and lively high notes on the happy.

Jesselynn took her knitting over to the circle, chuckling along with the rest of them until she sensed Wolf behind her. She dropped two stitches and had to stop because she couldn't see well enough in the near dark to pick them up again.

"What'd you go and do that for?" she hissed.

"What?" He leaned down to hear her better.

"Nothin'." She stabbed the needles back in the ball of yarn, not wanting to admit the desire to stab them into him. Where had all this violence come from? She who never wanted to hurt anyone, unless of course they were wearing a blue uniform—or any uniform, for that matter.

As the applause broke out, she knew she'd missed a good part of the story. That man. Not only would he not let her hunt buffalo, now he'd ruined a perfectly good evening as well. She turned and left, oblivious to the lack of good-nights directed her way.

Wolf, however, was not oblivious. He steamed instead, responding to a pleasant "Good night, Wolf" with a curt nod. *What a cluster of hypocrites.* His father had always said, *"Give me a straight-up Indian any day before a backbiting white."* Maybe there had been truth in that theory. Now that he could live comfortably in either world, all he could dream of was the life he'd lived as a child—before his mother died of the pox and his father took him back to civilization.

Meshach was still chuckling when he returned to their own fire. Sammy lay sleeping in Ophelia's arms, and Thaddeus clung to Meshach's hand. Ophelia put the two boys to bed while Meshach checked the meat hanging on the rack. He threw more chips on the fire to keep it smoldering all night to dry the meat. By the time the camp settled down, the moon had leaped from the horizon and floated like a silver disc in the heavens. After making sure everything was put away in their camp, Jesselynn rolled into her quilt on the ground under the wagon. Why had Wolf stood behind her like that? Silencing a yipping coyote would be easier than silencing her thoughts.

At a whine from Patch, Jesselynn rolled over, fully alert, listening with every nerve. She held still, wishing for Ahab, who was out with the remuda. Laying a hand on the quivering dog, she tried to see what he saw. A growl rumbled in his throat.

Could it be Indians?

Chapter Thirty-Seven

❧

EARLY JUNE 1863

Another dog barked.

Patch growled again, and the hair rose on the back of his neck.

Jesselynn slid out from the covers and to her feet as soundlessly as whoever or whatever was bothering the dogs. She stood at the end of the wagon, searching the flatlands around them. The grass wasn't deep enough to hide much.

A third dog barked. Patch, at her knee, growled again. This time the hair stood on her own neck. Something was out there, but what?

She knew Meshach was behind her without looking. "You think something's botherin' the horses?" She kept her voice soft so only he could hear it.

"I go see."

"Take Benjamin?"

"I'se here."

She strained, hoping to hear something, anything. Meshach and Benjamin looked like shadows flitting across the prairie. Patch streaked after them. She could hear others rustling. The dogs had sounded the alarm.

A shout! A rifle shot! All from the direction of the grazing animals.

Jesselynn grabbed her gun. If someone stole the horses, this long ordeal would have been for naught. "Stay here and guard!" she ordered Daniel and threw him a gun. A volley of shots and shouting made her run faster.

The hoofbeats of a running horse caught her attention, even above the thundering of her own heart. Another shot. Then a horse and rider in pursuit.

She met Meshach and Benjamin returning with the Thoroughbreds.

"Dey got Marse Wolf's Appaloosa and one other."

"Who?"

"Indians, we 'spect."

"Where was the guard?" She knew two men had been assigned to keep watch, as they always did. She swung atop one of the mares to ride back to camp.

Meshach's snort said what he thought of the guard. "Mos' likely sleepin'. He weren't on him horse, dat's for sure."

"Who?"

"Dat worthless Rufus Jones. He was mountin' when we got dere."

"Where was McPhereson?"

"Don' know. Got to look for 'im."

By now half the camp was awake and other men running out to join them.

"Where's Wolf?" several men asked at the same time. "What happened?"

"Indian raid. Got two horses, one Marse Wolf's."

At least our horses are safe. But guilt stabbed her as soon as the thought. Wolf and his horse were like one. She'd heard he'd raised the striking bay-and-white Appaloosa from a colt and never rode any other horse. But where was he?

She tied the mares to the wagon and waited for Meshach and Benjamin to return with the others. They'd gone to help round up the herd and bring it closer to camp. A shout said they'd found McPhereson. When they rode in with a body draped across the saddle, she knew.

Not only two horses, but they'd lost a good man. While Jones slept.

You don't know that for sure, she reminded herself.

A lantern flared and lit the circle where they lowered the body to the ground. The gash across his jugular glowed black in the light. His wife burst through the circle and dropped to her knees beside the body, her keening cry bringing tears to Jesselynn's eyes. Surely this was a death that could have been prevented.

"Where is Wolf?" one of the men growled.

"Mebbe gone after de horses?" Meshach dismounted and joined the circle.

"On foot?" The man snorted this time.

"Where's Benjamin?" Jesselynn spoke for Meshach's ears only.

"Out on guard."

"What about Jones?"

"Don' know. Just someone got to stand guard. I go back out. We bring dem all close to camp." Meshach headed back out to the herd.

The sound of galloping hoofbeats drew their attention to a rider, etched in the moonlight, coming into camp.

Jesselynn knew who it was as soon as she caught the white splashes on the lead horse. It was Wolf's horse, so Wolf must be the rider. A second horse raced beside them.

Silence greeted his halt at the edge of the camp.

"One brave—he won't steal horses again." He glanced around the circle. "Where's Jones?"

Several shrugged. The wife's keening continued, broken only by her gulps for air. Aunt Agatha knelt beside her, her murmurs of comfort lost in the sorrow.

"Shouldn'ta happened."

"High price."

The muttering caught Jesselynn's attention. Why were they blaming Wolf when Jones was to blame? If he'd been on watch like he was supposed to . . . but did they know that? Had her men kept that knowledge to themselves? Knowing Meshach, she was sure that's what had happened.

Edging closer so she could tell Wolf what had happened without announcing it to everyone, she caught her breath. His left arm wore a gash from shoulder to elbow, the blood dripping down over his hand. She turned to see Jane Ellen at her side.

"Get my medicine box, please." Still keeping her voice soft, she added, "And ask Daniel to build up the fire. We need hot water."

Her attention shifted back to the circle. Wolf stood at an angle so the men couldn't see his arm.

"I didn't sound an alarm because that was the job of the men on guard. If there had been more braves, more horses would have been stolen, but since I heard one set of hoofbeats, I knew . . ." His words wore the patient tone of a man explaining things to children.

"Didja know McPhereson was dead?"

Wolf shook his head. "No, but I suspected as much. What about Jones?"

"He was sleeping." Jesselynn raised her voice so everyone could hear. "Meshach found him just mounting his horse, his bedroll out by the fire."

"Ya sure about that?" A voice rose from the gathered men.

"Meshach never lies."

"That worthless—"

Jesselynn took a step forward, hands clenched at her sides.

"No, I don't mean your sla—er, man." The man with a full mink beard backed off, hands in front of him. "I mean that lowdown Jones."

"Good thing, Henry, he—er, she woulda dropped ya for sure." The air lightened at the general chuckle but for the keening that had now diminished to hiccupping sobs.

"Oughta just string those two brothers up. Save the woman a life o' trouble."

"There'll be no talk of stringing anyone up. We don't know the entire story yet."

Jesselynn took her box of medical supplies from Jane Ellen and, holding it with one hand, tapped Wolf's arm with the other. "How about I fix that arm of yours before you bleed to death?" Not that there was much danger of that. The bleeding had slowed, the dark river coagulating on the buckskin shirt.

Wolf glanced down at his arm, then at her. "It's fine."

"It will be after I get it bandaged. Once I see it in the light, I'll know better if you need stitches or not." She wasn't prepared for the tension that ran up her hand to her shoulder when she touched his arm. Like touching a hot stove, only in that case she was wise enough to pull back. Instead, she pointed to the hunk of oak they'd been toting across the plains. "Sit."

Jane Ellen held the lamp as she examined the wound.

"You need to take the shirt off, or I'll have to cut out the sleeve."

"You're givin' me a choice?"

She nodded.

Even in the lamplight, his face went white when he tried to raise his arm to pull his shirt over his head. Sweat broke out on his forehead and upper lip.

"Jane Ellen." Jesselynn nodded to her helper and between them they pulled off the shirt, cushioning the injured arm as best they could in the process. Firelight played over muscles that bunched when she touched a hot, wet cloth to the arm.

Trying to be gentle, she ordered her shaking hands to get the job done.

With the dried blood cleaned off, the slash started bleeding again.

"I'm going to have to stitch it." She paused, half expecting him to argue. But when he only nodded, she motioned for Jane Ellen to thread the needle.

The rest of the wagon-train folks faded away, heading back to their beds for what remained of a short night for sleeping. Jones had yet to enter camp.

"This is going to burn."

His grunt said only that he'd heard her.

She trickled the whiskey down from his shoulder, the length of the slash. The deepest section crossed the muscle from elbow to shoulder, but while it nicked the muscle, the cut didn't appear to have severed it.

"You're lucky."

Grunt or snort, she wasn't sure of his response, other than the white skin around his eyes and mouth.

"Had it severed this muscle, you'd have lost the use of the arm or hand." Holding the lips of the slash with one hand, she inserted the needle through the skin and drew the thread through, back and forth, until the gaping wound lay snugly shut. She knotted the thread, snipped it with the scissors, and stepped back with a sigh. At least somewhere in the stitching her hands had stopped shaking. She applied some of the salve from her medicinals and, taking a roll of two-inch-wide sheeting, bandaged the arm. "If you wear a sling for a few days, it will heal more quickly."

"Thank you." He didn't look at her.

"How is he?" Aunt Agatha returned from settling the new widow into her wagon.

"Good, if we can keep this from goin' putrid."

"Leastways, it wasn't your right." When he didn't answer, Aunt Agatha cocked an eyebrow at her niece, who shrugged.

Lord, get me outa here. Her hands burned him far worse than the whiskey or the wound itself. Her touch, firm but gentle, set him to twitching, which only the stiffest resolve kept him from succumbing to. What was happening? Ever since he'd realized she was a woman and the original rage wore off, he'd fought to keep his distance.

He tried working up that initial rage at her duplicity, but somewhere in the last few days he'd lost that as well. And now he was in her debt, all for a knife slashing that should never have happened. All he'd wanted was his horse back. Fool young buck, counting coup by stealing a horse. Cost him his life and the train a good man.

He clenched his teeth against the pain of the needle pulling the thread through his skin. Would she never be done? In spite of his steel resolve, his stomach roiled, and he blinked to clear the black spots from his eyes. Sure, all he needed to do was pass out now.

His arm might as well have been branded.

When she stepped back, the cool breeze of the coming dawn dried the sweat on his chest. He stared at the ground. Could he stand without making a fool of himself?

"Thank you." Never would she know what the two words cost him.

"You're welcome. Can you make it back to your bedroll all right?"

He glanced up at her to see her nod at Daniel, who had come to stand beside him.

Right now what he'd really like was a tote of that whiskey she had so carelessly poured down his arm. It might have done more good down his throat. Instead of answering, he lurched to his feet. Without a backward look he staggered once, then gained his equilibrium and strode off toward his simple camp. He could feel her gaze all the way. Calling himself all kinds of names did nothing to ease the holes she burned in his back.

"Well, if that don't beat all." Agatha planted her hands on her hips and stared after the retreating wagon master.

Jesselynn felt as if she had been horse whipped. Her shoulders ached, her hands ached too, but more for the touch of him than the weariness. She jerked her mind back from where it had wandered and began putting things to right in her box. Each stab of the needle through his flesh had been like piercing her own. *What in the world is the matter with me?*

"Good night," she said to Agatha, who was settling in the wagon. She tucked the box back in its place, and after checking on the herd of oxen and horses that now grazed near the circle of wagons, she crawled back in her bedroll, wishing for sleep for her burning eyes. The warmth seeped into her flesh and bones but did nothing to shut down the rampaging thoughts. She listened for the night noises—cattle and horses chewing the grass, an owl hooting, the cry of a nighthawk. Either of those last two could be an Indian signal. But surely they wouldn't come this close to camp. Agatha turned over above her with a sigh. Snores could be heard from the wagon in front of them.

Patch raised his head, setting her heart to thundering immediately, and it didn't stop when he sighed and lay back down. Since he felt his place was next to hers, she sensed his every move. He leaned into her stroking fingers, giving her wrist a quick lick in appreciation.

If one Indian got that close undetected . . . the thought made her stomach flutter. But all he'd wanted was a horse. Was that one horse worth the death of two men, one white, one red? *And would this be the last?* What if they were attacked by Indians? Other wagon trains had been, or at least she'd heard tell of it. Had Wolf ever fought off an Indian attack? Or was his being half Sioux an added protection for them?

Thoughts raced through her mind, circled, and came back for another attack. She turned over on her other side, Patch snuggled up against her back, his sigh a strong comment on her restlessness. Surely they had prayed for God's protection on their journey. Surely others had too, yet look what happened to some of them. She'd seen a blackened wagon or what remained of it. Had that been the work of Indians?

When the rooster, carried in a crate attached to one of the wagons, crowed, her eyes felt like burning coals, so intensely had she been staring into the darkness. Slowly, gently, dawn stole across the land, turning black to gray and washing the land in silver. By the time the sun broke the horizon, they were all near to ready for the wagons to pull out.

Didn't look to her like some of the others had had much more sleep than she had.

The second burial of the journey took more time for the digging, but the end results were the same. The slight mound of dirt would disappear under the wheels of the train.

"You seen that scum Jones?" Agatha asked in an undertone as they set the cooking things in the wagon box.

Jesselynn shook her head. "Don't care to neither. I just feel sorry for that poor woman to be married into such a shiftless bunch."

"I know. Poor white trash through and through." Agatha heaved herself up over the wagon wheel and settled on the seat she had padded with a quilt, thanks to Jesselynn's insistence. "You riding or walking today?" she asked.

"Depends on what Ophelia would like. Walkin', I guess. Most likely I'd fall asleep on the wagon. Could fall under the wheels thataway." Jesselynn touched the brim of her hat with one finger. "You get to be first today, so enjoy."

While she'd rather watch out across the ever changing prairie, she took her knitting out instead. Since the boys were playing in the back of Ophelia's wagon, she and Jane Ellen strode companionably along, both with their needles clicking as they turned wool into socks and sweaters for the winter. The cold in Oregon was more intense than that of Kentucky, or so they'd been told.

Jesselynn mulled over the events of the night before, her thoughts always returning to the feel of Wolf's skin under her fingertips. Knowing such thoughts were decidedly unladylike was no deterrent. She had to admit he'd been sneaking into her thoughts more and more lately, in spite of her good intentions.

She forced herself to think on the verse Meshach had given them for the day. *"Not by might, nor by power, but by my spirit, saith the Lord . . ."* That's all the further she got from memory. If only she could sit down with the journal and catch up on the letters she'd started for the family. The Lord himself had promised to watch over them. With that thought came another. But what about poor Mr. McPhereson? And his wife and family now left to fend for themselves? The Lord had promised to watch over them too.

She glanced up at the screech of a hawk, lost to her sight in the blue of the sky.

"Hey, you seen what's ahead?" Billy asked her from the back of his horse.

She shook her head, then looked to where he was pointing.

Far in the distant shimmering haze two rocks rose from the floor of the plain, one like a huge round table.

"Wolf says that's Courthouse Rock to the north, Jail House to the left. Immigrants been cuttin' their names in the sandstone for years. Like to be a hunk o' history right there for all to see. Mr. Wolf says maybe the Whitmans even signed it on their way to Oregon."

Jesselynn glanced up at the young man riding beside her just in time to catch one of the looks he slanted at Jane Ellen. Ah, no wonder he was paying such close attention to her. Another young pup sniffing around the females. She turned her attention to Jane Ellen to see her studying on her yarn, studying so hard she missed a hillock of grass and stumbled, catching hold of Jesselynn's arm to keep from falling.

Jesselynn kept a giggle inside. Indeed it must be spring.

Wolf rode back, stopping to talk with Aunt Agatha on the wagon, then rode over to her, his left arm hanging straight at his side.

"Keep a watch out. There's Indians trailing the train."

Her heart took up the staccato beat from the night before, but now she knew fear to be the culprit. Fear wore the same metallic taste as blood.

Chapter Thirty-Eight

CHIMNEY ROCK

The Indians trailing the wagon train kept everyone on edge.

"What do you s'pose they want?" Jane Ellen glanced over her shoulder, fear eating at the edge of her mouth.

"To drive us all stark ravin' mad." Aunt Agatha shuddered as she answered. "If a horse gets loose or an ox, they'll get it. They'll steal whatever we don't nail down."

"How can you say that?" Jesselynn stepped over the wagon tongue, carrying two buckets of water from Plum Creek that flowed into the Platte River. She hated skimming bugs off the Platte River water. Besides, many had come up with diarrhea from drinking from the South Platte. "What's come up stolen so far?"

Agatha *harrumphed* and shook her head again. "You mark my words." She wagged her finger for emphasis.

Jesselynn looked over to the Lyonses' wagon, where the children were gathered for their evening lessons. "I bet this is the only wagon train that carries a schoolmaster along with it."

Agatha harrumphed again, louder this time and, muttering under her breath, strode to the back of the wagon and stuck her head inside, ostensibly searching for something. Ophelia chuckled and shared a private glance with Meshach, who was repairing a piece of harness for one of the other wagons.

Sammy held a bug up for Ophelia to see, and Thaddeus brought one to Jesselynn.

"Grasshopper?"

"That's right. Daniel is using grasshoppers for fish bait."

"Dan'l catch fish for supper?"

"I sure do hope so. Buffalo and beans is getting a bit monotonous." At home the greens would be growing heartily in the gardens and the snap beans they started in the cold frames beginning to blossom. Here they didn't dare even go out looking for greens since the Indians began following them. Dandelions and poke would go far toward making the supper more palatable.

"We be thankful for good food. Leastways we get enough to eat." Meshach smiled up at her to take any sting out of his words.

"I know." She felt like snapping but refrained. The restrictions of camp made everyone restless, just knowing there was danger near and not being able to do anything about it. None of the women and children had been allowed out of camp for the last three days. Even picking buffalo and cow chips had been curtailed.

Wolf wasn't winning any popularity contest by the tighter rules. "Seems like they blame him." She said it without thinking.

"Who?"

"Wolf. Like the Indians following are his fault."

"Make no sense, do it?" Meshach hammered home the final rivet and slung the harness over his shoulder. "Be right back."

With the supper cooking, Jesselynn dug her writing case out of the storage box and made herself comfortable, or as comfortable as possible on the wagon tongue and the braces that bolted it to the wagon bed. Uncorking the ink, she made several entries in the journal before beginning a letter to her sisters. Since they would be in Fort Laramie in the next few days, she wanted the letters ready to go back east with the mail.

My dearest sisters. That part was easy, but how could she describe life on the trail so they would understand, when they had never done anything more exertive outdoors than go on picnics? Anytime the Highwood women traveled overnight, the carriage had stopped at inns and way stations with beds and hot meals, or they stayed with friends and relatives. Jesselynn looked up at the sky bowl above them, the sun edging toward the horizon, the flat shallow river over a mile wide, the valley, if one could call the slight depression of the Platte River Road a valley, and the wagons in their nightly circle with the herd grazing near enough to hear the oxen chewing their cud. Since the Indians had begun following them, Wolf ordered camp earlier at night because the herd couldn't graze out farther where the grass was better.

She stared at a heap of possessions that someone had dumped beside the trail—a trunk, a spinet piano, and a breakfront—apparently finding them too heavy to carry any longer. Furniture that had once graced someone's home now lay weathering in the prairie sun and rain. No one else had room to pick it all up. Thanks to the cave living they'd done all winter, they had no fine furniture to cart along. Just the bare necessities.

She read her opening words again. *Dearest sisters.* That sure covered it. She shook her head. *And brother.* How could she have forgotten Zachary? She brushed the feathered end of the quill pen across her chin. What was left of her dashing big brother? His wounds had sounded hideous. Missing his right foot, his right hand and right eye, along with a gash down the right side of his face. How he must be suffering.

She added his name in the salutation and continued.

> *We are still following the Platte River. Platte is French for flat, and it most certainly is that. Must be like Daddy said Louisiana is but without the levies.*

She told them about the Indian trying to steal horses and about Wolf's injury, not that it had slowed him down for long.

> *I am feeling hemmed in, which is hard to figure, since we can see forever. It took two days from the first sighting of Courthouse Rock until we drew near, and even though it looked close enough to touch, those who insisted on going out there took a day to get there and back. The air is so clear and the land so flat that distance is impossible to figure. Each day's journey looks pretty much like the day before. Never thought I'd be able to walk along, knitting and chatting, and not fall over my feet.*
>
> *We've buried two so far, a man and a little boy. The boy's mother was so stoic, grateful she had a nice outfit to bury her baby in. I wanted to run screaming, since none of the herbs and such I used to help him did any good. Death came so fast. The mother said our Father must have wanted her son up in heaven, but I think He has plenty of babies there already. Burying anyone is hard, but burying children is especially hard. If I didn't know there was a heaven, I might go stark raving mad.*
>
> *The horses are holding up well, much to everyone's surprise. I believe the real challenge will come when we get to the mountains. As Wolf says, "We are on the easy leg of the journey now."*
>
> *I hope and pray there will be a letter from you when we reach Fort Laramie. Thaddeus no longer asks to go home, and I am beginning to think he has forgotten Twin Oaks. He thinks he is old enough to join the other children in school, which is conducted by Mr. Nate Lyons in the evenings. Don't ever let on to Aunt Agatha, but I think Mr. Lyons is sweet on her. He brought her some wildflowers he had picked the other day. She still calls him Brushface, but I hope she can look beyond the wild hair and whiskers to see the value of the man within.*

She almost wrote more about Wolf, but after rereading what she had written, she realized she had mentioned him too much already. The thought made her pause. Did she write about him because he was on her mind so much?

> *May our God and Father keep you in his tender care and grant you peace.*
> > *With all my love,*
> > *Your sister Jesselynn*
> > *and all the rest*

P.S. I forgot to tell you that my secret is out. They all know I am a female in men's clothing, and many of the ladies will not forgive me for the deception. So be it. JH

She let the ink dry and folded the paper. She'd have to use another sheet of paper to make an envelope, since she had run out of that nicety.

Aunt Agatha invited Wolf to join them for supper.

Jesselynn made her way to the Lyonses' wagon and asked him to come too. *Tit for tat.* The thought made her smile.

"Thankee, but we already got an invite fer tonight." His eyes twinkled under brushy eyebrows. "We could come tomorrow." One eyebrow arched.

"That would be fine." She stopped herself from making the invitation a permanent one. As much as he was helping all those with children, he shouldn't have to cook his own supper on top of that. Maybe she should mention that to Wolf, and he could bring it up at one of the meetings. Sure as shooting, if she offered the suggestion, it would be voted down on general principles. Unless, of course, she took to wearing dresses.

Dusk shadowed the camp when Wolf joined them for supper. After Meshach said the grace, Ophelia dished the fried fish onto tin plates, and they all found a place to sit, mostly cross-legged on the ground.

Seemingly without his volition, Wolf found himself between two women — Jane Ellen with adoring eyes and Jesselynn who refused to look at him. *Now what have I done, or not done, as the case may be?* He slanted a peek to his right and saw Jesselynn helping her little brother cut his meat. How could he ever have bought her story that she was Marse Jesse? Surely if he had paid more attention he would have seen her tenderness with the children, her caring for her aunt, and the young woman on the other side whose doe eyes made him want to squirm.

"Seen anythin' of Jones?" Meshach looked up from his plate.

Even the thought of the worthless Rufus made his jaw tighten. "No. He most likely hightailed it on to Fort Laramie." *If the Indians didn't get him first.* Any day he expected to come across a carcass, minus the scalp. It would be a fitting end.

"Good fish."

"Thanks to Daniel." Meshach nodded to the young man sitting beside him.

"I strung out a trotline. Why don't de others?"

"Perhaps you could teach 'em how."

Daniel shrugged. "Mebbe." But his look said far more.

"We'll come on Chimney Rock soon, then a couple days to crossin' the South Fork of the Platte." *Because he's black, the others don't want to learn from him, then they mutter and grumble about how the Highwood wagons eat better than the rest. Yet they always share. I'm sick to death of this insane backbiting.* Visions of high country with cool winds singing through the pine trees, Indian tepees instead of white-sailed wagons, his people laughing and dancing after the day's hunt. Home. He could almost smell it on the air.

Could he leave the wagon train at Fort Laramie and head north? Who would take it on?

He looked up to see those around him staring at him. "Could you repeat that?"

"I asked how many days to Fort Laramie?" Aunt Agatha covered her hand with her apron and picked up the coffeepot. "Anyone else ready for this?"

Wolf held up his cup. "Should be there in four to six days, depending on how the river crossing goes. We'll be at the ford tomorrow. California Hill after that."

"I see to the caulkin' den."

"You have any grease left?"

"Yes, suh. We brought plenty like you said back to Independence."

If only the others had listened as well. He wouldn't ask anyone to share with the Joneses. But theirs was the wagon that would cause the most trouble. He was sure of it.

By late afternoon the sprinkles turned to heavy rain, so that by the time they circled the wagons near the ford, man and beast were sodden. With thunder rolling and lightning forking the sky, Wolf ordered everyone to bring in their own animals and tie them on long lines to keep them from stampeding.

Jesselynn clamped her legs to keep Ahab under control. Head high, the stallion snorted and shifted beneath her. "Easy, old son. You've been through a lightning storm before." The rain ran cold from the brim of her hat and down her neck. Could have been ice, the temperature had dropped so fast. She tied him to a rear wheel of their wagon and climbed inside to sit cross-legged on a box and eat dried biscuit and dried buffalo with the rest of them. There'd be no fires this night.

The rain continued through the night, raising the river a foot by morning. Brown froth rushed toward the east with the opposite shore shrouded in rain sheets.

Jesselynn rode up to the three men gathered on the bank.

"I vote we go on over. Two feet deep ain't much. We crossed deeper."

"I heard there could be holes runnin' deeper. Sure did pick up the pace some overnight." They both looked to Wolf.

Jesselynn tried to read some expression on either face or body, but Wolf stood still as a well-sunk fence post.

The sounds from the circled wagons were blurred just like her vision. Ahab snorted and dug in the mud with one front foot.

Wolf looked toward the west from where the storm blew in. He sniffed the air, turned slowly to study the sky in all four directions, then nodded. "Looks to be breakin' up. Give it an hour, and then we decide."

Two hours later the first wagon entered the rushing water. A whip cracked. The driver yelled orders to his four oxen. Two men rode by the lead team, one on either side.

Wolf gave last-minute orders. "Now, if your wagon starts to float, go easy with the current, but keep angling toward the shore. Just keep a steady hand on those reins. Your oxen can swim if they have to."

One by one, the wagons entered the river. Some floated, some angled upstream, some floated down. Jesselynn pulled up behind the Jones wagon. Benjamin on Ahab and Daniel on Domino rode point.

Wolf stopped his horse next to Jesselynn. "Wait until they get over that sandbar before you start in."

"Right." She watched the wagon ahead grow fainter in the mist. "Here we go." She flicked the reins when a shout went up from the wagon ahead. "Oh, God, no!" The wagon tipped and fell.

Wolf spun his horse and leaped into the river.

"Whoa!" Jesselynn pulled back on the reins. "Go help." She need not have said a word, for Daniel and Benjamin were already following Wolf.

"Oh, Lord above, much as I hate—no dislike—those folks, please protect them."

"Jesselynn, can you see anything?" Jane Ellen leaned on Jesselynn's shoulder.

"No." *Oh, Lord, this could be us. But it's not. There's justice, Lord. Jones is such a rotten man.* Guilt grabbed her by the throat and shook her. Such a thing to think. *Lord, forgive me, please. I'm sorry for even thinking such a thing. What kind of a Christian am I? Mother, what you would say to me?*

With all the ropes on the wagon, they had it righted and pulled it out of the river before Wolf came back to signal the next wagon.

With a prayer on her lips, Jesselynn started into the river.

"Swing to the upstream just across the sandbar. There's a hole off to the right."

"Are the Joneses all right?"

Wolf didn't answer.

With Daniel and Benjamin on either side of the lead team, the oxen pulled steady, up over the sandbar and back in the water. One bellowed. They drew closer to the shore. She popped the whip, her feet braced against the boot board. Throwing themselves against the yokes, the oxen hauled the wagon up the gentle incline and out of the river.

"We did it!" Jane Ellen threw her arms around Jesselynn. "Thank you, Lord. We made it."

Jesselynn wrapped the reins around the brake handle, stood on shaking legs, and climbed down over the wheel to stand on firm ground again. She went around the wagon and reached up to grab Thaddeus and squeezed him tight.

He patted her cheeks. "You good driver, Jesse." He looked over her shoulder. "Meshach comin'."

Jesselynn looked up at the sound of a keening wail from the Jones wagon. She glanced at Jane Ellen, who shook her head, eyes wide.

Meshach pulled up beside them and helped Aunt Agatha to the ground. "Never thought I'd be so grateful to stand on dry ground again." She stamped her foot to make the point. "Thank you, Lord above."

They stood and watched the crossing of the remaining wagons. Two men lassoed the ox horns to assist the next wagon, which was floundering, and the last one made it to the far shore without incident. They circled the wagons on the northern verge so some could hang things out to dry.

Jesselynn inspected their wagons and found no leaks, thanks to Meshach's careful caulking. She could hear others grumbling. The rain had let up somewhere during the crossing, and thanks to the sandy soil, the puddles had disappeared. Ophelia started a fire with the twigs Jane Ellen and the boys brought back from the brush along the river and added the cow and buffalo chips they'd collected during previous days' walks. With the kettle boiling, she added shaved dried buffalo meat, the last of the remaining vegetables, and the rice she'd been saving. The savory smell rose to tantalize while Ophelia mixed up dumplings.

Jesselynn made her way over to the Jones wagon, much against her better judgment. She wanted to leave them to their soaked fate, but the sobbing hadn't ceased. Everyone else seemed to be ignoring them.

Jesselynn drew even with the boxes stacked alongside the wagon.

"Shut up, woman! Just shut up!"

Jesselynn stopped. The crack of hand against flesh made her flinch. She stepped around the wagon to see Tommy Joe, hands clenched, standing over his wife. Mrs. Jones cowered on the ground, her baby clenched in her arms.

Tommy Joe reached for the soaked blanket-wrapped bundle. "He's dead."

"Leave her be!" Jesselynn stepped forward.

"Get outa here, you . . . you . . . interfering wench." Fists raised, he came at her.

With a growl like an attacking bear, Wolf grabbed Jones by the shoulder, spun him around, and planted a fist in Jones's face. Tommy Joe staggered, slumped to his knees, and toppled to the ground. Blood ran from his smashed nose.

Jesselynn knelt by the sobbing woman. She wrapped her arms around the thin shoulders and held her close, the wet bundle between them. *Oh, Lord, what can I say?* No words came, so the two women rocked together.

———

After the tragedy of the river they took the steep climb up and over California Hill with extreme care. The men braced against the wheels of each wagon to keep it from rolling over the oxen. Though it was grueling, Jesselynn knew it was just a foretaste of what was ahead for them when they reached the mountains. By the time they reached Ash Hollow, an extra day of rest was more than needed.

The morning they forded the river to Fort Laramie should have been a celebration, but discontent simmered beneath the surface like a kettle on slow boil. More than one family muttered that leaving the Joneses at Fort Laramie would be the best possible way to settle things.

They circled the wagons just south of the fort and made camp.

"Leastwise we don't have to worry about those Indians any longer." Aunt Agatha said what the others were thinking now that they were within the protection of the fort.

Jesselynn nodded. "Think I'll ride on in to the quartermaster tonight and see about ordering our supplies."

"Me go?" Thaddeus looked up from where he was digging a hole in the dirt with a stick.

"No, I—" But at the way his face fell, she changed her mind. "Why not? Come on, let's go get Roman."

The smile he gave her as he took her hand reminded her what little it took to make him happy. Riding with his big sister was one of those things. After bridling the mule, she set Thaddeus up on the bony back and swung herself up behind him. Handing him the reins, she nudged Roman forward. "You make sure you keep him goin' straight now, you hear?"

"I hear." His shoulders straightened as if she'd just asked him to take over the family.

At home he'd be riding a pony all by himself in the paddock by now. All the Highwood children could ride nearly before they could run, or at least it seemed that way. All but Thaddeus, another casualty of the war. Jesselynn dropped a kiss on his soft hair. He should be wearing a hat already too, but she had neither the time nor materials to make him one. So many things left undone, her daddy must be rolling over in his grave. Thoughts of her father made her shoulders slump. Sometimes the burdens got so heavy she could barely breathe.

As Meshach would say, "Time to put dem all back in de Lawd's hands —and leave dem dere." The leaving them there was the hard part.

"Ugh, bluebellies." Thaddeus snapped her back to attention.

"No. Don't you call them that." She gave him a gentle shake.

"You do."

"Not anymore. We've gone beyond the war. They are United States soldiers, and we are United States citizens. That's what your daddy always said."

"Bluebellies kill my daddy."

Oh, Lord, preserve us. What can I say? He is so right. Jesselynn sucked in a deep breath in the hopes it would help her think better. "Daddy was a casualty of the war, just like so many others. We have to forgive and forget." *So we aren't destroyed too.*

Jesselynn glanced up in time to catch the sight of a man disappearing behind one of the whitewashed buildings. "Jones!" *That scum is still alive.*

———

To tell Wolf or not dogged her all the way back to the camp. Thaddeus leaned against her chest, blissfully sucking on his peppermint stick. The hunk of cheese would bring cries of delight from those at the wagons, and the molasses would taste wonderful on pancakes in the morning. But if the others found out about Jones, would they demand a lynching?

Keeping the news to herself for now seemed the better part of wisdom, she had decided by the time they rode into camp. She lowered Thaddeus and his sack of peppermint sticks to the ground. "Now you go share those, you hear?"

He nodded and ran off, little-boy legs pumping, calling for Sammy and Jane Ellen.

She stripped the bridle off Roman and, with a swat on the rump, sent him galloping back to the herd. With the sack of supplies swung over her shoulder, she made her way back to the wagons, with each step wishing she hadn't seen what she had.

"Thought a trip to the store would take away that thundercloud sittin' on your head, not make it worse." Agatha studied her niece and lowered her voice. "Now, what is it botherin' you? No mail?"

Jesselynn shook her head. Seeing Jones had plumb driven the mail out of her mind. Another thing to hold against him. "Forgot to ask." She handed the tow sack to her aunt.

"What, then? You look blacker'n a bog at night."

Jesselynn sighed. She should have known better than to think she could pull off carrying a secret like that. "I saw Jones at the hostelry."

Agatha sighed and shook her head at the same time. "I know it isn't Christian, but I sure was hopin' the prairie or the Indians got him. You goin' to tell Wolf?"

Jesselynn shook her head. "Not unless I have to. Maybe the scum will just stay clear if he has any sense at all."

"Sure." Agatha rolled her eyes and opened the sack. "Ah, cheese. We can have it on biscuits for supper."

———

The camp had settled for the night when Jesselynn heard a shout. Rolling to her feet, gun already in hand, she stood beside the wagon searching the blackness for the reason. She could feel the warmth from Meshach right beside her.

"Hold 'im. He ain't gonna get away this time!" came the shout.

"Let's go," Jesselynn said, and together the two of them headed across the circle at a run.

Chapter Thirty-Nine

Fort Laramie

"Drop your guns."

Jesselynn spun at the guttural command. Wolf stood slightly behind her and off to the right, rifle in one hand, Colt in the other. She lowered her gun, realizing he wasn't even looking at her and Meshach. The men holding Jones stepped back from their captive, and those with guns holstered them.

"You can't be sticking up for the scum, Wolf. You know McPhereson died because this lowlife was too tired to stand watch properlike."

"He deserves a chance to say his piece to the military. They're in charge of the peace around here."

"I say let's just string 'im up."

"I din't sleep on watch. He hit me." Rufus whined like the bully-turned-weakling he was.

One of the men gave him a shove. "Then why'd that Indian not slit your throat too?"

Jones shrugged. "How should I know? I was just coming to when Highwood and her nigger run up."

"Then why'd ya run?"

"Reckoned they'd think I kilt Mac, that's why."

Jesselynn about choked on her rage. Meshach said he'd been lying on his bedroll or in it. Either way . . . "Don't believe a word he says," she hissed loudly enough for Wolf to hear.

"How'd you know Mac was dead?"

Silence.

"He's lyin', the dirty cur."

"Enough." Wolf took two steps forward. "Get some rope and tie his hands behind his back, then to a wagon wheel. We'll take him into the fort in the morning."

The men muttered and grumbled, but they did as he ordered. As soon as Jones was tied to the wheel, they moved off. Thunder rumbled in the distance, the smell of rain sweet on the breeze.

Jesselynn turned to head back to her bedroll. So Jones might get a bit wet. Far as she could see, more than his clothes needed washing. And some starch in his backbone wouldn't hurt neither. "You know he was lying."

"I knows. But de officer be de one to say, not us."

"I didn't think he'd be stupid enough to try and sneak into camp. What if his brother lets him go?"

"With Wolf guardin' 'im?"

"Oh."

A shadow by their wagon revealed a man as they neared. "Your turn on watch, Meshach."

"I know. Be right dere."

"You better get a slicker." She lifted her face to feel the first drops of the coming rain. Thunder rumbled again. "You want some extra help in case the storm spooks the cattle?"

"I go wid 'im." Benjamin handed Meshach a slicker. "I got Roman cotched already."

"Be careful." When she closed her eyes she could still see the dark slash of death across McPhereson's throat.

"Indians not come dis close to de fort." Meshach settled his hat more firmly on his head.

"I wouldn't want to bet your lives on it." She handed Benjamin her gun and drew more bullets out of her pocket. "As I said, be careful."

By morning everything not under canvas in camp was soaked, with water standing in puddles and the rain still sheeting down. The thunder and lightning had passed in the darkest hours without doing more than making the herd restless.

Jesselynn had heard Meshach singing during the night. The oxen seemed as comforted by it as she was.

With morning those assigned to the herd drove them down to water and then took them farther from camp for better grazing. Daniel made sure the Thoroughbreds stayed toward the center of the herd so as to be less visible to the officers at the fort.

Jesselynn had just finished washing Thaddeus's face when she heard a shout from the western rim of the camp where Jones had been tied the night before. "Go to Jane Ellen." She gave her little brother a push in the general direction, grabbed the gun she kept nearby, and headed for the fracas.

"Come any closer an' I drill 'im." Tommy Joe Jones stood with his gun barrel tight to Wolf's back.

Jesselynn could only guess at what happened. Wolf was going to take Rufus into the fort, and the good-for-nothing brother showed up.

"Now cut 'im loose like you thought to and let 'im go."

Wolf stood like a stone carving.

"You heard me!"

Jesselynn dropped back behind one of the wagons and, leaping the wagon tongue, circled from the outside. If she could get off a shot . . .

"Don't nobody move or he's dead."

"Come on, Jones, you won't make it outa here alive if you do that." Mr. Bronson spoke in an ordinary voice as if they were discussing the price of flour. "Ain't you had enough bad luck on this trip?"

Eyes wild, Tommy Joe pushed the gun more firmly into Wolf's back. "I'm warnin' ya."

Why didn't I kill him when I had the chance? Wolf refused to flinch. The barrel bit into his back. He could feel sweat trickling down from his armpits. He caught movement out of the corner of his eye but didn't dare shift to see who was the stalker.

"Now cut my brother loose, nice and easy." The rifle dug deeper with every word.

One of the men came forward, knife at hand. Keeping one eye on the rifle, he leaned down to release the bonds.

"See, told you I waren't gonna hang for somethin' I didn't do," Rufus hissed.

Holding steady took every ounce of determination Wolf owned. He stared burn holes in the man near his feet. One jab, one kick. Could he do it?

"Now help 'im up."

Bronson took Rufus's arm as if reaching for a rattler and pulled him to his feet.

Rufus swayed, then spat in Wolf's face. "Shoot 'im, brother. Dirty Injun like him ain't fit to live."

The gun barrel wavered. Wolf dropped. A gun went off. Men hollered. Someone screamed. A body hit the ground.

God above . . . Wolf never finished the thought as he rolled and surged to his feet.

Tommy Joe lay writhing on the ground. Rufus stood with his hands in the air. Jesselynn Highwood held a gun on the two brothers.

"Shoulda shot to kill." Jesselynn glanced at Wolf to make sure he was all right.

"My leg!" Tommy Joe stared at the blood welling from his thigh.

"Be glad that's all." One of the wagon men retied Rufus's hands. "You gonna stop the bleedin'?" He looked to Jesselynn, who shook her head.

"Take 'em both into the fort." She tucked her gun in the waistband of her pants. *Thank you, God, for a clean shot.* She knew that as soon as her heart quit racing, she might be able to move. This is if her knees held steady.

The men went about their business as if she weren't even there. Wolf nodded. Was that in gratitude? Or what? She sucked in a deep breath and swallowed hard. The burning at the back of her eyes warned her to get the blazes out of there. She spun on her heel and took the long way back to her own wagons. No way was she going to let anyone see her cry.

I shot a man! I shot a man! The words kept time with the beat of her feet. *Why didn't I aim for his head?* It had happened so fast. She tried to remember each move. By the time she got back to the wagon, her hands shook so hard that she about dropped the gun. Tears blurred her vision. Her teeth clicked together no matter how hard she clamped her jaw.

"Jesselynn."

She ignored Wolf, threw her gun in the wagon bed, and kept on going, breaking into a run when she cleared the wagons. Feet pounding the dirt, she tore across the prairie, heading for the willows that lined the river. Her breath tore at her sides, but she forced herself to keep on running. Was that someone behind her? She couldn't slow to look. Tears streamed. Breathe! Run!

Blood! She could see dark blood. Could hear again the rifle shot. *I shot a man!* She fell against the trunk of a tree and wrapped her arms around the rough bark to hold her up. Darkness covered the backs of her eyelids. Light-headed, she slumped forward as her whole body started shaking.

Suddenly solid arms held her from behind. Wolf gathered her to his chest when the shaking let up.

"Go away." She let her head drop to his chest. Holding it up was beyond her.

"No."

She could hear his heartbeat, thundering much like her own. "I . . . I . . . shot a man."

"I know. Thank you." The words rumbled in his chest. His breath teased her ear.

"You . . . could have . . . been . . . killed." Each word tore the lining on her throat.

"I know. Glad you had good aim."

She rested against him. He smelled of woodsmoke and man. She dug in her pocket. No handkerchief. Sniffing, she leaned back enough to look up into his face. Blood ran down the side of his head.

"You're hurt!"

"His bullet just grazed me. Might never hear right from this ear again."

With tender fingers she reached to touch his ear. The tip of it was gone and powder burns laced the side of his head. "Head wounds bleed bad."

He stripped some willow leaves from the branches and handed them to her. She compressed them in her hand and applied them to the wound along with pressure to stop the bleeding. All the while her eyes held steady on his.

"What are you lookin' at?" His breath fluttered her eyelashes.

"You." She took in a deep breath and let it out. His dark eyes shimmered, grew warm and warmer. Her heart took up a new rhythm. Heat pooled in her belly. Even with blood trailing down his neck, he took her breath away. *Is this what poetry means when it says "the heart sings"?* "I need to bandage you up."

"Not yet." *You are proud and strong, like a Sioux maiden.* He tightened his arms around her rib cage. *"Thou art beautiful, oh, my love . . . thy hair is as a flock of goats that appear from Gilead . . . my dove, my undefiled . . ."*

"Jesse! Jesse!"

Jesselynn swallowed again. "They're calling me."

"I know." Slowly, as though she was more precious than anything he'd ever held, he loosened his arms and, inch by inch, let his hands fall away from her until they stood separate once more.

A sound came from her throat. A whimper. She must stand alone again. Alone. The pain ripped through her. If she reached for him, would he hold her?

She blinked. Swallowed. And stepped back. Her legs trembled. Her belly quivered as if a cold wind nipped it. She took another deep breath. "Come." She reached for his hand, and together they turned and stepped out of the willow screen.

———

"I'm not going on with the wagon train." Three days later Wolf stood beside her again.

"What do you mean?" Jesselynn forced the words past the constriction in her throat.

"I have to go home."

"Home is going to be in Oregon."

"Not for me. I've already spoken with the men. They've agreed to go on with the train that arrived yesterday."

"Why wasn't I included in the meeting?"

"He's a good man — Jason Cobalt. He's led other trains west and plans on stayin' there himself this time. He'll get you all through." He kept his hands from clenching. And his teeth. *Don't look at me like that! You said you wanted to go to Oregon. I'm gettin' you there.*

"Why?"

"I must go home. To my people." *Come with me.*

She stared into his eyes, looking for the man who'd held her. Dark. Flat. Not even a flicker. Swallowing her tears, she took a step back. "Go with God."

———

Two days later, with the sun near to breaking the horizon, the order came. The wagons unwound from their circles and pulled into the long snake of white canvas and straining animals. Getting over the divide and into the South Pass lay before them.

Jesselynn drove one of her wagons, Meshach the other. She'd heard of the Rocky Mountains ahead. She didn't look back. She let the tears flow. *Lord, someday, some way, I will see him again. Surely you mean for that to happen. Surely.*

Off to the north, always on the opposite ridge, Wolf rode his bay Appaloosa, the white patches catching the sunlight. He didn't turn off until he saw they'd safely crossed South Pass. *Someday, my love—someday.*

The LONG WAY HOME

DEDICATION

The Long Way Home is dedicated to
the glory of God and to the gift
He has given me in my Round Robin Circle.
These friends help keep me sane and on track.

Chapter One

Gray Wolf Torstead, long dark hair tied back with a piece of latigo, topped the hill on his blood bay Appaloosa as the sun broke the horizon. Turning to look over his shoulder, he could no longer see the smoke from the campfires of the wagon train. Looking east he knew he could make it back to the fort with some days of hard riding, gather his supplies, and head home.

Home. Would his mother's tribe's tepees feel like home, or had he lived with the white men too long? Like he'd been trailing the wagon train too long. They didn't need him. Jesselynn didn't need him. Jesselynn—a much better name than Jesse. But he'd had to make sure the new wagon master knew what he was doing. They'd camped in the right places, kept watch at night, and grazed the herd. He'd even heard the fiddle singing one evening.

He knew the scouts had seen him, but then he hadn't been trying to hide. Just making sure they were safe.

He nudged his Appaloosa into a mile-eating lope and promised himself to put Jesselynn Highwood out of his mind. Out of his heart was another matter entirely. Questions that kept time with his horse's hooves circled round again. Why had he let her go? Why had he not at least asked her to stay, to marry him?

———

"Worryin' gots you lower den a turtle belly."

Jesselynn Highwood looked over at the smiling black face of Meshach, who used to be overseer at her home in Kentucky. Now he was a freedman and her friend. "I'm not worrying. I'm thinking." She tucked her slouch hat, which looked to have been wheel fodder, between her britches-covered knees and finger combed her shaggy hair back off her forehead. The hat kept her hair out of her eyes at least, dark blond hair now barely stained by walnut dye. Masquerading as a male to keep her people safe took a lot of sacrifices, especially for a nineteen-year-old Southern woman.

I thought you gave up lying. That little voice inside woke from a nap and, smirking, tapped her on the shoulder.

Jesselynn, her elbows propped on her knees, the reins to the two span of oxen loose in her fingers, stared out over the backs of her trudging bovines. Dust from the wagons ahead of her wore her face dry and crunched between her teeth. She'd lost the juice to swallow with, and the sun hadn't come on eleven yet.

"Whoa, son." Meshach gentled Ahab, the Thoroughbred stallion that would be the foundation of their horse farm when they made it to Oregon Territory and a new start—away from the war.

Right now, after weeks on the trail, Oregon seemed farther away than ever.

Meshach kept the horse even with the left front wheel of their lead wagon. "Looks like worryin' to me."

Jesselynn kept the bite out of her voice with great effort. "I said I'm not worrying." The emphasis on the last word rang hollow even to her own ears. If this wasn't worrying, what was it? She chewed on the thoughts like a hound dog with a knucklebone.

"I don't trust Jason Cobalt." She said the words loud enough for Meshach's ears alone.

"They say he be a good man."

"I don't doubt that. I just doubt his ability to guide this wagon train through to Oregon. Last night they were talking about taking a shortcut."

"I heard."

"Wolf said that shortcut was short on water and the hills steeper." That was her real problem—Mr. Gray Wolf Torstead, better known as Wolf. She knew it down to the stitching on her boots. Why had he left the train and his job as wagon master? She thought she understood the answer to that too, thanks to a conversation with an Indian scout. Wolf had felt a call to return to the land of his mother, an Oglala Sioux who died when he was a youth. However, understanding and agreeing were two entirely different things. She wished she understood all the scout had said.

But if she dug deep enough, and she did that only in the still hours of the morning before the rising sun dimmed the starlight, she knew the *real* question.

Why? Why had he left *her*? Thanks to that one embrace they'd shared, she'd dreamed of more. More embraces, perhaps a life together. After all, she didn't take embraces lightly, not when they made her breathless. Seemed like his had. She let her head drop forward like a heavy blossom on a slender stalk. Why had he left?

Meshach was entirely too perceptive. Aunt Agatha would be on her back next. Keeping her feelings from her nosy aunt would take some doing. Pious, upright, Southern to the smallest bone, Aunt Agatha would definitely not approve of the direction her niece's thoughts were taking in regard to a half-white, half-Sioux man named Wolf. No matter how much Agatha had changed since the early days of Springfield, with these woman-man thoughts, Jesselynn was seriously transgressing.

Jesselynn forced her head upright and a smile to her lips. Wolf was a moot point anyway. He'd left the train, left her, and all she had to do was keep her sights on Oregon.

Am I not sufficient for thee?

At the gentle reminder, she shook her head. *Of course you are, Lord, but you know what I mean. I . . . I thought maybe—okay, I don't know.* The sigh came from the balls of her feet. *He's a good man, and I hope and pray he will be happy up there with his mother's people.* She glanced ahead to see that Meshach now rode beside the McPhereson wagon. Something Mrs. Mac said made him throw his head back and laugh, a hearty laugh that said more about the man than the joke. Meshach laughed a lot more on the trail than she'd ever heard him laugh at Twin Oaks. His body-shaking laugh drew in others like bees to blossoms. One would have to be carrying a huge lump of a heart to not laugh along with Meshach.

Jesselynn saw it all and tucked it away to ponder later. Is this what freedom did to a man once enslaved? He'd told her once that Christ set him free long before she did, but she knew she witnessed the change.

Do others see that joy in me? The thought made her flinch. The last three days had been particularly empty of any emotion that bore even a fleeting reminiscence of joy. "Sorry," she said aloud and shook her head as she flipped a glance heavenward. *Praise ye the Lord.* Meshach had read that in a psalm the night before. She'd heard it with only half an ear. She had a feeling God would rather she not only heard but did as He commanded.

She could hear her mother too. *"No better time to change than right now."* Oh, *Mother, such wisdom you had. What would you say to all this that's gone on?*

"Marse Jesse, you all right?" Benjamin, another of her former slaves, looked at her out of the corner of his eye, as if afraid of intruding but caring enough to want to know.

"Yes, I'm right as a June bug." Jesselynn flashed him a smile that she'd dredged up somewhere out of her middle. "You want to drive awhile?" She grinned at the rolled-eye look he gave her. She knew he'd rather ride than drive any day, just like she would.

"Yes, suh." His sigh made her smile again. "I go tell Miss Agatha." He turned his horse and rode to the wagon behind hers. Jesselynn had become Jesse instead of Jesselynn and Sir or Suh or Marse to her family to keep them all safe when they were forced to leave Twin Oaks near Midway, Kentucky. When Benjamin returned, Jesselynn whoad the oxen and leaped to the ground, her feet sending tingles up to her knees. She swung easily into the saddle and waited while Benjamin climbed up on the wagon seat and hupped the oxen forward. The wheels creaked in protest. One of the oxen bellered.

Jesselynn dropped back to the end of the wagon train and crossed to the north side. No one had reported the Indian shadowing them in the last day or so. On one hand she felt the same relief the others expressed at his supposed departure, but on the other she wished she'd known who he was and what his purpose was. When Wolf had led the wagon train, she'd not wasted time thinking on such things.

Turning Ahab, she cantered back to the herd of horses and cattle that snatched grass along the way as they trailed the train. Daniel, another of her young freedmen, and two other young men from the train kept the herd moving, watching out for danger, be it Indian or beast.

"Anyone seen the Indian that followed us?" she asked as she drew even with Daniel riding Domino, her younger stallion. The two mares along with their foals kept to the center of the herd.

"No, suh." Daniel stood in his stirrups to stretch his legs. "We ain't seen nothin', not even a coyote. This sure do be empty land."

"Getting rougher too." Jesselynn looked westward toward the undulating hills that grew ever steeper. Black clouds billowed on top of the hills like frosting piled high on a three-layer cake, the sun stenciling the rims with silver. The cooling breeze felt welcome to her dry skin, but the thought of a thunder-and-lightning storm made her squint. Heat lightning speared the blackness.

Surely Cobalt would send others back to help with the herd.

Jesselynn saw Meshach cantering back toward them, but no one else.

"Is he going to circle the wagons?"

Meshach shook his head. "He say got to make up lost time. Keep dem wagons rollin'."

Jesselynn gritted her teeth. God help them if they had a runaway. Another lightning bolt streaked the sky, this time with a thunder rumble. Several of the herd leaders raised their heads, sniffing the wind. Bellows answered restless bellows.

Oxen lowed from the wagons ahead.

Meshach dropped back to speak with one of the young men and pointed out where he should ride, then did the same for the other. With the five of them circling the herd, perhaps they had a chance.

At the first heavy crack of thunder and lightning, Wolf had always circled the wagons with the herd inside. While restless at first, the herd had settled down, ignoring the rain, with the cattle chewing their cuds.

But now the pace picked up. More bawling. A horse whinnied.

Do I go confront Cobalt or not? Ice balled in her middle. The first drops spattered her hat brim and sprinkled her hands. Cold all right. It could turn to hail real easy.

"We need to settle the herd down in a low place. You want to take on Cobalt, or should I?" She knew better than to ask. Cobalt had already made his opinion of black men obvious. But then he'd ignored her also.

"We take care de herd first," Meshach said.

Jesselynn nodded. In a stampede her foals would be the first to go down. She turned and rode up beside one of the other young men with the herd. "Swing those ropes in front of the leaders and keep them calm. Whistle, sing, whatever you can do."

"Yes, sir." The boy—she couldn't remember his name—did as told. If only some of the others in the train were as cooperative.

"Over there!" She pointed off to what looked like a basin set among the hills. "Get the herd down there and off these hills."

Lightning lit the sky with blue light. She counted until the thunder crashed. Coming nearer. She drove Ahab into the center of the herd to cut out their mares. Daniel followed suit, and without adding turmoil to the tail-twitching, bawling herd, they each lassoed a mare and eased her and her foal out of the mass of animals. They still needed the filly and Roman the mule. Their loose ox would have to take his chances.

Meshach brought the filly out and handed his rope to Daniel. "I'll get de mule."

"No!" Jesselynn had to shout to be heard, close as they were. "Save the herd."

Never had she wished for another rope as much as now. Lightning flashed again, thunder rolled and boomed with another crack right after. The lead cow broke into a trot. Jesselynn handed her lead rope to Daniel and pointed to an arroyo that cut off to the north. "Get the horses up in that arroyo and hold them there."

Knowing he would follow orders, she whistled for Patch, their cow dog, and broke into a canter, heading for the leaders of the trotting herd. "Swing them in a circle. Now!" Thunder and splattering rain drowned out her shout. She whipped her hat off and waved it at the still-milling cattle. "Hai, hayup!" Patch headed for the leaders. Ahab shook his head but obeyed her squeezing legs and edged closer to the herd. Seeing what she and Meshach were doing, the other two herders followed suit, and the herd surged over the rise and down into the depression. With Patch barking and nipping when necessary, they turned the front-runners and got them circling with the riders loping around them. Sheltered by the hills in the shallow valley, Jesselynn breathed a sigh of relief. They could catch up with the train later.

Lightning turned the darkness into day, a blue day with the smell of lightning and rain on the air. The crack near to broke her eardrums. Ahab half reared, and only Jesselynn's hands clenched on the reins and her legs clamped to his sides kept him from bolting. She fought him back to a standstill, her voice calm in spite of the terror that set her heart to racing.

"That was a strike for sure. I'm goin' to check on the wagons. Can you hold them here?"

Meshach nodded, so Jesselynn reined Ahab away from the herd and trotted him up the rise, lightning flashes illuminating her way. Ducking her head to keep the rain from blinding her, she broke into a canter now that she was beyond the distance of panicking the herd.

This time she saw it. A forked bolt of lightning cracked the heavens, blued the world, and struck the ground up toward the front of the wagon train. The sound set the earth to ringing like an earthquake rolled through. Ahab leaped forward, his shrill whistle adding to the panic in Jesselynn's heart. She clung like a burr, her "Oh, God, oh, God" the only prayer she could offer.

Fire flared from the lead wagon. Screams rent the air. Teams broke loose from the train and drove ahead in all directions, wagons rocking and bucking over the rough ground.

Ahab slowed at her fierce hold on the reins, and they pulled even with the last of the wagons. The wagon drivers near the end of the train had gotten a strong enough hold on the reins that they were already stopping.

"Pull into a circle and unyoke!"

Aunt Agatha, white faced but able, pulled her oxen to the right, Benjamin right behind her. For once being at the rear of the train proved to be a blessing. She could hear Ophelia singing and praying loud enough to scare away thunder. The sound brought a smile to Jesselynn's face. She caught up with Nate Lyons, who waved when he saw her, and his grandson, Mark, clutching the seat beside him.

"Go on back. Benjamin and Agatha are circling."

"What we shoulda done some time ago, that . . ." Lyons, whom Agatha referred to as Brushface, cut off his sentence, but Jesselynn had a pretty good idea what he was thinking. He waved her on.

She pointed another wagon back to the circle and cantered on. A long storage box smashed open on the ground forced Ahab into the air in a jump that sent Jesselynn clinging upon his neck. She pulled him to a stop, settled herself in the saddle again, and peered through the sheeting rain, waiting for another heavenly candle to light the sky.

When it did, she blinked, trying to dislodge the eerie sight. Broken wagons and suffering oxen littered the land. Slowly picking her way among split barrels, soaked bedding, and a splintered rocking chair, she searched for injured people. One wagon missing a rear wheel stood upright, its driver unyoking the oxen, one down, one holding up a foreleg.

"Are you folks hurt?" Jesselynn paused by the man.

"Only shook up. Better'n some of the others."

Jesselynn touched her hat and nudged Ahab forward. The next wagon lay on its side, hoops crushed like paper. A limping man struggled to release the braces that held a thrashing ox to its still mate. A child's cries caught her attention from a nearby heap of debris.

"I'll be right back," she told the man and nudged Ahab forward. He snorted and trembled as they approached the shattered wagon bed. "Hello, anyone here?"

The cries rose louder.

Jesselynn dismounted and, looping Ahab's reins over her arm, dug into the mess. Lifting a soggy sack of grain, then assorted clothing, she found a young child dressed in the shift of all small children. She knelt beside the screaming, arm-flailing little one, seeing the right leg twisted at an angle.

"Easy, child, easy." The child opened its eyes and choked on a scream, reaching for her with both arms and a plaintive wail.

"Ma-a-a. Want Ma." A hiccup followed.

Jesselynn ignored the rain pelting them both and took the child's hands in hers. "Easy, baby. I can't pick you up until I make sure there's nothing else broken." The child's hands in one of hers, Jesselynn used her other to explore the child's body, watching for any signs of pain at her probing. "Now, you lie still and let me do something about that leg, you hear?"

But the child clung like mistletoe, refusing to let loose of her hand.

Jesselynn looked up, hoping and praying someone else would come by and help her. "Father, what do I do? I've got to get this child out of the rain, or we'll have more problems than just a broken leg." She glanced back to see if her wagons were in shouting distance. Barely able to see them through the curtain of rain, she figured not. A man shouted for help from some distance.

Thunder rolled again but heading east. The rain continued unabated. She pulled a piece of material from under more debris, ripped it in strips and, taking a piece of a shattered wagon board, folded part of the cloth around the board, then laid it beside the child's leg. "All right, little one, this is going to hurt again." With infinite gentleness, she slipped the board under the twisted leg.

The child screamed. Jesselynn bit her lip and whimpered herself. "Please, Father, guide my hands. Make this work. If you're near my mother, sure wish you could send her here to help." All the while she murmured soothing sounds to the child and reiterated in her mind her mother's instructions on setting a broken bone. *"Pull steady on the joint on either side until the break slips back in."* "Now we got to wrap this all the way up your leg, and then I can carry you to Ophelia. She'll help make it better. I know she will." With the last knot tied, Jesselynn slid her arms under the child's body and, holding the leg steady with the other hand, rose to an upright position. Trying not to jar the leg, she covered the ground to her wagon as swiftly as possible.

"Oh, dear Lord, what have we here?" Aunt Agatha, oilcloth cape over her shoulders, reached for the burden.

"No, I'll lay her down. I didn't set the leg. We'll have to do that later." She laid the child on top of a wooden box in the rear. "I've got to check on the others." She glanced up to see six wagons now in the circle and another approaching. "You seen Cobalt?"

Agatha turned from comforting the child whose weak "Ma-a" tore at Jesselynn's heart. "No, and don't say I care if'n I ever do," Agatha retorted.

"I know, me too." Jesselynn swung back on Ahab. "If Meshach comes, send him on to help me. Oh, and get my medicine box out when you can. We're going to be needing all the supplies we can find."

She made her way from wagon to wagon, assessing the damage. When she reached what had been the lead wagon, she asked one of the men what happened.

"Struck by lightning. Hit that first hoop, and the noise scattered all the critters. Never seen such a awful mess in all my born days."

"The driver's dead?"

"Umm. And the two rear oxen." He pointed to the two carcasses. "The others burnt some but alive."

Jesselynn studied the scorched wagon, burned at the bolts, the joinings, the wheels.

"The man have a family?"

"Uh, yup. Someone come and took the missus and the little boy. They was stunned bad but sittin' in the back outa the rain kept 'em alive."

"Better cut the throats of those two dead ox. Let them bleed out so they can use the meat."

"Uh, yup. That's what I come to do. Can't waste the meat in spite of all the tragedies." The man went about his task, and Jesselynn cantered off to help wherever she could.

The downpour continued.

She'd just checked the last wagon when Meshach caught up with her. "Herd safe. Good thing Daniel brought our horses back to the herd. Gully washer come through dat arroyo not long after."

"Thank the Lord above." Jesselynn reined Ahab so they rode knee to knee to be heard over the drumming rain. "At least there will be oxen able to pull the wagons that can go on. I think at least four are totally wrecked. Not sure how many people dead, or animals. Still haven't seen that so-called wagon master."

"He's sendin' folks back to the circle. Good thing you got them wagons turnin'."

"Only about an hour late. If he'd circled them at the first thunder roll, none of this would have happened." She indicated the area with a swept arm. "The man oughta be shot."

"You can't say for certain nothin' happen."

Jesselynn sighed. "I know. Let's get on and see how we can help."

Darkness fell with two wagons unaccounted for.

Jesselynn, Ophelia, and Aunt Agatha spent the evening bandaging wounds, comforting those who'd lost family members, and wringing out their mud-heavy skirts. Jesselynn was at least spared the skirt routine, since even after the others knew she was a female in men's clothing, she had never bowed to the pressure to give up her britches. When her box ran dry of rolled bandages, she set Jane Ellen to tearing up one of their few remaining sheets.

She and Benjamin strung a tarp off the rear of one wagon, and thanks to Meshach carrying dry wood in slings under the wagon, they got a fire going to heat soup and coffee. As the wagon folk ate and warmed themselves at the fire, Jesselynn heard comments about the wagon master, none of them good.

If I'd just followed my instincts and gone after Cobalt, this whole thing might have been averted. Wolf, where are you when we need you so bad? I sure hope you're happy with your family, tribe, whatever you want to call it.

"Anyone seen Cobalt?" She kept her voice low for Agatha's ears alone.

"I heard he's searching for any lost ones. If'n he had any sense, he'd be heading for the hills."

"Where Mr. Wolf go?" Three-year-old Thaddeus Highwood wrapped an arm around his sister's leg and leaned into her warmth.

"I told you he went north to his people."

"When he comin' back?"

Jesselynn squatted down to look her little brother directly in his blue eyes. "Thaddeus, he's not coming back. I reckon we just have to get used to that." She smoothed the honey-hued curls back off his forehead. "Do you understand?"

He nodded, one forefinger making its way to his mouth. "Where Patch?" The black shepherd-type dog had adopted them after his home and family went up in flames on the road before Independence. He took his job herding Thaddeus and Sammy seriously.

"Out with the herd, he was a big help in turning those critters into a circle."

"Did he bark?"

"Yup, and bit one old ox right on the shoulder." Jesselynn stood up, taking Thaddeus with her. He hugged both arms around her neck, his legs around her waist.

"Lightnin' scared me."

"Me too." She kissed his cheek. "But you were brave so Sammy didn't cry, weren't you?"

"Uh-huh. Sammy the baby." Dark as Thaddeus was fair, Sammy came to them when they found his mother dead in the Kentucky woods.

"He was mighty brave. Like an eagle, he was." Jane Ellen patted the little boy's bottom as she passed by. "Rain's done."

Jesselynn and Thaddeus both looked up to the canvas over their heads. Sure enough, not even spatters ticked the tarp. She hugged her little brother closer, and at the same moment they turned to listen, their smiles matching.

Someone had taken out a fiddle, and the plaintive notes of "Amazing Grace" floated across the circle.

Jesselynn blinked back the tears that burned at the back of her eyes. She hummed, stopped when her throat filled, swallowed, and picked up the words. "I once was lost, but now am found. . . ."

Jane Ellen's sweet soprano joined her. "Was blind, but now I see."

"Oh, Lord, help us find those who are still lost." Jesselynn set Thaddeus down on the wagon tailgate and motioned for him to stay there. She looked upward to see one star twinkling through the ragtag drifting clouds. "I'm going for Daniel. I'll stand guard so he can go look for the other two wagons." The notes of the song sang on in her mind, even after the fiddler segued into another tune. Lost and blind, that's what they were for certain sure out here on the Oregon Trail. What she wouldn't give for the friendly lights of a town or even one house. She stopped Ahab and looked back toward the camp. Two fires glowed now and a lantern or two, and hammers already rang in repair. Meshach's blacksmithing skills would be in great demand in the morning.

Coyotes yipped a hill or so away, sounding like they were behind the nearest rock. Most likely they smelled the blood of the dead and injured. "Oh, Lord, please send us a legion of angels to guard the camp tonight. We don't need an animal or Indian attack now."

Chapter Two

FORT LARAMIE, WYOMING TERRITORY

The storm broke as Wolf rode into Fort Laramie. Before he could dismount and tie his horse, he was soaked as if he'd stood under a waterfall, so he led his horse up the two steps to the porch with him. Lightning turned the evening into day in flashes close enough together to make a lamp unnecessary. The blue white light carried its own peculiar fragrance, and the ground failed to suck in the moisture quickly enough to keep from puddling.

Once under the overhang of the general store, he glanced back to the west. While he could see no farther than the water curtaining off the roof, in his mind he knew the wagons were circled in a hollow and the herd safely bedding down in the middle. Jason Cobalt surely had enough trail sense to do that, didn't he? *Of course he did*, Wolf answered his own silent question.

"Come on in out of the downpour," a man called to him from the door of the mess hall.

"Thanks, but I got to take care of my horse first."

"Down to the livery. Red'll put yer horse up, you too, if'n ye don't mind a hay pile for your bed. Then come on back. We got hot coffee in here that'll drive the damp out."

"Any food?"

"That too. Say, ain't you that wagon master called Wolf? Thought you was takin' a train west."

"I was. Long story." Wolf clucked his horse back down the wooden stairs, mounted, and trotted to the half-rock, half-wood hulk of a barn, recognized as such by the wide rolling door across the front. Wolf dismounted, slid the door open wide enough for his horse to follow him through, and stopped to drip. The roar sounded like the rain was intent on washing the shingles clear to Kansas City.

"Anybody here?" He shouted to be heard over the onslaught. When no one answered, he flipped the reins around a post and waited for the lightning to give him an idea where a door might be, other than the one he came in by. "Halloo."

Still no answer. He listened in the interval between thunder rolls. He could hear a horse chewing off to his right and a snort to the left. Figuring on stalls on both sides, he waited and, at the lightning flicker, saw an empty box ahead and to the right. Untying his horse, he led him to the place. One didn't need light to complete such a familiar task. Stalls were much the same everywhere. Hanging his saddle over the half wall between him and the main door, he tied a latigo around his horse's neck and to the manger, already filled with hay. He felt for the water bucket in the corner. It too was full.

"That Red runs a good barn. Now if we just knew where the grain bin lay." The horse nudged his elbow and nosed around him to drag out a mouthful of hay. The familiar sound of horses chewing gave the barn a cozy feeling. If his stomach hadn't rumbled about as loud as the last clap of thunder, he might have rolled up in his bedroll and slept out the remainder of the night.

Instead, he opened the door again, just enough to slip through, and headed for the mess hall, lights from the windows a friendly beacon. He pushed open the door and paused just inside. Two tables of poker, cigar smoke writhing above the players, appealed to him about as much as stepping back outside in the downpour, so he headed down the center aisle to trestle tables toward the back. Two men were writing letters, one reading in the lamplight.

"Grub's still hot." A sergeant motioned over his shoulder to the counter.

"Thanks." Wolf nodded as he spoke.

"You Gray Wolf Torstead?"

"Yes."

"Umm. Captain stopped by, said he wanted to see you first thing." When Wolf paused, the man continued. "You can eat first. They be closing up in here soon."

Wolf took the plate of stew and biscuits offered him and made his way to the end of the table, against the wall where he could see around the entire room. Not that there was much worth seeing.

"You want coffee?" The sergeant held up a steaming pot and two mugs.

Wolf nodded. The man plunked the cups down and filled them to the brim. Setting the gray coffeepot in the center of the table, he stepped over the bench and sat down.

With grizzled hair and a face that had seen more than man wanted or needed, the man sipped his coffee and let Wolf eat. When he'd scraped up the last of the juice with his remaining biscuit, the sergeant leaned forward on his elbows.

"What made you let the train go on with Cobalt?"

Wolf looked up to see the man studying him. "Why you asking?"

"Got me curious, that's all. I've heard nothing but good on you as a wagon master. . . ."

Wolf waited. If the man continued, fine. If not, he'd head for the captain's quarters.

"Not that I need to be nosy or nothin'."

Picking up his coffee mug, Wolf drank and set the mug down. "Anything I should know before I go talk with the captain?"

The sergeant shrugged. "Guess not. You know those Jones brothers?"

Wolf paused in the act of standing up. "Yes." Been some time since he was so close to killing a man as he had that Tommy Joe Jones.

"They took off outa here sometime after your train left. Said they was gonna catch up, like maybe the new wagon master would let them travel with him."

"I thought one of them was in the guardhouse."

"He was. Captain said to let 'im go on the condition they don't show their ugly faces around this fort again."

The words Wolf thought in regard to the Jones brothers went far beyond the biblical admonition to let your yes be yes and no be no. His father had added, "*No sense embroidering on what's right.*" Or wrong, as could be in this case. "I see." He almost asked if the sergeant knew what the captain wanted but stopped himself. No sense appearing concerned. After all, the army no longer held any control over him. Nor did the wagon train. Cobalt knew about the

Jones brothers, and if he didn't, the men of the wagon train did. They'd keep a close eye on those scums.

"Thanks for the food—and the information." He had no idea what he'd do with that information, but he now knew what a horse felt like with a burr under the saddle. The burr was named Jesselynn Highwood, and in spite of all his efforts, she clung closer than his skin. What a fool he'd been to let her go.

He dropped his dishes off at the window and exited to the captain's office. He didn't need to ask directions, although what the captain was doing in his office instead of being home with his family only brought up more questions. Was there more going on here than it had seemed when he had brought the wagon train through?

The orderly passed him on through, and Wolf shook hands with the blue-coated officer behind the desk. Obediah Jensen had a reputation as a spit-and-polish man, and his appearance this late in the day bore that up. He also had a reputation as a fair man who believed keeping the peace between Indian and white was his primary job. And supplying wagon trains, so they kept moving on through Indian territory, was only part of that.

"Have a seat," Captain Jensen said, indicating the chair with a sweep of his hand. "Thought you were going on home—to Red Cloud's tribe, wasn't it?"

"I was and am."

The captain reached for the humidor that reigned on a corner of his desk and held it out to Wolf. Then, at Wolf's gesture of refusal, he extracted a cigar, bit the tip off, and lighted it. After two puffs he leaned back and blew the smoke at the ceiling. "How long since you been up there?"

"Too long."

"Kept in touch?"

Wolf gave him a level stare. The captain knew the Oglala did not read or write. Those were two things Wolf hoped to change.

"I see." Captain Jensen appeared to be in deep thought.

Wolf sat as still as if he were hunting, his quarry in sight but too far for an arrow to hit. He never had cared for cigar smoke. Nor the chewing of tobacco. Nor the white man's firewater. His rifle, however, was another matter.

The captain leaned forward, forearms on the desk. "I have a proposition for you."

Wolf quirked an eyebrow.

"I need to know what Red Cloud's band is planning."

So do I, if I am going to help keep them alive.

"They have got to quit attacking wagon trains — not that it's been his band raiding the trains, but the Sioux in general."

"Red Cloud can't speak for all the Sioux."

"I know that, but he is gaining in leadership. I hoped you could be an influence on him."

"And come running to you if he chooses to wage war on the whites?"

"I wouldn't put it quite thataway."

Again the raised eyebrow. "The tribes have been warring on each other since time began."

"I know, and I have no trouble with that. Just leave the white men alone."

"But when white men settle on tribal lands —"

"Or kill off the buffalo — I know all the arguments, Torstead." The captain tapped off his ash in the pewter tray on the side of the desk. "Let me reiterate. I want to keep everyone alive. If the Indians steal horses or oxen from the wagon trains, the settlers won't get through to Oregon. They might choose to stay here instead. Can you understand me?"

The look Wolf sent him said he understood all too well and didn't much care for the tone the captain was taking.

"Well, you think on it. In the meantime, I wondered if you would take a couple of men out hunting. Our meat supply is running out, and I know you can locate elk far more swiftly than my men ever could. A couple days shouldn't make a big difference in your journey north."

When he could see Wolf was about to decline, he added, "I'll pay you in blankets, grain, whatever you want from the stores. Anything but rifles and whiskey."

"Done." Wolf extended his hand as he rose. "We leave at first light. Tell your men to bring packhorses."

But when he rolled up in his bedroll in the livery, visions of Jesselynn Highwood kept Wolf awake. Maybe after he got things going in the direction he knew was necessary for his tribe, he would make a trip to Oregon. And maybe the mountains would fall flat.

Chapter Three

Louisa Highwood heard them crying in her sleep.

"Dear, dear, Louisa, what is it?" Aunt Sylvania, mobcap askew, leaned over Louisa's bed. She laid a gentle hand along Louisa's cheek and patted softly.

"Wh . . . what's wrong?" Louisa shook her head and half sat up. She stared around the room into the corners that missed the light from the candle Sylvania held. Louisa flopped back on her pillows. "There's no one here. Oh, thank God." She turned to look at her aunt. "They wouldn't stop crying, the groaning . . . ah, there was nothing I could do." She rolled her head from side to side. "They're dying, Aunt. All the men are dying."

"There now. You've been having bad dreams is all. Go on back to sleep. You are doing all you can."

A groan floated up the stairs from one of the soldiers recuperating from war wounds, who were now sleeping on pallets in Sylvania's dining room and parlor. Many houses in the city of Richmond and across the South were being used for nursing homes for the soldiers, overflow from the heinously overcrowded hospitals.

Louisa started to throw back her sheet, but Sylvania laid a hand on hers. "Reuben will take care of them. You sleep."

Louisa knew Reuben was as exhausted as she, but that thought would not enter Sylvania's head. Kind as she was to her people, and though they were no longer slaves, she expected them to do all the heavy labor and the cooking and washing, just because that was the way it had always been. The blacks took care of the whites, and the whites provided homes and necessities for their people.

"Thank you, Aunt, I will. I'm sorry to have disturbed you." Tired didn't begin to describe how Louisa felt. And it wasn't just muscle tired. Weariness of body and mind had crept into her soul, and no matter how diligently she read her Bible, soul weariness took more than a night's sleep to restore. During the day she covered her inner turmoil with a smile and a sprightly step, but at night, when she was asleep, they would come to her. Her boys, her friends, her fiancé—all gone on to their heavenly home.

She'd begun to think that if the war kept on much longer, there would be no one left to bar the doors against the conquering bluebellies. "Oh, Lord, how long?" Her whisper seemed trapped within the mosquito netting, unable to ascend to the throne above.

While the Union troops had yet to enter Richmond, the capital of the Confederacy bore her battle scars from the repelled attack proudly. As Louisa well knew, pride was never lacking in the South. But the war that they'd thought to win in weeks had been raging for months and into years. Perhaps Christ would come again before it was over.

"Anytime, Lord, anytime." Her mother and father would be waiting to welcome her and the rest of them home. Home, where there'd be no sorrow, no tears, and no more war. Instead of going back to sleep, Louisa rose and crossed to the white-curtained window. The elm trees in the front yard whispered to one another, a nightingale warbled, the crickets sawed. A dog barked somewhere down the street. Night sounds, emissaries of comfort and peace. At least they no longer heard the rattle of rifles and the terrible cannonading of the heavy artillery.

The breeze cooled her skin. She laid her cheek on her hands crossed on the windowsill and fell immediately back to sleep until she slipped sideways and jolted awake. Crawling back in bed, she hugged her pillow. "And, Lord, please take care of Jesselynn and all the others."

Perhaps Gilbert will come today. Always her first thought on waking was of her first suitor and almost fiancé. She turned her face into the pillow. Gilbert Lessling would never come. He'd perished in a train wreck. *Lord God, you said you would gird me up with the strength of your right hand. Jesus, Savior, I need that strength—to even get out of bed.*

Staring in the mirror a few minutes later, she shook her head. Zachary, her brother, would take one look at the smudges beneath her eyes and send her up for a nap. In spite of losing a foot, a hand, and an eye in battle, he figured she shouldn't be working so hard. "Ha." She combed her hair back from her face and let the curls hang down her back. Two ivory combs held the masses back and out of her way. She should be wearing her hair bound in a snood, but the men appreciated her looking young like their little sisters back home.

She pinched some color into her cheeks, dusted powder under her eyes, and brushed any loose hairs off the shoulders of her day gown, which was so badly faded one could hardly see the tiny yellow and white daisies that graced a sky-blue background. Tying her apron, she realized the bow was bigger because her waist no longer needed a corset, even if there were such to be had. She'd used all the bone stays for wrist and finger and arm supports for her boys.

Louisa did not consider a lack of corsets a terrible deprivation of war, even though her baby sister, now nearly eight months pregnant, could hardly wait to be laced up again. But then Carrie Mae always did put fashion ahead of fact, even when they were girls growing up at Twin Oaks.

Ordering herself to let the past be just that, the past, she pasted a smile on her face and tripped gaily down the stairs. "Good morning, brother dear." She peeked into his study to find him already at his desk working on improving his handwriting, since he'd been forced to learn to write with his left hand. His right lay buried somewhere on a battlefield along with myriad amputated limbs.

Zachary, dark hair falling over his broad brow, nodded and continued to dip the quill in the ink and form legible letters.

"Can I get you anything?"

"Coffee?"

"I wish. Roasted oats with chicory will have to do."

"Just so it is hot." The frown pulled at the scar on the right side of his face, a scar that ended under the black patch he wore to cover the eyeless socket.

She almost crossed to rub his shoulders but knew that he would grumble until he got his coffee. "Did you sleep well?" *Why are you dallying here? Get going before he growls at you for something else.*

"Need you ask?"

"I'll get your coffee. Breakfast should be ready soon."

After they'd fed the five guests, those who could feed themselves helping those who couldn't, Louisa cleared the table and then set out the wool pieces that were slowly forming into a uniform coat. Those with two good hands learned to sew and knit. Those who had legs and at least one hand worked in the garden. She'd learned that the men recovered much faster if they could be busy and felt like they were doing something useful. The army always needed uniforms and wool stockings. The household always needed food.

Aunt Sylvania alternately read from either the Bible or Shakespeare and corrected their sewing before they would have to rip out their painful stitches.

Louisa took up a basket and escaped out the back door to the garden. While picking feverfew and other herbs to hang to dry, she encouraged her two garden helpers.

"Ned, if you will cut the potatoes so that each piece has an eye, we can replant that section over there." She pointed to the bare spot they'd dug the day before.

"Yes, Miss Louisa, be glad to."

"You want I should clean out the chicken house and turn it into the compost pile?" Due to a throat injury, her other young man sounded more like a rasping file than a man, but he made himself understood.

"Yes, that would be wonderful. Take the eggs in to Abby, if you please. Perhaps she'll make us lemon cookies for afternoon tea."

He nodded. "That be good." As he turned to go, Louisa felt a clenching around her heart. He'd be sent back to his unit, or some other, any day now. No matter that his wound had been near mortal, he was well enough to carry a rifle again and willing to do his duty.

Duty. How she was coming to hate that word.

About midmorning she heard a carriage stop in front of the house. Dusting off her hands, she smoothed her apron, just in case it was someone for her. She glanced down. She needed a clean apron.

"Is Louisa here?" Carrie Mae's voice tinkled through the open doors.

"I most surely am," Louisa called back. "Come out here and sit in the shade." She met her sister at the door. "How ever did you get away in your condition?" she murmured in her ear while giving her a loving hug. "Mama would take a switch to you for being out in public like that."

"I'm not in public. I'm here visiting my sister who never takes time to come to me so that I don't have to go out." Carrie Mae lowered herself carefully onto the lounge. "It will take three men and a pulley to get me up again, but ah . . ." She slumped into the comfort of the cushions. The shade from the ancient magnolia tree dappled her face as she removed her wide-brimmed straw hat. The strip of pink gauze bound round its crown hung over the edge of the settee.

"Is that new?" Louisa's voice squeaked on the final word.

"Yes, Jefferson insisted that I needed something new to perk me up." She fanned her face with the hat. "He heard that doldrums aren't good for the baby."

"And you have been in the doldrums?" Louisa eyed her sister's ankles, or rather where her ankles should have been.

"This heat. Our house is still not ready, and the flat gets no breeze at all." She pulled her dimity dress away from her bosom. "Do you have any lemonade?"

Louisa patted her sister's shoulder. "I'll be right back. I'll bring some cold cloths too." While on one hand she could tell Carrie Mae was indeed in distress, on the other, her lack of concern for the suffering soldiers went so far against their mother's teachings that Louisa wanted to shake her younger sister. She'd married an attorney, Jefferson Steadly, who'd lost an arm in the war, so one could not say he had not done his part. He was now an assistant to one of the local senators, and he and his young wife had become members of the congress with all the society obligations his position entailed. Balls, soirées, dinners, and teas kept Carrie Mae busy until lately, when one in her condition stayed home to knit booties or some such thing.

Carrie Mae never had been one for knitting. She painted lovely watercolors, played both piano and harp with wonderful skill, entertained ranking officers and politicians, and believed she was doing her best for the war.

Once in the kitchen, Louisa set the glasses on the tray with a bit more force than necessary, causing Abby, Aunt Sylvania's maid, to raise an eyebrow. "Have we any cookies left?"

"I'se got dem right here." Abby set a plate of molasses drops on the tray.

"The boys need them worse than we do." Louisa huffed one more time and lifted the tray. "Oh! Could you please bring a basin of cold water and a couple of cloths? Carrie Mae's ankles don't look good to me. But then what do I know about having babies?" *And at the rate I'm going, I might never get the opportunity to find out.*

Louisa used her hip to push open the screen door and set the tray down on a low table by the lounge. Carrie Mae lay fast asleep, her eyelashes feathered over purple shadows under her eyes. Perspiration gathered on her upper lip, and her body seemed dwarfed by the huge mound under her thin dress.

"Look like she have two in dere." Abby knelt beside the young woman and, wringing out the cloths, applied one to each swollen ankle.

Louisa brought out a collar to sew on while her sister slept. *Oh, Mother, if only I had listened more when you were trying to train us to be good wives and mothers and to care for all the people at Twin Oaks. I was so young, so terribly young.*

When Zachary came out some time later, he took a chair next to his youngest sister and picked up a fan, waving it gently. "She looks tired." His whisper made Louisa nod. "You think the baby is all right?" Another nod.

"Are you two talking about me?" Carrie Mae stretched and smiled up at her brother. "Doze off for a minute, and you get all worried."

"A minute?" Louisa smiled and shook her head. "You've been asleep for nigh unto two hours. I reckon you needed a good nap."

"It's the shade and the breeze and . . ." Carrie Mae inhaled deep. "And honeysuckle. I declare, that smells so fine." She reached for one of the glasses of lemonade and took a sip. "And this tastes even better." Her smile never quite reached her eyes. "I wish Mama were here."

Louisa gathered her close, knowing that tears were pooling in her own eyes just as they were in Carrie Mae's. "Me too, darlin', me too." She knelt by the lounger, holding her sister while she cried, and let her own tears flow unchecked.

Zachary cleared his throat when the shower started to abate. "I take it this is usual behavior for a young woman in her . . . in her . . ." He waved in the general direction of the mound.

"Oh, for mercy's sake, say the word, pregnant. As if having a baby was an embarrassment instead of a joy."

"Yes, well, I have some more correspondence to answer, so I shall leave you two to discuss female things." He beat such a hasty retreat for a man with one leg that both his sisters suffered an attack of the giggles in spite of their tears.

After Carrie Mae left, promising to send the carriage round the next day for Louisa to come visit her, Louisa ambled into Zachary's study, bedroom, meeting room, whatever he needed it to be. Ned, who shared the room at night, had gone next door to help Widow Penrod with her garden. The new men at her house were too ill to help out yet.

"Close the door, please."

Louisa did so and took the chair he nodded to. "Something has happened." Her words were more a statement than question.

"Yes, I have located enough funds for us to make another trip north. The Quaker folks who brought me home last time are willing to assist us again. Are you sure you want to go through the lines again?"

"Quinine or morphine?"

"Quinine. The malaria is killing our men fast as the Union bullets."

Chapter Four

WEST OF FORT LARAMIE
JULY 2, 1863

"You shouldn't be out here!"

"Mr. Lyons, since my animals are part of this herd, I have as much responsibility as anyone else to ride night watch."

Nate rode up beside her. "I know that, but this ain't no place for a lady."

At least the conversation made staying awake easier. Jesselynn knew she'd never live it down if she fell off her horse for sleeping. She was so far beyond tired that her hands felt numb.

"Come on, Mr. Lyons, you know about how long it's been since I got to think and act like a lady, let alone look like one. Besides, you're not relieving me but rather that young lad over there. Did you bring a rifle?"

"Yup." He slapped the gunstock on his right side. "Why? You see anythin' suspicious?'

"No, just a feeling." She whistled for Patch and started to ride on around the herd, then stopped. "Any sign of Cobalt yet?"

"Not that I know of."

Jesselynn shook her head and continued to circle the grazing herd. While the animals would normally have bedded down by now, the storm and ensuing panic had prevented them from filling their bellies. The coyotes yipped again, their wild music bringing the hair on the back of her neck to attention.

The hoofbeats of the young man heading back to camp told where he was. A dog barked from the circled wagons. Patch growled low in his throat.

"What is it, boy?" Jesselynn kept her voice to a whisper and her ears on full alert. Crickets sang, slowed to a hush, and then picked up their notes. The only part of Patch she could see was the one white cocked ear. Otherwise, his dark fur blended into the shadows. A cloud hovered over the half-moon, a reminder of the now passed storm.

She should have taken Meshach's advice and gotten some sleep before riding the herd. Doctoring the wounded and comforting the grieving took a toll on a body, but at the time she'd been too keyed up to even think about sleeping. She'd thought of moving the herd in sight of the circled wagons, but the cattle needed rest as bad as the people.

Patch growled again and, with a yip, took off around the edge of the herd. Jesselynn wheeled Chess, the gelding they'd saved from death by bullet wounds, and followed the dog. She yanked her rifle from the scabbard as Chess leveled out. Cocking the hammer with her thumb, she heard a yip and a snarl. She eased back on the reins, Chess slid to a halt, and she raised the rifle butt to her shoulder. More yips and snarls, and then Patch's barking.

"Coyotes." She nudged her horse back to a trot and followed her ears. The moon released its hold on the cloud in time for her to see three coyotes feinting and attacking the snarling dog. She took aim, fired, and levered another bullet into the chamber before firing again. A yelp, retreating yips, and Patch streaked after the two departing coyotes, one lying dead.

"Some shot." Nate Lyons rode up to stop beside Jesselynn. "How'd you see 'im good enough to hit?"

"Pure luck or heavenly intervention. I go for the latter." She whistled, and Patch came panting back to sit beside the horse, tongue lolling and tail wagging.

"Good dog." She dismounted and stooped to scuff his ears. Her nose took a licking, and Patch put his front feet on her knees. "Yeah, real good dog." She thumped him on the rib cage and swung back aboard her mount. Waving her arm, she sent the dog back to circling the herd.

"He's better'n two riders." Nate turned off in the other direction. "Think he can spot Indians like that?"

"I sure do hope he never has to." But the hair settled to where it belonged on the back of her neck, and the breeze kicked up signaling the coming day. Another rider came from the camp to tell her the camp news and take her place. She filled him in on what happened with the coyotes and headed back to her wagon—and bed.

At least the final wagon had been found, and Cobalt returned with it to camp.

————

Everyone spent the next day repairing what could be salvaged from the destruction. Meshach's forge ran from before sunrise to long after sunset. The dead oxen and one mule were hung and cut up, having been bled and gutted the night before. Tents of drying strips of beef hung over the fires, fueled by a couple of dead trees dragged down from the hills. The older children were set to keeping the fires smoldering to smoke the meat while it dried. The younger ones, under the supervision of Jane Ellen, were instructed to find dried cow or buffalo chips to supplement the wood supply.

Jesselynn awoke to the sound of two men arguing at the top of their lungs.

"I say that's my barrel and I kin prove it."

"Huh, got mine in the same store, same brand burned in the bottom."

"Why, you no good, sniveling dog's belly, if'n I din't know better, I'd—" The mushy thud of fist on face kept her apprised of their continued actions.

"Gentlemen, gentlemen." Cobalt was breaking up the fight.

Jesselynn lay in her bedroll, not even bothering to look out from under the wagon bed. At least the wagon master could break up fights. Of course if he'd done his wagon mastering right, there might not have been call for an argument.

"Soon as y'all can manage, I'd like to have a meetin' over by my wagon."

She knew he was speaking to the men, but the women would be there too. They had just as great, or greater, a stake in the trip ahead. Men decided to go. Women had to make the trip happen. But then, wasn't that the way of the world? She thought to the verses Meshach had read a few days before. God told Abraham to gather up his family and flocks and head out across the desert, but Jesselynn knew who did the gathering and the packing and the saying good-bye—Sarah. And Abraham couldn't even tell her where they were going or why, other than that the Lord told him to do so. Things didn't seem to have changed much in the years since then.

Some days Jesselynn felt sure the Lord was leading them to Oregon, and other days she wondered. Like today. She hauled herself out of the quilt, slammed her feet into her boots, and wished for a pitcher, nay a tub of hot water, to wash the dust from every inch of her body and clothing. Back home at Twin Oaks there had been lazy mornings to bathe and dress, but not for her since her mother died and even less since the war began.

She'd planned on spending some time with her journal and catching up on the bookwork, but now she'd have to be at that meeting, whether Cobalt wanted her there or not.

"Thanks." She accepted the mug of hot coffee Ophelia offered her and retrieved a strip of smoked meat from the drying rack. Steam rising from the bubbling kettle told her they'd have stew for dinner, same as everyone else. She gnawed on the stringy meat as she surveyed the bustling camp. Those that weren't repairing wagons and harnesses used the unexpected break to wash clothes. Nate Lyons had a group of children gathered at his feet as he explained the times tables. Ever since he took over the schooling of the young'uns, he'd not lacked for dinner and supper invitations.

She tossed the dregs in her cup into the coals and dipped a cup of cold water out of the barrel tied to the side of the wagon. They'd poured water from the Platte River through several layers of cheesecloth to strain out the bugs that coated the surface of the water. Most likely the river was higher, too, after that rainstorm. She studied the hooped canvas above the barrel. At home they'd run downspouts from the roof right into barrels to collect the soft rainwater for using in the house and especially for washing hair. Nothing felt better than long hair washed with soft rainwater. Her head itched for just such a treatment. The walnut dye she'd used as a disguise when she donned her men's britches had mostly worn off, and her hair had grown out nearly long enough to tie back with a thong. Soon she would be able to braid it. Soon she would look like a woman again.

Shame that Wolf wouldn't be there to see the transformation. The thought brought her up short, her teeth still implanted in the stringy slice of half-dried meat. Here, she hadn't been out of bed an hour yet, and she'd already thought about him. She sighed, and fetching her hat from under her bedroll, she clapped it on her head and tucked her deerskin-covered quilt into its customary place in the wagon. Like her mother always said, "*A place for everything, and everything in its place.*"

But her place had been a plantation named Twin Oaks. The memory of the big white-pillared house caught at her chest and burned behind her eyes. No way could she think of Twin Oaks being burned to the ground. It lived on in her memory, the fine white house shaded by ancient magnolia trees, a veranda for rocking chairs and neighborly chats, green rolling fields of grass, grain, and tobacco, and barns, wonderful old barns with box stalls for the Thoroughbreds raised there.

Jesselynn swallowed a sob and turned at the sound of Cobalt's voice calling them to the meeting. With a snort, she headed across the circle. Didn't take a college professor to figure what he was going to say. If he'd thought making time so important that he'd not circled the wagons, he'd surely be pushing for the shortcut now. The man just didn't understand that rushing and shortcuts most always took longer in the long run.

She let the others draw in closer, fairly certain that she'd be arguing with Cobalt before too much discussion commenced. Within moments Nate Lyons flanked her on one side, Mrs. McPhereson on the other. She could sense Meshach right behind her.

"I called you good folks here to say publicly how sorry I am we got caught in the rainstorm like that." Cobalt stood on a block of wood so he could be seen and heard by all.

Jesselynn waited for him to admit his mistake, but as he picked up his pace, she realized she'd wait until the hot place froze over. One more mark against Cobalt. He wasn't man enough to take the blame for three deaths, scores of injuries, and the destruction of wagons and goods.

Nate hawked and spat off to the side. Jesselynn knew it for the statement it was. If she were a man, she'd do the same.

"Easy now."

The whisper from behind her said she was doing something that gave Meshach a chance to read her mind. She dropped her hunched shoulders and sucked in a straightening breath. *God, help us, please, to do what's best.* Only through force of will did she keep her mouth shut and listen.

"I'm hoping we can be on the trail again by tomorrow. . . ."

Several groans met that statement, and many were shaking their heads.

"Or the next day at the latest. I know some of you disagree with me, but I think we have no choice but to take the shortcut. We can cut days off our travel time and—"

"What about water?" Jesselynn kept her voice deep in the hope he'd think someone else was talking.

"Far as I have heard, there is water shortage only in dry seasons. We all know this ain't been much for dry."

Someone snickered. Someone muttered. Another spoke up. "And the hills are steeper, the trail rougher."

"Now that's all a matter of opinion. I hear tell that there's been Indian trouble on the regular route."

Had there been? If so, how come none of the rest of them had heard that news?

"What you hear about savages?" This came from across the crowd.

"That they attacked one train. Got it from one of the soldiers at the fort."

More rumblings and mutterings, people talking with those around them.

"Now, y'all know that if you don't like what I propose, you can head on back to Fort Laramie and wait for another train, if another one comes along, that is."

"Or we could go it on our own."

Jesselynn strained on her tiptoes to see who was talking.

"True, but I been there and back two, three times. You got to admit experience counts for something."

"If he's so experienced, why didn't he circle the wagons and prevent the stampede?" Jesselynn spoke loud enough only for her friends around her to hear, but a couple in front of them turned to see who had spoken. A man, clad in a black leather vest over a once white shirt, nodded. The sling holding his right arm gave mute testimony to the tragedy of the night before.

"Any news about Indians on the route you want to take?"

"Not that I know of."

"The land's so rough even the Indians don't want it," Jesselynn muttered under her breath. She'd heard someone talking at the fort about how hot the area could get in July and August. Hot weather, no water, steep hills—didn't add up to her.

"So let's have a show of hands. How many of you are with me on takin' the shorter route?"

Hands raised slowly, as if unsure of the decision, but it looked like about everyone signed on.

"And those wantin' to go the usual route?"

Jesselynn shot her hand in the air, followed by those around her. The couple in front raised theirs too.

"Well, since we live in a democratic country where majority rules, guess we'll be takin' the shortcut, the safe route." The look he shot her made Jesselynn clench her fists. Had she been a man, he'd have taken her comments more seriously, she was sure of it. By the mutterings and stirrings she heard, she wondered if the answer would have been the same had the women been allowed a voice. Not that they couldn't yet put some pressure on their husbands.

"I'll be around to check on the repairs tonight. If we can leave in the mornin', so much the better. 'Bout sundown we'll have a buryin' service if'n y'all want to come. I asked Mr. Lyons if he would read a few words over the graves."

With that, the meeting broke up, and everyone went back to their chores. Meshach pumped the bellows to heat up the forge again and the sound of his hammer on the anvil rang through the camp.

Jesselynn headed back to their camp and found the mother of the girl with the broken leg, with a knot on her forehead the size of a pullet's first egg, waiting at the Highwood wagon. "Kin you come look on my little girl again? She be awful hot to the touch."

"Of course. Do you have some willow bark to make tea? That will help her fever come down."

The woman shook her head and blinked in obvious pain.

"Perhaps the tea will help you too." Jesselynn dug in her medicine box for the packet of dried willow bark.

"If'n you say so."

"How is your husband doing?" As she asked her questions, Jesselynn dug through her box for more supplies, but too many of the packets were empty. If only she could have Lucinda search the woods near Twin Oaks and send the medicinal herbs on to her. Fort Bridger was the next fort she could remember, and that was some distance away. Of course she had no way to mail a letter home either, so she might as well not waste her time thinking about it. Surely, many of the same things grew out here, if she only knew where to look.

She turned to look at the woman, only to find her weaving, her eyes rolling back in her head. Jesselynn caught her just as she collapsed. "Ophelia, Aunt Agatha, come help."

Together they spread a tarp and laid the woman on it.

"What do you think it might be?" Agatha straightened and scratched the end of her chin.

"That clunk on the head." Jesselynn indicated the swelling. "She needs to be lying down herself, not running around the camp. She's the mother of that little girl with the broken leg."

"*Tsk, tsk,* more's the pity. That baby gets the croup or some such from all that cold rain, and there won't be nothin' anyone can do for her."

"Thank you, Aunt Agatha." Jesselynn shook her head. Agatha did have a morbid streak in her, but this time she could be so right. "Come along, please. Let's bring the child back here where we can watch them both." As they made their way past two wagons, one where Meshach was just resetting a wheel he'd fixed, Jesselynn thought longingly of Ahab, grazing so free. She'd been thinking of going for a ride to help sort out her thoughts on whether they should go with the train or continue on the original route. Or should they return to Fort Laramie?

Every time she thought to get away, someone else came asking for help. By evening she gave it up. As the camp settled in for the night after the burying, Jason Cobalt made his rounds.

"We'll be pulling out first light," he said when he got to their fire.

"How many you leaving behind?" Jesselynn looked up from writing in her journal.

"Depends on who don't want to go." He rocked back on his heels. "You made up your mind?"

Jesselynn shook her head. "I just wish you'd take the regular route, the route most traveled by those who've gone before."

"I know that, but in good conscience, I got to get these people over *all* the mountains before snow flies." He nodded toward Meshach. "Sure hate to lose a good blacksmith like that if you go the other way."

"What about the Boltons?" Jesselynn now knew the name of the woman and child she'd spent the afternoon caring for.

"He says they'll be ready."

Jesselynn didn't even try to stop the snort that put paid to his comment. "You could give these people one more day of rest." She held up a hand when he started to answer. "I know, you got to get over the mountains."

Pushing against the unrest that weighed on her, she got to her feet with a sigh. "You know, I think we'll go the other way. Anyone wants to go with us, they'll be welcome." She pushed a coal back in the fire with the toe of her boot. "And you know what else? I sure do hope you learned your lesson about circling the wagons at the first roll of thunder. Might save a number of lives that way."

At his first move toward her, Meshach insinuated himself between them. "Time to be movin' on, suh." His voice, though gentle, held a flicker of steel.

"You think you know so much, I wouldn't let you come with my train if'n you paid double." His growl and scowl narrowed her eyes and drew her hand to the knife at her side.

"Good night, *Mr.* Cobalt. Go with God."

He glared again, spun on his heel, and strode away. Jesselynn wondered if he could feel the daggers she was sending him.

"You think I made the right choice?" She glanced up at Meshach.

"Yes, suh, I do."

"I sure hope so. Dear God, I hope so." *But what if I didn't?* The thought kept her staring at the stars, seeking an answer that never came.

Chapter Five

"I'm goin' back for Wolf," Jesselynn announced two days later.

"How will you ever find him?" Aunt Agatha stared at her niece with a look of utter confusion.

"Perhaps he stayed on at Fort Laramie. I know he needed to purchase supplies for his family."

"Maybe we should all go back with you. It safer'n stayin' here." Mrs. McPhereson stared around at the ridgetops, as if expecting Indians to ride down on them from all sides.

Jesselynn ignored Mrs. Mac's comment, looking instead to Meshach, who made no comment.

"But what if he ain't there?" Aunt Agatha said.

That was the hole in her bucket all right. What if Wolf had indeed gone north to only God knew where? Jesselynn looked around at her troop that had seemed adequate until the other wagons pulled out. Could they make it to Oregon with only five wagons? Surely there was safety in numbers, but this is what they had. Could they make it without a guide?

It would be hard to miss the trail.

"We could always wait for another train to come along. Could wait right here in fact." Aunt Agatha stirred the coals and moved the coffeepot back over the heat. "I can always think better over a cup of coffee. How about the rest of you?"

Meshach looked up from testing the shoes on the oxen. He'd already reset Ahab's. "You can't ride dere alone." He made the statement with a "no argument" look.

Why does everyone think they can tell me what to do? I'm supposed to be in charge here. Jesselynn looked up in time to catch a glance between Aunt Agatha and Meshach. What in tarnation did that mean?

"I can make better time on Ahab alone than with everyone else."

"Domino go just as fast." Meshach nodded at Benjamin. "Him too."

Jesselynn sighed. Of course he was right. But if something happened to her, the rest of them could go on, and they'd need Benjamin. But one glance at the set to Meshach's lower jaw and she knew better than to argue. When had he become their leader? She was the eldest Highwood.

She rubbed the side of her face where the mosquitoes had feasted the night before. Since no one had elected her wagon master, or mistress in her case, she realized she needed to ask everyone's opinion.

As soon as they all had cups of coffee, she cleared her throat. "Y'all know that I think I should ride back for Wolf. I need to know what you think." She looked to Nate Lyons, then to Mrs. McPhereson, and finally to the Jespersons, who were still having trouble with their wagon and had decided to join them at the last minute.

"Seems to me the choices are to wait here, head on west, all of us return to the fort, or you and Benjamin ride for help." Nate ran his tongue over his teeth and, squinting, nodded. "Guess now that you asked, I'm in favor of all of us returnin' to the fort. Just in case Wolf can't be found or, if he can, refuses to come." He looked to Mrs. McPhereson. "What say you?"

Mrs. Mac glanced over her cup at Jesselynn, then to her near-grown son. "I say wait a day and start back in the mornin'. Give the Jespersons here time to work on their wagon so two oxen can pull it. Perhaps they can find another span back at the fort."

"Thankee. That would be good." The husband and wife, he with a sling and her with a limp, both of them blue with bruises, nodded to each other and then to the others.

More people, Lord. You've added to our troop again. How will I feed them all, get them to Oregon safely? Jesselynn felt the weight of the load settle about her shoulders, heavy like a buffalo cape.

"Should pray 'bout it before doin' anythin'." Meshach's words carried the simple truth of all the ages. "We be in God's hands."

"We be in God's hands." *Thanks, Lord, for the reminder. I almost took it all on myself—like I used to. What do you want us to do?*

Meshach stood and, with an arm about Ophelia's shoulders, drew her into the circle that formed without conscious action on anyone's part. Heads bowed, and a silence settled over the group. Even Sammy, who jabbered constantly, stuck his finger in his mouth and leaned against his father's shoulder. Thaddeus one-armed Jesselynn's leg and leaned against her, Patch next to him. Jesselynn dropped her head forward, relief stealing from the top of her head to the heels of her boots. She closed her eyes, the better to concentrate. *Father God, thank you, thank you. I know I don't have to do it all, that you will. You are right here with us. You never left. No matter how big this land is, you are bigger.* She let the tears seep without wiping them. She wanted to hug herself, to sing and dance and shout for joy, to run up the hills and throw herself down in the grass to roll back down. The black anxiety that threatened had been blown away.

"God is in His heavens and on this earth, and all will be well. All will be well. We are His and the sheep of His pastures. He is the shepherd, and He guards the sheep. If anyone hear His voice and comes to Him, He will come in and . . ." Meshach's deep voice rose on eagle's wings.

Jesselynn sniffed and blinked hard. Music bubbled inside her, a meadowlark trilled on the breeze, the wind sang in the grasses. The sky arched above them and on forever, the deep blue of a rain-washed summer day.

" 'The Lord is my shepherd, I shall not want.' " Aunt Agatha began the psalm, and around the circle each one added a phrase.

" 'He maketh me to lie down in green pastures:' "

" 'He leadeth me beside the still waters.' "

" 'He restoreth my soul:' "

" 'He leadeth me in the paths of righteousness for his name's sake.' "

As one, their voices lifted. " 'Yea, though I walk through the valley of the shadow of death, I will fear no evil: for thou art with me; thy rod and thy staff they comfort me. Thou preparest a table before me in the presence of mine enemies: thou anointest my head with oil; my cup runneth over.' " The voices ebbed, then swelled. " 'Surely goodness and mercy shall follow me all the days of my life: and I will dwell in the house of the Lord for ever.' "

The meadowlark sang liquid notes, pouring peace over their heads and into their hearts.

"Amen." Thaddeus's voice rang out, strong and firm beyond his years.

Jesselynn picked him up and buried her face in his shirtfront. She sniffed again and used his sleeve to dry her eyes.

Thaddeus put a chubby hand on either side of her face and looked deep into her eyes. "Don't cry, Jesse. Jesus be here."

The tears burned again behind her eyes and filled her nose. "Yes, Thaddy, Jesus most certainly be here." She settled her little brother on her hip and looked to those around the circle. Everyone was either blowing or wiping, but their smiles wavered only a little. "Well, what do we do?" she asked.

"Go back to the fort. But you and Benjamin ride on ahead." Nate Lyons glanced at the others to get their nods of agreement. "If'n Wolf is leavin', you might could stop him, so's he can listen to us."

Jesselynn nodded. "We leave before sunrise, then?"

Again more nods.

Meshach tossed the dregs of his cup into the fire to sizzle and steam. "Mr. Lyons, you want I should check your oxen shoes?"

"If you would be so kind."

A humph came from Agatha, and she stuck her head in the back of the wagon, ostensibly searching for something. Jesselynn, leaning against the rear wagon wheel, could hear her muttering.

"Butter wouldn't melt in that man's mouth. 'If you would be so kind', indeed." She mimicked his rusty voice perfectly.

And here Jesselynn had thought perhaps a truce had been called, or that her aunt had finally realized what a fine man old Brushface, as she called him when he was out of earshot, really was. She'd heard Meshach and Ophelia laughing about them one night. Ophelia was sure Nate was sweet on Aunt Agatha and that all he needed was a little encouragement.

The look on Agatha's face brooked *no* encouragement. *Or doth the lady protest too much?* Jesselynn dug her knife out of the case and used the newly sharpened tip to clean her fingernails. What would happen if they threw Mr. Lyons in the creek along with a bar of soap and instructions not to come out until both he, including hair, and his clothing were scrubbed clean? Surely he had another pants and shirt in that wagon of his.

She pushed away from the wagon and went searching for Mark, Nate's thirteen-year-old grandson. Her fingers itched to use the scissors on Mr. Lyons' hair and beard. If her plan worked, Aunt Agatha would no longer be able to refer to him as Brushface.

"I ain't a'gonna! I look fine just the way I am!" Nate waved his arms, trying to grab hold of those behind him.

"Shush, you want her to hear you?" Jesselynn managed to speak around the laughter exploding around her.

"Don't care. Stop, please, I gotta get my watch out."

They let him dig his pocket watch and fob out of his leather vest, and his grandson accepted the offering with appropriate reserve. But the light dancing in his eyes earned him a sock on the shoulder from his glowering grandfather. With that taken care of, Meshach and Benjamin each grabbed an arm, Daniel pushed from behind, and Nate Lyons splashed into the waist-deep pool surrounded by drooping willows and whispering cottonwood.

"Here's the soap, Grandpa." Mark waded out to hand the spluttering man soap and a washcloth. "Your towel is up there." He motioned toward a tree limb. "Me 'n Patch, we gonna stand guard."

"Yer clean clothes are waitin' dere too." Benjamin pointed to the same tree limb.

"Bring him back here when he's dressed," Jesselynn hissed from behind the tree. They were far enough from camp to not be overheard, but she was taking no chances. She'd even found a stump for him to sit upon in her impromptu parlor. With ivory comb and sharpened scissors in her hands, she was ready to go to work.

When Lyons clumped through the brush, the look he sent her from under shaggy brows made her smile and swallow her laughter. His wet hair hung in curling locks to his shoulders, and his beard did the same on his chest.

"You sure you know how to cut hair properlike?"

"Learned at my mother's knee, just like I learned most everything else. Got so's my brothers would rather have me cut their hair than Mother, said I got it more even." Jesselynn studied the mass before her. "This is going to take some whacking."

"Whackin'! You said—"

"Just teasing." She clamped her elbows into his shoulders and pushed him back down. She leaned forward just a bit and whispered in his ear. "Don't you know I'm trying to help you?"

He cranked his head around to peer up at her. One hand came out to push back the locks that obscured his vision. "Help me what?" He huffed as he turned forward again.

Jesselynn lifted a lock and snipped, then repeated the action with the next, starting with the top of his head.

"Help me what?"

"Sit still or you're going to have a mighty funny haircut." She snipped as she spoke.

He sighed, a heavy sigh that rocked his shoulders. "Sometimes help is awful painful."

"You know, you have very nice hair, thick, and now that I can see it without the dust, a fine color." *How old are you? Maybe I shouldn't think of you as "old man."* There didn't seem to be much gray in the fox red mass.

"Thankee, I guess." His shoulders slumped. "You wouldn't mind tellin' me what kind a help I'm needin', would you?"

Now it was Jesselynn's turn to sigh. "Ophelia seems to think you are sweet on Aunt Agatha. . . ." She waited for some sort of answer. When he didn't respond, she shook her head and continued snipping. Now all the ringlets lay in a pool at her feet. With the comb she lifted the hair, held it between two fingers and cut. Slowly but surely, snip by snip, a well-shaped head appeared. "So are you?"

"Are I what?"

"Dear Lord, preserve us." She combed his damp hair back to reveal a broad forehead. The hair fell in waves, glinting in the sunlight. "Well, I'll be . . ."

"What in tarnation are we talkin' about?"

Jesselynn stopped her barbering, leaned forward, and whispered in his ear. "Are you sweet on Aunt Agatha?"

"The way she treats me? What kinda idjit you think I am?" He spun around to stare at her.

"You need your eyebrows trimmed too. I'll do them when I work on your beard."

"I kin cut my own beard."

"But you didn't, so I will." She leveled a gaze at him that would stop a charging buffalo. When he clamped his eyes shut, she tapped him on the nose. "Relax. I promise not to stab you."

" 'Sides, she don't like me."

"Maybe so, maybe no." She trimmed the sides of his face. "You want to keep the mustache?"

"Yes."

"Why? You have a well-formed mouth. You know, I think there's been a handsome man hiding behind all this hair."

His skin took on the tone of the hair and felt hot. He closed his eyes.

Jesselynn made one more pass with the comb and scissors, then stepped back. She tilted her head, studying him from all sides. Using her fingers, she fluffed the hair and combed the sides back. "Sure do wish I had a mirror here for you to see." She removed the sheet she'd tied around his neck and brushed the hair off his shoulders and shirtfront with it.

"There now, that didn't kill you, did it?"

He studied his hands before looking up at her. "You think there could be a chance for me? With Miss Agatha, I mean." His voice was so low, Jesselynn had to lean forward to hear him.

"I'm thinking there might. You read her some of that Shakespeare every night and just be your sweet self in general, and how could she not enjoy your company?" *And besides, she might have to beat off Mrs. Mac when they see what a handsome man we've been driving with.*

Nate nodded, slapped his hat against his thigh, flinched at the dust cloud that billowed, and let out a breath. "Guess I better wash the hat too. No tellin' what water might do to it." He stared at the relic that looked like mice had nibbled off nest lining from its brim.

Jesselynn stepped back. "Glad you see it thataway. Maybe a dunking would suffice. Get rid of the dust at least, though how your hat can be so dusty after that rainstorm we had—"

"Ingrained, I 'magine." He turned the hat in his hands, poking a finger through one hole. "Goin' to have to be soap." Shaking his head, he got to his feet. "Thankee, Miss Jesselynn. You done me a world a service."

Jesselynn ignored the "Miss". Nate Lyons had always called her Marse Jesse like the others. Looked like they'd become friends at last. After all, from now on, she could go by Miss Jesselynn again, britches or no britches. "Thank you, and you are most indeed welcome."

Agatha never said a word when Nate Lyons presented himself back in camp, but she poured him a cup of coffee and handed it to him without a harrumph or even that stitched look about her mouth.

Nate drank the coffee down and hung the cup back on the row of mugs.

"Where's your hat?" Agatha moved the coffeepot into the cooler coals.

"Gave it a drubbin'."

"Might be I could patch that hole in the crown." She didn't look at him as she spoke but studied the potholder twisting in her hands.

"Bein' as it's wool felt, you s'pose I could trim up that brim with a scissors?"

"Perhaps. But you might want to put it back on your head so the crown don't shrink."

"Thankee for the good advice. I'll go do that." Nate Lyons left the cook fire whistling.

Jesselynn, standing out of sight behind the wagon, used every bit of her self-control to keep from whooping and hollering. Those two had spoken more words to each other in the last five minutes than in all the rest of the trip combined.

She strolled out and, taking a mug off the rack, poured herself a cup of coffee. "Old Brushface surely is looking good."

For that she did get a humph but an exceedingly weak one.

Meshach winked at Jesselynn when she passed by his forge and anvil, and Ophelia giggled behind her fingers.

———

Jesselynn and Benjamin mounted up in the cool breezes before the stars left off their twinkling. The rest of the folks were just starting to shuffle around.

"God be wid you." Meshach's blessing lifted on the cool air. "We be prayin'."

"We too. See you back at the fort, if not before."

The two rode into the rising sun, watching it gild the hillcrests and paint the clouds in shades of joy. They kept the horses at a steady jog, stopping to rest midmorning, then pushing on. When they reached a wide creek, they dismounted and let the horses have a couple of gulps of water before pulling them back to graze. Jesselynn removed her boots and rolled up her pant legs before striding out in the creek. She dipped water and splashed it up her arms and over her face.

Ahab threw up his head, his nicker catching Benjamin unaware.

"Now, ain't this a purty sight." Tommy Joe Jones stepped from behind a tree, his rifle at the ready. A slouch hat shaded a face that might have been handsome had it not been mashed so many times by fists and even cut by a knife. To Jesselynn he was ugly as sin and ten times meaner, inside and out.

His laugh sent fear stampeding up Jesselynn's back. "What are you doing here?"

Chapter Six

"Why, we was just stoppin' fer a drink, same as you."

"We?" Anything to buy time.

"Oh, me'n my purty little wife."

The slitting of Tommy Joe's eyes told her much about his feelings for his "purty little wife." The way he knocked her around, she'd long before lost her "purtiness" to his heavy fists.

"No hope, I suppose, that your brother's dead?"

"Nope, none."

The leer he gave her sent more chills racing up Jesselynn's spine. While she had a pistol stuck in the waistband of her pants, reaching for it would be sure death. Without moving her head, she glanced sideways to see what Benjamin was doing. He had a rifle on the other side of his horse if he could get to it.

"Well, *Mr.* Jones, if you're lookin' for a drink, I'll move out of your way. Plenty of water here for everyone." She took a step toward the bank, but the end of the rifle now pointed directly at her.

"No, you don't." He stepped out farther and leveled the rifle, the grin on his lips nowhere near matching the flames in his eyes. "Take yer hat off."

"My hat?"

"You heerd me. Don't ya understand English? Take yer hat off—now!"

Jesselynn did as he asked, clutching the worn brim at her side.

"Ah, your hair, it's done growd some. Bet you was real purty afore you cut it all off."

Jesselynn narrowed her eyes, staring directly into his. Even across the distance she could see the spittle gathering at the corner of his mouth. *Oh, dear God, I'm in real trouble now. He knows I'm a woman, and he has just one use for women, other than knocking them around. Any time you want to send some angels in would be fine with me.* "How's that leg doing that I bound up for you?" The two Jones brothers had gotten into a shooting argument, and much to her disgust, she'd been on hand to patch them up.

"Good as new. Got a little somethin' else you can do fer me now, though. Take yer shirt off."

"Sorry, can't do that. Wouldn't be at all proper." Keeping her lips or any other part of herself from quivering took intense concentration. If those angels didn't show up, she'd need every bit of backbone she'd ever had.

He stepped forward. "I said, take yer shirt off—now!"

"Now, Tommy Joe, you know what your mama would say about such goings on."

"My mama is long gone, and even if she was right here, I knowed how to handle Mama." He waved the rifle. "Yer shirt."

In looking down to the buttons, Jesselynn glanced at Benjamin from under her lashes. He needed more time too. With shaking fingers she pulled her shirt out of her pants and freed the lowest button. Raising her head to stare at Jones with all the venom she could muster, she let her shirttails flap.

He licked his lips.

She slowly pushed the next button back through the fabric and, with fingers curled under the edges, held the shirtfronts apart so he could see her waistband. As she revealed the front, the gun at her back felt heavier.

"You're going to regret this." She kept her voice conversational while her fingers fussed with the third button. *Lord, if not angels, would you send Wolf? Please, I want to see him again.*

"Sure, who's goin' ter make me? You?" His laugh made the rifle bounce.

She shuddered. His finger had been so close to the trigger, he could have fired accidentally.

"You mind if I get a drink? I'm powerful thirsty."

He wavered. "I guess that won't hurt nothin'. Just make our little game last longer, that's all." He motioned with his head. "Drink away."

Jesselynn leaned forward to scoop water up in her hand. The other still held her hat. Could she shield her arm with her hat and retrieve her pistol? She dipped another handful and let some run down the front of her shirt.

Tommy Joe Jones stared at her, took two steps forward, his gaze burning into her shirtfront.

She sighed, an audible sigh that carried directly to his ears. "Ah, this water is so fine. Nothing quenches one's thirst like a clear flowing stream on a hot day." When she stood, she drank again and patted her cheeks with her wet hand. "Aren't you thirsty, Tommy Joe Jones?" Her voice carried a lilt put there by sheer desperation. Never in her life had she behaved like this, but if wanton would save their lives, wanton she could act. *Come on, Benjamin, get the gun.*

Keeping her gaze on the man with the rifle, she undid the next button, one to go. If she weren't wearing the strips she used to bind her breasts, he'd be staring at bare flesh. The thought alone made her skin tighten. Surely maggots crawling on her body couldn't feel any worse.

Tommy Joe took another step forward. The gun barrel pointed toward the ground.

"Ah, this water feels so good. You ever learned to swim, Tommy Joe?"

Another step. Benjamin took two and disappeared behind Domino.

She arched her back. *Lord, forgive me if actin' this way is against any of your commandments. It's not me doin' the lustin' here.* She splashed one hand in the water. The gun, if only she could get to her gun.

"Take it off!" He hawked and spat, his eyes never leaving her chest.

Jesselynn slid the final button through its hole and with both hands keeping the shirt closed, lifted the front of her shirt so that it fell back, revealing her shoulders.

Tommy Joe Jones took one more step forward. He never saw the brown arm that threw the knife, hitting him right between the shoulder blades. *"Arrrg."* His groan strangled in his throat as he pitched forward face first into the water. The barrel of his rifle smacked the edge of the stream, sending up a small spurt.

Benjamin slowly waded into the water and lifted Tommy Joe. "He be dead."

"It couldn't be helped, Benjamin. You had no choice. God knows." Jesselynn's hand shook a bit as she pulled her shirt back into place. Stuffing it in her waistband, she strode out of the creek. "I'll water the horses while you pull him back in the brush, and let's get out of here before his brother comes looking for him." While it seemed like hours since Tommy Joe Jones strolled back into their lives, she knew it had been only a matter of minutes.

Keeping her gun at the ready, she led the horses to the water. After staring across the creek for a few seconds, Ahab dropped his head and drank. Jesselynn breathed a sigh of relief. But how had the man gotten that close to them without her watchdog, or watchhorse in his case, letting them know? Unless he'd already been there and was downwind so Ahab didn't smell him.

She looked up to see Benjamin with a leafy branch brushing out the tracks the dragging heels had caused. He reset a stone that had been turned over and, standing, looked back to check his handiwork.

"Looks fine."

"I'se sorry I took so long, Marse Jesse. Had to wait till his back to me." Benjamin walked upstream and bellied down to get a drink. When he finished, he wiped his mouth and reached for the reins. "We go soon's you get your boots on."

I wonder where his no-good brother is. Not far, likely. We better get out of here. Jesselynn sat down to pull on her wool socks and then her boots, all the while checking over her shoulder in case Rufus showed up. Knowing him, he was most likely abusing his brother's wife, one way or another.

When Ahab dropped his head to snatch a few mouthfuls of grass, she breathed a sigh of relief. The thought of taking the body into the fort went out of her mind as fast as it came in. There was no way on God's green earth she was wasting any more horsepower, manpower, or even regrets on a man like Tommy Joe Jones. He'd earned the hell he'd be consigned to.

They crossed the creek and kept to the trees until they were far enough away so that Rufus Jones wouldn't see them, then picked up a lope to make up for some of the lost time. They covered five miles or so before either of them said a word.

"He were a bad'un." Benjamin finally broke the stillness.

Jesselynn could only think of one worse, Cavendar Dunlivey, who'd burned Twin Oaks to the ground and then come after her. While she hadn't pulled the trigger there, she had left him, gut shot, to die. Did war bring out the worst in men, or did they always harbor such cruelty behind a thin veneer of civility? Another one of those questions for which there were no answers.

"You all right, Marse?" Benjamin raised his voice in case she hadn't heard him before.

Jesselynn nodded. She could still hear the thunk the knife made, and she knew if she closed her eyes she would see the shock on Tommy Joe's face as he fell forward. *Lord, what if . . . How do I . . . ?* She couldn't even finish the thoughts. *Lord, am I becoming as callous as these men?* This thought gave her another case of the shakes. "Thank you for saving our hides back there," she finally responded to Benjamin.

"You done more'n me. If he hadn't been . . ." Benjamin let his words trail off. He shuddered.

Jesselynn knew that if anyone discovered who'd killed the man, Benjamin would be hung without judge or jury. *I can't let them at Benjamin. Father, I promised not to lie anymore. How? What? So many have died. Please, Father, protect us.*

"What we goin' do?"

"Nothing." Jesselynn sighed. "We're goin' to trust in God to protect us."

"Yes, suh." But the fear hadn't left his eyes.

———

When they finally reached Fort Laramie several days later, they heard the bugle blowing the evening call and saw the flag coming down for the night. The haunting notes floated over the valley. As they rode closer, Jesselynn searched the grazing horses to see if Wolf's Appaloosa was among them. She took in a deep breath and let it out. So much for that hope, but perhaps Wolf was within the quadrangle somewhere.

Or maybe he's long gone, and you've been building up false hopes. She ignored that reasonable sounding voice within her head and continued to hope. Just the thought of seeing Wolf again set her heart to thumping.

"What can we do for you?" The first soldier they saw wore the bars of a sergeant.

"I'm Jesse Highwood. We came through here with a wagon train, the one led by Gray Wolf Torstead, until Cobalt took over." The man nodded. "Our train met up with a terrible thunderstorm and a near stampede."

"Where's the train now?"

"Those that still trusted Jason Cobalt are on their way to Oregon Territory, taking a shortcut he talked them into."

"I take it you weren't part of that trusting group."

"No, sir. We have five wagons on their way back to the fort. We're hoping for another train." *Or for Wolf to come back to us.*

"How bad was the damage?"

"Three people killed, several wagons beyond repair, and probably half their supplies gone."

"And the oxen and horses?"

"We kept the herd safe." She noted his raised eyebrow. "The herd was some behind the wagons. Got them down in a hollow and running in a circle."

"That was good herding." He looked up at her, head turned slightly to the side. "Didn't Cobalt circle the wagons?"

"No, sir."

"Well, I'll be . . ." The man shook his head. "See any Indians?"

"Only one that trailed us for some days. I never saw him."

"Hmm. No new wagon trains shown up since you left. Nowhere near as many this year as in the past. Folks scared of the Indians, if'n you ask me."

"Have you seen Wolf?" She hardly dared look at the man when she asked the question that had been festering like a boil.

"Cap'n sent him out elk hunting with a squad."

"So he hasn't left for the north, then?" She kept her lips pressed together with an effort. Wolf hadn't left!

"Nope, but he didn't look any too happy at the setback. He'll go north soon as he can load his ponies."

Jesselynn touched her fingers to her hat brim. "Thank you, sir, you've been most helpful."

"What we gonna do now?" Benjamin rode beside her.

"Guess we get something to eat and ask where we can bed down. I'll go on over and talk with the captain's wife, Mrs. Jensen. She was real nice when we were here." They angled their horses across the parade grounds and dismounted in front of a two-story white house with porches across the front on both levels. The green trim looked freshly painted, and lace tieback curtains graced the windows. Flipping the reins over the hitching rail in front, Jesselynn mounted the two steps to the porch.

"I stay wid de horses."

Jesselynn nodded and crossed to knock on the green door. She'd barely raised her hand when the door flew open and Rebeccah Jensen took her hand and drew her inside.

"Land sakes, child, what a wonderful surprise. I thought you'd be halfway to Fort Bridger by now." She stopped her river flow of words and looked deep into Jesselynn's eyes. "Something bad happened, didn't it, to bring you back like this? Come, come in and sit down. Supper will be ready in a little bit."

"No, I can't . . ." Jesselynn motioned to her dusty pants and pointed to Benjamin out front. "We've been riding all day. I reckon you might let us have a plate of supper out on your back stoop or something. Or you could tell us where to go to get something to eat."

"You think I'm going to waste female companionship like that? Not on your sweet smile. Why, I reckon a bath might be something you'd enjoy. Then, while Clara is washing your clothes, you can wear a dress of mine. Bet you're dying to wear a dress again after all these months in those britches. I'll send my maid out to show your boy where to put the horses."

As she spoke, Rebeccah hustled Jesselynn up the stairs and into a guest room that had a hip bath in the corner. "I'll send water right up. There's soap and towels behind that screen. Oh, I am so excited to have you back. Are you thinking of staying here? Now that would be pure delightful."

Jesselynn hated to break in on this happy daydream, but she had to set the woman straight. "No, we're not staying. I came back to see if I could talk Wolf into taking our much smaller train on to Oregon."

"Oh, I see." From a chifforobe Rebeccah pulled a white cotton dress sprigged with blue forget-me-nots and the bodice laced with blue ribbon. She held it up against Jesselynn. "This should fit about right. You and I aren't too different in size."

"But . . . but this is too nice. An old housedress would do me just fine." In spite of what her mouth was saying, her fingers had a mind of their own, and that mind said to stroke the fabric and remember what a dress feels like.

Jesselynn could feel the heat creeping up her neck. "But I don't have any undergarments either. Please, this is too much."

"Nonsense." Rebeccah turned to a chest of drawers and pulled out the necessary camisole, pantaloons, and petticoats, all made of the finest lawn and trimmed with lace and ribbons. "I don't have an extra corset, but you are too thin to lace up anyway. I heard that corsets are going out of style."

"Water's here." A voice spoke from the hall.

"Come in." Rebeccah spun away to open the door. A black woman with a bucket of water in each hand led the way, followed by another.

Just the sound of the water swishing into the tub made a smile begin in Jesselynn's heart and spread quickly to her face. A bath, a real honest-to-heaven bath, with hot water and soap.

"Enjoy yourself. When you finish, if I haven't called you yet for supper, you can stretch out on that bed for a few minutes. Might feel real good." Rebeccah shepherded the two servants out ahead of her, then peeked back around the door. "Happy bathing."

Her light laugh trailed behind her as she descended the stairs.

Jesselynn needed no second invitation. Within moments she was stripped to the skin and stepping into hot water scented with rose petals. The fragrance rose with the steam, and no matter that the air temperature was hot as the water, she sank into the froth with a sigh. Leaning back against the slanted metal, she closed her eyes and inhaled to full lung capacity. When she let it all out, she took another breath, sank under the water, and came up blowing and wiping the wet hair from her face. She soaped herself, scrubbed her hair, and sank again. A sound made her open her eyes upon rising.

"Don't pay me no nevermind. I jest set this pitcher here for rinsing." The black maid left as silently as she'd come.

Jesselynn lay back and let the water lap her chin. If she moved too quickly, water swelled over the tub edges, so she soaped the cloth and extended one foot for scrubbing. When finished with both feet, she sighed. How wonderful it would be to lie back and float for a while. Let all the troubles take care of themselves, remember back when a bath like this was taken for granted, was a woman's right.

She stood up cautiously to keep from slopping water, reached for the pitcher, and poured a stream of cool water on her head. It gushed down over her shoulders, rinsing, cooling as it flowed. She hadn't felt so clean since before her father died.

Once dried, she discovered rose-scented powder on the shelf, and so she dusted herself before stepping into the bloomers and settling the camisole around her middle. She came out from behind the screen after folding the towel and looked longingly at the bed. Crossing the room, she stroked the pale yellow coverlet, quilted in a scroll pattern with stitches too tiny to count.

Such beauty in the midst of a harsh land. The fabric felt like silk beneath her fingertips. She pulled herself away and sat at the dressing table, a triple mirror showing her every feature. Her damp hair, freed from dust and grime, feathered about her face like a cloud of golden butterflies, tipped with walnut stain. Freckles dotted her slightly turned-up nose, causing her to shake her head.

"So much for soft white skin. Mine looks like old shoe leather, with spots." She ran a brush through her curls, rose, and slid the dress over her head. Lucinda would *tsk* if she saw her, but what Lucinda didn't know wouldn't hurt Jesselynn. Keeping her face from the sun had been the least of her worries, and now along with her hands and arms, it glowed golden brown, as if she were an octoroon.

The dress fit as though it had been sewn just for her. Puffed sleeves, a scooped neck filled in with a shirring of lace to be proper, and a full skirt gathered to a waist that dipped in front. She smoothed her hands down her sides. And stared at her boots. She daren't go barefoot. But boots with this dress?

Whirling in place so the skirt billowed and swished around her legs, she stretched her arms above her head.

A knock sounded on the door. "Jesselynn, I brought you some slippers."

"Come in. I'm decent." Slippers even. How would she ever repay Rebeccah for these luxuries?

Rebeccah came through the door and stopped, her eyes dancing in delight. "Oh, I knew you would be beautiful. How lovely." She crossed the room and handed Jesselynn the slippers. "I do hope they fit."

"Anything is better than those boots. Couldn't picture myself clumping down the stairs, trying to keep from stepping on the hem." She slid her feet into shoes that were a bit tight but certainly tolerable. "Thank you, dear Rebeccah. I'd almost forgotten . . ." She gestured to the dress, the hair. Further words refused to pass the lump in her throat. *If only Wolf could see me like this.*

"You are most welcome. My husband sent a note saying he was bringing company for supper, so as soon as you are ready, please join us in the parlor."

———

"Thank you for the invitation." Wolf leaned his rifle against the wall. "I need to wash first."

Captain Jensen pointed to the door leading to the back of the building. "There are basins and towels right out there. I'll give you five minutes. Rebeccah dislikes me being late, so when I can, I make sure I'm there early."

Wolf nodded and headed for the back of the building. While he had no clean clothes, he would wash off what dust he could. He shucked his shirt, washed, shaved, wet his hair, and combed it back for retying. With the latigo knotted in place, he shook the dust out of his shirt and pulled it back over his head. The wavy mirror only told him he had no dirt spots on his face, or razor cuts either.

Together the two men crossed the parade grounds and took the two steps as one. Captain Jensen held the door open and motioned Wolf to precede him. Just inside the door Wolf looked up to see a vision descending the stairs. The woman looked vaguely familiar, so he nodded and smiled.

He doesn't even recognize me. Jesselynn swallowed hard to get her butterflies back down to her middle. She lowered her lashes to keep him from seeing her soul. *He looks, he looks . . .* No words powerful enough came to mind. She trailed the banister with one hand and raised her chin just a mite.

"Hello, Mr. Torstead. How nice to see you again."

Chapter Seven

RICHMOND, VIRGINIA

"Take this note to Carrie Mae, please, Reuben, but don't let her know we're gone."

"Yessum." Reuben took the envelope, shaking his head all the while. "I knows dat what you do is good and is de Lawd's will, but dis ol' darky goin' to 'sail the gates of heaven dat He brings you back safe."

Louisa patted his arm. "I am grateful for any and all prayers. Our Father says He puts His angels in charge of us. I surely do hope He sent an entire brigade this time." Her stomach hadn't stopped fluttering since the afternoon a few days before when Zachary broke the news. Zachary nearly didn't come home the first time they went to Washington. While she'd made it straight through, his trip back had taken him three weeks. During that time, they didn't know if he was dead or alive. That after the months of not hearing from him when he was off fighting and then showing up in her hospital, wounded and unidentified.

With a black hat and veil, along with widow's weeds borrowed from a neighbor, she looked near like a spook, far as she was concerned. But there was no way to disguise Zachary's injuries, so they had capitalized on them instead. He sat hunched in a chair with wheels, his dark hair powdered white, his crutch bound to the handles, two boots in place on the footrests, with a blanket covering his knees and a shawl around his shoulders. He looked like an old man, a very sick old man.

"If only we had Meshach here to push this contraption." Louisa studied the handles on the back of the chair.

"This isn't all. There will be a coffin in the back of the buggy, with a dead possum in it to smell so bad no one will open it. We will be taking our dear brother home to Washington for burial. We have passes to get through both lines."

"How will we bring back enough quinine to do any good?"

"There's a false bottom in this chair and a false bottom in the floor of the buggy. And rocks in the coffin to make it weigh out like it carries a man, though he not be overly large. I heard that if you put pepper in your handkerchief, it will make tears a natural part of your demeanor."

Louisa returned to the kitchen to fix herself a small packet of pepper, tucking it into the edge of the basket filled with food for their journey. When they had the buggy loaded, she took up the reins and clucked their horse forward.

"Lord bless and keep you," Aunt Sylvania cried as they started out.

"He must, for there is no other," Louisa muttered under her breath.

The road to Fredericksburg seemed to speed by, as the Union lines were now north of Gettysburg. While they knew of the battle fought there, little information had come down before they left Richmond. Reaching the ferry at South Point, Zachary asked what anyone had heard of the battle.

"We done took a whuppin'," the man taking the money replied. "Three days fightin'—don't know how many kilt." He shook his head and spat a wad off to the side. "Lee done his best. Bet it nigh to broke his heart losin' so many of his boys like that."

Louisa blinked to stop the burning in her eyes. How many of the men they'd nursed back to health were now lying dead or injured again? And the supplies they would get wouldn't even fill a pinhole in the need.

She looked over at her brother. Mouth lined in white, Zachary thanked the man for telling them and clucked the horse forward as they loaded onto the ferry. Too late to plead for them to go home, but she knew it would do no good anyway. If their journey helped one wounded man, it was worth it.

As they neared the shore Louisa's heart picked up the pace always caused by the sight of blue uniforms. She could feel Zachary's gaze upon her.

"You all right?"

She nodded and forced her hands to relax in her lap.

"State your business, sir." The soldier held his rifle across his chest.

"We are taking our brother to be buried in the family plot."

"And where might that be?"

"North Church Cemetery. Generations of Highwoods are buried there."

Louisa held her handkerchief to her eyes, the pepper causing instant tears. She sniffed back a sob and laid a shaking hand on her brother's arm.

"I know, dear, this will soon be over." Zachary handed the sentry his papers. "You'll find them all in order."

The sentry glanced down at the signature and seal. "Pull your buggy over there while I show this to my superior."

Oh, Lord, preserve us. Louisa had no need to fake a sob. She instead fought for control of the fear that made her want to cry out. Oblivious to the traffic passing them by, she closed her eyes against the burning from the pepper and let her head droop against the seat back.

"Sorry to keep you waiting." The sentry handed back their papers and waved them forward.

Louisa nearly collapsed from relief.

"Thank you, Jesus" became her consistent prayer.

Since the procurement of the quinine and some morphine had been arranged ahead of time with sources of whom she knew nothing, they quickly packed the carriage, used their return passes at the Union lines, and faded into the morass of defeated and retreating Confederate soldiers, several of whom rode south with them unaware of the precious cargo accompanying them. Upon returning to Richmond, the supplies were dispersed among the hospitals. Their cargo was a mere drop in the vat of unimaginable misery, but Louisa felt she'd done something of value. If only she could do more.

Whenever she could, she canvassed Richmond homes, pleading for any small delicacy to give to the soldiers in the hospitals. She and Reuben picked peaches and apricots off trees badly in need of pruning but producing in spite of the war. Her regulars baked what they could, made puddings out of precious sugar and milk and eggs, shared jams and jellies, whatever they had been able to preserve.

With the rebels retreating from Gettysburg, every hospital was filled, including floor space with the overflow of the miasma of misery spilling into the churches. Thousands were buried where they fell on the battlefields, and those not buried were picked clean by scavengers, their bones bleaching in the hot summer sun. Louisa had an entire cadre of helpers who carried water to the suffering men, read to them, wrote letters home, eased whatever they could for the living. And a few chaplains came regularly to comfort the dying.

One night Reuben came to her, calling her gently to rouse her from sleep deeper than any well. "Missy Louisa." He touched her shoulder. "Missy Louisa."

"Yes."

"Dat young man dey brung today . . ."

Louisa threw the sheet back. "I'll be right there." She snatched her wrapper off the end of the bed and followed the old man down the stairs, tying her belt as she went. Automatically her prayers rose as she hurried into the dining room.

Zachary sat in the chair by the cot, dipping cloths into water and laying them back on the body burning with fever.

"Has he taken any tea?" Abby had steeped a tea from willow bark that usually helped with fever.

"Tried spoonin' it in, but he not swallow." The maid looked up from the bedside. "He choke."

"I tried to keep Reuben from waking you." Zachary glared at the old man.

"No, I told him to." Louisa laid a hand on the young soldier's forehead. So hot. What else could they do?

The boy's hands twitched, and his back arched in a shuddering convulsion. He went rigid, guttural sounds gagging on the humid air, with not even a breeze to ease the room. When he fell limp again, Louisa laid two fingers on the inside of his wrist to check his pulse.

"We've got to cool him down." She turned to Reuben. "Go get a clean sheet. We'll soak that and wrap him in it."

"It's not proper for you to be doin' all this." Zachary rubbed his forehead and sighed.

"Oh, dear brother, helpin' this young man live is more important than propriety. Our Lord . . ."

"Louisa, I don't much care what our Lord said or did." The sneer in his voice cut right to her soul. She'd known he no longer took part in church, but to say such things tore at her heart. He was her big brother, the one she looked up to.

"Zachary, how can you say such things, or even think them?"

"Look around you." Waving his hand, he tipped over the washbasin. Water sloshed over her bare feet. "You think God cares about which side wins this war?"

"I don't think He is on either side, but both sides. He doesn't want us fighting at all."

"You haven't seen the piles of dead bodies like I have. I lay on the field with a dead man across my legs for hours before help came. Two wounded men died right beside me, one callin' on his God to save him. No one saved him. No one saved him or the others. One wore a blue uniform. If God heard, He turned away."

Louisa's heart sprung a leak, and the tears flowed as she listened to his ragged voice. She put a hand on his shoulder, but he tried to shrug it off. Never before had he said anything about the time he was wounded. She'd known it had to be bad, for most men refused to talk about the battles, other than to mention where they'd been or whom they served under.

Father, help me help him. I hear him, but I don't know how to answer him.

The man on the bed convulsed again, his body bucking the cot, the legs scraping the floor. The sound of the scrapes ate into her like fingernails on a slate.

"Easy, son, easy." Zachary adopted the tone he would use with a fractious horse.

Reuben came into the room with a sheet soaked in a bucket of water, and together he and Louisa wound it around the gasping soldier. The sheet dried faster than if hung outside on a summer day with a hot wind.

"Mother?" The young man stared up at Louisa.

"No, dear, be easy now. Rest so you can get better." Louisa continued to stroke the hair back from his forehead, remembering how good her mother's hand felt when she had done the same.

"Mother . . . I . . . did . . . my . . . b-best, like . . . like you always . . ." He stared into Louisa's eyes. "Like you always . . . said." The pauses between words grew longer. "I will . . . see . . . you . . . in . . ."—Louisa bent her head to hear his fading voice—"in . . . the . . . mornin'."

Another breath. A long pause.

No, don't die like this. God, it's not fair.

But he was gone, the last gentle exhalation from lips that smiled, not a big smile but enough for Louisa to know that he saw something beyond and was no longer afraid.

Louisa and Reuben, both of them wiping away tears, nodded to each other. Again they, like him, had done their best. *My best wasn't good enough to keep him here, but how can I resent that, when I know he has gone on to a far better place? While he is in the arms of God, I am here and tired. So tired, Lord. I am so tired of the dying and the crying.* She stood and sighed. "I'll notify the hospital in the morning."

Zachary sat with his head propped on his hand, eyes closed, cheeks like carved marble. Louisa started to say something, but he waved her away, so she turned to Reuben. "You go on to bed, Reuben, you've not had a decent night's sleep in I don't know how long."

"Old man like me don' need much sleep. I cleans up here, den go to bed."

Knowing that arguing was as useless as trying to stop a rainstorm, Louisa made her way back up the stairs, each tread feeling higher than the last. At least Aunt Sylvania had slept through it all. Louisa fell across her bed, feeling the tears start again. The boy had never made it to manhood, yet had done a man's job. And died for it.

Oh, Lord, when will it all be over? She had no strength to stay awake for an answer that had yet to come.

———

Dusk was slipping in the window when she finally awoke. The birds twittered their good-night wishes outside her window. Not a sound came from downstairs. Up the street a mother called her son home. Louisa thought of the mother of the boy who'd died during the night. She would never call him home again.

A tear slid from the side of her eye and blotted her pillow. How many boys had she eased on their way, fighting to save them but blessing their passing? She didn't want to count. She crossed to the folding screen in the corner, stripped, and washed herself in the cool water of the pitcher. They should have wakened her earlier, but knowing her family, she imagined they decided she needed sleep more than anything. Once dressed, with her hair combed, she made her way downstairs, one hand trailing on the banister. Ignoring the dining room, knowing the body was gone and most likely another injured man in its place, she followed the sounds of laughter to the back veranda. She paused just inside the French doors that overlooked the backyard, a place now filled with laughter and teasing, perhaps trying to chase away the sorrow of the night.

She watched her brother as he told a story of their childhood, his good hand flashing to help in the descriptions. Was this the same man who hours earlier had said he no longer believed in a God who cared about the men fighting the war?

His words of the dark night felt like a vest of lead dragging at her shoulders, pulling her neck taut. Did he really believe what he'd said, or was his diatribe due to his grief at the death of the young boy and the frustrations of dealing with his own handicaps? Louisa rubbed her forehead where she could feel a headache starting. No one knew she was up yet. She could climb the stairs and sink back into oblivion, back where she had no worries about finding food for her men, or medicine, or even the simplest of comforts.

And if she felt that way, no wonder Zachary did. Perhaps he was more honest than she, admitting his doubts.

But I don't want to doubt you, Lord. All my life, you have been a part of me. If you were gone, would I not feel the amputation? I know you are here. I know you care. I know that you will see us through, for you said you would.

The ache in her head took up the cadence of a drumbeat leading the march. Turning, she headed back up the stairs and sank down on her bed. So much to do, and here she was lying down again. What would her mother say?

Oh, Mother, I need you so. You would have the wisdom to tell Zachary—to tell him what? I don't know, but . . . Louisa lay back on her pillows, the cool sheets blessing the back of her neck, her hand covering her closed eyes. The beat took up a place behind her eyes and pounded out the moments. *You would bring me peppermint tea and rub my neck and forehead. I can hear you singing. Ah, Mother dear, how I miss your singing. You sang when there was nothing to be joyful about, but you said singing and praising God made you feel joyful anyway.* A tear leaked from under her closed lashes and meandered down to the pillow. *You called it a sacrifice of praise. Is that what I need?*

Another tear joined the first. *My head hurts and I am so weary.* A tune trickled into her mind. *"Praise to the Lord, the Almighty, the King of creation."* She took a deep breath and let it all out, allowing her shoulders to sink back into the feathery softness. *"O my soul, praise Him, for He is thy health and salvation!"*

A bird twittered in the branches outside the window. A breeze lifted the once starched curtains and blew through the drape of mosquito netting. It kissed her cheeks and bathed her forehead with blessedly cool fingers, drying her tears as she drifted off to healing sleep.

———

There were times when Louisa almost asked Zachary if he really meant what he'd said, but courage failed her. She watched him, trying to decipher the pensive look he wore at times, the face he presented to the recuperating soldiers not matching the one she saw upon close scrutiny.

"Why are you always staring at me?" The snap in his voice lashed like the tip of a whip.

"I . . . I'm not. I . . ." She seized her courage with both hands and yanked it up to her heart where it belonged. "I'm just trying to figure you out."

"Well, don't bother. Just a waste of your time." He turned away and crutched out of the room, his stiff back sure evidence of his displeasure.

She hated people to be upset with her.

"Well, brother dear, two can play that game." With firm resolve, she kept herself from running after him.

But an hour later, he came up behind her where she sat sewing with her soldiers and dropped a kiss on the top of her head. She'd known it to be him by the sound of his crutch and stride.

"Forgiven?" he whispered.

She rolled her eyes heavenward. "Perhaps."

He proceeded to entertain the seamsters, keeping them laughing while their needles flew.

"Ouch!" One man stuck his finger in his mouth. "Now look what you did, made me laugh so hard I got blood on this coat."

I pray to God that's all the blood it ever gets! She had a bundle of coats in the other room that needed patches. Patches for the holes bullets had torn through the coat and into a body. By looking at the coats, she'd seen how the men had died or ended in a hospital. If only she could sew a lining that would withstand bullets and screaming shells.

"Mail done come." Abby brought several letters on a once-silver salver, now worn so that the lesser metal took precedence.

Louisa smiled her thanks, her mouth turning up further at the sight of Lucinda's laborious handwriting. "A letter from Twin Oaks."

Zachary looked up from his conversation, question marks all over his face, though he quickly wiped them away as he returned to his usual noncommittal expression.

With that brief glimpse of Zachary's pained expression, Louisa realized that she needed to look behind the mask on her brother's face to see his true feelings. What feelings he let himself have.

"Oh, and a letter from Jesselynn. How wonderful. Two in one day." She looked to the faces of her sewing group. "I will go over and see if any mail has come for you."

"I go see." Reuben nodded to the group before heading out the side gate.

Since black slaves were not supposed to be able to read and write, Louisa took out Jesselynn's letter first. Surely there would be parts in it she could share with all of them. She glanced down the page, wishing she were in her own room so she could savor every word.

She looked up to see expectant faces watching her, needles and thread lying idle. "My sister is on her way to Oregon in a covered wagon, along with others of our people. Much of Twin Oaks, our home in Kentucky, was burned last year. I'll read what she says.

" 'We have found a wagon train and are finally leaving Independence, Missouri. We were beginning to think we would have to remain there, but living in wagons is not my idea of a good way to spend a winter. The two foals are growing like weeds and making us all laugh at their antics. Living close to our horses, as we are now, has created a bond we didn't have before. Thaddeus is a born horseman, just like his daddy and older brothers. He has no fear around them, which can cause some of the rest of us plenty of fear at times.

'Aunt Agatha knits her way across the land. She has taken Jane Ellen under her wing, and the two of them are teaching the boys manners and correct speech, the kind of things I should be doing but have been too busy keeping us all together.

'The good news, Ahab can run as well as ever. While we lost the first race, I asked for more distance for the next one, and he did himself proud. The purse and selling the loser's horse back to him has caused our purse to swell to needed proportions again.' "

"Jesselynn raced Ahab?" Aunt Sylvania's eyes were as round as the lemon cookies on the plate near at hand. "That stallion?"

Louisa shrugged. "We all do what we must. I surely do wish I could see Thaddeus. He was just a baby, or so it seemed, when we saw him last. He won't even remember who we are." She hoped that changing the subject would derail Aunt Sylvania's horror.

"She rode sidesaddle?"

Louisa sent Zachary a pleading look that clearly cried *help*. His noncommittal shrug made her eyes narrow, sending darts his way.

"Here, she continues. 'The train we are joining is of a good size and the wagon master has a good reputation.' "

"Louisa, I asked you a question."

Louisa laid the letter in her lap. She sighed, shook her head, and looked up at her aunt. "Jesselynn wore britches, has been wearing them since she left Twin Oaks, because that is the only way she can keep all of them safe. She is doing what she has to do, just like the rest of us."

Aunt Sylvania shook her head and kept on shaking it. "The war, always the war. Life will never be the same again." She sniffed and dabbed at her nose with a bit of cambric. "Lord, have mercy on us all."

"Amen to that," one of the men muttered.

"Supper is ready." Abby stood in the doorway. "You want I should bring it out here?"

"No, we'll come in." Louisa stood and tucked the letters into her apron pocket. "My, that surely does smell fine."

But when she read the letter from Lucinda later in Zachary's study, she felt as though she'd been slugged in the midsection.

Chapter Eight

FORT LARAMIE

"See you again?" That voice?

Wolf stopped as if he'd hit a granite face at a dead run. "Jesselynn?"

She stopped on the second from the last riser. "I do believe so." Her accent thickened. She smiled, ordering her lips to not tremble, nor the tears behind her eyes to fall. *Ah, Wolf, how . . . why . . . I cannot bear this.* All her mother's and Lucinda's coaching about how a Southern gentlewoman behaved came to her aid.

"God be praised, you have come back." His whisper drove straight to her heart.

She took another step down, her gaze never leaving his, her mouth so dry she could not have spoken, even if an arrow were pointing at her.

Father God, she is most glorious, like the sun rising above the mountains or a lake with the kiss of evening upon it. And she has come back. Please, I beg of you, let her stay. Wolf stepped forward. If there were others in the room, he had no awareness of them. He took her hand, drew it up in the crook of his arm, and pressed it against his side. Could she hear his heart thundering like a spring cascade over a cliff?

Does he know what he is doing to me? Lord, I cannot go through the leaving again. He must come with us to Oregon. Can he hear my heart? Feel me tremble? Once in his arms was not enough. I want forever.

As the two of them walked into the dining room, Jesselynn glanced up in time to see Rebeccah wipe a pleased look off her face, the kind of look a cat wore when it had been in the cream uninvited.

"If you would sit here, Jesselynn, and Mr. Wolf, there." She indicated chairs on the opposite sides of the table, directly across from each other. When they all had taken their places, she nodded to her husband. "If you will say grace, Captain Jensen."

Jesselynn bowed her head but not so far that she couldn't see Wolf from under her lashes. He bowed his head, giving her a view of his broad forehead, the thick dark hair springing from it as if it had a life of its own. His shoulders filled out the shirt, the open collar framing his throat and upper chest, the cords of his neck strong beneath the skin. His skin reminded her of the Cordova leather that once bound her father's books. Neither brown nor red but some mix of the two that made a hue all its own, the richer for the joining.

"Jesselynn, would you like your meat sliced thick or thin?" Rebeccah spoke softly. Jesselynn could feel the heat flaming up her neck. She'd not heard one word of the prayer, not even the "amen." She dared not look at Wolf in case he realized where her thoughts had been. Never in her entire life had she lost herself like this, not even after her fiancé died, or her father. She'd always kept her wits about her.

Until today.

While she took part in the conversation, she had no memory of what she had said or eaten when they rose from the table. Clara, the second maid, served their coffee in the parlor.

"So what are your plans?" Captain Jensen turned to Wolf.

"I'll leave for the Oglala lands as soon as the general issues my requisition for blankets and supplies for my people. We brought in ten elk, which should help feed the fort for a while. The men now know the elks' range, and they can hunt again."

"And you, Miss Highwood?"

Jesselynn forced her attention away from Wolf and back to the captain. "My two wagons are returning to Fort Laramie. We have three others along. We are hoping that"—she drew in a deep breath, wishing for a private place to talk with Wolf—"Wolf, er . . . Mr. Torstead will change his mind and take our train west after all." She watched the shutter drop over his eyes and the rest of his face. Clearly, that wasn't what he wanted to hear.

"Ah, then I have a feeling you two could use some time alone to discuss your—um . . ." Captain Jensen turned to his wife. "Come, dear, we can go help Clara with the dessert." The two of them exited the room, leaving a curious silence behind.

Jesselynn studied her fingers, finding bits of dirt still under her fingernails. Without her knife, it would have to stay there. She snuck glances at Wolf, who stood looking out the parlor window. He hadn't moved since the Jensens left the room.

"How much damage did your wagons suffer?" *Lord, can I convince her to come with me?*

At the sound of his voice, her heart jumped into her throat. "Ah, not much. They were at the end of the train, and the stampede started when lightning hit the lead wagon. Aunt Agatha and Benjamin kept their oxen in hand." *Please, turn and look at me.*

"Where were you?" *I know I am rushing her, but we must have a camp for winter— if she will stay.*

"With the herd." She told him of the almost stampede and the hollow. "It could have been terribly tragic."

"You were wise to not take the shortcut with the others. They will lose more oxen that way." The silence deepened again.

Wolf, we need you. Please take us on to Oregon. We'll pay you double if you'll guide our train. Practicing what to say did not make the saying of it any easier. She knit her fingers so tightly together that they cramped.

"Why are you going to Oregon?"

"For the free land, so that Meshach can start a new life. He wants to be a free man where no one will look down on him or call him 'boy' again."

"So that is why Meshach is going. What about you?" He turned to study her with his dark eyes.

"They say the land will grow anything, horse feed included." She twisted her mouth to one side, sighed, and looked straight at him. "To get away from the war. I want nothing to do with slavery and war ever again."

"Why does it have to be Oregon?" The question hung in the stillness.

"I . . . I reckon I don't really know. We tried Missouri, and Daniel nearly got lynched. Kansas was worse with Quantrill's Raiders, so we decided on Oregon and went ahead with obtaining supplies. We hope Oregon is far enough away from the South that we can build a new life."

He took two steps across the room to where the lamplight burnished his face and threw his eyes into shadow. "You could have the same in Wyoming."

"I've heard the winters can be fierce in Wyoming." She stared into his eyes. *What is it you are saying?* Her throat dried. Her heart speeded up.

"My people know how to live through the winter. And after the snow comes spring. There are wild horses to be caught. Our herd would grow quickly that way."

Was it a slip of his tongue? Had he really said 'our'? "What are you saying?" Jesselynn's fingers shook, so she hid them in her skirt.

Wolf took two more steps, reached for her hands, and pulled her to her feet. With their hands clutched between them, he stared down at her. After taking a deep breath and letting it out, he spoke so softly she was forced to lean ever closer. "I am asking you to marry me. We can homestead in the hills above the Chugwater. The grass grows rich in the spring, and there are wild flowers the blue of your dress." He fingered the puff of one sleeve.

"Milady's eyes."

"What?"

"That's what some call these forget-me-nots." She waited. Would he ever say the words she so desperately longed to hear?

"Meshach would find it good there too."

"But he wants to go on to Oregon."

"And Aunt Agatha?"

Jesselynn closed her eyes. Taking a deep breath didn't help. *Aunt Agatha. Oh, my Lord, help me here—and there. How will I deal with Aunt Agatha? I know you are my life and you have the answers, but this man, Father, I love this man. Is there anything wrong with that? And I sense that if I don't answer now, he'll be gone.*

She opened her eyes to find Wolf watching her; his hands had not loosened their grip, his thumb stroked the back of her right hand. "I . . . I will talk with Aunt Agatha." *Oh, Lord, preserve me. Put words of wisdom in my mouth.*

"It is of her I must ask for your hand in marriage?"

Jesselynn shook her head. It should be Zachary. Now, if that wouldn't be a scene. She tried to take a step back, but he moved with her.

"No, I make my own decisions." She looked deep into his eyes, trying to read his soul. *Do you love me? Say it!*

She swallowed hard, cleared her throat. "Wolf, in my world words are important. . . ." *No, I'm saying it all wrong. This feels like love, looks like love, and acts like love. Can I trust that it is? Father, are you blessing this? I feel that you are.*

"Yes?" Now both his thumbs were sending messages screaming up her arms, setting her skin on fire, her heart to thundering.

Her head dropped forward, her forehead resting on his chest. His heart, too, beat faster, louder. When she looked up, she smiled into his eyes that carried a shadow. "Yes, Mr. Torstead, I will marry you."

The shadow fled, and the sun burst forth. He cupped her face with his hands and kissed her waiting mouth. As if that weren't enough, he tasted her nose, her chin, and returned to her mouth. When he drew away, he cupped her cheeks again, tenderly, as if holding a great and fragile treasure. "You are sure?"

"Yes. I am sure." She sucked in another breath and laid her hands over his. "I am sure that I love you. I am sure that I want to be with you for the rest of my life." *And I am sure that the next few days will test everything I am.*

"We will be married here at the fort?"

"If you want."

"I will go with you to bring in the wagons."

She now stepped back. "No, I will do that myself."

He studied her face, then nodded. "As you wish."

I can't have you wounded by her words. She will go berserk. "Not what I wish, but what I must do." She took another step back and realized they were no longer alone.

"Here's the dessert, Clara's chocolate cake with whipped cream. You've never tasted anything so delicious west of the Mississippi." Captain Jensen carried one tray, followed by his wife with another. When they set them on the low table, he looked up with a twinkle in his eye. "Your time was well spent, I gather?"

Wolf nodded. He took Jesselynn's hand. "She has agreed to marry me."

"A wedding! Oh, Captain, we will have it right here." Rebeccah beamed at her husband and then turned back to Jesselynn. "When? End of next week, of course. It must be soon if you are going to go north. Mr. Torstead, you *are* still going north, aren't you? This is the most wonderful news. Wait until I talk with the chaplain, I—"

Captain Jensen put his arm around his wife's waist. "You can tell we don't get a lot of opportunities to have a party here. Now, Rebeccah, you must let Miss Highwood do some of the planning." The smile on his face and in his voice brought matching smiles from the others.

"I . . . I haven't had time to think." *This is all so new. Oh, what have I let myself in for?*

Rebeccah took Jesselynn's hands in hers. "I would consider it a great honor if you would let me take care of the wedding. I have a silk dress you could wear that has been languishing in a trunk, needing just such an occasion as this. Why, wait until I announce this to the ladies here at the fort, not that there are many of us, but we will have a marvelous time."

Jesselynn could feel the warmth of Wolf standing right behind her. She leaned back just a mite to feel the solid wall of his chest holding her up. Getting control of the stampede seemed easier than this. At least those cows ran in a circle. The vibrations of a laugh in the wall behind her made a smile blossom, then bloom, and a matching laugh gurgled to the surface.

"Ah, I hate to tell you this, but when my wife gets hold of an excuse for a party, man the barricades, 'cause that party will happen." Jensen gave his wife the kind of look that brought a lump to Jesselynn's throat.

"Thank you." She accepted the plate Rebeccah offered and took a bite. Not since she left Twin Oaks had she tasted anything so fine. "This is wonderful."

"Thank you. Perhaps Clara will make your wedding cake from this recipe. But she makes a white cake that . . ."

Captain Jensen cleared his throat.

Rebeccah shrugged at the twinkle in his eye. "I'm doing it again?"

He nodded. She tipped her head to one side and shrugged again, the laughter in her eyes and the merry dimples on either side of her mouth mute testimony to her joy.

If planning a wedding brought such happiness to another, Jesselynn had no desire to deprive her of the privilege.

When he set his plate down, Wolf nodded to his host and hostess. "Thank you for a most enjoyable evening. Someday I hope to repay the hospitality, once our home is built."

Jesselynn hid a smile. Was this really the same man who so rarely strung more than five words together at a time? Another facet to the man called Wolf, the man she would spend her lifetime getting to know.

A tingle ran from her toes to the top of her head. After all this time, she was indeed going to be married. And at Fort Laramie—Indian territory, of all places. If God himself had told her in advance this would be happening, she would have had a hard time believing Him.

Since Wolf didn't let go of her hand, she followed him to the door and out onto the porch.

He took her in his arms and kissed her again. "That's to remind you that no matter what anyone says, you *will* be marrying me in ten days." With that, he stepped off the porch and strode away, fading quickly into the darkness.

Jesselynn leaned against the newel-post and watched him go, one fingertip resting against her lips, as if to keep the feeling intact. When she returned to the parlor a few minutes later, Rebeccah sat with the lamp pooling light on the rich colors of the tapestry she was working on, her needle flashing.

"Your bed is turned down and ready for you. Your Benjamin is sleeping out in our woodshed. Clara made him a pallet, even though he said he had his bedroll. Breakfast will be ready whenever you need to leave."

Jesselynn sank down in a chair and shook her head. "I cannot thank you enough."

"No." Rebeccah leaned forward. "It is for me to thank you. Life is plain on an outpost like this, and to be part of your life brings richness to mine. We never had any children, so this is my chance to pretend that I have a daughter who is marrying a fine man, and we will all celebrate." She took another stitch. "And to think that you will be living within two days or so of us. Why, we'll practically be neighbors."

Jesselynn hid a yawn behind her hand. With all that had gone on, sleep should be the last thing from her mind. However . . .

"Thank you again, Rebeccah, but I'm afraid I must excuse myself. This is so different from what I planned. I thought to sleep in a hay pile somewhere, and that would be a luxury after the ground all these months. Four walls and a roof, windows, and a real bed. And the bath. I can never thank you enough."

Someday, she thought. *Someday I will have a home again, a safe home with walls and children and . . .* The picture of the man who would lead that home made her face warm. She stood, bid her hostess good-night, and made her way up the stairs. A lamp on the nightstand made the room look even more welcoming than earlier. Her shirt and pants, washed and pressed, lay over the chair, and even her boots wore a shine. She hung the dress in the chifforobe, stroking down the skirt with a sigh. She pulled the nightdress that lay across the bottom of the bed over her head, and after blowing out the lamp, she slipped between sheets, real sheets, cool and crisp to the skin. Ah, such luxury. She was asleep after only three "thank-you's" to her God, and all of them concerned Wolf.

————

The ride back to the wagons gave Jesselynn plenty of time to stew over her upcoming discussion with Aunt Agatha. "Perhaps she has changed clear through, not just on the surface."

Ahab flicked his ears back and forth, listening to her and still keeping track of the surroundings. He snorted.

"I agree. I should have let Wolf come with me. Perhaps she will be happy for me." Now *she* snorted. Her shoulders curved forward as if to protect her heart. *He loves me.* The thought brought a rush of delight, like pure springwater in a dusty land. Then the gusher died. *He asked her to marry him, but never had he mentioned the word* love.

"You all right, Marse Jesse?" Benjamin rode up beside her.

"I'm fine. You get some of the prairie chickens?"

He held up a brace.

"Good. I reckon Ophelia will be right glad."

Father, this is becoming a muddle. Perhaps we should have just found the chaplain, said our vows, and presented this as a fait accompli. If only Aunt Agatha . . . She brought that line of reasoning to a screaming halt. "If only's" could drive one to distraction, and one isn't any further ahead after hours of worrying and stewing than at the beginning.

Jesselynn leaned forward and patted Ahab's arched neck. "Perhaps that is why our Father told us not to worry, you think?" How come deciding not to worry and actually not worrying were so far apart?

Ahab pulled against the bit, begging for a bit of a run. Ever since racing in Independence, he'd been begging to run again. She wanted to run all right — back the way she had come.

————

Jesselynn and Benjamin met the wagons late in the afternoon of the second day of hard riding. Counting the wagons, she shook her head. Who had they picked up now?

"Jesse back!" Thaddeus sang out his welcome, running ahead of Jane Ellen.

Jesselynn dismounted and knelt to meet his running welcome. He flung himself into her arms, almost knocking her over in spite of how firmly she was braced.

"Why you leave us? Where Mr. Wolf?" He looked over her shoulder as if she were hiding him, as if he might pop up like a jack-in-the-box.

Jesselynn scooped him up and set him in the saddle without answering. "Now, you hang on."

His stare of reproach made her smile up at him and jiggle his foot. "I know, you always hang on. A real Highwood you are when it comes to riding." Patch met her with a yip and a doggy grin, his teeth gleaming white against his black fur and pink tongue. Keeping a firm hand on the reins, in case something spooked Ahab, she ruffled the dog's ears, keeping her chin away from his lightning tongue. Anything to delay the coming confrontation with Aunt Agatha.

"You find 'im?" Meshach rode up on Chess.

"See me ride Ahab?" Thaddeus clutched a hank of matted mane.

"Lil Marse fine rider." Meshach answered the boy and at the same time sent Jesselynn a look pregnant with questions.

"I found him."

Meshach dismounted and fell in step beside her.

Jesselynn sucked in a deep breath. Might as well get it over with. She dropped her voice. "He wants us to go north with him. He says there is good land, two days' travel from Fort Laramie, where we could all homestead. He says there is a valley, good hunting, clear running streams, and . . ." She knew she was talking too hard and fast but couldn't seem to stop the spate.

When Meshach failed to answer her, she looked up into his face. "You would be a free man here too, with free land."

They stopped walking, the wagons drawing closer with every plodding step of the oxen.

"You don't have to decide immediately."

"What you not tellin' me?"

Jesselynn rolled her lips together. "He has asked me to marry him."

"Ahh." Meshach looked down at her, a smile splitting his ebony face. "Thank de Lawd, dat man done come to his senses." Meshach slapped his thigh with his hat, raising a dust cloud to equal that of a span of oxen. He stopped. "You did say yes?"

"I did. Mrs. Jensen is getting things ready. She's the captain's wife, my hostess for the night." *Please, Meshach, decide to stay. I don't want to lose you and the others.* Thoughts pelted around her mind like children just loosed from lessons. *Meshach, answer me.* The cry nearly broke from her heart, taking all her strength to suppress it.

"So, Jesse, how did you fare?" Agatha, driving the lead wagon, always wore her sunbonnet well forward to protect her face, so now she pushed it back the better to see her niece. After her careful scrutiny of Jesselynn's face, a frown wrinkled her forehead. But without commenting, she nodded over her shoulder. "Mrs. Jones has asked if she can travel with us. Both her husband and his brother seem to have met with some disaster, as they never returned to their camp. Strange, wouldn't you say?"

Jesselynn shrugged. "Fine with me, so long as she is alone. Either of the men show up, and none are welcome." At least she knew one of them wouldn't.

"I said the same, but she seemed fairly positive that would not be the case."

Jesselynn looked toward the last wagon. Most likely she should go talk with Mrs. Darcy Jones. Had she found her husband's body? And what happened to Rufus? For a moment, curiosity drove thoughts of Wolf right out of her mind.

"Me ridin'!" Thaddeus couldn't resist lording it over Sammy, who wriggled on the seat by Ophelia as she drove the second wagon.

Gratefully, Jesselynn switched her attention to her little brother. "Not anymore if you cannot be more considerate than that." She reached up and dragged him off the horse.

"Jane Ellen, would you please take him back?" She glanced over at Meshach. "And if you will give Sammy a ride, perhaps the young marse will learn better manners."

Meshach did as she suggested but without the smile that would ordinarily greet such a comment.

Sammy, sitting in front of his adopted father, crowed with delight. "Go, go." With one arm around his son, Meshach walked his mount alongside the wagon, where Ophelia said something that made both man and boy wear matching smiles.

Jesselynn remounted. "Think I'll go help with the herd." She could feel her Aunt Agatha's gaze drilling into her back, unspoken questions bombarding her like a flock of small birds chasing off an offending crow.

That night when they stopped for the evening camp, Aunt Agatha handed Jesselynn a cup of coffee and sat down on the wagon tongue beside her.

"Now, are you going to tell me what transpired at the fort?"

Jesselynn sipped at her coffee. "I stayed with Captain and Mrs. Jensen, had a real bath, and slept in a bed."

Agatha sighed. "Now that does sound like a long-lost privilege. No wonder you look so fresh. Just getting this dust off a body would be pure bliss."

How do I tell her?

"So, what did he say?"

"Who say?"

Agatha looked at Jesselynn as though she thought her niece had left her senses on the trail somewhere. "Mr. Wolf, that's who you went looking for, right?"

Jesselynn sat up straighter. "He asked us to go north with him instead of going on to Oregon."

Silence fell around them, as if everyone had quit breathing.

"Why ever would he do that?" Agatha turned slowly to stare at Jesselynn. "What is it you are not telling me?"

Jesselynn felt her stomach twist into a half hitch, then a double knot. "I agreed to marry him."

"Marry him?" Aunt Agatha sucked in a breath that wheezed around the constriction of her throat. "Marry a half-breed?" Her voice deepened. "A man of color?" Thunder rumbling in the distance could not have reverberated more. "No one! No woman in our family has evah"—her chest swelled. Her face mottled—"evah had truck with a man of colah!"

Chapter Nine

RICHMOND, VIRGINIA

"Taxes! Don't they know there's a war going on?" Zachary fumed.

Louisa was beginning to wish she'd never told her brother the news. What good did it do? He couldn't go back to Twin Oaks. If he entered Kentucky he'd be shot as a spy. And what did they have to pay the taxes with? Nothing. Unless he had some money stashed away, and that she very much doubted.

"I imagine they plan on financing the war with our tax money." Seeing the look on his face, Louisa wished she'd kept her mouth shut. If that were true, it would be a short war considering the state of their finances.

"We can't lose Twin Oaks." Zachary slumped in the chair as if all the air had gone out of him, or at least all the starch.

"Surely they wouldn't foreclose on someone who served in the army like you did, now wounded and not able to go home." She rose and paced to the other side of the room, her steps more agitated as she strode. "And both Daddy and Adam killed. And the place burned to the ground by a Confederate officer." She held up her hands to stop his objection. "I know we can't prove Dunlivey did that, but we all know it, sure as summer brings mosquitoes." She spun at the far wall and paced back again. "So what are we going to do?"

"*We* are going to do nothing. *I* am going to speak with our brother-in-law. Perhaps he can send a letter that will change their minds. He has high connections. He can use them for the family." Zachary levered himself out of the chair. "First thing in the morning. As for now, wasn't there some peach pie left over from supper? I think that would taste mighty fine."

"But—"

"No 'but's'. Let me at least handle this." He turned back after stumping to the doorway. "I think I will talk with Jefferson about a position with his firm. Surely they will realize their need to employ an ex-soldier who, while missing limbs, is every bit all right in his mind."

Louisa watched him leave the room. That surely did answer one of her questions, the one that asked how this recuperation time was affecting her brother. More questions buzzed in her mind like a nest of enraged hornets. How would he get to an office every day? What would he wear? Could he manage a job? And most of all, why hadn't Jefferson offered him one earlier, or at least promised something for when Zachary felt ready?

Like a hornet, she felt like stinging someone, anyone who crossed her path at the moment. If Zachary were working, how could they go on another mission?

Before going to sleep, she sat down to write Lucinda a message reassuring her that Zachary would find a way to meet the tax obligation. She only wished she felt as positive as she sounded. She'd thought earlier about the silver and other valuables buried in the rose garden. Jesselynn had written, in a roundabout way that took some deciphering, about the family treasures buried. She wanted Louisa to know about it for when the war ended. But in case someone intercepted the mail and read the letter, Louisa could think of no way to tell Lucinda to dig up and sell what she needed. And knowing Lucinda, she would starve first. So Louisa simply filled her in on the news, closing with . . .

> *Carrie Mae looks to be having twins. She is so large, but perhaps it only seems that way because she is typically so slender. We all wish you could be here to care for her and the baby and thus continue family traditions. Thank you for all the work you and Joseph are doing to keep Twin Oaks going. Someday, when the war is over, we will come home, and we will all be together again.*
>
> *With love and God's blessing, I remain*

Again she signed her name, this time including Zachary and Aunt Sylvania.

Louisa brushed the quill back and forth under her chin. Ah, if only she could get on a train and, no matter how roundabout the trip, return to Midway, and home to Twin Oaks. To walk again between the two ancient oaks at the end of the drive and on up to the big house. There was no way she could picture the house burned, with only the brick chimneys standing, as their neighbor had written. Or no horses grazing the pastures, or no rolling sweeps of tobacco fields.

After sealing the envelope Louisa knelt by her bed and opened her Bible to Psalm 91. *Ah, Lord, I know we are safe and secure under your mighty wings, but so many of our boys believed that and were killed anyway. Not that I'm not looking forward to heaven and your presence, you understand, but the agony has gone on and continues. And now Zachary disavowing his faith. O Father, do not let him go. Please hold him under your wings and in your camp with angels round about.* She read more about fiery darts not assailing and not even snakes or young lions. She closed her eyes and repeated the words from memory, branding them into her soul for when she needed them.

———

The next day, as soon as Louisa had her men working at their assignments for the day, she took her writing case out under the magnolia tree. Shaking the ink, she set the square corked bottle back in its holder, dipped the quill, and started the first of at least two letters for the day.

Dear Mrs. She stopped and forced her brain to remember the name of the young man who had died under their care. How she hated writing letters like this.

. . . Benson,

> *My name is Louisa Highwood, and I had the honor of knowing your son, Adam. He was brought to our house for care, but we were unable to quench the fever. He died praising you and his Lord. His last words indicated what a fine young man you raised. He said, "Mother, I did what you asked. I did my best." I am so sorry, Mrs. Benson, that our best was not good enough to save your son. Please know that he is in a far better place. The look on his face as he died made me sure of that. With this letter I am enclosing his personal effects.*

> *Sincerely,*

She signed her name and wiped away a wet spot from her tears. At least she had not smudged the ink.

Hearing a strange sound, she looked around her. Aunt Sylvania was reading from the local newspaper about how many Union prisoners had been exchanged for Confederate ones. Psalms would come next, and Shakespeare would be last. Yesterday one of the men had spoken the part of Petruchio that he'd memorized long before from *The Taming of the Shrew*.

After a few minutes Louisa heard the noise again. She turned to look under the peony bushes. Surely it sounded like a kitten. But seeing nothing, she returned to her letter writing.

In the letter to Jesselynn she told about her trip to Washington with Zachary, glossing over the frightening parts and trying to make her sister laugh about the dead possum.

> *I am concerned about our brother though, dear sister. He confesses to no longer believing in our God and Savior, and at times a black cloud hovers over him that makes me fear for his soul. One minute he can be nice and the next nasty. I sometimes feel I am walking on eggshells with him. Please keep him and us in your prayers, as we do you. Your journey sounds exciting, and I am grateful you found a good wagon train. How I will bear having you on one side of this country and us on the other is more than I can comprehend.*

> *There now, I am getting maudlin and I promised myself not to do that. Right now you would get a laugh here, for Aunt Sylvania is reading* The Taming of the Shrew, *and one of our guests is playing Petruchio from memory. I keep looking around for a kitten that seems to be crying, but perhaps it is a mockingbird.*

> *Give Thaddeus a hug and plenty of kisses from all of us. He will be half grown before I see him, so tall I will not even know who he is.*

She deliberately kept the "if" out of the sentence. Surely God would not be so cruel as to keep them apart forever. She signed her name, added the others, and prepared her letters for mailing.

The cry came again. This time it was so close at hand she put down her case and began to crawl on her hands and knees, the better to peek under the low-lying bushes.

"Oh, look." She parted the spirea boughs to reveal a ginger kitten, so small it could fit in her palm, hiding in the shadows.

"What is it?" One of the men stood and crossed to look down. "A kitten! Looks about six to eight weeks or so. How'd it get in here?"

"There are lots of places something so tiny could squeeze under our fence." Louisa reached to pick up the kitten, but it backed away, hissing like it were grown rather than teacup sized. One tiny paw struck, scratching her finger.

"Ouch! You little rascal." She grabbed the animal before it could strike again and cupped it in her hands.

"You want I should dispose of it?" The man beside her kept his voice to a whisper.

"No, I think not. We all need a baby around. He'll calm down, you'll see."

Louisa had to promise to scour the neighborhood looking for its owner before Aunt Sylvania agreed they could keep the kitten.

"Might help keep the mice at bay. Sure is a feisty little thing." Sylvania shook her head. "I don't cotton much to cats, but if no one claims it . . ." She shrugged. "I reckon it is yours."

While the kitten started out sleeping that night in a box in the pantry, it ended up with one of the soldiers sleeping on a pallet on the floor.

The next afternoon when Louisa petted the purring kitten on her lap, she lifted the sleepy, limp golden body and looked into the kitten's face. "I sure wonder why God brought you to us just at this time." She rubbed the kitten's pink nose with her own. "Bet He has something real important for you to do, hmm?" The little kitten yawned, his pink tongue curling, showing all the barbs that helped keep his short coat so shiny. "But you don't care, do you? Give you a nice lap, gentle hands, and you'll purr anyone to peace."

But the feeling wouldn't go away. Something was coming.

Chapter Ten

WEST OF FORT LARAMIE

The burn ignited in Jesselynn's middle.

Thaddeus started to cry. Sammy added a wail.

Ophelia threw her apron over her head. "Lawd, have mercy."

Meshach gathered the sobbing Sammy into one arm and his rocking wife into the other. "Shush now, both of you."

Thaddeus threw himself against Jesselynn's knees.

Why is it that everyone feels they can tell me exactly what to do? Jesselynn held Thaddeus close, patting his back while she studied on her aunt's words. She could feel the older woman's flaming-iron gaze burning into the top of her bent head.

Lord, right now I need wisdom beyond Solomon's. And I need a good answer right now. She wanted to stalk off into the darkness. She wanted to scream at her aunt. She wanted others to share the joy that she felt inside.

"Gray Wolf Torstead is a fine man." There, that was peaceable rather than incendiary.

"That is not what we are talking about!" The lash of the whip could not crack more fiercely.

Jesselynn set Thaddeus gently away from her, waiting until Jane Ellen took the little boy into her lap. Ordering her reluctant body to obey, she rose to her feet, as if locking each joint as she stood so that her body would hold her upright.

"Aunt Agatha, I know my mama and daddy would agree with you, but they are dead and gone—"

When Agatha started to interrupt, Jesselynn held up a restraining hand. "Please allow me to have my say." Agatha clamped her arms across her heaving bosom. Jesselynn nodded and continued, her voice as calm as if discussing the weather. "We left the South, and the war, to seek a new life. Part of that new life is to no longer judge men and women by the color of their skin." She paused, letting her words sink in, but continued with her answer when Agatha appeared about to interrupt again. "I am going to say this only once. Wolf and I will be married at the fort. I want your blessing, but I don't need it." She turned to the rest of the folks gathered around the fire. "You are all invited, both to the wedding and to continue north with us, if you would like to. If any of you would rather wait and go on with another train heading west, that is up to you. You have about three days to decide before we make it back to the fort, unless another train comes along in the meantime."

However, since she'd not seen a westward bound wagon train on her journey back to the fort, that was unlikely.

"I got a question." Nate Lyons leaned forward.

"Of course."

"I heard rumors of Indian trouble. The Sioux don't like all of us passin' through their huntin' grounds. We'd be up in their country, right?"

Jesselynn nodded. "But Wolf isn't concerned about that. Red Cloud, one of the more well-known chiefs, is a distant relative of his. That's who he was going to go live with."

"Has he talked with Red Cloud yet?"

Jesselynn shrugged. "I'm not sure. I know he wants to help his tribe with supplies and such."

"Seems, well, perhaps they would take offense at so many of us comin' in one party."

Jesselynn scratched under the sweatband of her hat. "I wish I knew the answer to that." *Why didn't I ask Wolf some of these things? Because all you could think about was him.* The two voices in her mind argued back and forth. "You'll be able to talk with Wolf about those things when you see him."

The silence coming from Aunt Agatha screamed a thousand protests.

Mrs. McPhereson cupped her coffee mug in both hands. "Seems we'll be seein' plenty of changes comin' ahead. Like a stout tree, if'n we don't bend we'll break. And you got to admit, life out here can be one big storm after another."

"So are you thinking on returning east to your folks now that . . ." Jesselynn let her voice trail off.

"Now that I'm widowed?" Mrs. Mac shook her head. "No, me and my boys here talked it over. There ain't nothin' for us back there, but in Wyoming or Oregon we can homestead and get our land for the workin'. That was Ambrose's dream for us, the land, that is. I don't pretend to think it will be free. We'll earn every rock and tree. But we ain't afeered a hard work. So we'll go where you go. Good friends is worth more than gold, as the Good Book says, and I do believe it."

"Well said." Nate Lyons nodded with a look over to where Agatha sat, her knitting needles screaming of her displeasure. "And this way, we'll get a jump on winter. Can even put up some hay for the horses, maybe." He turned to where Meshach sat working on softening a tanned hide. "What about you?"

Meshach continued pulling the hide back and forth over a chunk of wood he'd smoothed and laid in a frame of crossed poles. The silence stretched like the hide he worked.

Jesselynn tossed a couple of twigs from the ground into the fire, keeping her full attention on the orange-and-yellow dancing flames. She would not beg and plead. If Meshach felt going west was best for him, she would give him her blessing and one of the wagons along with the oxen to pull it. Daniel and Benjamin would have to make up their own minds too.

Meshach looked up from his handiwork. "Me and 'Phelia, we had big dreams for Oregon, but no reason why those dreams can't be here in Wyomin'. Free land is free land."

Jesselynn fought the burning at the back of her eyes, wiped her nose with the back of her hand, and cleared her throat. "Thank you, my friend. I wasn't sure how I was going to say good-bye to all of you."

"Daniel and Benjamin, dey say stay too. Be tired of travelin' wid no end in sight."

Mr. and Mrs. Jesperson looked at each other, and the mister shrugged. "We ain't made up our minds yet. Can I tell you after we get back to the fort?"

"Whatever suits you."

"Do y'all mind me comin' along? I ain't got no menfolk no more, but I can work hard. Won't be just another mouth to feed. I can sell my wagon at the fort or not, as you think." Mrs. Jones stammered over her last words.

Jesselynn kept from looking at Benjamin. Should she ask if Mrs. Jones found the body of her husband they had dragged into the bushes? And what happened to Rufus?

"I . . . I think I better tell you a little story, so's you know I . . . I'm a safe addition to the party." Darcy Jones hung her clasped hands between her knees, her ragged skirt bunched around her legs. "Few days ago Rufus, that's my husband's brother, ya know. Well, he come stormin' back into camp sayin' Tommy Joe be dead. Found his body in the bushes, been stabbed." She sniffed, but her eyes remained dry. "I could hardly believe it. I mean . . . But I"—she wiped her nose on her shirttail—"I was goin' to get him and give him a decent burial, ya know, when Rufus laughed like it were the funniest joke he ever heard. He come after me then, and I knew by the look in his eyes, he weren't goin' to stop until . . . well, you know. But afore he could throw me down, I ran. When he caught me, I grabbed the knife from the sheath at his side and . . . and . . ." She sighed and shook her head. "I hope the dear Lord can forgive me, but I couldn't go on livin' like that. I mean if'n he . . ." Her voice trailed away. "I dug one hole and buried them both." She hid her face in her hands. "C-Can I come with you?"

The snap of fire eating sticks sounded loud in the silence. They could hear the cattle grazing. Crickets sang in the grasses.

Jesselynn got to her feet, crossed the circle, and knelt down beside the woman who sat with hunched shoulders, the bones poking out like angel wings on her back. "Of course you can come with us. Why once we feed up your oxen, they'll be plenty strong enough to pull the wagon."

"Tommy Joe . . ." Darcy started and stopped, heaving a sigh that creaked her bones. She looked up to Jesselynn beside her. "He weren't bad back in the beginnin'. He just never seemed to have any luck, you know. He said the whole world was agin' him. He weren't bad unless he be drinkin'."

Jesselynn kept her thoughts to herself. Knowing how close she'd come to suffering some of Tommy Joe's rage herself, she could feel nothing but pity for the woman beside her. Maybe this just proved the old saw that true love is blind. *So, Lord, do I tell her? Wouldn't that be cruel?*

"Rufus said 'twas prob'ly Indians what killed Tommy Joe." Darcy shook her head. "An' I kilt *him*. Do you think the good Lord will ever forgive me?"

Jesselynn put her arm around the shivering shoulders. "I do believe He will. All we need do is ask. Jesus died to save sinners, and we all sin."

"But . . . not . . . l-like I did." The shuddering sobs sounded worse as she tried to subdue them.

Jane Ellen brought a square of cotton around for a handkerchief. "Here." She tucked it in the woman's hand.

Jesselynn let Darcy cry in her arms. No matter how much she'd despised the two brothers and could find no way in her heart to feel bad they were gone, sorrow was sorrow, and she'd felt a mighty lot of it herself. She glanced up to see Aunt Agatha wipe her own eyes and return to her knitting.

When the sobbing ceased, Jesselynn eased her leg out to release the cramp that had come from sitting on her foot all this while. "How about I take you back to your wagon, so you can go to sleep. Things always look better in the morning." She more felt than saw the brief nod.

After settling the woman, who was not much bigger than Jane Ellen, in her bedroll, Jesselynn strolled back to the fire. "Let's bring the herd in for the night."

Meshach folded the now softened hide and, after handing it to Ophelia, dismantled his roller and put it all back in the wagon bed. One more skin to sew into shirts or vests or whatever was needed most. "We do it."

"All right." Jesselynn looked around their small circle. Hardly room for all the oxen and horses, but they were much safer this way, and one person could stand watch rather than two.

"I'll take first watch," Nate Lyons said from just behind her.

"Good. Keep Patch with you. And watch Ahab if he gets restless. He's the best watchdog around." She wasn't sure why she was telling him all this. He'd stood watch countless times and knew it all as well as she did.

"She'll get over it." He kept his voice soft, for her ears alone.

"Mrs. Jones?"

"Her too, but I meant Miss Agatha. Give her time, and she'll come around." He hunkered down at Jesselynn's side. "She's been through some rough changes."

"As have we all."

"True, but it's harder for us older ones to adapt than you young'uns."

Jesselynn felt a chuckle rising. "Young'uns?" She shook her head. "I'm old as those hills around us. Leastwise it feels that way."

"You been through a lot. Now perhaps God is restorin' the years of the locust for you."

"The years of the war, you mean?"

"Them too. I got me a feelin' we're goin' to see that valley where He pastures His sheep. He'll have a place just for all of us, our new home."

"Mr. Lyons, I do hope you are right."

"Can't you call me Nate, my dear?"

"I guess, but I like Nathan better." Jesselynn smiled into his eyes, which were so much easier to see now that he'd been barbered. Such a fine-looking man they had found under all that hair.

"Nathan it is, then."

"Good night and sleep well. Tomorrow will be a better day."

Since she didn't have to take watch, she did just that, waking with the first sleepy birdsong. Three more days and she would see Wolf again. Her betrothed. What a wondrous word.

In the morning Aunt Agatha looked through Jesselynn like she was invisible. Jesselynn shrugged and went to saddle Ahab. Nathan's suggestion to give her aunt time echoed in her mind as she rode out of camp. From the way it looked, eternity might not be long enough.

The drive back to the fort passed uneventfully, just the way Jesselynn liked it. She rode much of the way, topping the crests of the hills away from the wagons, alone for the first time in what seemed like forever. Thoughts of Twin Oaks intruded at times, but mostly she thought of Wolf, of all that had happened in the time since she first saw him at the camps in Independence. They had come so close to not being allowed to join his wagon train.

That thought made her turn back to her small plodding wagon train. If only they could pick up the pace. She'd been engaged once before. But John went away to war before they could be married, and he never came back, his remains buried in some battlefield.

So many things could happen in the next few days. If only there were some way to hurry the wagons. And get Aunt Agatha speaking to her again.

Please, God, keep Wolf safe until we can be married. She thought about that prayer and shook her head. *God, please keep him safe for the rest of our lives.* Now *that* was a real faith-stretching prayer. But asking God to change Aunt Agatha's mind—that would take a miracle.

Chapter Eleven

FORT LARAMIE

Would she never return to the fort?

"Wolf, have you heard a word I said?" Rebeccah Jensen planted her hands on her hips and tapped her foot.

"I believe so." He turned back from staring out the window.

"Well, I'm sure your coffee is cold by now. Here, I shall warm it up." She extended a hand for his cup and saucer.

Instead of handing it to her, Wolf drained the cup and almost made a face. *Cold coffee, ugh. And weak enough to be tea.*

"I warned you." Rebeccah shook her head, rose, and poured him a refill. "Land sakes, you're worse'n kids nearin' recess." Rebeccah had been a schoolteacher before she married and still carried fond memories of her children. Since then she'd pretty much figured out that men were only boys grown larger.

"Sorry." Wolf sipped the new cup and nodded his approval, although it could still stand some backbone. "Now, what was it you wanted my opinion on?" His father had taught him white-man manners, along with those of the Sioux. One did not preclude the other.

"I asked if you wanted to borrow my husband's black suit for the wedding."

Wolf noted her discomposure and glanced down at the stained buckskin shirt he wore. He did have one shirt of what used to be white material. "I . . . I hadn't thought of that. Thank you for reminding me." *Do I go buy something? Or is my money better spent for supplies?* No question. "Yes, if you think it would fit me, I'd be more than pleased to borrow the captain's suit."

"It doesn't get worn much out here, so I shall have Clara brush it up." She held out the plate of cookies. "Have another. Now, regarding the food—"

"I thought we'd have the ceremony and then leave for the Chugwater."

Rebeccah shook her head. Her smile reminded Wolf of his mother's, warm and full of love.

"If you think we are goin' to miss this chance for a shindig, you, sir, are sadly mistaken. There will be supper and dancing and gifts and . . ."

Wolf held up a hand. "Whoa, slow down. When did all this come about?"

"When Jesselynn said she'd marry you. Now, how many weddings do you think we've had here at the fort?"

Wolf shrugged. Surely she didn't expect an answer.

"Two in all the years we've been stationed here. We have far more funerals than weddings, so this is an opportunity for you and your new bride to get to know more of us here at the fort. Two days' journey means we are neighbors, and neighbors do for each other. Captain Jensen says that when he leaves the military, he wants to establish a home right up the river from here. This valley and this land have snagged his heart, pure and simple."

Wolf kept one ear on the conversation and the other listening for the entry of a wagon train. He nodded. "Wyoming is a good land. Room here for both white man and Indians."

"Well, be that as it may, your wedding is what we were discussing." Rebeccah shook her head at Wolf's obvious restlessness. She clasped her hands in her lap and leaned forward. "May I make a suggestion, Mr. Torstead?"

"Wolf."

"All right, Mr. Wolf."

He shook his head but didn't stop her again.

"Would it be all right if we women here at the fort just do what we think best?" At his nod and sigh of relief, she continued. "I know Jesselynn will not be disappointed. Nor will you."

"Mrs. Jensen, I am deeply indebted to you for your thoughtfulness. I know that whatever you choose to do will be perfect and far beyond what we could have done." He set his cup and saucer on the whatnot table, sketched a bow, and with a "Thank you, ma'am" hightailed it to the door as if a pack of howling predators were on his trail.

He heard her chuckle float behind him.

He would head out to find them but for Jesselynn's admonition that this was something she had to do herself. Were they in trouble? Perhaps he should just ride out and see that they were all right. *I don't have to let them see me.* The thought flowed into the action, and within minutes he'd saddled his horse and trotted away from the fort, heading west.

———

Lord, what do I do about Aunt Agatha? The cold is so deep I'm afraid of frostbite. Jesselynn had insisted on taking first watch. She rode around the circled wagons, far enough off so as not to disturb those sleeping. Even Patch was curled up under the wagon, right next to where her bedroll would lie as soon as Mr. Lyons—she still had trouble calling him Nathan—came out to relieve her. With the moon in the dark phase, she had no idea of the time.

Ahab stopped, his head high, ears pricked. Patch tore past them, heading for the eastern hill. Jesselynn froze, not even breathing, in order to hear what roused the animals. Nothing. Patch hadn't even barked. She turned Ahab to follow where the dog had gone. Every few feet she stopped to listen. Was that Patch whining? He hadn't barked. Her stomach tightened, as if wrapped in drying rawhide.

She loosened the tie-down on the pistol at her hip and drew it from the holster.

Had whatever or whoever was out there killed her dog? Her mouth dried. Her scalp drew tight. She stopped Ahab again to listen. He lifted his head, nostrils flared to read the breeze. His intake of breath sounded loud as a steam whistle in the stillness.

When she heard his nostrils flutter in a soundless nicker, she glanced over her shoulder. Nothing had changed. No one had left camp, at least not that she could tell. Surely they would have told her. One did not go sneaking out of camp. They might get shot on the return. A necessary trip did not take one so far from camp either.

Short of Ahab's breathing, all was still, not even a cricket sang. Something was indeed amiss. Sure that someone was watching her, Jesselynn debated whether to rouse the camp, go get Meshach, or go look over the rise of the hill.

She'd just nudged Ahab forward when Patch came trotting up to her, tongue lolling, tail wagging. He glanced once over his shoulder, then sat by Ahab's front feet.

"So did you patrol the area and find nothing?"

Patch yipped and sat to scratch a flea. She could hear his hind foot thumping on the grass. Ahab lowered his head and snatched a few mouthfuls of grass before she tightened the reins.

"You can graze when I go to bed." She turned him back to circle the camp again, no longer feeling that someone was watching her. It was indeed a puzzlement, as she told Nate Lyons when he caught his horse and rode out to meet her.

"Ahab is trustworthy. I've never seen him give a false alarm." Nate studied the hill she'd pointed out.

"Whatever it was, he saw no danger. Patch neither. Had it been a rabbit, Patch would have barked and chased." Jesselynn yawned, quicker than her hand could cover her mouth. "I'm going to bed. At least the crickets are singing again. Strange."

"Which way was the breeze blowin'?"

"Not sure. Seems to kind of switch around at times. But both animals smelled something." Jesselynn walked Ahab back to camp, removed his saddle and bridle, and tied him on a long line so he could graze outside the circle of wagons. Long as Nate was on guard, the horse was safe. She could get some sleep.

"What do you think it might have been?" Jesselynn stood looking up at Meshach a few hours later. The sun had yet to rise above the horizon, but preparations to break camp were well under way.

"Don' know. I walked around, seen grass knocked down like someone or somethin' walk through dere, den lay down. Gone now."

"Indian?"

Meshach shrugged.

Jesselynn chewed on her bottom lip. She watched Aunt Agatha finish stirring the mush that had been simmering most of the night. *Lord, what am I going to do?*

"Any suggestions?" She nodded toward the fire.

Meshach took off his hat, scratched his head, and using both hands, settled the hat back in place. "Sure wish I did. But Bible say love those who persecute you. You be blessed dat way."

"What if she never comes around?"

"Never be long time."

"Breakfast is ready." Agatha straightened and kneaded her lower back with her fists.

Jesselynn knew that meant Agatha's back was bothering her. Sometimes chewing on willow bark helped. With that thought in mind, she turned away from the circled wagons and headed to the creek. Willow twigs she could supply in abundance. She tore off a couple of branches and brought them back to camp. Tying the bundle to the hoop right behind where Agatha sat, Jesselynn returned to the campfire. After dishing up her bowl of mush, she took a seat on the wagon tongue. Even Thaddeus ate quietly, sending furtive glances at Agatha.

Jesselynn reached over and tickled his ribs. "Hey, boy."

He giggled and squirmed.

Agatha turned away, her mouth pursed like she'd just sucked on green plums.

"I'll try talkin' with her later," Jane Ellen whispered. "We're all prayin' for her. She'll come around."

Mrs. McPhereson stopped right behind them and laid her hands on Jesselynn's shoulders, then brushed one along her cheek.

The tender gesture said more than ten minutes of talk.

After Meshach and Daniel finished hitching up the oxen, Agatha crossed around behind the wagon to climb up, so she didn't have to pass by her niece.

Mounting Ahab, Jesselynn swung out ahead of the wagons as they pulled into line.

———

In spite of Jesselynn's prayers for a return to the former ease of companionship, Aunt Agatha spoke to everyone but her all the next day. The closer they drew to the fort, the more Jesselynn wanted to ride ahead, away from the dust and the creaking wagons, away from her aunt's judging face and sniffs. Never before had she realized how effective a comment a sniff could be, a prolonged series of sniffs, to be exact.

While Jesselynn tried to work up a good mad, she understood how her aunt felt and what she believed. In the South, marriage between white and colored was not only a moral issue but a legal one as well. The law forbade intermarriage.

But was the law right? And was it biblical? Were those of white skin really better than the others? Didn't the Bible say all are the same, male and female, slave and free, no matter the color of skin or hair or eyes? *God, Father, how I wish*

I knew your Word better. I've heard the preaching for so many years that having slaves is right according to the Word—that the Bible says for slaves not to leave their masters. But the Bible also says we who are in Jesus are free.

So who's right? And does it matter?

Jesselynn crossed her hands on Ahab's withers, staring out over the valley below. Sod huts, smoke rising from a chimney, and grain bending in the breeze showed where someone had taken up the land to make it home. Sheets flapped on a clothesline.

She turned to watch their wagons start down the hill, angling so as not to let the wagons run over the oxen. Meshach and Benjamin had taken over the reins, and the women and children all walked, or rather the women walked and the children rolled down through the rich grass. Their shouts of laughter sang on the air, making her smile, especially when she saw Jane Ellen tumbling with the little ones.

If all of these folk decided to continue north with them, they would still be her family but no longer her responsibility alone. That thought brought a peace she hadn't felt since leaving Twin Oaks. Perhaps Aunt Agatha would choose to remain at the fort.

Jesselynn glanced up. No, there was no cloud in the sky. The cloud came from within. "Father, I don't want this cloud over my wedding. It should be a happy day for everyone." But as she well knew, "should" and "is" were not always the same.

And worrying wasn't what God wanted either. "So here it is, in your hands, and I will not think or worry on it again." Ahab flicked his ears back and forth and pulled on the reins. He hated to be left behind. "Amen, so be it. Come on, son, let's be going."

———

When they set up camp late that night, they were a quarter mile or so from the fort, with its lights in the windows, music and laughter, all the signs of civilization. Jesselynn planned on riding into the fort and finding Wolf as soon as the herd was set to grazing. She didn't care if she had supper or not, the desire to see him ate at her insides. She had her head in one of the boxes looking for her clean shirt and the skirt she'd packed so long ago, when Thaddeus came running.

"Jesse!" He jerked on her pant leg.

"I know I put that thing back in here. Where is it?" She pushed aside her journal, ignoring the reminder of how long since she'd written anything.

"Jesse!"

"Thaddeus Highwood, stop that. Can't you see I'm busy?"

"But Mr. Wolf . . ."

Jesselynn dropped the lid on her finger, yelped, stuck the wounded appendage in her mouth, and spun around.

"Hello, Jesselynn." The laughter in Wolf's dark eyes fueled her flurry.

"Don't you know it isn't polite to sneak up on a body like that?" Blood hammered in her smashed finger. Thaddeus looked as if she'd smacked him. Aunt Agatha harrumphed loud enough to wake a hibernating bear. Wolf continued to smile as he swung off his horse in slow motion and, locking his gaze into hers, crossed the few feet to stand in front of her. There he stood, all six feet of well-muscled, broad-shouldered, painter-lithe manhood, the man she'd been dreaming of for days, and now all she could think of was how much she wanted to smack him with a long board.

She pushed her hat back on her head, dusted off her britches, and pushed a small rock out of the way with the toe of her boot. *He's seen me all dressed up in forget-me-nots, and now look at me.* "Why couldn't you have waited?"

She's even more beautiful than I could picture. Wolf took another step forward. No, he shouldn't be seen kissing her, but her lips, now caught in a pout, begged him to. *Why are we waiting to get married? Why not tomorrow? I suppose women need time to prepare—even Jesselynn, who claims not to care about that sort of thing.*

Her question penetrated his concentration on keeping from sweeping her into his arms. "Waited? Why?"

"Because . . . because . . ." She dropped her hands to her sides. *Because I'm a mess, that's why.* She looked down at the source of the pressure on her leg and found Thaddeus staring up at her. He clung to her thigh, one finger in his mouth, staring from her to Wolf and back again. The puzzled look on his face banished her befuddlement like a breath blew away a dandelion puff. She reached down and swung her little brother up on her hip. She stuck out her other hand.

"Welcome, Mr. Wolf. You're just in time for supper." Her fingers clamped around his gave all the greeting her mind and mouth couldn't put into words.

What if Aunt Agatha treats him like she has me?

Chapter Twelve

"How'd she take your news?"

Jesselynn wished Wolf hadn't asked that. She'd been so careful to not allude to it, hoping she could pretend everything was all right.

Honesty, right? Lord, please keep him from being hurt. "Not too well."

"I didn't expect anything different. Will she go on to the Chugwater with us?"

Jesselynn could feel her jaw drop. "You want her to?"

"Can you see her going on west with the Jespersons?" Was that a twinkle she saw in his eyes?

"She could stay at the fort."

"What? And become a washerwoman or some such?" Wolf shook his head. "I knew what her feelings would be when I asked you to marry me. She can't help it. She has always lived that way."

"She can change. The rest of us have had to do a mighty lot of changing." Her flat tone said as much as her words.

Wolf took Jesselynn's elbow and pulled her behind the wagon so he could take her in his arms. "If you can ignore her actions, so can I."

Jesselynn laid her head against his chest. "I'll try." She looked up again. "Who said the Jespersons were going on west?"

"I heard them talking with Meshach. I think the woman would just as soon stay here, but he's got a burr under his saddle to see Oregon. They'll join up with the next train. I heard there's one about four days out."

"They could at least have told me."

———

The night before the wedding, Jesselynn woke gasping, fighting off a nightmare that threatened to strangle her. But when she tried to remember what it was, only nameless fears stirred her emotions. She crawled from under the wagon, wishing she had taken Rebeccah up on her offer of the guest bedroom.

Some insane sense of duty had kept her out here in the camp. Out of habit, she clamped her hat on her head and strolled to the perimeter of the circled wagons. Even here, within sight of the fort, she'd felt the necessity to do that.

Horses had been stolen before and would be again. She preferred it not be her horses.

Ahab raised his head and nickered. She could hear him coming to greet her, his footfalls soft on the grazed grass.

"All's well, old son." She stroked his nose when he hung his head over her shoulder. "What's keeping you awake, hmm?" He snorted and rested his head weight on her shoulder. She scratched his cheek and rubbed up around his ears, all the while knowing what was keeping her awake.

Getting married was a big step under the best of circumstances, but thanks to Aunt Agatha . . . Jesselynn changed her thought track deliberately. It wasn't just Aunt Agatha. It was a whole world that thought the color of a man's skin of more import than his character. Would she ever be able to take her whole family back to Twin Oaks? No closer to answers, she and Ahab watched the sun break free from the horizon to announce a new day. Her wedding day.

———

"Oh, Jesse, you look so purty." Thaddeus stared at his sister, eyes round as his mouth. When he started toward her, Jane Ellen grabbed him by the shirttails.

"No, don't touch her. You don't want to get her dress dirty, do you?"

Thaddeus looked down at his hands, up at Jesselynn, then over his shoulder at Jane Ellen. "I not dirty." For safe measure he wiped his hands on his new britches.

"Come here, little brother. Look in the mirror and see how fine you look." Jesselynn took his hand, and together they stared at the reflection in the oval, oak-framed floor mirror.

The rich cream silk showed off her shoulders and nipped in at her slender waist. Tiny pearl buttons ran from the dip in the sweetheart neckline to the point of the bodice an inch or two below her natural waistline. Wide enough for hoops, but buoyed by crinolines instead, the skirt hosted swirls of lace and seed pearls. The dress might have seen balls and cotillions in its early life, but like Jesselynn, it was far from a society that had use for such a garment.

Jesselynn bent over and kissed the top of her brother's head. "Don't you look handsome?" A blousy white shirt with a navy tie was tucked into deep blue pants cut just above his knees, one scraped from a fall over the steps not an hour before.

Would that her other brother would look at Wolf with the adoration of Thaddeus.

"You ready?"

He nodded.

"Then I reckon we better head for the chapel."

"Dearly beloved, we are gathered here in the sight of God . . ."

Jesselynn ached to turn around and see if Aunt Agatha came to the wedding, but instead she looked up at Wolf. The black suit he wore made him look like any other gentleman, Southern or Northern, only more handsome. Many of the French Creoles from Louisiana were darker skinned than he. She'd met them at Keeneland, the racetrack in Lexington. She brought her attention back to the black-garbed man in front of her, his deep voice saying the words she'd so longed to hear.

Mama, Daddy, I hope you're seeing this and giving us your blessing. Surely you know answers by now to some of my questions. And God, if you could put a bug in Aunt Agatha's ear, I'd sure be appreciative.

When the minister asked if anyone opposed this marriage, Jesselynn waited with her breath in her throat. Surely this was the time, but when no one answered, she let herself breathe again.

Wolf turned and took her hands in his. Thoughts of anything other than the light in his eyes fled her mind.

"I, Gray Wolf Torstead, take thee, Jesselynn Highwood, to be my wedded wife." He repeated the words after the chaplain, his voice strong and sure, his handclasp warm and dry. He looked deep within to her very soul as he finished the age-old words.

"Now repeat after me . . ." The chaplain nodded to her.

Jesselynn spoke the words, her lips trembling, but her voice even. "I, Jesselynn Highwood, take thee . . . to have and to hold from this day forward . . . and therefore I plight thee my troth." Safe and sure, their hands bound together along with their hearts, they bowed their heads to pray, repeated the "I do's," and turned back to the chaplain for the blessing. When he pronounced them husband and wife, she went into Wolf's arms like she'd been waiting for him all of her life. They held each other, then shared a kiss both chaste and full of promise.

"But, Jane Ellen, I got to go pee." Thaddeus's whisper carried to the front of the room.

Jesselynn could feel her face grow warm, knowing it was not due to the temperature outdoors or in the room.

As Jane Ellen scooted out the door with Thaddeus on her hip, chuckles flitted around the room like butterflies, and Jesselynn and Wolf turned to face the gathering. Mrs. McPhereson sniffed and honked into her hanky.

"Praise de Lawd and all Him handiwork," Ophelia sang from the rear.

Jesselynn smiled up at the man whose arm she held. "Well, Mr. Torstead, shall we go greet our guests?"

After shaking hands with everyone as they left the chapel, Jesselynn and Wolf followed Mrs. Jensen to the mess hall, where trestle tables groaned beneath the abundance of food. Elk haunches stood waiting to be carved, vegetables from the commissary gardens, fresh-baked bread, baked beans, and dishes of all kinds sat rim to rim so that the only tablecloth showing was that hanging down the sides. A white frosted wedding cake, decorated with wild asters, reigned on a separate table, as did the drinks next to it—coffee, tea, and lemonade. Bouquets of wild asters and daisies graced every table, and here and there nodded roses from the general's garden.

"Oh." Jesselynn stood in the doorway, gazing at it all and fighting the tears that had threatened during the ceremony. *All the work these women have done for us. What an amazing gift.*

"Right purty, isn't it?" Jane Ellen, Thaddeus in tow, squeezed in beside her.

"Me go play." Thaddeus looked up at Jesselynn. "Please?"

"We'll eat first." Wolf swung the child up into his arms. Now that Thaddeus could see, he spotted the cake immediately.

"Look, Jesse, cake." He pointed to the white confection in the corner.

"I know. I'm surprised you remember what one is."

"Come on up here so we can have grace and serve our bride and groom. Then the line forms to the right." Captain Jensen waited until all was quiet before raising his voice for all to hear. "Heavenly Father, we come before thee this day with joyful hearts. Thank you for blessing all of us with this wedding and with the food our folks have prepared. We ask that thou will bless this union and bring health and happiness to this couple. In thy holy name we pray, amen."

By the time everyone had helped themselves, the room fairly rocked with laughter and buzzing conversation. Children ran in and out, Patch barked from the front step, and before long a fiddle tuned up out on the parade ground.

After cake and drinks, they followed the music outside for the dancing to begin. Jesselynn and Wolf danced the first waltz.

"I think I've about forgotten how to dance." Jesselynn lost herself in Wolf's dark eyes.

"Then we can stumble together. I never had much time for dancin' on the wagon trains, and my people didn't exactly dance this way when I was growing up."

Jesselynn leaned back in his arms, the better to study his face. "When will you tell me about growin' up in the tribe?"

"Someday. You will meet my relatives one day."

The thought made her pause, only a fraction of a moment, but still he caught it. "You need not fear them."

Fear wasn't a word she had applied so far, but horror stories were whispered about Indian attacks and how they hated whites. Getting her family through to Oregon had taken up too much of her time and energy to worry about something that might or might not happen. Meshach's admonition that they trust the Lord for their protection carried over to other things besides Indian attacks.

"As you say, my husband." Ah, what pleasure to say such words. *My husband.* She repeated the words several more times in her mind.

"I say so, my wife." He drew her closer and rested his chin on the top of her head. "My wife." His voice deepened, warmed, licked at her senses.

The music ended with a flourish, and those gathered around clapped, and someone whistled. Jesselynn felt the red creeping up her neck. She'd forgotten they danced in such a public place. It seemed there'd been only the two of them and that the music might go on forever.

The fiddle sang into a reel, and men and women lined up on opposite sides. Every time she passed Wolf, he winked at her. About the third time, she started to giggle, and with each additional wink, it grew worse. By the end of the dance she collapsed against a hitching post, out of breath from both the fast footwork and the giggles.

"Me dance." Thaddeus stood beside her.

"Of course." She picked him up, and they whirled away together, he with his legs locked securely around her waist, she with her arms around his middle. They dipped and swirled until Wolf tapped her shoulder and took the little boy off with him, this time riding on his tall shoulders.

Jane Ellen's gaze followed Wolf around the dancers. "He do be one fine figure of a man."

"That's for sure." Jesselynn waved her hand in front of her face to create a breeze of some sort. "But I've been noticing a certain young man looking your way."

"Who?" Jane Ellen glanced around the gathered people.

"He's wearing a blue uniform, and now that he thinks I'm looking at him, his cheeks are as red as the roses on the table." Jesselynn nodded over to a young private who doffed his visored cap and blushed even more. "You're going to dance with him now that he's coming, right?"

"I guess. Do you know his name?"

"No, but I'm sure we will in a moment." Jesselynn dropped her voice so he wouldn't hear.

The young man doffed his hat, half bowed, and in a voice that cracked only once, said, "I'm Private Henry Workman." Even his ears turned red. "And canIhavethisdance?"

Jesselynn gave Jane Ellen a nudge in the back. "This is my friend, Jane Ellen."

"Pleased to meet you, Miss." He extended his hand.

Jane Ellen shot Jesselynn a look of panic, swallowed, and stepped forward. "I don't dance too good."

"Me neither." The two started off, stiff as two porch posts.

Jesselynn glanced around the assembled folks in the hope that Aunt Agatha had changed her mind and at least enjoyed some of the festivities.

"She won't be comin'." Nate Lyons spoke softly from behind her. "I tried, Miss Jesselynn. I surely did, but that Miss Agatha is one stubborn woman."

"I know." *But I do hope she comes around.*

"She said 'twere none of my business, but it really is. I care about that woman, if you haven't already surmised that." He hung back, as if not wanting to look Jesselynn in the face.

"I had me an idea."

"I'm a-fixin' to ask her to walk out with me. You think she will?"

"I'm a poor one to ask at this point. She won't even speak to me, nor come to my wedding."

"I told her that times are a-changin', and what used to be in the South won't be in the West."

"I'm sure that made her very happy."

His chuckle turned into a snort, then a guffaw. "Not hardly, Miss Jesselynn. Not hardly a'tall. But you mark my words, she'll marry me before winter."

"Lord's blessing to you, Mr. Lyons. Now, will you look at that." She nodded to Jane Ellen and her young man. "I reckon she's growing right up." *At least perhaps this young man can help her get over her crush on Wolf.* While Jane Ellen had never said a word, the way she leaped to serve him and spoke his name with a mixture of gentleness and awe had announced her admiration of Wolf as surely as if she'd blown a trumpet.

"Ah, my dear, you make a lovely bride." Mrs. Jensen strolled up with her arm through her husband's.

"Thanks to your lovely gown." Jesselynn stroked down the sides of the creamy silk with both hands. The skirt and petticoat swished against her legs as she whirled through the dances, making her grateful that hoops weren't *de rigueur* out on the plains. And since she'd not been laced into a corset, she could enjoy the dancing without a near faint.

"No, it is not just the gown. Your face shines with happiness. We do"—she glanced up at her husband, who patted her hand on his arm—"wish you all the best in God's blessings."

"Thank you." Jesselynn sketched a curtsy. Her gaze automatically searched out Wolf, and when he smiled at her, she felt a quiver clear inside. That fine-looking man dancing with one of the officers' wives was *her* husband. Would that she would never get over the joy of it. She remembered her mother telling her how, even after all their years of marriage, her heart still leaped when her husband entered the room. *Oh, Father, to love like my mother and daddy is all I ask.*

"Come, Captain, surely you have the energy to dance with your wife. And, my dear"—Rebeccah leaned closer to Jesselynn—"I see a certain fine young man is coming to claim his bride for this dance."

Jesselynn and Wolf whirled away to the fast pace of a polka, their feet following the dance steps while their eyes made promises and their hands spoke only of love.

Later, when the musicians took a much needed break, Jesselynn and Wolf stood with the Jensens in the shade of one of the buildings sipping lemonade and the women fanning their faces.

"The women of the camp have prepared the guest quarters for you to spend the night. We thought, well . . ."

The captain broke in with a laugh. "Rebeccah, your cheeks are as pink as Miss Jesselynn's. I'm sure they appreciate the thought."

"Yes, I . . . we . . ." Jesselynn glanced up at Wolf, who smiled down at her and nodded. "Thank you, and please thank all the others for us. You all worked so hard to make this day one to remember." She tucked her arm in the crook of Wolf's elbow.

"I'm just sorry your aunt felt unable to attend. Do you think if one of us were to go talk with her?" Rebeccah's question was hesitant.

Since Jesselynn had made no mention of Aunt Agatha, she wondered how they knew, or if they knew the real reason. Shaking her head, Jesselynn sighed. "I don't know what will change her mind. Mr. Lyons tried, and I know Mrs. McPhereson spoke with her too." The urge to tell the entire story almost made Jesselynn continue, but she stopped, knowing that Wolf did not need to hear it all. Instead of making up an excuse for her aunt and thus adding another lie to her long list, she just said Agatha was staying in camp.

Before taking her wedding vows, Jesselynn had made a vow of another sort, this one only between God and herself. The vow to never lie again, to always tell the truth, made her feel fifty pounds lighter. Guilt was a heavy burden, one she no longer desired to carry, not that it had ever been her desire. Living the lies had been necessary to keep them safe, but no longer.

Does Wolf realize what a burden he has assumed, all these people that make up our train? Widows, black folk learning to be free, a woman who has played the role of a man and liked a great deal of that role, a small boy with a temper like the other males in his family, and all the others. Good thing this man has broad shoulders.

"Do you have all of your supplies for the Oglala?" Captain Jensen turned to Wolf.

"Those that were available. And two packhorses to carry it all." Wolf crossed his arms. "I still have more credit at the store. I'll be bringing the horses back before winter."

Jesselynn listened to the conversation. If they could catch wild horses, perhaps they would be bringing some of them in at the same time. *If.* So many "if's."

The party broke up after dark, with folks going back to their quarters or wagons and Jesselynn saying good-night to Thaddeus.

"But why you not come?" Thaddeus planted his fists on his hips, a banty rooster set to fight.

"Because Wolf and I are staying here at the fort."

"Why?"

"Because . . . because . . ." She looked up to Wolf from her kneeling position in front of Thaddeus. She could feel heat creeping up her neck. *Little brother, sometimes . . .*

"Because she is my wife and is going to stay with me." Wolf leaned over and swung the boy up to sit on his arms.

Thaddeus studied the man who held him. Blue eyes dueled with dark. "Tomorrow you come back?"

Wolf nodded. Thaddeus smiled and motioned to be set down. "Good." Feet again on the ground, he ran to Jane Ellen and, taking her hand, waved as they left.

As the crowd dispersed, Wolf and Jesselynn thanked everyone for coming and strolled over to the guest quarters, where a white bow hung on the door. Jesselynn could feel panic begin to bubble in her middle. Her feet didn't want to climb the steps. She stumbled on the second one, saved from a fall by Wolf's strong arm.

Lord, I hardly know this man!

Chapter Thirteen

RICHMOND, VIRGINIA

"We'll leave in the mornin'."

Louisa stared at her brother, questions rioting through her mind. How had he gotten a leave of absence when he started the position with Jefferson's firm not a week before? Where were they going, and what route would they take? And most important, what disguise would they use this time? The coffin trick had worked so well, but did they dare try it again?

She waited, trying to be patient, but her foot tapped in spite of her. Zachary did not like to be questioned or rushed.

When he resumed his writing, she cleared her throat.

"Yes?"

From the look he gave her, she knew he'd forgotten her presence. How could he do that—concentrate on what he was doing and forget the rest of the world existed?

"Have you nothing further to inform me regarding the trip?"

"I will tonight after I meet with—" He cut off the remainder of his thoughts, always careful to keep as much information to himself as possible. That way if they were ever questioned, she could say she didn't know, without lying. Though he had explained that to her, she still felt he treated her like . . . like someone too young to trust.

The entire family knew what a poor liar she was, although she had lived another persona for several months at the hospital, playing the part of *Mrs.* Highwood, instead of Miss. When he was released to his aunt's house, Zachary had refused to play along, ordering her home as soon as he was able. His concept of what a proper young lady should be allowed to do was hopelessly outdated.

Knowing that further questioning would be futile, she turned and left the room, resisting the urge to stamp her feet just a little. Or slam the door.

Instead, Louisa picked up the kitten mewing at her heels and took herself outside to assist their newest patient in the intricacies of stitching a fine seam. He'd resisted the idea of knitting, but when she switched the focus to sewing and reminded him that men made good tailors, he'd accepted the needle and thread. After all, his lack of legs didn't take away the ability of his hands. She set the kitten down in the lap of a soldier who had not as yet smiled.

"Miss Louisa, you make this sewing look so easy, but it ain't, not in the least." The young man, who'd served as a lieutenant, pointed to his uneven stitches.

"Hmm. It could be the light."

"It could be the needle, or the thimble, or the . . ." The glare was more for the material in his hands than for her.

"When you first shot a gun, did you hit the target all the time?"

"Well, no, but—"

"When I first held a needle, I was five, maybe four, years old. My stitches were far worse than yours, and I had far less patience. But my mother refused to let me quit, no matter how hard I begged. Sometimes I near to wore out the thread, I had to take it out so many times." She held his work up to see better. "Just remember, the smaller the stitches, the less likely the seam will rip. All the difference between a soldier being warm enough or freezing in the winter."

"I understand." He made himself smile, for her sake, she knew. Learning to live without legs sent some men into such depression that they were unable to continue living. This man was trying.

Louisa wanted to hug him. Surely he was older than she, but he seemed like a baby brother. Even though she was only eighteen, she felt ancient. Ever since her Lieutenant Lessling died, she knew she'd aged years. She glanced over to see the ginger kitten purring beneath a stroking hand.

She patted the young legless man's shoulder. "You'll make it. Our Father will see you through."

He sighed. "Not so sure I believe in 'Our Father' anymore. Not after all the things I saw."

Louisa knelt beside his chair. "If we give up, Satan wins the battle. Remember, the Bible says 'If God be for us, who can be against us.'"

"I know." He looked into her eyes, searching her soul. "But do you really believe God is still for us?"

Louisa swallowed. "I believe God is for each one of us, and when we trust in Him, He never fails."

"But what if I don't trust no longer?"

"God never changes." *But please don't ask me if I believe God is on the side of the South. I can't say that any longer.* "Excuse me, I see that Abby needs me for something. You keep on practicing those stitches. You'll do fine." Before he could ask her another question she left the veranda. Thank God for Abby.

"Missy Louisa, Miss Sylvania, she don' look too good. I made her go up and take a lie-down."

"Thank you, Abby. I didn't realize she'd returned from her sewing circle."

Twice a week Aunt Sylvania attended the sewing circle at her church. While she'd given up asking her niece to join her, she still faithfully attended. Louisa knew she enjoyed the gossip as much as the sewing. Together the group sewed for the war effort, just like they did at home.

"I'll go check on her." Louisa made her way up the stairs to her aunt's room. She tapped on the door. "Aunt Sylvania, may I come in?"

"Of course, dear."

Crossing the sunny room, Louisa stifled a gasp.

Sylvania lay against the pillows, her face nearly as white as the pillow slips. She raised a hand, trembling like a leaf in the wind.

"What happened?" Louisa took her aunt's frail hand in hers. "Your hand is freezing."

"I . . . I just felt dizzy, and now my head aches." Sylvania's voice sounded fretful, like a confused child.

Louisa felt her aunt's forehead, the skin papery beneath her fingertips. A faint sheen of perspiration had formed, but she was not hot with fever.

"I think we should call the doctor."

"Oh, pshaw, he's too busy with really sick folks. I'll just have me a lie-down for a while. I didn't sleep too well last night."

"How about if we make some willow bark tea for you?"

"I don't know." Sylvania closed her eyes and sighed. "My stomach doesn't really feel like anything. Perhaps a cold cloth would help."

"I'll get it." Louisa paused at the doorway. "Anything else?"

Sylvania fluttered her hand in dismissal.

"What you think?" Abby met her at the bottom of the stairs.

"I think we should send Reuben for the doctor. But in the meantime, a cool cloth, some willow bark tea laced with honey, and a rest should help."

"I gets the tea made. She ain't been eatin' 'nough to keep a bitty bird alive. No wonder she done feel poorly." Abby bustled off, muttering all the while.

After sending Reuben on his way, Louisa took the cool cloth back upstairs and laid it across her aunt's forehead. Gentle snores never changed cadence with the attention. Louisa studied her aunt's slack face. Was there something wrong with the right side? Surely it was only a shadow.

Her stomach clenched. *Dear God, please let nothing be wrong with Auntie.* She crossed to the other side of the bed where the light was better. Sure enough, the right eye drooped, the skin of the cheek slacked, the mouth pulled downward like wax slightly melted. "Oh, Lord, apoplexy."

A bit of drool slipped from the right side of the older woman's mouth and pooled on the pillow slip.

Louisa darted from the room and down the stairs. "Abby, come quick."

"Tea most ready." Abby stuck her head around the doorframe.

"No, come now."

Drying her hands on her apron, the black woman hurried up the stairs, muttering, "Lawd, have mercy. Lawd, have mercy."

She knelt by the side of the bed. "Ah, Missy Louisa, look at her face."

"I know. I hoped . . ." *I hoped I was just seeing things. That's what I hoped.* "Do you know of anything to be done?" Louisa took her aunt's hand and stroked the back of it. Sylvania slept on.

"No. Nothin' to do but wait. See how bad. I helped wid a neighbor. Some get better, some get worse." Abby swiped at a tear on her cheek. "Please, Lawd, let her get better."

Louisa echoed the simple prayer. "I'll stay with her, you go send Reuben up as soon as he returns. Perhaps the doctor will have something to help her."

Abby left, shaking her turbaned head, her sniffing audible over the sound of Sylvania's breathing.

––––––

When the doctor finally came just before supper, he only shook his head. He lifted the old woman's eyelids, listened to her heart and lungs, and counted her pulse.

"Her heart is strong, but all we can do is keep her comfortable. Has she tried to speak since this happened?"

"No, she's been asleep since shortly after she lay down. We talked briefly then. She said she'd felt dizzy at church and her stomach was so upset, so she came on home early. She mentioned a headache, so I set Abby to making willow bark tea. She never woke up to drink it." Louisa stepped back from the bed and motioned to the doctor to follow. Lowering her voice, she asked, "Will she wake again?"

"Oh my, yes. Unless she gets much worse, I feel this is a minor case of apoplexy. We'll know more in the next few days how severe the damage is."

"Can you tell me what happened?"

"A blood vessel has burst in her brain. The damage depends on how large a vessel and the location. Sleep is the best thing for her right now. When she wakes up, if she has a hard time speaking, reassure her that it likely won't stay this way. She can learn to speak again. The same with the use of her hands and feet. As I said, this seems like a light one."

"Can you give her anything?"

"If she were real restless, I would suggest some laudanum, but . . ." He shrugged and raised his hands, only to drop them again at his side.

Louisa knew both the gesture and the situation. If she could find some laudanum on their next trip, she would keep some for her aunt.

The thought of the journey triggered panic to flutter her stomach. She and Zachary were supposed to leave tomorrow.

"Thank you for coming so quickly." She showed the doctor out, wishing, as he did, that the diagnosis had been different.

"I've known Miss Sylvania for twenty years or more, doctored her husband and her children, poor thing. She lost them all. She hasn't had an easy life, and now to have this happen to her. Hard to understand the Lord's will at times." He patted her arm. "You take care of yourself now, with all these folks to care for."

"Of course, and the same for you." The two of them exchanged a look of secret commiseration, both recognizing the polite deception. They'd often met each other coming and going on errands of mercy all hours of the night or day.

Before he reached the street, she thought of something and dashed out the door. "Doctor?"

He paused and turned to wait for her.

"If I have to be gone for a few days, would Abby and Reuben be able to care for my aunt?"

"Of course, my dear. I'm counting on her to be up and about as early as tomorrow. If there are any further developments, send Reuben for me immediately."

"Thank you again, Doctor." She watched as he climbed into his black buggy and clucked to his horse. Why was caring for wounded soldiers easier than for her own aunt? But as she returned to the house, she knew the answer. While she cared about the soldiers, she loved her aunt, her father's last remaining sister. And besides, the men were under orders to mind her, while Aunt Sylvania had never minded anyone, if Louisa's father's stories were to be believed.

Louisa made her way out to the veranda, where the men were enjoying their afternoon lemonade and cookies.

"How is she?" The question came from all directions at once.

"We'll know more by tomorrow."

"Is there anything we can do?" The lieutenant asked for the four of them.

"Pray."

He arched an eyebrow, and from their earlier discussion, Louisa knew what he was thinking.

"Sometimes we find it easier to pray for someone other than ourselves. If I could think of anything else, I would tell you."

"Thank you, Miss Louisa. My prayers, for whatever they are worth, will be rising for Miss Sylvania. We all miss her sweet voice as she reads to us."

"I will tell her so." *Oh, Lord, let her return from her slumbers with a mind to understand how we love her and appreciate all that she does.*

Louisa ambled back inside, offering to help Abby with the supper preparations.

"You just go on up and sit by Miss Sylvania till I calls you. Reuben done taked my place. I need his old worthless hide down here to carry water to the washtubs. After supper I wash de sheets. Take dat kitten with you."

Louisa knew better than to argue. Abby felt strongly on issues of what the missies of the house were allowed to do. Washing was not one of them. She swooped up the kitten, setting him to purring when she stroked his head, and headed upstairs.

"She not move yet." Reuben rose from the chair, speaking softly, as if in a house of worship.

"We need to talk normally. Perhaps she can hear and needs to know we are here." Louisa sat in the chair and took her aunt's frail hand in her own. The little kitten snuggled down next to the sleeping woman, his purr loud in the stillness. How could her aunt look so fragile so quickly, or had this been going on for a time and none of them noticed? If only there were ways to find some answers.

Chapter Fourteen

"So what actually happened to Aunt Sylvania?"

"The doctor says she has apoplexy. We will know how severe in the next few days. He seemed to think it's fairly mild."

"And we are to leave in the morning." Zachary thumped on the desk with his only hand.

"I cannot do that, Zachary. I will not leave her."

Zachary stared at her, the intensity of his gaze burning into her mind. "You would put an old woman ahead of helping our wounded men?"

"Zachary Highwood, how can you say such a thing? Aunt Sylvania isn't some old woman we are talking about. This is our aunt, who has opened her house and heart for us all this year. She has taken us in and shared everything she has." Anger swelled at the sight of his appearance of disinterest. Had he lost all concern for his own family, all semblance of Christian love even?

Louisa squared her shoulders. "Yes, brother dear." She honeyed her words. "I would put an aunt I dearly love ahead of wounded soldiers." *And as titular head of our family, you should too.* She kept the thought from registering on her face, along with the urge to slap the supercilious look off his face. Surely he must be putting on an act to convince her to leave. "I will make this compromise. If Aunt Sylvania is much better by the morning, we can leave on Tuesday." Surely one more day wouldn't make a difference.

"But I have tickets for tomorrow's train."

"We're taking the train?"

"Yes, west."

"You'll have to find someone else or put off this trip. I'm not leaving our aunt like this." There, she'd had her say.

She waited for him to say more, but when he leaned back in his chair and closed his eyes, she realized the discussion was over. "Is there anything else I can get you?"

A headshake, so brief she'd have missed it had she not been glaring at him, sent her to the doorway. She paused. "I take it I am dismissed?"

A slight lifting of a corner of his mouth let her know he knew what she was doing.

Louisa and Abby took turns sitting with Aunt Sylvania through the night. Toward dawn, on Louisa's shift, Sylvania opened her eyes and looked around. Bewilderment etched the good side of her face. Louisa moved from the chair to the edge of the bed.

"Can I get you something?" She took her aunt's hand in hers, feeling a slight quiver.

"Thirsty, so thirsty." The words came slowly, as if Sylvania were unsure of her tongue.

"Oh, dear Aunt, you can speak, thank our good Lord."

Sylvania quirked her left eyebrow, a familiar sign that she questioned her niece's good sense.

"What is so, so . . ." A look of total confusion caused lines to deepen on the left side of her face, but little happened on the right. "I . . . I can't find the word." She tried to raise her right hand to her face, and it lay flaccid on the coverlet. She stared at the hand, and then her gaze darted to Louisa like that of a child pleading for mercy.

"What . . . what has happened?"

"You've a mild case of apoplexy." Louisa smoothed the wisps of gray hair off her aunt's forehead. "It has affected your right side, your face a bit, and now we know your right hand. Can you move your foot?"

Sylvania looked toward her feet and smiled, making Louisa more aware of the distorted face. "It moves—that's good, right?" She stared at her hand, which finally lifted off the bed but fell back limp, like wet laundry.

"Good, very good." Louisa stood and walked to the pitcher of water sitting on the commode. She closed her eyes and breathed a prayer of thanksgiving. Taking a cup of cool water back, she held it for her aunt to drink.

"My mouth . . . not workin' right." The tone became petulant, like a small child in need of a nap.

"I know, but I think it will get better again. Doctor said he would be back today when he could."

"He came?"

"Yes."

Sylvania nodded. "He would." Her eyelids drifted closed. "Sleepy, so sleepy."

"You rest now, and when you wake we'll bring some breakfast." Louisa realized her patient was already asleep.

When Louisa entered the kitchen, Abby already had the iron stove plenty hot for biscuits, grits steaming in a kettle, and syrup warming on the back of the stove. For a brief second, Louisa craved ham. How long since they'd had ham and redeye gravy for breakfast. A thick slice of ham that needed cutting with a knife. Thoughts of such a ham brought memories of home, memories salt and sweet, just like the meat. The smokehouse at Twin Oaks, the walls standing impregnated with salt and smoke and the dripping grease of untold delicacies, meat taken for granted, a smokehouse part and parcel of the ongoing life.

She sighed as she stepped out onto the veranda. Would life ever be the same again?

Silly question, she chided herself. *Of course it won't. It can't.* Another sigh. She leaned against the brick wall and gazed over what was once Aunt Sylvania's glorious rose garden. Now vegetables were planted between the few remaining roses. Where once only blossoms reigned, now green beans climbed poles and lettuces made borders, along with feathery carrot tops. Dewdrops glistened on petals and leaves, while bitty bushtits gleaned the roses of aphids. A mockingbird sang through its repertoire. A wren twitted from the magnolia.

"You're out early." Zachary spoke from behind her, startling her, since she hadn't heard his crutch step.

She waited a moment for him to ask about their aunt. And when he didn't, she felt like shaking him.

"Aunt awoke."

A cardinal sang for his mate, rich notes threading the rising humidity. Louisa rubbed her forehead with her fingertips.

"We'll talk when I return."

Zachary turned and crutch-stepped his way back through the kitchen. His position at the law office kept him away until dusk, and many times, he had meetings in the evening. He never asked a single question about Aunt Sylvania's condition. *Mama would have given him a lecture,* Louisa thought. *Not only a lecture on his lack of manners, but one on his Christian duty. If he weren't my brother, I don't think I'd even like him anymore.*

The thought made her gasp. Here she was criticizing him for lack of Christian duty, and look at her. She picked up her basket and shears from the shelf by the door and headed out to the rosebushes to cut flowers for the breakfast table and find a special bud for Aunt Sylvania. She did love her roses, and waking to the scent of roses in her room might make her feel a bit better.

When the doctor arrived after dinner, he greeted Sylvania with a broad smile.

"You are looking much better, my dear, far better than I feared." He took her hands. "Now, then, squeeze with your left. Good. Now the right. Umm." He nodded. "Now let's get you out of that bed and see how well your feet and legs work."

"But I am in my nightdress."

His smile and her consternation made Louisa smile. Here they were concerned about the lingering affects of apoplexy and her aunt was worried about a man, a doctor, for pity's sake, seeing her in her nightdress.

Together, an arm on either side of her, they helped Sylvania up on her feet.

"Oh, I'm dizzy."

They let her sit back on the edge of the bed.

"Better now?" The doctor rubbed Sylvania's hands. He glanced to Louisa. "You can help her by rubbing her hand and foot, even the side of her face, gently at first and then with more strength as she improves."

Abby nodded from her position at the foot of the bed. "We does that."

"Still dizzy?"

"No."

"Let's get you vertical then." Slowly they eased her to her feet. Louisa watched her aunt's face for any signs of faintness. They stood still, waiting for any sign from Sylvania. When she nodded, Louisa tightened her grip on her aunt's waist.

"Left foot first." The three took one step at the same time. A small step, but movement nonetheless.

"Right foot." The doctor's glance warned Louisa to be on guard. Another small step.

"I did it." Sylvania gripped Louisa's hand with a strength born of fear.

"And another." They tottered as far as the brocade chair and settled her into it.

"I feel like I walked clear downtown." Sylvania slumped against the chair back, her left hand on the padded arm, her right lying in her lap. She looked up at the doctor standing by her side. "Now, what happened to me?"

She started to turn to the mirror, but Louisa nonchalantly stepped in front of it. The visible damage could be seen later, when Sylvania grew stronger.

Right now Louisa could believe that would happen. Memories of a neighbor at home who'd never been able to speak nor feed herself after such as this skulked back into the lair from which they came.

While Abby and Louisa changed the bed and fluffed up the pillows, Sylvania and the doctor visited, him telling her a story that brought out a chuckle.

"All right, now I reckon it's about time you walk back to bed. I expect you to get up every day. The more you walk, the stronger you will become."

After they settled Sylvania in her bed again, with a sigh of relief on her part, Louisa followed the doctor down to the front door.

"Sure you wouldn't like to stay for some lemonade?"

"No, I must get on. Fill an old sock with dried beans or rice and make her —"

At the raising of Louisa's eyebrow, he chuckled.

"I know, making Miss Sylvania do anything is a miracle in its own right, but she needs to squeeze that sock over and over if she wants to regain the use of that hand."

"We'll keep reminding her. Thank you for coming by." She watched as he strode down the walk and climbed into his buggy. With his shoulders rounding and the slight limp, he looked to have aged ten years in the last twelve months. He was good at telling others to take care of themselves, but what about him?

Louisa looked up toward Aunt Sylvania's window. Not being able to sew or knit with only one hand would make her downright cantankerous. Or drive her to work her hand harder.

Could she leave right now? Could Abby and Reuben take care of not only their soldiers but also Miss Sylvania? Who could she find to come in and help? *Ah, if only Lucinda were here.*

Chapter Fifteen

FORT LARAMIE

There was knowing, and then there was knowing.

Jesselynn stretched her hands above her head and watched the dust motes dance on the sunbeams lilting in the window. Sheer white curtains billowed in the breeze, a breeze that felt cool as springwater on her arms. She glanced to the side to see the dished place where her husband's head had lain on the pillow. She stretched again, enjoying the lassitude.

Wolf had kissed her good-bye sometime after dawn, with the birds still twittering their morning wake-up call. He'd said she should sleep as long as she wanted. No one would come by to disturb her, or they would answer to him. The remembered growl in his voice made her smile again.

Smiles came easy this morning, her very first morning as Mrs. Gray Wolf Torstead.

She could hear soldiers marching out on the parade grounds where the wedding guests had danced the day before. Most likely she had danced with some of the men out there. Her feet reminded her that she'd danced with most everyone west of the Missouri. Or at least it seemed that way.

Ah, the only thing that would have made the day shine more brightly was if Louisa and Carrie Mae could have been here. And Lucinda. That thought brought an immediate dimming to the smile that echoed clear through her. They would most likely feel the same as Aunt Agatha. At least Zachary would. That was for certain sure.

She threw back the covers and reached for the dressing gown that Rebeccah had so thoughtfully provided, along with the nightdress, the pins for her hair, and the rose water she'd splashed on before retiring.

She closed her eyes. Yes, Wolf had liked the rose water. Dressing gown belted in place, she ambled out to the kitchen of the quarters, where a loaf of bread, a hunk of cheese, butter, and milk sat under cheesecloth on the counter. The coffeepot was still warm, pushed to the back of the stove. She sliced off two pieces of bread and enough cheese to cover them and poured herself a cup of milk. Who needed coffee anyway on a morning like this?

Once she'd finished eating and washed up her knife and cup, she peeked out the window, standing off to the side so no one would see her. No Appaloosa in sight. He'd said she should sleep until he came to wake her. By the angle of the sun, the morning was half gone, and she had a pile of things to do if they were to leave for the Chugwater in the morning.

Within minutes she was dressed in a shirt, britches, and boots. Clapping her sorry hat on her head, she headed out the door, smack dab into a broad chest that rumbled with laughter.

"Whoa." Wolf steadied her by grasping her upper arms. "You look to be in a real hurry, ma'am. Is there somethin' I can help you with?"

Her hat fell behind without her notice as he captured her lips with his.

"Wolf, people will see us." She murmured the words against lips that drew back only a little.

"I know. So how about we back up a couple of feet and close the door. That way . . ." Their feet obeyed. Their eyes spoke in paragraphs. The next kiss lasted longer, ending on her sigh.

"You sure this is the way newly married folk behave?"

"If they can." He drew her over to a chair and pulled her down in his lap. "Now, Mrs. Torstead, where were you goin' in such a rush?"

"To find you, I think. Or was it back to my wagons? You get my head all mixed up." She clasped her hands around the back of his neck. "I like that Mrs. Torstead name."

"Good thing. It's yours now."

"I like that Mr. Torstead name too." Would it be too forward if she kissed him first? She did so without hesitating. He didn't seem to mind.

"So what have you been doing?"

"While you slept, you mean?"

"Um." She hid a yawn behind her hand. "I haven't been this lazy since . . ." The sun dimmed for her. *Since Mother died, and I had to take over the managing of Twin Oaks.* A sigh slipped out before she could catch it.

She opened her eyes to see him studying her. Laying her head on his shoulder, she picked up one of his hands and placed hers against it, palm to palm. "My mother taught me how to be a good wife. I can manage a plantation, keep the slaves busy and in order, keep up the household accounts, the entire plantation accounts if need be. I know how to cook, put up food for the entire plantation, garden, sew a fine seam, entertain the kinfolk and the men who come calling on the husband, read Greek and Latin. My father taught me to ride, along with how to shoot a gun, and raise tobacco—from field preparation to drying, shipping, and selling." She ticked off each skill on her fingertips.

"She taught you well."

She jerked up right. "How do you know?" At the look on his face, she thumped him on the chest, a saucy grin tickling her cheeks. "Wolf! You taught me that." She nestled her cheek back into his shoulder. "Thank you for this morning."

"You are very welcome." He leaned forward. "Now, I have work to do, and Meshach has already been by to see what you wanted him to do."

"But of all those things I know to do"—she shook her head, her hair teasing his chin—"not many are needed out here in the wilderness."

"No, but you already have added many more things. You can tan hides, sew shirts out of either buckskin or cloth, cook over a campfire, drive a wagon, train horses or oxen, skin a rabbit or deer or whatever needs skinning, including a buffalo, birth foals, and while there'll be no call for harvesting tobacco"—he kissed the tips of her fingers—"you have made one man bone-deep happy and sometime, God willing, you'll be raising sons and daughters along with those foals that will pay for the things we can't raise."

Jesselynn could feel the blush start below her neck and flame its way up to her forehead.

"I declare, Mr. Torstead, the way you talk." She fingered the fringe on his buckskin shirt. "There is something I haven't told you."

"We have our entire lives to find things to tell."

"I know, but this is different." She sat up straight and looked into his eyes. "Someday, when that cursed war is finally over, I want to take breeding stock back to Twin Oaks."

"Domino?"

"Perhaps. But if the colt develops like he looks to be, him for sure, maybe the two fillies. Both mares took." She tipped her head slightly to one side. "That means fewer for sale in the next couple of years."

"We'll send all the horses we can, but keep in mind that I, you and I, cannot live in Kentucky."

"I know, and someone famous once wrote, 'You cannot go back.' The life I knew will never be there again. Even if someday Zachary can rebuild the big house, it will not be the same. The war has destroyed life as we lived it." She could feel the tears burning the backs of her throat and eyes. "I wish you could have seen it."

"Had you stayed there, you would not be here." His hand stroked the nape of her neck.

"I know." She dredged up a grin so that she would not cry. "God sure does work in mysterious ways." She leaned forward and butterfly-kissed his smiling lips. When she started to stand, he held her back.

"I am grateful every day to our God and Father that you came west."

"Even if you almost refused us passage with your wagon train?"

He groaned. "That was business."

"Bad business." She shook her head. "I will never understand why you allowed the Jones brothers to join up but almost refused us." She looked at him again, her head continuing to move from side to side.

"Me neither." He set her on her feet and rose. "Let's be on out to the wagons."

"I have to return my dresses first." She gazed at the creamy silk hanging on a hanger. "That most surely is a lovely dress." She caressed the material again. "Wolf, I do have a skirt in the wagon."

"Good. Let it stay there. You can use it when we come into the fort if you like. Britches are much more practical where we are going. Oglala women wear deerskin leggings under a deerskin shift. No skirts to get in the way." He thought a moment. "At least they used to. My mother did beautiful bead and quill designs on her clothes, and my father's too. Even moccasins testified to her love of beauty."

Jesselynn held perfectly still. For once, she had a glimmer into his life as a child. A life so foreign to her that she wondered if she would ever understand it anymore than he would understand life at Twin Oaks. After a moment she folded the garments over her arm so that nothing dragged and went out of the door ahead of him.

Someday they'd have a house too. But for now . . . She sucked in a deep breath. For now she must go back to the real world, of Aunt Agatha, slow plodding oxen, dust, and distances. "I'll hurry."

———

They left in the morning as planned, waving good-bye to the Jespersons, who figured on waiting for the next wagon train heading west. Scouts reported there was another train three days out. Jesselynn rode Ahab, she and Wolf at the head of their small train, the two packhorses on lines behind the last wagon, driven by Meshach. Aunt Agatha managed to lead the train without talking to either Jesselynn or Wolf. When Jesselynn gave thought to her aunt, she caught herself sighing.

This could be a long trip and a hard winter if Agatha kept her mouth pursed like that and went out of her way to avoid sitting by them or joining in conversation. But how could Jesselynn uninvite her along? There was no place for her at Fort Laramie.

Lord God, this is beyond me. I've done everything I can, short of not marrying, and she will not bend an inch. Yet I know she respected Wolf as the wagon master, thought he was a fine man. Fine for everything but marrying into the Highwood family.

She knew Zachary would feel the same way, so the letters she sent to Richmond and Twin Oaks made no mention of the wedding. She just said they had decided to go north instead of on to Oregon. Not a lie, but certainly not the whole truth either.

Riding with Wolf certainly beat riding alone or driving a wagon. He pointed out buffalo wallows, places where deer spent the daylight hours, and a slide for river otters. Benjamin fished the deep pools of the Chugwater River that snaked across a valley belly-deep in rich grass. Daniel's snares netted rabbits.

"Why don't we settle here?" Jesselynn looked back over her shoulder at grass shimmering in the sun as it turned from green to gold. "There's hay aplenty and—"

"And the river floods in wet years, and we would be forced to build all over again. There is grass also in the valley I know of. And we will be bothered less up the river."

"Bothered?"

"My tribe travels through here from summer to winter hunting. I do not want to be in their way."

"Oh."

"Other tribes too, and sometimes they war on one another."

"I see." But she didn't. The word "war" made her want to head south again to the Oregon Trail. Would she never be free of war?

The second day they left the verdant valley and traveled between hillocks as they followed the south branch of the river, now more like a creek. Willows and other brush lined the waterway, and grass grew deep on the flats, but the hills around them wore sparser blankets of golden grasses. Hawks and eagles screed above them, huge ravens announced their passage, grouse thrummed in the evenings. Deer and pronged antelope leaped the hills while Wolf promised elk in the mountains ahead.

The great sky arched in changing shades of such blue as to take one's breath away. They saw no other humans but themselves.

"Come, I have something to show you." Wolf mounted his Appaloosa and waited for her to mount Ahab. "Just follow along the creek," he instructed Benjamin who, mounted on Domino, scouted ahead for the wagons. "We won't be gone long. We'll be at camp before nightfall."

"Yes, suh." Benjamin touched one finger to the brim of his hat. "That be good."

Nudging the horses to a lope, the two riders edged the creek a ways before Wolf set the Appaloosa at a hill. Up and down they walked and trotted until Wolf stopped with a raised hand. "See."

Jesselynn stopped and looked ahead to where he pointed. A small valley, shaped like a bowl, lay before her, hills mounding on all four sides. On the face of the tallest hill three caves faced south. "While I hadn't planned on this many people, we can make do. Brush fences can keep the horses in the valley. See there and there." He pointed to low places, like small ravines, that led into the bowl. "We can bring logs from up in the mountains, or use rock, to build walls. This will keep us through the winter."

Jesselynn nodded. "We spent last winter in caves around Springfield, Missouri. Guess this won't be much different."

"Plenty snow here, but"—he drew a circle with his arm to encompass the area—"good protection. Game nearby. Water. We will do well."

"Will the creek freeze over?"

"Sometimes yes, sometimes no. We can cut hay and bring it back on the wagons."

Jesselynn thought to the bags of oats she had purchased at the fort. Enough to feed the mares through their foaling? Enough to plant next summer?

"Come, I will show you more."

Not many minutes later they trotted around a corner with a rock face perhaps twenty feet high. Jesselynn felt like she'd stepped into a dream. The valley widened out, the creek deepened, lined by willows and cottonwood with deep green pine climbing the gentle sides of the hills. Grass rippled like a green lake under a breeze.

A slap echoed in the valley.

"What was that?"

"Beaver. They dammed the creek. That's why the pond. They're just announcing visitors."

"Why can't we winter here? This is beautiful."

"No caves. But here is where we build a house out of that rock we came around. You saw the square stones. Like using bricks."

Jesselynn leaned on her arms crossed over Ahab's withers. "This is some beautiful."

"When the red bark of the low brush shines through the snow or ice, then too this valley has beauty."

"You have stayed here in the past?"

"In the caves one winter, my father and I, after my mother died."

"No wonder you wanted to come back here." She looked to the west where hills covered with oak and evergreens climbed to the mountains hidden in the distance. "Let's get the others, Mr. Torstead. Our new life is about to begin."

Chapter Sixteen

RICHMOND, VIRGINIA

"We'll still be going then?"

"I can put it off three more days, but no longer."

"What about disguises?"

"We're working on that."

Louisa wondered who he meant by "we." Who was providing the money for this trip, and who was getting them the quinine on the other end? Why did her brother see the need to be so secretive here at home? She could understand out in public, but at home? The "why's" could stretch on forever.

Secret missions brought up another thought. She'd heard rumors of secret missions before her lieutenant told her he had to return to his family home. Who had blown up the train that took his life? Did they ever search for or catch the fiends that did such things? Or was that a natural part of war?

The war. Everything always came back to the war.

"And when will I be informed as to what I am to do?" She didn't bother to keep the sarcasm from her voice.

Zachary shook his head, a smile flirting with the corners of his mouth.

"I've been a bit of a dolt, haven't I?"

"Now that I won't argue with." Louisa knew she'd forgive him anything when he turned on the Highwood charm. "You've been treating Aunt Sylvania most shabbily, and you know she dotes on you."

He had the grace to look ashamed.

Thank you, Lord, there is hope for my brother yet.

"I will go up and see her."

"I know the stairs are hard for you, but—"

He interrupted her before she could finish her sentence. "But not impossible."

"That wasn't what I was going to say."

"Perhaps not, but you've thought it."

Louisa looked down. "I stand condemned."

"No, Louisa, don't ever even think such things." He reached for her hand. "Never, do you hear me?" His voice shook, the whisper cutting to her heart.

She looked into his eye, past the fire to see—what? Fear?

Zachary shrugged his shoulders and leaned back in his chair. When she looked at him again, the man she'd come to dislike gazed back at her.

"I need to go sit with Aunt Sylvania. When you come to see her, bring that charming man with you, the brother I used to know." Pivoting so her skirts swished, she sailed out the door, her teeth clenched at all the other words she would like to have said.

Dear Lord, what do I do with him? I want to strangle him one minute and hold him the next. I know he's in pain much of the time, but this cruelty—that's not my brother. And if it's not my brother, who is it? What is it?

The sharp edges that jutted and jabbed all around downstairs had not made it up the stairs. Peace, soothing and gentle, reigned in Aunt Sylvania's room. The evening breeze danced with the sheer white curtains, wafting the fragrance of the roses out through the open door.

Aunt Sylvania sat in her chair, pulled up by the window to catch the morning sun and any errant breeze. Her Bible lay open on her lap, her lips moving silently as she read.

In the three days since the incident—Louisa had had a hard time using the word apoplexy—Aunt Sylvania had regained some use of her hand, and her smile could faintly move the right side of her mouth. Louisa encouraged her to smile often. While her walking gained strength daily, she had yet to venture downstairs.

The ginger kitten with a white patch on its chest brought smiles to the faces of all who lived there. When Aunt Sylvania dragged a piece of string for the kitten to chase, Louisa said she had to use her right hand to do so. And when the kitten was played out, he snuggled in any lap available but preferred Sylvania's, his purr lion-sized. Excusing herself, Louisa returned downstairs when Zachary made his way into Sylvania's room.

One of the soldiers fashioned a lopsided ball of wood that the kitten batted around, his antics making everyone laugh.

Louisa wished she had thought of a pet sooner. She also wished the kitten would stay a kitten, since it brought such pleasure.

They had yet to choose a name for it.

"We need a name for our kitten," Louisa mentioned after grace at the supper table.

"I think Spot or Patch," one of the men said.

Another shook his head. "Too ordinary."

"Fluffy?" Everyone made a face.

"We had one we called Cat." The lieutenant shrugged. "Just a thought."

"What is Spot or White in French? That would sound exotic."

"Blanc."

"Nah, he's a cat. Blanc would embarrass him. I say we call him Bones."

"Bones?" Louisa wrinkled her nose. "What kind of name is that?" But looking around at the grinning faces, she couldn't help but smile back. "Bones it is, I reckon."

When the doctor came the next morning, he decreed this was the day Aunt Sylvania went downstairs.

Louisa breathed a sigh of relief. She'd been both dreading and anticipating this day and praying it would happen before she had to leave.

She had yet to tell Aunt Sylvania she would be leaving. But every evening since she and Zachary had their discussion, he had forced himself to stump-hop up the stairs to visit with his aunt, no matter how late he arrived home from his job.

He said very little about working in the law firm and even less about his evening meetings, but he made Aunt Sylvania laugh, and that was all that mattered to Louisa.

───────

"Aunt, I have something I need to tell you." Sitting together while Aunt Sylvania read and Louisa stitched, the afternoon had passed pleasantly.

"You're leaving again, aren't you?" The accusation chased the peace to hiding in the corners.

"Yes. Zachary cannot do this alone."

Louisa looked up to see a tear leak from the down-pulled eye. Louisa fell to her knees at the side of Sylvania's chair. She laid both hands on her aunt's arm, which was already shrunk thin from the illness. If she left, would Sylvania keep on squeezing the sock and strengthening her arm?

Bones stretched and stirred in Sylvania's lap, yawning wide to show a pink tongue and tiny white teeth.

"Oh, you poor little thing. Louisa disturbed you." Sylvania stroked the kitten with her left hand until she caught Louisa's eye and switched. "See, I nee—" She cut off the word.

Louisa felt like Zachary had her by one arm and Sylvania the other, and that they were pulling her apart like medieval torturers.

Sylvania patted Louisa's hand. "Nothing is more important than helping our soldiers. You go on with Zachary. There are plenty here who will help me. By the time you g-get back, I will be my old self."

Louisa stared into her aunt's eyes. If only the sorrow-filled eyes matched the commonsense mouth.

The kitten arched his back and rubbed against Sylvania's chest. His straight-up tail tickled her under the chin. When the old lady stroked his back, his purr could be heard clear downstairs.

"Besides, I can go down and read to the boys again and encourage them in their stitching. We will keep busy until you return."

Was there a trace of the former Sylvania coming out again?

With desperation in her soul, Louisa prayed so.

————

When Louisa and Zachary drove off in the predawn, she looked back at the house. *Protect them, please, dear Lord.* It was all she could do to not plead with her brother to make him turn around.

No one gave a second glance to the old man with his octoroon maid when they boarded the westbound train at Richmond. One old darkie helped her with the trunk she wrestled from the back of the buggy.

"Thankee, suh," she muttered, keeping her head down in an attitude of submission. No one could see her blue eyes that way, and the white bandana tied round her hair, like any mammy or slave, hid her dark blond hair. Walnut dye changed her skin to the octoroon hue.

Again their papers took them through both lines, although Louisa chewed the metallic taste of fear each time.

————

When they returned after two weeks, Aunt Sylvania greeted them at the door. While she carried her right arm closer to her body, Louisa could hardly detect the damage to her aunt's face, as the smile she welcomed them home with stretched both cheeks and her hug felt as of before.

Thank you, Lord, thank you. Louisa collapsed on her bed and slept round the clock. The trunk full of quinine and morphine disappeared like hoarfrost in the sun.

Summer dragged on under a mantle of humidity that wilted both men and beast. The wounded troops from Gettysburg still filled the hospitals, the churches commandeered as hospitals, and the homes that had taken in recovering patients.

A knock at the door early one morning sent Abby scurrying to answer and Louisa looking to see how they could accommodate another pallet.

"Come quick," a black maid pleaded. "Missy Carrie Mae done be havin' her baby. She be cryin' for you." She nodded to Louisa. "She say she be dyin'." The young woman's black eyes rolled white with fear.

"Has she called a midwife?" Louisa asked as she loaded a basket with a Bible, the layette she had stitched, and smelling salts, along with other things. She followed the maid out to the buggy waiting at the curb.

"I don' know."

"Give her our blessings," Aunt Sylvania called from the front porch.

Louisa waved back and turned to the maid. "How long has she been in labor?"

"She woke up before cockcrow sayin' her back hurt."

"Where is Mr. Jefferson?"

"Gone somewhere. I don' know."

"What is your name?" Louisa hadn't seen this particular maid before.

"I'se Becca, and I be new. I don' never seen a baby born before."

"I'm sure Carrie Mae is doing just fine. Women been having babies since time began." Louisa tried to sound as comforting as possible. After all, she remembered how Carrie Mae couldn't stand pain of any kind and would carry on until their mother lost patience. For their gentle mother to say, *"Land sakes, Carrie Mae, you carry on worse than a just-weaned calf"* sent Louisa and Jesselynn out of the house to snicker at their sister's expense.

Lord, please let that be the case here. While I attended one baby's birth with Mother, I've not helped on my own. "Why didn't Carrie Mae call for the midwife?"

"I don' know she did or din't."

And what happened to that French maid? "Is Elise still with my sister?"

"Yes'm, but she don' know nothin' 'bout birthin' no baby neither."

"Oh."

———

Three hours later, Carrie Mae was still carrying on, the pains coming closer and harder.

Louisa wanted to stuff a rag in her sister's mouth. "Carrie Mae, you get up here and walk with me right now!"

"I want Jefferson here."

"Mama always said the only thing men were good for at a birthing was lowering the level of whiskey in the cupboard." She hoisted Carrie Mae off the bed and, with one arm around her, forced her to keep walking.

"Now sing with me. 'O, I wish I was in the land of cotton.' Sing, Carrie Mae, sing." They went on to "Amazing Grace" and "Rock of Ages." Each time a contraction came they stopped walking and singing for Carrie Mae to double over and cry.

"Breathe, Carrie Mae. Pain is always less if you ride it, not fight it. Now take a deep breath and let it all out."

They kept on walking.

"Oh! Oh no." Carrie Mae stared down at the puddle widening around her feet.

"Not oh no, oh good. Now we can get on with this." Louisa nodded toward the two maids alternately cowering in the corner and helping walk their mistress.

"Becca, you are going to sit on the bed with your back against the wall, and Carrie Mae will lean against you. You puff with her. Elise, tie these sheets to the end of the bed for her to pull on." Louisa handed her the sheets she'd had them knot earlier. "We're going to have a beautiful little son or daughter here by the time Jefferson returns, and that is just how it should be."

As the pains came faster and harder, she finally allowed Carrie Mae to climb on the bed, her back braced against Becca and her hands knotted into the sheets.

"Now, relax between these, and . . ."

Carrie Mae scrunched her face, gritted her teeth, and groaned as another wave rolled over her. "You give instructions . . . so well here . . . and you've never been through this." Her panting between words made Louisa smile.

"That's the way. Get angry at me if it will help you." With the next contraction that arched Carrie Mae right off the bed, Louisa checked. Sure enough, she saw a small circle that showed the baby's head.

"I can see it, dear sister. I can see the hair, dark like Jefferson's. When you feel like pushing, you just push away. We're almost there."

Another three good hard contractions, along with a scream through each, and Louisa assisted her niece into the world, turning her gently as her shoulders slipped through the opening.

"Ah, Carrie Mae, Mama would say you were made for bearing babies." She laid the already squalling infant on her mother's chest. "See, isn't she beautiful?"

Carrie Mae laid back against Becca's arms, panting, tears streaming down her cheeks, one finger tracing her daughter's cheek. "She's so tiny."

"I surely do hope so. Any bigger and you'd have had real problems."

Elise handed Louisa a warmed towel. "You want to wrap her?"

"Not yet. Mama said never cut the cord until it lays flat." Louisa used the towel to dry off her own face, including tears, and then her sister's.

"Ah, Carrie Mae, you did splendidly."

"I did, didn't I?" Her face scrunched again. "Ow."

With the cord cut and the afterbirth delivered, Louisa washed the baby, who seemed to be looking right at her.

"Look at you, already studying on the world. I can tell you are one smart little girl, going to be pretty as a daisy." She kept up the soft whispers as she swished the tiny body in a pan of warm water. She dried her and, after diapering and swaddling, laid the baby back in Carrie Mae's waiting arms.

While she'd been caring for the baby, the two other women cleaned up Carrie Mae, changed the bed, and dressed her again.

When Jefferson walked in an hour later, he saw his wife, all lovely with her hair combed, sleeping sweetly with his equally beautiful daughter asleep in her arms.

"Now, if that isn't about the prettiest picture I ever did see." He leaned over to kiss his wife on the forehead.

"What have you decided to name her?" Louisa kept her voice low so as not to disturb the sleeping pair.

"Her?"

"Yes, you have a daughter."

"Oh, well, ah . . ."

Louisa felt like smacking him. What was so all-fired important about having a son first? "Mother and baby are doing just fine."

Jefferson recovered himself and turned to Louisa. "I do believe we should name this little darlin' after her maternal grandmother. How does that sound to you?"

"Miriam Amelia, wouldn't that be lovely?" Louisa knew Jefferson's mother would want her name used too. No sense creating discord in the family. She smiled at her brother-in-law. "That's very kind of you, Jefferson. I'm sure Carrie Mae will be most happy."

"Jefferson?" The sleepy voice brought their attention back to the bed. He crossed and knelt beside his wife, his stump around her head, his hand clasping hers.

"She's beautiful, wife, just like you." He kissed her cheek and the baby's head. "I'm sorry I couldn't get here any sooner. I was out to dinner, but they told me as soon as I returned to the office."

Louisa stepped out of the room. "I'll let them be," she said to the maid. "Tell Carrie Mae that I'll come by to see her tomorrow."

"I call de buggy for you." Becca went out the door before Louisa had time to argue.

She arrived home just in time for supper being served out on the back veranda, where everyone hoped for a bit of breeze.

"We have a beautiful baby girl named Miriam Amelia. Mother and baby are both doing fine." She clasped her hands to her bosom and smiled at Sylvania. "I have now joined the exalted ranks of auntyhood."

"Does that make us honorary uncles?" The young private missing a leg and an eye smiled as he asked.

"But of course. Although as honorary uncles, you might need to hold her at times."

"I'm the oldest of eight. I've held lots of babies." He held up the knife he used to carve handy spoons. Abby used them all the time now. "Think I can do a rattle, you know, with a little ball within a sphere, with a handle. Made one for my baby brother. You know where I could get me some cherrywood? Even babies can't gnaw on that."

Louisa kept her astonishment to herself. He'd never said more than "please" and "thank you" and "yes, ma'am" up to now. "I'm sure I can find you some, or Reuben will." *If I have to turn Richmond upside down, I'll find it.*

Two days later Zachary came to her and announced another trip.

Louisa felt her heart knock around her kneecaps. Weren't they testing God's providence to try for a fourth trip?

Chapter Seventeen

෨ා

ON THE CHUGWATER RIVER
AUGUST 1863

Cave living hadn't changed much, just more people, more animals, and smaller caves.

Jesselynn stared out at the curtains of rain. Rain falling so hard she could barely see across their little valley. Sammy and Thaddeus both had a bad case of the squalls this morning, perhaps due to the weather.

"Thaddeus, give that back to Sammy." Jesselynn didn't even bother to turn around. With all she had to do, standing watching the rain fall could be called a direct waste of time.

The squall going on within her looked about as gray as the rain. They'd been in camp three weeks now, and Aunt Agatha still hadn't spoken a word to her. With the sour look on her face, even the little boys had taken to giving her a wide berth.

"Thaddeus, I said give that back to Sammy—now!" Where in heaven's name was Jane Ellen? Most likely with Mrs. Jones. For some reason the two of them had taken a shine to each other and had become the best of friends.

Patch came in from a check on the herd and shook himself, soaking Jesselynn before he sat down at her feet. Tongue lolling out one side of his mouth, he looked up for her pat or words of approval. When they didn't come, he whined.

"I know. You're a good dog. I'm surprised the mares didn't come back with you to stand here under the shelter of the cave." She leaned over to give him the expected and well-earned pat. All the animals looked as if they'd put on weight with the rest and good pasture. The rain of course would help that pasture remain green, but Jesselynn and Mrs. Mac had planned on washing clothes today. She had set water to dripping through wood ash to make lye, not that they had much fat to make soap with, but if Wolf and Benjamin brought back deer and elk with plenty of fat, she'd use that.

"Jesse, me go outside?" Thaddeus leaned against her leg.

"You'll get wet."

"Patch is wet."

"Patch was herding the cattle."

"Where Meshach?"

"Over making scythes and rakes."

"Go see?" He looked up at her, hope written all over his face.

"No. You'll get in the way." She looked down to see Sammy stuck to her other knee. "Where's Ophelia?"

Thaddeus pointed to the back of the cave. "There."

Jesselynn looked over her shoulder, but the way the cave curved around an angle, she could see nothing. "You two play with Patch. Get a stick of wood and throw for him." She snatched Thaddeus back as he headed outside. "No, get one from the woodpile."

She ignored the smoke floating out along the low ceiling and blinked in the dimness lit by the slow fire with racks of venison drying on A-frames along both sides of the shallow trench. A caldron of stew bubbled on a separate and more substantial fire. They'd decided to use this cave for all the storage, cooking and sleeping outside until the rain drove them into the other caves. Good thing they'd brought in plenty of dry wood. Daniel and Nathan, along with his grandson, Mark, and the McPhereson boys, had taken two ox teams and wagons up into the hills to bring back more wood. By winter they hoped to bring down logs to extend the fronts of the caves into a cabin or two with rock fireplaces and chimneys for cooking.

"You go help Ophelia. I need to talk with Meshach." Jesselynn gave her little brother a pat on the seat and sent him to the rear of the cave.

"Me go." Her little brother's plaintive plea tugged at her heart.

"Not this time." She settled her hat firmly on her head and, grabbing a cape off a peg, ducked out into the downpour. The gray sky looked to be sitting right on top of them, with enough rain tucked into the lowering clouds to last the proverbial forty days and nights.

Meshach sat just under the lip of the cave so he could use the available light, carving pegs for the three-foot rake he'd fashioned from slender willow saplings. A completed one leaned against the cave wall.

"What's that bar across the handle?"

"Get a better grip dat way." Meshach eyed the peg and laid it beside him, picking up another piece of wood and commencing to whittle it to the right size.

Jesselynn looked toward the rear of the cave where another fire and drying racks matched those in the storage cave. Aunt Agatha was laying strips of venison in place. *If only she would talk with me.*

Meshach raised an eyebrow and shrugged.

Jesselynn took in a deep breath. Just because her aunt was being stubborn gave her no excuse to act the same. "Good morning, Aunt Agatha. Looks to be raining forever, doesn't it?"

Agatha laid a final strip in place, wiped her hands on her apron, and strode on out of the cave without even glancing in Jesselynn's direction. She turned to the left and trotted on over to the easternmost cave where Darcy and Jane Ellen were sewing soft buckskin into shirts for the men for the winter.

"Give her time."

Jesselynn turned back to Meshach. "Not much else I can do, short of snatching her by the shoulders and shaking her." The thought brought a smile to lighten Jesselynn's outlook. That would be something all right.

"God work slow, it seem to us, but we don' see de whole picture. Bible say let de day's own trouble be sufficient for de day."

"I know, Mama used to say that so often."

"She teached me."

"But, Meshach, think what the winter will be like in these close caves if she continues to act like this."

"De winter long ways off."

"I know, today's trouble." *So what is today's trouble? Agatha didn't talk to me— that's nothing new. It's raining. So, we need the rain. I can't do the wash, so I'll do it tomorrow or when the rain stops.*

So here I am in a grumbling mood when we have so much to be thankful for. Father, forgive me.

"Thanks, Meshach. Think I'll go fishing. They should be biting good in weather like this, right?"

He nodded, giving her a slow smile that drew forth one in return. "Fried fish taste mighty fine. Take de rifle."

As she darted back out in the rain, she heard him pick up the tune he'd been humming when she arrived—"Way Down Upon the Swanee River." No, they weren't on a deep river here, but the creek sure was a welcome part of their new home.

Back in the main cave, she called to Ophelia. "I'm going fishing." She dug into one of the boxes for the fishhooks. "Should be biting good in this weather." Fishhooks and line in hand, she stopped. "You want I should take the boys over to play with Jane Ellen?"

"No, they be fine here."

Jesselynn checked her lye drip. She'd fashioned a skin to make a water bag with a slow leak and hung that above a pan of wood ashes. The pan had a hole drilled in the bottom and dripped the lye into an iron kettle. Oh, the things she'd taken for granted at Twin Oaks, useful things like soap and candles and a smokehouse and a cellar in the ground for storing the bounty they'd put by. Digging an outhouse was another thing they needed to do, and soon.

"You boys go on back in the cave." She snagged Sammy back from his dash out in the rain. "I told you to stay inside." The urge to swat his fat little bottom went down to setting him on his feet with a gentle shove pointed in the direction of his mother. "Here they come, Ophelia. I think they need to break up kindling for a while. I'll be up by the beaver pond."

Ignoring the look Thaddeus sent her, Jesselynn swung the waterproof cape over her shoulders again, pulled her hat down snug and the hood up. She'd just stepped out in the rain when Ophelia, rifle in hand, called from behind her. "You need gun."

"I have the pistol."

"You take gun." She and Meshach sure thought alike.

Jesselynn shook her head and took the rifle and the powder horn. "I'm just going fishing right around that hill."

Ophelia shrugged. "Fish be good for supper."

Rifle in the crook of her arm, Jesselynn struck off toward the creek to follow the trail that bordered it. While originally a game trail, they'd ridden back there enough now to make it more visible, even in the rain.

A pouch with worms in moist dirt hung at her belt, along with her skinning knife and the holster for the pistol. While tempted to leave the rifle propped in a tree, she carried it under the cape to keep it dry. Wet powder never did anyone any good. Of course, if she saw deer or elk coming to drink, she'd be ready. Now wouldn't that be a good joke if she got something and the men didn't. Right close to home too.

She stopped often, peering ahead, trying to see and hear if anything but fish and beaver had visited the pond or taken up residence there. Nothing. The rain splatting on the cape drowned out any sounds but itself.

Leaning her rifle against a hefty cottonwood tree trunk, she deftly cut a willow sapling, skinned off its branches, and tied her string to the tip. Knotting the hook took some concentration with wet hands, but within minutes she was seated on a rock on the bank with the worm floating on the top of the water ten feet out. She sighed. Should have tied a rock on for a sinker. Raising the tip to pull it back in, the pole bent and a flopping fish broke the surface of the rain-pecked pond. Jesselynn gave a jerk, and the fish flew through the air to land with a splat in the grass behind her.

"*Whooa-ee.* Let's do that again." Jumping to her feet, she heard a whoof, much like a big dog. She turned and froze. Her heart thundered in her ears, her mouth dry as cave dust. A black bear rose on his hind legs and whoofed again. He raised his snout, sniffing the air, forepaws relaxed against his chest. The falling rain shimmered like a gauze curtain graying the bear to apparition.

If he doesn't know human smell, he knows fish smell. Only her eyes moved as she measured the distance to the rifle. Without a sound, she pulled the pistol from the holster, all the while keeping her gaze on the bear. When she smelled a rank odor, she knew the wind was protecting her. If she could smell him, he couldn't smell her.

Dear God, keep him blind. Make him go away. Never had any animal looked so big. Surely he was taller even than Wolf.

Her hands shook so she could barely grip the pistol. She'd have to be close enough to smell his breath to kill him with that. But the rifle. One shot she'd have. Would have to be right in the eye. Keeping her mind at work on how to kill the monster freed her feet to ease her to the side. Barely moving, one foot and pause.

The bear continued sniffing, his big head moving from side to side, testing the air currents.

Jesselynn licked her dry lips.

A dog barked from the trail back to the camp. The bear swung in that direction. Jesselynn took two steps and grabbed the rifle, putting the massive tree trunk between her and the bear. The dog barked again, coming closer, growling.

"No! Patch, go back!" She might as well try to stop a waterfall. She stepped from behind the tree. The bear swung back in her direction.

A flash of black and Patch was at him, snarling like he was as big as the bear.

Jesselynn raised the rifle, sighted, and with the muzzle, followed the bear's weaving head.

The bear and dog snarled at each other. Patch dodged under the massive swinging front paws and slashed the bear's rear leg. The bear roared.

Patch danced out of reach, barking all the while.

"Patch! No!" She'd never trained him to "No." Not that she'd had to train him.

The dog charged again. The bear swiped and knocked the dog high in the air. Patch landed with a thump.

"No!"

The bear swung to face her shout. Jesselynn pulled the trigger, and the bear rocked back, half his head gone with the blast. He started toward her.

She drew her pistol and dodged behind the tree again. She listened. No sound but the rain on the leaves above her.

Then a crash. She stepped from behind the tree to see the bear fall face forward, crushing the brush, twitching but not trying to rise.

Jesselynn ran around the brush, leaping an overturned log where the bear had been digging grubs, and searched for her dog.

"Patch!" She screamed his name, listened, and called again. Nothing.

Ten feet farther, Patch lay on his side in the flattened grass, as still as the huge black bear. Jesselynn knelt beside him, tears streaming down her face. "Oh, Patch, not you too."

Chapter Eighteen

Jesselynn laid a hand on the dog's ribs.

"Come on, Patch, you can't let a little ol' bear knock the life outa you." She knelt and laid an ear to the same place. Sure enough, though faint, the dog's heart beat on. She wiped away her tears with the back of her hand. "God, you have to save him. He was just trying to save me."

She glared at the bear, half expecting him to rise and charge her again. Back to the dog. Was that a twitch of his eye? The tip of his tail lifted also. Once, twice. She raised his lip to look at his gums. White gums meant internal bleeding, but his teeth gleamed white against pink flesh. "Thank you, Jesus." She felt his legs, looked for blood, none. Pushing gently on his rib cage, she heard a slight crackle. "Ribs. He broke your ribs." She rocked back on her heels to think. "But all we have to do is get you back to camp without poking one through a lung. Even dogs can heal of broken ribs." She kept up the soothing words, not sure who needed them most, her or the dog.

"You wait right here, Patch. I'll be right back." Taking her knife from the sheath on her belt, she rose and returned to the bear, nudging his hind foot to see if he moved. Nothing. No rise and fall of the back. Swiftly she twisted the massive head just enough to reach the neck and, with a slash, left him to bleed out. They couldn't afford to waste the meat, the hide, nor the fat.

"You'll make good soap, you fool critter. All over that measly fish." She glanced skyward to realize that the rain had let up. Now, how to carry Patch and the rifle? She pulled off her cape and laid it on the ground by the dog with the rifle beside him. She folded it over and, kneeling, slid both hands underneath the package.

Patch whimpered, so faint she wouldn't have heard it had she not started to lift him. She pushed to her feet, swaying against the weight. A rhythmic thudding caught her attention. "Horse's hooves. Ah, Patch, help is on the way." She turned to see Jane Ellen, skirts a-flying, riding astride on Dulcie, one of the mares. The colt ran right beside her.

"What happened?" Jane Ellen called over the clop of hooves.

"Bear."

At that same moment the mare scented blood and plowed to a stop. Jane Ellen kept right on going over the mare's neck and flat out to thud on the grass, water causing her to slide before coming to a halt. The colt snorted and retreated behind his dam.

But before Jesselynn could put the dog down and get to Jane Ellen, the girl groaned. She gagged and finally sucked in a breath. "Knocked . . . my . . . breath out." She shook her head and looked up at the mare snorting at the end of the reins still clenched in her fist. "Fool horse."

"Just sit there a minute." Carrying her burden carefully, Jesselynn approached the wild-eyed mare. "Come on, Dulcie, behave yourself."

The mare backed up, dragging on the reins. Jane Ellen rolled over on her belly, glared at the horse, and commanded, "Stop now, you hear me?" She tugged on the reins at the same time, then coughing again, got to her feet. "Nothin's gonna hurt you."

"Patch has broken ribs, so we got to carry him real gentlelike. Thanks for coming."

"We heard the shot, and it took me a minute to catch this stubborn horse." Jane Ellen looked around. "So what happened to the bear?"

"I shot it."

Jane Ellen's eyes widened, her jaw dropped. "Kilt it?"

Patch whimpered again, more strongly this time.

"We'll come back for it. We can use my cape as a sling. You lead the horse and carry this end. I'll take the other and the rifle."

"It weren't a mama bear with cubs, were it?"

"Never saw any." Jesselynn adjusted the sling, and they started off. "Saw the log where it had been eating. Think the blood smell from the fish is what caught its attention."

"You ever eat bear?"

Jesselynn shook her head. "Not a lot of them left in Kentucky, leastways not around Twin Oaks."

"It be right good. Greasy. Good for makin' soap like you started with the lye. My pap used to grease his boots with it too. Kept out the wet real good."

"All I know was it looked like a mountain, standing up sniffing the wind like it did. Then Patch came running and tore off a strip of his hide. That bear near went crazy." Jesselynn stopped walking to shift hands. "When he walloped Patch like he did, why, that dog flew through the air like a rag doll."

Jesselynn shuddered again. "Thank the good Lord he's still alive. He was trying to save me." She swiped at her eyes again and sniffed. "Fool dog."

They stopped several times to rest, and unconcerned now, Dulcie snatched mouthfuls of rich grass. The colt danced around them, inspecting flowers and brush, snorting at something on a branch.

Jane Ellen laughed heartily at the colt's antics. "We got to name him. He can't be called Colt forever."

"He'll be registered as Ahab, with the second name beginning with J — since he's the tenth colt. Ahab's been throwing mostly fillies."

"What about Joker? He is one, you know. Makes us all laugh."

Jesselynn stopped to switch hands again. "Ahab's Joker of Twin Oaks. I like that. A good handle for such a strong colt."

"That the way your daddy kept track of the get?"

"Umm. Long time tradition at Twin Oaks. Haven't used Domino for stud yet. Had planned to be racing him this year. He did all right as a three year old but was a late bloomer. Not much chance for him to race now."

"What they gonna do about the books for registerin' the Thoroughbreds?"

Jesselynn shook her head. "No idea. Not too many Thoroughbreds left in the South, that's for sure. Lot of the Northern studs were stripped too, I imagine. Those officers like fine horses to ride on." The thought of all the slaughtered horseflesh made her skin crawl. Men at least had a choice. The poor animals had no option but to go where their rider wanted. She watched Joker leap in the air and take off, his brush tail a flag in the breeze. *Thank God, I got you all out of there. We at least have something to start over with when that vile war does finally cease.*

"It can't go on forever, can it?"

"What?"

"The war. Seems they're going on until all the men and horses are dead, nothing left to fight with."

"Jesse comin'." Thaddeus yelled loud enough to be heard across the meadow.

"He can call you Jesselynn now, can't he?" Jane Ellen stopped to get her breath. "Never thought this dog could weigh so much. He ain't that big."

"Got a mighty big heart, though."

"Easy now." Jesselynn cautioned Thaddeus as he ran up to them. "Patch is hurt right bad."

"What happen?" Thaddeus eyed the sling. "He alive?"

"Yes, a bear took a swipe at him. You go get Ophelia."

Thaddeus took off as fast as his legs would pump. " 'Phelia, come help." He stumbled over something, got back up, and kept on running.

By the time they reached the entrance to the cave, Ophelia, waddling behind her big belly, met them, shaking her turbaned head. "A bear? Thaddeus say a bear."

"He's dead. Let's lay Patch on a pallet by the fire. Bear broke his ribs, or hitting the ground did."

Ophelia reached for Jane Ellen's side of the sling. "Go ask Aunt Agatha for strips to wrap him ribs. Bestest way to help."

"Thaddeus, where's Meshach?"

"Gone."

"Where?"

Thaddeus pointed up toward the hills. "To woods."

"Him went lookin' for wood for de rake. Need hardwood, him say."

"Wonderful." All the men were gone.

Jane Ellen came back with a roll of narrow strips of cloth.

After telling them all what happened, Jesselynn and Ophelia knelt on the sandy cave floor, and with gentle fingers, wrapped the strips around the dog's rib cage, tight enough to hold broken ribs in place but not so tight he couldn't breathe.

"Thaddeus, get Patch a bowl of warm water."

Someone dipped for him, and Thaddeus carried the bowl back, both hands cupped firmly on the side, his tongue firmly clamped between his teeth. The water sloshed as he set it down by the dog's muzzle.

"Drink, Patch." He stroked the white ear. "Please, Patch, drink."

"Here, like this." Jesselynn dripped some of the water on the side of Patch's muzzle. He licked it away. Thaddeus repeated her action.

"Look, he likes it." He drizzled more and giggled when Patch quickly licked his fingers.

"Good. Let off awhile and let him sleep, then do the same again until he can drink from the bowl." Jesselynn stood and stretched. "We've got to get that bear back here before some varmint comes in and takes it." But how to get the carcass up on a wagon?

"We could use one of the canvases to drag it on." Jane Ellen followed Jesselynn toward the mouth of the cave.

"Good idea. Let's yoke up a span of oxen. They won't be so flighty with the smell. You go get them, and I'll get the canvas. We'll set the yoke together."

"You need some more help?" Mrs. McPhereson met them in front of the cave. "I can get Mrs. Jones too."

Jesselynn noticed the omission of Aunt Agatha. Far as she knew or seemed to care, the bear might have gotten her. "Thanks, I'd appreciate that." When the others left to do their part, Jesselynn stood shaking her head. *What will it take, Lord? We can't go on like this forever. You say to forgive as we have been forgiven. How do I forgive someone who won't even look me in the eye, let alone talk with me? This is beyond me. You're going to have to fix it. And I'd appreciate it done soon. Life's too short to carry noxious things like this.* At the remembered sight of the bear standing upright, its heavy head swinging from side to side testing the air for scents, her mouth dried again. If that didn't bring on nightmares, not much else would anymore.

Within minutes they were striding out across the meadow to the creek and around the rock face to the pond.

Jesselynn had to tell her story one more time, since Darcy Jones hadn't heard it. Ophelia pronounced, "De Lawd done take good care of her."

"Wait until the men hear about this. They'll never let us go beyond the creek." Mrs. Jones hefted the saw over her shoulder.

"Just make sure you don't go without a gun. And don't let it get out of arm's reach. That's where I made a big mistake. I leaned it up against the tree behind me. Never again, no matter how cumbersome."

Three turkey vultures, their red heads naked of feathers, lifted off from where the carcass lay in the grass and low brush. Ravens scattered, their hoarse voices scolding at the intrusion.

"Good thing we didn't wait. They've announced the kill to the entire forest." Jesselynn stopped the oxen a ways away. "Let them graze while we dress the bear out."

Knives and saw in hand, the women approached the bear.

"He's so big." Jane Ellen stopped, her eyes as big as her voice sounded small.

"You should have seen him standing." Jesselynn stood over the carcass. "Let's roll him over. Can't be much different than dressing an elk."

"Look at his claws." Mrs. Mac hefted a forepaw.

"And teeth." Jane Ellen stepped backwards. "I never seen anythin' so fierce."

"Can we eat him?" Mrs. Jones wrinkled her nose. "He smells rank."

"Bear meat is good. My pa brought some home." Jane Ellen ran her hand over the fur. "Be a good hide."

Jesselynn sharpened her skinning knife on the whetstone she'd brought along, yet still, sawing through the hide took time, even on the tender underbelly. As soon as she'd slit the belly, the others dug in to help her. By the time they'd gutted the beast, they were all dripping wet, though the rain had stopped and a breeze now swept across the pond.

"The wind is keeping the mosquitoes down at least." Mrs. Mac sat back on her heels and wiped her forehead with the back of her hand, leaving a streak of blood across it. Her bleached calico sunbonnet hung down her back out of the way.

"Do we want to wash these intestines like we do a pig for sausage?"

"I don't know. Might be different for meat eaters. We used them from the buffalo and the elk." Jesselynn turned her head away to get a breath of fresh air. "And to think that all I wanted was fresh fish for supper."

"You got a nice perch over there." Jane Ellen nodded toward the bank where Jesselynn had been fishing. "You want I should try for some more?"

"Why not." Jesselynn untied the pouch with worms from her belt and handed it to her. "No sense letting the worms go to waste. The pole I cut is right there too."

The three women finished cleaning up the carcass and, leaving the hide on to protect the meat, rolled the bear onto the canvas. They lashed the two sides together and across the end to form a pouch, tied the open end to the single tree, and started the oxen back to camp.

"Come on, Jane Ellen, no one is staying out here alone again."

"Just one more? They're biting like . . . like . . ."

"Come on." Jesselynn turned to Mrs. Mac. "You start on back, and I reckon we'll catch up before you get to the caves."

Taking the rifle with her, Jesselynn strolled on over to lean against the tree. Jane Ellen jerked the pole, and a fish flew back. Jesselynn ducked.

"You nearly got me."

"Sorry. I never had so much fun fishin' in my entire life." Jane Ellen dug in the pouch, turned it inside out, and shook her head. "Out of worms." She sighed and crossed her arms on her knees. "Right purty place, isn't it?"

"Sure enough is. No wonder Wolf remembered it."

"He and his daddy stayed here one winter, right?" Jane Ellen wrapped the string around the pole, then leaned forward and pulled her forked branch lined with fish out of the water. She held it up for Jesselynn to see. "You want to help carry 'em?"

———

Meshach was the only man in camp when they returned; he'd just come back with several cottonwood trunks and branches, which were now leaning against the cave wall. He helped unwrap the bear and whistled his surprise. Looking up at Jesselynn, he shook his head slowly, as if he couldn't believe what he saw.

"I be thinkin' you got some story to tell. Wait till Wolf see dis."

For a second Jesselynn froze. Would Wolf be angry? After all, it wasn't like she'd gone hunting; she'd just done what he'd always told her. Be prepared to shoot, and when you shoot, shoot to kill.

"We better hang dis in back of de cave where it's cooler."

"How?"

"Put up a bar, I be thinkin'."

"Have we anything strong enough to hold 'im?" While she talked, Jesselynn disengaged the oxen and loosed them to rejoin the herd.

"Mebbe one trunk I bring in." He ducked into the cave and brought out a stout trunk. "I get de brace up."

"Good, and we'll skin him and cut off the head and paws."

They all set to their jobs, and by the time the hunters returned, the bear was hanging in the back of the cave. Aunt Agatha was frying fish for supper, and Mrs. Mac was making corn pones from cornmeal, flour, bacon fat, and water. She patted them together and laid them in the frying pan to sizzle in more bacon grease.

Wolf had a deer thrown across the back of his horse, as did Benjamin.

"More skinnin'." Jane Ellen and Mrs. Jones looked at each other and shook their heads.

"More skinnin'?" Wolf turned from untying the deer.

Jesselynn kept from smiling. "Nice deer." She touched the four prongs on the antlers. "These will come in handy."

Benjamin looked at Wolf, then around the circle of women and back to Wolf. Meshach turned away.

"Need more bars."

Wolf narrowed his eyes and, after lowering the deer to the ground, looked full at his wife. "What is goin' on?"

Jesselynn shrugged. "Nothing now."

"Now?"

She shrugged. "Well, we got him all skinned and hung. And just in time, looks like, since you brought in more. I reckon we're going to be doing a lot of smoking, that's for certain sure."

"Keep those little boys breakin' kindlin'." Jane Ellen kept a straight face too. Mrs. Mac turned away, a cough covering her laughter.

"Think I'll go help Ophelia." Mrs. Jones scurried into the cave like something was after her.

"Jesselynn, I got me a feeling . . ." Wolf took one step toward her.

"Well, Mr. Wolf, he's only a little bear." Jesselynn rolled her lips together.

"A bear. Meshach shot a bear?"

"No, sir." She stuck her hands in her pockets and studied the design her boot toe sketched in the dirt.

"Who shot the bear?" His voice deepened.

"Me." She shrugged and looked up at him from under her lashes.

His face wore that cut-granite look she knew meant trouble.

"I had the rifle along, and the bear smelt the fish, I think, and Patch came charging to the rescue, and I shot the bear before he could finish off Patch, and so we"—she indicated the women with a sweep of her hand—"gutted him and Meshach hung him, and . . ." She felt impaled to the cave wall by his stare.

"Supper ready," Thaddeus called from the mouth of the cooking cave. "Wolf, you back."

"The rest of you go on and eat. We'll be there in a moment."

"Should we wait grace?" Meshach shoved the stick he'd been carving through the tendons on the rear legs of one of the deer and threw it over his shoulder with a grunt. "I hang dis."

"No, yes . . ." Wolf shook his head. "Show me the bear, Mrs. Torstead. Perhaps we should name you She Who Kills Bear." He slung his arm over her shoulder, and they entered the cave. "Thank God, you are safe. Shooting a bear. And here I thought I left you safe in camp."

"All I did was go fishing."

Chapter Nineteen

RICHMOND, VIRGINIA

Dear Jesselynn, Thaddeus, and all the others,

I am writing a quick letter so you can be aware of what is going on here. I'm sure Carrie Mae has written to tell of her beautiful little daughter. They named her after our mother and Jefferson's, Miriam Amelia. Carrie Mae had a fairly easy birthing, even though to hear her you'd think she was in labor for all of August instead of only hours. But little Miriam is precious, and I go to see her as often as I can. Would that it were more so, but we had a major crisis here. Aunt Sylvania suffered a minor apoplexy that scared us all, especially her. But she is recovering well, and we are all grateful. Our new kitten, named Bones by one of our guests, is her delight.

I must tell you that I am concerned about Zachary. Please pray that he not turn his back on his Christian upbringing. I know Mama and Daddy are beseeching our Father before the throne, but I covet all earthly prayers too. He has become so cynical, I hardly recognize him any longer. Yet, every so often he's as nice as can be. I just don't know what to do about him.

Our boys here at the house are sewing and knitting for those still on the march.

I must tell you that Zachary and I are making another trip. Each one stretches my faith as I pray for our Father's protection, both for us and for those at home.

Oh, sister, I want this despicable war over and done with, so we may get on with our lives. I want to go home, no matter how damaged Twin Oaks is. We received a letter from Lucinda saying the taxes are due. How can they levy taxes on those who have given so much for the cause of the South? I struggle with this like the straw that broke this woman's back. Zachary has said he will take care of it, but since he has said nothing further, I have my doubts there too. The thought of losing Twin Oaks is intolerable. My heart bleeds again and again, until I fear I shall have nothing left to give. How much can our Lord expect of us? I know the answer—He has said we will never be tried beyond our strength. But, enough of my whining.

How are all of you? Where are you? I am so anxious for a letter from you. How big is Thaddeus now? I pray you tell him about us and our lives at Twin Oaks, so he knows whereof he came.

We all send our love and our prayers, as I know you pray for us. Someday we will all live together again at Twin Oaks in dear Kentucky. Lord bless and keep you, my dear sister and brother.

I know I am including love from all the others here.

A tear just missed blotting the page as she signed her name and let the ink dry while she addressed the envelope.

With the letter ready to send, she blew out the lamp and climbed into bed. Any day now and she and Zachary would be on the road.

————

"We'll do a grieving mother and father this time, using a coffin again and that false-bottomed buggy. I've had a foot carved to fit in a boot so it won't be so obvious I've lost mine." Zachary had made plans for another trip to the North.

"Where will we be going?"

"Washington."

Louisa flinched inside. She still had nightmares about the time Zachary was missing. All alone in that hotel, not knowing if he were alive or dead, captured or shot for treason.

She hadn't heard from her friend Mrs. Hinklen, who'd come south to retrieve her husband's body. He'd died of injuries during one of the battles. Talking with her had made Louisa realize that Northern women and Southern women suffered the same thing in losing their men to the war. Mrs. Hinklen hated the war as much as Louisa.

But her husband had done his duty, just as had Louisa's father and brothers.

If only it were over, and they could all go home.

"Zachary, have you heard anything regarding the taxes on Twin Oaks?" The question popped out before she had time to think it through.

The look he gave her said quite clearly that she should stay out of men's affairs. She'd learned to read that look well.

"You know what?" She leaned forward, staring him right in the eye. "Twin Oaks is my home too, and I have every right to inquire about it." She made each word distinct and forced herself to not draw back.

"You know, dear sister . . ."

She refused to flinch at the sarcasm.

"You are sounding more like Jesselynn every day. Mother would chide you for becoming so unfeminine."

Louisa stared him right back. "Be that as it may, dear brother . . ." Two could play at that game. "But if I waited around for men to do for me, we would starve here, along with our guests." She kept her voice low so their guests wouldn't hear them. *And considering you have not contributed one dollar to the upkeep of this house, you do not have a lot you can say.* Surely they were paying him for working in the law office, but he had never mentioned how much or when. Another very unchristian thought flitted through her head, made a hairpin turn, and returned to roost.

What was he doing with his money? Had he paid the taxes? Had he even written a letter in response to the one Lucinda had sent them? When he said he would deal with it, she had trusted him to do so. No longer was she so certain that was wise.

Lord, if I can't trust my own brother, whom can I trust? But she knew the answer there too. As her mother always said, *"In God alone do I put my trust."*

Now the real question. *Do I?* She heard herself arguing, or rather remonstrating, with herself as if she were another person standing back and eavesdropping on a conversation.

"You will be ready?" Zachary's question stopped her internal discussion. His voice had softened.

"Yes."

"Making you look old enough will be difficult."

A compliment. Zachary had paid her a compliment. Veiled or not, one had to take compliments when offered.

"Thank you, dear, I will manage." Now how would she tell Carrie Mae that she would be gone?

———

"But where are you going? I need you here." Carrie Mae stared at her sister as if she had left a portion of her mind at home.

"Carrie Mae Highwood, er, Steadly, some of us have more important things to do than wait on you hand and foot."

Carrie Mae slumped as though she'd been slugged in her still-tender midsection. Tears sprung from her eyes like downspouts after a rainstorm.

Even though Louisa knew Carrie Mae could put on tears as easily as she put on a shawl, she felt as if she'd tried to drown a kitten.

"I'm sorry, dear, but I must do this. I'll be back as soon as I can, and—"

"It's that dumb old war again, I just know it. I am so sick and tired of hearing about the war I could throw up." The baby let out a wail. "Now see what you've done."

Louisa hid a smile. While she wasn't the one who'd been shouting, she knew her sister well enough to know who would get the blame. "I'm sorry." Louisa walked through the archway and picked her niece up from the basket where she slept. "There now, sugar, you don't need to cry. How long since you fed her?"

"Two hours or so. She's like a little pig, eating constantly. That's all I do, feed the baby, change the baby, feed the baby. I feel like an old milk cow." Carrie Mae threw herself down on the sofa.

Louisa nuzzled the now quiet infant. "Ah, you precious little one, if only your grandmother were alive to see you. She loved babies so." She looked up to see her sister mop away tears. At the bereft look on Carrie Mae's face, Louisa knew they were thinking the same thing. Some days, even after these years she'd been gone, the ache to see their mother again cut clear to the heart.

Louisa crossed the polished floor to sit beside her sister. "I'd stay home if I could."

"I know that. Forgive my childish tantrum. I . . . I just didn't realize babies took so much time, and I'm tired clear to the bone. Jefferson suggested a wet nurse, and now I'm beginning to think I made a mistake in refusing him." She glanced at her daughter, who was now engaged in conversation with her aunt. She watched in silence. "You are so good with her."

Louisa turned to look at her sister. "So are you."

"I get impatient."

"I didn't have to get up with her every two hours during the night. Why don't you feed her and go take a nap? I'll stay awhile."

"No, I'd rather visit with you." When the baby screwed up her face, Carrie Mae picked up a blanket to throw over her shoulder and unbuttoned her waist. "Can Elise get you anything?"

"No thanks." Louisa watched as Carrie Mae set her daughter to nursing, all the while smiling and whispering to the baby.

"Lucinda would say she's sweet as sugar and pretty as a rose."

"I know. I always thought I would have my babies at Twin Oaks. Funny, I never thought I would have to go with my husband wherever he lived. Just never entered my mind." She smiled at Louisa. "Life certainly is different than we dreamed, isn't it?"

———

Back at Aunt Sylvania's, working on her disguise, Louisa kept thinking about Carrie Mae's comment. Sometimes the only thing that kept her going was the thought that God knew what was happening and was not surprised. No matter how severely her world was torn apart, He was still in control. *Lord, help me to remember that, no matter what.*

———

Louisa reminded herself that God was in control when she and Zachary climbed into their rather odoriferous buggy.

She reminded herself again when the Union officer studied their papers. One of her prayers had been answered. He wasn't the same man who had passed them through on the earlier trip.

Union uniforms painted Washington blue. From the troops camped to the south of the city to the officers who took part in the life of the capital, one could not step out the door without seeing uniforms.

As Zachary and Louisa drove to a house in the northern outskirts, heads turned away at the putrid effluence of their coffin. Riding with the foul odor so long had deadened their sensitivities, so they could look suitably grief stricken. Pepper in her handkerchief helped as before. Red eyes only added to her appearance of age.

"Zachary, dear, I keep getting the feeling someone is watching us." Louisa had hesitated to say anything, for due to the stench, many watched them.

"I think not. I've been observing carefully." Zachary tied the reins to the whip handle, and using the armrest and his crutch, carefully lowered himself to the ground.

"Don't go lookin' around like you are frightened or some such." He barely moved his lips while giving instructions.

"I know." She climbed from her side of the buggy and followed her brother up the walk. Staying at a hotel had been hard enough but with strangers would be worse.

Zachary knocked at the door that had missed a few paint jobs, as had the porch. A curtain dropped back into place, the only indication someone was home. Within moments the door opened, and a man in a black coat and trousers invited them in.

"Were you followed?" His first words sent ripples chilling up Louisa's back.

"No, at least not that I could detect. Why would anyone follow me?"

"Just bein' careful. We have the box ready to transfer. I will take your buggy inside my barn and do so while the two of you have a bite to eat. Then you must be on your way again."

Without even a night's sleep? Louisa wished her brother would look at her so she could question him. But he ignored her, keeping his attention on their host.

"That will be fine. Perhaps you have a place my wife could rest and wash a bit?"

"Of course, follow me."

Louisa did as asked and was shown into a bedroom with a pitcher of water set on the commode. When their host left the room, she sank gratefully down on the bed and removed her hat. After using the necessary, she washed her hands and face, brushed her hair, and wound it back in a bun. Lying down on the bed, she closed her eyes, sinking into the softness of the feather bed. The night before had been spent at an inn where the only available bed had been boards with a thin pallet. Her shoulder still ached.

"Mrs. Highwood, are you ready?" The voice came far too soon, but Louisa answered yes. She rose, tucked stray wisps of hair into the bun, donned her hat, and after straightening the bed, left the room.

Zachary met her at the front door, their host beside him with a basket over his arm.

"I dislike hurrying you off like this, but we have been informed we must leave this house and find another immediately."

Louisa took the basket. Chills raced each other up and down her spine like a hawk after chickens. One look at her brother's face and the mask covering it, and she knew he was as edgy about the situation as she. Why, then, had they been sent here?

"I'm sorry there was no time to inform you of any changes." The man hustled them out the door and into the buggy. "If I were you, I would go further north and west before heading south."

"Thank you. All is loaded as needed?"

"Yes, and Godspeed."

Louisa climbed into the buggy and waited for Zachary to accomplish the same. But when he clucked the horse into a trot down the street with no difficulty, she let herself rest against the back of the seat.

The odor seemed even more pervasive.

Zachary threaded their way among the wagons, buggies, and riders clogging the streets, making Louisa wonder how he could possibly find their way.

They spent the night at an inn and left again early in the morning. A drizzle grayed the road and set the trees to dripping. At one point they pulled off the road and watched a battalion of Union soldiers pass with fully loaded provision wagons and wagons with red crosses painted on their sideboards. If only they could appropriate the supplies therein, but instead she kept her head down, handkerchief to her nose. Since no one gave them a second glance, they followed some distance behind until they met the Union lines.

"Halt!" A young soldier, rifle across his chest, stepped into the roadway.

Zachary dug in his breast coat pocket and held out his papers. "We are taking our son home to be buried." He enunciated clearly, sounding as Northern as possible.

"And where is that?" The man folded the papers and handed them back.

"Not far down the road, at Manassas."

"I've been instructed to have all civilians vetted by my superior officer. You will have to come with me."

Louisa felt her stomach tighten, then loosen, like a snake preparing to strike. *Please, God.* She looked up with tear-filled eyes.

"Please, as you can smell, we must get him home, or we will have to bury him along the road." One sniff of her handkerchief and the tears ran.

"I'm sorry, ma'am, orders is orders." He beckoned to another to take his place at guard and motioned them forward.

They stopped in front of an officer's tent.

"Please leave your buggy and come inside."

"My poor husband has a difficult time getting out of the buggy. Is it possible for us to talk out here?"

"One moment." He disappeared in the tent.

"Do not say any more than necessary." Zachary spoke without moving his lips.

The young man returned. "Sorry, ma'am. Follow me, please."

Louisa controlled the shaking of her hands with the greatest effort. She stumbled as she stepped down, but the soldier caught her arm before she fell.

"Easy there, ma'am."

She recognized the discomfort in his face and voice at forcing them to do this. Knowing how old and frail they appeared, she let herself lean on his arm, then rounded the buggy to assist Zachary.

As they hobbled into the tent, the officer behind a desk looked up and commanded, "Search their buggy."

Chapter Twenty

"Sir, the body . . ." Louisa dabbed at her eyes with her handkerchief and the tears rose immediately. "Our son . . ." Her sniff was as genuine as her fear. "The smell is . . . is bad. Has . . . has he not been through enough?"

"Ma'am, we've seen enough war that the sight of one more decomposing body won't be a shock."

No, but what isn't in that box may be. She turned and hid her face on her brother's shoulder, the sobs real.

"Now, dear, please, don't carry on so." Zachary patted her back with the stump of his arm. "Now see what you've done." He shook his head sadly. "Too much. This has all been too much." His voice sounded old and feeble, as if the very life were being drained from him also.

"Here, both of you, have a seat. This won't take but a few moments, and you can be on your way." The officer, who wore the maple leaf of his rank, motioned to two chairs to the side of his field desk.

Oh, God, please make them blind or willing to accept the coffin for what it is. Please help us. Louisa could hardly sit for the shaking, her prayers skittering through her mind like desiccated cottonwood leaves before a winter wind.

"Sir." One of the men beckoned the major from the tent door. He nodded to the two of them and left.

Louisa closed her eyes. They were discovered. She knew it with every bone in her body.

When the major reentered the tent, the look on his face said it all. No longer a hint of apology, but now the steel of accusation.

"Put these two under arrest for running contraband. And bury that raccoon. He has more than served his purpose."

Zachary sat straight in his chair, one arm resting on his crutch.

The major took his seat and leaned slightly forward, his voice soft but laced with steel. "Now, would you like to tell me who you *really* are?" He glanced down at their papers on the desk in front of him. "I believe Mr. and Mrs. Tyler to be as false as that body out there."

"Captain Zachary Highwood, Confederate States of America, discharged due to war injuries. This is my sister, Miss Louisa Highwood. The contraband, as you call it, is quinine and morphine, not for resale, not for pleasure, but to ease the suffering of men who fought nobly."

"I see." The major leaned back in his folding chair, one arm cocked over the leather back. "So after fighting you Southerns for every hill and valley, I should now alleviate your suffering?"

"Some of them are your men too. Cannonballs show no partiality."

"So you can send them to rot in Libby Prison or Andersonville?" Narrowed eyes glared across the distance.

Zachary shrugged. "If we have nothing to care for our own, how can we care for yours? Besides, many prisoners are paroled almost as soon as they arrive."

"Take them away." The major waved at the young man standing at attention at the open tent flaps. "And put them in separate quarters. Manacled wrists."

"For both?" The rosy-cheeked young man raised an eyebrow.

"Both."

He used his rifle to indicate they should precede him.

Louisa went out first, followed by Zachary, the young soldier, and another who fell in beside them. Both soldiers held their rifles at the ready.

What? They think we shall run? Zachary hardly able to walk and me looking like a woman far beyond her prime, older even than Aunt Sylvania? Louisa tottered some for good effect, not that anything they said or did would make any difference.

Spies were shot. She would argue they weren't spies, only angels of mercy, but she had a feeling the major would hardly accept that.

Shame such a fine-looking man had been so harsh.

As if it would be easier were he ugly? The little voice snickered. *What are you doing noticing he is a fine-looking man? He's the enemy.*

Louisa turned into the tent indicated and sat down on the cot.

"Sorry, ma'am." Another soldier entered. "Please hold out your hands."

Louisa did as requested, a knot forming in her stomach as the iron manacles were snapped about her slender wrists. The sound of it sent waves of horror rolling through her body. She stared up at the blue-clad man in front of her. "Is this really necessary?" Her voice cracked, her throat so dry she couldn't have spit if ordered.

"Only obeying orders, ma'am." He dipped his head, a mere sketch of good manners, and left, dropping the tent flap behind him.

Any semblance of breeze died with the dimness. And with the heat trapped in the tent, her fear rose from a mewling kitten to a roaring tiger.

Oh, Lord, no matter how much I look forward to heaven, I'm not ready to leave this earth yet. What about those at Aunt Sylvania's, and Jesselynn? Please, Lord, I want to see her again. I want to see Twin Oaks. I want to be married and have babies. God help me, I don't want to be shot. I can't do this, Lord, I can't. The manacles weighted her hands like the fear weighted her heart. She curled up on the coarse blanket that covered the cot into a shivering ball in spite of the heat.

What have they done with Zachary? The thought brought the tears from her heart to her face. He'd already been through so much. Why should he have to face a firing squad? *Why, God, why? He says he is only doing his duty. And Lord, I was trying to follow your precepts, caring for the wounded.* She didn't need to use her peppered handkerchief; the tears flowed no matter how much she tried to staunch them.

A soldier with brushy whiskers brought her food on a tray but said not a word and refused to look her in the eye. When she held out her hands so he could take off the manacles, he looked the other way and left the tent.

"At least they gave me a fork." Louisa eyed the bowl, then the distance between her hands. No room for manners here, no napkin, nothing to drink. *So I won't eat,* she thought, then canceled that immediately. If there was to be any chance of escaping, she would need every bit of strength she could summon.

Escape, what a silly thought. *Zachary cannot escape, and I surely won't go without him.* But the stew caught in her throat, making her gag and wish for a drink.

By dark, her stomach growled and twisted. The smell of cooking fires and food teased her nostrils. *If you want something, get off this bed and go ask for it, you ninny.* Food she could do without but not water.

She tried arranging her hair, but the chain caught in a wayward tress, and she flinched. She finally pulled her hands free, stifling a yelp in the process. Instead of neatening her hair, she brushed off the front of her black skirt and aged yellowing waist and forced herself to not lie back down and hide.

When she opened the tent flap, the length of a rifle stopped her from moving farther. "Excuse me, but would it be possible for me to have a drink of water, please?" She almost neglected the please but reminded herself that she was a lady, no matter the treatment she received. Her mother's voice had comforted her in the long hours of her confinement. She could hear her quoting Scripture clear as if she were right here in the tent with her. *"Blessed are they which are persecuted for righteousness' sake: for theirs is the kingdom of heaven."*

In her case, righteousness was a matter of point of view.

"Let me ask the major."

"For water?" Her voice squeaked. She heard him move off, but the clearing of a throat made her aware someone else had taken his place.

A few minutes later a water jug was slipped through the tent flaps.

"Thank you. You are most kind." Ah, how sweet she could speak, honey more sweet than sugar in her tone.

No answer.

Had they been ordered not to talk with her, or was this normal for captives?

After drinking, another need became obvious.

"I'm sorry to bother you again." She almost choked on the words. Anger was fast replacing fear. If she was condemned after all, what was the need for civility? "But the afternoon has been long, and I sincerely need to use the . . . the facilities." How more specific could she be?

"I'll ask the major." A different voice, more gruff.

A few minutes later a chamber pot appeared at the tent door.

"Thank you."

No response.

The next day passed much the same. By the time the sun hit the zenith, her temper had reached the boiling point.

"Excuse me, but I demand to see the major or whoever is in charge."

A mumbled discussion followed, and again she could hear someone walk away.

Oh, Mama, my mouth has gotten me in trouble again. You would not be proud of me now. She looked down at her clothing, wanting nothing more than a cloth and water to wash with, a brush for her hair, and a breeze. *Oh, dear Lord, what I would give for a bit of breeze.*

The tent opened, and a hand beckoned her out. Feeling all eyes were on her, she followed the pole-straight back to the major's tent.

"Good afternoon, Miss Highwood." The major pointed to a chair.

Louisa elected to stand. Knowing how shabby she appeared, she straightened her spine and raised her chin. "Major . . ." She paused, hoping he would fill in his name. Referring to him as "Major" seemed in her mind to give him more importance than she desired he be given.

He cocked an eyebrow, waited, then finally supplied his name. "Major James Dorsey."

Insolent, bluebellied . . . She cut off the string of names, fearing she may say more than she should.

"Major Dorsey, is there some reason you are treating me with such contempt? Surely there are rules for dealing with prisoners."

"Yes, there are. Spies may be shot at will."

She tried to breathe around the punch to her stomach and sought the chair instead.

"Then I believe we are having a problem with semantics. I am not a spy. My brother is not a spy. We are not carrying messages of any sort, only succor for injured men."

"Miss Highwood, did you or did you not pick up your contraband at . . ." He named the address of the house they'd been to.

"Why, yes, but only morphine and quinine." She kept her head high.

"You are certain no messages were passed on to your brother?"

Louisa thought to the time she'd spent lying down. Zachary had not been with her.

He fingered a piece of paper on the desk before him. An envelope lay beside it. "Does this look at all familiar?" He held it up.

Louisa shook her head. "No, not at all."

"This is not a letter from your sister?"

Louisa knew she'd been trapped. "How can I tell? I have not read the letter."

He handed it across the desk.

She let the chain of her manacles clank on the wooden desk top as she reached for the letter. Her gaze dropped to the bottom. The signature read, "Your loving sister." No way was this Jesselynn's handwriting. And glancing quickly through the message, it didn't make any sense.

She looked at the envelope. No return address. No, this was not from Jesselynn, and who the writer was, Louisa had no idea.

"You don't recognize it, do you?" Was there a note of sadness in his voice?

Louisa looked up, tried to come up with a lie, and shook her head.

"We'll be leaving for Washington in the morning. Corporal, show Miss Highwood to her quarters."

Louisa held her head high until the tent flap dropped behind her.

Zachary, what have you done now? She collapsed on the cot. *Oh, Lord, how will you get us out of this one?*

Chapter Twenty-One

Zachary wasn't really a spy, was he?

Riding in the back of a wagon with a soldier between them kept Louisa from questioning her brother.

Tarnation. If only she could ask him about the letter. Surely there was a reasonable explanation.

The gray look Louisa saw on Zachary's face as she was helped into the wagon let her know his accommodations had been no better than hers, most likely more severe. Not shaving for three days added to his disheveled appearance, and she was certain he thought much the same of her. While they'd attempted to look old, now they looked dirty along with it. She'd never worn the same underthings this long in her life, and picking a flea off her skin this morning told her what made her itch. All over. She most likely had picked up a few lice too.

The thought made her shudder.

If only I could have a bath. Hot water had never before seemed so precious. And soap. *All those things you've taken for granted,* she scolded herself. *If nothing else comes of this, perhaps you will be more grateful.* Keeping her mind on such mundane matters kept her from thinking the darker thoughts that sent her mind into a black hole of fear, peopled with specters of despair.

Her shin itched. Her mother would have said a lady never, ever, scratched in public. Right at that moment, Louisa was no longer sure she cared what her mother had said. If only she could talk with Zachary. She shifted on the hard boards. The wagon hit a bump, and she figured she now had a bruise that would only get worse on the trip to Washington, considering the state of the roads.

A tune ran through her mind, "My Old Kentucky Home." She leaned back against the boards with a slight smile. *Ah, Kentucky home. Lord, please help us make it that long.* All she'd ever heard about how spies were treated made release doubtful. *But I will not doubt, Lord. I believe you can protect us. I believe you will protect us. I don't know how, but you kept Daniel from burning in the lions' den.* She stopped. No, He kept Daniel from burning in the fiery furnace and from being eaten in the lions' den. She sighed, shaking her head. *Keep your stories right,* she chided herself, then sighed again. Here she was on a prison wagon to Washington, trying to keep track of Bible stories she learned at her mother's knee. If only she could talk with Jesselynn. *Lord, I want to see my sister again. Father, how do I keep the fear from eating me alive? Jesus. Jesus. Jesus.* Only repeating his name kept the terror at bay.

Another bump, strong enough to throw her against the guard. The leer he gave her shuddered up her spine. She pulled as far away as her manacles would allow. Besides, he smelled riper than their discarded raccoon.

She wished she could melt into a puddle when they entered Washington. She kept her gaze on the tailgate of the wagon, looking neither to the right nor left.

When they pulled up in front of the prison, the major climbed over the wagon wheel and stepped to the ground, signaling the driver to take the wagon on through the heavily barred gate that swung open just for them. The look he gave her made her skin ripple, much like the thought of lice had.

I was just doing what needed to be done, she wanted to tell him. *Just like you are.*

The gate clanged behind them, sending a scream of despair echoing through her mind. *Lord, save us!*

The guard leaned closer to her. "You'll like it here, missy. They takes good care of female prisoners." His chuckle made her want to shrivel up and disappear. Would she be thrown in a cell with all the men, or was there a separate place for women? Surely there would be. *Oh, Lord, surely.* She gritted her teeth. *I will trust you, O Lord. I am trusting you, Jesus, in your precious name.* Only repeating those words kept her from screaming.

The driver wrapped the reins around the brake handle and leaped to the ground, coming around to let down the tailgate.

"Come on, you two vermin." The guard they were manacled to scooted to the end of the wagon, dragging them along with him.

Louisa sneaked a peek at her brother only to see his mouth set in a straight line, bracketed by commas of pain. She reared back against the pressure on her wrist, dragging the guard off-balance.

He cursed at her, turning with tobacco juice spitting from his snarl.

But her stunt took the pressure off Zachary, allowing him to move more at his own crablike pace.

She reached over with her free hand and grabbed his crutch, dragging it behind her. Her wrist felt as though she'd held it above a flame.

The driver took Zachary by the arm, and between the two men, they jerked him to his feet where he sagged between them.

"Give him his crutch, you sorry excuses for men!" Louisa deliberately rammed the handle of the crutch into her tormentor's side as she reached around him to hand it to Zachary.

A slight grunt helped her endure the savage jerk on her wrist that sent her to her knees.

The driver snarled at both of them and dug in his pocket for the key. "You take her. I'll keep this'un."

"My pleasure."

Louisa read the full meaning of the word *lascivious* in the look her guard gave her. She felt stripped, as if she stood shivering in her bloomers, or less. She stared around, searching, pleading for someone to come to her rescue. Two men leaning against a wall laughed. A prisoner shouted from a barred window above them.

Another answered.

The guard jerked her in front of him wrapping his free arm around her chest.

"Keep it up, girlie, I likes it when you squirm." If his words hadn't frozen her, his breath would have.

Louisa willed herself to hold perfectly still. The pressure across her breast made her want to scream, but she swallowed the horror.

"Little, that's enough!" The major's order cut through the air.

Little released Louisa with a curse, muttering softly so that his commanding officer couldn't hear him.

"We are not animals, Little, so don't act like one."

Louisa sucked in a breath and then another, anything to deny the blackness hovering near the edge of her mind. She clutched her dignity like a staff, sketched a nod of appreciation to the major, and shivered in spite of air so thick with humidity she could scarcely breathe.

Thank you, Lord, thank you. She wanted to shout the words, but her lips were so clamped against the roiling in her stomach, she didn't dare move them.

"Unlock her."

"Yes, sir."

Even during the unlocking, Little managed to rub his upper arm against her breast. Without thought, Louisa stamped her heel down on his toes and flinched back as he raised his hand to strike her.

"Little!"

The order stopped the guard in midswing. He jerked the manacle off her wrist with a snarl, drawing blood.

Louisa wrapped her fingers around the deep scratch to staunch the bleeding. She took two steps back to get out of his breathing range and swallowed hard again. The blackness hovered, leering as wickedly as Little.

"Come with me." Major Dorsey touched her elbow.

Louisa blinked and clamped her arm against her side, her other hand still protecting her wrist. What in the world was the matter with her now? One man ripped her wrist, and a touch from the major made her elbow burn.

"Wh-what have you done with my brother?"

The major nodded to a soldier who opened another door for them, then let it clang shut after they passed through. The sound echoed and reechoed through her bones. With each clang, she felt diminished, as though the sound sliced off another strip of flesh.

Men waved and whistled from cells on either side as she followed at the major's side. When he showed her into a small room, empty but for a cot and a commode, she kept the tears of relief at bay by biting her lip.

"Thank you."

"Someone will come with your supper." He glanced around the room, nodded, and left, closing the door behind him, the sound of a key turning in the lock reverberating in the stillness.

Quiet, such a blessed relief after the din of her march through purgatory. She sank down onto the cot, releasing her fingers from her wrist to inspect the damage. Dirt crusted the blood, promising infection if she didn't get it cleaned, and soon. The sight of the wound reminded her of Corporal Little. She needed far more than water to wash away the horror of that man.

Lord, I thank you for your care. I know you can see through prison walls. Please, could you remind someone to bring me water? She crossed the short space to the window and, resting her forehead against the glass, stared out through steel bars to the yard below. Men paced along the cut block wall, others played cards in the shade, some slept, others talked in small groups. She wished she could hear what they said. While the noisy gauntlet she had traversed as she was led to this room had made her ears ring, now she wished for any voice. A fly landed on her wrist. Before brushing it away, she watched as it nibbled on the crusted blood. Another landed. And another. Three blue black creatures crawling on her wrist. When one deposited an egg, she shuddered and brushed them away. *Oh, Lord, I know you made the flies too, but what is becoming of me when I watch them feasting on my blood?* She walked back to the cot and lay down. The smell of rot and mildew filled her nostrils as she fell asleep, her opposite hand protecting the wound from the persistent flies.

When a rattle of keys woke her, Louisa noticed the room had dimmed. The door swung open, and a man entered carrying a tray with food and a pail of water.

She blinked. Was he an apparition? He looked gray enough to be so.

"Th-thank you." Her throat rasped so dry she could barely talk. His nod would have been missed had she not been staring at him. "Don't tell me. Let me guess—you've been ordered not to talk with me." Again that millisecond nod. "Well, there's nothing that says I cannot talk to you."

Was that a twitch of the sides of his mouth?

A bit of encouragement, all that she needed.

"Is there the smallest chance you could bring me a bit of bandaging?" She held up her wrist. "I really need to clean this and wrap it. Place like this must breed infection." She held out a hand. "Not that I'm criticizing, mind you."

An eyebrow twitched this time. How could the man say so much with such tiny motions? Or was she reading more into him than was there?

He set the tray on the end of her bed, reached into his pocket and drew out a small roll of bandage, set it on the tray, and pointed at a smear of ointment on a bit of paper.

Louisa clasped her hands at the base of her neck. Fighting back the tears that clogged her throat faster than she could think, she whispered, "Thank you." It had to be the major. No one else knew of the slice on her wrist. "And thank Major Dorsey for me also. And tell him you never said a word, for you haven't. Our Lord will bless you for this kindness."

He sketched a sign of the cross on his chest, dipped his head in the briefest of bows, and left the room, shutting the door with a click behind him, not a clang. She heard the key turn, but at the moment, it mattered not.

Bread, stew with meat, even a cup of coffee. Soap, small but real. She sniffed the tiny sliver, inhaling the sharp fragrance of clean. And a bucket of water.

Lord, O Lord, I am the most blessed of women. Thank you. How can I thank you enough? She tore a bit of the bandage off, dipped it in the water, and then with caution born of need scrubbed at the dirt around the wound. She could hear her mother's admonition, *"Use plenty of water to cleanse an open wound, the hotter the better."* Hot she had no control of, but a bucketful was plenty. Quickly she drank the lukewarm coffee and used the tin cup to dip out more water. Finally she rubbed the soap on the rag and scrubbed all over the cut, causing red to well up again.

"Good. Bleed. That will help." Finally she smeared the ointment on the cut and wrapped the cloth around it with her other hand. She used her free hand and her teeth to rip the end of the bandage to create two tails, wrapping them in each direction. Knotting took teeth and fingers working together, but she made it.

Eating cold stew was worth every minute of the time she took to ward off infection. *Thank you, Father, thank you* repeated through her mind like the metronome that counted time for her piano lessons in that life long ago at Twin Oaks.

Louisa paced her cell in the darkness, the stink from the chamber pot mingling with all the stenches that seemed to permeate the very walls. Unwashed bodies, sicknesses of both body and soul, vermin, mildew, hate, all imbedded in the stones and carried on the air. Mosquitoes droned and hummed in her ears, a scratching from a corner was surely a mouse, or more likely a rat. A squeak.

Her heart leaped into a pace used for running. But where could she run? She paced back again, this time banging her shin on the cot.

All her life she feared being alone in the dark. Her brothers had teased her, leaped out at her often enough. Now with no effort on their part, terrifying creatures haunted the corners and under the cot. Fear sucked her mouth dry.

She crept onto the cot, drawing her legs to her chest, leaning her back into the corner walls so nothing could reach her. *Mother, I need you.* She chewed the knuckle of the bent finger she kept at her mouth to still the screams that threatened to erupt.

Like a gentle breath, verses came into her mind. *"I will never leave thee, nor forsake thee . . . and, lo, I am with you alway. . . . Thou shalt not be afraid for the terror by night; nor for the arrow that flieth by day. . . ."*

Louisa lay down. *"I will never leave thee, nor forsake thee. I will never leave thee, nor forsake thee."*

Lord, please go to Zachary as you have come to me. Please keep him safe, and I pray they fed him as well as they have me. If he is alone . . . a song came into her mind as she drifted off to sleep.

A scream woke her sometime later. Could that be Zachary? Would they be interrogating him? She'd heard of brutality being used to get answers. Oh, *Lord, please — not Zachary.*

Chapter Twenty-Two

❧

ON THE CHUGWATER RIVER
AUGUST 1863

"You be careful now." Jesselynn knew she sounded like a worrying wife, but, oh, how she wanted to go along.

Wolf looked down at her, shaking his head. "I've trapped wild horses before."

"I know." Sure he'd trapped horses before, but his helpers hadn't and neither had she. "Why don't you trade some of those goods with your people"—she nodded toward the laden packhorses—"for horses." She stroked the bloodred neck of his Appaloosa. *I don't want you to go off without me.*

"Because all the blankets and supplies are my gift to them." His voice wore the longsuffering tone of one who had said all this before.

"Will Red Cloud know where the wild horses are?"

"Perhaps. Now it is my turn to say be careful. Don't go off hunting or fishing by yourself." He added a "please" when her jaw squared off.

"We're going to cut hay."

"I know." His dark eyes twinkled. "But you seem to have an uncanny ability to find trouble."

"I think trouble finds me. I don't go looking for it." *How long will you be gone? Will Red Cloud be glad to see you? What if he isn't?* The questions piled on top of each other in her mind. She'd known since Fort Laramie that he would be going, but the knowing and the doing were two separate things. "God bless, and we'll all be praying for you." She squared her shoulders and lifted her chin, forcing a smile to lips that would rather tremble.

After giving Thaddeus a hug and whispered instructions, Wolf mounted, without using the stirrups, and checked out his helpers. Benjamin, Daniel, and Mark Lyons stood by their horses, their bedrolls with supplies rolled up inside and tow sacks hanging behind their saddles and at their horses' shoulders. Each had a rope of braided latigo and hobbles tied to his saddle also. They'd spent the last days making hobbles and ropes, and practicing their throwing skills.

While she and Wolf had said their good-byes privately before rising, Jesselynn felt an ache the size of Wyoming in her heart as they rode out of camp. Something could happen to them so easily, just like the near tragedy with the bear. Feeling an arm around her leg, she looked down to see Thaddeus, one hand on Patch's head, the other around her knee, staring out after the riders.

"Come home soon." His whisper brought forth the rush of tears she'd been holding back all morning. She picked him up and used his shirt to wipe her eyes.

"Yes, Thaddy, please God, they come home soon." *All in one piece and with plenty of horses.*

"How soon you be ready?" Meshach stood right behind her, Ophelia at his side.

"Whenever you are."

"I still think I should go with Meshach." Nate Lyons spoke around the stem of the pipe he chewed on more often than smoked. "I could cut more hay."

"You heard the man." Jesselynn indicated the disappearing Wolf with a nod of her head. "A man stays in camp at all times." The slightly sarcastic tone of her voice implied more than she said. The bear incident had made Wolf far more cautious than before, and he had always been extra careful. But the bear story had a happy ending after all. They'd made plenty of soap, kept grease for waterproofing boots and leather jackets, eaten and dried the meat, kept the hide to make a robe, and she'd saved the claws and teeth to trim buckskin shirts and moccasins. The porcupine quills she had kept after killing a four-footed scavenger added to her stash of trimmings. They'd found the porcupine chewing a pair of leather gloves someone had left lying on a log. Wolf had said the porcupine had chewed them for the salt.

Killing the bear had made Jesselynn truly aware that no matter how civilized the caves were becoming, they still lived in the wilderness. And many of the other wilderness dwellers were bigger, faster, and perhaps hungrier than they.

She set Thaddeus back down and patted his rear. "You and Patch stay right by the cave, you hear? No going to the creek or anywhere else by yourself." She knelt in front of him so he would see how serious she was. When his lower lip came out, she poked at it with a loving finger. "No, don't you go getting in a huff, or we'll put you on a long line like we do the horses sometimes."

Thaddeus cocked his head to one side. "Put Sammy on long line."

Chuckling, Jesselynn hugged him and stood. "Now, Darcy, you and Jane Ellen will bring the other wagon out in three days. We'll turn the hay then."

"Yes'm." Since they'd left the fort, Darcy Jones seemed to be getting younger every day. She laughed with Jane Ellen and played with the two little boys, and was once even heard singing when off doing the wash down at the creek.

Jesselynn smiled in return. What a difference.

Now if only the same miracle could happen to Aunt Agatha.

As soon as Nate and Meshach finished removing the sides of the wagons, the two McPhereson boys helped load up the supplies needed in the hay camp. They yoked the oxen and hitched them to the wagons.

"Me come?" Thaddeus wore a look of hope.

"No, you need to stay here and take care of Aunt Agatha."

The look Thaddeus gave his sister said very clearly what he thought of that idea. Jesselynn hugged him again and handed him to Jane Ellen.

"We'll see you soon, I reckon." Without another backwards look, her haying party headed out the curving creek to the Chugwater basin. Jesselynn studied the lay of the land more this time, searching out small valleys where they would be able to graze the herd in the winter so as to not use up their hay. That would be saved for the mares in foal and for emergency rations in case of a blizzard. Wolf's stories of blizzards that kept everyone in camp for days at a time made her dread the coming winter.

She eyed the thickets along the creek. If deer and elk could winter on the branches when the snow got too deep for foraging, so could their cattle and horses.

They arrived at the valley on the afternoon of the second day. While Jesselynn set up camp, Meshach and the boys started directly on cutting grass. With Meshach's height and long arms, wide swaths of grass fell before him and the scythe that he stopped to sharpen regularly. After hobbling the oxen, finding wood for the fire, and setting a trotline baited with bits of smoked bear in the creek, Jesselynn took up the shorter scythe and started her own swath.

Meshach made it look a lot easier than it was. Getting the correct angle of the blade took practice. Convincing her arms to continue swinging after the first hour took sheer teeth-clenching guts, and resisting the urge to slap mosquitoes was harder than anything. No wonder animals rolled in the mud to keep bug free.

Her shoulders ached, her hands — in spite of wearing leather gloves — sported a blister or two, and her back screamed as though she'd been stuck with a hot poker. Meshach kept on swinging, the grass falling in smooth sweeps with nary a blade missed. She looked back at her own rows — and sighed. But when she looked at those of Aaron and Lester McPhereson, she didn't feel quite as bad. Height and experience seemed to play a big part.

When dusk sneaked across the land and the red-winged blackbirds began their evening arias, Jesselynn leaned the scythe against a wagon wheel and staggered to the banks of the Chugwater. Kneeling, she splashed her face, shook her head, and after removing her boots, waded out in the gentle current. When even that wasn't enough, she dove in and flipped over on her back. Floating with the eddies, she felt every screaming muscle in her body begin to relax. Ducks flew overhead and quacked somewhere in the near distance. For the first time since she couldn't remember when, she was alone, and her responsibilities floated on along with the river.

Walking back to find her boots was a combination of swimming and slipping on the mossy rocks in the riverbed. The water weighed down her clothing, but she resisted the urge to strip to her undergarments. The fellas would be wanting a bath or a swim too.

" 'Bout to come lookin' for you." Meshach sat with his feet in the water where she had left her boots and gloves. He nodded upriver to the trotline. "Plenty fish for supper."

"Good. Where are the boys?" She plunked herself down on a rock with her feet still in the water.

"They be gettin' the oxen."

"Go on and take a swim. The water is lovely." Swallows and flycatchers dipped and skimmed above the water, making their meal on the flying insects. The setting sun washed the water in gold leaf and tipped the grasses pure gold.

One of the oxen bellowed.

"I better get the fire going." Jesselynn waited a minute or two longer before drying her feet with her wool socks and putting her boots back on. "This sure is one pretty place."

"That it be." Meshach lowered himself into the water with a sigh.

While the boys cleaned up after their supper of fried fish, Jesselynn took out her journal to catch up on the happenings. The last entry concerned the bear. She wrote of Wolf leaving, of camp details, and of cutting hay. She prayed for wisdom in dealing with Aunt Agatha. Meshach took out his Bible and hunkered down by the firelight to read. When Jesselynn closed her journal, she looked across the fire. "Read aloud, please."

His deep voice awoke the beauty of the psalms as he read one after another. Jesselynn marveled at how many he read with his eyes closed. He finished with the twenty-third, so they all said it together. " 'The Lord is my shepherd . . .' " Jesselynn sure felt cared for. " 'I shall not want.' " *Please take care of Wolf.* " ' . . . beside the still waters.' " *Just like here.* " ' . . . and I will dwell in the house of the Lord forever.' " A hush fell. Jesselynn looked up at the stars embroidered like French knots across the deep velvet sky. Crickets sang, a bullfrog harrumphed. *"The house of the Lord"—I'm in it. Thank you, Father.*

———

Picking up the scythe again in the morning, even though she hadn't shared the watch with Meshach and the boys, took strength of both body and character. She couldn't remember ever aching so much. Cutting tobacco was far easier than this, as was the walking plow when they turned the tobacco fields.

The August sun beat down, mosquitoes sucked blood, and the swaths from the day before were already drying. Only looking toward winter and knowing she would save her horses through her sweat and screaming muscles kept her going.

By the time the others rode up on the fifth day, Jesselynn and the scythe had become intimate friends instead of screaming enemies. While her swaths were nowhere near the width of Meshach's, the grass lay smooth, she honed her blade with ease, and by evening she could still stand up fairly straight.

Several days later, after Meshach laid a frame of willow trunks across the wagon beds to extend them to hold more hay, they loaded what was dry, and Jane Ellen and Darcy Jones headed the wagon westward. By the time they returned, Meshach and his helpers had the second wagon loaded, with more cut.

"Wait till you see our haystack back at the caves." Jane Ellen, looking more boy than girl since she, too, switched to britches, dashed across the field, leaping the rows of grass raked and turned for drying. "Mr. Nate and Aunt Agatha are fencin' it off."

Jesselynn leaned on her scythe handle. "Well, I'll be. She's working with Nathaniel Lyons."

Jane Ellen pulled a piece of grass and nibbled on the tender stalk. "I think he's winnin' her over." Her eyes danced at sharing the news.

"You got to admit, the man is persistent." Jane Ellen stepped closer, her eyes sparkling like the sun kissing the river ripples. "We brought you a present, a real surprise."

Knowing how much Jane Ellen enjoyed surprises, both gotten and given, Jesselynn widened her eyes. "All right, what is it?" Hands on hips added to the fun.

"We brought bread. Ophelia baked bread."

"Real, yeast-risen, wonderful bread?"

Jane Ellen nodded.

"Not biscuits?"

Jane Ellen shook her head. "We can have it for supper. Ophelia started sourdough from milk and flour she got at the fort. It bubbles in a crock like nobody's business. Now that it is going good, she can use flour and water to keep it goin'. Ain't, I mean, isn't that just . . . just . . ." Jane Ellen threw her hands in the air, the best word not coming.

"When did all this come about?"

"Oh, when you was moonin' after Mr. Wolf."

"I wasn't mooning."

"Sure was, just like a lovesick cow." Jane Ellen dodged the swat Jesselynn sent in her general direction.

"What lovesick cow?" Darcy pushed her sunbonnet back to wipe her forehead. She'd hobbled the oxen before joining Jesselynn and Jane Ellen. "Whooee, be hotter here than up at our place."

Jesselynn noted the "our place." She was willing to wager that Darcy Jones had never had a place to call home in her entire life. When Wolf returned he planned on staking out property lines for each of the settlers, so when the day came that they could file on their homesteads, they'd be ready.

She hoped when they returned to the fort for winter supplies, they would have horses to sell, the first of many.

The bread was all Jane Ellen had promised, even though a couple days old. That along with boiled cattail tubers and wild onion made the fried fish a banquet.

———

Wolf had no idea leaving camp would be so difficult. How he'd wanted to bring Jesselynn along, both to meet his relatives in Red Cloud's tribe and to see the beauty of the country. She, who thought it wonderful where they camped, would be amazed at the mountains to the north. Besides, he wanted to show her off to his friends. If they were still his friends. Ten years was a long time to be gone, and much had happened in the meantime.

While they saw several Indian camps, none of them were Red Cloud's. He asked if the tribes knew where Red Cloud was, but the answer was always a shaking of the head. Some said Wind River country, others said Powder, and some said he'd gone south.

No one had horses to trade either.

As he and his helpers climbed higher, the trees grew larger, the creeks dashed more swiftly, and herds of elk grazed in the valleys. Scouting ahead one afternoon, Wolf found traces of another Indian band. He secreted his three young helpers, along with the packhorses, in a dense forest.

"Wait here until I return. If I don't come back in four days, head on home."

"We can make a fire?" Benjamin leaned his crossed arms on the pommel of his saddle. "And hunt?"

"Snares yes, but no guns. And keep the fire smokeless." Along the way he'd taught them how to cook over a small, nearly smokeless fire, how to shoot with a bow and arrows, and how to identify wild things that were edible. The bow he'd made during camp at night needed more arrows, which was their job when on watch during the wee hours. So far they'd sharpened, burned, and sharpened again the ends of the arrows to make them hard as flint since they'd not had time to make arrowheads.

"If you are found, they will steal our horses and the goods, so be on guard." Wolf looked each of them directly in the eyes, extracting their promises.

He rode slowly, following the trace, checking over each crest of the hill on foot before proceeding. When he finally looked down into a valley deep in grass, with tepees spaced between the trees and the sparkling creek, the familiarity of it all stabbed him in the chest. How he'd missed this simple way of life. He'd been gone far too long.

He hoped not too long.

Wolf watched the camp for several hours, realizing most of the braves were gone. He was too far away to recognize faces, but the longer he watched the more certain he was that this was Red Cloud's band. When a hunting party rode back into camp from the opposite direction, he continued to watch. Finally he mounted his horse and rode down into camp.

Chapter Twenty-Three

Oglala Camp

Gray Wolf kept his horse to a slow walk as he entered the Oglala camp.

Two dogs barked around his horse's leg. One of the packhorses kicked back and snorted. Two braves, rifles across their chests, stepped in front of him. Wolf stopped his horse and nodded a greeting.

"I am Gray Wolf, son of Laughing Girl. Red Cloud is my uncle." He sat on his horse without moving, waiting for them to acknowledge his greeting. Speaking the language of his mother felt good and proper.

At a grunt from one of the braves, the dogs slunk off.

"You have been gone a long time."

"Yes. Too long. Is it you, Dark Horse?"

The brave on the right nodded, a smile starting in his eyes. "I did not expect to see you again." The two had been best friends from the time they tumbled in the grass together as babies.

"I said I would return." Wolf glanced around the camp. Children peeked from the entrances to tepees, and some of the women had joined the men standing at attention throughout the camp. Cooking fires with racks of meat drying looked just like those at the caves.

"You were but a boy, and the white man's ways are different from the Oglala."

More than you would ever know. "Is Red Cloud here?"

"Yes. He is head chief now." Dark Horse turned to a young brave behind him and ordered him to announce the visitor to the chief. He crossed to stand at Wolf's knee. "You are indeed welcome, my brother." He looked at the Appaloosa. "One fine horse. You want to trade?"

Wolf shook his head. Leave it to Dark Horse. "No, but I brought gifts." He swung to the ground and indicated the two packhorses.

"Come, Red Cloud is waiting."

Wolf knew that another youth, a bit older than he, had taken the name of Red Cloud when he earned the position as chief of the Oglala. There had been chiefs named Red Cloud before him, but he was winning a place in the Sioux nation as both a warrior chief and one with wisdom. Braves followed him into battle because he always won. His camp was strong because he was adept at stealing horses from other tribes. So far he counseled peace with the white man.

So far. One of the reasons Wolf wanted to talk with him. One of the reasons the general at Fort Laramie wanted to talk with him.

A woman came running from a tepee set across the camp from him and stopped at his side, staring up with a smile that lit her entire face. "Gray Wolf, is this really you?"

"Yes, Little Squirrel, my mother's sister, I have come back."

"To stay?"

Leave it to her to ask the questions right in the beginning. Wolf shook his head. "No, but I will come again. I have a wife. We live on the Chugwater."

"A white man's house?" She patted his arm. "You married a white woman?"

"Yes. You will like her. She can tan a deer hide almost as soft as you do."

"You go now. Red Cloud is waiting."

———

The celebration of his return lasted far into the night, with feasting, singing, and dancing. He dispensed the goods from his packs, making sure that his aunt received both a red-and-black striped wool blanket and lengths of red print calico. When the packs were empty, he joined Red Cloud in his tepee.

"We need more guns." Red Cloud sat cross-legged on a pile of skins on the other side of the fire.

"I cannot help you there. The general refused to sell me guns and whiskey."

"We all eat better because of the rifles. Hunting is easier."

"So is war." Gray Wolf studied the flickering flames. Should he mention letting the white man pass through on their way to Oregon without attacking them?

"Buffalo are becoming scarce. Not like in the days when we were young."

"I know." Gray Wolf also knew that battles between tribes had been going on for as long as the Indian roamed the land.

"Rifles bring down the buffalo."

"And the elk and deer. But I cannot help you there. I'm sorry."

Red Cloud nodded, smoke circling his head from the pipe he smoked. He raised the bowl in a salute. "Good tobacco. Very good." He nodded again and studied the fire. The silence in the tepee made the drums sound distant.

Wolf waited, knowing the manners of his people.

"You have a camp on the Chugwater?"

"No. Homesteading." Wolf knew none of his people would think of declaring ownership of land. "White men have laws about land. To farm, raise horses, cattle, and food, I must seek to own the land."

Red Cloud shook his head, indicating his opinion of such foolishness.

"Do you have any horses to sell?" Wolf broke another long silence.

"Some to trade for guns."

Wolf smiled at his old friend. "You never give up, do you?"

Red Cloud shook his head, and his smile acknowledged the joke. "Why?"

"My wife brought Thoroughbred horses to our marriage. We will raise horses to sell." He didn't mention their plan to sell the horses to the military. "I need good mares."

"When we raid again, I will find you some."

The cessation of the drums announced the end of the entertainment. Not long after that, Wolf made his way to the tepee of his aunt, where he would spend the night. He fell asleep remembering times from his childhood. Perhaps bringing Jesselynn to meet his people would help her understand more about him.

The next two days were spent recalling both ancient tales and those from their youth, as all the men had gathered to talk. They watched the boys trying to be men and the girls trying to attract the boys. The men agreed that things didn't change much except for the inroads the white men made. Talk always came back to the white man.

"You come again and bring your wife." His aunt's words sounded more like an order than a request.

"I will. And her little brother." Wolf nodded before mounting his horse, the packhorses now carrying a buffalo robe, a present from Red Cloud, a necklace of dyed quills for Jesselynn from another aunt, Swims Like a Beaver, and a small bow and arrows for Thaddeus.

"You teach him to hunt," Dark Horse said when he handed Wolf the bow. "Then he will never be hungry."

"Unless the white man chases away all the game."

Wolf heard the subdued growl of one of the younger braves. Wolf hoped Red Cloud could keep them calm as he'd said he would.

"Thank you." He grasped Dark Cloud's hand, then waved to his aunt, now standing back with the women. Several of the young boys ran alongside as he rode out of camp, shouting their farewells as he trotted off.

When he returned to his own encampment, he found the three young men roasting prairie chickens over the near smokeless fire.

"One more day and we would have headed on home. Say de Indians got you." Benjamin took the lines to the packhorses and prepared to hobble them to graze.

"I'm here now. We head for horse country in the mornin'."

Chapter Twenty-Four

❧

WASHINGTON PRISON

Only the gray ghost, as Louisa came to call him, appeared for the next three days. Never did he say a word as he delivered food and water and removed the chamber pot, bringing it back rinsed clean.

But she gleaned plenty of information from him just the same. It all depended upon her skill in asking questions. To some, like "When will I be released?" he only shrugged. He knew no more than she.

But of "Zachary, my brother, have you seen him?" the right eyebrow rose. She'd learned that meant yes. "Is he well?" Slight shrug.

"Ah, is someone mistreating him?" She scoured her brain, frantically searching for a way to learn what she needed.

Nothing. Either he didn't know or couldn't answer.

"Has he been moved to a cell of his own yet?" His gaze roved around her walls. "I take it that means yes." The eyebrow rose.

He ducked his head and backed out the door. The interview was over.

Louisa paced the floor again as dusk grayed the window and darkness, along with the rats, crept into the room. No matter how carefully she ate her bread, crumbs would still fall to the floor for her nighttime visitors to squeak over. She'd learned to wrap her skirt up around her head and tuck her petticoats around her legs. Bare flesh was an open invitation to both rats and mosquitoes.

Forcing herself to wake with the daylight grew harder. At least in sleep she worried about neither those in Richmond nor Zachary in prison. Day after day passed much the same. Rising, eating, pacing, praying, singing, only to repeat it over and over. She tried to keep track of the passing of days by scratching a line on the wall, as many others had done before her. When August passed into September she began to despair. *Oh, God, where are you? I know you will deliver us, but when?*

———

"Miss, they be ready for you." Gray Ghost could talk. Louisa snapped her mouth closed.

"They who?"

"The military court."

"And I am to go before them looking like this?" She gestured to her filthy clothes.

He shrugged. "I wouldn't make 'em mad, if'n I was you." The longest sentence he'd spoken yet made good sense.

But after two weeks of solitary confinement, rather than breaking Louisa, their summons sent her into a fury.

"There must be some kind of a law against such behavior."

"They *is* the law."

Louisa's starch left her in a whoosh. With shaking hands, she tried to give some semblance of order to her hair and brush out her skirt.

"Please, miss. Don't want the sojers to come."

She nodded. *"I will never leave you nor forsake you."* She repeated the verse in cadence to her steps following the slightly stooped man.

Silence greeted her as she walked between the cells on both sides.

"God bless," a voice called, others echoed. Someone started clapping in time to her steps. Others picked it up, a cadence of respect and good wishes.

"Why are they doing that?" she asked as they passed through another slamming door.

"You a hero to the men, once they learned who you were. You and your brother."

Louisa took a deeper breath and straightened her shoulders. *Father, give me strength.*

Three men in blue, with an abundance of gold bars and braid, sat behind a long table. Major James Dorsey sat apart from them, off to the side. While he stood when she entered the room, the others didn't.

"State your name, please." The officer in the middle, the one with the most gold, wore the mask of power.

Louisa wanted to melt into a puddle and trickle out the door, but instead she ordered iron into her backbone, straightened her shoulders, and answered with all the assurance she could muster.

"Miss Louisa Marie Highwood."

"Your home is where?"

"Richmond at the time."

"And before that?"

"Twin Oaks near Midway, Kentucky." Her lips quivered, but her speech held steady.

"The charge before us is treason. How do you answer to that?"

At the horrifying word, her stomach lurched and bile rose in her throat. She swallowed hard to settle it back, then coughed into her handkerchief at the burning. She swallowed again, but the coughing refused to be pacified.

"I . . . ah . . ." Another coughing spell.

The interrogator waved at a soldier near the door. "Get her some water."

After a drink, she wiped her mouth. "Thank you." She cleared her throat again, sending pleas heavenward all the while.

"General, if trying to alleviate the suffering of wounded men is treason, then I believe you would have to convict me. I'd rather have you convict me of treason than have our Lord convict me of not caring for his sons."

"Answer only the question."

"I did." A slight narrowing of his eyes let her know she'd hit home.

"Miss Highwood." He leaned slightly forward, his hands clasped on the table in front of him. "Do you realize I can have you shot to death?"

"Yes, I do." No way was she going to call him sir, no matter what her mother had drilled into her all those years earlier.

One eyebrow twitched and settled back into a straight line with the other.

"But that will only serve to send me home to my Father." Where had that come from? She kept herself from licking her dry lips and reached again for the cup of water that had been left for her. She observed her shaking fingers as if they belonged to someone else.

He leaned back, his eyes drilling into hers. "Did you know your brother was carrying a letter that confirms our suspicions that he spied for the Confederate army?"

Her head shook before she could stop it. "N-no." *Stand straight, don't you buckle now. Why, Zachary, you promised me we were only coming for medicines.* But even while asking it, she knew the answer. He would do anything to assist the Confederacy, anything to feel he was still of use, still a man.

The general nodded to the man at the door. "Take her away."

At the look on her face, he added. "You'll be informed of our decision."

"Sir, what about my brother?"

"You are dismissed."

She shot a glance at the major, who returned it without as much as a blink.

Louisa squeezed her hands shut until she could feel the pain of her fingernails digging into her palms. *Lord, hold me up until I get to my cell.* But as she walked between rows of well-wishers, it was all she could do to keep from stumbling. She nodded, tried to smile.

"Hang in there, missy. They won't never shoot a lady."

Oh, God, make him right. "Thank you."

"I be prayin'." With that Gray Ghost shut the door behind him, and she heard the lock turn.

She just made it to the chamber pot before the bile erupted, burning her throat, searing her heart. She rinsed her mouth from the water bucket and collapsed on the cot. *Lord, I cannot take any more. I cannot.*

Though her eyes burned as though she'd been in smoke, she could not cry. She could not lie still either and paced the cell until darkness wrapped her like a shroud. Sinking onto the cot, she performed her nightly ritual, including, with no thought or will on her part, her evening prayers. *Unto thee, O Lord, do I lift up my heart, my gratitude for all thy mercies. . . .* A trickle of a song, so faint she had to strain to hear it, seeped into her despair. *I thank thee for sending thy dear son to die for me. . . .* The song swelled like a tiny creek after rain. *I thank thee that . . .* Tears broke from their dam, washed her cheeks, and cleansed her soul. She hummed the tune, the words building to be sung. "O God, our help in ages past." A whisper, but a song. "Our hope for years to come." She sat up, wiped the tears, swallowed, and continued. "Our shelter from the stormy blast, and our eternal home." She sang it again, pacing to the window and shouting it out the bars. An echo, no, someone else was singing. She started again. "O God, our help . . ." The music swelled as voice after voice from around the quadrangle picked it up. "Before the hills in order stood, or earth received her frame, from everlasting thou art God, to endless years the same." When she reached the final line of the last verse, her throat clogged. "Be thou our guide while life shall last, and our eternal home."

"Thank you," she called when the song died away, hoping the men couldn't hear the quiver in her voice.

"And you," echoed around the brick walls.

The next morning a key turned in the lock after Gray Ghost had already brought her breakfast. She watched as the door swung inward to reveal the major standing there.

"C-come in." As if he needed an invitation.

"The decision has been made. You are free to go."

"Free?" She stared at him, unable to believe it. Reality fell like a log on her shoulders. "What about Zachary, my brother?"

"He will be shot at dawn."

Chapter Twenty-Five

September 1863

"Would they take me and let him go?"

The major shook his head. "You weren't the courier."

"But what if he didn't know what he carried?" Her mind raced, banging from reason to reason like a wild thing in a cage.

"He knew."

Somehow she believed the major wished things could be different. She stared at him, willing him to look at her face instead of her hands. Hands that knit together, snarled like bad yarn. When he finally looked up, she saw anguish puddling his eyes.

"Is there anything . . . anything I can do?" Louisa swallowed the pending tears.

"Pray for his soul."

"His soul is not what is in jeopardy. Is there anything I can do in this life?"

The man hesitated, then lowered his voice, so she had to strain to hear him. "You could appeal to President Lincoln."

"Could the execution be postponed long enough for me to get an interview with him? If he would see me, that is?" Hope glimmered, an infinitesimal flame down a long tunnel.

"I'll see what I can do." He breathed what sounded like a sigh of relief.

At least she'd be off his hands. Why did that make her feel a pang of regret? If only they had met at another time, another place.

"Why, Major? Why do you care?"

He studied her, as if unsure he should answer. "You grew up at Twin Oaks, a Thoroughbred stud farm near Lexington, Kentucky."

She could tell it wasn't a question. "Yes. What do you know of Twin Oaks?"

"You have a sister named Miss Jesselynn?"

"Yes." Her heart picked up the pace.

"I was there the day of your father's funeral. Someone had told us there were horses hidden there, so I was ordered to verify the rumor."

Louisa closed her eyes. She could see a few men in blue trotting up the long avenue of oak trees that led to the big house, a house that no longer lived but in her heart.

"Miss Jesselynn, she is one fine woman. She let me know that we were intruding, and yet she served us lemonade on the front porch. A big black, shoulders this broad"—the major held out his hands to demonstrate—"he stood by the door, and an older black woman let us know we were in no wise welcome but served us anyway. Your sister made her."

"Did you find any horses?"

He shook his head. "Nary a one. Only two mules, but Miss Jesselynn made me feel so guilty, I didn't dare requisition them. We weren't in the habit of depriving citizens of their livelihood then."

And you are now? No longer is there room for feelings and manners. On either side. Lord, please keep me from losing the heritage my mother taught me, from losing the grace you taught me. "I'm glad you were treated well at my home." *Oh, God, how I wish I were there right now.* She looked up. The major had schooled his face back to officer lines. His jaw looked to be chiseled from stone.

She tried anyway. "Can you tell me any more about getting an appointment with Mr. Lincoln?"

A shake of his head so brief as to be nearly nonexistent.

"Can you promise—" She cut off the sentence. She knew he couldn't. Only the general could give stay of execution orders. To stand before that man again . . . Her hands clenched automatically. But for Zachary? She rose, hiding her now shaking hands in her skirt folds.

"Could you please take me to see the general?"

One raised eyebrow told her he questioned her sanity, but he nodded. "Follow me."

"Tole ya so," a prisoner called as she traversed the long walk between cells full of butternut-clad men. The cadence of clapping picked up again, buoying her spirits. "God bless you all." She nodded at the faces crammed between bars, hands reaching toward her. Their well-wishes followed her past the slamming door.

If only Zachary had been one of them so she could see his dear face. *But he's better off in a cell like mine,* she reminded herself. Thinking of him kept her from dwelling on her own predicament. Where would she stay? How could she force an appointment with the president? How would she get home to Richmond?

She didn't have to wait long for the audience.

"I take it you are not pleased with my decision." The general sat behind a walnut desk, campaign maps on the walls, brocade curtains at the tall windows. She thought to the tents of the men in the field. Some had it harder in war than others, that was for sure.

"Regarding myself, I am most grateful, but I have a favor of mercy to ask for my brother."

"Don't even bother asking me to pardon him. Military law states that spies are to be executed."

"I understand that. I plead for a few days' grace. That is all."

"Even heaven cannot save him now." The general narrowed his eyes, eyes that glittered like blue ice.

"Then what would hurt with putting it off for a week even?"

He thumped the desk. "I don't know what you hope to gain, but I will give you three days, no more."

"Thank you."

"Did Major Dorsey give you the money from your brother yet?"

"No, sir."

He nodded to the major who stood off to the side. "Do so and show her out." He waved a hand as if shooing a bothersome fly.

Louisa dipped her head in a semblance of a nod, turned, and followed the straight back of the major from the room. *Thank you, God* warred in her mind with *that insufferable pig*. She wanted to fall to her knees in gratitude. She wanted to shoot the general between the eyes. Instead, she thanked the major politely when he gave her Zachary's leather money pouch.

"I have something further for you." He stepped behind a shelf and brought out her satchel.

"Oh, Major." She looked up at him, at a loss for words in her delight.

"We removed the bottom."

"Oh." She shrugged. "All that money down the river."

"Oh, the quinine will be put to a useful purpose, as will the morphine. My men don't always get enough either."

Louisa refused to let his words bother her. She'd done her best, and God didn't require more. "Thank you, Major, both for this and the other."

"Good luck." He opened the door for her.

She stepped outside and, when the door closed behind her, stood in the sunshine, letting it soak in and begin to burn out the dregs of prison. Wishing she'd asked him which way to a boardinghouse or hotel or some place where she could scrub herself clean before making her way to the White House, she glanced up the street, then the other way. Which way?

She looked down at her satchel. While she had to brush and scrub at her skirt, she now had a clean waist and drawers, a gift beyond measure.

Feeling as though she'd been granted a new life, she set out up the street. Three days, that's all. What could she say to the president of the United States to make him take pity on her and release her brother?

At a hotel she located, a maid brushed her skirt while she scrubbed from head to toenails, rinsed, and scrubbed again. Her skin burned when she finished, wondering if she would ever feel really clean again. But dressing in clean clothes helped, and fashioning her still damp hair into a bun, so she looked neat and womanly again, helped even more. After asking directions from the man at the desk in what could almost be called a lobby, she set out for the White House nearby.

She knew she'd seen it before. Officers in blue and men and women in street clothes flowed in and out the wide double doors guarded by tall white pillars. She took a seat in a room full of chairs, wishing for her knitting. If she had something to do with her hands, the time would pass more swiftly. Studying the gilded wallpaper, the heavy velvet drapes, and the walnut moldings failed to occupy even a fraction of the many hours.

One after another, the people seated around her rose when their names were called and disappeared through one door or another, and others took their places. By the time she was the only one left, dusk was falling and the man in charge shook his head.

"I'm sorry, miss, but the president will not be seeing any others today."

"So then I can make an appointment for tomorrow?"

The man glanced down at a book in front of him. "You can come again, and I will try to fit you in, but his appointments are all taken."

"I see." Louisa sighed. "And the next day?"

"The same."

"Sir, I don't think you understand the urgency of my visit. A man's life is at stake." *My brother's life.* But she had a feeling that telling the entire story to this tight-lipped minion would only earn her a hasty exit. And no return.

———

The second day passed as the first. Louisa trudged back to her bare room at the hotel with a heart so heavy as to tip her into the sewer drain running alongside the street. She barely missed being run over by four brawny horses pulling a dray. Ignoring the shouts of the driver, she mounted the hotel steps.

Lord, what do I do? What am I doing wrong? Please, is it your will that my brother should die? But you say to ask for what we desire, and above all else on this earth, I desire my brother's freedom. Hoarding her few remaining coins, she spent the evening on her knees pleading before the throne of grace, rather than eating.

Trusting for everything, including her daily bread, was an unusual predicament. Never in her life had she gone hungry. Never in her life had she pleaded so for another.

———

Striding along the streets in the morning, she could think of nothing but that this was Zachary's last day on earth if something didn't happen to stay the execution.

The hours passed like the tolling of the bells for a funeral. People came and went. She only got up to use the necessary.

"Have you even told Mr. Lincoln that I have spent three days here waiting?" She asked the man for the third time.

"He's busy."

"I know that, but surely there are two minutes that he could spare."

"I will do what I can."

That hasn't been very much. But she returned to her seat, praying all the while.

Oh, Lord, have you turned your face away from me? Have you closed your ears? I have trusted you all my life, but I am left hanging here. Is there something else I could do? Oh, Lord, hear my prayer.

As the afternoon waned, her spirits faded with it.

Three people, including her, remained in the room. One by one the other two were admitted to the place they desired. She sat alone again.

When the man at the desk left the room on some errand, Louisa sucked in a deep breath, rose, and slipped through the door the others had used. Down the hall, peeking into each room, she prayed no one would see her and bodily throw her out. Just as Louisa was about to give up, she heard two men talking, and one said, "President Lincoln . . ." She heard no more but was certain she knew which room was the president's office. Hovering around a corner, she waited until the man left, then opened the door and slipped inside.

The president sat in a swivel chair behind an immense desk covered in papers. He was turned facing the tall narrow window. Brocade drapes were gathered to the sides with gold cord and a heavy tassel. She heard a sigh, but all she could see was a head of dark hair, struck every which way by hands that had plundered it. After a few moments long-fingered hands smoothed the hair down, and the president turned the chair back to face the desk.

Weariness dragged at the skin of his face, and dark eyes held a sorrow that didn't lighten when he saw her standing just inside the door.

"I thought I was finished for the day."

"I wish you were, but I need to talk with you, but only for a moment, for you can save a man's life today."

He beckoned to the chair by his desk. "And this man is your husband?"

"No, my brother." She sat on the edge of the seat, her shaking hands clenched in her lap.

Lincoln leaned back in his chair. "Tell me."

"My brother is to be shot at dawn as a spy." She swallowed, tried to clear her throat.

"And is he a spy?"

"My father did everything he could to keep Kentucky in the Union, but too few would listen. He and my other brother both died in battle. Zachary is my only brother . . ." She paused. "Other than my baby brother who is out west somewhere." *Stay with the story,* one side of her mind screamed. Get on with it.

"I see."

How can you see? "Zachary was wounded terribly—he's lost a hand, a foot, and an eye. We thought we would lose him too." Her throat clogged up again.

Mr. Lincoln poured a glass of water from a carafe on his desk and handed it to her.

"Thank you." Her stomach growled so loudly she was sure he could hear it. She blinked back the blackness that lurked at the edges of her mind like vultures waiting for the death rattle.

"How long since you've eaten?"

"Ahh." She had to think. Was it the day before yesterday? "Some time ago, I believe, but that is not what is important. Our family has lost everything, and while I know others have given all too, I beg of you, please spare my brother's life."

"Was he spying?"

She paused. Something in his face told her only the most simple truth would be tolerated.

"I . . . we came to Washington for quinine and morphine. Mr. President, sir, I volunteer at the hospital, and we are treating wounded men in our home. I cannot bear to see and hear them suffer—if there is something I can do. So many of them young boys, boys like my brothers. I didn't know he carried a letter."

"Did he?"

She looked at him, questions in her eyes.

"Did he know?"

"I . . . I believe so."

"Why should I spare him?"

"Because he is my brother." Despair loosened the starch in her neck and spine. Her head fell forward. There was no reason he should spare Zachary. This was all a waste of her time and that of the man with whom she spoke.

"Thank you, sir, for the water and for listening to me."

A servant entered with a tray of bread and cheese, cookies, and an apple. He set it on the edge of the desk.

"Anything else, sir?"

"No, that is all."

When he left, the president leaned forward, moved the tray to in front of her, and nodded. "Help yourself."

With hands shaking so badly she could hardly hold the knife, she buttered a piece of bread, laid slices of cheese on it, and took a bite.

As if no longer aware of her presence, the man before her took a paper and pen and began writing.

"What prison is your brother in? And what is his name?"

Did she dare hope?

Chapter Twenty-Six

THE WHITE HOUSE

"Do you promise not to spy again?"

"I wasn't spying, sir, I was . . ."

He waved a hand. "I know, I know. But your brother was. Can you speak for him?"

"An oath by any member of the Highwood family is honored by all." Louisa brushed crumbs from her skirt, her heart leaping with hope.

President Lincoln signed the paper, dusted it with sand, and leaned forward. "Miss Highwood, this letter will release your brother into your keeping. I abhor this war more than you can know, and this is perhaps not the wisest thing I can do, but . . ." He paused. "Would that we all had women like you to plead our cause." He nodded to the remaining food on the tray. "Wrap that up in a napkin and take it with you. It wouldn't help if you were to faint on the way to set him free."

"Y-yes, sir. Th-thank you." She looked into the president's sad, dark eyes and couldn't help reaching a hand to touch him. "I will pray for you, sir, and flood the floors of our Lord's throne room with my gratitude. I think I could not have gone on any longer had you not had the grace to save my brother."

"You are welcome." A smile tugged at the corner of his mouth and lightened his eyes. "Just keep that brother of yours out of Washington and be strong to rebuild our land when this heinous war is over."

"Yes, sir." Louisa settled the remainder of the food in her bag and rose, extending her hand. "Thank you again."

Her hand disappeared in his, and he tucked it in his arm as he walked her to the door. "Go this way and no one will bother you." He indicated a door in the opposite direction of the way she had come.

Louisa squeezed his hand again. "God bless you, Mr. President."

Her feet never touched the cobblestones as Louisa hurried along the now gaslit streets. She looked to neither side, her mind focused on another meeting with the general. Any thoughts of "what if" she banished with a snort. "Deceiver, you have no hold over me. God himself has set my brother free." When she finally arrived at the prison, a light rain had begun to fall. But she ignored the chill and pounded on the heavy wooden gate.

A sentry opened a square port and peered out. "Who do you wish to see?"

"The general."

"He is not here."

"Then I will wait in his office." She paused. "Where is he?"

"That is none of your business, ma'am. Come back in the morning." He shut the portal.

Louisa staggered, leaning against the wet wall for support. *Now what? Lord, where are you? Surely you wouldn't let all this happen and not free Zachary?*

She pounded on the door again.

The portal opened.

"I have an order from President Lincoln to give to the general."

A hand came out. "Let me see it."

Did she dare let go of the lifesaving piece of paper?

"It is only for the general." *Please, God, please.*

The portal slammed shut, and the door swung open.

Fear gripped her by the throat and made her gag. What if she never came out again? What if they took the paper and threw it away? What if, what if?

Lightning couldn't strike faster and more severe than fear.

God, help! The door began to close.

She stepped through the portal, clutching her bag, and her faith, like a shield.

The man in blue pants and shirt, no jacket, led her into a small room. "Wait here." He left a lamp on the table and exited the room.

Louisa shivered in the dampness of both clothes and room. No one would ever know if she disappeared now. Like two pieces of flotsam on a river, she and Zachary could be swept out to sea and never heard from again.

Chapter Twenty-Seven

WASHINGTON

Praying and shivering, Louisa waited out the hours. Every time footfalls sounded outside the door, she sat up straighter, only to slump again as they passed on by. Her head ached, her stomach grumbled. She dug out the bread and cheese to nibble on, but her stomach rebelled, roiling and threatening to erupt.

Thirsty. Lord, how can I be so thirsty? She felt as though she'd been trapped in the room for days rather than hours when the door finally opened.

"Come with me."

She followed the stiff back up the stairs and into the general's office.

"You have something for me?" The general held out his hand.

She laid the paper in it and fought off the shivers, of fear or freezing, she knew not which.

"I see." The look he sent her over the edge of the letter made her take a step back. Malevolent. She'd never understood that word before, but now she even felt it. When she looked again, his face had assumed a look devoid of any emotion.

His words came softly. "You had better pray that I never see either one of you again." He rang a handbell on the side of his desk. An aide entered.

"Release Highwood and show both him and his sister out."

"Thank you."

The general did not respond.

Louisa nodded, turned, and followed the aide to the hall and back to the room she'd memorized before.

Within a few minutes she heard Zachary's crutch-and-thump gait. She met him in the hall, faced his icy stare, and in moments the two of them stood outside the gate; the door thundering shut behind them.

How could Zachary walk as far as her hotel? Why didn't he say something?

"This way." She pointed up the street. "Perhaps we can find a buggy."

He stumped beside her, his false foot swinging in the peculiar gait he had developed.

"I have a hotel room. In the morning you can get a bath before we leave for home."

Still no answer. She tried to see his face in the lamplight as they passed another lamppost. The light threw shadows that made her shiver.

She paced her steps to his. Did he not care to know what had happened?

The rain picked up again, but at least now they were free. The drops fell like a warm, cleansing shower.

At one corner, Zachary stopped and raised his face to the downpour. The streetlight showed his good eye closed. He took a deep breath, and they started off again.

Louisa could endure his silence no longer. "Zachary, dear brother, what is it? Why are you not rejoicing to be freed from that . . . that"—she shuddered— "that terrible place?"

He stopped with a turn. "Would that you had let me die there." He swung his crutch and clumped onward.

Would she ever forget the look in his eye? The gargoyle sneer on his dear face? The scar from eyebrow to chin glittered like a lightning strike in the lamplight.

Sometime later, when Louisa felt sure Zachary could go no further, as his steps had grown slower and slower, she touched his arm and pointed at the hotel where she'd been staying. "In here."

Without even a nod, he staggered up the steps. She sprang ahead of him to open the door, receiving only a glare for her efforts. Instead of following her to the stairs, he arrowed for the desk.

"Send up a bottle of Kentucky bourbon, and make sure you don't water it down." Zachary stared at the desk clerk as if daring him to argue.

"But . . . but we have no . . ." The young man with mutton-chop whiskers gestured to the single room furnished with the desk, one chair under a gaslit lamp, and a brass spittoon badly in need of a polishing.

Zachary leaned forward. "Am I to understand you don't know how to buy a bottle?"

"N-no, sir, that's not it." The man took a step backwards. "But I . . . I cannot leave my post, sir."

Louisa thought to stick up for the clerk, even so far as to take a step forward, but she restrained herself. If her brother chose to act like an overbearing boor, so be it. She turned instead and started up the stairs. *Lord, what has gotten into him?* At the scowl on his face, even she had not wanted to cross him, let alone a poor desk clerk who was only doing his job.

The sound of a fist slamming on wood made her look back over her shoulder.

The clerk scurried out from behind the desk and headed out the door they'd entered. Louisa knew he would be back within minutes, for there was a saloon only two doors down.

Zachary crossed the room and started up the stairs, left hand on the railing pulling himself up, while his right arm clutched the crutch to his side. He hopped to each step on his good leg.

"Shame you couldn't get a room on the first floor."

Louisa ignored his comment and made her way down the hall to the room she'd stayed in for the last few nights. The single bed would not do for the two of them, certainly, but she'd ask for another quilt and make up a pallet on the floor. Every time the question arose in her mind as to how they would get home, she shoved it aside. *Let Zachary worry about that,* she commanded herself. *He's the one spending money like the bag will never run empty. God took care of the widow with the oil, but I think liquor doesn't count.* She felt like slamming the door and locking it before he could get there, but with the mood he was in, he'd pound on every door in the building.

The bottle arrived shortly after he did.

"Pay him!" His order cut through her tender skin.

Without a word, Louisa removed the leather pouch from her reticule. "How much is it?" She gasped at the price.

Zachary thumped his cane on the floor. "You suffering mess of a man. What kind of fool do you take me for? You doubled the price. Now, how much did you really pay?"

Louisa stood with her eyes closed. *How can I bear even being in the same room with him?*

"A-a dollar, ma'am. I'm sorry, but the boss says that other is what to charge."

"I understand." Louisa gave him the dollar bill. "However, this is the best I can do."

"Don't just stand there, bring it here." Again the crutch thumped.

The clerk thrust the bottle at Zachary and scuttled from the room.

Louisa shut the door behind him. *I will not open the bottle for him.* She leaned her forehead against the door, listening to him curse the cork, the clerk, and life in general.

The pop of the cork and the glugging of the liquid told her he'd succeeded without her help.

Moving to the window, she studied the street below, the pools of yellow light from the gas lamps glittering the rain. *How will we get home?* Without other distractions, the question took over. The few remaining coins wouldn't buy two good meals, let alone two train tickets or rental for a horse and buggy. *Lord, you have said you will provide, that you will take care of our needs.*

The bottle glugged again. She clenched her teeth at the sound. Sure, the booze would give Zachary momentary solace, but it wouldn't do anything for their situation. He needed a clear mind to figure what they should do next. Her stomach rumbled. Thank God for President Lincoln. Without his concern, she'd have fainted from lack of food. Taking the napkin-wrapped bread and cheese out of the reticule hanging from her wrist, she nibbled it while keeping her concentration on the street below. Anything rather than turning to face her brother. Time dragged at her like her wet skirt. The bread gone, she leaned her forehead against the cool windowpane.

"Louisa?" His words had already started to slur.

"Yes."

"How much money is left?"

At least he was still thinking.

"A couple of dollars in coins."

"They give it all to you?" He coughed, spluttered, and took another swallow.

"How should I know? You were very careful to keep from telling me anything. I was grateful to get any money back. Thanks to that pouch, I've at least had a roof over my head for the last few days."

"You could have gone to dear cousin Arlington."

"I could have. And if I were starving, I might have." She ground her teeth again, fighting the eruption pushing at her control. "I had the audacity to think it important to do all I could to keep you alive."

He lifted the half-empty bottle, drank, and lowered it to stare at her across the chasm yawning between them. "I'd be better off dead."

"Yes, you informed me of that already. Pray, come up with something new." She clamped her arms across her chest to hold in the shivering.

"You think I want to live like this?" He gestured to his leg, then raised his stump and turned his head to show his patch.

"Others do. You can be a man about it."

"What do you know?" His voice cracked. "Everything I do takes ten times as long. I can hardly dress by myself. I can no longer ride a horse—how will I manage Twin Oaks when the day comes we can return? I slave in that office on the grace of my brother-in-law, Steadly—what a misbegotten name."

"Other men would be grateful to have a place to work."

"But I'm not other men! I'm not even a man anymore. I'm a caricature! I thought I could at least be a courier, but I couldn't even do that." He stared at her out of his reddening eye. "What did you have to promise to keep me from the firin' squad?"

"That we would not make another trip like this."

"How *could* you do that?" He leaned on his crutch. "How could you take away the one thing I can contribute to the cause?" He lifted the bottle to his mouth again.

Louisa knew she should just keep her mouth shut. He wouldn't remember what he'd said in the morning anyway. "Haven't you had enough?"

He held up the bottle, shook it, and took another swig. "There's still some left." He wiped his mouth with the sleeve that covered the stump of his arm. "Worthless, that's what I am."

Louisa watched him, anger warring with pity. Might as well ask the question, or rather one of the questions that had been bothering her. "Zachary, did you pay the taxes on Twin Oaks?"

He looked up at her from under his eyebrows. "With what?"

Louisa closed her eyes. *Lord, please, don't . . .*

"Rest easy, dear sister. Steadly took care of the matter. One more thing we owe to dear Jefferson."

His words slurred even more, coming in bursts punctuated with silences. The scar gleamed against the deepening red of his face. Jaw slack, head back, drool slipping out the side of a mouth no longer flattened with rage.

"Twin Oaks, all for you . . ." Silence and a snore.

Louisa brushed at the tears she'd not realized were trickling down her cheeks. Zachary had been the best looking of the two brothers, the laughing, dashing brother who charmed the acorns off the trees and cookies from Lucinda. The brother who fetched kittens from trees and bonbons from the confectionary, who assisted his mother in teaching the slaves to read and write, who first promised Louisa she would be beautiful when she felt ugly with the chicken pox. While their mother insisted she had no favorites among her children, Zachary was the one who wrote her letters from college and made her smile.

Ah, Mother, I hope you cannot see him now. It would break your heart as it has mine. So what to do, leave him in the chair or try to get him to bed? She eyed the distance she would all but have to carry him.

She knelt beside him and took the bottle from his lap, easing it out from under fingers that clutched the bottle's neck like a life preserver.

"Zachary, dear brother, let's get you to bed."

"No, no. Leave me—no more." He cringed back as though she'd struck him. "I . . . I don't know. Can't you . . . understand? I don't know."

She could barely hear his words. She studied the back of his hand, realizing that what she thought to be dirt was instead a festering sore. She pushed his sleeve up to reveal more sores crusted with dried blood.

Had they beaten him? She pulled up the pant leg on his good leg only to find the same. "Those . . . those vermin from hell." The other words that marched through her mind were beyond even thinking. She didn't mean the four-footed kind, although they must have done their share.

She smoothed back the hair that fell over his forehead. A snore flapped his lips, and the smell of both unwashed flesh and booze-burdened breath made her gag, swallow hard, and nearly gag again.

"Zachary." She shook his shoulder, then dodged back as he flailed a hand in her direction. "All right, sleep in the chair." Surely he would rest better there than he'd done at the prison.

Dear Lord, make this night like a lanced boil. Let the pus flow out and the healing begin. She unbuttoned the top two buttons of his shirt and left him to sleep off the alcohol. Worn beyond endurance herself, Louisa crawled into bed and fell asleep halfway through "Our Father, who . . ."

When she woke, Zachary was gone.

Chapter Twenty-Eight

RETURNING FROM THE HARVEST

Jesselynn, Meshach, and the boys cut hay for ten days. By the time the last cutting was dry and loaded, they were exhausted and more than ready to head home.

Jesselynn glanced up at the thunderclouds looming over the western foothills. "The rain held off right well, wouldn't you say?"

Meshach leaned on his three-pronged pitchfork. After Jesselynn finally convinced him he could sell them at the fort, he and his students had quickly carved four of them and were working on others. Finding the perfectly pronged branches was half the battle, but Aaron and Lester were getting adept at spotting them.

"Dis load done be topped as much as I can. Rain run right off it. We should have brought de canvas."

Jesselynn studied the hay load. Both it and the two piles they'd stacked to come back for later looked like golden bread loaves with combed hair, all the strands lying curved toward the sides so the water would run off. She'd seen pictures of thatch-roofed cottages in England that looked much like these. And England was a wet country, so the thatching must work.

"Looks mighty fine to me. We could cover some miles before dark."

Meshach slid to the ground and forked back up the hay that slid off with him. He stuck his fork in behind the wagon front where they'd built a vertical frame like the wide flat one they'd built for the bed. The oxen looked dwarfed in comparison to the load.

Clouds scudded overhead as the westerly wind picked up. The oxen leaned into their yokes, and with a creak the wagon started forward. Jesselynn and Meshach walked beside. The boys were scouting good rake trees and fishing for supper. Jesselynn took out the mitten she was knitting and, other than watching for holes, continued to knit one row and purl the next. Mittens were easier to do while walking than gloves.

While the sky looked ominous, the rain held off but for a spatter or two. They covered about five miles before dark and set up camp within minutes. While Jesselynn hobbled the oxen and started the fire, Meshach tossed out a grasshopper on the hook where the river eddied and whispered in the deep dusk. Fireflies dipped and twinkled, and bats swooped for their evening meals.

Jesselynn dug out of her pocket the rose hips she'd picked as they passed a patch of pink roses. Using her knife handle and a flat rock, she pounded them into bitty pieces. She mixed them with the last of their cornmeal and water, then patted the mixture into flat cakes and laid them in the pan to bake. When the water boiled in the deep pot, she poured in the grains she'd pulled off marsh grasses. Wolf had shown her which ones tasted the best. After they cooked, she would add the greens she'd picked as they walked—dandelion, pigweed, and watercress from the river.

Her heart said Wolf had been gone forever. *Father God, please take good care of him. I know getting horses and meeting with his people are important to him, but his coming back is more important to me. I don't want to be a pest, but can you help him hurry? We have a mighty lot to do before winter.* As the wind tugged at her shirt she shivered and laid a couple more sticks on the fire.

A stick cracked, and Meshach stepped into the ring of light with enough fish for supper and breakfast hanging from a forked stick.

"Dis land got food enough for de grabbin'. Never seed such good fishin'."

Jesselynn stirred her gently boiling pot and set the cover back in place. "Wolf says the Indians use far more that the land offers than the whites do. All we have to do is learn what's good and what isn't. I think I saw a plum tree on the way down. Might be ripe enough to pick on our way home. He said something about chokecherries, but I don't know what the tree looks like." As she talked, she pulled back the frying pan and slid the cakes out onto the tin plates.

Meshach scaled the fish he'd already gutted at the river and, along with the last of their grease, laid them in the frying pan. The smell of frying fish rose with the smoke, the sound of sizzling pleasing as well.

"Seems strange, doesn't it, to be out here all this time, and to have no one else come by? Like we're the only ones on the earth." Jesselynn poked another stick into the coals so the kettle would continue to simmer. Watching the flames held the usual fascination.

"De Good Book say who be man dat God be mindful of him."

"I know. And under skies as big as these, I feel pretty small."

"But He hold us in de palm of Him hand." Meshach cupped his big hands, hands that could swing a scythe for hours or bend metal at the forge, yet also be gentle and still enough to let a gold and black butterfly, wings fanning, sit on his brown fingers. Sammy and Thaddeus had been delighted speechless when Meshach showed them the butterfly.

Now he held his cupped hands out to her. She peeked inside to see a firefly winking at her. He opened his hands, and the bitty blob of light flew off. "Dat what we do."

"But we can come back." Jesselynn turned the fish to brown on the other side.

"I know. Thank de good Lawd we can come back."

Lifting the lid of the kettle, she gave the grains a stir, then added the greens. "Supper be ready in a minute." With future rake handles on their shoulders, the boys caught up just as she was ready to serve the supper. Aaron pulled a wild onion from one pocket and tubers of cattails from the other. Together they enjoyed a feast granted them by the generous land.

The closer they drew to home, the more Jesselynn felt like that firefly that flew away. No matter how hard she tried to push them from her mind, thoughts of Aunt Agatha shoved aside concerns about Wolf. Jesselynn didn't want to call them worries, but they sure made for an unhappy state of mind.

Meshach walked along whistling. She felt like telling him to shut up. The thicket of plums hung purple, still hard, but she knew they'd ripen once picked.

But she had nothing to carry them in.

Meshach studied the plums, then pulled his shirt over his head. "We knot de sleeves . . ." His hands followed his words, and within moments they had a bag of sorts. By the time they'd filled that and the kettle, she knew what to do. Tomorrow she'd send Jane Ellen and Darcy back down on the mares. The foals were old enough to be weaned anyway. She stopped picking and turned to Meshach.

"We could come here to have a picnic. How far are we from home?"

"By horseback, two hours. By wagon, four. About in dere somewhere."

"Oh." Another idea shot down before flight.

"Leave early in de mornin' and get home late. 'Phelia love a picnic."

As they prodded the oxen to lean into the yokes again, Jesselynn remembered picnics at Twin Oaks. Lucinda would load the wicker baskets, starting with a white-and-red checkered cloth. Fried chicken, biscuits, her lemon cake, sweet pickles, corn relish, bean salad. Ah, the good things that came out of Lucinda's kitchen. There'd be a jug of lemonade or cold buttermilk, blankets to sit on, and parasols to keep the sun off. Dimity dresses with ribbon sashes, broad straw bonnets, and laughter. Darkies singing and the buggy wheels spiraling behind the high-stepping bay team.

She stumbled into a hole and fell nearly to her knees, one knitting needle stabbing into the heel of her hand. "Oh!" *So much for dreaming, you silly thing. Pay attention to life now, and don't get all weepy.* She sucked on the red spot from the needle. At least it hadn't broken the skin, and she didn't break a leg or something walking along daydreaming like that.

"You all right?"

She nodded. The oxen kept plodding along.

Oh, if only Wolf would be in camp when they got there. *Now, don't go wasting your time on stupid "if only's." That'll only get you bad feelings, and yours are too close to that already.*

If only the talking to herself would work. If only Meshach would quit whistling.

Chapter Twenty-Nine

❦

Horse Hunting on the Powder River Range
September 1863

"There they are."

Mark looked where Wolf pointed. "I don't see anything."

"Look in that thicket of aspen, the trees with the silver trunks. The stallion is off to the left, higher up. You can see his head above the rocks."

Benjamin and Daniel chuckled. "You got to look close if you want to see wild things."

"You can be sure he sees us." Wolf backed his horse under the shade of a grandfather cottonwood. "Study the trees until you see shapes that don't fit."

"If'n they're there, they ain't movin' much."

"They're there. We're downwind of them or that stallion would have them moving already."

"How many you think?" Benjamin kept his attention on the wild horses.

"Not sure. Perhaps twenty head."

"Including young?"

"No, that would be the cream. Remember, we're looking for mares, yearlings of either sex. Might be some two- or three-year-old young bucks the stallion hasn't driven out of the herd yet. Those are the ones we can break and sell this fall." Wolf studied the lay of the land.

"Benjamin, you head on up the north rim. Daniel, go to the south. See if there are any box canyons heading off this main one that we can run them into. I doubt this one here is a box. That old stallion would be too wily to be trapped that easily."

"Do the Indians catch the wild horses?"

"Not usually. They find stealing them from another tribe easier. Besides, the horse is totem for many."

"And yours is the wolf?"

"Um." Wolf concentrated on the horses. "He knows something is here."

The stallion whistled, and the horses dozing in the thicket shifted and trotted out. A buckskin mare loped off toward the mouth of the wide canyon, followed by the rest of the herd, the stallion charging off the cliff above and nipping at the rumps of any stragglers.

"Oh, I never saw anything so purty in all my life." Mark's eyes shown, the smile near to cracked his ears.

"Thirty anyway. Some nice lookin' horses in that bunch. That stallion throws good colts."

"Where'd they come from?"

"The Spanish brought them into Mexico when they came to conquer the New World. They traded some to the Indians, gave some away, and many ran away, and when they got back on their ships to leave, the horses stayed here. Changed the life of the Indian from dogs and people as pack animals to the horse. Been in the last hundred years or so.

"We'll make camp over this ridge while you two go on and scout. If we're lucky, this valley is that stallion's favorite grazin' grounds."

As the other two trotted off, Wolf took Mark to the place he'd chosen for camping, left him there to build camp, and returned to scout the valley floor. A small lake mirrored the rocky cliff above and the aspen leaves already touched by gold. This high in the mountains, winter would come soon.

Ah, Jesselynn, how you would love to see this. One day I'll bring you back here.

An eagle *screed* from high against the blue, and another answered. As a young boy he had found eagle nests in the cliffs above the valley floors. He'd known where the elk wintered and where the mountain sheep with the curly horns raised their young. His father had trapped all over these mountains in the years before he loved Laughing Girl. Then her tepee became his, and he lived with Red Cloud's tribe, the uncle of the Red Cloud who now led the Oglala band, selling his trappings to the white man and making sure they were not cheated by the fur traders.

Visiting the tribe made Wolf feel that he'd come home, the language rippling music to his ears, the laughter, the smells. But especially the laughter. He knew white men thought the Indian stoic, hard of face and heart. But none enjoyed a good joke like an Indian, often playing pranks to make the entire tribe laugh. He had yet to meet a storyteller better than his uncle, Brown Bear Who Limps. Not even Nathan Lyons, who could spin a good yarn.

Lord, make Jesselynn see these people as I do. Let her not be afraid, nor angry and hateful like some. He stopped and studied the grazing area. From the varied heights of the grass, the horses had been here some time, or left and returned.

That night around the campfire, Benjamin drew a picture in the dirt with a stick. Up the canyon about a mile, a box canyon led off to the right. "It about half mile long, narrowing, den cliffs, waterfall dat be big in spring, now not."

"How wide is the main canyon beyond the one you mean?"

"Narrower, gettin' wider further up. Like big landslide sometime fill in part way." He drew that in too.

"Could we fence it off?"

Benjamin nodded. "Take some work."

"But they can't get out of the box canyon?"

"Not dat I see. Go tomorrow and ride up it."

By the time they laid out their bedrolls, with Wolf taking the first watch, they'd detailed out their plan. Now if only the horses would cooperate.

————

Building a brush fence across the main canyon took them two days, working from before dawn until well past moonrise. They cut poles to drag across the mouth of the small canyon as soon as the horses galloped into it. When finished, the hunters headed for the lake and fell into the water.

The next morning they set out in search of the herd again. Following their trail took little skill. When they located them again a day later, Wolf reminded them of the plan.

"Remember, we want to move them slowly, but keep them on the move. No time to graze or drink until they get to the canyon." He looked to Mark. "You'll take the far side, Benjamin next, then me and Daniel closest to the other rim. Just showing yourselves will be enough to keep them moving."

They swung into position. The stallion discovered them, and the buckskin mare took the lead. When she tried to head a different direction, one of the four men appeared and sent her back toward the canyon shaking her head and snorting. By taking turns watering and grazing their own horses, they kept the herd on the move. All day, all night. In the morning they reached the canyon and took up their places. The wild horses headed for the lake, took a few swallows, and the riders showed up again, moving them on.

When she reached the brush fence, the lead mare stopped, trotted first one way, then the other. The riders held their mounts, still in view. The horse herd tried to turn around, but the stallion nipped rumps and drove them back away from the riders. The mare saw the open canyon and headed for freedom.

"Got 'em." Wolf reached down for one of the poles and dragged it into place, as did the others. Some of the poles they bound to tree trunks, others to posts they dropped into already dug holes. Within an hour, the fence was up and sturdy enough to corral the horses.

Benjamin removed his hat and wiped the sweat from his forehead. "Dat some slick herdin'."

"There's even water and grass in there for them, though that spring isn't very big." Mark climbed up on the fence to better see the herd, screened now by brush and rock faces.

"What next?" Benjamin glanced skyward. "I get fish for supper?"

"Good idea. Dried venison and canteen water puckers your mouth after a while." Wolf watched as the horses, but for the stallion, settled down to grazing. The big bay trotted to the end of the canyon, checked all the walls and returned to stand on a mound of rubble and trumpet his displeasure. The challenge ricocheted round the walls of the box canyon.

"Him know he trapped."

"But he'll fight to the death." Wolf chewed on a stem of grass. "We'll let him go as soon as we choose which horses to keep."

"Him keep de lead mare?"

"I think so. She's most likely beyond foaling anyway."

Early the next morning they started roping the horses they wanted to keep and tying them tight to tree trunks. Five young stallions were the first, five mounts for the army. The stallion seemed not to mind so much as they were led out of the gate, but when the men began taking the mares, he lunged at Wolf on his Appaloosa, giving the horse a vicious bite on the rump.

"Haiya!" Wolf swung his coiled rope and slashed the stallion across the nose, sending him running off shaking his head.

"We get 'im outa here?" Benjamin rode up to check the bite. "He near to got you!"

"I know. You got to admire him. He's fightin' for his life." Wolf knew by the thudding of his own heart how close he had come to disaster.

When the stallion screamed again, they heard an answering trumpet from Ahab, tied high up the hillside in the trees.

"All we need is a stallion fight. Ahab be dead in no time." Benjamin shook his head.

"Those Thoroughbreds have done well, as Jesselynn said they would. I didn't think they'd make it to Fort Kearney, let alone up here."

"They be strong. Mostly heart, no, all heart."

"Well, let's get the mares and fillies out of there. Do we have enough rope?"

Before nightfall they had eight mares, five with foals, and three fillies snubbed to more trees and the fence posts. With the setting of the sun, they took down the bars and freed the stallion and his greatly reduced band. He drove them out of the enclosure, the buckskin mare leading the way, her ears laid back as if she, too, would tear anyone who touched her limb from limb. The stallion stopped a hundred yards out and trumpeted his challenge, but this time Benjamin had a hand over Ahab's nostrils to keep him quiet.

After they released the captured horses back into the corral so they could eat and drink during the night, Wolf had Mark build camp right outside the bars to the enclosure.

"This way that stallion can't come and steal his horses back."

"He would do that?" Mark turned from dumping a load of dead branches for firewood on the ground.

"Oh yes. Wild stallions have been known to steal horses from tame herds and drive them off. We'll have to pay close attention on the way home for both thieving Indians and a thieving stallion."

"But you met your people."

"I know, but there are other tribes in the region, and stealing horses is a good way to prove your manhood." Wolf pulled the saddle off his own horse and tied the hobbles around his front legs.

"You don't usually hobble him."

"I know, but like I said, tonight is different. Hey, Benjamin, put the others in the corral with the wild ones. That way they'll all be safe."

———

By the time they reached the banks of Chugwater Creek, Wolf was able to ride three of the young stallions, and Benjamin could ride two of the mares. Daniel sported a black eye, and young Mark was favoring his left wrist. But all the horses had been haltered and led part of the way, so they were ready for training.

Jane Ellen, who'd been assigned watch, scrambled down from the highest hill and ran yelling into camp. So out of breath, she could hardly talk, she yelled again, "They're coming! With the horses. They're almost here!"

"How many did you see?" Jesselynn grabbed Jane Ellen by the shoulders. "How far out are they?"

"Lots of horses and maybe half a mile." Jane Ellen hugged Jesselynn. "Wait till you see 'em."

"You're sure it's our men?" At the look on Jane Ellen's face, Jesselynn shook her head. "Sorry, I apologize. I'm just so . . . so—oh my, I've got to comb my hair." She looked down at her shirt, streaked with dirt from helping dig postholes for the corral. While it wasn't finished yet, another day's work, and it would be.

"You look fine. You think Wolf would care about your shirt?"

"No, I guess not." But Jesselynn darted into the cave anyway and returned with hair combed and a clean shirt buttoned and tucked into her britches.

Thaddeus and Sammy ran back and forth below the caves, from post to post of the corral, out to the haystack and back.

"You two stay back from the horses now, you hear?" Jesselynn put an extra dose of command into her voice, which only upped the giggles.

Meshach strode after them, snatched one boy under each arm, and returned to plunk them on the ground next to Ophelia. "Now, don' you move."

Jesselynn wanted to run just like the little ones. Run to show Wolf the three stacks of hay, the fenced draw, the corral, and the stack of poles where Mrs. Mac had been stripping off bark. She glanced around. Sure enough, Aunt Agatha hadn't come to join the party.

"Don't fuss about her. She's comin' around." Nathan Lyons had read her mind again.

"I hope so. I miss her something fierce." *If someone had told me back in Springfield that I'd be feeling like this, I would have had a laughing fit. Lord, please convince Agatha that the color of a man's skin is not the judge of his heart. I don't know why I think she should change. The whole war is being fought over just that principle.* She looked around at the folks who'd become closer than family. Together they were carving a home out of this new land.

She heard Ahab whinny and could wait no longer. She tore her hat from her head and ran across the grazed land toward the creek, where they would come around the curve of the hill. She reached the shade of a grand old cottonwood just as Benjamin on Ahab led in the herd.

"We done it, Marse Jesse, we done brung home de horses." He leaped to the ground and gave her a leg up. "Marse Wolf, he be back dere." Benjamin flipped a loop over the nose of the horse he'd been leading, swung aboard, and used the lead rope as a rein. "You go on and find 'im. He be right glad to see you."

Jesselynn allowed the stream of horses to pass, saluting both Daniel and Mark as they waved, her attention on the man bringing up the rear. As always, he and his horse moved as one while keeping the new stock moving ahead. She could feel his eyes on her. Shivers ran up her arms and down her back. Her belly warmed. She leaned forward to pat Ahab's neck. He shifted, sensing her tension.

"Hello, wife." Wolf's voice sent shivers chasing the others.

Thank you, God, for bringing him home safe. She searched him for the war wounds she'd seen on the others. None. "Hello, husband. Looks like you've been busy." *So how did Red Cloud treat you? Was the country as wonderful as you remember?* She noticed that his medicine pouch now hung outside his shirt. Was there a reason for that?

Chapter Thirty

☙❧

RICHMOND, VIRGINIA

Louisa found him. That's all that mattered.

"Lemme go." The man on the buggy seat beside her thrashed at his invisible demons. Obviously he'd tried to drown them in whiskey and failed.

So, Lord, what do I do now? How do I pay for this conveyance even? Zachary must have been on his way back to the hotel. That's all she could figure.

The driver stopped at the hotel she'd indicated and peered over his shoulder.

"Could you help me, please?" She gritted her teeth. How was she to haul this sorry heap of humanity up to their room?

"Yes ma'am." The man climbed down and came around to Zachary's side. "Here, sir, let me help you."

"Are we there?"

"Yes." She blinked. How had he sobered up so quickly?

Zachary dug in his watch pocket and handed the driver a dollar. "Keep the change."

"Yes, sir." With the driver assisting, Zachary gained his balance. Louisa followed as the two men made their way up the steps, through the lobby, and up to the room. With Zachary in the chair again, the driver tipped his hat and closed the door on his way out.

"A driver will be here for us in the morning. Make sure you are ready," Louisa said to her brother.

He closed his eyes and refused to answer the questions that boiled within her.

The Quakers had come to their assistance again.

If Zachary remembered any of his dark nights of raving, he never alluded to them. And other than curt orders, he didn't speak to Louisa again. Though taciturn, he was at least polite to those who assisted them.

Louisa swung from anger to fury to hurt, clear to her deep insides. Over and over she pleaded with the Lord to repair the rent in their family, but Zachary refused to even look at her, as if she were a pariah or had leprosy.

Throughout the trip home, while often she felt like hitting him with his crutch, she kept a gentle smile on her face and prayed for love and patience. Never was she happier to see Aunt Sylvania's house and to crawl into her own clean bed.

When Louisa woke after sleeping round the clock, she washed and washed again, dressed in clean clothes, and wandered out to the back veranda to visit with those gathered there.

After returning the greetings, she asked her aunt, "Where's Zachary?"

"Gone to work. He will be staying with Carrie Mae and her family now that they have moved into their new house. That way the poor boy won't have to travel so far."

Poor boy, my liver. Good thing Aunt Sylvania wasn't a mind reader.

But at the sweet smile on her aunt's face, Louisa knew Zachary had said nothing about their ordeal.

"I was getting so worried when you didn't return as soon as you said you would."

The statement obviously needed a reply. What should she say? Louisa cleared her throat and leaned close to her aunt's chair. "We ran into some difficulties, but as you can see, we are all right now." *Or at least I am. Lord, only you know what's on my brother's heart.*

"I feared that. We all prayed for you, even our soldiers here. You haven't met Charles, Corporal Saunderson yet." She took Louisa by the arm. "Come meet him. He's such a sweet boy."

Louisa stopped at the chair where a man, all bones and angles, sat staring straight ahead. A lock of dark hair fell over his forehead. Tall and thin as he was, he reminded her of Lieutenant Lessling. Louisa couldn't help thinking that a sweet boy he was not, as a deep, resonant voice answered her aunt's question.

"I am doing well, ma'am. You are not to worry."

"I'd like you to meet my niece, just back from . . ." Aunt Sylvania glanced at Louisa, who stepped forward and touched the man on the shoulder.

"I'm glad to welcome you to our home. I was . . . I mean, the trip took longer than I expected, or I would have been here to greet you." She glanced over his body, looking for injuries but found none except that it appeared he couldn't see. He held out a hand in her direction, but his eyes never tracked her nor showed emotion. He held his head still, as though he thought it might fall off if he moved too fast.

"The surgeon general thought perhaps, since you have helped others who lost their sight, you could help me." The tone of his voice told her what the words cost him, for his face registered nothing. Blank like a freshly washed blackboard was all she could think of.

"I'll be glad to help you. Where is your home?" She settled herself on a chair that Reuben set behind her.

"It was in Fredericksburg but no longer stands. So far I have not been able to locate any of my family." He lifted a hand to his face. "This, this has made everything impossible." He dropped his voice as he did his hand.

"I could write letters for you."

"I would be most grateful."

Louisa gave the corporal as much attention as she could in the next few days, teaching him how to feed himself, shave, and find his way around the house. They moved him into Zachary's room, along with one of the men who'd been at the house for some time. He had no legs and was fashioning himself a low cart that he could ride in and propel with his hands.

"Better'n draggin' meself along the floor. Can't abide feelin' sorry fer meself. Bad 'un that."

Louisa smiled at her legless friend. "Thanks, Homer, you always brighten my day." As she left the two together in the room, Louisa paused in the hall at the sound of Corporal Saunderson's voice.

"Describe Miss Louisa for me, please."

She could feel the heat flame her face as she headed for the kitchen. Now, what had brought that on?

That evening she was putting away the sewing supplies when Reuben brought an envelope on the once-silver tray.

"This comed to de door. For you." The grizzled black man wore an air of curiosity as he glanced back over his shoulder to the front of the house.

"Who brought it?" Louisa took the letter and studied the handwriting. Only her name. She looked up to see Reuben shaking his head.

"Don' know who brought it. Knock on de door, I goes to answer, no one dere, but dis on de mat."

Louisa slit the flap open with her fingernail and withdrew a single sheet of paper. She leaned closer to the lamp.

Dear Miss Highwood. She glanced to the bottom of the sheet and caught her breath. It was signed by Major James Dorsey.

"Who's it from?" Aunt Sylvania glanced up from her knitting.

"A-a man who assisted me on . . . on this last trip."

Sylvania cocked her head to the side. "You know, both you and Zachary have been most evasive about details of this last trip."

"Someday I'll tell you." Louisa drew in a breath to slow her thudding heart and read the remainder of the letter.

> *I hope and pray this not only finds you, but finds you well and recovered from your experience. I have been transferred back to my company in the field and am grateful, as I'm sure you were, to leave Washington behind. Please know that I do not bear you and your brother the rancor that the general does. We were all just doing our duty. Please remember me to your sister when you write to her.*
>
> *I am proud to know two such fine Southern ladies. May our loving Lord bring you safely through this abominable war and home again to your beautiful plantation.*
>
> *Sincerely,*
> *Major James Dorsey*

Louisa folded the letter and tucked it back into the envelope, shaking her head all the while. What a surprise! Nay, what a shock.

Several nights later, after she'd visited Carrie Mae, she wrote to Jesselynn, telling her not only of their escape and all that happened but also of the major, reminding her sister where and when she had met the man.

> *It seems a shame to me that we should meet under such reprehensible circumstances. If only it had been another time and another place, not on opposite sides of this abominable war. I am eternally grateful God brought us safely back to Richmond, but I have not seen Zachary since I returned.*

She told Jesselynn about the new men in the house and then continued with news of the family.

> *Carrie Mae and the baby are settled into their new home, or as settled as anyone can be at this point. Her house is lovely, and our baby is a bright spot, like a nodding daisy in a field of thistle. The war colors everything. Sister, dear, I hate this war with such a passion. And fear strikes clear to the bottom of my heart for our brother, who is bitter and angry beyond description. I do not know what to do but pray for him. I know that God can bring our brother back to himself, but will Zachary allow that to happen?*
>
> *Forgive my rantings here and give Thaddeus hugs and kisses for me. He is growing up without knowing his sister Louisa, who loves him dearly. One day we will meet again at Twin Oaks, God willing.*

She signed her letter, then added a postscript. *Aunt Sylvania is back to being her old self but for a slight limp, and her eye droops when she gets tired, which also happens more easily.*

She didn't tell her sister about the rush of joy she'd felt when she saw the major's signature.

If only James Dorsey were not in the Union army.

Chapter Thirty-One

ON THE CHUGWATER RIVER

"Fall is on the way."

Jesselynn stopped beside her husband at the mouth of the cave and leaned against him. He put his arm around her shoulders so she could fit right next to his heart. "How do you know?" she asked.

"Smell the air, and the geese are flying south."

Jesselynn inhaled, sorting the smells as she became aware. Horse manure, dust, skunk, the grasses down by the water. She inhaled again. Her husband's special scent, woodsmoke, meat drying over a low fire. Nothing else.

"So what does fall smell like?"

"That bite in the air, turning leaves—there's a difference between growing and turning—you can smell the pine. . . ." He glanced down at her. "Maybe after a few more years here, you'll know what I mean."

Jesselynn sniffed again. "Guess I haven't been paying enough attention to the smells."

"Do you know that to the Indian, the white man has a peculiar odor? Can smell one coming if the wind is right."

"And if your Indian family uses bear grease, I know what they'd smell like." At the flash of something, she wasn't sure what, across his face, she wished she'd not brought that up. However, moccasins soaked in bear grease really did repel water, as did boots soaked in bear grease.

"So you want another lesson in training horses today?" Wolf looked down at her. "You have a talent along that line."

"Lesson?" She cocked an eyebrow. "I gentle 'em. You and Benjamin train 'em."

"Works well. Another couple of weeks and we can take them to the fort. That'll give us seven horses to sell. What about selling some of the oxen too? They could use them for beef, if nothing else."

"I've been thinking. What if we give one or two of ours to Red Cloud's people?"

Wolf nodded and smiled down at her. "Guess we better ask everyone else what they want to do. Can't see how we can winter over this many oxen though. They can't dig down to the grass like buffalo and elk, or eat the willow tips."

"And yet we'll need them for breaking ground in the spring. Some of this bottom land ought to grow oats real well." She slipped her arm around Wolf's waist. They so seldom had time alone together without sixteen interruptions. She treasured moments like these, perhaps more so because they were rare.

"This is why the Indian bands keep on the move. Graze off one patch and move to the next. Summer near the rivers and winter where the trees protect the tepees and the snow is not so deep the horses can't dig through to graze. Easier, I think."

"Some of the tribes are raising gardens down along the river, I heard someone talking about that at the fort. Then the other tribes come trade for pumpkins and squash and such."

Wolf sighed. "I know. Times sure are changing."

"Will being a farmer be hard for you?" She bit her lower lip, waiting for his answer.

"Not as long as we raise horses. If training horses is my work, I'll play all my life."

Jesselynn smiled up at him. "We have to feed them too."

"Ah, wife, ever practical." He tipped her chin to share a kiss when they heard from the cave behind them, "Jesse, I got to pee."

"Today we'll put those young pups to diggin' an outhouse." Wolf sighed. "Civilization has indeed come to the high country."

"So we'll have the first latrine. Will that make us famous?" Jesselynn reached up and kissed him quick. "I'm coming, Thaddeus."

As soon as they'd eaten, Jesselynn brought another mare into the corral and began her training. She followed the mare around the circle for a time to keep her moving. When the mare lowered her head and turned to face her, Jesselynn stopped and waited. When she took a couple steps backward, the mare came toward her. They continued the dance until the mare came right up to her, head lowered, acknowledging Jesselynn as leader of the herd. Jesselynn stroked her ears and rubbed down the dark neck. If only she'd learned this easy way of working a horse years ago, although the Thoroughbreds at Twin Oaks were handled from the day they were foaled and never had to be broken.

She slipped the loop around the mare's neck and walked her around the circle, then turned the other way and walked figure eights. Always the mare followed. The only time she hesitated was when she heard her colt cry. They'd weaned the babies as soon as they arrived in camp, much to the consternation of both mares and offspring. Some were being more stubborn than others.

Stroking the mare, rubbing her with a cloth, then putting the saddle blanket in place—nothing bothered the mare, as long as Jesselynn stopped and backed up a step as soon as the horse began to tighten up.

Wolf leaned against the top bar of the corral. "You sure do have the touch."

"Thank you. You can probably ride her tomorrow." She crossed the corral, the mare following. "How are the geldings doing?" They'd gelded the five young stallions two days earlier.

"You'd hardly know they'd been cut. Meshach is a man of many talents."

"He says all you need is a sharp knife and someone to hold the horse down."

"Benjamin sitting on their heads did that trick. No bleeders, no infection." Wolf stepped back from the rail. "Ahab took care of the mare that came in heat. She's good and sturdy, should make a good colt." Since they had no idea how many of the wild mares were already bred, they were watching them carefully. They couldn't afford to winter over a mare that hadn't taken.

"Think I'll go up and see how Nate and Daniel are doing with the loggin'. You want to ride along?"

"Oh yes." Jesselynn stopped. "No, I can't. I promised Jane Ellen that we'd go looking for hazelnuts, herbs, and such as soon as I finished with the mare. She works so hard, she deserves a treat like that."

"You're riding?"

"Dulcie and Sunshine."

"Agatha rode up with Nate and Daniel. Nate said she can snake a tree out good as any man. Those oxen do just what she tells them."

Jesselynn smiled up at him. "Is that what he says? I think he just wants to spend time with her away from all the prying eyes."

"Up loggin'?"

"Heard tell she fixed a special basket for dinner. Even some molasses to spread on the corn bread."

"Well, I knew he was sweet on her, but looks like it goes both ways."

I just hope her happiness spills out on the rest of us. Jesselynn knew she particularly meant on her and Wolf, but others in the party had borne the brunt of Agatha's displeasure too.

She'd just turned back to the mare when two rifle shots echoed down from the tree line. Two shots were a signal for help.

Wolf whistled. His Appaloosa broke free from the herd and galloped toward him. He swung aboard and galloped on around the bend up toward the hill.

"Get my medicine kit!" Jesselynn called into the cave. "Something's wrong up on the hill." Benjamin had Domino saddled and ready for her, along with Dulcie for himself, by the time she had grabbed her small kit with extra bandages and had run back out to the corral.

"Dear God, take care of them, whoever's hurt." She muttered the prayer over and over, both inside and out, as she galloped up the hill.

"This way!" Nate hollered down the hill, waving his arm at the same time.

Jesselynn urged her horse straight up the incline rather than following the zigzags used to skid the logs down. Domino was heaving by the time they got to the site, but Jesselynn ignored that, dismounting and running for the body she saw lying on the ground. Aunt Agatha. Something had happened to Aunt Agatha.

"The chain slipped and caught her hand." Wolf kept his voice low. "She's lost some fingers and fainted, I think from the pain."

Jesselynn dropped to her knees beside the pasty-faced woman. Blood everywhere told a story all its own.

"I done de best I can." Daniel had clamped his fingers over the blood vessel in her wrist so that the bleeding had stopped. He looked up at her with tears in his eyes. "I shouldn't a let her do de chain."

"Hush, Daniel, no one lets Aunt Agatha do anything. She does what she thinks best."

"But she saved my life in dat town."

"Thanks to your quick thinking, she's not goin' to die. So you returned the favor." As Jesselynn spoke, she inspected the mangled hand. Two fingers gone, another might have to go by the looks of the shredded flesh, a deep gash at the base of the thumb. She looked up to Nate, who now cradled the woman's head in his lap. "How long she been out?"

"Since before Wolf got here." He sniffed, his thumb stroking Agatha's cheek.

Jesselynn bound the hand, tying a tight knot over the wrist. "You can let go now." She glanced up at Daniel, who sat with closed eyes and mouth moving without sound. She knew he was praying. "Daniel."

The young man slowly opened his eyes. "You sure, Marse?"

"I'm sure." She watched her aunt's hand as he released his thumb. No gusher. She sighed, relief evident in every line of her body. "Aunt Agatha." She patted the woman's cheek. "Aunt Agatha, can you hear me?"

A slight nod of the head. Nate leaned over and laid his cheek against her forehead.

"You'll be all right, my dear Agatha. You'll be all right."

Agatha murmured something and turned her face into the cupping hand, her eyes slowly opening. "Hurts some bad."

Jesselynn uncorked the small flask of whiskey she kept for emergencies. "Here, drink some of this. It will help."

"I don't drink spirits."

"Today you do." A note of command in Nate's voice caused Jesselynn to look up to Wolf, who smiled back at her.

A slight nod and Agatha swallowed several times. Her eyes flew open and her good hand went to her throat. "Oh! You are tryin' to kill me!" She coughed and gagged. "Water." Wolf held the canteen to her mouth for several more swallows.

"We can dilute that with this."

Agatha shuddered. "No, thank you. I'm done with fainting now." She tried to sit up, but before she could do more than make a motion, Nate had her propped against his knees and leaning back against his chest. Agatha looked at the bound hand and closed her eyes for only a moment. "How bad is it?"

"We'll know more after we get you to camp and clean it up."

"Then we better go."

"Do you think you can ride?"

"If I must."

"If you will ride in front of me, I can hold you secure." Wolf looked her directly in the eyes when he offered. "Otherwise we will go for a wagon."

Agatha looked up to Nate, and at his nod, she did the same. "Th-thank you. I will ride."

Jesselynn knew her aunt well enough to know what this was costing her. "Daniel, switch my saddle to the Appaloosa." She turned back to her aunt. "I'm going to bind that hand up to your shoulder, so you can't bump it. All right?"

Agatha nodded, her face still white from the pain, her lower lip quivering the slightest bit.

Jesselynn wanted to wrap her arms around her aunt and hold her close, but now was not the time for that.

"I'll go ahead and get things ready."

Agatha reached for Jesselynn's hand with her free one. "Be careful."

Fighting the tears that threatened to flood her, Jesselynn raised her aunt's hand and kissed the fingers. "I will."

By the time Wolf made his way down the hill and into camp, Agatha was near to fainting again. Her eyes fluttered open when they stopped, and she slumped into Meshach's waiting arms.

"God be takin' good care of you," he whispered as he carried her to a pallet laid by the outside fire pit. "Me 'n 'Phelia been prayin'."

Jesselynn had water boiling with her needle, thread, and scissors in it. Jane Ellen stood with the bottle of laudanum in one hand and the whiskey in the other, fighting the tears that seeped in spite of her efforts.

"We takes good care of you." Her smile wavered, but her words held firm.

"I know." Agatha lay down with a sigh. "Such a bother I am. But I wasn't bein' careless." A trace of her normal asperity flavored her words.

"I want you to drink some more of that whiskey. We can dilute it with water if you like." Jesselynn shook her head. "Wish I had some honey for it to make it more palatable, but—"

"I can drink it if I must." Agatha glared at the silver flask. "Let's get this over with." She held it in her own hand, swigged as much as she could before her eyes watered so bad she had to sniff, and her throat closed. She choked and coughed. "More?"

Jesselynn nodded. "Just think, Daddy and Uncle Hiram thought this the best sipping whiskey anywhere."

"Well, Joshua and Hiram weren't always known to have the best of sense." Agatha took another swallow and sucked in a lungful of air. "Huh." She blinked and closed her eyes. "I burn so bad inside, I won't feel you work on my hand."

Jane Ellen chuckled and rocked back on her heels. "You one fine, strong woman, Agatha Highwood."

"I'm ready." Agatha lay back and closed her eyes. "Don't worry about gentle. Just get it done."

Jesselynn handed her a bit of clean rag. "Bite down on this if you have to. It can help."

With Nathan Lyons holding Aunt Agatha's other hand and Wolf and Meshach ready to hold her down if necessary, Jesselynn unwrapped the mangled hand. Carefully she cleaned all the dirt and debris away and washed it with whiskey. She then sewed flaps of skin over the severed fingers and stitched up the slash on the thumb. While the third finger looked bad, once it was cleaned, she was able to set the broken bone, grateful to not see bone splinters. It didn't look like the tendons had been severed either. When finished, Jesselynn poured more whiskey over the entire hand, took the thin wrapped board that Meshach handed her, and bound the hand to the splint.

"Please, God, make this heal with no infection, so Agatha can have full use of her hand again. Thank you, this wasn't worse."

"Amen," Agatha murmured from between clenched teeth. "Now, if I can have some of that laudanum, I will gladly and gratefully go to sleep. Thank you, all."

Jesselynn stumbled when she stood, for her feet had gone to sleep. Wolf caught her and held her against his chest.

"You did a fine job. No doctor could have done better, and most of them not as well."

Jesselynn leaned against him. "That was a close one."

"Yes, but as Agatha said, 'tweren't her fault. She was bein' careful."

She could hear his chuckle down in his chest. What a miracle that this man could still care for Aunt Agatha in spite of the way she'd treated him and his wife. She looked up into his eyes. "You know, Mr. Torstead, you are one fine Christian man, and I am right proud to know you."

"Thank you, Mrs. Torstead," he whispered in her ear. "And I'm glad to *know* you, and the more often the better."

She could feel the heat start low and race to engulf her face. "I better see to my patient." She poked him in the chest. "And you, sir, mind your thoughts." Her whisper was for him alone. His chuckle made her warm all over.

———

Several days later Jesselynn walked into the cave and stopped, placing her hands on her hips. "Aunt Agatha, what happened to your sling?"

Agatha straightened from laying strips of venison across the drying racks. "It was in my way." She poked her board-bound hand back into the sling of white muslin tied behind her neck. "There. Now are you happy?"

"Yes, although I'd be happier if you were to take it easy for a few more days."

"I *am* takin' it easy. If I went any slower, I'd be sittin' down, and since I can't knit or sew, I won't sit."

"As you wish. But the more you bump it, the longer it might take to heal." Jesselynn left the cave before her aunt could have the last word. At least she was talking to them, oh happy day. And there was no sign of infection. *Ah, Lord, you are so good to us.*

————

Sunday, after Meshach read the Scriptures and they'd sung several songs, Nathan spoke. "I would like to say somethin', if'n you don't mind."

Agatha, sitting beside him, tugged on his shirt sleeve. "I'd like to speak first."

Nate patted her hand. "If you want."

Agatha stood up. "I have a confession to make, since the Bible says that we must confess our sins to one another so that we might be healed." She held her wounded hand to her breast with the other. "All of you know how hateful I have been to Jesselynn"—she nodded toward Jesselynn—"and to Wolf." Another nod. "In my own defense, I have to say that I only believed what I was born and raised in. But Meshach, with his wisdom of the Word, and Na—ah, Mr. Lyons, with his persuasive tongue, have forced me to look at other parts of Scripture. Jesus said to forgive as we are forgiven and to love like He loves, with no mention of skin color or anything else, just to love our neighbor as ourselves." She paused and looked skyward, a ploy that helped fight unwanted tears. Taking a deep breath, she continued. "I want to love God with all my heart, strength, and mind and my neighbor as myself. Therefore, Jesselynn and Wolf and each of you that I have wronged with my self-righteous ways, please . . . forgive me?"

Jesselynn stood and crossed to her aunt. "I forgive you if you will forgive me for being so angry at your bullheadedness." The two hugged and sniffed together. Jesselynn took a square of calico from her pocket and wiped her aunt's eyes. "I'm so glad to have you back. I've missed you terribly."

"And I you." Agatha turned to Wolf, who stood right behind Jesselynn. "And you, nephew, will you forgive an old lady blinded by color?"

"Most certainly. And I am honored to hear you call me nephew."

Sitting back down, Jesselynn felt as if she were so light she could hover above the block of wood on which she sat. It seemed that if Wolf didn't hold on to her, she might float away and go dancing with the breeze.

Mr. Lyons stood beside Agatha. "And now I get to speak." He took Agatha's left hand in his. "I have asked Miss Agatha to be my wife, and she has said yes. We thought perhaps we could be married at the fort when we go for supplies."

Jesselynn flashed an I-told-you-so kind of grin at her husband and rose to be the first to wish the couple well. Everyone crowded around, shaking hands, hugging, and laughing at one another's teasing.

"Where's Ophelia?"

Jesselynn looked around. When had Ophelia left their gathering?

Chapter Thirty-Two

RICHMOND, VIRGINIA

"Has Zachary said anything to you about our trip north?"

Carrie Mae shook her head. "Not to me. I just know he is real unhappy."

Unhappy doesn't begin to describe our brother. But Louisa just nodded. No sense making Carrie Mae worry. It was unlikely they could do anything about Zachary, anyway, other than pray for him, of course. Why did that lately feel like such an exercise in futility?

Louisa cocked her head. "Think I hear the baby crying." She rose before Carrie Mae could move. "I'll get her."

Louisa admired the silk damask wall coverings and the walnut wainscoting as she made her way down the hall to the nursery. After the one cry Miriam had chosen to play with her fingers instead of setting up her "I'm hungry" howl.

"You sweet thing." Louisa lifted the baby from her crib and kissed the side of her smile. "Miriam, what will we do with you? You get prettier every day." Laying her down on the padded dresser, she changed the baby's diapers, dusting the little bottom with cornstarch and blowing on her rounded belly.

Miriam cooed and waved her fists, legs pumping like she was ready to run.

I wonder what my baby would look like if I— She stopped the thought in shock. *Why, Louisa Highwood, you were going to add the major's name. Whatever has come over you?* She could feel the heat rising up her neck.

"You won't tell anyone, will you, sugar?" She patted the baby's hands together and tickled her toes. "Ah, baby dear, I hope and pray you never have to go though a war like we've been having. Lord, please, please bring peace. I want a baby like this, a husband, a home. I want to go home to Twin Oaks."

"So do I." Carrie Mae stood in the doorway. "Not fair sharin' secrets with her. She can't pass them on."

How long has she been standing there? A moment of concern about what Carrie Mae might have heard flickered through Louisa's mind, but she brushed it away. Cuddling Miriam to her cheek, she turned to her sister. "Who better to share with?"

"Me." Carrie Mae leaned against the doorjamb. "I feel like I live all alone in this big old house."

"You have a brand-new house, servants, and a husband, and—"

"A husband who is never home, a brother likewise, and a baby who, sweet as she is, doesn't carry on much of a conversation yet."

Louisa studied her younger sister. Frown lines aged her forehead. While she'd regained her figure, her bounce had yet to return.

"You know what, Carrie Mae?" *Oh, Lord, here I go again. Give me the right words, please.*

"No, but I have a feeling I'm about to learn." She crossed the room and pulled at the cord in the corner. "I'll order tea so we have the sustenance to continue."

"I'm not joking."

"Neither am I. You take the baby. She's going to want to eat any minute now." Carrie Mae gave the maid who appeared at the door her instructions and motioned her sister down the hall. "You know, sometimes you sound so much like Jesselynn that I have to stop and remind myself you aren't."

"I think I'll take that as a compliment."

"And then I remember that she is clear off in the wilderness somewhere, and I prob'ly won't see her again in this lifetime, and I get sorry for all the mean things I said to her."

"She was just trying her best, like all the rest of us." *If only our best were good enough.*

When they were settled back in the parlor, with tea poured and Miriam making her little pig noises at her mother's breast, Louisa stirred sugar into her tea with a silver spoon, wondering where such things came from anymore. She laid the spoon on the china saucer and, propping her elbows on her knees in a decidedly unladylike manner, sipped from her cup and studied her sister.

Might as well say what she was thinking.

"Carrie Mae, I reckon your trouble is this. You have entirely too much time on your hands."

"Why, Louisa Marie Highwood, however can you say that? You have no idea how much time this baby takes. I'm just an old milk cow far as she's concerned, and running a house like this—you know how hard Mama worked at Twin Oaks."

Louisa sighed. "I know Mama worked hard. She ran an entire plantation along with the big house and made sure close to fifty people had food in their bellies and clothes on their backs."

"Well, I have to entertain too, you know. Jefferson is always bringing home friends for supper, sometimes without even having the grace to let me know beforehand."

"And how often have you cooked supper for these guests or cleaned up afterward?"

"My word, why would I do that? We have servants—and let me remind you they are not slaves—to do those things. Jefferson says we are doing our part giving these people a place to work, and"—her voice rose—"I think you are just horrid to talk to me like this."

"You could knit, sew uniforms, and roll bandages like the rest of us." Louisa cringed inside at the tone of her own voice. *Whatever happened to "A soft answer turneth away wrath"?*

"Is that all? Why, you silly, I sent an entire box of rolled bandages over to the hospital just yesterday."

And who did the rolling? But Louisa had a notion that those who worked in the Steadly home did the rolling in order to make their mistress look good and thus keep their positions. She'd not taken time to count the number of personal maids Carrie Mae had employed in the time since she and Jefferson had been married.

Louisa sighed. "I'm sorry, dear sister. You just look unhappy, and I hoped to help that sad look go away."

Carrie Mae put the baby to her shoulder and patted her back. A big burp made both women smile.

"There now, sweet thing. That's what we think of your mean old auntie's ideas. We work real hard for the cause, don't we?" In spite of the sugar-sweet words, the glare Carrie Mae sent around her daughter's head could have ignited coal.

"I'm sorry, Carrie Mae, I don't know what's gotten into me lately." But Louisa knew that was an untruth. She did know what had gotten into her. She was sick of the war, sick of Zachary acting like he was, sick of being so far from home. When would it ever end?

"You needn't look so sad yourself." Carrie Mae handed Louisa the baby. "Look at that smile and tell me anything in this whole wide world is more precious than that."

Louisa cupped the baby with her hands and lower arms, elbows propped on her knees. Miriam smiled, her full, rounded mouth open, her eyes intent on her auntie's. Rosy lips thinned as she struggled to make a sound, not a scream, but an answer to Louisa's gentle baby murmurings.

"That's right now. You can talk with me, of course you can." She nodded slowly, smiling and cooing back.

"You two certainly can carry on some kind of conversation. Why, I'd think you knew exactly what she was sayin'."

"She's saying 'I love you, Auntie Louisa.' Can there be any doubt of that?"

Carrie Mae sat down on the horsehair sofa beside her sister and, leaning her chin on Louisa's shoulder, watched her baby's efforts. "Isn't she the smartest, most beautiful baby you ever did see? Why, Mama would bust her buttons over this baby, and can you think what Lucinda would say?"

"I reckon Daddy would have been carrying her out to the barn already to make sure she loves the horses from the beginning."

"Carrying, my right foot! He'd have had her up in the saddle with him." Carrie Mae traced the outline of her daughter's cheek with a gentle fingertip. "Sometimes I want to go home and see Mama and Daddy again so bad that I near to run out that door and call for the carriage."

"I know." Louisa sniffed back the tears. No matter that their parents had gone ahead to heaven, when she thought of home, they were still there. The big house and all the barns, the slaves' quarters, the trees, the rose garden, all were still there.

"Miss Carrie Mae, message from Mr. Jefferson." The maid paused in the doorway, waiting to be acknowledged.

"Thank you." Carrie Mae took the envelope, and with a slight shrug to her sister, slit it open.

"Oh, bother." She heaved a sigh. "Is he waitin' for an answer?"

"Yes, ma'am."

"Tell him I'll be ready." Carrie Mae turned to Louisa. "Jefferson says I have to accompany him to a soirée tonight. President Davis and General Lee will be the guests of honor." She tapped the envelope on the edge of her finger. "How would you like to come with us?"

Louisa shook her head. "No, I wasn't invited. And besides, I have nothing to wear to something like that. I'll just go on home and—"

"And you'll do nothing of the kind." Carrie Mae studied her sister. "You've lost so much weight we might have to take in one of my dresses. I'll have Lettie do your hair. She is the best with a hot iron and pins. Come on, we haven't played dress-up in years."

Louisa looked down at the baby now blinking her eyes to stay awake.

"I'd much rather stay here and take care of Miriam. She and I can have a fine time."

"No, we'll put her down to sleep, and you and I are going to get ready."

"But Aunt Sylvania is expecting me." Louisa now had a pretty good idea what a drowning victim felt like. Getting enough air in the face of Carrie Mae's whirlwind tactics took extra doing.

"I'll send her a note." Carrie Mae picked up the baby. "Besides, maybe you'll meet the man of your dreams there."

I think maybe I've already met the man of my dreams, but no one will ever know that.

Chapter Thirty-Three

"Is that really me?" Louisa stared at the figure in the full-length mirror.

"It most surely is. I knew there was a beauty hiding under that mouse look of yours. I know you do good works, but you don't always have to look so . . . so . . ." Carrie Mae made a face.

"Should I take that as a compliment?" Louisa touched one of the springy curls that lay over her shoulder. Lettie had gathered the curls up in back with diamanté clips and waved the hair on top of her head. The clips caught the light every time Louisa moved her head. She touched the strands of gold and sapphires around her slender neck and smoothed down the sides of the blue silk overskirt that flared from her narrow waist and was gathered into scallops by small nosegays of single roses. The pleated underskirt of cream lace was threaded by matching narrow ribbon.

"Here." Carrie Mae handed her a silk fan. She stepped back and studied her sister. "You look lovely."

"So do you." Louisa turned from her image. "Wouldn't Daddy be proud of his girls?"

"The cab is here, ma'am."

"Do you need a shawl?" Carrie Mae held out a diaphanous drape.

"Maybe I should." Louisa looked again at the amount of flesh showing above the low cut of the bodice.

Carrie Mae draped the shawl around her sister's shoulders, stood for Lettie to do the same for her, and the two of them sailed out the door.

Louisa swallowed the butterflies that threatened to take wing. What on earth was she doing all dressed up like this when she should be home taking care of her boys? What if something happened to Aunt Sylvania? What if—

"Now you just quit your worryin' and have a good time. You deserve a good time for a change. You've been workin' like a servant ever since we left home. And before then."

But Louisa knew better—it was Jesselynn who had worked so hard to keep Twin Oaks going. While she and Carrie Mae could be excused because they were young, she knew they could have been more help. Should have been more help.

The driver halted the cab under the portico of the Ambergine Mansion, and a doorman stepped forward to assist the two women. Louisa shook out her skirt, reminded herself to quit chewing on her lower lip and, head held high, followed her sister through the doors. *Oh, Lord, here we go. Are you sure this is where I belong?*

Light danced among the crystals on the chandeliers as they waited in the receiving line. Within moments Jefferson Steadly joined them, kissing his wife on the cheek and smiling at Louisa.

"What a pleasure to have two such beautiful women to introduce around this evening. I'm glad you could join us, sister Louisa." He bowed over her hand and led the two sisters forward.

"Is that who I think it is?" Louisa tried to hang back.

"Of course." Jefferson stepped forward again. "President Davis, may I introduce you to my sister-in-law, Miss Louisa Highwood?"

"Why, most certainly. I am delighted." Jefferson Davis, president of the Confederate States of America, took Louisa's hand and bowed, his neatly trimmed beard brushing the back of her hand.

"I-I'm honored, Mr. President." Louisa tried swallowing, but her words still sounded breathless.

"No, I am the one honored. I have heard tales of a lovely young woman who, with her brother, dons various disguises and ventures north to bring back medical supplies for our suffering men. Someone even told me of a nefarious raccoon. . . ."

Louisa couldn't contain the smile. "The poor creature who gave its life to assist us was a possum, sir."

"Ah." He nodded, eyes twinkling. "So it is you." He turned. "And that is your brother over there?"

"Yes, sir."

"Besides these mercy trips, Zachary has proven a great help since he came to work for me."

As if sensing he was being spoken of, Zachary turned. At the sight of his sisters, he straightened, then ordered his face into a semblance of a smile and nodded.

"Thank you, sir. I am truly grateful that we could help our wounded." *But please make this war stop.* But she kept the smile on her face as they were handed to the next man in line.

"I heartily concur with our president's comments." General Robert E. Lee, hair now fully white, bowed over her hand.

Louisa glanced at Carrie Mae, seeking support. "Th-thank you, General. I-I never . . ." She swallowed and sucked in a breath of air, air now grown sultry with perfume and cigar smoke.

The general leaned closer, speaking more softly for her ears alone. "In spite of what a certain young man believes, I am grateful for your efforts to keep him alive. We need his talents to help bring our country through this war and out on the other side."

I cannot believe these men know about what we did. "Thank you, sir."

With a hand at her back, Jefferson eased the sisters through those trying to talk with the two famous men and on toward the table set up with food that far surpassed anything Louisa had dreamed of in the past years. Hams and roasts of beef, salads, bite-sized vegetables, hors d'oeuvres of delectable colors and shapes. Young men in white jackets walked about the room with trays of fluted glasses that Louisa knew contained spirits.

She declined a beverage and allowed herself to be propelled to the end of the table where the serving began. Full plate in hand, she seated herself at the table Jefferson indicated, all with the feeling she was up high in one of the corners looking down on some stranger who had assumed her name.

She studied the food on her plate. If only she could take these delicacies home to her boys, how they would delight in the tempting fare.

"Now don't you go thinkin' of others right now. Just enjoy what you have before you, now hear?" Carrie Mae leaned close enough to whisper in Louisa's ear.

"Are you a mind reader or what?"

"Never you mind, but I was right, wasn't I?"

Louisa nodded. Since she was sitting with her back to the damask draperies, she could watch the room, or what she could see of it between groups of people. Zachary remained on the other side of the ballroom, one man staying by his side. The two of them were in deep discussion, interrupted by brief interludes of conversation with other men and women. She could tell by watching him that he greeted these interruptions out of necessity but would rather have talked only with the one man.

And that man looked familiar. Where had she seen him before? Trying to figure that out, Louisa ate most of her supper without much attention to the conversations around her.

"Sister, come back. Where are you?" Carrie Mae tapped Louisa's arm with her fan.

Louisa started, nearly dropping a bite of ham. "Why? What?" She dabbed at the corner of her mouth with her napkin. "Did you say something?"

Carrie Mae giggled behind her fan. "I wondered if you noticed."

"Noticed what?"

"That man over there with Zachary. He keeps lookin' our way. Do you know who he is?"

"No, but he does look familiar."

"Well, I thought sure you must know him, the way he's been starin' at you."

"Well, if he's a friend of Zachary's, he—"

"Look, he's comin' this way. Jefferson, dear, do you know who he is?"

"Who?" He followed his wife's gaze. "Oh, of course, that is Wilson Scott, recently recovered from his war injuries. He was a year or two ahead of Zachary at college." Steadly stood to extend his hand. "Welcome back to Richmond, Wilson. Glad to see you are looking so well."

"Thank you, good evening." He stopped in front of the table. "Miss Highwood, Mrs. Steadly, I'm sure you don't remember me."

Louisa felt like someone was cracking open a door in her mind but wouldn't open it to reveal the secret hiding there. Then the door swung wider.

"Willy?" Louisa laughed in delight. "You visited Twin Oaks one summer with Zachary. I remember that—"

"Oh, please. I know what you are going to say. I fell off one of your horses, smack dab into a slough. Your older sister laughed so hard I thought she might fall off, but—"

"It would take more than laughter to unseat Jesselynn."

"Join us. Please sit down." Jefferson swung a chair next to the table. He waved to a waiter. "Bring this man a drink."

Louisa watched as Wilson sank into the chair with a sigh of relief that she knew she wasn't supposed to notice. By the way he moved, she guessed he'd suffered a back injury.

While he answered Jefferson's questions, she noticed other things, like well-cut lips that smiled so readily, hazel eyes with creases at the edges that spoke of either laughter or lots of time in the sun. A patch of hair on the right side of his head had turned white, stark against the rich cordovan of the rest. A slight bead of sweat on his clean-shaven upper lip made her think he might be in pain, even now. While he wasn't a tall man, his broad shoulders filled out the dark coat and gave him an imposing air.

Louisa brought herself back into the moment. "And what rank will you return as?"

"Major."

Ah, another major in my life. The thought made her sigh. And from the sounds of things, this one would be gone as soon as the other. She felt her sister's foot nudge hers under the table.

"Can I get you anything, Major?" She nodded toward the table of food.

"No, thank you, but I'd best be going on." He looked Louisa directly in the eyes. "But I would like to call on you tomorrow, Miss Highwood. If that is not too forward. I mean . . . I know . . . if times were different . . ."

Louisa smiled. Now would be the time to use her fan, to open it and fan herself oh so delicately. But she kept her fan closed on the cord about her wrist.

"That would be fine." She could hear the squeal that Carrie Mae didn't utter. Had this all been a setup? She wouldn't put such a thing past her baby sister, not for one minute.

Chapter Thirty-Four

ON THE CHUGWATER RIVER

Jesselynn found Ophelia kneeling by the drying racks.

"Are you all right?"

"Soon be." She laid more strips in place as the smoke shrank the former. She groaned and clutched her belly.

"The baby is coming?" Jesselynn knelt beside her.

"Yessum. Be soon now, I be thinkin'."

"I'll get Mrs. Mac." Jesselynn could feel her heart speed up already. While she'd helped at many birthings, she'd never done one herself.

"Not yet."

"You'll tell me when?"

Ophelia's laugh turned into another groan. She got up and walked around the fire to move more strips around. "Dis baby in a hurry to be borned."

"I'll have Jane Ellen take the boys to play in the other cave and get Mrs. Mac. My medicine box is . . ." She glanced up at the shelf. "Right here." Jesselynn laid a hand on Ophelia's shoulder. "Do we have time for that?"

Ophelia nodded and started slicing more strips off the elk haunch.

Jesselynn headed back outside to the gathering and, drawing Meshach aside, whispered the news to him. Then she made her way to Jane Ellen.

"Please watch the two little ones. Ophelia is having her baby."

Jane Ellen jumped to her feet. "You want I should help?"

"You will be by keeping them out of the way. I'm getting Mrs. Mac."

Jesselynn stood just behind Mrs. McPhereson, who was talking with Aunt Agatha. "Mrs. Mac, Ophelia is having her baby," she whispered. "Come when you can."

"I'll be right there. Let me get my things."

"Is she all right?" Aunt Agatha had obviously overheard.

"I hope so. She keeps working at the drying rack."

"You want to take her to one of the other caves and let the rest of us see to dinner?"

Jesselynn stopped. Aunt Agatha had indeed spoken to her, just like she used to. *Thank you, Lord.* The forgiveness was a reality.

"How far along is she?"

"No idea."

Though Jesselynn hadn't been gone more than five minutes, when they returned they found Ophelia lying on a pallet, pushed up against the wall so she had a backrest.

"It comin'," she groaned, panting between contractions.

Mrs. Mac dashed to her side, and Jesselynn fetched her medical kit off the shelf. At least she had scissors and tincture of iodine in it. The baby had slipped out and lay in Mrs. Mac's hands by the time she returned.

"A girl. You have a baby girl." Mrs. Mac sniffled between the words. "She is so perfect." The baby let out a squall loud enough to be heard over thunder, making all three women chuckle. "She sure has a healthy set of lungs." She laid the baby on Ophelia's chest and turned to Jesselynn. "You can cut the cord after we tie it off. You brought some string?"

"No, but a fine piece of latigo should work." Jesselynn knelt at Ophelia's side. "You did fine, 'Phelia, just fine. And now we got a little girl in camp. Just think, she's the firstborn of our new life." She kept up the comforting words as she waited for the cord to cease pulsing, knotted the latigo, and cut the cord.

"De baby borned already?" Meshach stopped just inside the curve of the wall.

"You have a baby girl, and she is not happy with any of us at the moment." Jesselynn smiled up at the big man. "We'll get things cleaned up here, and you can come visit."

Ophelia held out her hand. "Come see our baby."

Within minutes, Ophelia was sitting propped against Meshach's chest, their daughter tugging on a nipple like she'd been nursing for weeks.

"She just like a little pig." Meshach traced his daughter's skull with a gentle forefinger. "What shall we name her?"

"Lucinda."

"Ah, such a fine name. Lucinda be pleased she have a namesake."

"And what name will you use for your surname, now that you are free?" Jesselynn knelt beside the family and offered a cup of water for Ophelia to drink. "You must drink lots now to make milk for the baby." She glanced back to Meshach to see a look of pure fear masking his usual smile.

"You don' want us to be Highwood?"

"Oh, Meshach. That's not what I meant at all." She shook her head and held out her hand. "No, Meshach, I would be proud if you want to keep the family name. But some . . . some . . ." She turned her slightly cupped hands palm up. "Some freedmen never want to hear their old name again."

"But some freedmen had massahs what beat dem. Marse Joshua was one fine Christian genneman. He more like a father to me den my own father."

Thank you, Lord, for giving me a father like mine. Times like this I miss him so much I could bawl like a baby. Daddy, if you can hear, be proud of us. Be glad for us, for our new life out here.

"Thank you, Meshach, we will never mention this again." Jesselynn cupped the baby's head. "Do we call you Lucy, for Lucinda is such a big name?"

One by one the others tiptoed in and admired the baby. Sammy and Thaddeus stood back until Ophelia beckoned them to her.

"See our baby girl?"

"Can she run?" Thaddeus leaned closer to Jesselynn.

Ophelia shook her head. "No."

"Can she go fishin'?" The day before Thaddeus had been fishing with Daniel and caught five fish.

"No. But someday."

"Can she play with sticks?"

"No. Not yet."

He looked up at Jesselynn. "Is she broke?"

Jesselynn stooped down beside him. "She's not broken. She was just born, Thaddeus. She has to grow some."

He shook his head, disgust in every line of his sturdy body. "We eat now?"

"Yes, dinner will be ready very soon. You two go on out and help Mrs. Mac."

Meshach chuckled and laid his cheek against Ophelia's head. "I reckon dey don' think much of de baby." He looked down to see his wife and daughter both sound asleep.

———

Two nights later, Jesselynn and Wolf were just falling asleep in the tent they'd pitched down in the meadow near the grazing herd, when Jesselynn heard a voice. She crawled out of the tent and, looking up the hill, saw Meshach standing with something in his hands. She paused in the shadow while moonlight outlined him in silver.

He raised his cupped hands and looked heavenward, his arms strong and unwavering, his face radiant with glory.

"Lord God, see my daughter, my daughter who is free. No slave but free!" His voice rolled over the land, his words ringing like cathedral bells. Like the angels who came to the shepherds, his voice spoke of freedom from fear. "My daughter, Lord, who is born free, named Lucinda after your servant, Faith after you, Highwood after our family, she be yours. She be yours."

The baby cried once but stopped as soon as her father gathered her to his bosom.

Jesselynn crept back to lie beside her sleeping husband, the tears continuing to wet her pillow long after she fell asleep.

———

Getting ready for the trip to the fort took weeks. October stayed warm with chilly nights as they all worked toward winter preparations. The horses to be sold were well trained and groomed to look their best. Trade goods, such as carved pitchforks, willow baskets, knitted stockings, buckskin shirts, braided rawhide bridles, and ropes took up wagon space. The three fattest oxen were chosen to sell for beef, and seven horses formed the herd to be sold.

The night before they left, the temperature plummeted, leaving the ground white for their early morning departure.

Nate and Aunt Agatha drove one wagon, Benjamin another, and Jesselynn the third. Wolf rode his Appaloosa, and Mark Lyons mounted one of the new mares. Daniel and Meshach stayed in camp with the others.

Jesselynn laughed at the sight of her breath in the air. The rising sun sprinkled the ground with gemstones, glittering every color of the rainbow.

"Lord bless and keep thee." Meshach raised his hand in benediction.

"And you, also." Jesselynn raised her gloved hand in return. "Be watching for our return in a week." If it weren't for the wagons, the trip would take two days each way, but because they needed to haul so much back, it would take longer.

"We'll throw a wedding party when you return," Mrs. Mac promised.

Aunt Agatha laughed and ducked her head against Nathan's shoulder.

As the wagons creaked out of the meadow, Jesselynn looked back over her shoulder. What a beautiful valley. Now to just keep it peaceful.

The closer they drew to the fort, the more traffic they encountered—army patrols, fort Indians, and other settlers who occupied land near the fort.

"Sakes alive, never saw so many people," Agatha said loud enough for Jesselynn to hear as she rode the mare alongside the wagons.

Jesselynn laughed. "We used to see twenty wagons all day every day."

"I know, but that seems in another life. Like Springfield is a dreamland that I made up."

"At least everyone will be reminded we are still alive." Jesselynn patted her saddlebag that carried the letters she and the others had written. The next stagecoach would take them all east, and hopefully there would be letters with news from Richmond and Twin Oaks to collect at the post office.

Jesselynn paused for a moment. She'd started to think *home* in reference to Chugwater, but her mind often changed it to Twin Oaks. It was confusing. Had this outpost already become home to her? She pondered the question. *Maybe it is that wherever Wolf is, is where my heart now calls home.*

She looked across the herd to Wolf, who rode so effortlessly. As if he felt her gaze, he turned to look at her. Her stomach clenched, and her cheeks grew warm. Always his look had that power over her. She touched the brim of her hat with one finger. He touched his brim in return, a signal of love across the bobbing heads of horses. In her second saddlebag were rolled her skirt and a new waist sewn by Aunt Agatha. Wolf had yet to see her in her new finery. She'd been saving it for Aunt Agatha's wedding.

Since the sun was about to set, they made camp a quarter mile from the fort, and Jesselynn and Wolf rode on in to make arrangements for the wedding and the trading. Bugle notes floated on the air as they rode into the parade ground. They stopped their horses and watched the Stars and Stripes ripple in the breeze as the soldiers brought it down for the night.

After folding the flag, the detail tied down the halyard and stepped back. They saluted, pivoted, and marched off in precise time with their officer's orders.

As one, Jesselynn and Wolf signaled their horses forward, then stopped in front of the store and tied their horses to the hitching rail.

"I'll go see when the captain would like to inspect the horses while you place our order. Meet you at the Jensens'." At her nod, he strode off to the quartermaster's office, and she climbed the two narrow risers to the roofed porch. The bell tinkled over the door when she pushed it open, and the cornucopia of smells that said "store" greeted her entrance.

"Why, Mrs. Torstead, good to see you. Y'all makin' out all right up in that Chugwater country?" Sam Waters came from behind the counter to greet her.

"We most certainly are." She handed him her list. "Takes a lot to feed and care for all those people."

"Like a village all your own, ain't it?" He read down her order. "Why, looks like we got about everything. You need it all tomorrow?"

"Yes, thanks. There's something else, though. You know anyone who has a milk cow for sale? I'd like a couple of chickens too."

"Hmm." Sam scratched his chin. "You might could ask out at the Breckenridge place. He raises and sells oxen to the folks goin' west."

"Where is that?"

"Off east of the fort. Cross back over the river and head due east about a mile or so—no, more like two. Tell 'im I sent you." Sam looked down at her list again. "He and his family live in a sod house and dugout."

"Thanks. Sure would like to have milk for the little ones."

"You might could use a goat if he don't have no milk cow. Goats is cleaner and don't take so much feed. My wife runs goats out back. You could talk with her."

Jesselynn nodded, then swung her saddlebags off her shoulder. "I got mail to go out. Anything come for us?"

He took her letters with a smile. "You goin' to be right pleased." Moving behind his counter, he pulled a thick packet of letters out of a cubbyhole. "I put McPheresons' in with this too, along with Mr. Lyon's. If'n you let me know about where you live, I could sometimes send mail out with an army patrol, if they're goin' thataway."

"Thank you, we'll do that. Oh, and I have a lot to trade too. We'll bring the wagons in early in the morning."

"Fine by me." He walked her to the door. "You might want to take time to look through our new shipment of cloth too. Just came in t'other day."

Jesselynn slid the packet of letters into her saddlebag as she left the store. She'd wait until they could all hear them together. But the temptation to peek dogged her all the way to the Jensens' home.

————

Aunt Agatha and Nathan Lyons stood before the chaplain the next morning, with Jesselynn standing up for her aunt, and Wolf for Nate. As they said their vows, Jesselynn leaned forward enough to see Wolf, only to find him doing the same. The smile he gave her sealed their own vows all over again.

Strange, Jesselynn thought as she heard her aunt making the same vows she'd repeated so recently. *A month ago she wouldn't speak to us, and now we're standing up for them. Lord, you sure do have a sense of humor.* The word "cherish" leaped out at her. To cherish one another. Love, honor, and cherish. *Lord, please show me how to cherish Wolf. I get so busy that I overlook things, things that might be important to him. How am I to know them?*

She brought herself back to the matter at hand.

"And now, may the Lord, who gives us so abundantly more than we think to ask, bless and keep thee in the way everlasting."

So all I have to do is ask?

"I now pronounce you husband and wife." The chaplain smiled at the newlyweds. "You may kiss your bride."

Jesselynn turned enough to see the red creeping up Aunt Agatha's neck. Turning further, she caught Wolf's wink at her. Now her own neck was heating up.

"The guesthouse is ready for you," Mrs. Jensen said after congratulating the couple. "I made sure there is food for your supper all ready."

"Land sakes, you didn't have to go to all that trouble." Aunt Agatha shook her head. "It's not as if we're young like—"

"Agatha, let us thank these wonderful friends of ours and be on our way." Nathan took her by the arm, thanked them all, and away they went.

Jesselynn looked at Wolf, then at Mrs. Jensen. "Well, I'll be. Did I really hear a 'Yes, dear'?"

They swung by the guesthouse shortly after dawn with the wagons loaded, including a pair of gray goats and a trio of chickens, the young rooster missing the stewpot by only a day. The way home didn't seem so long when they had so many wonderful surprises to share.

Jesselynn was pretty sure her secret would get told soon. Each day made her more certain. She hugged her midsection with joy, hoping Wolf would be as delighted as she.

Chapter Thirty-Five

RICHMOND, VIRGINIA

October 1863
Dear Jesselynn,

Thank you so much for your letter. I was beginning to think you had fallen off the face of the earth. The poor mail service is frustrating at times, but I suppose it is one more thing for which we can blame the war.

Thank you for telling me such wonderful things about Thaddeus. It sounds like he has his uncle Zachary's sense of humor. At least the way our brother Zachary used to be. Since our return from our last mission north — I wrote you about that time when Zachary was saved by a pardon from Mr. Lincoln — our stubborn, hardheaded brother cannot seem to get over the experience. When I revealed our angel in disguise to be President Lincoln, I thought Zachary was going to explode right then and there. At times I think he hates me for getting him released. He doesn't seem to want to live anymore, at least that's what he told me. Please help me pray that the brother we once knew will come back to us.

My news here is that I have met a man, thanks to the conniving of our sneaky little sister. She dressed me up one evening in a dress the likes of which I haven't seen since before the war, and off we went to a soirée, where I was introduced to President Jefferson Davis and my hero, General Lee. My heart nearly jumped out of my chest when they both commended me for helping Zachary on our missions. I hoped their approbation would please Zachary too, since he received the brunt of it, but I wouldn't know, because he hasn't spoken to me since. The glares he sent my way gave me an indication of his feelings, however.

But in spite of all that, Major Wilson Scott asked to be introduced to me and then asked if he could call on me. We met him years ago, when Zachary brought him home from college to visit Twin Oaks. Carrie Mae was so excited she couldn't quit talking about him.

He did come to call and charmed Aunt Sylvania all a-twitter. He is recuperating from a back injury and hopes to be rejoining his company soon.

Isn't that the way of it? He seems a fine man, the kind Daddy would be proud to have come calling. Major Scott is from Tennessee. His father raised Tennessee Walking Horses, and like most of our horses, they were sacrificed to the war.

Louisa reread what she had written. *Hmm, sounds like I'm enamored of Major Scott, and here I've only seen him three times.* She continued her letter with bits about the men staying at Aunt Sylvania's, Miriam's antics, and her hopes for them to all be together again.

We miss you, and think of you every day. It pains me to think of how quickly life is changing. We have so little control. Therefore I commend you to the keeping of our Lord and Savior, who is far more able to keep you safe than I ever could.

Be assured that I pray for you all every day and always look forward to seeing your dear faces again.

Your loving sister

She signed her name and caught the tear that would have blotted the paper. If only she could share good news about their brother. If only the distance were not so great as to be impossible.

No, she reminded herself, *with God all things are possible. Even bringing this family back together again. Even bringing Zachary back.*

Somehow the latter seemed far more difficult than the former.

"Miss Louisa, dat genneman be here to see you," Abby announced from the French door leading out to the veranda where Louisa had escaped in hopes of finding a bit of breeze.

"Show him out here." Louisa looked down at her waist. Should she change? She shook her head. Perhaps it was time for Major Scott to see her as she really was, not all groomed and polished like a horse readied for auction. She tucked a strand of hair back in the chignon she wore most of the time, since it was cooler, and wiped beads of perspiration from her upper lip. "Please bring out a pitcher of lemonade when you can."

"He talkin' wid de sojers."

"Good. Perhaps he can cheer them up. Tell the men that lemonade will be served out here shortly."

Abby shook her head. "I don' think dat a good idea. Why, de major come all dis way to be wid you, not all de others."

"Oh." Louisa sighed. "All right. I will show him the roses or something. I can't keep the entire backyard for myself, now can I?"

"Not every day a fine genneman come callin'." Having stated her obvious disagreement with Louisa, Abby spun fast enough to make her skirt swirl and returned to the house.

Louisa shifted her gaze from outer to inner. Was her heart beating just a mite faster? Her cheeks warmer? Unbidden, Major Dorsey strolled into her mind.

Lord, I cannot pay attention to that man. After all, he's a Northerner, he's military, and besides, I'll never see him again. I loved Gilbert and he died. That's what the war does — kills the good men. She amended the thought to men in general.

I don't want to fall in love with an army man again.

But when Major Scott walked through the door, she had to admit he was a fine-looking man, with a voice deep enough to send shivers up her back.

"I'm sorry to intrude like this, but I cannot stay more than a few minutes."

"You are in no way intruding. I've just finished a letter to my sister who now lives in Indian territory not too far from Fort Laramie." Louisa knew she was babbling. She took a deep breath. "I take it you have news?"

"Yes, both good and bad, depending on how you look at it." He tucked her hand through his arm. "Shall we walk and talk?"

Louisa started to draw her hand away, but at the look of supplication on his face, she kept it on his arm. She hoped he couldn't feel the way her heartbeat picked up.

Under the magnolia tree in the far corner of the garden he turned to look down at her. "My good news is that I've been reassigned to my regiment."

"Oh." What more to say? "I'm glad" would be a lie. "How sad" would hurt his feelings.

"The sad news is that right now I'd rather stay in Richmond. I never thought I'd feel this way." He took her hands in his. "Miss Louisa, would it be all right if I wrote to you?"

"Of course, sir, I'd be right honored."

"And . . . and would you write back?"

Louisa nodded. "I would. I know there is no guarantee my letters would get to you, but I will do my best."

"That is all one can ask." His eyes said far more than his lips, and the gentle pressure on her fingers added a third dimension.

"Thank you, Miss Louisa, you have made me a happy man." He sighed. "I leave as soon as I can get packed. Say a prayer for me, please. I feel I need all the prayers I can get."

"Of course. Let me wrap some cookies for you to take along."

The two strode swiftly back to the house, and within minutes he was gone, a package of lemon cookies tucked under his arm.

Louisa leaned against the pillar post on the front porch. Was she always destined to send men off to battle?

————

November 1863
Dear Jesselynn,

You are married? Tell me more! How? When? And you must tell me more about your husband. You have been rather enigmatic concerning this great event in your life. How did he come to be called Wolf?

I am so glad to hear that you had horses to sell to the quartermaster at Fort Laramie. I am not at all surprised that you have become a trainer of horses and the methods you described make such good sense. I still have a hard time picturing you in britches and Daddy's old felt hat.

I love your descriptions of Wyoming and of those you claim have become like family. I am jealous, you realize, that others can visit with you and enjoy your company when I cannot. But I am coming to realize that loss is a part of life, and we just need to do our best to weather the changes.

I am glad you were able to write good news, but I am not so fortunate. Remember the man I met at the soirée with Carrie Mae? Major Wilson Scott called on me several times and then announced that he was being sent back to his regiment and asked if he could write to me and would I return the favor. Of course I said yes, but after three letters I heard no more from him. Jefferson told me last evening that Major Scott had been killed in the line of duty. Such barren words. Please don't ask me if I loved him, for I am no longer sure I know what that means. I was beginning to care for him, however, and I now am grieving for what might have been.

She didn't mention another letter she had received only two days earlier, this one signed *Major James Dorsey.* She told no one about the letter that Reuben again found on the mat at the front door.

I am beginning to believe that I am destined to be an old maid, caring for my sister's children. And yes, that means what you think. Our Carrie Mae is in the family way again, and Jefferson is sure it will be a boy this time. As if any boy could be more lovable than our baby Miriam. I must close and go assist with the sewing bee. Two of our men were released to return home, so I must train others. May God hold you close and protect you and those you love from all harm.

Your loving, but sad, sister

Louisa picked up Bones and cuddled him under her chin. When he began to purr, she sank down in a chair and let her tears dampen his fur. Major Dorsey had written that he thought of her often and prayed that God was keeping her safe. Wishing she could write back, she shivered in the cold. They had no coal nor wood to heat the house, so all their work was done in the kitchen where the cooking fire devoured any sticks they could find. Some folks were cutting down the big old trees that lined the streets and provided shade in backyards. Another sacrifice to this wretched war. Louisa shivered again. When would it end?

Chapter Thirty-Six

RICHMOND, VIRGINIA

April 1865

Dear Jesselynn,

The war is over. I cannot begin to describe my feeling of relief that there will be no more killing. While I know some in the Confederate government were eager to fight on, all I can think of is that we can go home. Home to Twin Oaks, if I have to walk all the way. Though that is such wondrous good news, I have news of the other kind, which brings me to frequent tears. Aunt Sylvania went home to be with our Lord a week before the surrender. She went to sleep one evening and never woke up. I know she is happy, for there was a look of such peace on her face that Jesus must have met her right there himself, instead of sending any angels.

Louisa wiped away the tears that still fell when she thought about her aunt who'd become so frail in the final months of the war.

We will be leaving for home soon. Zachary has not given me a specific date, but I have our things all packed, and tomorrow will go to say good-bye to Carrie Mae. Little Miriam is the one I shall miss the most. She is such a delight, chattering away. Though

I cannot always understand her, she has a large vocabulary for one so young. I shall miss her dreadfully. Please write to us at Twin Oaks. Perhaps now that the war is over, the mail will go through on a regular basis. I do so love to hear from you. Is there any chance at all that you will come back to Kentucky? I can tell that you love Wyoming and your life there, but along with seeing you and Thaddeus, I want to meet the husband you speak so highly of, and my other niece and nephew also.

With love always from your sister,
Louisa

As she sat rereading the letter, Zachary strode into the room.

"If you want to go along, be ready in the mornin'." He turned away without waiting for her answer.

"But what about . . . ?" Louisa didn't bother to finish her question. Zachary didn't care one whit what happened to Reuben and Abby, or Aunt Sylvania's house. Should she deed them the house? After all, it had been their home for much of their lives. But what would they live on? Reuben was far too old to find a position easily, and while Abby might find one as a cook or maid . . . Louisa shook her head. Should she take them with her? Or at least ask them if they wanted to go? *Oh, Lord, what am I to do? What will they eat if they stay here?*

Why do I have to be the one to make these decisions? This thought ignited a spark of anger. If Zachary was head of the Highwood family, why didn't he act like it? *Daddy, you would never have made Mama handle all of this.*

Her sigh came from so deep inside that it took all her strength out with it. *Lord, I cannot handle this. What am I to do?* She wondered if her mother had felt the same way, and now that she reconsidered, she realized the Highwood women always made the major decisions, even long before the war, when the men were off trying to either start it or keep it from happening.

Louisa wandered out to the back veranda where their remaining two guests were enjoying the sun, weak as it was. Actually, the air felt warmer outside than in.

"Y'all want a cup of coffee?" Louisa asked as she stopped between their chairs. Since they had no more sewing to do, Louisa had finished the last jacket and given it to one of the men to wear home. They were talking about what they'd do when they got home.

Samuel looked up, his smile creasing a face too young to have seen all he had. "That sounds mighty fine, Miss Louisa. Looks like we'll be headin' out tomorrow. I do thank you for keepin' us as long as you have."

"You're more than welcome. Coffee coming right up." She returned to the house in time to meet Abby carrying a tray out to the veranda.

"You read my mind."

"You gonna sit a spell and drink wid dem?"

"No, I think not. Could you and Reuben meet me in the parlor as soon as you've served them?"

Abby gave a brief nod and continued on out the French doors.

Louisa stood by the lace-draped windows, fingering a hole where the sun-rotted threads had separated. Who would have money to buy a house like this one? And what was it worth? She heard movement behind her and turned to find Reuben entering the room right behind Abby.

"What you be needin', Miss Louisa?"

"Nothing, thank you, but we need to talk." She laced her fingers together, then unwound them. "Abby, Reuben, Zachary and I will be leaving for Twin Oaks in the morning."

"So soon?" The two in front of her exchanged glances.

"I know. He's not giving me any time to make arrangements."

"You don' need to worry none about us." Abby took a step forward. "We gots kin to go to."

"You're sure?" Louisa felt like a smashing weight had just lifted.

"We be all right." Reuben nodded.

"Then I shall ask Mr. Steadly if he can sell this house for me. I would be grateful if the two of you could live here until that happened, if you wouldn't mind."

"Makes no nevermind. I keep up de yard, Abby de house. We keep it lookin' nice."

"Is . . . is there anything here you would like to take with you when you go?" Louisa looked around at the walnut highboy on one wall and the carved arms of the horsehair sofa. They could use all of these things at Twin Oaks if . . . She knew the "if" didn't mean a thing. The big house at Twin Oaks was no longer, and that was that. No matter how much she dreamed it to be different. They would need furniture eventually, but there was no way to transport these furnishings from here to there, nor any place for proper storage.

"Well, if you think of anything, let me know, and I will not include that in the list I shall make up for Jefferson." She sighed again and straightened her spine, squaring her shoulders as if for battle. "I need to go say good-bye to Carrie Mae and the babies. Perhaps Zachary has told them more than he has me." Keeping the bitterness from her voice was hard, and from her thoughts even more difficult.

"You want I should borry Miss Julie's buggy?"

"Thank you, Reuben, but I need the walk." As she strode toward the door-way, she caught the sheen of tears in their eyes, and instantly tears ran down her own cheeks. "I . . . I am so sorry it has to be like this, so rushed and—" She wrapped an arm around each of them, and the three stood in the embrace, wiping their eyes and reassuring one another that all would be well.

When Louisa left the house, she had one more stick she wished to beat her brother with, his hurting those two gentle people who had worked so hard caring for them all, including all the soldier guests they had helped bring back to health.

"Zachary Highwood, if Mother could see you now, she would take a willow switch to your bare legs." Another sob caught in her throat. He only had one leg to switch. The old Zachary would have made a joke about it all and had everyone laughing.

———

By the time Carrie Mae's buggy had returned her home, Louisa felt like she had no more tears to shed. Or at least hoped so.

Carrie Mae had promised to come visit as soon as the trains were rolling regularly again.

Louisa hadn't added the "if." Somehow she doubted life would ever again be what it used to be.

But when Zachary and the buggy stopped in front of the house in the predawn stillness, she was ready, her clothing packed in one bag, bedding in another, and a basket of food that Abby prepared, salted with her tears.

"God be wid you," Reuben whispered as he placed her things in the lidded box in the rear of the buggy.

"And with you." Louisa gave Abby and Reuben each a hug and, with the old man's hand assisting, climbed up in the seat.

"Did you bring water?" Zachary asked, voice abrupt as ever.

"Yes." She settled her skirt and wrapped her shawl more closely around her shoulders. She wasn't sure if the chill came from the air or from the agony of leaving. But either way, it crept into her bones, setting her teeth to chattering.

The buggy started forward, and Louisa waved once more to her two old friends. As long as it remained in sight, Louisa gazed at the house that had been her home for five years. *Dear Lord, keep them safe, please.* She fought the tears that clogged her throat, knowing that if Zachary heard her, she would receive one of his looks that stripped flesh off her bones. Maybe she should have stayed in Richmond, at least until . . . at least until what? She knew there were no good answers to any of her questions.

Zachary never looked back.

———

The trip passed in a morass of despair, with soldiers clumping their way home, stepping back off the road to let the buggy by. More than once she was grateful for the rifle Zachary had prominently displayed. Hungry men would do whatever was needed to eat.

Any time she tried to start a conversation, Zachary acted like he didn't hear her, only giving orders—to get down or to hand him whatever he needed at the moment. At least the harness was light, and she was adept at backing the horse into the shafts and hooking the traces. Every time she had to do something he would have been doing had he been able, she made sure not to look at his face. Icy or flaming, rage was rage.

The contents of the silver flask seemed to be his only antidote. She came to think on it as a friend.

Trees were donning new leaves as they drew close to Lexington. And the rolling green hills looked no worse for the war, except for the burned-out shells of houses in some areas and the battlefield at Richmond, Kentucky. As they drew closer to home, places looked much the same, but they didn't stop to talk with anyone. When they turned on Home Road, Louisa could hardly swallow, her throat was so dry. The Marshes' house and barns stood, needing paint and general fixing up, but smoke rose from the chimney. If she squinted, she could make herself believe it looked no different.

Ahead she saw the two ancient oaks at the end of their lane. *Oh, Lord, we are home. Thank you, thank you, we are home.*

Zachary turned the horse in between the green-furred sentinels and stopped.

No white house with green shutters and welcoming portico beckoned from the slight rise at the end of the lane. No big barns that had once looked to have been placed there when God created the earth. The brick chimneys poked skyward like skeletal fingers.

Louisa crumbled within, her heart faltering. No matter that she'd known this to be true, still some small part of her had hoped, dreamed, that Twin Oaks still stood.

She sneaked a peek at Zachary. He sat frozen, like a bronzed statue, a single tear sliding down his cheek.

Chapter Thirty-Seven

Twin Oaks

May 1865
Dear Miss Highwood,

I have been assigned to Kentucky to assist in the reparations now that this horrible war is over. I hope that I might call on you at Twin Oaks, as I am hoping you have returned there. I called at the house in Richmond, only to learn of your loss. Please accept my condolences on the death of your aunt.

Yours truly,
Colonel James Dorsey

Louisa read the letter for the third time. James Dorsey, a Union colonel, was coming to Twin Oaks. Of course she had seen blue uniforms in Midway, and rumor had it that Frankfort and Lexington were well populated with blue-and-gold soldiers, along with their wives and families. While shopkeepers disdained serving them, the truth was, they were the only ones with money to spend.

What will Zachary say? More important, what will he do? Louisa climbed back up in the buggy and clucked the horse homeward. At least they had a horse and buggy, thanks to Jefferson, or she, like most of the area folk, would be walking to town. She'd stopped by the neighbors to see what they needed, but with Confederate money being worthless and a frightening shortage of gold coin, everyone was getting along with what they had or going without.

The knot in her stomach that tightened whenever her brother raised his voice twisted now. When would Colonel Dorsey call? Should she warn Zachary? She glanced down at her faded and well-patched skirt. She had one dress in less deplorable condition. Thoughts of all the lovely garments that Carrie Mae took so for granted roused the little demon of jealousy. Perhaps if she had asked, Carrie Mae would have shared some of her things, but pride had kept her quiet. Her sister should have volunteered. Carrie Mae wasn't intentionally selfish, just thoughtless.

Once out of town, she clucked the horse to a trot. Perhaps the mail addressed to Zachary would lift his mood. While she'd been hoping for letters from Jesselynn and Carrie Mae, she couldn't deny the tingling joy brought by the one she received.

"I will see him again and have a chance to thank him properly." The horse flicked his ears, listening to her and keeping track of all around him.

————

When she returned to the log cabin that Lucinda and Joseph had built behind where the summer kitchen used to stand, she tucked the letter away in the box where she kept her writing things. Zachary never came up in the loft where she had a pallet, as climbing the ladder would be next to impossible for him. She hung her bonnet on a peg in the wall and donned her apron. Best get to hoeing. Dreaming over a handsome man never did put victuals on the table.

As each day passed and the warmth of May caused the tobacco plants to shoot up, along with the corn and beans in the garden, Louisa kept one eye on the long drive, waiting for a man in blue to ride up. She trimmed the roses back and weeded the rose garden, in between hoeing the tobacco. In spite of the wide-brimmed straw hat, ventilated by mice, that she had found in the cabin, her face and arms took on the golden hue of one who worked outside.

Two of their former slaves returned, and as they hoed and mended fences, the place took on a more kept appearance.

Everyone walked on tiptoe around Zachary, for no one ever knew what might ignite him in a roaring rage.

"I don' know what to do wid dat boy." Lucinda watched Zachary's back as he stomped and stumbled back down to the shed where he kept his bottle under his sleeping pallet. If he slept at all.

"Wish I knew. I'd sure enough tell you." Louisa kneaded her aching back. The weeds in the garden grew far more quickly than the carrots. Before that she'd been out hunting greens so they would have a noon meal. She eyed the rose garden, knowing what still lay deep beneath the soil. Zachary had no idea that the family silver and their mother's jewelry lay boxed and safe. She had no intention of telling him until the day they could be used again or were needed to save Twin Oaks.

Some days it was harder than others to be thankful for what they did have—food to eat, a roof over their heads, and work that would pay off in the fall. All Zachary could see was what was gone, not what they had. And it was eating him alive.

"You gon' write to Jesselynn and ask her to bring de horses back?" Lucinda sank down on a stool, rubbing her gnarled fingers.

"No. She will do so when she can. Besides, what use would stallions be when we have no mares?"

"Dey be runnin' at Keeneland dis year?"

"I don't think so. At least I've not heard of it. But then, if Zachary knew, he wouldn't tell me anyway." Keeping the bitterness out of her mind and voice took real gumption at times. *Lord, forgive my judging spirit. You sure have to love this brother of mine for me, 'cause at times like this, all I want to do is haul off and smack him with that crutch—or something heavier.*

She turned to wash her greens when movement down the lane caught her attention. The sun glinted on gold buttons and bars on a blue uniform.

"Oh!" She looked down at her skirt, knees dirty from grubbing in the dirt. "I have to change clothes. We have company coming." She dashed inside, disappeared behind the screen in the corner, and whipped off her skirt and waist. She'd hung her remaining dress on a hook, just in case, and now pulled it over her head. Her fingers shook as she fastened the buttons, while her mind told her it could be someone else coming down the road.

But her heart knew differently.

She stepped out the door as he dismounted from a horse that looked as if it could have been bred and raised at Twin Oaks. Reins over his arm, he removed his gray felt hat. The smile that carved his cheeks seemed only for her. He was more handsome than she remembered.

"Miss Highwood, good day."

"Yes, it is a fine day." Her tongue adhered itself to the roof of her mouth. She knotted her shaking hands in her skirt. *Say something, you ninny.*

"I'm sorry for all your losses."

Was he having as much trouble talking as she?

"Yes, thank you."

Lucinda cleared her throat behind her. "Ah . . ." What could she offer him? "Would you like a drink of fresh springwater?"

"Yes, thank you." A smile tugged at the side of his mouth.

"Ah, good. Have a seat, please."

Lucinda harrumphed. "Here he come." While a whisper, the shock of it sent Louisa into a panic. Why did Zachary have to see this? Why couldn't he be sleeping off his drunk like he so often did?

"Louisa, get in the house!" The war injuries hadn't affected her brother's voice. It cut like glass.

Louisa tucked her chin, forced a smile to her trembling lips, and nodded to the bench beside the house. "I'll get that drink for you."

"You needn't, you know."

"Yes, but I do." She lifted the cheesecloth from the drinking bucket they kept in the shade and dipped him out a cupful, handing it to him with a steadier smile.

"What are you doin' here, you—?"

Louisa's ears turned hot at the name he'd used. "Forgive my brother, sir, he knows not what he does."

"Oh, I think he does." Dorsey handed the empty cup back to her. "I had to make sure you were all right."

"We are doing the best we can."

"Get off my land, you—" More epithets.

Louisa tightened her jaw and straightened her spine. "Zachary, I ask you to be polite to a guest here. Mama would—"

"Our mother is dead and gone, and I won't have any murderin', thievin' bluebelly contaminatin' this soil." Zachary stumbled and caught himself. "Get out of here before I get my gun, and you'll never leave." His words slurred, and spittle flew in front of him. Unshaven, hair sticking every whichway, he looked as deranged as he acted.

"Zachary Highwood, Colonel Dorsey only came to inquire as to how we are. If you can't keep a civil tongue in your head, just return to your room until this visit is over." Louisa couldn't believe those words had come out of her own mouth.

But when Zachary raised his crutch as if to strike her, she stepped back, only to find herself staring into a blue-clad back.

"You strike her, and cripple or not, I'll see you don't strike anyone ever again."

Zachary caught himself and propped his crutch firmly back under his arm. "Get off my land."

"The war is over. I'm here to help you Southerns—"

"You're not here to help nobody. You bled us on the battlefield, and now you'll bleed us again." Zachary took two steps forward.

Louisa stepped from behind the blue wall and looked up at the man beside her. "You had better go. As you can see, we are doing as well as can be expected."

"May I call on you again?" The look in his eyes set her heart to fluttering.

"No, you may not!" Zachary screamed the words. If he'd been a cotton-mouth, he would have struck.

"Yes!" She swallowed hard.

"You lyin' witch. You see this man again, and I'll kill you."

"Would he?"

"No." But the uncertainty must have shown on her face.

"I can get you protection in town."

"Go with him, then. Who needs you here, anyway?" Zachary swayed on his feet and lurched forward. "I'll kill you both."

"I cannot leave you like this."

"Just go. We'll be all right."

Dorsey turned toward his horse, then back. "No, come with me now."

"I . . . I can't. Please, don't ask me to."

"This wasn't the way I hoped to do this, but Louisa, I love you. Come with me, and we will be married in the morning."

Louisa felt her jaw drop. Her clasped hands flew to her throat. Her heart raced as though she'd been running for hours. "M-marry you?"

"Go with him, then. And don't ever come back. You are dead to me. Get out!"

Oh, Lord . . . She took one more look at her brother, nodded, and met the warm gaze of James Dorsey. "I'll get my things."

"You take nothin'. Just get."

Louisa turned to Lucinda, whose tear-tracked face wore the sorrows of forever. "Please get my Bible for me and the packet of letters." She lowered her voice. "I will keep in touch."

They rode out the long lane with Zachary shouting imprecations after them. By the time they reached the ancient oaks, Louisa could no longer hold back the tears. Up the road a piece, James Dorsey swung his leg over the pommel and dropped to the ground, reaching up to lift Louisa into his arms. Murmuring comfort and endearments, he stroked her hair until her sobs lessened. She nestled against his chest, hearing his strong heartbeat against her ear.

"You know that every man I've become attached to has been killed in the war?"

"No, I didn't know that. But now that I have you, I'll be sure to watch my back."

"How about your front?" She drew back to see a water stain the size of a dinner plate on his uniform. "Good thing this is wool, so my tears won't show." She looked up to see his eyes crinkle in a smile so tender, she caught her breath. "You were really serious about loving me? That wasn't just to chase off Zachary?"

"Oh, no, ma'am. I've been wanting to come find you since that day at the prison. I figured any woman who would offer to give her life for her brother's would make a wonderful wife and mother. That you are so beautiful and sweet and caring and—"

She laid a finger against his lips. "I believe you."

"Do you think . . . ah, that perhaps . . . ah . . ."

She watched red heat travel up his neck and face. "Why, Colonel, you're blushing." Her laughter tinkled like wind chimes on the breeze.

He sighed. "What I want to say is . . ." He paused again. "Do you think you could learn to love me?"

"Oh, I think the learning has already begun, some time ago, in fact. When your letters made my heart go pitty-pat, I told myself to stay away from military men, because they always get shot. Made me begin to think I was the kiss of death, not that all of them kissed me, mind you, but it's the thought." She sighed and in the sigh let go of all the fears she'd been holding in. "Could you hold me close again, sir? Your arms are indeed most comforting."

They were married late that afternoon by a chaplain known to Colonel Dorsey.

––––––

June 1865
Dear Sister,

I have both wonderful news and terrible news. In fact there is much to be thankful for. We planted five acres of tobacco, thanks to some seed Zachary was able to find. And thanks to Jefferson and Carrie Mae, the taxes are paid. So we will be able to keep our home.

Or rather, Zachary will. I'm sorry to say that he has banished me from Twin Oaks. When Colonel Dorsey came calling, Zachary threw him off the place. And when I stood up for the man who helped save our brother's life on that horrible trip to Washington, our dear brother, and I say this with great sorrow, threw me off the place too. James and I were married that afternoon, and now I shall accompany him west where he will be stationed at Fort Kearney, Nebraska. His orders were changed so quickly. I can't help but believe God's hand is directing us. How far is Fort Kearney from where you live? Is there some way we can meet together? I would so love to see your family. As I said, I am both sad and happy.

Please pray for Zachary, as he is drinking far more than is good for him, and he is so bitter that he is driving all his friends away.

        Love from your married sister,
        Louisa

P.S. I cannot wait for you to meet James again. He speaks so well of you, and sometimes I tease him that he married the wrong sister. Isn't it strange the directions our lives have taken, and all because of the war.

        Your loving sister,
        Mrs. James Dorsey

––––––

July 1865

Dear Louisa,

I am so glad for your joy and happiness. Reading a letter from you reminds me so much of Mama that I can scarce read for the tears. At Fort Kearney you are half of Nebraska and part of Wyoming away. Should you ever be quartered at Fort Laramie, I could ride there in two days. That is how long it takes us to deliver the horses we sell to the army and to get supplies.

Things are tense here due to the battles between the army and the Indians. I pray that your colonel will be safe and not have to fight again. This war, like the other I believe, could be stopped if men would learn to sit down and talk instead of shooting off both their mouths and their guns. Wolf does what he can to help our Sioux friends and family have enough to eat and adapt to the white man's ways. I know that God made us all equal, none better than another because of skin color or family, but all loved by our Father in heaven.

I have not received any letters from Carrie Mae since the war ended, not that she was a regular correspondent before then, either.

Thaddeus has grown so big, and Peter John, at fifteen months, follows him everywhere, on unsteady little legs. Mary Louisa is three months old and such a joy. Wolf dotes so on her. I am busy training horses when I get the chance. You would be amazed at the things I have learned about horses since I married Wolf.

We have our own little community here. Jane Ellen is married to Henry Arsdale, a fine young man she met at the fort. He joined her here on the piece she had homesteaded, so they are our neighbors to the north. Meshach and Ophelia send their love. He has pretty much taken over as our pastor and to some of the members of Red Cloud's tribe also. I do hope and pray that we will be together one of these days. Always remember that I love you.

Jesselynn

Chapter Thirty-Eight

WYOMING TERRITORY
SPRING 1867

"*Now, Thaddeus, you have to sit still.*"

"I know. I'm tryin'." Thaddeus blew the hair off his face and sneezed as some tickled his nose.

Jesselynn lifted another curl with the comb and snipped it off. Since they would soon be leaving for Cheyenne to catch the train east on their journey to Twin Oaks, she wanted him to look his best. While the letter from Zachary had demanded she bring Thaddeus back to Twin Oaks to live, she had no intention of leaving him there, not unless he really wanted to stay. She knew that would break her heart, but right was right.

"The horses are ready." Wolf stopped in the doorway of their stone house, built three summers before.

"Thaddeus, if you keep squirming like that, it'll be tomorrow before we leave." Jesselynn ran the comb through his hair again and trimmed another spot. "There." She untied the towel from around his neck. "Go outside to brush off." She reached down to pick up Mary Louisa, who'd been playing with the curls of hair on the floor. Jesselynn brushed her off and kissed her freckled cheek. "Whatever will we do with you?" She kissed her daughter again.

"Now don't you go worryin' about the young'uns. They'll be fine with me." Mrs. Mac swung Peter John up on her hip. "Won't you, honey?" When he screwed up his round face readying to wail, she handed him a cookie. Sunshine returned.

———

Jesselynn had knit a sweater for Wolf and started a matching one for Peter John by the time the train pulled into Frankfort, Kentucky. What they thought would take three or four days took more than a week. They'd changed trains so many times, she'd come to the point she wasn't sure where they were going. At times she envied Wolf and Daniel in the boxcars with the horses. Thaddeus had alternated between the horses and sitting with her. As they drew further east, he'd chosen the men and horses over the boring sitting. When the train finally screeched to a stop, they unloaded the horses, and Wolf went to find a buggy. *I'd rather ride in on horseback than a buggy,* Jesselyn thought, but here in civilization she had to be proper. No britches and no riding astride.

She chewed on her bottom lip. *Lord, what are we heading into this time? Has that brother of mine improved any?* Not according to Lucinda's last letter, but they'd all been praying for a miracle. And miracles did still happen, did they not?

She answered that question with a smile. After all, she and Louisa had seen each other not once but twice. Surely that counted as miraculous.

A tall shadow brought her out of her reverie. She looked up to see Wolf blocking the sun. "We're ready then?" she asked.

"The bags are loaded." He held out his arm, and when she put her hand through the crook of his elbow, he patted her hand. The smile he gave her warmed her heart and put starch in her backbone.

The nearer they drew to Twin Oaks, the more Jesselynn's heart speeded up.

"The trees are still here." She pointed to the two ancient oaks that held sentinel on either side of the drive. But when they trotted the rented buggy between them, she had to shut her eyes. No white house stood at the end. While she'd been preparing herself, still the pain caught in her throat. The big house of Twin Oaks really was gone.

Wolf stopped the buggy to give her time to recover. "Even though the house is not there, I can see it clearly, thanks to your descriptions."

"Don' look de same, do it?" Daniel leaned on his horse's withers. "But dere's tobacco growin' green."

"Zachary must have more help now." Jesselynn tucked her handkerchief back in her bag. "Let's go."

Wolf clucked the horse, and they trotted between the trees that still lined the drive, grown some bigger since she left.

A dog ran out to bark at their arrival. Smoke rose from a log cabin set back behind where the summer kitchen used to stand. But while Louisa had told of the brick chimneys remaining upright, they were now only piles of bricks.

A thin black woman came to the door of the cabin, shaded her eyes, then threw her apron over her head.

"Lucinda, we've come home." Jesselynn didn't wait for the buggy to come to a full halt before leaping to the ground and running to throw her arms around the turbaned woman. Together they laughed and cried, hugging, stepping back, and then hugging again.

"I din't think dis day would ever come." Lucinda wiped her eyes with the edge of her apron as Thaddeus and Wolf came to stand beside Jesselynn. "And is dis big boy my baby, Thaddeus?" She put her hands up to her cheeks. "Lawd above, he near to grown."

"Lucinda, this is my husband, Gray Wolf Torstead." Jesselynn slipped her arm through her husband's and finished the introductions. Then looking around, she asked, "Where's Zachary? Didn't he get the telegram?"

"Oh, he did." Lucinda's face lost its smile.

"Has he a place ready for the horses?"

"He do." She nodded to where the barns used to be. "Down dere."

Something's sure wrong here. Jesselynn turned to Wolf. "You and Daniel want to take the horses down there?"

Wolf looked from Lucinda to the pole building he took to be the barn.

"You better go wid." Lucinda shook her head. "I have supper ready when you comes back."

"I'm comin' too." Thaddeus kept within touching range of Jesselynn's arm, as if sensing things weren't quite what she had promised him.

Each of them leading one of the horses, they walked on down the track to what looked more like sheds than barns. Rosebushes so overgrown they were hardly recognizable still bloomed pink and white in what had been the rose garden. Louisa said she trimmed them back before she left. Looks like Zachary cares not a whit for beauty.

"Perhaps I can take some cuttings back with me. How I would love to have one of Mama's roses growin' by our house. See that old burnt tree there by the house, Thaddy? That's a magnolia. I used to climb out my window and down that tree when I wanted to be at the barn."

"Why not use the door?"

"Because my mother didn't want me down riding Ahab or the other Thoroughbreds. She said that wasn't ladylike, and Lucinda was worse than Mama." Jesselynn started to laugh but stopped when she saw a man leaning on a crutch step out of the pole building.

"Zachary?" *Oh, dear Lord, can that really be my handsome brother?* She forced a smile to lips that quivered and ran forward to greet him.

Hugging him was like hugging a stone. She stepped back. Lines crevassed his face, his eye bloodshot, the black patch slightly askew. He smelled like he'd taken a bath in a whiskey barrel.

"We brought you pure Thoroughbreds, no crossbreeding."

"Only four?"

"The two mares are bred to Domino. I couldn't come until we weaned their babies, and those two fillies were too young to have made the trip well. Joker is the older stallion. He's by Ahab, Dulcie's foal when we were traveling west. Their papers are up in my bag."

"Tie 'em in there." He turned to look down at Thaddeus. "Can you ride?"

"Yes, sir."

"Like all the Highwoods, he is a natural horseman." Jesselynn nodded to Thaddeus. "Come tie your horse in that stall."

After settling the horses, the four of them stepped back out into the soft air of late afternoon. One of the horses whinnied.

"I'll feed and water them if you like." Wolf nodded to the man still standing in the same place as though the post might fall over if he moved.

"Why? You think I can't?"

"Just being neighborly." Wolf took a step closer to Jesselynn.

"So you a breed, then?"

"Zachary!" Jesselynn only stopped because of Wolf's hand on her arm.

The one eye burned into her. "I had three sisters, and now I got one. One married a Northerner; one a breed. I ain't got no truck with Northerners nor breeds. You can leave Thaddeus. He belongs here."

Jesselynn squeezed the small hand that had crept into hers. "We'll be up at the cabin if you have any questions about the horses." She turned and, taking Wolf's arm, led the way back to the cabin. "Daniel, if you want, you can stay here."

"No, not to work for the likes of him. I got land in Wyomin', free land."

"For a free man." Jesselynn finished the quote they all used from Meshach. She imagined daggers assaulting her shoulder blades but kept on walking. In spite of all Louisa had said, she'd hoped and prayed the return of the horses would melt the anger her brother carried. After all their work to bring the horses back, he didn't even say thank-you or comment on how wonderful they looked.

"I don't have to stay here, do I?" Thaddeus tugged on her hand.

"No, darlin', you don't have to stay here."

She stopped to gaze over the growing tobacco fields and the green, shimmering pasture. Tears made her sniff. "I . . . I'm sorry, Wolf."

"Not your fault. Nothing to apologize for. Like Meshach warned us, we got to pray for our brother Zachary, pray that someone or something will help him see what he's doing. We've got room in our hearts for that."

Jesselynn looked up at the man beside her. "How come I am so blessed to be married to you?"

"Because you had the foresight to hook up with a wagon train going to Oregon, whether the fool wagon master wanted you to or not."

Thaddeus giggled beside her. The story had been told many times, always to his delight.

Jesselynn glanced over her shoulder to see that Zachary no longer leaned against the post. "How will he handle those horses, take care of them?" She'd seen his hands shaking in spite of the tough show he put on. And the look of despair that flashed across his face so quickly she almost missed it spoke louder than his words. Northerners and breeds, eh? She sighed, this time for him. She and Louisa were both so happy, and Carrie Mae too, still in Richmond.

"Someday we'll be back. God says He answers the prayers of His people. Zachary will come out of this. We must believe it," Wolf said, taking her arm.

"God willing," she responded.

"Yes, God willing."

After eating the meal Lucinda prepared, they gathered their things. "I do wish you would consider coming with us. We have plenty of room for you, Lucinda," Jesselynn entreated.

"I stay here in my home. 'Sides, dese old bones need warmin', not cold winters like you tole me."

"Write to me and tell me if you need anything, promise?"

Lucinda nodded, and the two women hugged as if they'd never let go. Lucinda stood waving as they climbed back in the buggy. Daniel and Thaddeus squeezed in between the bags in the rear.

Jesselynn waved again, then looked toward the barns. Sure enough, Zachary stood there watching them leave. "I love you, brother, no matter what. We all do." She sighed. "Please, Lord, heal my brother." She wiped her eyes and blew her nose.

"It's a long way home." Thaddeus leaned on the seat back in front of him.

"Not really. With the fine trains and all, we'll be there before you know it." Wolf slapped the reins on the horse's rump. "Get up there, horse. We got to get on home."

Epilogue

FALL 1872

"Wolf brought a letter," twelve-year-old Thaddeus shouted as he pelted into the stone house, where Jesselynn was cutting corn off the cobs to spread it on trays where it could dry in the Wyoming sun. With the excellent corn crop, she'd canned and now dried bushels.

"I'm in the kitchen."

Thaddeus skidded to a stop. "It's from Twin Oaks."

Jesselynn dried her hands, her heart picking up a beat. She took the letter, reaching for a knife to slit it open at the same time. She'd begun to wonder if anyone was still alive at the homeplace, it had been so long since anyone had written. Or answered her own infrequent letters.

"It's from Lucinda." Thaddeus, nearly as tall as she, glued himself to her shoulder.

"I know." Lucinda's penmanship would be recognized anywhere. Why did she feel so certain it was bad news? Jesselynn pulled the paper from the envelope and unfolded it.

"Read it aloud."

"Where is Wolf?"

"Putting the horses away."

Should she wait? Her curiosity proved stronger than hesitation.

"Dear Miss Jesselynn,

I know I should have wrote more often, but Mr. Zachary forbid us to. And now I must tell you our sad news. Mr. Zachary passed this life on de last day of August. I prayed for him that he let go the bitterness that ate at him. I know you was praying for him too and Carrie Mae and Louisa. God did answer your prayers, for de last night when I sat by his bed, he turn to me and say, "I don't want to go to hell. I've already been there." He look so sad, then he say, "You believe God save a sinner like me?" I tells him yes, and he smile. First time I see that smile since he left for de war. Den he say thank you. His face smooth out, and his smile stay. We buried him in de plot with the rest.

Someone must come and see to de place and de horses. I send letter to each of you. Please come soon.

Lucinda"

Jesselynn stared at the paper. What could they do? She smoothed her hand over the round belly that carried their fourth child. Twin Oaks was a long trip for a woman in her condition.

"Do we have to go?" Thaddeus asked, studying her, trying to figure out what she would say.

"Someone has to." *And I'm the oldest. But Louisa is closer. Carrie Mae said she never wanted to return to Kentucky, but someone has to.*

Unless she wrote to one of their old neighbors and asked them to sell it. But to whom? Would anyone want the land? What about the horses? Surely Zachary had taken care of the horses. The real question was, did anyone have any money to buy the land?

Wolf entered the kitchen and dipped water out of the cheesecloth-covered bucket. He took a long drink, eyeing her over the rim of the long-handled dipper. When he finished, he asked, "Good news?"

"Not so's you'd notice."

"Zachary died, and Lucinda wants someone to come to see to the place." Thaddeus took the letter and handed it to Wolf.

Wolf stared at his wife, who had crossed her arms over her belly and was chewing on her bottom lip. A single tear meandered down her cheek. He read the letter then looked up. "We can be ready to leave in two or three days."

"That place belongs to Thaddeus."

"I don't want it. I live here in Wyoming," Thaddeus said.

"Unless Zachary deeded it to someone else."

"I thought of that." She shook her head slowly. "Guess we better go see."

"You want me to take Thaddeus, and you stay home?"

Leave it to Wolf to try to make things easier for her. The one time he'd been there had not been pleasurable.

"No, I better go along." She reached for the letter and read it again. "I wonder if Lucinda ever showed him where we buried the silver."

————

Ten days later, trotting up the drive in a borrowed buggy, Jesselynn felt as though they'd stepped back in time. The trees had grown in the last five years, but the big house had never been rebuilt. Horses grazed in the pasture off to the right near a barn of sorts. Tobacco fields stretched to the left.

"He must have sold enough horses to keep food on the table."

"And whiskey."

Another buggy waited under a magnolia tree. She'd written Louisa to say when they'd arrive, so she must have gotten the letter. Two outcast sisters coming home, and the one who'd not been banished never cared to return.

Wolf helped Jesselynn down, and she rubbed the cramp in the small of her back. She'd not sat so long since the return home from delivering the horses. Louisa came running to greet her and, after a hug, stood back and gave her an up-and-down inspection.

"You shouldn't have come in your condition."

"It'll be a few weeks yet."

The two sisters locked arms and strolled to where Lucinda, grizzled hair peeking from her turban, waited.

"Ah tried, Miss Jesselynn, but he one stubborn man."

"But the end was good."

"Jesus, He be good. He take His wandering son home." She wiped her eyes with an apron corner. "What we to do now?"

Louisa and her husband exchanged glances, then Louisa nodded. "If no one else wants to farm this land, we do." She smiled at Thaddeus. "If we can work that out with you, since I believe you are the legal heir."

Thaddeus spun to grin at Jesselynn. "Does that mean I can go back to Wyoming?"

Jesselynn smiled. "I'm sure there are legalities we need to follow, but we can do that."

"If one day you decided you wanted to come back, we could make provisions for that." James nodded to his wife. "I will turn in my resignation, and we can be moved here before winter, or as soon as we can get a house built." He looked from Wolf to Thaddeus and Jesselynn. "If this meets with everyone's approval." At their nods, he turned to the old woman. "All of you will have homes here for as long as you live or want."

"Praise de Lawd." Lucinda clasped her hands together.

Jesselynn breathed a sigh of relief. Here God had been at work answering her prayers again, even before she was sure what to pray for. Paving the way before them all.

"Let's go down to see the horses and the graveyard." She ruffled Thaddeus's hair. "I'm sure there is a track down there where I used to ride. My mother and Lucinda were adamant that a young girl did not ride racehorses or wear her brother's britches." She paused. To think how simple life had been—before the war. But had it not been for the war, she would not have met Wolf or traveled to Wyoming and have the life they now had there. She paused to breathe around a healthy kick in the ribs. Hopefully this baby would wait until they got home before making its arrival.

Locking her arm through Wolf's, she grinned up at him. No, they would not do well at Twin Oaks, but Louisa, her officer husband, and their children would. So Twin Oaks would go on, and maybe even the house, or a smaller but lovely one, would wait for visitors at the end of the drive. And Twin Oaks Thoroughbreds would once again be sought after for breeding stock and for the tracks. As Lucinda had said, "Praise the Lord."